medieval
russia's
epics,
chronicles,
and tales

St. George in the garb of a medieval Russian knight. A sixteenth-century icon.

medieval russia's epics, chronicles, and tales

Edited, Translated, and with an Introduction by,

SERGE A. ZENKOVSKY

Vanderbilt University

REVISED AND ENLARGED EDITION

A MERIDIAN BOOK

MERIDIAN
Published by the Penguin Group
*Penguin Books USA Inc., 375 Hudson Street, New York, New York
10014, U.S.A.*
Penguin Books Ltd, 27 Wrights Lane, London W8 5TZ, England
Penguin Books Australia Ltd, Ringwood, Victoria, Australia
*Penguin Books Canada Ltd, 2801 John Street, Markham, Ontario,
Canada L3R 1B4*
*Penguin Books (N.Z.) Ltd, 182-190 Wairau Road, Auckland 10,
New Zealand*

*Penguin Books Ltd, Registered Offices:
Harmondsworth, Middlesex, England*

*Published by Meridian, an imprint of New American Library,
a division of Penguin Books USA Inc. Previously published in a
Dutton paperback edition.*

20 19 18 17 16 15 14 13 12 11

ACKNOWLEDGMENTS

*Grateful acknowledgment is made to the following for permission to
quote from copyright material:*

Selections from The Russian Primary Chronicle *as translated by
Samuel H. Cross in Harvard Studies and Notes in Philology and
Literature, Volume XII, 1930, reprinted by permission of the Harvard
University Press. Copyright 1930, © 1958, by The President and
Fellows of Harvard College.*

Selection from The Correspondence Between Prince A. M. Kurbsky
and Tsar Ivan IV of Russia *translated by J. L. I. Fennell, 1955, reprinted
by permission of the Cambridge University Press, London and New
York.*

PREFACE

IN PREPARING this volume for publication, I felt that at the present level of American and British scholarship in the field of Russian studies the time has come to offer readers and students a comprehensive anthology of Russia's medieval literature in translation. The works of modern Russian writers of the nineteenth century, especially those of the age of the great Russian novel as represented by Dostoevsky and Tolstoy, have long since become an inalienable part of American and British curricula of literary studies and of collections in public and school libraries. Also rather well known are the contemporary writings of Russia's Soviet period. Very different is the situation regarding the literature of previous centuries, especially that of the Russian Middle Ages, which lasted until the beginning of the eighteenth century. Indeed, there are available in English translation such masterpieces of medieval Russian letters as the *Primary Chronicle*, the *Lay of Igor's Campaign*, some adaptations and translations of the *Life*, or autobiography, of Avvakum, and of some other works written from the eleventh through the seventeenth centuries. Most of these translations, however, are either out of print or not readily available, having appeared in rare or expensive editions. Moreover, the tremendous remaining part of Russian medieval writings has never been translated either into English or into any other Western language.

The present anthology is therefore a pioneering effort to present to Western readers the finest works, a few in excerpt, of Russian literature from its very beginning, in the early eleventh century, through the seventeenth century, when Peter the Great forced Russia to rejoin the European family of nations and discard its medieval culture.

Russian medieval literature is very extensive. According to incomplete statistics, for example, there are over seven thousand versions of lives of saints written during Russia's Middle Ages, and many thousands of chronicles and tales. Therefore, the task of selecting for translation the most outstanding of these was not easy. I attempted to solve this problem by offering here as many recognized masterpieces of that period as possible, together with some lesser-known works that also contribute to an understanding of the mentality, culture, and literary manners of Old Russia. My guiding principle was to offer entire works whenever possible, or at least complete narrative passages from such longer writings as the chronicles, in order to give the reader an opportunity to grasp the style and spirit of the Russians of that age. In a few cases—as, for instance, the long historical and polemical writings of the sixteenth and early seventeenth centuries—I decided, owing to the limitations of this volume, to include the most characteristic and interesting passages, in order to convey a more complete picture of the evolution of Russian letters.

When possible, already existing translations have been used; but the major part of the works published in this book appear for the first time in English. The translation of medieval Russian letters presents a number of technical difficulties. Their syntax, structure, and style are very different from the methods and devices of contemporary writers. Therefore, the translation of many passages required some adaptation to the mode of expression of modern English for them to be comprehensible to readers. For the sake of those who are not well acquainted with Russian medieval history, geography, and terminology, the words "prince," "city," or "river" have been added to avoid possible confusion. Since the Russian medieval calendar was 5,508 years behind the Western one, the corresponding Western dates have been supplied where necessary.

A customarily difficult problem is that of the transliteration of Russian names. For the titles of original Russian sources the system of the Library of Congress has been used, except for the diacritical signs. In the transliteration of Russian names and terminology, the Library of Congress system underwent some minor modification: for instance, the initial Russian soft vowels rendered by *ia* or *iu* have been changed to the more readable *ya* or *yu* (that is, "Yaroslav," not "Iaroslav"); the final *ii* and *yi* have been replaced by *y* (that is, "Kurbsky" instead of "Kurbskii"); and the final *iia* has been rendered by *ia* ("Dobrynia" in place of "Dobryniia"). Most of the proper names are given in their Russian form. Those of the clergy, such as "Theodosius" or "Sergius," are usually given in their original Greek or Latin version, and those of foreign rulers and writers in their original form, while common Christian names, such as "Alexander," "Nicholas," "Andrew," or "Helen," are given in the usual English manner.

Of the works previously translated into English and incorporated in the present collection, many have been revised against the original Russian texts and their transliteration of Russian names altered for the sake of consistency. It is my pleasant duty to acknowledge my gratitude to the following publishing houses, persons, and institutions for their permission to reproduce here the material listed:

1. to Harvard University Press, Cambridge, Massachusetts, for permission to reprint passages from *The Russian Primary Chronicle*, translated by Samuel H. Cross; copyright 1930 by Harvard University Press;

2. to G. P. Putnam's Sons, New York, and London, for permission to use portions of Leo Wiener's *Anthology of Russian Literature;* copyright 1902 and 1903 by G. P. Putnam's Sons;

3. to the Editorial Board of the *Slavonic and East European Review*, London, for permission to reprint *Adam's Address to Lazarus in Hell*, translated anonymously and published in Volume X (1932), pp. 145–152; copyright 1932 by Cambridge University Press;

4. to Mr. Nicholas Zernov and The Society for the Promotion of Christian Knowledge, London, for permission to reprint *The Acts and Miracles of Our Dear and Holy Father, Sergius,* by Epiphanius the Wise, from *St. Sergius, Builder of Russia*, translated by Nicholas Zernov; copyright 1939 by The Society for the Promotion of Christian Knowledge (London);

5. to Cambridge University Press, London and New York, for permission to reprint J. L. I. Fennell's translation of Prince Andrew Kurbsky's "First Epistle to Ivan IV," from *The Correspondence between Prince A. Kurbsky and Tsar Ivan IV of Russia;* copyright © 1956 by Cambridge University Press;

6. to Miss U. M. Lane and The Hogarth Press, Ltd., London, for permission to use *The Life of Archpriest Avvakum by Himself*, translated by Jane Harrison and Hope Mirrless; copyright 1929 by L. and V. Woolf (London).

In the preparation of this volume I was assisted by students in my graduate seminar on ancient Russian literature at the University of Colorado. The Reverend George Benigsen helped in translating *The Life of Yuliania Lazarevsky*, and Mr. Dan B. Chopyk translated Bishop Serapion's *Sermon on the Merciless Heathens*. The remaining translations were made by myself in cooperation with my graduate student and assistant, Mr. Richard White. It is evident, however, that I am the only person responsible for all possible errors or shortcomings in selecting, translating, and commenting on the works in this book.

I am grateful to the Graduate School of the University of Colorado for financial help toward the completion of this volume when I was Professor of Slavic Languages and Literatures at that University.

Only I can fully appreciate the contribution made by my wife and colleague, Betty Jean, whose interest and editorial skill were so helpful in the planning and completion of *Medieval Russia's Epics, Chronicles, and Tales.*

SERGE A. ZENKOVSKY

April 10, 1963

PREFACE TO THE SECOND EDITION

THIS SECOND, revised edition of *Medieval Russia's Epics, Chronicles, and Tales* differs considerably from the first. Many works have been added, among which such important Old Russian texts as the *Instruction to His Children* of Vladimir Monomakh, the *Lives* of St. Theodosius, Alexander Nevsky, Prince Dovmont, and Dmitry Donskoy, the *Writing of Daniil the Prisoner*, the *Travels of Afanasy Nikitin*, the epic of Sukhan, one of the earliest recorded *byliny*, and several poetic works from the seventeenth century should be singled out. Whereas in the earlier edition the texts were organized primarily in chronological order and historical periods, now the governing literary school has determined the classification of the selections. The original order has been changed to accord with a new division of the texts into the literary school of the Kievan era; epigones of the Kievan school in the thirteenth and fourteenth centuries; the age of Muscovite ornamentalism; and the wane of medieval letters and beginning of the Baroque. The translations have been checked, revised, and sometimes changed substantially to agree more closely with new and better editions of the Old Russian literary "monuments."

This is a pleasant opportunity for the editor to express his gratitude to several students in his seminars on Old Russian literature at Vanderbilt University who lent their very considerable help in the preparation of this new edition of *Medieval Russia's Epics, Chronicles, and Tales*. Among them he would like particularly to thank his graduate assistant, David L. Armbruster, as well as Messrs. James Hadra, Robert Patterson, and Robert Bowie. He also thanks his wife, Betty Jean, for her editorial assistance.

Despite the generous help of these and several other persons, the editor, himself, is of course responsible for any omissions, misjudgments, errors, or inaccuracies found herein.

Since medieval Russian syntax and stylistics were very different from today's, sometimes the editor has had to supply some additional words in order to make the text more readable: these words are in brackets. In other cases some *explanatory* words were likewise added to the text: in this case these words are in parentheses.

SERGE A. ZENKOVSKY

Vanderbilt University

CONTENTS

ILLUSTRATIONS

СЛЫШАТИ ДА СЛЫ
ШИТЪ ⁙

ЦА МАРТА · СТРА
СТЫХЪ МКЪ · И

ЕVА ОТЪ МАТ ГЛА С ⁙

РЕЧЕ ГЬ ПРИТ
VЖСНИЖ ПОДО
БЬНО ЕСТЬ ЦРЬ
СТВИИ НБСЬНОЕ
VЛКОV ДОМОВН
ТОV ИЖЕ НЗИДЕ
КОVПЬНО ЗАОVТРА

A page from the Gospel of Ostromir written in 1056. It is the oldest Russian book in existence.

INTRODUCTION

The Literature of Medieval Russia

1. BEGINNINGS

THE TERM "Middle Ages" has a somewhat different connotation and time span for Russia than for Western Europe. In the West the Middle Ages began in the fifth century, when the Western Roman Empire fell under the blows of Germanic barbarians. They ended there at the close of the fifteenth century or the beginning of the sixteenth, when Columbus discovered the New World, Luther broke the spiritual unity of the West, and secularized thought put an end to the "Age of Faith." The Russian Middle Ages began much later, in the ninth century, and her Age of Faith came to an end in the late seventeenth century, when Russia adopted the secularized culture of Western Europe.

During the years that witnessed the fall of Rome, the Slavic tribes inhabiting the territory of present Russia were still in the age of prehistory. Only scattered data about the apparently Slavic "Antes" point to the inception of a loosely organized statehood in that area. Four additional centuries were needed for the appearance of a more solid national structure among the Eastern Slavs and for their emergence on the stage of history. The first indications of a firmly founded government among the Eastern Slavs, in the cities of Novgorod and Kiev, can be observed only in the ninth century when, in 862, according to legend, a certain Rurik became the prince of Novgorod. Since that time the word "Rus," or Russians, rapidly won a place in the pages of historical annals. In the tenth century the Russian prince and conqueror, Sviatoslav, built a vast empire spreading from the Volga to the Dnieper and Danube rivers, and from Kiev to Novgorod. Despite these military and political successes, however, the culture of this early Russian state remained at a modest level. Only after the Christianization of Russia in 988 or 989 by Sviatoslav's son, Vladimir, did literacy and literature appear among these Slavs, and only from that time can historians observe the first blossoming of early Russian culture.

2. CHRISTIANIZATION AND CHURCH SLAVONIC

Christianity came to Russia from Byzantium, or, as it was often called, the Eastern Roman Empire, at that time a powerful and culturally highly developed nation. Its flourishing capital, Constantinople, was still the most important political and cul-

tural center of Europe and commanded a vast empire comprising the Balkan Peninsula, the Aegean Archipelago, all of Asia
Minor, and parts of Italy. Its literary and state language was
Greek, and Byzantium, as the preserver of both Christian
thought and Greco-Roman arts and letters, was the main lumi-
nary for still "dark" Western Europe. Despite Russia's conversion
to Byzantine Christianity, however, Greek never won a position
in Russia similar to that of Latin in the West, where for centuries Latin continued to be the exclusive liturgical and educa-
tional medium for medieval Catholic Europe. Indeed, from the
very beginning of evangelization in Russia, the Mass was read
there in Slavic, not in Greek. This does not mean that the Byzantine Greeks were not nationalists. To be sure, they always placed
their language, the tongue of Homer, Plato, and the Gospel,
above all others. Still, the wealth of the native cultures of the
non-Greek provinces of Byzantium compelled them at an early
stage to permit the churches of the Middle East to use languages
other than Greek. Later, when in 863 the Moravian prince
Rostislav asked Constantinople to send missionaries for the
Christianization of his realm—which occupied the present territories of Slovakia and Hungary—the Byzantine Church did not
hesitate to permit the use of the Slavic tongue in these new
churches.

The tasks of creating an alphabet for the Slavs and forming
out of the primitive Slavic vernacular a suitable language for the
Mass and Gospel was undertaken by two brothers, Cyril and
Methodius, Greek monks from the city of Saloniki. Linguists of
genius, Cyril and Methodius created a Slavic alphabet (commonly called "Cyrillic") on the basis of the Greek one. They
translated the ecclesiastical literature into one of the dialects of
the Slavs of Macedonia, using Byzantine Greek stylistics and
syntax. This new, somewhat artificial literary language—now
called "Church Slavonic"—was Slavic in its vocabulary and grammar but rather Byzantine in its stylistic aspect.

Transplanted to Russia as a liturgical and literary language,
Church Slavonic, which was very close to Old Russian, proceeded to absorb specific features of this Eastern Slavic language.
Thus there developed a very colorful Russian literary language
composed of Church Slavonic, with its original South Slavic
linguistic features, interspersed with purely Russian characteristics. Surviving some periods of Russification, this adopted
language remained the official literary language of Russia until
the end of the seventeenth century, and the literary monuments
written in it often have an elevated, solemn, even esoteric,
coloration. As there were in medieval Russia no definite stan-

dards for the literary language, an erudite or sophisticated writer or cleric would couch his literary prose exclusively in Church Slavonic—which strongly reflected the refined and adorned stylistics of Byzantine letters—while in the same given period private correspondence, state documents, and even some simpler literary works were written in an almost pure and stylistically more naïve Old Russian vernacular. The possibilities for interweaving these two very close yet contrasting linguistic strata were innumerable and, since strict linguistic rules for the written language were established only in the eighteenth century, many Old Russian texts have a particular charm owing to a mingling of the vernacular with Church Slavonic. Unfortunately, this aspect of Old Russian literary monuments cannot be reproduced at all in translation.

3. ADVANTAGES AND LIMITATIONS OF CHURCH SLAVONIC

Most of the subsequent development of medieval Russian culture and literature was thus determined by the introduction and example of the Byzantine literary legacy in Church Slavonic translation. Initially, such adoption of a new culture in a linguistically comprehensible version offered a very considerable advantage for the Russians, who, contrary to the experience of the Catholic Germans or Poles, had not to learn a difficult foreign language, that is, Latin or Greek, in order to absorb the new religion and civilization. Byzantium's ecclesiastical, and some of its secular, literature, with all its stylistic patterns and genre models, became readily available to the Eastern Slavs in translation, and Russian letters were given a rapid start. Their beginnings appear even spectacular when compared with the literary destinies of the Western Slavs—the Czechs and the Poles —who, having been Christianized by Rome, were obliged to adopt Latin in their Mass and in their writing. Poland's first literary work in its native language did not appear until some three hundred years after its conversion to Christianity, and even five hundred years after evangelization the Poles continued to write in Latin more often than in Polish. A very similar delayed development can be observed among the Czechs. The first original Russian writings, however—some sermons by the Novgorodian and Kievan preachers, Bishop Luka Zhidiata and Metropolitan Hilarion—appeared as early as forty or fifty years after Russia's conversion. The *Primary Chronicle*, a significant work of literary, historical, and ideological interest, came into being just a little over a century after the appearance in Kiev of Christian priests and Church Slavonic manuscripts, and the *Lay of Igor's Campaign*, Russia's greatest monument in the heroic epic tradition, had already been written within two centuries after her Christianization.

The spread of Byzantine culture to Russia in its Church Slavonic versions, however, also had negative aspects. Because Russian priests officiated in Church Slavonic, they were not obliged to study Greek, so the knowledge of this language and of antique, classical, culture for centuries remained extremely limited in Russia. Although Western Europe did not forget Vergil and classical Latin even during the darkest years of its cultural dormancy—the fifth to eighth centuries—during the Russian Middle Ages knowledge of the Greek language and an acquaintance with Byzantine literature in the original was restricted to only a few representatives of the upper cultural strata. Numerous translations from Greek into Church Slavonic were made in Russia but most of these were of theological or historical works. Neither the wealth of pagan Greek literature nor the entirety of Byzantine secular writings became known to medieval Russians. The Russian clergy apparently was afraid to translate and propagate the works of pagan writers, while the Greeks themselves were not especially interested in spreading education and their cultural heritage among the Slavs. It can be surmised that Byzantium was content to keep Russia as a cultural colony not expected to attain the level of civilization of its cultural "mother country." In any case, the Greeks sent to Russia neither teachers for the purpose of forming a sophisticated cultural elite nor the works of ancient Greece. Moreover, they preferred to appoint Greeks to the head of the Russian Church rather than to prepare Russians for such positions, and did very little to raise the intellectual standard of the native Russian clergy. Thus, the humanistic, scientific, and philosophic traditions of Byzantium put down no substantial roots in Russia, and Byzantium's influence there remained limited primarily to the religious, political, and artistic spheres. The bulk of classical Greek, as well as Latin, thought and letters remained rather unknown to Russians until the late seventeenth century.

I. LITERARY SCHOOL OF THE KIEVAN ERA (ELEVENTH TO MID-THIRTEENTH CENTURY)

4. KIEVAN RUSSIA

As has been pointed out, the cultural history of Russia begins largely with its Christianization at the end of the tenth century. Although an early Russian state had existed at least since the mid-ninth century, and some scattered information concerning the national-state organization of the Russian, or Eastern, Slavs

can be traced from the seventh century after Christ, or even the
fifth (the state of the Antes), disappointingly little is known
about the life of the pagan Russians and their culture. Judging
from the quick flowering of their letters, art, and architecture
after Christianization in 988–989, it can be presumed that the
earliest contacts of the Eastern Slavs with Greece, Byzantium,
the Caucasus, and peoples of the Eurasian steppes led to the
formation in Eastern Europe of a very definite cultural type
even before Christianity and letters came there. The trade routes
from Scandinavia to Byzantium, from Central Asia and the Far
East to Western Europe, passed through the territory of this
early Russian state and certainly contributed to its cultural
growth. The city of Kiev was at the crossroads of these two
important trade routes, and its rise as the capital of a Russian
state was largely due to the prosperity brought it by merchants
who traveled to or through the city. After the Russians' conversion to Christianity at the insistence of the Kievan Prince Vladimir (ruled 980–1015), Byzantine culture in its Slavicized forms
won the dominant position among the Russians for the next
seven centuries, and the years from A.D. 1000 to 1700 can be
called the medieval period, or the era of "Byzantinized" Russia.

Kiev, itself, became one of the wealthiest and most animated
cities of medieval Europe, richer and more brilliant than Paris
or London of the time. It was adorned with innumerable
churches, and by the time of the reign of Vladimir's son, Yaroslav (ruled in Kiev 1019–1054), there were already numerous
schools, hospitals, and libraries. In the eleventh and twelfth
centuries Russia was an integral part of Europe, and Kievan
princes maintained close dynastic ties with the ruling houses of
Western countries. Their children married the sovereigns or
princesses of England, Germany, France, Sweden, Hungary,
and Byzantium. A daughter of Prince Yaroslav, Anna, married
King Philip of France and was the only literate member of the
French royal family, for whom she signed state documents herself. Prince Vladimir Monomakh (who ruled in Kiev from 1112
to 1125), the grandson of Yaroslav, married Princess Gita,
daughter of the last Anglo-Saxon king, Harold, whose family
had been obliged to abandon England after the Norman Conquest and to live as émigrés in Kiev, where there were many
foreigners. Western chronicles often mention the wealth and
beauty of this early Russian capital. The German chronicler,
Thietmar, bishop of Merseburg, remarks that during a fire over
four hundred churches burned in Kiev. The city's main cathedral,
St. Sophia (Holy Wisdom), was richly decorated with exquisite
frescoes and mosaics. A northern counterpart to Kiev was the

city of Novgorod, a natural gate to northwestern Europe. Novgorod developed its own distinct variety of architecture, painting, and writing.

The Kievan era, however, was short-lived: from the late tenth
century to the early thirteenth. Yaroslav's children and grandchildren sundered the unity of Kievan Russia by indulging in
fratricidal feuds and Vladimir Monomakh was the last Kievan
ruler to be obeyed by most of the Russian princes. After his
death the Kievan state disintegrated into a number of large and
small principalities that competed and fought with one another.
In the face of increasingly frequent raids into the South Russian
territories by Turkic nomads—Pechenegs and, later, Kumans
(Polovtsians)—the Slavic population began to migrate from the
southern area of Kiev to the forests in the north, or westward to
the plains of Galicia and the Carpathian Piedmont. The prosperous merchant city of Novgorod in the northwest, Galich—the
capital of Galicia—in the extreme southwest, and the cities of
Suzdal and Vladimir—precursors of Moscow—in the northeast
outgrew Kiev in prominence. With the conquest of the Holy
Land and Constantinople by the Crusaders, new trade routes
opened up from West to East and Kiev's importance as a trading
center rapidly diminished. The Mongol (Tatar) invasion that
took place in 1237–1240 under the leadership of the heirs of
Genghis Khan dealt the final blow to the dying Kievan state.
Kiev itself was sacked and burned, not to recover for centuries;
most other Russian cities were also devastated, and some two-
thirds of the Russian population perished. Thus weakened, most
of western and southern Russia then fell to the Lithuanians and
Poles, while the rest of Russia remained a vassal state of the
Mongol (Tatar) Empire for the following two centuries.

5. THE BYZANTINE LITERARY HERITAGE OF EARLY RUSSIA

When Russia was Christianized by Prince Vladimir, some
Christian literature and several secular Byzantine works had al-
ready been translated from the Greek into Church Slavonic
by Cyril and Methodius or by Bulgarians, who formed a powerful Slavic state in the Balkans in the ninth and tenth centuries.
Bulgaria's proximity to Byzantium stimulated both the knowledge of Greek among the Bulgarians and an active translation of
Greek works into Church Slavonic, as well as the transmission of
Byzantine literary patterns from the Greeks to the Slavs. These
South Slavic translations from Greek became the first writings
available to the Russians. Later, a considerable number of Byzantine writings were translated in Russia itself. Among the
former, of capital importance were, of course, the Gospel and

parts of the Old Testament, particularly the Psalms, which in Church Slavonic were readily understandable to all Russians who attended the Church service. Many of the liturgical texts had been composed by Byzantine theologians who were at the same time talented religious poets, such as St. John Damascene. Their aesthetic perfection, so clearly reflected in the ornate beauty of the Russian Church service itself, greatly influenced the subsequent spiritual and artistic development of the Russian people, while the stylistic and compositional influence of patristic writings on all genres of ancient Russian literature remained very great.

Among the translated literature, of prime importance also were writings of the early Christian Fathers and the "lives," or *vitae* (*zhitie*), of early Christian and Byzantine saints. Of the former, the most popular in Russia were the writings of St. John Chrysostom, which were continually translated and recopied throughout the whole seven centuries of the Russian Middle Ages. The spirit of this great Antiochian preacher of Christian social teachings influenced Russian religiosity almost as much as the Gospel itself; in any case, much more than the Old Testament, which, with the exception of the Psalms, was not often read by Russians. A collection of St. John Chrysostom's sermons, *Marguerite* (*The Pearl*), was printed in the 1630s long before the publication of the first full text of the Bible.

Saints' lives, often enhanced by fictional elements, were compiled in special collections, in which the *vitae* were arranged in the order of the calendar. They remained for centuries the most edifying reading for Russians. Even as late as the nineteenth century, Greek, Syrian, Egyptian, and Russian *vitae* found an echo in the works of Tolstoy, Dostoevsky, Leskov, Turgenev, and other Russian authors, and for early Russian writers, especially the compilers of the *vitae* of native Russian saints, translated Byzantine hagiography constituted the main source for stylistic and spiritual inspiration.

Of similar attraction for the Russian reader were the Apocrypha—writings on subjects of the Old and New Testaments not recognized by the Church as authentic or canonic, translated from Greek into Church Slavonic either in Bulgaria or in Russia. Among them the apocrypha on King Solomon—whose wisdom eclipsed for Russian minds that of Aristotle and Plato—as well as the apocryphal tale, *Descent of the Virgin into Hell,* particularly absorbed the Russian reader. The latter was apparently considerably reworked in Russia and, in its content, was something of an Eastern counterpart to Dante's *Divine Comedy.* Russians liked especially its spirit of compassion for sinners, shown by the

Holy Virgin's intercession on behalf of the souls condemned to perpetual torment. The Jobian theme of man's discontent with his fate was treated, in the form of a dialogue, in the apocryphal tale, *Adam's Address to Lazarus in Hell.* This theme was taken up some six centuries later in an autobiographical *vita* by the Monk Epiphany, a follower of the famous martyred Archpriest Avvakum.

A few works from Byzantine scholarly literature became known in Kievan and, later, in Muscovite Russia, such as the historical chronicles of John Malalas and George Hamartolas and the *History of the Jewish War* by Josephus Flavius. The style and manner of these writers were followed by the early Russian chroniclers.

Secular tales received by Russia from Byzantium included the legends of *Barlaam and Josaphat* and *Digenes Akrites,* as well as the *Alexandria.* The first, of Indian origin, gives an account of the life of Buddha, who is presented as Prince Josaphat, a fictitious Christian hero and saint. It was reworked in Byzantium and Russia many times, and in the sixteenth century a Russian hymnologist, Markel Bezborody, composed a poetic church service in honor of this prince. The legend of *Digenes Akrites* originated within the confines of Byzantium and Persia and related the heroic deeds of Christian knights fighting the infidels. Although this Byzantine forerunner of the Spanish epic of El Cid was almost the only knightly tale known to Kievan Russia, its entire romantic element was expurgated by the austere Church authorities, who were probably also responsible for the fact that none of the great works of pagan Greek literature and philosophy found its way into Old Russia. Only occasional quotations and passages from such authors can be found in early Russian miscellanies, as, for instance, *The Bee.*

Of paramount importance for the development of medieval Russian writings, also, was the native oral folk tradition. Epic tales, popular lamentations, and even anecdotes were a very early influence on Russian literature, which from the very beginning developed its own national coloration, clearly differentiated from the writings of the Byzantines or the Balkan Slavs.

6. EARLIEST RUSSIAN SERMONS AND THOUGHT

In the cultural life of every newly converted land the clergy always occupies a position of preeminence. Therefore there is nothing astonishing in the fact that the first Russian writers and learned men were predominantly representatives of the Church. In Novgorod, soon after his elevation to the bishopric there in 1036, Luka Zhidiata wrote his *Instruction,* which is usually considered the oldest dated work in Russian literature. This is a didactic, rather dry homily consisting of admonitions and reminders concerning Church ritual. It is written in very simple language and can hardly be considered an inspiring piece of rhetoric.

Of completely different intellectual and literary value is the sermon of Metropolitan Hilarion, the first Russian—not Greek—head of the Russian Church, elevated to this position in 1051 by Yaroslav the Wise. Hilarion was a well-trained theologian and skillful writer who apparently knew Greek and was well versed in Byzantine religious literature. His main work, the *Sermon on Law and Grace,* is especially pointed and convincing, and despite its elaborate allegorical language the thought is clear and readily understandable. It begins with a treatment of the problem of the spiritual superiority of the New Testament over the Old: of the teachings of Christ over the law of Moses. Hilarion then switches very astutely from this topic to the thesis of the equality of newly converted Russia with older Byzantium. He considers that Russia has gained an honorable position in the Christian world because the religion of grace, ". . . the fount of the Gospel . . . overflowed upon our land . . . and, together with all Christians, we glorify the Holy Trinity." Hilarion presents the destiny of Russia in the general framework of world history and interprets it in the light of the divine plan for the general salvation of mankind. Strangely enough, this earliest Russian metropolitan is rather a philosopher of history than a preacher of purely religious, moralistic truths, and the appearance of a thinker of such depth of historical vision in the first decades of Russian Christian history is one of the most amazing phenomena of the early development of Russian culture.

Whereas Hilarion is primarily anthropocentric, more concerned in his writings with the fate of man on earth or of the nation than with purely theological problems, Cyril of Turov, a preacher of the mid-twelfth century, is entirely theocentric. A member of a rich noble family, Cyril preferred the life of a monk to a military or court career. He subsequently became bishop, but he always remained a man of contemplation, meditating on the mystical relation between God and man. Of his numerous works, his sermons won the particular admiration of his contemporaries and of later generations. Their main concern is the problem of salvation, which he treats with great erudition and oratorical skill. Perhaps he often exaggerates in the use of complex allegories and metaphors, but it is precisely this perfect command of ornate Byzantine stylistics that lends his writing great charm and elegance. For long centuries his sermons remained the best example of elevated rhetoric in Russian literature, and Cyril can be called, without exaggerating, the greatest preacher of medieval Russia.

A rather humanistic trend in the Russian sermon was represented by the works of Metropolitan Clement, a native of Smolensk who was elected to the metropolitan see in Kiev in 1147. His contemporaries accused him of quoting more often from Plato, Aristotle, and Homer than from the Bible or the Church Fathers. The only fragment of his works that has been preserved is an impressive example of early Russian scholarship in the best Byzantine tradition. Clement's knowledge of Byzantine Greek learning seems to have been very extensive, and there is reason to believe that he completed his education not in Russia but in some Greek monastery or school.

Very close in his cultural background and spirit to these prelates of the Russian Church was Prince Vladimir Monomakh (died 1125), grandson of Yaroslav the Wise. Monomakh's father had spoken five languages, and he, himself, was well read, and left some significant writings. Among them, his *Instruction*, addressed to his children, stands out for its penetrating moral and spiritual portrayal of the author himself. The work of a wise layman, a stern though benevolent, indefatigable, and farsighted ruler, the *Instruction* was written for the practical purpose of advising his children. In his admonitions Vladimir shows himself to have a profound understanding of Christian teaching and illustrates his advice with examples from his own life. According to Monomakh, humility, contemplation, and the examination of one's own mind and life are the main instruments in the hard task of the self-perfection of a ruler. He follows the general patterns of the instructions of Byzantine and even Anglo-Saxon rulers (it may be recalled that his wife was an Anglo-Saxon princess). His ideas concerning a prince's obligations to his people and to himself are, however, original, yet appropriate to the general framework of the developing Russian spirituality: a ruler should never forget the teaching of Christ, for humility is one of the outstanding qualities of a Christian man and prince.

Among the erudite men of Kievan Russia was also a certain Daniel, styled "the Exile," who was the author of a *Supplication* written *circa* 1200 and addressed to the prince of Suzdal, Yaroslav. More adroitly than any other stylist of the dawn of Russian writing, Daniel plays gracefully with quotations from the Bible and Greek writers, Russian folk sayings, and his own pointed witticisms. Apparently intended as a petition for patronage, Daniel's *Supplication* displays his superior command of literary Church Slavonic and contemporary learning.

7. CHRONICLES

The chronicle (*letopis*) forms the most important and sizable part of Russian literature of this early era. These chronicles—or, more precisely, annals, since they consist usually of annual entries organized chronologically—contain very heterogeneous material. Along with concise entries giving in one or several lines information on a ruler or an event in a city, there can be found various historical and diplomatic documents, treaties, and admonitions, as well as longer stories about the deeds, adventures, and campaigns of a prince or the prose recordings of heroic legends. The Russian chronicles were not the product of a single author but a complex and continuously maintained work that was copied, completed, and often re-edited by successive writers. The initial Russian annals are the *Primary Chronicle*, or *The Tale of Bygone Years*—the most interesting and best written of them. There can be discerned various distinct layers in the *Primary Chronicle*, which was begun about 1040 and continued through 1118 by at least six different annalists, among whom the most remarkable were its first writer-editor, Monk Nikon, who worked on it in the 1060s, and Monk Nestor, one of its last editors and compilers, who practically completed the writing of this work. It is very difficult to determine now which of its various writers gave the chronicle its general tenor and main ideological line, but in any case this "collective" work, the compositional elements of which are so heterogeneous, still produces a very unified and sustained impression. The annalist, or annalists, consistently stress the necessity of preserving the unity of the Russian state, appeal repeatedly to the princes to give up their fratricidal feuds and live in brotherly love because they are members of the same dynasty, "brothers who have the same father and the same mother," who are supposed to preserve, not destroy, the fruits "of the heavy labor" of their forefathers. In the Prolegomenon to the *Primary Chronicle*, the annalist discusses the origin of different peoples and races, all of whom were the offspring of Noah, and succeeds in finding among them the Slavs, the descendants of Japhet, thus establishing an honorable biblical background for his own nation. Describing the legendary visit to Russia by the Apostle Andrew, the annalist does not fail to claim that this disciple of Christ predicted the forthcoming blossoming of Christianity in Russia. Very cleverly interweaving the actual fabric of historical material with legendary accounts and reminiscences, the annalist succeeds in creating a religious and political tradition for his newly emerged country, and points out that Russia has won a respectable status among the other nations of the Christian world.

A considerable amount of historical information covering the centuries preceding the rise of Russia was evidently taken from Byzantine chronicles, but it is reworked stylistically and ideologically. The very structure of the Russian annals—their chronological yearly entries—is different from that of Byzantine historical works, which are usually organized into chapters covering the reigns of the emperors.

Stories and tales integrated into the historical entries convey considerable freshness and charm to the *Primary Chronicle*. Many of these accounts, as, for instance, of the death of Prince Oleg or the revenge of Princess Olga, have a clearly legendary background and were probably taken from the epic tradition. Others have the character of actual eyewitness accounts, as, notably, the dramatic story of the blinding of Vasilko, written by Priest Vassily, or the narratives about the life of the monks of the Kievan Crypt Monastery.

The *Primary Chronicle* was the earliest and most literary, but not the only, historical work of the Kievan period. Most leading cities, as well as certain branches of the Rurik dynasty, which then ruled Russia, maintained their own annals from the twelfth century. Among these, the *Kievan Chronicle* (the continuation of the *Primary Chronicle*) and the *Galician-Volynian Chronicle* are the more skillfully written, and contain many passages that were the work of gifted writers. Most of the chronicles were written by members of the clergy, mainly monks; only the *Galician-Volynian* and perhaps the twelfth-century *Kievan* chronicles, which emphasize details of army and court life, were composed probably by a member of the princes' retinue. The northern chronicles, on the other hand, especially those of the city of Novgorod, are much drier and more concise, and are characterized by their businesslike, even abrupt, style.

The heroes of the chronicles are predominantly princes. Sometimes the chronicler mentions commanders, knights, or priests, but such characters are certainly secondary. The annalists of the Kievan Era gave simple yet impressive sculptural— even monumental, in the words of Dmitry S. Likhachev—portrayals of their hero-princes, who are divided clearly into positive characters and villains. The portrayals are frequently stereotyped: a good prince is usually described as "a good man of war," "handsome of face," "mild of habits," or "detesting wrong and loving right." The main positive attributes are defense of the Russian land, protection of the Church, and generosity toward his subjects. Few feminine figures appear in the chronicles, indeed, in general, in all of early Russian literature. Those that do are either faithful wives or affectionate mothers, but never a participant in a romantic love intrigue. Contrary to the Western tradition, Russia's austere Middle Ages do not know any amorous or erotic themes such as can be found in the *chansons* of the troubadours, not to speak of such manuals on the art of love as *De arte honesti amandi* (1170) or *La clef d'amour* (1250), which were completely unthinkable in Kievan and early Muscovite letters. No traces even of innocent romantic courtship can be found in Russian chronicles or tales until the seventeenth century. The rare exception, the tale of *Peter and Fevronia of Murom,* written in the fifteenth century, stands out strikingly in pre-seventeenth-century Russian literature for its unusual love theme, but even here the motif is one of the affection and devotion between a husband and wife. The other case with a very different theme of love can be found in the story of Moses, the Hungarian, of the Kievan Crypt *Paterikon.* Its ending is not happy at all. Moses, who was loved by a Polish woman but who did not, himself, respond to her advances, was finally castrated on her order.

8. LIVES OF SAINTS AND PATERICS

Narrative writing with extensive biographical, occasionally fictional or legendary, content can be found in Kievan literature in the *vitae* (*zhitie,* saints' lives or hagiography) and paterics (monks' lives). Although these two genres, especially the *vitae,* adhered to strict compositional patterns, they were nevertheless often embellished with interesting details mirroring medieval psychology and the author's own imagination.

The tragic fate of the Princes Boris and Gleb, sons of Vladimir, Christianizer of Russia, who were killed in 1016 in a fratricidal feud by order of their elder brother, was described in *vita* form as well as in two other narratives. Written by Nestor, one of the authors of the *Primary Chronicle,* the *vita* version of the brothers' martyrdom is most detailed and realistic, and it places the fratricide within the framework of Russian religious history. In Nestor's eyes Boris and Gleb were martyrs for peace in Russia, preferring death to participation in internecine strife. Their pathos is heightened by the touching laments Nestor puts in their mouths in anticipation of their murder. The anonymous author of the *Legend* (*Skazanie*) about Boris and Gleb emphasizes less their desire to preserve peace in Russia than their voluntary acceptance of death after the example of Christ. Meditating just before his murder, Boris recalls, "The Lord resists the proud and gives his grace to the humble." In these lines, written toward the end of the eleventh century, appears for the first time one of the leading characteristics of Russian Christianity—humility and the acceptance of fate in imitation of the deeds of Christ. This idea can be traced through subsequent Russian literature even into the early twentieth century. *Skazanie* is the best work on the martyrdom of Boris and Gleb but it is not included in this volume because of its considerable length.

Another masterpiece of early Russian hagiography is the *Life of St. Theodosius,* cofounder of the Kievan Crypt Monastery. This work, also written by Nestor, is probably his best. He furnishes not only abundant material on the life of Abbot Theodosius, which makes the *vita* a vivid and realistic narrative, but also tries to convey the religious philosophy of this great Russian saint: simplicity in life, humility of attitude before God and people, and Theodosius' gentle, loving care toward the monks and his spiritual children.

The early *vitae* and stories of the paterics have many structural features in common, and usually consist of a number of episodes loosely woven into one continuous narrative. Although both were intended as edifying religious literature for the Christian education of their readers, their final purposes are, however, different. The *vita* is the devotional biography of a saint, explaining his role in the development of Orthodox saintliness and the religious mind, and giving the reason for his canonization. It is always solemn, often begins and ends with a prayer or hymn, and, much more than the pateric narrative, stresses the spiritual aspect of its hero's life. The *vitae* were traditionally constructed according to a stereotyped pattern, with the ideal of sainthood outweighing an accurate presentation of the details of the saint's actual life, since the aim of the hagiographer was not to present the life story itself but rather the saintly example, for the edification of believers. The stories of the paterics, on the other hand, were instructive tales about the lives of monks, many of whom were never canonized. The pateric described the life and deeds of the monks of a given monastery, and consequently the name of the monastery was usually included in the title.

These two genres are not always clearly distinguishable, and some biographies of noncanonized monks are very similar to the hagiographic *vitae.* Toward the end of the Russian Middle Ages the *vita* lost its strict hagiographic purpose and developed into a new genre of secular biography. The narratives of the pateric, likewise, gradually assumed the form of a not strictly religious short story. Both the *vitae* and paterics were the most popular reading of medieval Russia, and innumerable versions of the lives of Russian saints were written and rewritten from the eleventh through the seventeenth centuries. Together with Byzantine paterics and hagiography, they formed the major part of the libraries of Russian monasteries and of private collections, since they were the medieval equivalent of modern short stories and novels and intermingled descriptions of everyday life, edification, and sometimes even ebullient Oriental fantasy.

9. HEROIC EPICS

The greatest literary work of Kievan Russia is the *Lay of Igor's Campaign* (*Slovo o polku Igoreve*), which describes an unsuccessful raid by Russian princes against the nomadic Turkic tribe of Kumans, who, in the twelfth and thirteenth centuries, inhabited the plains north of the Black Sea. This raid, which took place in 1185 under the leadership of Igor, Prince of Novgorod-Seversk, became the subject of the only epic and purely poetic work of Kievan Russia, written probably within a year or two after Igor's return from Kuman captivity.

Against the rather uniform and undiversified background of the chronicles and religious literature of the Kievan period, the *Lay of Igor's Campaign* stands out as an exceptional specimen of strictly secular poetic letters. Its lyric pathos, rich imagery and symbolism, noble national spirit and pagan references contrast strikingly with the rest of the preserved wealth of early Russian literature. Literary historians usually classify the *Lay* as a typical example of epic poetry, but its loose structure, lyric and rhetorical digressions, and the author's addresses to his audience rather suggest its classification as a work of mixed genre in which the epic content is strongly diluted by lyric digressions and allusive admonitions.

The origins of the Russian epic tradition still remain in darkness despite decades of intensive research. Since the end of the eighteenth century a tremendous wealth of Russian epic songs, the *byliny*, have been discovered and collected. Much of this epic folklore deals with the time of Kievan Russia and the court of Prince Vladimir, "the bright sun," Christianizer of Russia, and his valorous knights—Ilia Muromets, Alyosha Popovich, Dobrynia Nikitich, and many others—who formed around Vladimir a Russian counterpart of King Arthur's Round Table. Scholars, however, cannot agree in their estimates on the actual age of the *byliny*. Indeed, Dobrynia was the real uncle of Vladimir, and is well known from the chronicles. The name of Ilia, "the Russian knight" or "cousin of Vladimir," can be found in Scandinavian and Lombardian epics penned as early as the eleventh and twelfth centuries. Moreover, while the oldest Russian work containing a reference to the *byliny* epics and their heroes dates only from the sixteenth century, the narrative parts of the *Primary Chronicle* itself, as well as such later works as, for instance, the *Tale of the Destruction of Riazan*, show very definite traces of the epic tradition. Hence, it is possible to assume that the Russian epic tradition goes back as far as the time of Kievan Russia, although its exact form and poetic devices can hardly be determined at the present stage of scholarship. It may only be surmised that at the time when the *Lay of Igor's Campaign* was written, the Russian poetic and epic tradition already had rather deep roots, especially since the *Lay* refers to the songs of a former bard, Boyan, who previously glorified the valor of Russian princes.

The subject and treatment of the *Lay* may be compared to some extent with the French *Chanson de Roland*. Both have for their topics a Christian army's fight for the honor of its country and its defeat by non-Christian, Moslem or pagan warriors. Both treat nature as an almost animate participant in the military and national drama. Also, both use fixed epithets extensively in characterizing their heroes. Recently Professor Roman Jakobson showed the *Lay*'s similarity to its contemporary Western counterpart in the use of pagan, pre-Christian motifs. He also showed the similarity of the poetic devices of the *Lay* to those studied and described by the Byzantine scholar Choiroboskos, whose treatise on poetic tropes and figures had been known in Russia since 1073. In view of these parallels with West European and Byzantine writings, it is possible to state that the *Lay* did not evolve exclusively from the Russian epic tradition but might also have been influenced by the general poetic environment of Western Europe and the Balkans, with which Russia was so closely connected at that time. In any event, the *Lay of Igor's Campaign* will probably continue to be an enigma for many more generations of scholars because it remains a unique specimen of unusually high quality in Kievan poetics.

The narrative part of the *Lay* is not very developed. Instead of reporting in detail the successive stages and episodes of the campaign, the author really only alludes to events and persons supposedly familiar to his audience or readers. Instead of communicating the minutiae of the battle, he impresses on his audience his own sorrow over the Russians' defeat and his desire to see Russia once again powerfully united in order to prevent further national calamity. The work strongly mirrors Russia's and the author's sorrow over the princes' feuds, their perpetual warring, and the political decline of Russian power.

The narrative structure given the *Lay* by its author, whose intent was apparently not so much to narrate as to warn his contemporaries of the perilous consequences of princely feuding, differs from that of most Western or later Russian epic works, whose usual purpose is to recall past deeds and glory. This might be explained by the fact that the *Lay* was composed almost immediately after Igor's stunning defeat, while the episodes of the campaign were still vividly preserved in the reader's memory.

The *Lay of Igor's Campaign* did not considerably influence Russian literature in the next decades and centuries. It was too different from the generally functional, didactic, and religious tenor of the other writings of the newly Christianized Russians. Its reference to the pagan Slavic gods, moreover, probably seemed to the clergy too hazardous to warrant any wide circulation, and the topic of defeat could not have been particularly popular among the princes, especially since in the very near future the relatively minor misfortunes of Igor's campaign were vastly overshadowed by a catastrophe of immensely greater magnitude. Therefore, it is not too surprising that the *Lay* was preserved only in a single manuscript and that only one other medieval Russian poetic work definitely reflects the strong stylistic and structural influence of the *Lay of Igor's Campaign*. This is *Zadonshchina*, written two hundred years later on the occasion of the first major Russian victory, in 1380, over the nomads, Russia's historical enemy.

II. EPIGONES OF THE KIEVAN SCHOOL (MID-THIRTEENTH TO FOURTEENTH CENTURY)

10. THE MONGOL INVASION

The foreboding of the author of the *Lay of Igor's Campaign* and his apprehensions for Russia's future were soon justified by historical events. In 1223 the vanguards of Genghis Khan's Mongol army, after a successful Caucasian campaign, unexpectedly crossed the Don River and inflicted a crushing defeat on regiments of the South Russian princes at the Kalka River. At this time the Mongols did not proceed to the conquest of Eastern Europe but crossed the Volga and disappeared into the Central Asian plains. In 1237, however, exactly half a century after the writing of the *Lay*, the Mongol hordes reappeared on the Volga and in the following three years subjugated and devastated all of Russia.

It might have been expected that the Mongol, or Tatar, Yoke

("Tatar" was the name of one of the Mongolian tribes of the Horde but became applied by the Russians to all of these Asian nomads) would leave a widespread influence on Russian culture and letters. Apart from the fact that Russian civilization was set back two centuries, however, this was not the case. Russian spiritual, artistic, and literary development remained entirely immune to the culture of these illiterate horsemen, and only a few political and military patterns of the Mongol Empire modified the previous Russian organizational forms. The Asian nomads—cattlemen and shepherds—did not settle in the Russian territories, but preferred the nearly uninhabited plains and grazing lands of the eastern and southern confines of present Russia to the forests and marshes of its central and northern parts, where most of the Slavic population lived. The tremendous differences in language, religion, and way of life between the sedentary Christian Slavs and the pagan (only subsequently Moslem) Asian nomads prevented the Russians from indulging in any widespread contacts with their conquerors, and there were few intermarriages between Russians and Tatars in the Middle Ages.

The century following the invasion was one of marked cultural decline but hardly of any perceptible changes in the basic features of Russian civilization. Monasteries and palaces had been burned and the cultural elite decimated or abducted into slavery, but the surviving representatives of the Russian clergy and aristocracy managed to preserve the essential elements of Russia's cultural heritage, although they were hardly able to develop them. The cultural decline was further intensified by the conquest of western Russia by Poles and Lithuanians and the splitting up of Russian territories under the Mongols into innumerable small principalities that competed and fought among themselves. Only northern Russia, the republic of wealthy Novgorod, preserved the integrity of its immense territory, and the city itself became the center for burgeoning new forms in the arts, especially of architecture and painting.

11. MILITARY TALES

Although no stylistic changes are perceptible in Russian writings of the first century after the Mongol conquest, their topics clearly evidence whether they were written before or after the collapse of Kievan Russia. One of the most popular subjects for thirteenth-century works was, of course, the Tatar invasion and therefore the military tale—already well known in Kievan literature, as seen from the *Lay of Igor's Campaign* and the chronicles—now became much more widespread. Of the new ones, two, the *Orison on the Downfall of Russia* and the *Tale of the Destruction of Riazan,* give an exceptionally artistic treatment of the invasion and the feelings of its survivors.

Still enigmatic in its origin, the *Orison on the Downfall of Russia* seems to be only an introduction to some now lost longer work. It speaks of the previous grandeur and glory of the realm founded by Vladimir and Yaroslav and is highly pathetic, but, unfortunately, the preserved fragments end exactly with the words that begin a description of the catastrophe.

Tales of the capture of various cities are poignant and numerous. Riazan, a city in the extreme southeast of Kievan territory, was the first to fall to the Tatar armies, and the description of its destruction is the most dramatic account of this type. The *Tale of the Destruction of Riazan* is a complex work in which four separate episodes and various genres are interwoven. The episode dealing with Evpaty Kolovrat, a *bogatyr* (knight) who challenged the Mongol army, has strong motifs of the oral epos, and is no less impressive than Western tales of heroic knightly deeds. Folklore elements can also be found in the laments of the princes. The narrative is considerably more vivid and dynamic than that of the *Lay of Igor's Campaign* or of earlier military tales. While some of the symbols and tropes have a close connection with those of the *Lay,* however, the *Tale* is far behind the *Lay* in its poetic and stylistic excellence. The dominant idea of the *Tale* is the juxtaposition of the Christian Russian army to the Tatar "infidels," and more than any other work of early Russian literature the *Tale* conveys the concept of Russia as the bulwark of Christian civilization against the hordes of pagan Central Asian nomads. Other military tales of the time deal with the conquest of Kiev and of other Russian cities that fell to the Tatars, as well as the first battle, in 1223, between Russians and Mongols on the Kalka River.

During these difficult years the Tatars were not the only conquerors of Russian lands. Poles and Lithuanians succeeded in occupying extensive regions in the west, from the Neman to the Dniester rivers and from the Carpathian Mountains to Kiev and Smolensk. German knights of the Livonian Order took over present Latvia and Estonia and pushed against the ancient city of Pskov. Swedes appeared on the Nevá River, attacking the confines of the territory of Novgorod. The defense of this northern border is the subject of many episodes of the *Life of Prince Alexander Nevsky* (called "Nevsky" for his defeat of the Swedes on the Nevá River). In the manuscripts his *vita* usually follows the *Orison on the Downfall of Russia,* and some scholars even believe that the *Orison* was intended as an introduction to the

life of this courageous prince who was so largely responsible for
Russia's gradual rehabilitation after the Tatar conquest. Alexander, who died in 1263, was canonized primarily for his devotion to the cause of the Russian land and Church rather than for
exceptional spirituality. Therefore, his *vita* is more a work of
secular biography incorporating military tales than a piece of
hagiography. The author widely used biblical portrayals and
stylistics in Alexander's *Life*, and treated many events in the
manner of the Byzantine chronicles and military stories. Alexander is compared to Roman emperors and biblical patriarchs.
The *Life* ends with a touching miracle: when, during Alexander's
burial, the metropolitan wanted to put in Alexander's hand a
parchment remitting his sins, in accordance with Church ritual,
the dead hero extended his hand to take it.

The defense of Pskov against the Lithuanians forms the background of the *Narrative of the Pious Prince Dovmont and His
Courage*, written in the thirteenth century, while the miraculous deliverance of the city of Smolensk from the Tatars is
related in *The Heroic Deeds of Mercurius of Smolensk*, written
in the fourteenth, or even fifteenth, century. In no other Russian
military tale does the miraculous element play such importance
as in this story, which is treated in the hagiographic manner:
beheaded by the Tatars, Mercurius returns to the city he had
saved, holding his severed head in his hands.

The great battle in 1380 at the Don River, where the Russians
inflicted their first decisive defeat upon the Tatars toward the
end of the Tatar Yoke, supplied rich material for several literary
works. *Zadonshchina* (*The Deeds Beyond the Don*), the best
known of these, written by Sofony of Riazan, is to a large extent
patterned after elements of the *Lay of Igor's Campaign*. Indeed,
Sofony appropriated many of the compositional and poetic devices of the *Lay*, and in places *Zadonshchina* adheres almost
literally to the figures of speech and symbolism of the *Lay of
Igor's Campaign*. Like the author of the *Lay*, Sofony had re-
course to poetic generalization rather than to a minute description of the details of battle and let the lyric laments of Russian
women express the sorrow of the Russian land at the losses suffered by the Russian army. Still, the narrative of *Zadonshchina*
is somewhat more detailed, realistic, and sustained in plot than
the great twelfth-century Russian lay. Its spirit is entirely Christian and it lacks the pagan tendencies of the former. Although
not so adept poetically, Sofony was no less skillful in expressing
his ideas than was the anonymous bard of Kiev. Both gave voice
to Russia's hopes, sorrows, and expectations: the *Lay* deplored

the princes' disunity; *Zadonshchina* praised their successful united effort to cast off the foreign yoke.

Two other works that treat the same Russian victory, less poetic but more informative than *Zadonshchina,* are the *Tale of the Battle on the Don* in the *Simon* and *Ermolinsky* chronicles and the *Legend* (*Skazanie*) of the *Rout of Mamai* (khan of the Tatar Horde). In the latter are some beautiful, highly poetic descriptions of the Russian army and of the night preceding the battle.

With *Zadonshchina* the era of the Kievan tradition in Russian literature came to a close. During the cultural revival that ensued in Russia in the late fourteenth and fifteenth centuries, new problems, topics, and literary methods came to the fore.

12. CHRONICLES OF THE FOURTEENTH AND EARLY FIFTEENTH CENTURIES

The writing of annals was almost completely interrupted by the Mongol invasion. Kiev and Vladimir, Russia's northern capitals, were so thoroughly sacked by the invaders that cultural life there was entirely suspended. Therefore the main chronicles of the thirteenth and fourteenth centuries are those of Novgorod, Tver', and Rostov; in the fourteenth century, when Moscow arose as a new political rival, chronicle-writing also commenced there and the transfer of the Russian metropolitan see to Moscow in 1325 made out of this previously insignificant princedom an important religious and cultural center. The Muscovite chronicles of the late fourteenth and early fifteenth centuries—the *Simon* and *Trinity* (*Troitsky*) chronicles—include the ancient *Primary Chronicle,* and use widely the annals of such other cities as Novgorod, Smolensk, Riazan, Tver', and others. They cultivate insistently the idea of Russian reunification under the aegis of the Muscovite prince, but the fact that they are only compilations necessarily deprives them of inner unity and of the stylistic uniformity that characterizes the *Primary, Kievan,* and *Galician-Volynian* chronicles, and they often grow into tremendous codices since they were supposed to contain ever-growing new material besides the wealth of early historical information. Although the chronicler's task became increasingly difficult in these centuries, he continued to work according to the originally elaborated methods: yearly entries and the inclusion of heterogeneous material. Among the codices of the era the most important are the *Laurentian,* written in 1377 for Great Prince Dmitry of Suzdal and Nizhny Novgorod; the *Hypatian,* compiled in the early fifteenth century; and the *Radzivil,* or *Königsberg,* completed in the late fifteenth century and given by Prince J.

Radzivil to the Königsberg library. All of these contain the entire text of the *Primary Chronicle* and rich later material.

III. ERA OF MUSCOVITE ORNAMENTAL FORMALISM (FIFTEENTH TO BEGINNING OF THE SEVENTEENTH CENTURY)

13. LIVES OF SAINTS

At the end of the fourteenth century Russian letters came
under the influence of a new spiritual and literary movement
that had arisen among the monks of Byzantium and the Balkan Slavic states. The participants in this movement, who called
themselves "Hesychasts" (from *hesychia*—quietude, silence, indirectly, contemplation), taught self-perfection and domination
of the passions. According to their views, a believer could
achieve direct vision of the Divine Light, a visual contemplation
of the Creator. This teaching, which to a large extent was
conditioned by renunciation of the passions and the pleasures
of this world, led its followers away from the realities of this
life and resulted in the field of literature in the development
of a highly artificial and rhetorical style. At first primarily in-
fluencing hagiography, in the fifteenth and sixteenth centuries
this style spread to other types of writing. For a Hesychast
writer, not the recorded biography but the ideal truths of the
saints' lives were important. Their *vitae* depict not the everyday
deeds of the heroes but rather the supreme truths and eternal
significance of the saints' actions. Like the modern impressionist
or even contemporary abstract painter, the writer conveyed a
portrayal of the saint as he visualized him and not as he necessarily was.

In their search for a medium worthy of describing spiritual
perfection, the Byzantine and Balkan Slavic Hesychasts developed a highly ornate language. Its elements were bookish words,
compounds (*composita*) consisting of two or three words, complex syntactical structure with a multitude of subordinate clauses,
numerous epithets, repetition of the same sound at the beginning of each rhythmic unit of the sentence, and archaic grammatical forms. These devices conveyed to the *vita* an especially
elevated and solemn tone. Many of these stylistic methods can
be found in the earlier Byzantine and Slavic works, but rarely
if ever before can such heavy ornamentation be observed as in
this period.

Callistos (Patriarch of Constantinople from 1350 to 1363) was
the first writer to apply widely this formal, sophisticated, and

ornate style which, from Byzantium, spread to Serbia and Bulgaria and, at the beginning of the fifteenth century, to Russia. The Balkan Slavic writers of this period considerably reformed their literary language by reviving outlived ancient grammatical forms of Church Slavonic. When the Hesychast literary vogue came to Russia, it also became instrumental there in restoring to the literary language the archaic Church Slavonic grammar and phonetics. This "neo-Byzantine" literary influence in Russia, whose duration is referred to as the second Balkan, or South Slavic, period in Russian literature, dislodged from Russian letters purely East Slavic vernacular forms, renewing the archaic Church Slavonic. The outstanding Russian representative of this new ornamental formalism, which Russians termed "weaving of words," was Epiphanius, called "the Wise" (died in 1422). His masterpieces were the well-known *Lives* of St. Sergius and St. Stephen, evangelizer of Perm, a Finnic region west of the Urals. Despite his rich stylistics, Epiphanius successfully conveys a realistic portrayal of the saints, adorned with prayers, eulogies, and laments, and his writings remained for some two centuries the most imitated specimens of the formal, ornamental style in Russia. In the mid-fifteenth century his work was continued by Pachomius the Serb, an émigré from the Balkans who reworked some of Epiphanius' *vitae* and composed numerous new ones.

Ornamental formalism reigned in Russian literature until the seventeenth century. Not all the literary works of these two centuries were written in this style, but it became almost compulsory in hagiography, sermons, and historical writings. The result was the transformation of the *vita* into a uniform enumeration of the saint's virtues, and lengthy eulogies that frequently completely overshadowed the actual story of his life. In the mid-sixteenth century Metropolitan Macarius, tutor and adviser of the young Ivan IV, undertook a compilation (*Chetyi Minei*) of the finest works in Russian spiritual literature, and at that time a great many *vitae* were reworked according to the exigencies of ornamental formalism.

Side by side with the erudite writers of rhetorical *vitae* and chronicles, however, there were other writers of the late fourteenth and fifteenth centuries who used a simple, almost vernacular, language without any particular embellishment. A good example of such unsophistication and even naïve narration are the early versions of the *vita* of St. Michael of Klopsko (its later versions were reworked by the Muscovite writers of ornamental style) in which the hagiographer concentrates on interesting episodes in the saint's life rather than on epithets and eulogies.

Also in the same unadorned, yet expressive, language is the *vita*-tale of Prince Peter of Murom and his wife, Fevronia. This is the rare medieval Russian literary work with some romantic content, and it supplies many everyday details from the life of these saint-spouses. Fevronia, a peasant girl by origin, is placed against the background of rural life. The composition of this narrative is complex, containing legendary folklore motifs interwoven with the narrative. This charming story, which ends with a description of the hero's and heroine's death and posthumous miracles, may be considered a Russian counterpart of the Western legend of Tristan and Isolde.

14. POLITICAL LEGENDS AND TALES

From the mid-fourteenth to the mid-fifteenth century two principalities, Tver' and Moscow, competed for supremacy and attempted to unify around themselves the central regions of Russia on the upper Volga and Oka rivers. The victor was Moscow, which subjugated Tver' and won leadership over all central Russia. The subsequent unification of all of Great Russia was completed in 1478, when Ivan III (1462–1505), the founder of Muscovite power, forced Novgorod also to accept the suzerainty of Moscow.

Eager to justify their claims to the political leadership of Russia, the Muscovite dynasty and its ideologists elaborated, according to the medieval tradition, a number of political legends, most of which had their origin in Byzantine and Western historical myths. Among them, the *Legend of the Babylonian Kingdom* and the *Legend of the Princes of Vladimir* propagated the idea that only a powerful ruler could guarantee the security of the nation. The latter legend aimed, moreover, at providing the Muscovite princes with a respectable genealogy: according to this legend, the Muscovite dynasty descended not only from half-mythical Rurik but had its origins much deeper in history— its founder was said to be Prus, a wholly imaginary brother of the Roman Emperor Augustus.

The narrow purpose of the Muscovite political legends—to establish the prestige of the Muscovite dynasty and gain support for its political claims—to a large extent limited their circulation and popularity. More widely read was the Novgorodian *Tale of the White Cowl*. Novgorod, Moscow's main adversary, also sought historical tradition in defending its independence and republican institutions against encroachment by the Muscovite princes. The central idea of this tale is Russia's selection by God as the defender of Orthodoxy: the final kingdom of the Holy Spirit, which will replace both the Old Testamentary kingdom of law and the New Testamentary kingdom of grace, would become manifest in the Russian land. Novgorod and its archbishop are singled out in this legend as the heirs to one of the most sacred symbols of pure Christianity, the White Cowl, the possession of which endowed this old republican city with spiritual superiority and placed it on a level with Moscow in the sphere of Church tradition. The *Tale of the White Cowl* became particularly popular in the seventeenth century and had a profound influence on the subsequent development of Russian ideology. In connection with this legend there arose in the early sixteenth century the theory of Moscow, the Third Rome. This concept, however, differed considerably from that of the *Tale of the White Cowl*, which taught that the entire people of Russia, not only Moscow and its ruler, bore historical responsibility for the guardianship of true Orthodoxy.

15. NEW MILITARY TALES

In 1478 Ivan III, by annexing the tremendous territory of the Republic of Novgorod, completed the main stage of the unification of Russia, which for centuries had remained divided into small feudal principalities. Two years later the Russians shook off forever the Tatar Yoke, and the Golden Horde disintegrated. Some seventy years later, in 1547, Ivan IV was crowned the first Tsar of Russia by the wise and erudite Metropolitan Macarius. Feudal Russia, with its endless fratricidal feuds and princely warring, was replaced by one, powerful, unified autocratic state. This process of unification and the rise of autocracy required considerable military effort to preserve the new unity and defend the young tsardom, as well as the further elaboration of a new political philosophy justifying this newborn power. It is therefore understandable that throughout the late fifteenth and sixteenth centuries, during the reigns of Ivan III (1462–1505), Vassily III (1505–1533), and Ivan IV (1533–1584), Russian literature was dominated by two basic genres: the military tale and political polemics.

In the late fifteenth century there appeared a new type of military tale—narratives about the siege and defense of fortresses or cities. One of the first of these was the *Tale of the Taking of Constantinople*, which fell to the Turks in 1453. It was written by a certain Nestor Iskander, a professional Russian soldier who had been captured by the Turks, forced to accept Islam, and to join the Ottoman army. He was a writer of considerable talent, and, as an eyewitness, colorfully described the siege and storming of the city. Although he is highly rhetorical, he nonetheless conveys a detailed picture of the battles. His original narrative was apparently reworked by some Muscovite writer who added an ideological introduction and a conclusion: after the conquest of the Balkans and the fall of the capital of Orthodoxy, Russia was to take over the role of protector of Orthodoxy and become responsible for its fate.

The siege of the Tatar capital, Kazan, which was taken in 1552 by Russian troops under Ivan IV, supplied the topic for two very different narratives on the subject. One, the *Kazan History,* was written in the 1560s by an anonymous Russian who, similarly to Nestor Iskander, became prisoner of the Tatars and spent two decades in Moslem captivity. He observed the military operations from within the city, on the Tatar side, and after the Russians' victory joined Ivan's army. His work, besides depicting the siege, covers an extensive period of time, studies Russo-Tatar relations, the life of Russians in Tatar captivity, and the preparations for war. His literary devices are patterned considerably after Iskander's tale. Although he depicts the heavy fighting and storming of Kazan in long and ornate sentences, he provides very lively descriptions. Particularly impressive is his account of the tsar's return to Moscow and the capital's jubilation. Another treatment of the same siege was given by Prince Andrew Kurbsky, one of Ivan's commanders, in his *History of Tsar and Grand Prince Ivan Vassilievich.* Kurbsky is much more matter of fact, and uses the rich stylistics of his era with considerable economy.

The *Story of Stephen Bathory's Campaign Against Pskov* exceeds all previous military tales in the extended employment of intricate, ornamented stylistics, allegory, metaphors, and epithets. The author belonged to a particularly sophisticated current in Russia letters, and had perfect command of all the subtleties of ornamental formalism. The use of compound words, figures of speech, and elaborate sentences makes this tale one of the best specimens of the heavy, embellished style of early Muscovite literature.

From the late fifteenth century there developed in Russia a new type of historical work, the so-called chronograph, in which the material was organized into article-chapters in place of the customary yearly entries and in which surveys of world events were usually included along with events in Russian history. They were written in the new ornamental style with heavy panegyrics to the rulers and Church leaders, a style that spread to the chronicles themselves, whose compilation continued into the late seventeenth century.

16. POLEMIC LITERATURE

Beginning in the early fifteenth century, polemics on theological and political problems form a prominent part of Russian letters of the early Muscovite era. The first polemic arose over the heresy of the Strigolniks, a movement for Church reform that denied the necessity of some sacraments and of an ordained clergy and that grew very strong in Pskov and Novgorod around 1400. A century later appeared the rationalistic Judaizers, who to some extent followed the teachings of the Strigolniks but also denied veneration of icons and the dogma of the Trinity, thus preceding by half a century the emergence of the West European Unitarianism of Servetus and Socinius. This movement spread to Moscow, and Ivan III himself was strongly suspected of being a secret sponsor of the sect. In any case, the main opponent of the Judaizers, Abbot Joseph of Volok, who finally won the struggle and succeeded in destroying the movement, clearly hinted at the "pernicious" role in Church affairs played by Ivan III, the founder of Russian political unity. The lively polemics for and against the heresy of the Judaizers lasted several decades and produced a number of important works.

The struggle against the Judaizers was not yet over when a new conflict arose between the supporters and opponents of monastic estates. Joseph of Volok once again came out forcefully in favor of the estates of the monasteries, which he called "the wealth of the poor" and which in his eyes were fundamental for maintaining and educating the clergy as well as for the Church's social work. In Joseph's opinion the Church was responsible for the souls and well-being of believers and was supposed to take the necessary action for preserving their spiritual condition. His adversaries were the contemplative hermit-elders from the hermitages of northern Russia beyond the Volga, who taught that the Church's wealth leads to corruption of the clergy and diverts the attention of the monks from their spiritual tasks. They opposed Church intervention in the inner life of believers, and considered that only a Christian's personal action may lead to his salvation. Their leader, Nil Sorsky, a pupil of the Greek Hesychasts, insisted that the way to God can be found only through suppression of the passions, self-perfection, and a believer's individual effort to understand and follow the divine commandments. His teaching had some common points with Western Protestantism. He stressed primarily the importance of faith for salvation and to some extent de-emphasized ritualism and the mediatory role of the priesthood. The polemics between the followers of Joseph, called the "Josephites," and the Trans-Volga elders was largely a discus-

sion of the necessity for discipline and the enforcement of
Church law against spiritual freedom and an individual approach
to God.

In the 1550s there arose in Moscow and northern Russia still
another religious movement, this time under the very definite
influence of the Western Reformation. Like the previous non-
conformist sects, its leader disputed the value of the sacraments
and the Church hierarchy. This new threat to Orthodoxy, however, was rapidly liquidated and did not leave many traces in
Russian spirituality. The controversies around these various
teachings led to the growth of a prolific polemic literature
which, although neither fictional nor even particularly artistically
written, is nonetheless an important witness to an intense
spiritual and intellectual life in the first century of the Muscovite
era.

Purely political polemics are best seen in the *Story of Sultan
Mehmed*, by Ivan Peresvetov, and in the correspondence between Ivan IV ("the Terrible") and Prince Andrew Kurbsky. In
his story, written about 1550, Peresvetov describes conditions in
Russia under the guise of those in the Ottoman Empire, and
argues against the excessive power of the boyar aristocracy. He
was a firm supporter of autocracy, in which he saw the best
instrument for consolidating national power: "When the Tsar is
gentle and weak, his Tsardom declines and his glory diminishes.
When the Tsar is dread and wise, his Tsardom grows and his
name is glorified on the earth," writes Peresvetov. It can be considered that the autocratic rule of Ivan IV was to a certain extent
the result of Peresvetov's writings, in which the latter suggested
breaking the power of the feudal lords.

Prince Andrew Kurbsky represented a completely different
viewpoint. He defended the political role of princes, boyars, and
the aristocracy in general, which he regarded as the bearer of
national stability, conservatism, and wisdom. According to
Kurbsky, autocratic rule necessarily leads to excesses, and a
proud ruler becomes instrumental in the decline of his nation. A
well-trained dialectician and writer, Kurbsky cleverly and con-
vincingly presents his views in his correspondence with Ivan
IV. He appeals to the tsar to cease persecuting the aristocracy
and to pardon the victims of his wrath. Ivan was hardly less
erudite than the prince, but he did not command his passions
and pen as well, and exploded in vituperative replies to Kurbsky,
his former friend and commander in chief of the Russian armies.
Ivan is sarcastic and biting, and does not shun using the most
offensive language in speaking of his enemies. The tsar's strong-
est argument is the boyars' misrule, which he describes in

recollecting his childhood. Whereas Kurbsky is always concise and to the point, Ivan is verbose, accumulating one argument after another to prove his views. Very different in their respective styles, Prince Kurbsky and Tsar Ivan are certainly the most outstanding of Russian sixteenth-century polemists, and their letters are the best example of the Muscovite epistolary art.

17. ENCYCLOPEDIC WORKS

The greatest literary undertaking of the reign of the dread Tsar Ivan IV were the encyclopedic compilations of various types of Russian writings, initiated and conducted under the supervision of Macarius, Metropolitan of Moscow from 1530? to 1554. The most important of these works were the *Reading Meneae* (*Chetyi Minei*), a collection of *vitae* and other spiritually edifying readings arranged for each calendar day. Altogether, there are in these *Meneae* some thirteen thousand folio pages, the equivalent of thirty or forty modern volumes; most of the existing *vitae* were rewritten for this new compilation in the official style of ornamental formalism.

The other encyclopedic work, written in the same ornamental manner, was the *Book of Generations* (*Stepennaia kniga*), an extensive rewriting of the chronicles and chronographs in which special attention was paid to the biographies of Russian rulers. The main literary interest presented by this historical work consists in the small stories and anecdotes incorporated in them (often taken from oral folklore), which herald the nascence of the fictional short story. Both of these works abound in neological compounds, epithets, and long rhetorical constructions.

The third important encyclopedic work of this time was the *Nikon Illustrated Codex of Chronicles,* a monumental historical encyclopedia covering not only Russian but also world history as far as it was known to sixteenth-century Muscovites. It consists of twelve enormous volumes richly illustrated with over ten thousand miniatures.

The completion of these catenae apparently exhausted the energies of Russian writers of the late Byzantine tradition and the talent of the ornamental formalists. After codifying and rewriting nearly all of previous Russian literature in these series, it was difficult and almost purposeless to invent any new sophistications in the adorned and heavy style. Thus, the *Reading Meneae, Book of Generations,* and *Illustrated Codex* became the final monuments of the period of prevalent Byzantine domination over Russian literature. Although ornamental stylistics lasted into the seventeenth century, undergoing a final blossoming from 1615 to 1630, new currents and literary genres began to appear.

This last century of the undisputed domination of medieval
stylistics over Russian writing was simultaneously the last century of the Rurik dynasty, which, according to legend, had
ruled in Russia since 862. After the death of Ivan IV, his son,
the last offspring of this dynasty—Tsar Theodore—reigned for
some fifteen years, but with his death in 1598 the Rurik dynasty
was extinguished. During the following fifteen years (1598-
1613), called the "Time of Troubles" (*Smuta*), Russians witnessed four legitimate tsars from three new dynasties, two tsar-
impostors, grave social disturbances, the breakdown of central
government and foreign intervention, all of which brought the
nation to the verge of another complete catastrophe. Only in
1613 was a new tsar, Michael (ruled 1613–1645), elected. Tsar
Michael was the first of the Romanov dynasty, which reigned for
the next 304 years, disappearing only with the revolution of
1917. His task was to rehabilitate the state, put an end to Polish
and Swedish intervention, and bring social order to the nation.
These tasks were fairly soon accomplished and order restored,
but Russian culture and letters survived this historical trial
considerably changed.

IV. THE WANE OF MEDIEVAL PATTERNS AND RISE OF
THE BAROQUE (SEVENTEENTH CENTURY)

Erosion of the traditional medieval patterns in ancient Russian literature becomes perceptible from the second part of the
sixteenth century. In historical works authors tend to prefer
narration of the mythical legend in the manner of the Polish
chroniclers to the down-to-earth style of early Russian annalists.
Prose becomes more and more frequently interspersed with
fragments of rhymed couplets. Job, Russia's first patriarch (from
1589 to 1605), included even in his *vita* of Tsarevich Dmitry
long versified passages. One of the best, but now almost completely forgotten, medieval Russian hymnologists, Abbot Markel
Bezborody, soon after his retirement in 1557, wrote a memorial
church service to the saints Barlaam and Josaphat in the unusual
form of a dramatic poem with vivid dialogues. Many hagiogra-
phers, especially those who did not belong to the official school
of ornamental formalism but who wrote in a simple, unadorned
manner, began to include the autobiographical reminiscences of
their heroes, thus conveying a more realistic tenor to their *vitae*.
The writers of these *vitae* even began to lift the veil of ano-
nymity, providing the reader with more information about themselves. Along with the steady growth of autobiographical
elements in both the *vita* and in historical narratives, the West-

ern picaresque tale and knightly novel became translated into
Russian for the first time. Finally, fictional characters and a
satirical portrayal of Russian life make their appearance, as in
the short tale of *Shemiaka's Judgment,* written probably around
the end of the sixteenth century.

This inauguration of new ways in Russian letters and the
passing of the old literary tradition were accelerated by the
events of the Time of Troubles, when large numbers of foreigners—Poles, Lithuanians, and Swedes, as well as German and
French mercenaries—came to Russia in the ranks of invading
armies. At the same time many representatives of Russian
society became closely acquainted with Western modes of life
during their captivity in Poland, Lithuania, and Sweden. The
reunion of "Little Russia" [1] with Muscovy in 1654 intensified
Western, especially Polish, cultural influences. Moreover, the
alienation from the hierarchy and the state of the conservative
Old Believer wing of the Church [2] considerably weakened the
influence of traditionalists with the government and the cultural
elite, and facilitated the further secularization and modernization
of the Russian state, its culture, and letters.

To be sure, many Russian writers still continued until the
middle of the seventeenth century to use the previously established literary manners, methods, and devices, but the more
important and interesting part of literary production comes now
from writers seeking new ways of expression. From the beginning of this century the *vita* was gradually replaced by secular
biography, autobiography, and first-person confession. Ever-
growing attention is given to the psychology of the heroes, and
purely fictional characters come into being. The occasional
rhymed couplets and versified fragments grow into larger poetic
works, and lyric and epic songs open a new era in the expression
of feelings. The vernacular plays an increasing role.

18. HISTORICAL WORKS OF THE TIME OF TROUBLES

During the decades immediately following the Time of
Troubles, historical works describing the calamities of social
disturbance and foreign intervention played a dominant role in
Russian letters. Both old and new literary methods characterize
this transitional period. Although some seventeenth-century
writers achieved a high perfection in the employment of ornate
stylistics, behind their rhetorical facade can frequently be found

---

[1] The southern part of Russia, with Kiev, now called "the Ukraine."
[2] For more detailed information on this movement, see the introduction to *The Life of Archpriest Avvakum by Himself* in this volume.

detailed portrayals of the character and psychology of their
contemporaries as well as analyses of the reasons for the great
cataclysm. The best stylist of the time was the *dyak* (high
official) Ivan Timofeev, author of the well-known *Vremennik*
(*Book of the Times*). His sentences are often built of rhythmic
units with occasional rhyme, and are extremely rich in epithets,
compound words, and a symbolic interpretation of names: for
instance, "artillery" becomes "artifacts for the destruction of
walls"; "boats"—"transporters over the water"; "Theodore"—"the
gift of God"; "John"—"the Grace." The abundance of stylistic
devices and allegories makes a reading of this clever analytical
work—his study of the time of Ivan IV is particularly penetrating
—extremely difficult. Timofeev's ideology is strictly conservative,
the Time of Troubles being, in his mind, the result of the disappearance of the ancient dynasty and the rise of new social
groups. Still, his conservatism does not preclude a severe judgment of the boyars, the upper class of this semifeudal society,
whom Timofeev accuses of political irresponsibility and lack of
civic virtue.

Other authors of historical works on the Time of Troubles—
Avraamy Palitsyn, Ivan Khvorostinin, Ivan M. Katyrev-Rostovsky,
Prince Simon I. Shakhovskoy—use predominantly the same literary devices but, being more modest in displaying their stylistic
ability, their works are more accessible to contemporary readers
and translators. The most distinguished of these works is the
Povest' (*Story*) written by Prince Katyrev-Rostovsky around
1626. Despite frequent rhetorical digressions, effusions of sympathy and indignation, he provides a well-organized, clear, and
rather simply written account of events of the Time of Troubles.
His versified fragments are skillfully rhymed and refresh the
prose recital of events. He should be remembered as the first
seventeenth-century writer to present physical and psychological
depictions of his heroes, as well as descriptions of landscape.
Palitsyn's *Skazanie* (*Narrative*), the main part of which deals
with the siege of the Holy Trinity and St. Sergius Monastery
near Moscow, is remarkable for its powerful and severe philippic
against the ruling classes of Russia, which, in his eyes, neglected
their Christian and patriotic duties and, instead of caring for
the nation and Church, indulged in the accumulation of personal
power and wealth. The works devoted to the Time of Troubles
are so numerous that it is hardly possible even to enumerate
them here, but at least one other such work should be mentioned, the *Tale on the Death of Prince Skopin-Shuysky*. It is
notable for the touching laments uttered by the prince's relatives
after his poisoning. The author made in these laments extended

use of folklore motifs, cleverly weaving them into the fabric of
his tale.

19. LATE MUSCOVITE *vitae* AND AUTOBIOGRAPHY

The drastic changes in the traditional genres are particularly
visible in the seventeenth-century *vita*. One of the earliest of
this century was written by Kallistrat Druzhina-Osoryin, who,
soon after the death of his mother in 1604, Yuliania Lazarevsky,
wrote the story of her life. The matter-of-fact, simple, and
realistic narrative style of this *vita* opened a new era in Russian
hagiography. Yuliania, who later was canonized, is presented
against a background of the everyday life of rural Russia. In
place of the habitual eulogies and stereotyped enumeration of
the saint's virtues, Druzhina-Osoryin supplies details of family
relations, of his mother's daily household occupations, her
generosity toward the poor and the sick, and her help to the
peasants during the famine that struck Russia under Boris
Godunov. Of course, there are in this *vita* some descriptions of
miracles performed by St. Yuliania, but for the first time the
heroine of a hagiographic work is neither a nun distinguished
by her holy life nor a pious princess, but the simple and devout
wife of a small nobleman. The story's language is simple and
unadorned, very fitting for a description of the life of this charitable and unobtrusive woman.

Close to the realistic descriptions found in the *vita* of Yuliania
Lazarevsky are the *vitae* of St. Dionysius, Abbot of the Holy
Trinity and St. Sergius Monastery, of Ivan Neronov, of boyarinia
Morozova—the two latter being important leaders of the Old
Believers—and of Theodore Rtishchev, boyar and close friend of
Tsar Alexis (1645–1676). Although they preserve some features
of traditional hagiography, most of these works are secular
biographies of people of exemplary religious life, particularly
the last, the story of a boyar noted for his welfare work and his
role in promoting enlightenment in Russia. These *vitae* are
almost completely devoid of rhetorical stylistics, and frequently
employ the vernacular language.

In the 1670s leaders of the schismatic Old Believers wrote
the first true Russian autobiographies. *The Life of Archpriest
Avvakum by Himself* belongs among the most significant works
of medieval Russian literature, and modern Russian literary
historians are unanimous in considering Avvakum one of the
greatest masters of the Russian tongue. Concise, expressive,
biting, and sarcastic, Avvakum broke radically with the old
formalist tradition and the centuries-long use of Church Slavonic
as the written language of Russian letters. D. S. Mirsky (in his

History of Russian Literature) writes that Avvakum was the only Russian writer to use satisfactorily a pure Great Russian vernacular (the spoken language of Muscovy, present central and northern Russia) for a literary purpose: "Avvakum molded it into a new form for his own purpose, revamped it, widened its use and gave to this language new, purely literary, importance. His style is active, original, literary, creative." Avvakum reduced the length of the sentence, renounced the use of subordinate clauses, participles and gerunds, multiple epithets and compounds. He saturated his short, dynamic phrases—usually some eight to twelve words in length—with nouns and verbs. This leader of the Old Believers was not only a consummate stylist and expressionist but also a master of psychological delineations, and from his pen issued concise, pointed characterizations of his contemporaries. When appropriate, however, Avvakum knew how to use rhetorical stylistics in descriptions of his cobelievers, as, for instance, in that of boyarinia Morozova. Although his *Life* was the best of his numerous works, in most of Avvakum's writings can be found his vivid, colorful, colloquial language and his unusual gift for observation.

Another outstanding autobiography, or, rather, confession, came from the pen of Avvakum's spiritual father, Monk Epiphanius, who recorded his martyrdom and spiritual experiences during the persecutions inflicted upon the Old Believers by the Church and government. Whereas Avvakum's *Life* treats his sermons, tribulations, and struggle for the old faith, Epiphanius' *Confession* presents the powerful, moving story of the writer's inner life, his doubts and visions, mystical experiences, and spiritual recoveries. This "Jobian" monologue is the first instance in Russian literature of the "exposure of the soul," which later became so famous in the works of Dostoevsky and Tolstoy.

The emergence of secular biography, autobiography, and the literary confession signaled the end of medieval literary patterns. With secularization, literature turned away from religious and historical biography. New ways of life, together with freer cultural and spiritual criticism, demanded a new type of letters, greater realism, and a more penetrating portrayal of character and human psychology. A fictional hero replaced the historical or hagiographical one, and the novella and satirical tale made their appearance.

20. THE BIRTH OF FICTION

The rise of fiction was the most spectacular literary event of the last century of Muscovite Russia. Many literary historians classify all the fictional works of this time under the term *povest'* (tale, long story, or novella), but among these numerous works with fictional heroes and plots can be distinguished two different genres. One, of the novella type, centers upon the deeds of the main character. In the other, the satirical tale, the social aspect and a criticism of conditions and mores overshadow the narrative part and character delineation. Both of these types of *povest'* arose under a certain influence of Western picaresque novels that were translated into Russian in the seventeenth century, as, for instance, *Peter of the Golden Keys, Brunswick, Prince Bova, Basil the Golden-Haired, Eruslan Lazarevich* (of Oriental origin), or the *History of Apollonius of Tyre.* The seventeenth-century Russian novella, however, has a simpler structure than Western picaresque novels. It is much more concise, contains fewer characters and adventures, and the narrative is provided a purely Russian sociohistorical setting. The most interesting aspects of this new genre are its unexpectedly wide range of topics, its moral appraisals, linguistic facets, and manners of treatment.

The *Tale of Savva Grudtsyn,* which to some extent resembles the story of Dr. Faust's temptations, is probably the oldest Russian novella, the earliest version dating from the middle of the seventeenth century. Written in heavy Church Slavonic and interwoven with hagiographic motifs, the tale depicts Savva's amorous adventures, and its realistic, even naturalistic, descriptions of the worlds of the merchant and soldier are strikingly novel. Savva's adventures are placed against an actual historical background, and even the name of this fictitious hero belongs to a well-known merchant family. The same theme—the downfall and moral recovery of a youth—is the basis of another charming novella, this one in verse form, *Misery-Luckless-Plight,* which, for its choice use of the vernacular, the extensive inclusion of figures of folk speech, and its impeccable structure, can be considered one of the finest works of late medieval literature

Shifting still further away from the earlier literary manners is the tale of *Frol Skobeev, the Rogue.* Any moral element is entirely absent from this work, and the author obviously enjoys relating the successful adventures of another new hero—a rogue from the lower nobility whose swindles finally open the door to the society of the upper aristocracy for him. Whereas Savva Grudtsyn is the victim of his own passions and of sorcery, Frol Skobeev is simply an adroit, cynical scamp who cares nothing for true love and for whom the seduction of aristocratic Annushka is merely the means to social success. The tale's language shows a new stage in the development of literary Russian: in place of the heavy Church Slavonic of *Savva Grudtsyn,* the author of *Frol Skobeev* uses the vernacular extensively and does not shun vulgarity.

An intermediate stage among these three novellas is represented by the tale *Karp Sutulov*, the story of a merchant's virtuous wife who cleverly maintains her virtue during her husband's absence on a business trip. A contrasting evolution of amorous motifs can be found in the touching *Novel in Verse*, written probably toward the very end of the century, about a young girl whose father forces her to break with her true love and marry another man. This tale is rich in colorful details of everyday life during this culturally and socially transitional period. The *Tale of Solomonia, the Possessed,* on the other hand, is the most striking Russian medieval horror novella because of its demonological scenes. In most of these novellas the plots and characters are given a precise setting as to locale and time.

No less rich is seventeenth-century satire, often written in rhymed verse. Its oldest specimen, *Shemiaka's Judgment,* a social satire, is charming for its naïve and abrupt style. The judicial system of medieval Russia suffered strongly from the partiality and graft of the judges, and supplied abundant material for satire. Shemiaka is the classic type of venal judge, and this story, which became extremely popular in seventeenth- and eighteenth-century Russia, is known in innumerable prose and verse redactions. A similar theme appears in the various prose and verse versions of the satire *Yorsh Yorshovich* (*Ruff, Son of Ruff*): *Proceedings of a Suit Brought by the Bream Against the Ruff in the Case of the Lake and Rivers of Rostov.* This theme of the partiality or impartiality of judges goes far back into history, to Buddhist, Tibetan, and Indian legends, Arabic tales, or ballads on the judgments of Charlemagne. Similar tales were certainly popular in oral form in Russia for centuries, but only now, with the relaxation of state and Church control over literature and the breakdown of a purely spiritually oriented culture, did they become available in written form. Other satirical poems and prose narratives have as their heroes drunkards, corrupt clerics, and monks (as, for instance, in the *Supplication of Kaliazin* and the *Novella of Priest Savva*); the virtuous man and the sinner (as in the *Legend of the Rooster and the Fox,* the rooster being the symbol of polygamic man); or the debauched aristocracy, a jealous husband, and inefficient administrators. The number of novellas and satires penned in the seventeenth century is extremely large and they clearly reflect the secularization of Old Muscovy and the collapse of its traditional mode of life and mentality.

21. THE RISE OF POETRY

In the nineteenth century the beginning of Russian poetry was usually ascribed to Simeon Polotsky (1629–1680), a West Russian scholar and poet of Polish training and culture who, after coming to Moscow in 1664, became the writer of odes to the court and tutor to Tsar Alexis' children. Later research has discarded Polotsky not only as the initiator of Russian poetry but also as the first poet of the syllabic school of versification.

In 1608, a nobleman, Ivan Funikov, wrote an ironical versified epistle, full of puns and folk witticisms, the *Message of a Nobleman to a Nobleman*. With this oldest dated Russian work in verse not only Russian rhymed poetry began, but also its satirical and ironic ramifications—which later, after the middle of the century, produced verse versions of such satirical tales as *Shemiaka's Judgment, Yorsh Yorshovich,* or *Foma and Erema.* All of them use the vernacular, folk witticisms, and the rhymed couplet of the *skomorokhs,* folk jesters and entertainers. As every product of folk poetics, which abound in rhymed puns, colloquial sayings, and vulgarisms, such works, unfortunately, are not easily rendered into another language.

At the same time, also in the beginning of the seventeenth century, there appeared the so-called presyllabic versification, of a more formal type, which was characterized by a regular use of rhymed couplets in a line of undetermined length, vacillating usually between eight and sixteen syllables, but with no specific meter. Patriarch Job in his *vita* of Tsarevich Dmitry, mentioned above, used a wealth of such couplets for the first time in a hagiographic work. Numerous similarly versified fragments can be found in the historical writings of the Time of Troubles, especially those of Katyrev-Rostovsky and Shakhovskoy, as well as in *The New Story About the Glorious Muscovite Tsardom* (*Novaya povest*) written around 1610. One of these earliest poets was Prince Ivan A. Khvorostinin, who in 1624 wrote the first large, formal poetic work, *Epistle Against Blaspheming Heretics,* a monumental theological poem abounding in autobiographical digressions. Directed against the propagation in Russia of Western religious beliefs, Khvorostinin's *Epistle* numbers over three thousand versified lines. The vogue for versification (*stikhobesie*) spread rapidly to various genres of Muscovite letters, and Khvorostinin's example was followed by scores of Russian versifiers who compiled their theological and political treatises in rhymed form. Even many of the Old Believers, usually the staunch enemies of all new spiritual and cultural currents, succumbed to the temptations of this new vogue and also wrote some of their protests in verse form.

Thus, we can trace two different roots of early Russian poetry. One grew out of Russian folklore, the other out of the literary tradition. In the case of the former, we can find, from the very beginning of Russian history, indications of the existence of various oral poetic works. These were laments, wedding songs, and other songs of folk rituals, as well as the songs and rhymed witticisms of the jesters (*skomorokhi*). As has been seen, this folk tradition frequently influenced Russian letters although its metric structure was little preserved. The strict church and government censorship did not permit this oral folk poetry to be recorded and, probably, even if some was recorded, it was later destroyed since the scribes and keepers of book and manuscript collections were almost exclusively clergymen. With the breakup of the old social order and a new approach to culture, which resulted in the wake of the upheavals of the Time of Troubles in the early seventeenth century, the recording of folk poetics was initiated and it even began to influence literature.

The second source for the development of poetry was the medieval literature, itself. Over the entire period of Old Russian letters, from the eleventh to the sixteenth centuries, there can be found various attempts at the poetic organization of creative writing. Many medieval Russian prose writings contain long rhythmic sections that consist in the arrangement of groups of short semantic-syntactical units with a similar number of stresses —usually two or three—in each unit, all couched in the prose text. The best examples of such early rhythmic prose can be seen in the *Lay of Igor's Campaign*, the *Orison on the Downfall of Russia*, some *vitae*, and certain excerpts from the chronicles. Another type of such attempt at poetic organization consists of anaphoric arrangement and/or rhymed endings of short prose units. For instance, the *vita* of St. Stephen of Perm by Epiphanius the Wise contains many such rhymed passages. Out of the use of such rhymed passages and under the influence of Polish poetry and of some Kievan works, there developed in Moscow the poetic school of the abovementioned presyllabic versification.

An attractive aspect of seventeenth-century Russian poetry can be found in lyric verses in which writers gave expression to their feelings, hopes, and sorrows. The earliest of these were recorded, surprisingly enough, by an English traveler in Russia in 1619, a certain Richard James, in whose transcriptions have been preserved the oldest known specimens of Russian lyric verse. The above-mentioned *Novel in Verse*, a huge work organized in alphabetic form with each chapter beginning with a consecutive letter of the alphabet, is partially a novella, partially a love poem. To the same transitional type also belongs *Misery-*

Luckless-Plight. Toward the end of the century some remarkable lyric songs were written or recorded by Peter Kvashnin, Simon Pazukhin, and other poets of this new Muscovite school. Most of them show the strong influence of folklore and are in the meter of folk lyrics, although some use the rhymed endings that developed under Western poetic influence, and a rather novel and sophisticated vocabulary.

The final stage of seventeenth-century Russian poetry is represented by the appearance of "syllabic" versification, which had come into ascendance in Polish poetry and made its way to Russia. The prosodic foundations of syllabic verse were a fixed number of syllables in each line, exclusively feminine rhyme, and a caesura, or break, in the middle of each line. This method of versification was perfectly suited to the Polish language because of its constant accent on the penultimate syllable, but was inappropriate for Russian with its unstable stress. Therefore syllabic verse lasted only a short time in Russia and syllabic poetry completely disappeared from Russian letters in the second quarter of the eighteenth century, leaving very few traces in Russia's further poetic development. It was important, however, for acquainting Russians with the formal techniques of prosody.

This syllabic versification came to Muscovy from western and southern Russia (the Ukraine), where scholars and poets during the century of Polish domination were strongly influenced by Polish culture. The earliest syllabic poems appeared in Russian as early as the 1650s but the first significant Russian syllabic poet was Simeon Polotsky, mentioned above, who was also the first Russian poet whose poems were printed during his lifetime. An erudite scholar and accomplished technician of *ars poetica*, Polotsky was not a man of real poetic inspiration. His copious work falls into two categories: odes written in his capacity as court panegyrist, and didactic poems revealing to Muscovites either ancient mythology or some achievement of Western scholarship. Skillfully constructed and often formed in geometric shapes and figures, in accordance with the mode of the time, his verses are dry and uninspiring and should be classified rather as the writings of a leader of the enlightenment than of a genuine poet.

From the point of view of the development of the Russian literary language, Polotsky's verses—written in an artificial admixture of the Muscovite and Kievan versions of Church Slavonic—were a step backward, away from the increasingly simple, vernacular language of the novellas, satires, and autobiographies. Polotsky's importance in Russian literature is primarily historical because his work, which belongs more to Baroque than to medieval literature, brought Russia entirely into the new literary sphere of the West. In the Baroque period of the late seventeenth century, which signaled the end of the centuries-long medieval tradition, a prominent literary role was played by Polotsky's Muscovite followers, Kariot Istomin, Sylvester Medvedev, and Mardary Khonikov, and later in the eighteenth century by Antioch Kantemir. Their language is somewhat easier than that of Polotsky, and they reveal more genuine poetic inspiration than did their teacher, but they do not excel him in erudition and poetic techniques.

The emergence of poetry was one of the most obvious manifestations of the profound changes in Russian literature. Western modes of life and culture rapidly won a place in Russia, and Muscovy, in the second half of the seventeenth century, was very different not only from what it had been in the sixteenth century, but even in the *first* half of the seventeenth. The reunion of southern, formerly Kievan, Russia with Muscovy in 1654, as well as the Russian-Polish War of 1654–1668, were both instrumental in effecting these changes, since thousands of Kievan and West Russian scholars, noblemen, and merchants moved to Moscow or to the northern and eastern cities of the empire, carrying new Polish and Western modes with them. The Russian court was quick to adopt them, and in 1672 the first theatrical troupe performed in the palace of the tsar. Fourteen years later, in 1687, the first institution of higher education, the Muscovite Slavo-Greco-Latin Academy, was founded, and when, at the beginning of the eighteenth century, Peter I introduced his reforms—many of which only continued further the trends that had been taking place in preceding years—he, in effect, merely formalized the transformation of medieval Muscovite Russia into a Westernized empire and European power.

PART I

Literary school of the kievan era

(Eleventh to Mid-Thirteenth Century)

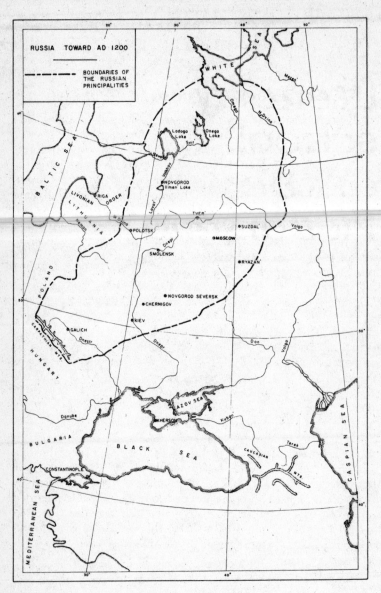

Russia toward A.D. *1200*

A. EPICS AND STORIES FROM THE CHRONICLES

a. Stories from the *Primary Chronicle*

THE *Primary Chronicle,* or, as it was called by its authors, *The Tale of Bygone Years,* is structurally a very complicated work compiled by various writers in the course of some three-quarters of a century, from about 1040 to 1118. After a short introduction, which forms a prolegomenon to Russian history, the *Chronicle* starts with the year 852 (6360, according to the old Byzantine and Russian calendars) and is organized strictly on a yearly basis. Even when the chronicler had no event to record for a given year he recorded the year, leaving a blank space after it. Some of the entries are extremely laconic and are written in an almost telegraphic style, for example: "In the year 6376 (868) Basil [Emperor of Byzantium] began to rule. In the year 6377 (869) the entire Bulgarian land was Christianized. In the year 6378 (870) . . ." (no entry).

Besides these telegraphic entries, however, the *Chronicle* contains many colorful accounts of the deeds of the Russian princes, of legal documents—such as treaties between Russia and Byzantium, and the *Testament,* or *Instruction,* of Vladimir Monomakh—and lengthier descriptions of the feuds, wars, and other events that took place in old Russia.

According to the renowned Russian philologist Alexis Shakhmatov, whose opinion is generally accepted by most contemporary investigators of *The Tale of Bygone Years,* the first draft of this chronicle was composed between 1037 and 1039. From 1060 to 1073 the task of its continuance was assumed by Nikon, a monk of the Kievan Crypt Monastery. Nikon recorded many events to which he was an eyewitness and also re-edited the earlier entries. From 1093 to 1095 this version of the *Chronicle* was reworked in the Kievan Crypt Monastery and the resulting redaction is usually referred to as the "Beginning Version" by literary historians. Around 1113 another monk of the Kievan Crypt Monastery, Nestor, rewrote the "Beginning Version" and it was probably he, also, who added the introduction with its historical and philosophical discussions. It was at this time, apparently, that the work received its present name, *The Tale of Bygone Years.* Nestor's version of the *Chronicle* also underwent redaction between 1117 and 1118 and this became the final form of the *Primary Chronicle.* As such, it was used as the initial part of most other Russian annals through the fourteenth and fifteenth centuries, as in the *Laurentian Chronicle,* the *Hypatian Chronicle,* and the *Troitsky* (Trinity) *Chronicle,* the most important early Russian annals.

The text of the Prolegomenon and various stories taken from the *Primary Chronicle* are presented here in the translation by Samuel H. Cross. Some editorial changes as well as changes in transliteration of geographical and historical names have been made for the sake of consistency in spelling throughout this volume.

1. PROLEGOMENON

THIS IS THE TALE OF BYGONE YEARS:
FROM WHENCE CAME THE RUSSIAN LAND, WHO
FIRST RULED IN KIEV, AND FROM WHICH SOURCE
THE RUSSIAN LAND HAD ITS BEGINNING

LET us begin this tale in this way: after the Flood the sons of Noah—Shem, Ham, and Japheth—divided the earth among them. To the lot of Shem fell the Orient, and his share extended lengthwise as far as India and breadthwise (from east to south) as far as Rhinocorura, including Persia and Bactria, as well as Syria, Media (which lies beside the Euphrates River), Babylon, Cordyna, Assyria, Mesopotamia, Arabia the Ancient, Elymais, India, Arabia the Mighty, Coelesyria, Commagene, and all Phoenicia.

To the lot of Ham fell the southern region, comprising Egypt, Ethiopia facing toward India, the other Ethiopia out of which the red Ethiopian river flows to the eastward, the Thebaid, Libya as far as Cyrene, Marmaris, Syrtis, Numidia, Massyris, and Mauretania over against Cadiz. Among the regions of the Orient, Ham also received Cilicia, Pamphylia, Mysia, Lycaonia, Phrygia, Camalia, Lycia, Caria, Lydia, the rest of Moesia, Troas, Aeolia, Bithynia, and ancient Phrygia. He likewise acquired the islands of Sardinia, Crete, and Cyprus, and the river Gihon, called the Nile.

To the lot of Japheth fell the northern and the western sections, including Media, Albania, Armenia (both little and great), Cappadocia, Paphlagonia, Galatia, Colchis, Bospore, Maeotis, Dervis, Sarmatia, Tauria, Scythia, Thrace, Macedonia, Dalmatia, Molossia, Thessaly, Locris, Pellene (which is also called the Peloponnese), Arcadia, Epirus, Illyria, the Slavs, Lychnitis, Adriaca, and the Adriatic Sea. He received also the islands of Britain, Sicily, Euboea, Rhodes, Chios, Lesbos, Cythera, Zacynthus, Cephallenia, Ithaca, and Corcyra, as well as a portion of the land of Asia called Ionia, the river Tigris flowing between the Medes and Babylon, and the territory to the north extending as far as the Pontus and including the Danube, the Dniester, and the Caucasian Mountains, which are called Hungarian, and thence even to the Dnieper. He likewise acquired dominion over other rivers, among them the Desna, the Pripet, the Dvina, the Volkhov, and the Volga, which flows eastward into the portion of Shem.

In the share of Japheth lie Russia, Chud, and all the gentiles: Meria, Muroma, Ves, Mordova, Chud beyond the hills, Perm, Pechera, Yam, Ugra, Litva, Zimegola, Kors, Setgola, and Liub. The Liakhs, the Prussians, and Chud border on the Varangian Sea. The Varangians dwell on the shores of that same sea and extend to the eastward as far as the portion of Shem. They likewise live to the west beside this sea as far as the land of the Angles and the Italians. For the following nations also are a part of the race of Japheth: the Varangians, the Swedes, the Normans, the Rus [Russians], the Angles, the Gauls, the Italians, the Romans, the Germans, the Carolingians, the Venetians, the Genoese, and so on. Their homes are situated in the northwest and adjoin the Hamitic tribes.

Thus Shem, Ham, and Japheth divided the earth among them, and after casting lots, so that none might encroach upon his brother's share, they lived each in his appointed portion. There was but one language, and as men multiplied throughout the earth, they planned, in the days of Yoktan and Peleg, to build a tower as high as heaven itself. Thus they gathered together in the plain of Shinar to build the tower and the city of Babylon round about it. But they wrought upon the tower for forty years, and it was unfinished. Then the Lord God descended to look upon the city and the tower, and said: "This race is one, and their tongue is one." So the Lord confused the tongues, and, after dividing the people into seventy-two races, he scattered them over the whole world. After the confusion of the tongues, God overthrew the tower with a great wind, and the ruin of it lies between Assur and Babylon. In height and in breadth it is 5,433 cubits, and the ruin was preserved for many years.

After the destruction of the tower and the division of the nations, the sons of Shem occupied the eastern regions, the sons of Ham those of the south, and the sons of Japheth the western and the northern lands. Among these seventy-two nations, the Slavic race is derived from the line of Japheth, since they are the Noricians, who are identical with the Slavs.

For many years the Slavs lived beside the Danube, where the

Hungarian and Bulgarian lands now lie. From among these Slavs, parties scattered throughout the country and were known by appropriate names, according to the places where they settled. Thus some came and settled by the river Morava, and were named Moravians, while others were called Czechs. Among these same Slavs are included the White Croats, the Serbs, and the Khorutanians. For when the Vlakhs attacked the Danubian Slavs, settled among them, and did them violence, the latter came and made their homes by the Vistula, and were then called Liakhs.[1] Of these same Liakhs some were called Poles, some Lutichians, some Mazovians, and still others Pomorians. Certain Slavs settled also on the Dnieper, and were there called Polianians. Still others were named Derevlians, because they lived in the forests. Some also lived between the Pripet and the Dvina, and were known as Dregovichians. Other tribes resided along the Dvina and were called Polotians on account of a small stream called the Polota, which flows into the Dvina. It was from this same stream that they were named Polotians. The Slavs also dwelt about Lake Ilmen, and were known there by their own original name. They built a city which they called Novgorod. Still others had their homes along the Desna, the Sem, and the Sula, and were called Severians. Thus the Slavic race was divided, and its language was known as Slavic.

When the Polianians lived by themselves among the hills, a trade route connected the Varangians with the Greeks. Starting from Greece, this route proceeds along the Dnieper, above which a portage leads to the Lovat. By following the Lovat, the great lake Ilmen is reached. The river Volkhov flows out of this lake and enters the great lake Nevo. The mouth of this lake opens into the Varangian Sea. Over this sea goes the route to Rome, and on from Rome overseas to Constantinople. The Pontus, into which flows the river Dnieper, may be reached from that point. The Dnieper itself rises in the upland forest, and flows southward. The Dvina has its source in this same forest, but flows northward and empties into the Varangian Sea. The Volga rises in this same forest, but flows to the east, and discharges through seventy mouths into the Caspian Sea. It is possible by this route to go eastward to reach the Bulgars and Khorezm, and thus attain the region of Shem. Along the Dvina runs the route to the Varangians, whence one may reach Rome, and go on from there to the race of Ham. But the Dnieper flows through various mouths into the Pontus. This sea, beside which taught St. Andrew, Peter's brother, is called the Russian Sea.

---

[1] Original Slavic name for Poles.

2. THE APOSTLE ANDREW COMES TO RUSSIA

In the tenth or eleventh century the belief was held, based on the writing of Eusebius, that the Apostle Andrew, during his trip to the Greek colonies on the Black Sea, had visited the territories that were later to become Russia. This legend became very popular with the Russians and laid the foundation for the later-developed theory of Russia as the guardian of the Orthodox Christian faith. According to the *Primary Chronicle,* Andrew crossed through Russia from the mouth of the Dnieper River, passed the hills on which Kiev was later founded, and went as far north as the ancient city of Novgorod.

When Andrew was teaching in Sinope and came to Kherson (as has been recounted elsewhere), he observed that the mouth of the Dnieper was nearby. Conceiving a desire to go to Rome, he thus went to the mouth of the Dnieper. Thence he ascended the river, and by chance he halted beneath the hills upon the shore. Upon arising in the morning, he observed to the disciples who were with him: "See ye these hills? So shall the favor of God shine upon them that on this spot a great city shall arise, and God shall erect many churches therein." He drew near the hills, and having blessed them, he set up a cross. After offering his prayer to God, he descended from the hill on which Kiev was subsequently built, and continued his journey up the Dnieper.

He then reached the Slavs at the point where Novgorod is now situated. He saw these people existing according to their customs, and on observing how they bathed and drenched themselves, he wondered at them. He went thence among the Varangians and came to Rome, where he recounted what he had learned and observed. "Wondrous to relate," said he, "I saw the land of the Slavs, and while I was among them, I noticed their wooden bathhouses. They warm them to extreme heat, then undress, and after anointing themselves with tallow, they take young reeds and lash their bodies. They actually lash themselves so violently that they barely escape alive. Then they drench themselves with cold water, and thus are revived. They think nothing of doing this every day, and actually inflict such voluntary torture upon themselves. They make of the act not a mere washing but a veritable torment." When his hearers learned this fact, they marveled. But Andrew, after his stay in Rome, returned to Sinope.

3. THE FOUNDING OF THE CITY OF KIEV

The story of the founding of Kiev by three brothers, Kii, Shchek, and Khoriv, constitutes one of the oldest historical legends of Russia. An Armenian historian of the seventh century, Zenob Glak, knew of a similar legend concerning the founding of the city of Kuar (Kiev) in the land of Poluni (Polianians) by three brothers, Kuar, Mentery, and Kherean. It is possible that this legend arose from the actual merging of three settlements that archaeological evidence shows to have existed within the limits of present-day Kiev.

The Polianians lived apart and governed their families, for thus far they were brethren, and each one lived with his gens on his own lands, ruling over his kinfolk. There were three brothers, Kii, Shchek, and Khoriv, and their sister was named Lybed. Kii lived upon the hill where the Borich Trail now is, and Shchek dwelt upon the hill now named Shchekovitza, while on the third resided Khoriv, after whom this hill is named Khorevitza. They built a town and named it Kiev after their oldest brother. Around the town lay a wood and a great pine forest in which they used to catch wild beasts. These men were wise and prudent; they were called Polianians, and there are Polianians descended from them living in Kiev to this day.

Some ignorant persons have claimed that Kii was a ferryman, for near Kiev there was at that time a ferry from the other side of the river, in consequence of which people used to say: "To Kii's ferry." Now, if Kii had been a mere ferryman, he would never have gone to Constantinople. He was then the chief of his kin, and it is related what great honor he received from the emperor when he went to visit him. On his homeward journey, he arrived at the Danube. The place pleased him, and he built a small town, wishing to dwell there with his kinfolk. But those who lived nearby would not grant him this privilege. Yet even now the dwellers by the Danube call this town Kievetz. When Kii returned to Kiev, his native city, he ended his life there; and his brothers Shchek and Khoriv, as well as their sister Lybed, died there also.

4. THE BEGINNING OF THE RUSSIAN STATE AND THE ARRIVAL OF RURIK

The expansion of the Norsemen in the ninth and tenth centuries was not limited to northwestern Europe—Germany, France, and England. Long before the Vikings established themselves in France and, under William the Conqueror, in England, other Norse warriors from Norway, Sweden, and Denmark had penetrated to the Mediterranean Sea and built strong principalities in southern Italy and Greece. Some of these Norsemen entered the service of Byzantium in Constantinople. Simultaneously, another current of Norse expansion extended into eastern Europe. Skillfully utilizing the river systems of Russia, with the Dnieper playing the most important role, the Vikings—or, as the Russians called them, the Varangians—crossed through Russia and began to attack Byzantium, their bands being reinforced by Slavs.

According to both the *Primary Chronicle* and archaeological evidence, some of these Varangians settled in various places on Russian territory. It is difficult to determine now how important their role was in the subsequent organization of the Russian state, but the *Chronicle* records that Rurik, the leader of a group of Varangians, was invited to rule over Novgorod in 862, and legend has it that Rurik became the founder of both the Russian state and the dynasty that ruled Russia until 1598, when Fedor, the son of Ivan IV, died without an heir. The legend of Rurik's founding of the Russian state has been contested by many distinguished scholars and has divided most Russian historians into the Normanists, or "Norsemanists," who believe the legend to be true, and the anti-Normanists, who reject it and consider the Russian state to have been founded long before the arrival of Rurik.

6367 (859)   The Varangians from beyond the sea imposed tribute upon the Chuds, the Slavs, the Merians, the Ves, and the Krivichians. But the Khazars imposed it upon the Polianians, the Severians, and the Viatichians, and collected a squirrel skin and a beaver skin from each hearth.

6370 (862)   The Slavs, the tributaries of the Varangians drove them back beyond the sea and, refusing them further tribute, set out to govern themselves. There was no law among them, but tribe rose against tribe. Discord thus ensued among them, and they began to war one against another. They said to themselves: "Let us seek a prince who may rule over us, and judge us according to the law." They accordingly went overseas

to the Varangian Rus: these particular Varangians were known
as Rus, just as some are called Swedes, and others Normans,
Angles, and Goths, for they were thus named. The Chuds, the
Slavs, and the Krivichians then said to the people of Rus:
"Our whole land is great and rich, but there is no order in it.
Come to rule and reign over us." They thus selected three
brothers, with their kinfolk, who took with them all the Rus,
and migrated. The oldest, Rurik, located himself in Novgorod;
the second, Sineus, in Beloozero; and the third, Truvor, in
Izborsk. On account of these Varangians, the district of
Novgorod became known as Russian (Rus) land. The present
inhabitants of Novgorod are descended from the Varangian race,
but aforetime they were Slavs.

After two years, Sineus and his brother Truvor died, and
Rurik assumed the sole authority. He assigned cities to his followers, Polotzk to one, Rostov to another, and to another Beloozero. In these cities there are thus Varangian colonists, but
the first settlers were, in Novgorod, Slavs; in Polotzk, Krivichians; at Beloozero, Ves; in Rostov, Merians; and in Murom,
Muromians. Rurik had dominion over all these districts.

With Rurik there were two men who did not belong to his
kin, but were boyars. They obtained permission to go to Constantinople with their families. They thus sailed down the
Dnieper, and in the course of their journey they saw a small
city on a hill. Upon their inquiry as to whose town it was, they
were informed that three brothers, Kii, Shchek, and Khoriv, had
once built the city, but that since their deaths, their descendants
were living there as tributaries of the Khazars. Askold and Dir
remained in this city, and after gathering together many Varangians, they established their domination over the country of
the Polianians at the same time that Rurik was ruling at
Novgorod.

6374 (866) Askold and Dir attacked the Byzantine capital
during the fourteenth year of the reign of the Emperor Michael.
When the emperor had set forth against the Saracens and had
arrived at the Black River, the eparch sent him word that the
Russians were approaching Constantinople, and the emperor
turned back. Upon arriving inside the strait, the Russians made
a great massacre of the Christians, and attacked Constantinople
in two hundred boats. The emperor succeeded with difficulty
in entering the city. The people prayed all night with the Patriarch Photius at the Church of the Holy Virgin in Blachernae.
They also sang hymns and carried the sacred vestment of the
Virgin to dip it in the sea. The weather was still, and the sea
was calm, but a storm of wind came up, and when great waves

straightway rose, confusing the boats of the godless Russians,
it threw them upon the shore and broke them up, so that few
escaped such destruction. The survivors then returned to their
native land.

5. PRINCE OLEG'S CAMPAIGN
AGAINST CONSTANTINOPLE

According to the *Primary Chronicle*, Rurik died in 879, leaving
the conduct of state affairs to his relative, Oleg, in view of the
infancy of Rurik's son, Igor. Oleg was the first nonlegendary
ruler of Russia. In 882 he moved the capital from Novgorod to
Kiev, and consolidated most of the Russian and Eastern Slavic
tribes under his rule. A successful warrior and cautious ruler,
Oleg became a popular figure in Russian historical tradition, and
was called "the Seer" by his contemporaries. His campaigns
against the Byzantine Empire, referred to by the writer of the
Chronicle as the "Greek Empire," were particularly successful.

The tribes mentioned in the following text are primarily of
Slavic origin. The Krivichians were a Slavic people who inhabited the entire northwestern Russian territory between the
present cities of Moscow, Tver', Pskov, and Minsk. The Chuds,
Merians, and Ves were Finno-Ugric tribes of northern Russia.

6415 (907) Leaving Igor in Kiev, Prince Oleg attacked
the Greeks. He took with him a multitude of Varangians, Slavs,
Chuds, Krivichians, Merians, Polianians, Severians, Derevlians,
Radimichians, Croats, Dulebians, and Tivercians as the guides.
All these tribes are known as Great Scythia by the Greeks.
With this entire force, Oleg sallied forth by horse and by
ship, and the number of his vessels was two thousand. He
arrived before Constantinople, but the Greeks fortified the strait
and closed up the city. Oleg disembarked upon the shore, and
ordered his soldiery to beach the ships. They waged war around
the city, and accomplished much slaughter of the Greeks. They
also destroyed many palaces and burned the churches. Of the
prisoners they captured, some they beheaded, some they tortured, some they shot, and still others they cast into the sea. The
Russians inflicted many other woes upon the Greeks after the
usual manner of soldiers. Oleg commanded his warriors to make
wheels, which they attached to the ships, and when the wind
was favorable they spread the sails and bore down upon the city
from the open country. When the Greeks beheld this, they were
afraid, and, sending messengers to Oleg, they implored him not

to destroy the city, and offered to submit to such tribute as he should desire. Thus Oleg halted his troops. The Greeks then brought out to him food and wine, but he would not accept it, for it was mixed with poison. Then the Greeks were terrified and exclaimed: "This is not Oleg, but St. Demetrius, whom God has sent upon us." So Oleg demanded that they pay tribute for his two thousand ships at the rate of twelve *grivnas* per man, with forty men reckoned to a ship.

The Greeks assented to these terms, and prayed for peace lest Oleg should conquer the land of Greece. Retiring thus a short distance from the city, Oleg concluded a peace with the Greek emperors Leo and Alexander, and sent into the city to them Karl, Farulf, Vermund, Hrollaf, and Steinvith, with instructions to receive the tribute. The Greeks promised to satisfy their requirements. Oleg demanded that they should give to the troops on the two thousand ships twelve *grivnas* per bench, and pay in addition the sums required for the various Russian cities: first Kiev, then Chernigov, Pereiaslavl, Polotzk, Rostov, Liubech, and the other towns. In these cities lived princes subject to Oleg.

The Russians proposed the following terms: "The Russians who come hither shall receive as much grain as they require. Whosoever come as merchants shall receive supplies for six months, including bread, wine, meat, fish, and fruit. Baths shall be prepared for them in any volume they require. When the Russians return homeward, they shall receive from your emperor food, anchors, cordage, and sails, and whatever else is needful for the journey." The Greeks accepted these stipulations, and the emperors and all the courtiers declared: "If Russians come hither without merchandise, they shall receive no provisions. Your prince shall personally lay injunction upon such Russians as journey hither that they shall do no violence in the towns and throughout our territory. Such Russians as arrive here shall dwell in the St. Mamas quarter. Our government will send officers to record their names, and they shall then receive their monthly allowance, first the natives of Kiev, then those from Chernigov, Pereiaslavl, and the other cities. They shall not enter the city save through one gate, unarmed and fifty at a time, escorted by soldiers of the emperor. They may purchase wares according to their requirements, and tax-free."

Thus the emperors Leo and Alexander made peace with Oleg, and after agreeing upon the tribute and mutually binding themselves by oath, they kissed the cross, and invited Oleg and his men to swear an oath likewise. According to the religion of the Russians, the latter swore by their weapons and by their god

Perun, as well as by Volos, the god of cattle, and thus confirmed
the treaty.

Oleg gave orders that silken sails should be made for the
Russians and linen ones for the Slavs, and his demand was
satisfied. The Russians hung their shields upon the gates as a
sign of victory, and Oleg then departed from Constantinople.
The Russians unfurled their silken sails and the Slavs their sails
of linen, but the wind tore them. Then the Slavs said: "Let us
keep our canvas ones; linen sails are not made for the Slavs."
So Oleg came to Kiev, bearing palls, gold, fruit, and wine, along
with every sort of adornment. The people called Oleg "the
Seer," for they were but pagans, and therefore ignorant.

6. THE DEATH OF OLEG

The life of Oleg, the Seer, furnished material for several
popular legends, one of which treats his death as predicted by
the magicians.

6420 (912)   Thus Oleg ruled in Kiev, and dwelt at peace
with all nations.

Now autumn came, and Oleg bethought him of his horse that
he had caused to be well fed, yet had never mounted. For on
one occasion he had made inquiry of the wonder-working
magicians as to the ultimate cause of his death. One magician
replied: "O Prince, it is from the steed which you love and on
which you ride that you shall meet your death." Oleg then reflected, and determined never to mount this horse or even to
look upon it again. So he gave command that the horse should be
properly fed, but never led into his presence. He thus let several
years pass until he had attacked the Greeks. After he returned
to Kiev, four years elapsed, but in the fifth he thought of the
horse through which the magicians had foretold that he should
meet his death. He thus summoned his senior squire and inquired as to the whereabouts of the horse which he had ordered
to be fed and well cared for. The squire answered that he was
dead. Oleg laughed and mocked the magician, exclaiming:
"Soothsayers tell untruths, and their words are naught but false-
hood. This horse is dead, but I am still alive."

Then he commanded that a horse should be saddled. "Let me
see his bones," said he. He rode to the place where the bare
bones and the skull lay. Dismounting from his horse, he laughed,
and remarked: "Am I to receive my death from this skull?" And
he stamped upon the skull with his foot. But a serpent crawled

forth from it and bit him in the foot, so that in consequence he
sickened and died. All the people mourned for him in great
grief. They bore him away and buried him upon the hill which
is called Shchekovitza. His tomb stands there to this day, and it
is called the Tomb of Oleg.

7. IGOR'S DEATH AND OLGA'S REVENGE

After Oleg's death, Igor became the ruler of Russia. He was
neither successful in his military enterprises nor popular with
the people. A campaign undertaken by him against the Slavic
tribe of Derevlians, who lived between Kiev and the present-
day Polish border, resulted in his death. His clever widow, Olga,
cruelly revenged the death of her husband. Folklore motifs are
evident in this story of her revenge, which is one of the most
colorful narratives of *The Tale of Bygone Years*.

6453 (945) In this year, Igor's retinue said to him: "The
servants of Sveinald are adorned with weapons and fine raiment,
but we are naked. Go forth with us, O prince, after tribute, that
both you and we may profit thereby." Igor heeded their words,
and he attacked Dereva in search of tribute. He demanded additional tribute, and collected it by violence from the people
with the assistance of his followers. After thus gathering the
tribute, he returned to his city. On his homeward way, he said
to his followers, after some reflection: "Go forward with the
tribute. I shall turn back, and rejoin you later." He dismissed his
retainers on their journey homeward, but being desirous of still
greater booty, he returned on his tracks with a few of his
vassals.

The Derevlians heard that he was again approaching, and
consulted with Mal, their prince, saying: "If a wolf comes
among the sheep, he will take away the whole flock one by one,
unless he be killed. If we do not thus kill him now, he will
destroy us all." They then sent forward to Igor inquiring why he
had returned, since he had collected all the tribute. But Igor
did not heed them, and the Derevlians came forth from the city
of Izkorosten, and slew Igor and his company, for the number
of the latter was few. So Igor was buried, and his tomb is near
the city of Izkorosten in Dereva even to this day.

But Olga was in Kiev with her son, the boy Sviatoslav. His
tutor was Asmund, and the troop commander was Sveinald, the
father of Mistisha. The Derevlians then said: "See, we have
killed the Prince of Russia. Let us take his wife Olga for our

Prince Mal, and then we shall obtain possession of Sviatoslav, and work our will upon him." So they sent their best men, twenty in number, to Olga by boat, and they arrived below Borichev in their boat. At that time, the water flowed below the heights of Kiev, and the inhabitants did not live in the valley, but upon the heights. The city of Kiev was on the present site of the palace of Gordiat and Nicephorus, and the prince's palace was in the city where the palace of Vratislav and Chud now stands, while the ferry was outside the city. Without the city there stood another palace, where the palace of the Cantors is now situated, behind the Church of the Holy Virgin upon the heights. This was a palace with a stone hall.

Olga was informed that the Derevlians had arrived, and summoned them to her presence with a gracious welcome. When the Derevlians had thus announced their arrival, Olga replied with an inquiry as to the reason of their coming. The Derevlians then announced that their tribe had sent them to report that they had slain her husband, because he was like a wolf, crafty and ravening, but that their princes, who had thus preserved the land of Dereva, were good, and that Olga should come and marry their Prince Mal. For the name of the Prince of Dereva was Mal.

Olga made this reply: "Your proposal is pleasing to me; indeed, my husband cannot rise again from the dead. But I desire to honor you tomorrow in the presence of my people. Return now to your boat, and remain there with an aspect of arrogance. I shall send for you on the morrow, and you shall say: 'We will not ride on horses nor go on foot; carry us in our boat.' And you shall be carried in your boat." Thus she dismissed them to their vessel.

Now Olga gave command that a large deep ditch should be dug in the castle with the hall, outside the city. Thus, on the morrow, Olga, as she sat in the hall, sent for the strangers, and her messengers approached them and said: "Olga summons you to great honor." But they replied: "We will not ride on horseback nor in wagons, nor go on foot; carry us in our boat." The people of Kiev then lamented: "Slavery is our lot. Our prince is killed, and our princess intends to marry their prince." So they carried the Derevlians in their boat. The latter sat on the crossbenches in great robes, puffed up with pride. They thus were borne into the court before Olga, and when the men had brought the Derevlians in, they dropped them into the trench along with the boat. Olga bent over and inquired whether they found the honor to their taste. They answered that it was worse than the death of Igor. She then commanded that they should be buried alive, and they were thus buried.

Olga then sent messages to the Derevlians to the effect that, if they really required her presence, they should send after her their distinguished men, so that she might go to their prince with due honor, for otherwise her people in Kiev would not let her go. When the Derevlians heard this message, they gathered together the best men who governed the land of Dereva and sent them to her. When the Derevlians arrived, Olga commanded that a bath should be made ready, and invited them to appear before her after they had bathed. The bathhouse was then heated, and the Derevlians entered in to bathe. Olga's men closed up the bathhouse behind them, and she gave orders to set it on fire from the doors, so that the Derevlians were all burned to death.

Olga then sent to the Derevlians the following message: "I am now coming to you, so prepare great quantities of mead in the city where you killed my husband, that I may weep over his grave and hold a funeral feast for him." When they heard these words, they gathered great quantities of honey, and brewed mead. Taking a small escort, Olga made the journey with ease, and upon her arrival at Igor's tomb, she wept for her husband. She bade her followers pile up a great mound, and when they had piled it up, she also gave command that a funeral feast should be held. Thereupon the Derevlians sat down to drink, and Olga bade her followers wait upon them.

The Derevlians inquired of Olga where the retinue was which they had sent to meet her. She replied that they were following with her husband's bodyguard. When the Derevlians were drunk, she bade her followers fall upon them, and went about herself egging on her retinue to the Massacre of the Derevlians. So they cut down five thousand of them; but Olga returned to Kiev and prepared an army to attack the survivors.

6454 (946) Olga, together with her son Sviatoslav, gathered a large and valiant army, and proceeded to attack the land of the Derevlians. The latter came out to meet her troops, and when both forces were ready for combat, Sviatoslav cast his spear against the Derevlians. But the spear went between the ears of his horse, and struck its feet, for the prince was but a child. Then Sveinald and Asmund said: "The prince has already begun battle; press on, vassals, after the prince." Thus they conquered the Derevlians, with the result that the latter fled, and shut themselves up in their cities.

Olga hastened with her son to the city of Izkorosten, for it was there that her husband had been slain, and they laid siege

to the city. The Derevlians barricaded themselves within the
city, and fought valiantly from it, for they realized that they
had killed the prince, and to what fate they would in consequence surrender.

Olga remained there a year without being able to take the
city, and then she thought out this plan. She sent into the town
the following message: "Why do you persist in holding out? All
your cities have surrendered to me and submitted to tribute, so
that the inhabitants now cultivate their fields and their lands in
peace. But you had rather die of hunger, without submitting to
tribute." The Derevlians replied that they would be glad to
submit to tribute but that she was still bent on avenging her
husband.

Olga then answered: "Since I have already avenged the misfortune of my husband twice on the occasions when your messengers came to Kiev, and a third time when I held a funeral
feast for him, I do not desire further revenge, but am anxious
to receive a small tribute. After I have made peace with you, I
shall return home again."

The Derevlians then inquired what she desired of them, and
expressed their readiness to pay honey and furs. Olga retorted
that at the moment they had neither honey nor furs but that she
had one small request to make. "Give me three pigeons," she
said, "and three sparrows from each house. I do not desire to
impose a heavy tribute, like my husband, but I require only this
small gift from you, for you are impoverished by the siege."

The Derevlians rejoiced, and collected from each house three
pigeons and three sparrows, which they sent to Olga with their
greetings. Olga then instructed them, in view of their submission, to return to their city, promising that on the morrow she
would depart and return to her own capital. The Derevlians re-
entered their city with gladness, and when they reported to the
inhabitants, the people of the town rejoiced.

Now Olga gave to each soldier in her army a pigeon or a
sparrow, and ordered them to attach by a thread to each pigeon
and sparrow a match bound with small pieces of cloth. When
night fell, Olga bade her soldiers release the pigeons and the
sparrows. So the birds flew to their nests, the pigeons to the
cotes, and the sparrows under the eaves. Thus the dovecotes,
the coops, the porches, and the haymows were set on fire. There
was not a house that was not consumed, and it was impossible
to extinguish the flames, because all the houses caught fire at
once. The people fled from the city, and Olga ordered her
soldiers to catch them. Thus she took the city and burned it,
and captured the elders of the city. Some of the other captives

she killed, while she gave others as slaves to her followers. The
remnant she left to pay tribute.

She imposed upon them a heavy tribute, two parts of which
went to Kiev, and the third to Olga in Vyshegorod; for
Vyshegorod was Olga's city. She then passed through the land
of Dereva, accompanied by her son and her retinue, establishing
laws and tribute. Her residences and hunting preserves are
there still. Then she returned with her son to Kiev, her city,
where she remained one year.

8. SVIATOSLAV'S EARLY CAMPAIGNS

Mention of the campaigns and deeds of the first Russian em-
pire-builder, Prince Sviatoslav, can be found in different entries
of the *Primary Chronicle*. Although scattered, these entries offer
a heroic image of this knightly prince-conqueror. Ruling Russia
from 956 to 971, Sviatoslav not only united all the Eastern
Slavs, including the tribe of the especially primitive Viatichi,
but also annexed to Russia the powerful state of the Khazars
and the north Caucasian tribes of Yassians and Kassogs. Moreover, he undertook a daring military campaign into the Balkans,
whither he was attracted by the wealth and brilliance of Byzantine civilization.

6472 (964) When Prince Sviatoslav had grown up and
matured, he began to collect a numerous and valiant army. Stepping light as a leopard, he undertook many campaigns. Upon
his expeditions he carried with him neither wagons nor kettles,
and boiled no meat, but cut off small strips of horseflesh, game,
or beef, and ate it after roasting it on the coals. Nor did he
have a tent, but he spread out a garment under him, and set
his saddle under his head; and all his retinue did likewise. He
sent messengers to the other lands announcing his intention to
attack them. He went to the Oka and the Volga, and on coming in contact with the Viatichians, he inquired of them to
whom they paid tribute. They made answer that they paid a
silver piece per plowshare to the Khazars.

6473 (965) Sviatoslav sallied forth against the Khazars.
When they heard of his approach, they went out to meet him
with their prince, the Kagan,[1] and the armies came to blows.
When the battle thus took place, Sviatoslav defeated the Khazars

---

[1] A Turkic word for emperor.

and took their city of Belovezha. He also conquered the Yassians and the Kassogians. [2]

6474 (966)   Sviatoslav conquered the Viatichians and made them his tributaries.

6475 (967)   Sviatoslav marched to the Danube to attack the Bulgarians. When they fought together, Sviatoslav overcame the Bulgarians, and captured eighty towns along the Danube. He took up his residence there, and ruled in Pereiaslavets, receiving tribute from the Greeks.

9. THE SIEGE OF KIEV AND OLGA'S DEATH

During Sviatoslav's Balkan campaign, a new and dangerous horde appeared in the south Russian prairie—the Pechenegs, Turkic nomads from Central Asia. Cruel and dynamic, these warriors commenced raiding Russian territories and in 968 they besieged Kiev. Their incursions continued until 1036, when Yaroslav defeated them. Soon thereafter, however, a new Turkic horde appeared—the Kumans, who continued the raiding of Russia. Some Pechenegs merged with these Kumans, and others settled among the Russians under the name of "Torks" and served the Russian princes, later becoming Slavicized.

6476 (968)   While Sviatoslav was at Pereiaslavets, the Pechenegs attacked Russia for the first time. So Olga shut herself up in the city of Kiev with her grandsons, Yaropolk, Oleg, and Vladimir. The nomads besieged the city with a great force. They surrounded it with an innumerable multitude, so that it was impossible to escape or send messages from the city, and the inhabitants were weak from hunger and thirst. Those who had gathered on the other side of the Dnieper in their boats remained on that side, and not one of them could enter Kiev, while no one could cross over to them from the city itself.

The inhabitants of the city were afflicted, and lamented: "Is there no one that can reach the opposite shore and report to the other party that if we are not relieved on the morrow, we must perforce surrender to the Pechenegs?" Then one youth volunteered to make the attempt, and the people begged him to try it. So he went out of the city with a bridle in his hand, and ran among the Pechenegs shouting out a question whether anyone had seen a horse. For he knew their language, and they thought he was one of themselves. When he approached the river, he

---

[2] Tribes in the northern Caucasus.

threw off his clothes, jumped into the Dnieper, and swam out. As soon as the Pechenegs perceived his action, they hurried in pursuit, shooting at him the while, but they did not succeed in doing him any harm. The party on the other shore caught sight of him, and rowed out in a boat to meet him. They then took him into their boat, and brought him to their company. He thus reported to them that if they could not relieve the city on the next day, the inhabitants would surrender to the Pechenegs.

Then their commander, Pryetich by name, announced: "To-morrow we shall approach by boat, and after rescuing the princess and the young princes, we shall fetch them over to this side. If we do not bring this to pass, Sviatoslav will put us to death." When it was morning, they embarked before dawn in their boats, and blew loudly on their trumpets. The people within the city raised a shout, so that the Pechenegs thought the prince himself had returned, and accordingly fled from the city in various directions. Thus Olga went forth with her grandsons and her followers to the boats. When the prince of the Pechenegs perceived their escape, he came alone to Pryetich, the general, and inquired who had just arrived. Pryetich replied that it was the army from the opposite bank. The prince of the Pechenegs inquired whether Pryetich was the prince himself. The general then replied that he was the prince's vassal and that he had come as a vanguard but that a countless force was on the way under the prince's command. He made this statement simply to frighten the Pecheneg. So the prince of the Pechenegs invited Pryetich to become his friend, to which request Pryetich assented. The two shook hands on it, and the prince of the Pechenegs gave Pryetich his spear, saber, and arrows, while the latter gave him his own breastplate, shield, and sword. The Pechenegs raised the siege, and for a time the inhabitants could no longer water their horses at the Lybed on account of the retreating enemy.

But the people of Kiev sent to Sviatoslav, saying: "O prince, you conquer and defeat foreign lands. But while you neglect your own country, the Pechenegs have all but taken us captive, along with your mother and your children as well. Unless you return to protect us, they will attack us again, if you have no pity on your native land, on your mother in her old age, and on your children." When Sviatoslav heard these words, he quickly bestrode his charger, and returned to Kiev with his retinue. He kissed his mother and his children, and regretted what they had suffered at the hands of the Pechenegs. He therefore collected an army, and drove the Pechenegs out into the steppes. Thus there was peace.

6477 (969) Sviatoslav announced to his mother and his
boyars: "I do not care to remain in Kiev, but should prefer to
live in Pereiaslavets on the Danube, since that is the center of
my realm, where all riches are concentrated: gold, silks, wine,
and various fruits from Greece, silver and horses from Hungary
and Bohemia, and from Russia furs, wax, honey, and slaves."
But Olga made reply: "You behold me in my weakness. Why
do you desire to depart from me?" For she was already in pre-
carious health. She thus remonstrated with him and begged him
first to bury her and then to go wheresoever he would. Three
days later Olga died. Her son wept for her with great mourning, as did likewise her grandsons and all the people. They thus
carried her out, and buried her in her tomb. Olga had given
command not to hold a funeral feast for her, for she had a
priest who performed the last rites over the sainted princess.[1]

Olga was the precursor of the Christian land, even as the
dayspring precedes the sun and as the dawn precedes the day.
For she shone like the moon by night, and she was radiant
among the infidels like a pearl in the mire, since the people
were soiled, and not yet purified of their sin by Holy Baptism.
But she herself was cleansed by this sacred purification. She put
off the sinful garments of the old Adam, and was clad in the
new Adam, which is Christ. Thus we say to her: "Rejoice in
the Russians' knowledge of God," for we were the firstfruits of
their reconciliation with him.

She was the first from Russia to enter the kingdom of God,
and the sons of Russia thus praise her as their leader, for since
her death she has interceded with God in their behalf. The
souls of the righteous do not perish. As Solomon has said: "The
nations rejoice in the praise of the righteous, for his memory is
eternal, since it is acknowledged by God and men" (Proverbs,
29:2; Wisdom, 3:4). For all men glorify her, as they behold
her lying there in the body for many years. As the prophet has
said: "I will glorify them that glorify me" (I Samuel, 2:30). Of
such persons David also said: "The righteous shall be had in
everlasting remembrance, he shall not be afraid of evil tidings.
His heart is fixed, trusting in Jehovah, his heart is fixed, and
will not be moved" (Psalms, 112:7–8). And Solomon said:
"The righteous live forever, and they have reward from God
and grace from the Most High. Therefore shall they receive
the kingdom of beauty, and the crown of goodness from the
hand of the Lord. With his right hand will he cover them, and
with his arm will he protect them" (Wisdom, 5:16–17). For

---

[1] By that time Olga had become a Christian.

he protected the sainted Olga from the devil, our adversary and our foe.

6478 (970)   Sviatoslav set up Yaropolk in Kiev and Oleg in Dereva. At this time came the people of Novgorod asking for themselves a prince. "If you will not come to us," said they, "then we will choose a prince of our own." So Sviatoslav promised them that a prince should be designated, but Yaropolk and Oleg both refused, so that Dobrynia suggested that the post should be offered to Vladimir. For Vladimir was son of Malusha, confidante of Olga and sister of Dobrynia. Their father was Malk of Liubech, and Dobrynia was thus Vladimir's uncle. The citizens of Novgorod thus requested Sviatoslav to designate Vladimir, and he granted their request. The Novgorodians took Vladimir to be their prince, and he went forth to Novgorod with Dobrynia his uncle. But Sviatoslav departed thence to Pereiaslavets.

10. SVIATOSLAV'S WAR AGAINST BYZANTIUM AND HIS DEATH

Rapidly defeating the Bulgars in the Balkans, Sviatoslav planned to annex their territory to Russia. His intentions were thwarted, however, by the Byzantine emperor, John I Zimisces (969–976), educator and co-emperor of the minor legitimate emperors, Basil II (963–1025) and Constantine VIII (963–1028). After a long siege of Dorostol (now Silistria), where Sviatoslav's army was concentrated, the Greeks forced the Russians to give up Bulgaria. On his way back to Russia Sviatoslav was ambushed and killed by the Pechenegs, who were probably paid for this deed by the Greeks. The *Primary Chronicle's* report of Sviatoslav's war in Bulgaria is confirmed by a Byzantine description of it in the *Historia* by Leo the Deacon. The wording of Sviatoslav's speech in the Deacon's version differs, however, from that in the Russian chronicle.

6479 (971)   Sviatoslav arrived before Pereiaslavets, and the Bulgarians fortified themselves in the city. They made one sally against Sviatoslav; there was great carnage, and the Bulgarians came off victors. But Sviatoslav cried to his soldiery: "We seem to be doomed to die already. Let us fight bravely, brothers and companions!" Toward evening, Sviatoslav finally gained the upper hand, and took the city by storm. He then sent messages to the Greeks, announcing his intention to march against them and capture their city, as he had taken Pereiaslavets. The Greeks replied that they were in no position to offer resistance, and therefore begged him to accept tribute instead for himself and his soldiery, requesting him to notify them how many Russians there were, so that they might pay so much per head. The Greeks made this proposition to deceive the Russians, for the Greeks are crafty even to the present day. Sviatoslav replied that his force numbered twenty thousand Russians. So the Greeks armed one hundred thousand men to attack Sviatoslav, and paid no tribute.

Sviatoslav advanced against the Greeks, who came out to meet the Russians. When the Russians perceived their approach, they were terrified at the multitude of the Greek soldiery, and Sviatoslav remarked: "Now we have no place whither we may retreat. Whether we will or no, we must give fight. Let us not disgrace Russia, but rather sacrifice our lives, lest we be dishonored. For if we flee, we shall be disgraced. We must not take flight, but we will resist boldly, and I will march before you. If my head falls, then look to yourselves." Then his warriors replied: "Wherever your head falls, there we too will lay down our own!" So the Russians went into battle, and the carnage was great. Sviatoslav came out victor, but the Greeks fled. Then Sviatoslav advanced toward the capital, fighting as he went, and destroying towns that stand deserted even to the present time.

The emperor summoned his boyars to the palace, and inquired what they should do, for they could not withstand Sviatoslav's onslaught. The boyars advised that he should be tempted with gifts, to discover whether Sviatoslav liked gold and silks. So they sent to Sviatoslav gold and silks, carried by a clever envoy. To the latter they gave command to look well upon his eyes, his face, and his spirit. The envoy took the gifts, and went out to Sviatoslav. It was reported to the prince that Greeks had come bringing greetings, and he ordered that they should be introduced. They then came near and greeted him, laying before him the gold and the silks. Sviatoslav, without noticing the presents, bade his servants keep them. So the envoys returned before the emperor; and the emperor summoned his boyars. Then the envoys reported that when they had come before Sviatoslav and offered their gifts, he had taken no notice of them, but had ordered them to be retained. Then another courtier said: "Try him a second time; send him arms."

This suggestion was adopted, and they sent to Sviatoslav a sword and other accouterments, which were duly brought before him. The prince accepted these gifts, which he praised and admired, and returned his greetings to the emperor. The envoys went back to the emperor and reported what had occurred.

Then the boyars remarked: "This man must be fierce, since he pays no heed to riches, but accepts arms. Submit to tribute." The emperor accordingly requested Sviatoslav to approach no nearer, but to accept tribute instead. For Sviatoslav had indeed almost reached Constantinople. So the Greeks paid him tribute, and he took also the share of those Russians who had been slain, promising that their families should receive it. He accepted many gifts besides, and returned to Pereiaslavets with great acclaim.

Upon observing the small number of his troops, Sviatoslav reflected that if haply the Greeks attacked him by surprise, they would kill his retinue and himself. For many warriors had perished on the expedition. So he resolved to return to Russia for reinforcements. He then sent envoys to the emperor in Silistria (for the emperor was then at that place) indicating his intention to maintain peaceful and friendly relations. When the emperor heard this message, he rejoiced, and sent to Sviatoslav gifts even more valuable than the former ones. Sviatoslav accepted these gifts, and on taking counsel with his retinue declared: "If we do not make peace with the emperor, and he discovers how few of us there are, the Greeks will come and besiege us in our city. Russia is far away, and the Pechenegs are hostile to us. So who will give us aid? Let us rather make peace with the emperor, for the Greeks have offered tribute; let that suffice. But if the emperor stops paying tribute, we shall once more collect troops in Russia in still greater numbers, and march again on Constantinople." His speech pleased his followers, and they sent their chief men to the emperor. The envoys arrived in Silistria, and reported to the emperor. He summoned them before him on the following day, and gave them permission to state their errand. They then replied: "Thus says our prince, 'I desire to maintain true amity with the Greek emperor henceforth and forever.'" The emperor rejoiced, and commanded his scribe to set down on parchment the words of Sviatoslav. One envoy recited all his words, and the scribe wrote them down. He spoke as follows:

"In accordance with the previous treaty concluded by Sviatoslav, Prince of Russia, and by Sveinald, with John surnamed Zimisces, written down by Theophilus the secretary in Silistria during the month of July, in the year 6479 (971), the fourteenth of the indiction, I, Sviatoslav, Prince of Russia, even as I previously swore, now confirm by oath upon this covenant that I desire to preserve peace and perfect amity with each of the great Greek emperors, and particularly with Basil and Constantine, and with their successors inspired of God, and with all their subjects. In this resolve concur all Russians under my sway, both boyars and commons, forever. I will therefore contemplate no attack upon your territory, nor will I collect an army or foreign mercenaries for this purpose, nor will I incite any other foe against your realm or against any territory pertaining thereto, and particularly against the district of Kherson, or the cities thereto adjacent, or against Bulgaria. But if any other foe plans to attack your realm, I will resist him and wage war upon him. And even as I have given oath to the Greek emperors in company with my boyars and all my subjects, so may we preserve this treaty inviolate. But if we fail in the observance of any of the aforesaid stipulations, either I, or my companions, or my subjects, may we be accursed of Perun the god in whom we believe, and Volos, the god of flocks, and may we become yellow as gold, and be slain with our own weapons. Regard as truth what we have now convenanted with you, even as it is inscribed upon this parchment and sealed with our seals."

After making peace with the Greeks, Sviatoslav journeyed by boat to the cataracts of the Dnieper, and the general, Sveinald, advised him to ride around the falls on horseback, for the Pechenegs were encamped in the vicinity. The prince did not heed him, but went on by boat. The people of Pereiaslavets informed the Pechenegs that Sviatoslav was returning to Russia after seizing from the Greeks great riches and immense booty but that his troop was small. When the Pechenegs heard this news, they ambuscaded the cataracts, so that when Sviatoslav arrived it was impossible to pass them. So the prince decided to winter in Belobereg, but the Russians had no rations, so that there was a severe famine, and they paid as much as half a *grivna* for a horse's head. But Sviatoslav wintered there nevertheless.

When spring came, in 6480 (972), Sviatoslav approached the cataracts, where Kuria, Prince of the Pechenegs, attacked him; and Sviatoslav was killed. The nomads took his head, and made a cup out of his skull, overlaying it with gold, and they drank from it. But Sveinald returned to Yaropolk in Kiev. Now all the years of Sviatoslav's reign were twenty-eight.

11. VLADIMIR CHRISTIANIZES RUSSIA

Vladimir, son of Sviatoslav, reigned from 980 to 1015, and solved the important problem of Russia's cultural orientation. He was faced with the need to choose a religion for his state, and vacillated among several: Islam, which had been carried to Central Asia by Arab armies and to the Upper Volga [1] by Arab missionaries; Judaism, to which belonged the upper class of the Khazars on the Lower Volga; the Christianity of the West, professed by the Germans; or the Christianity of the East, professed by Byzantium. Preachers of each of these religions were present in Kiev, and each tried to convert Vladimir to his particular faith. Finally, the Christianity of the East prevailed. This is not surprising, since for centuries Russia had been in close contact with Byzantium and, even earlier, with the Hellenic world. As early as the sixth and seventh centuries B.C., the Greeks had founded prosperous colonies in the Crimea, such as the important city of Kherson, and others at many places on the northern coast of the Black Sea, all of which became the focal point for Greek, and later, Byzantine, influence in eastern Europe. Lively trade relations between Kiev and Constantinople had been maintained for centuries, despite intermittent interruptions by Russian military campaigns against Constantinople —or, as the Russians of that time called it, "Tsargrad," the Caesar (ruler) of all cities, or the City of the Caesars.

6495 (987)   Vladimir summoned together his boyars and the city elders, and said to them: "Behold, the Bulgarians came before me urging me to accept their religion. Then came the Germans and praised their own faith; and after them came the Jews. Finally the Greeks appeared, criticizing all other faiths but commending their own, and they spoke at length, telling the history of the whole world from its beginning. Their words were artful, and it was wondrous to listen and pleasant to hear them. They preach the existence of another world. 'Whoever adopts our religion and then dies shall arise and live forever. But whosoever embraces another faith, shall be consumed with fire in the next world.' What is your opinion on this subject, and what do you answer?" The boyars and the elders replied: "You know, O prince, that no man condemns his own possessions, but praises them instead. If you desire to make certain, you have servants at your disposal. Send them to inquire about the ritual of each and how he worships God."

Their counsel pleased the prince and all the people, so that they chose good and wise men to the number of ten, and directed them to go first among the Bulgarians and inspect their faith. The emissaries went their way, and when they arrived at their destination they beheld the disgraceful actions of the Bul-

---

[1] To the realm of the Volga Bulgarians, a Turkic state not to be confused with the Slavic Bulgarians of the Balkans.

garians and their worship in the mosque; then they returned to
their own country. Vladimir then instructed them to go likewise
among the Germans, and examine their faith, and finally to visit
the Greeks. They thus went into Germany, and after viewing the
German ceremonial, they proceeded to Constantinople where
they appeared before the emperor. He inquired on what mission
they had come, and they reported to him all that had occurred.
When the emperor heard their words, he rejoiced, and did them
great honor on that very day.

On the morrow, the emperor sent a message to the patriarch
to inform him that a Russian delegation had arrived to examine
the Greek faith, and directed him to prepare the church and
the clergy, and to array himself in his sacerdotal robes, so that
the Russians might behold the glory of the God of the Greeks.
When the patriarch received these commands, he bade the
clergy assemble, and they performed the customary rites. They
burned incense, and the choirs sang hymns. The emperor accompanied the Russians to the church, and placed them in a
wide space, calling their attention to the beauty of the edifice,
the chanting, and the offices of the archpriest and the ministry
of the deacons, while he explained to them the worship of his
God. The Russians were astonished, and in their wonder praised
the Greek ceremonial. Then the Emperors Basil and Constantine
invited the envoys to their presence, and said: "Go hence to
your native country," and thus dismissed them with valuable
presents and great honor.

Thus they returned to their own country, and the prince
called together his boyars and the elders. Vladimir then announced the return of the envoys who had been sent out, and
suggested that their report be heard. He thus commanded them
to speak out before his vassals. The envoys reported: "When we
journeyed among the Bulgarians, we beheld how they worship
in their temple, called a mosque, while they stand ungirt. The
Bulgarian bows, sits down, looks hither and thither like one
possessed, and there is no happiness among them, but instead
only sorrow and a dreadful stench. Their religion is not good.
Then we went among the Germans, and saw them performing
many ceremonies in their temples; but we beheld no glory
there. Then we went on to Greece, and the Greeks led us to the
edifices where they worship their God, and we knew not
whether we were in heaven or on earth. For on earth there is
no such splendor or such beauty, and we are at a loss how to
describe it. We know only that God dwells there among men,
and their service is fairer than the ceremonies of other nations.

For we cannot forget that beauty. Every man, after tasting
something sweet, is afterward unwilling to accept that which is
bitter, and therefore we cannot dwell longer here." Then the
boyars spoke and said: "If the Greek faith were evil, it would
not have been adopted by your grandmother Olga, who was
wiser than all other men." Vladimir then inquired where they
should all accept baptism, and they replied that the decision
rested with him.

After a year had passed, in 6496 (988), Vladimir marched
with an armed force against Kherson,[2] a Greek city, and the
people of Kherson barricaded themselves therein. Vladimir
halted at the farther side of the city beside the bay, a bowshot
from the town, and the inhabitants resisted energetically while
Vladimir besieged the town. Eventually, however, they became
exhausted, and Vladimir warned them that if they did not surrender, he would remain on the spot for three years. When they
failed to heed this threat, Vladimir marshaled his troops and
ordered the construction of an earthwork in the direction of
the city. While this work was under construction, the inhabitants
dug a tunnel under the city wall, stole the heaped-up earth,
and carried it into the city, where they piled it up in the center
of the town. But the soldiers kept on building, and Vladimir
persisted. Then a man of Kherson, Anastasius by name, shot
into the Russian camp an arrow on which he had written:
"There are springs behind you to the east, from which water
flows in pipes. Dig down and cut them off." When Vladimir received this information, he raised his eyes to heaven and vowed
that if this hope was realized, he would be baptized. He gave
orders straightway to dig down above the pipes, and the water
supply was thus cut off. The inhabitants were accordingly overcome by thirst, and surrendered.

Vladimir and his retinue entered the city, and he sent messages to the Emperors Basil and Constantine, saying: "Behold,
I have captured your glorious city. I have also heard that you
have an unwedded sister. Unless you give her to me to wife, I
shall deal with your own city as I have with Kherson." When
the emperors heard this message, they were troubled, and replied: "It is not meet for Christians to give in marriage to
pagans. If you are baptized, you shall have her to wife, inherit
the kingdom of God, and be our companion in the faith. Unless
you do so, however, we cannot give you our sister in marriage."

---

[2] The city of Kherson was located in the Crimea, near present-day
Sebastopol.

When Vladimir learned their response, he directed the envoys of the emperors to report to the latter that he was willing to accept baptism, having already given some study to their religion, and that the Greek faith and ritual, as described by the emissaries sent to examine it, had pleased him well. When the emperors heard this report, they rejoiced, and persuaded their sister Anna to consent to the match. They then requested Vladimir to submit to baptism before they should send their sister to him, but Vladimir desired that the princess should herself bring priests to baptize him. The emperors complied with his request, and sent forth their sister, accompanied by some dignitaries and priests. Anna, however, departed with reluctance. "It is as if I were setting out into captivity," she lamented; "better were it for me to die here." But her brothers protested: "Through your agency God turns the Russian land to repentance, and you will relieve Greece from the danger of grievous war. Do you not see how much evil the Russians have already brought upon the Greeks? If you do not set out, they may bring on us the same misfortunes." It was thus that they overcame her hesitation only with great difficulty. The princess embarked upon a ship, and after tearfully embracing her kinfolk, she set forth across the sea and arrived at Kherson. The natives came forth to greet her, and conducted her into the city, where they settled her in the palace.

By divine agency, Vladimir was suffering at that moment from a disease of the eyes, and could see nothing, being in great distress. The princess declared to him that if he desired to be relieved of this disease, he should be baptized with all speed, otherwise it could not be cured. When Vladimir heard her message, he said: "If this proves true, then of a surety is the God of the Christians great," and gave order that he should be baptized. The Bishop of Kherson, together with the princess' priests, after announcing the tidings, baptized Vladimir, and as the bishop laid his hand upon him, he straightway received his sight. Upon experiencing this miraculous cure, Vladimir glorified God, saying: "I have now perceived the one true God." When his followers beheld this miracle, many of them were also baptized.

Vladimir was baptized in the Church of St. Basil, which stands at Kherson upon a square in the center of the city, where the Khersonians trade. The palace of Vladimir stands beside this church to this day, and the palace of the princess is behind the altar. After his baptism, Vladimir took the princess in marriage. Those who do not know the truth say he was baptized in Kiev,

while others assert this event took place in Vasiliev, while still
others mention other places. . . .

Hereupon Vladimir took the princess and Anastasius and the
priests of Kherson, together with the relics of St. Clement and
of Phoebus his disciple, and selected also sacred vessels and
images for the service. In Kherson he thus founded a church on
the mound which had been heaped up in the midst of the city
with the earth removed from his embankment; this church is
standing at the present day. Vladimir also found and appropriated two bronze statues and four bronze horses, which now
stand behind the Church of the Holy Virgin, and which the
ignorant think are made of marble. As a wedding present for
the princess, he gave Kherson over to the Greeks again, and
then departed for Kiev.

When the prince arrived at his capital, he directed that the
idols should be overthrown and that some should be cut to
pieces and others burned with fire. He thus ordered that Perun
should be bound to a horse's tail and dragged along Borichev
to the river. He appointed twelve men to beat the idol with
sticks, not because he thought the wood was sensitive, but to
affront the demon who had deceived man in this guise, that he
might receive chastisement at the hands of men. Great art thou,
O Lord, and marvelous are thy works! Yesterday he was honored
of men, but today held in derision. While the idol was being
dragged along the stream to the Dnieper, the unbelievers wept
over it, for they had not yet received Holy Baptism. After they
had thus dragged the idol along, they cast it into the Dnieper.
But Vladimir had given this injunction: "If it halts anywhere,
then push it out from the bank, until it goes over the falls.
Then let it loose." His command was duly obeyed. When the
men let the idol go, and it passed through the falls, the wind
cast it out on the bank, which since that time has been called
Perun's Bank, a name that it bears to this very day.

Thereafter Vladimir sent heralds throughout the whole city to
proclaim that if any inhabitant, rich or poor, did not betake
himself to the river, he would risk the prince's displeasure. When
the people heard these words, they wept for joy, and exclaimed
in their enthusiasm: "If this were not good, the prince and his
boyars would not have accepted it." On the morrow the prince
went forth to the Dnieper with the priests of the princess and
those from Kherson, and a countless multitude assembled. They
all went into the water: some stood up to their necks, others to
their breasts, the younger near the bank, some of them holding
children in their arms, while the adults waded farther out. The

priests stood by and offered prayers. There was joy in heaven and upon earth to behold so many souls saved. But the devil groaned, lamenting: "Woe is me! how am I driven out hence! For I thought to have my dwelling place here, since the apostolic teachings do not abide in this land. Nor did this people know God, but I rejoiced in the service they rendered unto me. But now I am vanquished by the ignorant, not by apostles and martyrs, and my reign in these regions is at an end."

When the people were baptized, they returned each to his own abode. Vladimir, rejoicing that he and his subjects now knew God himself, looked up to heaven and said: "O God, who hast created heaven and earth, look down, I beseech thee, on this thy new people, and grant them, O Lord, to know thee as the true God, just as the other Christian nations have known thee. Confirm in them the true and unalterable faith, and aid me, O Lord, against the hostile adversary, so that, hoping in thee and in thy might, I may overcome his malice." Having spoken thus, he ordained that churches should be built and established where pagan idols had previously stood. He thus founded the Church of St. Basil on the hill where the idol of Perun and the other images had been set, and where the prince and the people had offered their sacrifices. He began to found churches and to assign priests throughout the cities, and to invite the people to accept baptism in all the cities and towns.

He took the children of the best families, and sent them to schools for instruction in book learning. The mothers of these children wept bitterly over them, for they were not yet strong in faith, but mourned as for the dead. When these children were assigned for study, there was thus fulfilled in the Russian land the prophecy which says: "In those days, the deaf shall hear words of Scripture, and the voice of the stammerers shall be made plain" (Isaiah, 29:18; 32:4). For these persons had not ere this heard words of Scripture, and now heard them only by the act of God, for in his mercy the Lord took pity upon them, even as the prophet said: "I will be gracious to whom I will be gracious" (Exodus, 33:19).

12. YAROSLAV THE WISE

Fratricidal warring among the sons of Vladimir ended in 1016 with the victory of Prince Yaroslav, who established a firm rule over Russia for nearly forty years, from 1016 to 1054. This was the "golden age" of Kievan Russia, the age when material, intellectual, and artistic achievements were particularly brilliant.

Prince Yaroslav, called "Yaroslav the Wise" by his contemporaries because of the peace and prosperity that marked his reign,
maintained lively relations with Byzantium and Western Europe,
and his children and grandchildren married the royalty of various western European nations. His daughter, Ann, became
queen of France, and ruled that country in the name of her
son after the death of her husband, Henry I, the Capet. It is of
interest to note that Ann was the only literate member of the
French royal family, and signed most of the state documents for
her husband and son.

6545 (1037) Yaroslav built the great citadel at Kiev, near
which stand the Golden Gates. He founded there also the
metropolitan Church of St. Sophia, the Church of the Annunciation by the Golden Gates, and also the Monastery of Sts. George
and Irene. During his reign, the Christian faith was fruitful and
multiplied, while the number of monks increased, and new monasteries came into being. Yaroslav loved religious establishments
and was devoted to priests, especially to monks. He applied
himself to books, and read them continually day and night. He
assembled many scribes, and translated from Greek into Slavic.
He wrote and collected many books through which true believers are instructed and enjoy religious education. For as one
man plows the land, another sows, and still others reap and
eat food in abundance, so did this prince. His father Vladimir
plowed and harrowed the soil when he enlightened Russia
through baptism, and this prince sowed the hearts of the faithful with the written word, and we in turn reap the harvest by
receiving the teaching of books. For great is the profit from book
learning.

Through the medium of books, we are shown and taught the
way of repentance, for we gain wisdom and continence from
the written word. Books are like rivers that water the whole
earth; they are the springs of wisdom. For books have an immeasurable depth; by them we are consoled in sorrow. They are
the bridle of self-restraint. For great is wisdom. As Solomon
said in its praise: "I (Wisdom) have inculcated counsel; I have
summoned reason and prudence. The fear of the Lord *is the
beginning of wisdom.* Mine are counsel, wisdom, constancy, and
strength. Through me kings rule, and the mighty decree justice.
Through me are princes magnified and the oppressors possess
the earth. I love them that love me, and they who seek me shall
find grace" (Proverbs, 8:12, 13, 14–17). If you seek wisdom
attentively in books, you will obtain great profit for your spirit.
He who reads books often converses with God or with holy men.

If one possesses the words of the prophets, the teachings of the evangelists and the Apostles, and the lives of the Holy Fathers, his soul will derive great profit therefrom. Thus Yaroslav, as we have said, was a lover of books, and as he wrote many, he deposited them in the Church of St. Sophia, which he himself had founded. He adorned it with gold and silver and churchly vessels, and in it the usual hymns are raised to God at the customary seasons. He founded other churches in the cities and districts, appointing priests and paying them out of his personal fortune. He bade them teach the people, since that is the duty which God has prescribed them, and to go often into the churches. Priests and Christian laymen thus increased in number. Yaroslav rejoiced to see the multitude of his churches and of his Christian subjects, but the devil was afflicted, since he was now conquered by this new Christian nation.

13. THE BLINDING OF VASILKO

Like the Middle Ages in western Europe, the feudal period in Russia was characterized by cruel power struggles among the princes of the ruling house. The first victims of such a struggle were Boris and Gleb, whose story was recorded in the entry for the year 1015. No less tragic was the struggle between Princes Sviatopolk and David against their cousin, Prince Vasilko, who ruled Volynia and Galicia in western Russia. The struggle ended with the blinding of Vasilko by his cousins. This story was told to the chronicler by the priest Vasily, and is one of the most dramatic narratives in *The Tale of Bygone Years*.

6605 (1097) Satan now incited certain men to report to David son of Igor that Vladimir was conspiring with Vasilko against Sviatopolk and against himself. David gave credence to their false words, and endeavored to stir up Sviatopolk against Vasilko, saying: "Who killed your brother Yaropolk? Now he plots against me and against you, and has conspired with Vladimir. Take thought for your own head."

Sviatopolk was thus perturbed, and wondered whether these allegations were true or false. He was uncertain, and replied to David: "If you speak aright, may God be your witness. But if you speak from motives of jealousy only, God will punish you for it."

Sviatopolk was concerned for his brother and himself, and wondered whether the rumor were true. He finally believed David, who thus deceived Sviatopolk, and the two of them set out to plot against Vasilko. Now Vasilko and Vladimir were ignorant of this fact. David remarked, however, that if he and Sviatopolk did not seize Vasilko, neither of them could be sure of the domains they then held. And Sviatopolk believed him.

Vasilko arrived on November 4th, crossed over to Vydobychi, and went to make his reverence to St. Michael in the monastery, where he also supped. He pitched his camp on the Ruditsa. At evening, he returned to his camp. When it was morning, Sviatopolk urged him by messenger not to depart before his name day. Vasilko refused, urging that he could not wait that long, or there would be disorder in his domain. Then David begged him not to depart, but rather to obey his elder kinsman. Vasilko, however, was still reluctant to comply.

Then David remarked to Sviatopolk: "See, he sets no store by you, though he is in your power. If he departs to his domain, you shall see whether he does not seize your cities of Turov and Pinsk, and other towns which belong to you; then you will perhaps remember my words. Call the men at once and take him prisoner; then deliver him over to me."

Sviatopolk followed his advice, and sent word to Vasilko, saying: "If you are unwilling to remain until my name day, at least come and embrace me now, and then we shall meet with David." Vasilko promised to go, and did not perceive the treachery which David was planning against him. Vasilko thus mounted his horse and rode off. One of his servants then met him and urged him not to go, because the princes were plotting to take him prisoner. But Vasilko heeded him not, as he thought to himself: How can they intend to take me prisoner? They joined me in the oath that if any one of us should attack another, the holy cross and all of us should be against him. Having thus reflected, he crossed himself, and said: "God's will be done."

He thus rode with a small escort to the prince's palace. Sviatopolk came out to meet him, and they went into the hall. David entered, and all sat down. Then Sviatopolk begged Vasilko to remain until the day of St. Michael (November 8th).

Vasilko replied: "I cannot remain, kinsman; I have already ordered my camp to move forward."

David sat silent as if struck dumb, till Sviatopolk invited Vasilko to breakfast with them, and Vasilko accepted. Then Sviatopolk said: "Remain seated here a moment while I go out and make certain dispositions." He thus went out, leaving David and Vasilko alone together. Vasilko tried to open a conversation with David, but there was no voice nor hearing in him, for he was afraid, and had treachery in his heart. After he had sat awhile, he inquired where his kinsman was. The answer was

given that he was standing in the vestibule. David then rose and
asked Vasilko to remain seated while he went in search of
Sviatopolk. He thus stood up and went thence. When David
had thus gone out, others seized upon Vasilko and fettered him
with double fetters, setting guards over him by night. This
treachery took place on November 5th.

In the morning, Sviatopolk assembled the boyars and the men
of Kiev and informed them of what David had told him, to the
effect that Vasilko had been responsible for his brother's death,
was plotting with Vladimir against him, and intended to kill him
and seize his cities. The boyars and the populace replied: "It
behooves you, O Prince, to protect your own life. If David
spoke aright, let Vasilko suffer the penalty. If David has spoken
falsely, let him suffer the vengeance of God and answer before
God."

When the abbots heard of the circumstances, they interceded
with Sviatopolk in Vasilko's behalf, but he protested that it was
all David's affair. When David heard of all this, he urged that
Vasilko should be blinded, on the ground that if Sviatopolk did
nothing and released Vasilko, neither he himself nor Sviatopolk
would be able to retain their thrones much longer. Sviatopolk
was in favor of releasing him, but David kept close watch over
him and would not consent.

During the night, they thus took Vasilko to Belgorod, which
is a small town ten *versts* from Kiev. They transported him
fettered in a cart, and after removing him from the vehicle, they
led him into a small house. As he sat there, Vasilko saw a Tork [1]
sharpening a knife, and then comprehending that they intended
blinding him, he cried out to God with loud weeping and groaning. Then came the emissaries of Sviatopolk and David: Snovid,
the son of Izech, the squire of Sviatopolk, and Dmitry, David's
squire, and they laid a rug upon the floor. After they had spread
it, they seized Vasilko and endeavored to overthrow him. He
offered a violent resistance, so that they could not throw him.
Then others came and cast him down. They bound him, and
laid upon his chest a slab taken from the hearth. Though Snovid,
the son of Izech, sat at one end and Dmitry at the other, they
still could not hold him down. Then two other men came, and
after taking a second slab from the hearth, they too sat upon
him, and weighed upon him so heavily that his chest cracked.
Then a Tork, Berendi by name, a shepherd of Sviatopolk, came
up with his knife, and though intending to strike him in the eye,
missed the eye entirely and cut his face. This scar Vasilko bears

---

[1] Torks were a Turkic tribe of southern Russia.

Blinded Prince Vasilko asks for water.

A miniature from the Radzivil Chronicle of the fourteenth century.

to this day. Afterward, however, he struck him in one eye, and
took out the pupil, and then in the other eye, and also removed
the pupil of the latter.

At that moment Vasilko lay as if dead. They raised him in
the rug, laid him fainting in the wagon, and carried him off to
Vladimir. While he was being thus transported, they happened
to halt with him at a marketplace after they had crossed the
bridge at the town of Zvizhden. They took off his bloody shirt,
and gave it to a priest's wife to wash. After she had washed it,
the woman put it on him while the others were eating, and she
began to weep, for he was as if dead. He heard her weeping,
and inquired where he was. They replied that the town was
Zvizhden. He then begged for water. They gave him some, and
after he had drunk the water, full consciousness returned to him.
He remembered what had occurred, and feeling his shirt, he
lamented: "Why did you take it from me? I had rather have
met my death and stood before God in this bloody shirt."

When they had eaten, they rode on swiftly in the cart with
him, and over a rough road, for it was then the month of
Gruden, called November. They arrived with him at Vladimir's
on the sixth day. David accompanied them, and behaved as if
he had captured some prize. They quartered Vasilko in the
Vakeev palace, and placed over him a guard of thirty men, as
well as two servants of the prince named Ulan and Kolchko.

b. Tales from the *Novgorodian Chronicle*

IN southern and central Russia the princes eventually established their undisputed rule over the Russian cities and principalities, and the ancient people's assembly, the *Veche,* which
had played an important role in many Russian cities before the
twelfth century, gradually declined in importance. But in the
cities of Novgorod and Pskov, in northwestern Russia, the power
of the princes was curbed and the *Veche* became the principal
ruling institution. The princes, who served as commanders of
the army, the *posadniks,* who headed the civil administration,
other administrators, and the bishops were all elected by the
Veche, and often removed by it if its members became dissatisfied with them. Like such European merchant cities as Venice,
Genoa, Hamburg, and Lübeck, both Pskov and Novgorod had a
powerful merchant class. Novgorod became a member of the
Hanseatic League and maintained lively trade relations with
Germany and other nations of northern Europe.

The style of the *Novgorodian Chronicle* strongly reflects the commercial atmosphere that prevailed in these two cities. The entries tell little about political events, but furnish details concerning matters of commerce, such as the state of the harvest, the prices of merchandise, trade activities, and climatic conditions that might have a bearing on the economic situation. Most of the longer stories in these northern annals are of southern origin, have been taken from the Kievan or central Russian chronicles.

The translation of the *Novgorodian Chronicle* presented here is based on *Novgorodskaia pervaia letopis,* Second Version, published by the Academy of Sciences of the U.S.S.R., Moscow and Leningrad, 1950.

14. LIFE IN THE CITY OF NOVGOROD

6636 (1128)   Kiriak, the Abbot of St. George, died. In the same year John, son of Vsevolod, grandson of Mstislav, died on the 16th of April. In the same year Zavid Dmitrevich was made *posadnik* in Novgorod. This was a cruel year: an *osminka* of rye cost a *grivna;* the people ate lime leaves, birchbark; they ground wood pulp and mixed it with husks and straw; and some ate buttercups, moss, and horseflesh. And the corpses of those who had fallen from starvation were in the streets, the marketplace, the road, and everywhere. And they hired men to carry the dead out of town, for the stench was poisoning the air. Sorrow and misery befell all. Fathers and mothers would give their children as gifts to merchants or put them to death. And many people went to other lands. Thus a blight was brought upon our land for our sins. And this year the water of the river Volkhov was very high, and it carried away many houses. And Prince Boris Vsevolodovich of Polotsk died, and Zavid Dmitrevich, *posadnik* of Novgorod, died.

6651 (1143)   All this autumn was rainy; from Our Lady's Day of Nativity until the winter solstice it was warm and wet. The water was very high in the river Volkhov, and it carried away hay and wood. The lake froze, and there was great coldness in the night. And the wind broke up the ice and carried it into the river Volkhov, where it broke the bridge and carried away four of the bridge piles. In the same year Sviatopolk married in Novgorod. He brought his bride from Moravia between Christmas and Epiphany. And in the same year the Korelians campaigned against the Yamians, but were forced to retreat.

6664 (1156)   The Novgorodians expelled Sudilo, the *posadnik* of the city, and he died five days later. And they gave the position of *posadnik* to Yakun Miroslavovich. In the same spring, on April 21st, Archbishop Nifont passed away. Before he died he went to Kiev to oppose the metropolitan bishop, but many people say that he went to Constantinople after having plundered the Cathedral (St. Sophia in Kiev). They say many things about him, but it is their sin for doing so. We should remember that he was the one who embellished the Cathedral (St. Sophia of Novgorod), who decorated the porches, who made the icon case, and who adorned the church on the outside. He also built the Church of the Holy Savior in Pskov and the Church of St. Clement in Ladoga. I believe that God, because of our sins, did not desire that we should have his grave for our consolation and so he sent him to Kiev, where he died. And he was buried in the Crypt Monastery.

In the same year the whole populace of the city gathered and decided to elect as bishop a holy man, Arkady, who was chosen by God. And all the people went to the Monastery of the Holy Mother of God and took him, Prince Mstislav, the entire clergy of the Cathedral of St. Sophia, and all the priests, abbots, and monks of the city and brought them to the court of St. Sophia. And they entrusted the bishopric to Arkady until the Metropolitan of Russia should arrive and consecrate him. And in the same year the merchants from over the seas erected the Church of Good Friday on the market square.

6665 (1157)   There was malice among the people, and they rose against Prince Mstislav Yurievich and began to drive him from Novgorod, but the merchants took up arms for him. And brother quarreled with brother. The bridge over the river Volkhov was seized. Guards took their stand on either side of the town gates, and it nearly came to the shedding of blood between them. And then Sviatoslav Rostislavich and David Rostislavich arrived. That very night Mstislav fled from Novgorod. And in three days Rostislav himself arrived. And the brothers came together, and no harm came of it.

In the spring Prince George died at Kiev, and the people of Kiev set Iziaslav Davidovich on the throne. In the same year Andrew, Abbot of the Church of the Holy Mother of God, died. And Alexis was appointed in his place. And in the fall the weather was fearsome with thunder and lightning, and on November 7th, at five in the night, there was hail of the size of apples.

15. NOVGOROD AT WAR WITH SUZDAL

The chronicle entries for the years 1169 and 1170, which follow below, give a clear picture of the struggle between the princes of Novgorod and those of central Russia. First the princes of Suzdal and later those of Moscow tried to unify all Russia and to bring the prosperous merchant city of Novgorod under their sway. The struggle described in these two entries is against the armies of Suzdal, led by the autocratic Prince Andrey, and their allies, led by Prince Roman and Prince Mstislav. At this time the troops of Novgorod were commanded by young Prince Roman. These entries are written in short, telegraphic style. For a better understanding of the text some explanatory notes have been added in parentheses.

6677 (1169) Danislav Lazutinich went with his troops beyond the Volok [1] to collect tribute, but (Great Prince Andrew) sent his army against them. And it came to a battle. There were only four hundred men of Novgorod against seven thousand soldiers from Suzdal, but God helped the Novgorodians, and the Suzdalians suffered thirteen hundred casualties, while Novgorod lost only fifteen men. Novgorod retreated, but then returned and collected tribute (beyond the Volok), and received tribute also from the peasants of Suzdal. And all returned home in good health.

In the same year in the winter the army of Suzdal, under the command of the son of Prince Andrew, Prince Mstislav, and Prince Roman, and with troops from Smolensk, Toropets, and Murom; the armies of Riazan led by two princes, the Prince of Polotsk with his armies, and men from the entire Russian land all approached the city of Novgorod. But the people of Novgorod were firmly behind their leader, Prince Roman, and their *posadnik*, Yakun. And so they built fortifications about the city. On Sunday (the emissaries of the princes of Suzdal) came to Novgorod to negotiate, and these negotiations lasted for three days. On the fourth day, Wednesday, February 25th, the day of St. Tarasy, Patriarch of Constantinople, the Suzdalians attacked the city and fought the entire day. Only toward evening did Prince Roman, who was still very young, and the troops of Novgorod manage to defeat the army of Suzdal with the help of the holy cross, the Holy Virgin, and the prayers of the Right

---

[1] Volok (Portage) was the name of the region that formed the watershed between the West Dvina and Dnieper.

Reverend Bishop Elias. Many Suzdalians were massacred, many were taken prisoner, while the remainder escaped only with great difficulty. And the price of Suzdalian prisoners fell to two *nogatas*.

6678 (1170)   There were high prices in Novgorod. A barrel of rye cost four *grivnas*, bread cost two *nogatas*, and honey ten *kunas* a *pood*. After deliberations, the Novgorodians decided to renounce Prince Roman. And they sent their emissaries to Great Prince Andrew Bogoliubsky (of Suzdal), suing for peace. They asked Prince Andrew to give them another prince who would preserve their liberties. In the same year on the 4th day of October, St. Erofey's day, Prince Rurik Rostislavich (the prince sent to Novgorod by Prince Andrew) arrived in Novgorod. This same year the God-loving Archbishop Elias and his brother, Gabriel, founded a monastery and erected the Church of the Annunciation of the Holy Mother of God. And this year Prince Mstislav Iziaslavich, the grandson of Vladimir, died. In the same year Prince Gleb Giorgivich died at Kiev, and (the Kievans) put in Vladimir Mstislavovich.

16. THE ELECTION OF ARCHBISHOP MANTURY, AND NOVGOROD WARS AGAINST THE UGRIANS

The entry for the year 1193 gives an interesting account of the election and consecration of a new archbishop. The second part of the entry is concerned with the description of a Novgorodian campaign against the people of Ugra (kinsmen of the present-day Hungarians) who occupied the area both east and west of the northern Urals. The Novgorodians began building their colonial empire in what is now northern Russia. By the fifteenth century, when this empire was nearing its end, it extended into Siberia and covered an area the size of present-day France, Germany, and Italy combined.

6701 (1193)   The Archbishop of Novgorod, Gabriel, passed away on May 24th, the day of our holy Father St. Simon. And he was solemnly buried in the porch of the Cathedral of St. Sophia next to his brother whose name was George after he took the holy vows. And then the people of Novgorod, the abbots, the Chapter of St. Sophia, and the clergy began their deliberations as to who should be the new archbishop. Some wanted to elect Mitrofan, while others wanted to elect Mantury, and still others wanted Grichina in this office. There was a great feud among them, and they decided to cast lots after High

Mass in the Cathedral of St. Sophia. And they prepared the lots, and after the service they sent for a blind man and he was given to them by God. And with the help of Divine Grace the blind man cast, and Mantury was chosen. And they sent for Mantury and they brought him to the court of the Archbishop.

And they announced his election to the Metropolitan of Kiev, and he sent for Mantury with great honors. And Mantury went to Kiev with the patricians of Novgorod. And he was received there with love by Prince Sviatoslav and the metropolitan. He was consecrated on the 10th day of December, the day celebrated for the deaths of the holy martyrs Mina, Hermogen, and Eugraph. And Mantury returned to Novgorod on January 16th, the day of the Falling Off of the Fetters of the holy Apostle Peter.

In the same year the Novgorodian troops under Voevoda Yadreik reached the land of Ugra and took a town. And they went to another town and besieged it. And they remained there five weeks, and the people of Ugra sent the Novgorodian forces a deceitful message saying the following: "We are collecting silver and sables and other valuables for you, so that you should neither destroy us nor your own tribute." And in the meantime the Ugrians began collecting their forces, and when their army had been gathered, the city sent a message to Voevoda Yadreik saying the following: "Come to the city bringing with you twelve men."

And Voevoda Yadreik went to the city, taking with him the priest John Legena and other leading men, and they were cut to pieces by the Ugrians on the eve of St. Barbara's day. And then they took thirty of the best Novgorodian warriors prisoner and cut them to pieces. And later fifty more Novgorodian warriors were cut down by the Ugrians.

And then Savka (apparently a Novgorodian) came to the Ugrian prince and said: "Prince, if you don't kill Jacob Prokshenich (presumably the second-in-command of the Novgorodian forces), but let him live to reach Novgorod, he will bring more warriors and will devastate your land." And the Ugrian prince called Jacob Prokshenich before him and ordered that he be killed, but Jacob said to Savka: "Brother, God and Holy Sophia will judge you if you have in mind the spilling of your brothers' blood. And you will appear before us and God, and you will be responsible for our blood." And after he said this he was killed, for Savka had secret connections with the Ugrian prince.

And then the army of Novgorod was starving because they had remained for six weeks, being induced to do so by Ugrian deceit. And on the Holy Day of St. Nicholas they broke camp

and were all cut to pieces by the Ugrian army. And there were
sorrow and misery among those who remained alive, and there
were only eighty of them. During the whole winter there was
no word in the city of Novgorod as to whether the men of the
army of *Voevoda* Yadreik were dead or alive. And in Novgorod
the prince, the archbishop, and the entire people of the city
grieved.

In the same year a son, Rostislav, was born to Yaroslav in
Novgorod. And they built a wooden church called Zhivoglozha
to the holy Apostles, and another church to St. Joan the Merciful at the Gates of Resurrection.

c. Stories from the *Galician-Volynian Chronicle*

17. PRINCE ROMAN, KHAN OTROK,
AND THE WORMWOOD

THE *Galician and Volynian Chronicle*, from which this tale is
taken, gives a rather detailed account of the fate of southern
Russia in the thirteenth century. The authors of the first part
demonstrate an unmistakable talent for narration and some
poetic inclination. The present excerpt gives a short but poetic
account of the circumstances under which Khan Otrok returned
to his native land.

The text upon which this translation is based is the *Ipatiev-
skaia letopis, P.S.R.L., Volume II*, St. Petersburg, 1908, pages
715–716.

Great Prince Roman, the unforgettable ruler of all Russia,
died. He was the one who conquered all the heathen nations
and with wisdom fulfilled all the divine commandments. He
would strike against the infidels (Kumans) like a lion. He could
be as full of wrath with them as is a lynx. He annihilated them
like a crocodile. Many were the times he crossed their lands
like an eagle. He was as courageous as an aurochs. He continued
the deeds of his grandfather, Prince Vladimir Monomakh, who
destroyed the infidel sons of Ishmael, who are usually called
Kumans. He drove Khan Otrok from the steppes to beyond the
Iron Gates (of the Caucasian Mountains) into Abkhasia.[1] Only
the horde of Khan Syrchan remained on the river Don, and he
had only fish for food. It was that time when Prince Vladimir

---

[1] A small nation on the eastern shores of the Black Sea.

Monomakh drank water from the river Don with his golden helmet. He conquered the entire Kuman land and drove away these accursed sons of Hagar.[2]

After the death of Prince Vladimir Monomakh, Khan Syrchan sent his bard, Oria, to his brother, Khan Otrok, who was still in the land of Abkhasia. And Syrchan told Oria to tell his brother: "Vladimir is dead. Come back, brother; return to your native land." And he added to Oria: "Tell these words I have spoken to my brother and sing him our Kuman songs. But, if he does not want to return, let him smell the fragrance of our prairie grass that is called wormwood."

When Khan Otrok wanted neither to return nor to listen to the songs of his brother's bard, the bard presented him a bouquet of wormwood from the prairie.

And when Khan Otrok inhaled the fragrance of the prairie wormwood, he began to weep, and said: "It is still better to die in one's native land than to win glory in a foreign one." And thus Khan Otrok decided to return to his native land.

---

[2] Following the Byzantine tradition, the Russians considered all nomads to be the descendants of Ishmael, the son of Hagar.

B. HOMILETIC AND DIDACTIC WORKS

18. METROPOLITAN HILARION: SERMON ON LAW AND GRACE

THE *Sermon on Law and Grace* is arranged in two distinct parts: "The Sermon on the Law of Moses Given to Him by God and on the Grace and Truth Brought to the Earth by Jesus Christ," and "The Eulogy to Our Kagan, Vladimir."

This famous sermon by Metropolitan Hilarion is the oldest Russian literary-philosophical work and one of the earliest Russian sermons preserved. It was written several decades before the *Primary Chronicle* and the most ancient Russian *vitae*, probably between 1037 and 1050. Its author, Hilarion, became in 1051 the first Russian (non-Greek) head of the Russian Church and Metropolitan of the city of Kiev. He was one of the most erudite and brilliant Russian preachers and writers of the Kievan age. Despite his clearly Byzantine cultural background, he manifests the Russian national spirit.

Besides the *Sermon on Law and Grace*, there has also been preserved Hilarion's *Confession of Faith*, in which he emphasizes the Trinitarian foundation of Christian dogma and the dual nature of Jesus Christ. In this work he wrote: "He suffered for me as a man. . . . He revived as God, . . . and after three days he arose from the dead, as a victor, Christ, my King."

In his *Sermon on Law and Grace* Metropolitan Hilarion reveals himself to be an astute preacher. The central idea of the sermon is the juxtaposition of the faith of the Old Testament with that of the New Testament. For the sake of comparison, he uses the story of the two sons of Abraham: the first, Ishmael, who was not free, but the son of Hagar, Sarah's handmaid; the second, who was free, being the son of Abraham by his wife, Sarah. For Hilarion, Christianity is the faith of freedom and liberation, whereas the religion of the Old Testament was one of law, compulsion, and strict obedience.

Hilarion's attitude toward the problem of salvation is very characteristic of early Eastern Christianity: salvation through "baptism and good deeds," through Christian mercy and charity. This is remote from Luther's and Calvin's teachings of salvation solely through faith and, concomitantly, moral behavior.

This sermon, despite its clear tendency to raise the prestige of the Russian nation and the Russian Church, was composed in a typical Byzantine style, and is saturated with repeated parallels between Hagar and the Old Testament, and between Sarah and the New Testament. When Hilarion wrote that "Divine Grace announced to God" and that "the Father did as he was told by Divine Grace," he apparently referred to "Holy Sophia," that is, the Divine Omniscience of the three hypostases of the Trinity. The teaching of "Holy Wisdom," or "Holy Sophia," was widespread throughout Byzantium and Russia at that time, and is attested to by the fact that cathedrals in Constantinople, Kiev, and Novgorod were dedicated to "Holy Sophia."

Having adroitly presented his view of the fundamental doctrine of the Christian faith, Hilarion turned to the destiny of the Russian people. In his eyes, when the Russians adopted Christianity they became the equal of all Christian peoples, including the Greeks. He regarded the Russian Church as having the same dignity, status, and rights as the Byzantine Church. It must be remembered that both Yaroslav and Hilarion attempted to liberate the Russian Church from Byzantine supervision and that Hilarion was the first native Russian to head the Russian Church and to defend its autonomy from Constantinople.

Hilarion ends his sermon with a highly rhetorical panegyric to Prince Vladimir, whom Russians consider a saint for having Christianized Russia. Optimistic, bright, even triumphant notes can easily be discerned in Hilarion's treatment of history. Russia had become enlightened by the Christian faith, and therefore its future would lie in Christ's hands.

The following translation is based upon the text of Metropolitan Hilarion's sermon published by A. B. Gorskii in *Pamiatniki dukhovnoi literatury vremeni velikogo kniazia Yaroslava I-ogo*, Moscow, 1844.

THE SERMON ON THE LAW OF MOSES GIVEN TO HIM BY GOD, AND ON THE GRACE AND TRUTH BROUGHT TO EARTH BY JESUS CHRIST

Blessed be the God of Israel, the God of Christianity who visited his people and brought them salvation. He did not disdain his creation, which was for ages possessed by pagan darkness and by worship of the devil, but he enlightened the Children of Abraham by giving them his Law tablets, and later he saved all nations, sending them his Son, his Gospel, and his Baptism, and by giving them resurrection to eternal life. . . .

Law was the precursor and the servant of Grace and Truth. Grace and Truth were the servants of the future life and immortal life. Law led its people of the Old Testament toward the blessing of Baptism, and Baptism led its sons to the life eternal.

Moses and the prophets announced the coming of Christ, but
Christ and the Apostles announced resurrection and the future
age. . . .

And what could the Law achieve? And what could Grace
achieve? First was the Law and then Grace. Hagar and Sarah
are the pictures of Law and Grace: Hagar was a handmaid and
Sarah was free. First comes the handmaiden and then the free
woman. And he who reads (the Bible) must understand this.
Abraham, since his youth, had Sarah for his wife and she was
free and not a slave, and so God decided before all ages to send
his Son into the world that Grace might appear through him
(but sent him to man only later). But Sarah was restrained
from bearing children, since she was unfruitful. But she was not
actually unfruitful, but was chosen by Divine Providence to bear
in her old age. The wisdom of God was not revealed to anyone,
but concealed from both angels and men. This wisdom was not
shown, but was concealed to be revealed at the end of the age.
It was Sarah who said unto Abraham: "Behold now, the Lord
has prevented me from bearing children; go in to my maid; it
may be that I shall obtain children by her."
And so the Divine Grace (of the Son) announced to God, the
Father: "It is not yet my time for descending to the earth and
to save the world. Descend to Mount Sinai and give them the
Law."
And, just as Abraham did as Sarah told him and went into
Hagar, so God, the Father, did as he was told by the Divine
Grace and descended to Mount Sinai.
And Hagar, the handmaid, bore from Abraham a servant (not
a truly free man), and Abraham gave him the name Ishmael.
And Moses brought from Mount Sinai the Law and not the
Grace, the shade and not the Truth.
When Abraham and Sarah were old, God appeared to Abraham by the oaks of Mamre, as he sat at the door of his tent in
the heat of the day. And he ran to meet him, and bowing lowly
to the earth, he hastened into the tent (to Sarah). And so, when
the end of the age was nearing, God appeared to the humankind, descended to the earth, and blessed the womb of the
Virgin. And he was received by the Immaculate Virgin into the
tent of the flesh. And the Virgin said to the angel: "Behold I am
the servant of the Lord; let it be to me according to your word."
Once the Lord gave Sarah to bear a child, and she begat
Isaac, the free son of a free mother. And, when once more our
Lord visited the humankind, he appeared unknown and hidden

from men and then was born Grace and Truth, but not the Law. And now it was the Son and not the servant.

And the child grew up and was weaned; and Abraham made a great feast on the day that Isaac was weaned. And when Christ was upon the earth Grace did not reveal itself and Christ was hiding himself until he was thirty. And when he had grown and was weaned, then there, in the river Jordan, Grace was revealed by a man. And Our Lord invited many and made a great feast and offered up the fatted calf of the age, His beloved Son, Jesus Christ, and God then called to this feast many of heaven and earth and they the angels and men into one (Church). . . .

This blessed faith spreads now over the entire earth, and finally it reached the Russian nation. And, whereas the lake of the Law dried up, the fount of the Gospel became rich in water and overflowed upon our land and reached us. And now, together with all Christians, we glorify the Holy Trinity, while Judea remains silent. . . .

THE EULOGY TO OUR KAGAN VLADIMIR

Rome, with voices panegyrical, praises Peter and Paul through whom they came to believe in Jesus Christ, the Son of God; Asia, Ephesus, and Patmus praise John the Theologian; India praises Thomas; Egypt, Mark. All lands, cities, and men honor and glorify their teacher who brought them the Orthodox Faith. Thus, let us, through our own strength, humbly praise our teacher and mentor, the great Kagan of our land Vladimir, the grandson of Igor of yore and son of glorious Sviatoslav, who ruled in their day with courage and valor, becoming famed in many lands for their victories and fortitude. And they did not reign in a poor and unknown land, but in Russia, which is known and celebrated by all to the ends of the earth. . . .

A good attestation of your devotion, blessed one, is the Holy Church of the Blessed Virgin, the Mother of God, which you build on the Orthodox foundation and where your valorous body now lays at rest and awaits the archangel's trumpet.

A good and certain attestation is your son, George (Yaroslav's Christian name), whom God has made the heir to your throne,
who does not destroy your laws, but confirms them,
who does not diminish works of piety, but extends them,
who does not undo, but strengthens,
who finishes that which you have left unfinished'
even as Solomon finished the works begun by David;
who has built a great and holy temple to God's omniscience
that it may hallow your city;
· who has embellished with all manner of things beautiful,

with gold and silver and precious stones
and with sacred vessels;
so that the church is a wonder to all surrounding lands
and so that the like cannot be found in all the northern land,
nor in the east nor the west;
who has given your famous city of Kiev the crown of glory,
who has turned your city and its people
to all-glorious Mother of God,
who is always ready to succor Christians
and for whom he has built a church with doors of gold
in the name of the first Holy Day of the Lord of the Annunci-
    ation,
that the veneration, which the archangel will offer to the
    Virgin,
may also be upon this city.
To her he speaks, saying:
    "Rejoice, Blessed One, the Lord is with you!"
And to the city he speaks, saying:
    "Rejoice, faithful city, the Lord is with you!"

Arise from your grave, venerated prince,
arise and shake off your sleep.
You are not dead,
but only sleep until the day of resurrection of all.
Arise! You are not dead,
for it is not right that you should die,
for you have believed in Christ,
the Sustainer of the whole world.
Shake off your deep sleep
and lift up your eyes
that you might see what honor the Lord has granted you,
and you still live upon this earth,
unforgotten through your sons.
Arise! behold your son George, your child, your beloved one!
whom God has brought forth from your loins.
Behold him embellishing the throne of your land.
Rejoice and be of good cheer!
Behold the pious wife of your son, Irina.
Behold your grandchildren
and your great-grandchildren.
Behold how they live and how they are cared for by God.
Behold how they preserve devotion in your tradition,
how they partake of the Sacraments of the Holy Church,
how they glorify Christ,
and how they venerate his Holy Name.

Behold your city radiant with majesty.
Behold your blossoming churches,
behold Christianity flourishing.
Behold your city gleaming,
adorned with holy icons and
fragrant with thyme,
praising God and filling the air with sacred songs.

And beholding all this, rejoice and be of good cheer, and praise the Lord, the Creator of all . . .

19. CYRIL OF TUROV: SERMON ON THE FIRST SUNDAY AFTER EASTER

Among Russian writers of the Kievan period, Cyril, Bishop of Turov, was probably the most accomplished master of Orthodox theology and the Byzantine style of writing. He had an excellent command of Greek and his literary achievements surpass those of any other Russian man of letters of that era. He wrote numerous epistles, prayers, and sermons, all of which are distinguished by their elegant and elaborate style. They show clearly the author's gift for composition and his extensive knowledge of the Bible and early Church history. In his works he quotes the patriarchs and prophets of the Old Testament with unusual adroitness for that time. Though full of symbolism and allegory, his writings are nonetheless lucid and fully comprehensible, and they gained the admiration of endless generations of Russians. Even as late as the seventeenth century, many of Cyril's stylistic patterns were still popular with writers of the conservative literary tradition. Of all his works, Cyril's sermon with the triumphant description of spring as the symbol of the Resurrection was the most popular.

Very little is known of the author's life except that he lived in the middle of the twelfth century and was Bishop of Turov. His best-known works are eight sermons delivered on the occasion of the eight Sundays beginning with Palm Sunday. The *Sermon on the First Sunday After Easter*, his most famous single work, is offered here in a translation by Leo Wiener.

The Church needs a great teacher and a wise orator to celebrate the holiday properly, but we are poor in words and dim in mind, not having the fire of the Holy Ghost—the enjoyment of words useful to the soul; yet for the love of my brethren who are with me, we shall say something about the renewal of the Lord's Resurrection. In the past week of the Easter there were joy in heaven and terror in the nethermost regions, a renewal of life and liberation of the world, a destruction of hell and victory over death, a resurrection of the dead, and annihilation of the enticing power of the devil; a salvation of the human race by the Resurrection of Christ; an impoverishment of the Old Testament and enslavement of the Sabbath; an enrichment of the Church of Christ, and enthronement of the Sunday.

Last week there was a change of all things, for the earth was opened up by heaven, having been purified from its satanic impurities, and the angels with their wives humbly served at the Resurrection. All creation was renewed, for no longer are the air, the sun, the fire, the springs, the trees, thought to be gods; no longer does hell receive its due of infants sacrificed by their fathers, nor death its honors, for idolatry has come to an end, and the satanic power has been vanquished by the mystery of the Cross. The Old Testament has become impoverished by the rejection of the blood of calves and sacrifices of goats, for Christ has given himself to the Lord as a sacrifice for all. And with this, Sunday ceased to be a holiday, but the Sunday was sanctified on account of the Resurrection, and Sunday is now supreme, for Christ arose from the dead on that day. . . .

Today the heavens have been cleared from the dark clouds that enshrouded them as with a heavy veil, and they proclaim the glory of God with a clear atmosphere. . . .

Today the sun rises and beams on high, and rejoicing warms the earth, for there has arisen for us from the grave the real sun, Christ, and he saves all who believe in him. Today the moon descends from its high place and gives honor to the greater lights. The Old Testament, as had been prophesied, has stopped with its Sabbath, and with its prophets gives honor to the Testament of Christ with its Sunday. Today the winter of sin has stopped in repentance, and the ice of unbelief is melted by wisdom. Today spring appears spruce, and enlivens all earthly existence; the stormy winds blow gently and generate fruits, and the earth, giving nurture to the seed, brings forth green grass. For spring is the beautiful faith in Christ which, through baptism, produces a regeneration of man, and the stormy winds are the evil, sinful thoughts that, being changed to virtue through repentance, generate soul-saving fruits; but the earth of our being, having received the Word of God like a seed, and, passing through an ecstatic labor, through the fear of him, brings forth a spirit of salvation.

Today the newborn lambs and calves frisk and leap about joyfully and returning to their mothers gambol about, so that the shepherds, playing on their reeds, praise Christ in joy. The lambs, I say, are the gentle people from among the pagans, and the calves—the idolaters of the unbelieving countries who, having accepted the Law through Christ's incarnation and the teachings of the Apostles and miracles, and having returned to the holy Church, suck the milk of its teachings; and the teachers of Christ's flock, praying for all, praise Christ, the Lord, who had collected all the wolves and sheep into one herd.

Today the trees send forth buds and the fragrant flowers bloom, and behold, the gardens already emit a sweet odor, and the workers laboring in hope acclaim Christ the giver of fruits. We were before like the trees of the forest that bear no fruit, but today the faith of Christ has been grafted on our unbelief, and those who already held to the roots of Jesse have burgeoned with the flowers of virtue and expect through Christ a regeneration in heaven, and the saints who labor for the Church expect a reward from Christ. Today the plowman of the Word leads the oxen of the Word to the spiritual yoke, sinks the plow of baptism into the furrows of thought and deepening them to furrows of repentance plants in them the spiritual seed and rejoices in the hope of future returns. Today everything old has taken an end, and all is new for the sake of the Resurrection. Today the apostolic rivers are full, and the pagan fish let out their broods, and the fishermen, having examined the depth of the divine incarnation, drag in full nets into the Church. . . . Today the industrious bees of the monastic order show their wisdom and set all to wonder, for, living in the wilderness and providing for themselves, they astonish both angels and men, just as the bee flies upon the flowers and forms combs of honey in order to furnish sweetness to man and what is needed in the Church. . . .

Today there is a feast of regeneration for the people who are made new by the Resurrection of Christ, and all new things are brought to God: from heathens, faith; from good Christians, offerings; from the clergy, holy sacrifices; from the civil authorities, God-pleasing charity; from the noble, care for the Church; from the righteous, humility; from the sinners, true repentance; from the unhallowed, a turning to God; from the hating, spiritual love.

20. VLADIMIR MONOMAKH: INSTRUCTION
TO HIS CHILDREN

By the end of the eleventh century the Russian princes, the heirs of Vladimir, were continually struggling to enlarge their own patrimonies to the detriment of those of their brothers and cousins. It was at this time that Vladimir Monomakh, grandson of Yaroslav the Wise, came to power and succeeded in assuming leadership among the princes. He maintained order and peace for several years, and during his reign the Golden Age, which had been initiated by Yaroslav the Wise, reached its height. The feudal wars ceased and the united forces of the Russian princes were able to contain the Kumans, a Turkic nomadic people who by this time occupied most of Russia south of Kiev.

The son of Prince Vsevolod and of a Byzantine princess of the house of Monomakh, Vladimir married Gita, the daughter of the last Anglo-Saxon king, Harold, who was defeated at the Battle of Hastings in 1066. After this defeat the surviving members of the Anglo-Saxon royal family lived as émigrés in Vladimir's court at Kiev. Vladimir Monomakh, continuing the tradition of Yaroslav the Wise, maintained lively relations with Western Europe: his sister, Eupraxy, became the wife of the German Emperor, Henry IV; and his children married into various royal houses, including those of Hungary, Sweden, and Byzantium. He lived from 1053 to 1125 and became the prince of Kiev in 1113.

The *Testament*, or *Instruction*, of Vladimir Monomakh is recorded in the *Laurentian Chronicle* under the year 1096, apparently having been interpolated into the chronicle after the prince's death. Vladimir had considerable erudition and an excellent knowledge of the Scriptures and writings of the Holy Fathers. His *Instruction* is one of the best examples of early Russian letters and was written as a moral and political instruction for his children. The *Instruction* is imbued with a real Christian spirit: in it Vladimir Monomakh instructs his children not how to be cunning princes or successful conquerors, but rather teaches them the duties of good Christians who are supposed to care for their own souls as well as for the welfare of their subjects and people around them. It can be easily divided into three distinct parts: (1) admonition to the children; (2) autobiographic notes; (3) final advice. It may be added that Vladimir Monomakh was the first Russian ever to write about his own life, and in this way laid the foundation for the Russian autobiographical tradition.

The translation follows the text published in *Polnoe sobranie russkikh letopisei*, Volume I, Leningrad, 1926, cols. 240–256. Because of the limitations of the size of this book, some passages of the *Instruction* have been omitted.

I. ADMONITION TO THE CHILDREN

I, wretched one, named at my baptism Vassily by my blessed and glorious grandfather, Yaroslav, but commonly known by my Russian name of Vladimir,[1] and who . . . (lacuna) . . . by my beloved father and my mother, who was from the family of Monomakh . . . whom, for the sake of Christian people He has preserved many times from all distresses thanks to His mercy and thanks to my father's prayers.

As I approach the end of my life I meditate in my heart and praise God, who led me, a sinner, to these days. My children or anyone else who happens to read this message should not laugh at it, but those who like it should take it to heart and should not be disposed to laziness but to hard work.

First of all, for the sake of God and for the salvation of your own souls, retain the fear of God in your hearts and give alms openhandedly, for generosity is the source of all virtue. If this message displeases anyone let him not laugh, but just say: "On the eve of his last journey, approaching the end of his life, he talked nonsense."

Once on the Volga I was met by my brothers' envoys, who told me: "Hurry to join our forces, and let us expel Rostislav's children[2] and take their principalities. If thou dost not join us, we will do it by ourselves, and thou wilt get nothing." And I answered: "You may grow angry with me, but I can neither go with you, nor break my oath." And I sent the envoys away and I took the Psalter; I opened it in my sorrow and came across (the following text): "Why art thou cast down, O my soul? and why art thou disquieted within me?" (Psalm 43:5). I collected these noble words, and arranged them in order, and copied them. If the last passage does not please you, then accept the first: "Why are thou cast down, O my soul? and why art thou disquieted within me? I hope in God: for I shall yet praise him, who is the health of my countenance, and my God" (Psalm 43:5). "Fret not thyself because of evildoers, neither be thou envious against workers of iniquity. For evildoers shall be cut

---

[1] In the eleventh and twelfth centuries Russians often used to have two names: one Christian, given them at baptism, which was mostly of Greek or of biblical origin; and another Russian name, which was commonly used in addressing people.

[2] Rostislav's sons, Princes Volodar of Peremyshl and Vasil'ko of Terebovl', cities and principalities in Galicia, the southwestern part of Russia located on the western slopes of the Carpathians and the neighboring plains.

off: but those that wait upon the Lord, they shall inherit the earth. For yet a little while, and the wicked shall not be: yea, thou shalt diligently consider his place, and he shall not be. But the meek shall delight themselves in the abundance of peace. The wicked plotteth against the just, and gnasheth upon him with his teeth. The Lord shall laugh at him for he seeth that his day is coming. The wicked have drawn out the sword and have bent their bows, to cast down the poor and needy and to slay such as be upright in their ways. Their sword shall enter into their own heart and their bows shall be broken. The little that a righteous man hath is better than the riches of many wicked. For the arms of the wicked shall be broken, but the Lord upholdeth the righteous. They shall not be ashamed in the evil time and in the days of famine they shall be satisfied. For such as be blessed of him shall inherit the earth; and they that be cursed of him shall be cut off. The steps of a good man are ordered by the Lord and he delighteth in his way. Though he fall, he shall not be utterly cast down: for the Lord upholdeth him with his hand. I have been young and now am old, yet have I not seen the righteous forsaken, nor his seed begging bread. He is ever merciful, and lendeth; and his seed is blessed. Depart from evil, and do good; and dwell for evermore" (Psalm 37:1, 9–17, 19, 22–27). "If it had not been the Lord who was on our side, when men rose up against us: then they had swallowed us up alive, then the waters had overwhelmed us, the stream had gone over our soul" (Psalm 124:2–4). "Be merciful unto me, O God: for man would swallow me up; his fighting daily oppresseth me. Mine enemies would daily swallow me up, for they are many that fight against me, O thou Most High" (Psalm 56:1–2). "The righteous shall rejoice when he seeth the vengeance: he shall wash his feet in the blood of the wicked. So that a man shall say, Verily there is a reward for the righteous: verily there is a God that judgeth the earth" (Psalm 58:10–11). "Deliver me from mine enemies, O my God: defend me from them that rise up against me. Deliver me from the workers of iniquity, and save me from bloody men. For, lo, they lie in wait for my soul" (Psalm 59:1–3). "For his anger endureth but a moment; in his favor is life: weeping may endure for a night, but joy cometh in the morning" (Psalm 30:5). "Because thy loving-kindness is better than life, my lips shall praise thee. Thus will I bless thee while I live: I will lift up my hands in thy name" (Psalm 63:4–5). "Hide me from the secret counsel of the wicked; from the insurrection of the workers of iniquity" (Psalm 64:2). "Rejoice, all ye righteous in heart. I will bless the Lord at all times: his praise shall continually be in my mouth" (Psalm 34:1).

It was Basil [3] who used to gather young men of pure heart and untainted body and approach them with a short and meek talk and with a right measure of divine words: "Do not be noisy when you eat and drink. Remain silent in the presence of your seniors. Listen to the wise men; obey your superiors; love those who are your equals and your inferiors. Speak without guile, but try to understand. Be moderate in your language. Do not insult other people with your words. Have awe for the aged. Refrain from chatter with shameless women, and cast your eyes downward but your souls and words upward. Don't hesitate to warn those who seek power. Avoid flatterers. If some one of you may be of help to the others, he can accept his divine recompense and he shall enjoy eternal salvation." (And Basil also taught:) "O Our Lady, Mother of God, take away the pride and violence from my poor heart, lest I be exalted in the empty life by the vanity of this world."

Let the faithful learn to strive for pious effort, since according to the words of the Bible:

Learn to control your eyes,
to curb your tongue,
to moderate your temper,
to subdue your body,
to restrain your wrath,
to cherish pure thought,
exerting yourself in good works for the Lord's sake.
When robbed, avenge not,
when hated or persecuted, endure,
when affronted, pray,
destroy sin,
render justice to the orphan,
protect the widow,

" 'Come let us reason together,' saith the Lord: 'though your sins be as scarlet, they shall be as white as snow' " (Isaiah, 1:18).

"The dayspring of fasting shall shine forth, and likewise the light of repentance. Let us purify ourselves, my brethren, from every corporal and spiritual blemish, and, as we call upon our

---

[3] Basil: in this case Monomakh means St. Basil the Great, Bishop of Caesarea (330–379), one of the greatest early Christian theologians, preachers, scholars, and poets.

Creator, let us say, Glory to thee, lover of mankind!" In truth, my children, understand how merciful, yea, how supremely merciful is God, the lover of mankind. Being of human stock, we are so sinful and mortal that, when anyone does us evil, we desire to destroy him and to shed his blood speedily. But Our Lord, the ruler of life and death, suffers our sins to be higher than our heads, and yet he loves us all our lives as a father loves his son whom he chastens and then summons once more to his embrace.

As you read these divine words, my children, praise God, who has shown his mercy. The continuation of this letter is the advice of my own poor wit. Give heed to me and if you are not disposed to accept all my advice, at least accept one-half of it. When the Lord softens your heart, shed tears for your sins and pray: "As thou hast taken pity upon the adulteress and the publican, have pity upon us, sinners." And say these words in the Church and before going to bed.

Fail not, if it is possible, one single night to kneel to the ground three times, in the case that you cannot do so more often. Forget not, nor be remiss in this observance, for by his nightly worship and hymn man conquers the devil, and by this means expiates what sins he has committed during the day. When you are riding forth upon your horse, if you have not anything special to discuss with a companion and do not know other prayers, then exclaim without ceasing: "Kyrie eleison!" within yourselves. This is the best prayer of all, and infinitely better than thinking evil thoughts while riding horses.

Above all things:
Forget not the poor,
but support them to the extent of your means.
Give to the orphan,
protect the widow,
and permit the mighty to destroy no man.
Take not the life of the just or the unjust,
nor permit him to be killed.
Destroy no Christian soul,
even though he be guilty of murder.

When you speak either good or evil, swear not by the name of God, nor cross yourselves, for that is unnecessary. Whenever you kiss the cross to confirm an oath made to your brethren or to any other man, first test your heart as to whether you can abide by your word, then kiss the cross, and after once having given your oath, abide by it, lest you destroy your souls by its violation.

Receive with affection the blessing of bishops, priests, and abbots, and shun them not, but rather, according to your means, love and help them, that you may receive from them their intercession in the presence of God. Above all things, admit no pride in your hearts and minds, but say: "We are but mortal; today we live and tomorrow we shall be in the grave. All that thou hast given us is not ours, but thine, and thou hast but lent it to us for a few days." Hoard not the treasures of earth, for therein lies great sin. Honor the ancient as your father, and the youth as your brother.

Be not lax in the discipline of your homes, but rather attend to all matters yourselves. Rely not upon your steward or your servant, lest they who visit you ridicule your house or your table. When you set out to war, be not inactive, depend not upon your captains, or waste your time in drinking, eating, or sleeping. Set the sentries yourselves, and take your rest only after you have posted them at night at every important point about your troops; then take your rest, but arise early. Do not put off your accouterments without a quick glance about you, for a man may thus perish suddenly through his own carelessness. Guard against lying, drunkenness, and vice, for therein perish soul and body. When journeying anywhere by road through your domain, do not permit your followers or another's company to visit violence upon the villages or upon the dwellings, lest men revile you. Wherever you go, as often as you halt, give the beggar to eat and to drink. Furthermore, honor the stranger, if not with a gift, at least with food and drink, whencesoever he comes to you, be he simple, or noble, or an emissary. For travelers give a man a universal reputation as generous or niggardly.

Visit the sick and accompany the dead, for we are all but mortal. Pass no man without a greeting; give him a kindly word. Love your wives, but grant them no power over you. This is the end of all things: to hold the fear of God above all else. If you forget all my admonitions, read this counsel frequently. Then I shall be without disgrace, and you shall profit thereby.

Forget not what useful knowledge you possess, and acquire that with which you are not acquainted, even as my father, though he remained at home in his own country, still understood five languages. For by this means honor is acquired in other lands. Laziness is the mother of all evil; what a man knows, he forgets, and what he does not know he does not learn. In the practice of good works, you cannot neglect any item of good conduct.

II. AUTOBIOGRAPHIC NOTES

I now narrate to you, my sons, the fatigue I have endured on journeys and hunts for fifty-three years. First I rode to Rostov through the Viatichi,[4] whither my father had sent me while he himself went to Kursk, in 1073. Second, to Smolensk with Stavko the son of Skordiata; he then went to Brest with Iziaslav, and sent me to Smolensk. From Smolensk, I rode on to Vladimir.

In the same winter my brethren sent me to Brest to the place which the Poles had burned, and there I beheld the city in peace. Then I went to my father in Pereiaslavl; and after Easter, from Pereiaslavl to Vladimir to make peace with the Poles at Suteisk. Thence back to Vladimir again in the summer. Then Sviatoslav sent me to Poland; after going beyond Glogau to the Czech forest, I traveled four months in that country.[5]

(Omitted: an enumeration of some thirty other campaigns in which Vladimir Monomakh participated.)

I concluded nineteen peace treaties with the Kumans with or without my father's aid, and dispensed much of my cattle and my garments. I freed from their captivity the powerful Kuman princes, including two brothers of Sharukan, three brothers of Bagubars, four brothers of Osen, and one hundred of their foremost nobles. Of other chieftains whom God delivered alive into my hands, I took captive, killed, and had cast into the river Saenia, Koxus and his son, Aklan Burchevich, Asgului Khan of Tarev, and fifteen other young chieftains, and at the same time not less than two hundred of the important prisoners were likewise killed, and cast into the same river.

I ruled in Chernigov and made journeys from that city. Until the present year, in fact, I without difficulty used all my strength in hunting, not to mention other hunting trips around Turov, since I had been accustomed to chase every kind of game while in my father's company.

I even bound wild horses with my bare hands or captured ten or twenty live horses, and besides that, while riding through the plains, I caught these same horses with bare hands. Two buffaloes[6] tossed me and my horse on their horns; a stag once

---

[4] Viatichi: a Russian tribe in western Russia.

[5] Vladimir fought extensively against the Kumans and Poles and even campaigned in the Czech lands. Sviatoslav was the son of Yaroslav the Wise and father of Prince Oleg of Chernigov, who fought Monomakh and was responsible for many fratricidal feuds among the Russian princes.

[6] In the eleventh and twelfth centuries there were still many wild horses and buffalo in southern Russia, especially in the steppe.

gored me; one moose stamped upon me, and another tossed me with his antlers; a boar once tore my sword from my thigh; a bear on one occasion bit my knee; and another wild beast jumped on my hip and threw my horse with me. But God preserved me unharmed.

I fell many times from my horse, fractured my skull twice, and in my youth injured my arms and legs when I did not reck of my life or spare my head. In war and at the hunt, by night and by day, in heat and in cold, I did the same as my servant had to do, and gave myself no rest. Without relying on stewards and envoys, I did whatever was needed; I looked to every problem in my household. At the hunt, I posted the hunters, and I looked after the stables, the falcons, and the hawks. I did not allow the powerful lords to distress the poor peasant or the unfortunate widow, and I myself cared for ecclesiastical administration and Church service.

III. FINAL ADVICE

Let not my sons or whoever else reads this epistle criticize me. I do not commend my own courage, but I praise God and glorify his memory because he guarded me, a sinful and a wretched man, for so many years in these mortal dangers, and did not make me inactive or useless for all the necessary works of man. As you read this writing, prepare yourselves for all good works, and praise God among his saints. Without fear of death, of war, or of wild beasts, do a man's work, my sons, as God gave it to you. If I suffered no damages from war, from wild beasts, from flood, or from falling from my horse, then surely no one can harm you and ruin you, unless it is God's will. And when God will send death to you, then neither your father nor your mother, nor your brothers can help you to escape its hands. It is good to be on one's guard; the divine guardianship is better, however, than man's.

(Some additional advice has been omitted.)

C. THE LIVES OF SAINTS AND MONKS

a. Stories from the *Primary Chronicle*

21. THE MARTYRDOM OF BORIS AND GLEB

AFTER the death of Vladimir, a fratricidal struggle broke out among his sons. The eldest, Sviatopolk, seized power and began plotting the elimination of his brothers, Boris, Gleb, and Yaroslav. The murder of Boris and Gleb in 1015 is described in a touching manner by the chronicler: the two refused to take up arms against their elder brother in order to prevent further bloodshed. They decided to accept their fate passively, following the example of Christ. The story of their tragic death was the first instance in Eastern and Western medieval ecclesiastic tradition of the imitation of Christ as a humble martyr dying for the sins of man. In both Western and Byzantine Christianity at that time, Christ's image was that of a pantocrat: an awe-inspiring, omnipotent ruler of the universe, to be dreaded. The humble aspect of Christ was stressed neither in Byzantine nor in Western Christianity until the time of St. Francis, some two hundred years after the martyrdom of Boris and Gleb.

The text presented here is the Samuel H. Cross translation.

Sviatopolk settled in Kiev after his father's death, and after calling together all the inhabitants of Kiev, he began to distribute largess among them. They accepted it, but their hearts were not with him, because their brethren were with Boris. When Boris returned with the army, not having met the Pechenegs, he received the news that his father was dead. He mourned deeply for him, for he was beloved of his father before all the rest.

When he came to the Alta, he halted. His father's retainers then urged him to take his place in Kiev on his father's throne, since he had at his disposal the latter's retainers and troops. But Boris protested: "Be it not for me to raise my hand against my elder brother. Now that my father has passed away, let him take the place of my father in my heart." When the soldiery heard these words, they departed from him, and Boris remained with his servants.

But Sviatopolk was filled with lawlessness. Adopting the device of Cain, he sent messages to Boris that he desired to live at peace with him, and would increase the patrimony he had received from his father. But he plotted against him how he

might kill him. So Sviatopolk came by night to Vyshegorod.
After secretly summoning to his presence Putsha and the boyars
of the town, he inquired of them whether they were whole-
heartedly devoted to him. Putsha and the men of Vyshegorod
replied: "We are ready to lay down our lives for you." He then
commanded them to say nothing to any man, but to go and kill
his brother Boris. They straightway promised to execute his
order. Of such men Solomon has well said: "They make haste
to shed blood unjustly. For they promise blood, and gather evil.
Their path runneth to evil, for they possess their souls in dishonor" (Proverbs, 1:16–19).

These emissaries came to the Alta, and when they approached,
they heard the sainted Boris singing vespers. For it was already
known to him that they intended to take his life. Then he arose
and began to chant, saying: "O Lord, how are they increased
who come against me! Many are they that rise up against me"
(Psalms, 3:1). And also: "Thy arrows have pierced me, for I
am ready for wounds and my pain is before me continually"
(Psalms, 38:2, 17). And he also uttered this prayer: "Lord, hear
my prayer, and enter not into judgment with thy servant, for no
living man shall be just before thee. For the enemy hath crushed
my soul" (Psalms, 140:1–3). After ending the six psalms, when
he saw how men were sent out to kill him, he began to chant
the Psalter, saying: "Strong bulls encompassed me, and the
assemblage of the evil beset me. O Lord my God, I have hoped
in thee; save me and deliver me from my pursuers" (Psalms,
22:12, 16; 7:1). Then he began to sing the canon. After finishing vespers, he prayed, gazing upon the icon, the image of the
Lord, with these words: "Lord Jesus Christ, who in this image
hast appeared on earth for our salvation, and who, having voluntarily suffered thy hands to be nailed to the cross, didst endure
thy passion for our sins, so help me now to endure my passion.
For I accept it not from those who are my enemies, but from
the hand of my own brother. Hold it not against him as a sin,
O Lord!"

After offering this prayer, he lay down upon his couch. Then
they fell upon him like wild beasts about the tent, and overcame
him by piercing him with lances. They also overpowered his
servant, who cast himself upon his body. For he was beloved
of Boris. He was a servant of Hungarian race, George by name,
to whom Boris was greatly attached. The prince had given him
a large gold necklace which he wore while serving him. They
also killed many other servants of Boris. But since they could
not quickly take the necklace from George's neck, they cut off

his head, and thus obtained it. For this reason his body was not
recognized later among the corpses.

The murderers, after attacking Boris, wrapped him in a
canvas, loaded him upon a wagon, and dragged him off, though
he was still alive. When the impious Sviatopolk saw that he was
still breathing, he sent two Varangians to finish him. When they
came and saw that he was still alive, one of them drew his
sword and plunged it into his heart. Thus died the blessed Boris,
receiving from the hand of Christ our God the crown among the
righteous. He shall be numbered with the prophets and the
Apostles, as he joins with the choirs of martyrs, rests in the lap
of Abraham, beholds joy ineffable, chants with the angels, and
rejoices in company with the choirs of saints. After his body had
been carried in secret to Vyshegorod, it was buried in the
Church of St. Basil.

The impious Sviatopolk then reflected: "Behold, I have killed
Boris; now how can I kill Gleb?" Adopting once more Cain's
device, he craftily sent messages to Gleb to the effect that he
should come quickly, because his father was very ill and desired
his presence. Gleb quickly mounted his horse, and set out with
a small company, for he was obedient to his father. When he
came to the Volga, his horse stumbled in a ditch on the plain,
and broke his leg. He arrived at Smolensk, and setting out
thence at dawn, he embarked in a boat on the Smiadyn. At this
time, Yaroslav received from Predslava the tidings of their
father's death, and he sent word to Gleb that he should not set
out, because his father was dead and his brother had been murdered by Sviatopolk. Upon receiving these tidings, Gleb burst
into tears, and mourned for his father, but still more deeply for
his brother. He wept and prayed with the lament: "Woe is me,
O Lord! It were better for me to die with my brother than to
live on in this world. O my brother, had I but seen thy angelic
countenance, I should have died with thee. Why am I now left
alone? Where are thy words that thou didst say to me, my
brother? No longer do I hear thy sweet counsel. If thou hast
received affliction from God, pray for me that I may endure the
same passion. For it were better for me to dwell with thee than
in this deceitful world."

While he was thus praying amid his tears, there suddenly
arrived those sent by Sviatopolk for Gleb's destruction. These
emissaries seized Gleb's boat, and drew their weapons. The
servants of Gleb were terrified, and the impious messenger,
Goriaser, gave orders that they should slay Gleb with dispatch.
Then Gleb's cook, Torchin by name, seized a knife, and stabbed

Gleb. He was offered up as a sacrifice to God like an innocent lamb, a glorious offering amid the perfume of incense, and he received the crown of glory. Entering the heavenly mansions, he beheld his long-desired brother, and rejoiced with him in the joy ineffable which they had attained through their brotherly love.

"How good and fair it is for brethren to live together!" (Psalms, 133:1). But the impious ones returned again, even as David said, "Let the sinners return to hell" (Psalms, 9:17). When they returned to Sviatopolk, they reported that his command had been executed. On hearing these tidings, he was puffed up with pride, since he knew not the words of David: "Why art thou proud of thy evildoing, O mighty one? Thy tongue hath considered lawlessness all the day long" (Psalms, 52:1).

After Gleb had been slain, his body was thrown upon the shore between two tree trunks, but afterward they took him and carried him away, to bury him beside his brother Boris in the Church of St. Basil. United thus in body and still more in soul, ye dwell with the Lord and King of all, in eternal joy, ineffable light, bestowing salutary gifts upon the land of Russia. Ye give healing to other strangers who draw near with faith, making the lame to walk, giving sight to the blind, to the sick health, to captives freedom, to prisoners liberty, to the sorrowful consolation, and to the oppressed relief. Ye are the protectors of the land of Russia, shining forever like beacons and praying to the Lord in behalf of your countrymen. Therefore must we worthily magnify these martyrs in Christ, praying fervently to them and saying: "Rejoice, martyrs in Christ from the land of Russia, who gave healing to them who draw near to you in faith and love. Rejoice, dwellers in heaven. In the body ye were angels, servants in the same thought, comrades in the same image, of one heart with the saints. To all that suffer ye give relief. Rejoice, Boris and Gleb, wise in God. Like streams ye spring from the founts of life-giving water which flow for the redemption of the righteous. Rejoice, ye who have trampled the serpent of evil beneath your feet. Ye have appeared amid bright rays, enlightening like beacons the whole land of Russia. Appearing in faith immutable, ye have ever driven away the darkness. Rejoice, ye who have won an unslumbering eye, ye blessed ones who have received in your hearts the zeal to fulfill God's only commandments. Rejoice, brethren united in the realms of golden light, in the heavenly abodes, in glory unfading, which ye through your merits have attained. Rejoice, ye who are brightly irradiate with the luminance of God, and travel throughout the world expelling devils and healing diseases. Like beacons supernal and zealous guardians, ye dwell with God, illumined forever with light divine, and in your courageous martyrdom ye enlighten the souls of the faithful. The light-bringing heavenly love has exalted you, wherefore ye have inherited all fair things in the heavenly life: glory, celestial sustenance, the light of wisdom, and beauteous joys. Rejoice, ye who refresh our hearts, driving out pain and sickness and curing evil passions. Ye glorious ones, with the sacred drops of your blood ye have dyed a robe of purple which ye wear in beauty, and reign forevermore with Christ, interceding with him for his new Christian nation and for your fellows, for our land is hallowed by your blood. By virtue of your relics deposited in the church, ye illumine it with the Holy Spirit, for there in heavenly bliss, as martyrs among the army of martyrs, ye intercede for our nation. Rejoice, bright daysprings, our Christ-loving martyrs and intercessors! Subject the pagans to our princes, beseeching our Lord God that they may live in concord and in health, freed from intestine war and the crafts of the devil. Help us therefore who sing and recite your sacred praise forever unto our life's end."

22. THE BEGINNING OF THE KIEVAN CRYPT MONASTERY AND ITS FOUNDER, ST. ANTONIUS

The Crypt Monastery, located on the hilly banks of the Dnieper River on the outskirts of the city of Kiev since its foundation in the eleventh century, became the main spiritual and cultural center of early Russia. Its founders, Sts. Antonius and Theodosius, were remarkable religious leaders whose lives and teachings inspired endless generations of the Russian people. Until the revolution of 1917, the Crypt Monastery remained the principal place for Russian devotional pilgrimages, and even now its churches and crypts attract numerous pilgrims.

Works describing life in the monastery are collected either in the *Primary Chronicle,* their author apparently being one of the monks of this monastery, or in the *Kievan Crypt (Monastery) Paterikon* (the Greek word *paterikon* means a collection of lives of saints or stories about the life of monastery inhabitants). The *Kievan Crypt (Monastery) Paterikon* was written in the first quarter of the thirteenth century by Bishop Simon and Monk Polycarpe, both having been monks of this monastery. Later, more stories were added to the *Paterikon* by other writers. Despite the fact that Simon and Polycarpe lived more than one hundred years after the final compilation of the *Primary Chronicle,* the style of their work differs very little from that of the chronicle. In both collections can be found historical accounts of life in the monastery, edifying tales about its inhabitants, some half-legendary stories with considerable mystic or fantastic elements, and finally demonological narratives describing the struggles of the monks with the devil.

The stories of the Kievan Crypt Monastery were entered in the *Primary Chronicle* under the years 1051 and 1074. However, as often happens in the *Primary Chronicle*, these tales were not necessarily connected with the given year but describe life in the monastery over most of the second half of the eleventh century. The author apparently belonged to the monastery, and witnessed many of the events described by him.

The text of this work is that of Samuel H. Cross as translated by him in the *Primary Chronicle*.

6559 (1051) Yaroslav, after assembling the bishops, appointed Hilarion Metropolitan of Russia in St. Sophia.

Let us now relate why the Monastery of the Crypts bears this name. Prince Yaroslav was fond of Berestovoe and the Church of the Holy Apostles there situated. He gathered a large company of priests, among whom was a presbyter named Hilarion, a virtuous man, learned and ascetic. Hilarion used often to walk from Berestovoe toward the Dnieper to a certain hill, where the old Crypt Monastery now is, and made his orisons there. He dug a little crypt two yards deep, and often went thither from Berestovoe to chant the hours and offer his prayer to God in secret. Then God inspired the prince to appoint him Metropolitan in St. Sophia; and the crypt remained as it was.

Not many days afterward, there was a certain man, a layman from the city of Liubech, in whose heart God inspired the desire to go on pilgrimage. He made his way to Mount Athos,[1] beheld the monasteries there, and, upon examining them and being charmed by the monastic life, he entered one of the local monasteries, and begged the abbot to confer upon him the monastic habit. The latter complied with his request and made him a monk, calling him Antonius, and after he had admonished him and instructed him in his monastic obligations, he bade him return to Russia accompanied by the blessing of the Holy Mount, that many other monks might spring from his example. The abbot blessed him and dismissed him, saying: "Go in peace." Antonius returned to Kiev, and reflected where he should live.

---

[1] Mount Athos, or the "Holy Mount," has long been the most important monastic center of Eastern Christianity. It is located in Greece in the vicinity of the city of Saloniki.

He went about among the monasteries and liked none of them, since God did not so will, and subsequently wandered about among the hills and valleys seeking the place which God should show him. He finally came to the hill where Hilarion had dug the crypt, and liked this site, and rejoiced in it. He then lifted up his voice in prayer to God, saying amid his tears: "O Lord, strengthen me in this place, and may there rest upon it the blessing of the Holy Mount and of the abbot who tonsured me." Thus he took up his abode there, praying to God, eating dry bread all the day long, drinking little water, and digging the crypt. He gave himself rest neither day nor night, but endured in his labors, in vigil, and in prayer. Afterward good men noticed his conduct, and supplied him according to his necessities. Thus he acquired distinction as the great Antonius, and those who drew near to him besought his blessing.

When the Great Prince Yaroslav died, Iziaslav his son inherited his domain and settled in Kiev, while Antonius was celebrated throughout Russia. Iziaslav observed his manner of life, and came with his retainers to request his blessing and prayers. The great Antonius was thus remarked and revered by everyone. Brothers joined him, and he welcomed and tonsured them. Brethren thus gathered about him to the number of twelve. They dug a great crypt and a church, and cells, which exist to this day in the crypt under the old monastery. When the brethren had thus assembled, Antonius said to them: "God has gathered you together, my brethren, and ye are under the blessing of the Holy Mount, through which the abbot at the Holy Mount tonsured me, and I have tonsured you also. May there be upon you first the blessing of God and second that of the Holy Mount." And he added this injunction: "Live apart by yourselves, and I shall appoint an abbot; for I prefer to go alone to yonder hill, as I formerly was wont when I dwelt in solitude." So he appointed Barlaam their abbot, and betook himself to the hill, where he dug a grotto, which is under the new monastery, and in which he ended his life, enduring in virtue, and for the space of forty years never issuing forth from the crypt in which his bones lie to the present day.

The brethren thus abode with the abbot, and as the number of monks in the crypt increased, they considered the establishment of a monastery outside the original crypt. Thus the abbot and the brethren approached Antonius and said to him: "Father, the brethren have increased in numbers, and we can no longer find room in the crypt. If God and thy prayers so direct us, we might build a small church outside the crypt." Antonius then bade them so to do. They obeyed him, and built a little chapel

over the crypt and dedicated it to the Assumption of the Holy
Virgin.

God continued to augment the number of the brotherhood
through the intercession of the Holy Virgin, and the brethren
took counsel with the abbot as to constructing a monastery. The
friars again visited Antonius, and said: "Father, our brethren
increase in numbers, and we are desirous of building a monastery." Antonius rejoiced, and replied: "Blessed be God for all
things, and may the prayers of the Holy Virgin and of the
fathers of the Holy Mount be with you." Having thus spoken,
he sent one of the brotherhood to Prince Iziaslav with the
message: "My prince! Behold, God strengthens the brotherhood,
but their abode is small; give us therefore the hill which is
above the crypt." When Iziaslav heard these words, he rejoiced,
and sent his servant, and gave to them the hill. The abbot and
the brethren founded there a great church, and fenced in the
monastery with a palisade. They constructed many cells, completed the church, and adorned it with icons. Such was the
origin of the Crypt Monastery, which was so named because
the brethren first lived in the crypt. The Crypt Monastery thus
issued from the benediction of the Holy Mount.

23. ST. THEODOSIUS, ABBOT OF THE CRYPT MONASTERY

Now, when the monastery was completed during the abbotship of Barlaam, Iziaslav founded the Monastery of St. Demetrius, and appointed Barlaam abbot therein, since he intended, by
virtue of his material wealth, to make it superior to the ancient
monastery. Many monasteries have indeed been founded by
emperors and nobles and magnates, but they are not such as
those founded by tears, fasting, prayer, and vigil. Antonius had
neither silver nor gold, but accomplished his purpose through
tears and fasting, as I have recounted.

When Barlaam had departed to St. Demetrius', the brethren
held a council, and then once more visited the ancient Antonius
with the request that he should designate them a new abbot. He
inquired whom they desired. They replied that they desired
only the one designated by God and by his own selection. Then
he inquired of them: "Who among you is more obedient, more
modest, and more mild than Theodosius? Let him be your abbot."
The brethren rejoiced, and made their reverence before the old
man. Being twenty in number, they thus appointed Theodosius
to be their abbot. When Theodosius took over in the monastery,
he began to practice abstinence, fasting, and tearful prayer. He

undertook to assemble many monks, and thus gathered together brethren to the number of one hundred.

He also interested himself in searching out the monastic rules. There was in Kiev at the time a monk from the Studion Monastery named Michael, who had come from Greece with the Metropolitan George, and Theodosius inquired of him concerning the practices of the Studion monks. He obtained their rule from him, copied it out, and established it in his own monastery to govern the singing of monastic hymns, the making of reverences, the reading of the lessons, behavior in church, the whole ritual, conduct at table, proper food for special days, and to regulate all else according to prescription. After obtaining all this information, Theodosius thus transmitted it to his monastery, and from the latter all others adopted the same institutions. Therefore the Crypt Monastery is honored as the oldest of all.

While Theodosius lived in the monastery, following a virtuous life and the monastic rule, and receiving everyone who presented himself, I, a poor and unworthy servant, came to him, and he accepted me in my seventeenth year. Hence I have set down and certified what year the monastery came into being, and why it is named the Crypt Monastery; but to Theodosius' life we shall recur later.

6582 (1074)   In this year the Church of the Crypts was founded by the Abbot Theodosius and the Bishop Michael, while George the metropolitan was absent in Greece and Sviatoslav was reigning in Kiev.

Theodosius, the abbot of the Crypt Monastery, passed away. We shall therefore supply a brief account of his assumption. When the Lenten season approached, upon the eve of Quinquagesima Sunday, Theodosius was accustomed, after he had embraced the brethren according to his practice, to instruct them how to pass the Lenten period in prayer by night and by day, and how to guard against evil thoughts and the temptations of the devil. "For," said he, "demons incite in monks evil thoughts and desires, and inflame their fancy so that their prayers are impaired. One must combat such thoughts when they come by using the sign of the cross and by saying: 'Lord Jesus Christ our God, have mercy on us, Amen!' With this end in view, we must practice abstinence from many foods, for evil desires develop out of excessive eating and immoderate drinking, and by the growth of such thoughts sin is caused. By this means," said he, "oppose yourselves to the influence of the demons and their malice, guard against laziness and too much sleep, be zealous in churchly song, in the traditions of the fathers, and in the reading of the Scriptures. For it befits monks above all things to have upon their lips the Psalter of David, and thereby to expel the weaknesses caused by the devil. It befits all young persons to show toward their elders love, obedience, and attention, and it behooves all older persons to offer the younger brethren their love and admonition, and to be an example by their continence and vigil, their self-restraint and humility, to counsel and console the youthful, and to spend Lent in such pursuits.

"For," he added, "God has given us these forty days in which to purify our souls. This is a tithe given to God by the body. For the days of the year are three hundred and sixty-five, and giving to God each tenth day as a tithe makes a fast of forty days, during which the soul is cleansed and happily celebrates the Resurrection of the Lord as it rejoices in God. For the Lenten season purifies the heart of man. In the beginning, fasting was first imposed upon Adam, so that he should not taste of one tree. Moses fasted forty days to prepare himself to receive the Law upon Mount Sinai, and then he beheld the glory of God. During a fast, Samuel's mother bore him. Through their fasting, the Ninevites averted the wrath of God. By his fasting, Daniel prepared himself for great visions. After his fast, Elijah was taken up to heaven to receive celestial sustenance. Through their fasting, the Three Children quenched the violence of the fire. And Our Lord, by fasting forty days, made known to us the Lenten season. By means of their fasting, the Apostles rooted out the teaching of the devil. By virtue of their fasts, our fathers appeared to the world as beacons that continue to shine after their decease. They exhibited great labors and continence; for example, the great Antonius, Euthymius, Savva, and the other fathers. Let us imitate them, my brethren."

After thus instructing the brotherhood, he kissed them, calling each by name, and then left the monastery, taking with him but a few loaves of bread. He entered a crypt, closed the door behind him, and covered himself with dust. He spoke to no one, unless some object was needful to him, and in any case he conversed only on Saturday and on Sunday through a small window. Upon other days, he remained in fasting and in prayer, maintaining strict abstinence. He returned to the monastery on the eve of Friday, St. Lazarus' day. For on this day ends the forty days' fast, which opens on the first Monday after the week of St. Theodore and concludes on Friday, the feast of St. Lazarus. Holy Week is then observed as a fast on account of Our Lord's passion. Theodosius thus returned according to his custom, embraced the brethren, and with them celebrated Palm Sunday.

When Easter Day came, he celebrated it brilliantly as usual, and then fell ill. When he was taken ill, and had been sick for five days, he bade them carry him in the evening down into the courtyard. The brethren laid him upon a sled and set him before the church. He then desired that the whole brotherhood should be summoned, so the brethren struck upon the bell, and all assembled together. Theodosius then said to them: "My brethren, my fathers, and my children! I now depart from you, for God made known to me, while I was in the crypt during the Lenten season, that I must now quit this world. Whom do you desire for your abbot, that I may confer my blessing upon him?"

They made answer: "You have been a father to us all. Whomsoever you yourself select shall be our father and our abbot, and we shall obey him even as we obey you." Then our father Theodosius said: "Go apart from me and designate him whom you desire, except the two brothers Nicholas and Ignatius: but choose from the rest whomever you prefer, from the eldest down to the youngest."

They obeyed his behest, and upon withdrawing a short distance in the direction of the church, they took counsel together, and then sent two of the brethren back to Theodosius to beg him to designate the one chosen by God and his own holy prayer, and who should be agreeable to Theodosius himself. Theodosius then made answer: "If you desire to receive your abbot from me, then I will appoint him not so much from my own choice as by divine disposition," and he designated the presbyter James. This nomination did not meet with the approval of the brotherhood, who objected that James had not taken orders in the monastery, since he had come thither from Letetz with his brother Paul. They demanded rather Stephen the cantor, who was then a pupil of Theodosius, and therefore said: "He has grown up under your hand and has served with you; appoint him as our abbot."

Then Theodosius said: "By the commandment of God, I designated James, but you prefer that the appointment should coincide with your own wishes." He gave way to their desire, however, and appointed Stephen to be their abbot, and blessed him, saying: "My son! I give over to you this monastery. Guard it with care, and maintain what I have ordained in its observances. Change not the traditions and the institutions of the monastery, but follow in all things the law and our monastic rule."

The brethren then raised him up, carried him to his cell, and laid him upon his bed. At the beginning of the sixth day, while he was seriously ill, Prince Sviatoslav came to visit him with his son Gleb. While the prince was sitting beside him, Theodosius said: "I depart from this world and entrust this monastery to your guardianship in the event that some disorder arises in it. I confer the abbotship upon Stephen; desert him not in his hour of need."

The prince embraced him, and after promising to care for the monastery, departed from him. When the seventh day was come, while Theodosius was steadily growing weaker, he summoned Stephen and the brotherhood, and spoke to them these words: "Upon my departure from this world, if I have found favor with God and he has accepted me, then this monastery, after my decease, will grow and prosper through his help. In that event, know that God has accepted me. But if, after my death, the monastery begins to lose in membership and income, be assured that I shall not have found favor in the sight of God."

When he had spoken thus, the brethren wept, saying: "Father, intercede with God for us, for we know that he will not scorn your labors." They thus sat out the night with him, and at the beginning of the eighth day, being the second Saturday after Easter, in the second hour of the day, he commended his soul into the hands of God, upon May 3rd, in the eleventh year of the indiction. The brethren thus mourned for him.

Theodosius had given command that he should be buried in the crypt where he had performed many good works. He had also directed that his body should be buried by night, and they followed his injunction in this respect. When evening was come, the brethren took up his body and laid it in the crypt, after conducting it thither in all honor with hymns and candles to the glory of our God Jesus Christ.

24. BROTHER ISAAC AND THE DEMONS

There was also another monk, named Isaac. While still in the world, he was very rich, since in the secular life he was by birth a merchant of Toropets. But he resolved to become a monk, and distributed his fortune to the needy and to the monasteries. He then approached the great Antonius in the crypt, and besought him to receive him into the order. Antonius accepted him, and put upon him the monastic habit, calling him Isaac, for his secular name was Chern. Isaac adopted an ascetic mode of life. He wrapped himself in a hair shirt, then caused a goat to be bought, flayed it, and put on the skin over his hair shirt, so that the fresh hide dried upon him. He shut himself up in a lonely gallery of the crypt in a narrow cell only four ells across, and there lamented and prayed to God. His sustenance was one wafer, and that only once a day, and he drank but moderately of water. The great Antonius carried it to him, and passed it in to him by a little window through which he inserted his arm. Thus Isaac received his food. He subsisted thus for seven years without seeing the light of day or even lying down upon his side, for he snatched what sleep he could in a sitting posture.

Once, when evening had fallen, he had knelt till midnight singing psalms, as was his wont, and when he was wearied, he sat down upon his stool. As he sat there, and had as usual extinguished his candle, a light suddenly blazed forth in the crypt as if it shone from the sun, and strong enough to take away man's vision. Two fair youths then approached him. Their faces were radiant like the sun, and they said to him: "Isaac, we are angels; Christ is drawing near to you. Fall down and worship him."

He did not understand their devilish artifice nor remember to cross himself, but knelt before the work of the demons as if to Christ himself. The demons then cried out and said: "Now, Isaac, you belong to us."

They led him back into his cell and set him down. They then seated themselves around him, and both the cell and the aisle of the crypt were filled with them. One of the devils, who called himself Christ, bade them take flutes and lyres and lutes and play, so that Isaac could dance before them. So they struck up with flutes, lutes, and lyres, and began to make sport of him. After they had tormented him, they left him half alive, and went away when they had beaten him.

The next day at dawn, when it was time to break bread, Antonius came to the window according to his custom and said: "May the Lord bless you, Father Isaac." But there was no answer. Then Antonius said: "He has already passed away," so he sent into the monastery in search of Theodosius and the brethren. After digging out the entrance where it had been walled up, they entered and lifted him up, thinking him dead, and carried him out in front of the crypt. They then perceived that he was still alive, and Theodosius the prior said: "This comes from the devil's artifice." They laid him upon a bier, and Antonius cared for him.

About this same time it happened that Iziaslav returned from Poland, and was angry with Antonius on account of Vseslav, so that Sviatoslav caused Antonius to escape by night to Chernigov. When Antonius arrived there, he was attracted by the Boldiny

Hills, and after digging another crypt, he settled there. At that spot in the Boldiny Hills, there is a monastery dedicated to the Virgin even to this day. When Theodosius learned that Antonius had fled to Chernigov, he came with his brethren, took Isaac, and bore him to his own cell, where he cared for him. For Isaac was so weakened in body that he could not turn from one side to the other, nor rise up, nor sit down, but he lay always upon one side, and relieved himself as he lay, so that numerous worms were caused under his back by his excrement. Theodosius washed and dressed him with his own hands, and for two years cared for him thus. It is wondrous and strange that he lay thus for two years, tasting neither bread nor water nor any other food nor fruit, nor did he speak with his tongue, but lay deaf and dumb for the whole two years.

Theodosius prayed to God in his behalf, and offered supplications over him by day and by night, until in the third year he spoke and heard, rose upon his feet like a babe, and began to walk. He would not go faithfully to church, but the brethren carried him thither by force; they also taught him to go to the refectory, but seated him apart from the rest of the brethren. They set bread before him, but he would not take it unless they placed it in his hand.

Theodosius then said: "Leave the bread before him, but do not put it in his hand, so that he can eat of his own volition."

For a week he ate nothing, but gradually he became aware of the bread, and tasted it. Thus he began to eat, and by this means Theodosius freed him from the craft of the devil.

Isaac then assumed severe abstinence. When Theodosius was dead and Stephen was abbot in his stead, Isaac said: "Demon, you deceived me once when I sat in a lonely spot. I must not confine myself in the crypt, but must vanquish you while I frequent the monastery." He then clad himself in a hair shirt, and put on over this a sackcloth coat, and began to act strangely. He undertook to help the cooks in the preparation of food for the brotherhood. He went to matins earlier than the others, and stood firm and immovable. When winter came with its heavy frosts, he stood in shoes so worn that his feet froze to the pavement, but he would not move his feet till matins were over. After matins, he went to the kitchen, and made ready the fire, the water, and the wood before the other cooks came from the brotherhood.

There was one cook who was also named Isaac, who mocked at Isaac and said: "There sits a black crow; go and catch it." Isaac bowed to the ground before him, then went and caught the crow, and brought it back to him in the presence of all the cooks. They were frightened, and reported it to the abbot and the brotherhood, who began to respect him. But not being desirous of human glory, he began to act strangely, and to play tricks, now on the abbot, now on the brethren, and now on laymen, so that others dealt him blows. Then he began to wander through the country, acting like an idiot. He settled in the crypt where he had formerly lived, for Antonius was already dead. He gathered young men about him and laid upon them the monastic habit, so that he suffered blows from the Abbot Nikon as well as from the parents of these youths. But he suffered these hardships, and willingly endured blows and nakedness and cold by day and by night.

One night he lit the stove in a cabin by the crypt. When the stove was heated, fire began to issue forth from the crevices, for it was old and cracked. Since he had nothing to put over the stove, he braced his bare feet against the flame till the stove burned out, and then left it. Many other stories were told about him, and I myself witnessed some such occurrences.

Thus he won his victory over the demons, holding their terrors and apparitions of as little account as flies. For he said to them: "You did indeed deceive me the first time in the crypt, since I did not perceive your craft and cunning. But now that I have on my side the Lord Jesus Christ and my God and the prayers of my father Theodosius, I hope to vanquish you." Many times the demons harassed him, and said: "You belong to us, for you have worshiped us and our leader." But he replied: "Your chief is Antichrist and you are demons," and signed his countenance with the cross. At this they disappeared. Sometimes, however, they came upon him again by night, and frightened him in his dreams, appearing like a great company with mattocks and spades, and saying: "We will undermine the crypt, and bury this man within it," while others exclaimed, "Fly, Isaac, they intend to bury you alive." But he made answer: "If you were men, you would have come by day; but you are darkness and come in darkness, and the darkness shall swallow you up." Then he made the sign of the cross against them, and they vanished.

On other occasions, they endeavored to terrify him in the form of a bear, sometimes as a wild beast and sometimes as a bull. Now snakes beset him, and now toads, mice, and every other reptile. But they could not harm him, and said to him: "Isaac, you have vanquished us!" He replied: "You conquered me in the image of Jesus Christ and his angels, of whose sight you are unworthy. But now you rightly appear in the guise of beasts and cattle or as the snakes and reptiles that you are, repulsive and evil to behold." Thereupon the demons left him, and he suffered no more evil at their hands. As he himself related, his struggle against them lasted for three years. Then he began to live still more strictly, and to practice abstinence, fasting, and vigil.

After thus living out his life, he finally came to his end. He fell sick in his crypt, and was carried in his illness to the monastery, where he died in the Lord upon the eighth day. The Abbot John and the brethren clothed his body and buried him.

Such were the monks of the monastery of Theodosius, who shine forth like radiant beacons since their decease, and intercede with God in behalf of the brethren here below, as well as for the lay brotherhood and for those who contribute to the monastery in which to this day the brotherhood abides together in virtuous life amid hymns, prayers, and obedience, to the glory of Almighty God, and protected by the intercession of Theodosius, to whom be glory, Amen.

b. *Monk Nestor*

25. LIFE OF OUR BLESSED FATHER THEODOSIUS, ABBOT OF THE CRYPT MONASTERY

THE *Life of Theodosius* is certainly one of the most significant works of early Russian literature. Written by Monk Nestor in the 1080s soon after the death (in 1074) of this first abbot of the Kievan Crypt Monastery, it has preserved the freshness of an eyewitness account. The details of Theodosius' childhood, for instance, were supplied by his own mother and provide us with a fascinating description of Russian life and monastic habits in the first century of Russian Christianity. Nestor's vivid narrative manner, the wealth of realistic description and skillful use of dramatic effect testify to his literary abilities. Monk Nestor came to the Crypt Monastery some years after the abbot's death and obviously made a careful selection of the brethrens' and other witnesses' recollections of Theodosius' life and activities. When he started writing this *vita* he had already read some early Christian and Byzantine hagiographic works, especially those of St. Cyril of Scythopol and Athanasius the Great. These helped him organize the structure of his biography and supplied a number of rhetorical devices. Yet, the entire style of Russian life was so different from that of the Sinaitic and Egyptian desert fathers that Nestor was bound to write quite an original piece of hagiographic literature.

St. Theodosius, together with the real founder of the Crypt Monastery, St. Antonius, was the creator of this oldest and most important Russian monastic center, which also became the cradle of Russian culture and letters. His deep, sincere piety, humility, and meekness, as well as his love and care for men, won him respect in the minds and memories of generation upon generation of Russians; and even after World War II, when the Kiev Crypt Monastery was reopened, many thousands of pilgrims flocked there to venerate his holy relics.

The translation follows in excerpts a twelfth-century text preserved in the so-called *Sbornik moskovskago uspenskago sobora*, published in Moscow in 1899, pages 40–97. (This *Sbornik*, re-edited by Dmitry Chizhevsky, was reprinted by Mouton & Co., The Hague, 1957.)

I. PROEM

I thank thee my Master, Lord Jesus Christ, that thou hast made me worthy to be the undeserving narrator of the lives of thy holy saints. For lo, when I was first writing about the life, the murder, and the miracles of the holy and blessed martyrs Boris and Gleb, I felt compelled to come to yet another narration, which is above my strength and of which I was not worthy, being ignorant and unlearned, the more so since I had not been taught in any arts. But I recalled, O Lord, thy word, saying: "If you have faith even as a mustard seed, and you say unto this mountain, 'Move and cast yourself into the sea,' straightway it will obey you."

And lo, I, the sinful Nestor, keeping in my mind these words and being comforted with the faith and the trust that all things are possible through thee, I started writing this story, which is about the life of our most blessed father Theodosius, late abbot of this monastery of Our Holy Lady the Mother of God. We celebrate and remember now his day of passing.

For lo, brothers, when I recalled that the life of one most blessed had not yet been written down by anyone, I was gripped for days by sadness and I prayed to God to make me worthy to write down everything in an orderly way about the life of our pious father Theodosius; so that caloyers [1] coming after us, having received the account, having read it, and having seen the deeds of this man, would praise God and, honoring this saint, would be strengthened for greater dedication to God, the

---

[1] Caloyer: from Greek "kalogeros," a medieval word for a monk of the Eastern Orthodox Church.

more so that in this very land such a man and saint of God had appeared.

For about this the Lord himself prophesied thus: "Many will come from the east and the west and will sit down with Abraham and with Isaac and Jacob in the Heavenly Kingdom." And again: "Many that are first shall be last; and the last shall be first." And indeed, this last one has shown himself to be greater than the first fathers, imitating in his life the holy first superior of the monastic order—the great Antonius I mean.[2] And even more wonderful is the fact that it is written in the books of the fathers that the last of the kin will be glorified. And lo, Christ has led this last of the kin to be his follower and a shepherd to the monks.

For he was from youth adorned with a pure life, good deeds, with faith, and great purpose. Now, from this time I shall begin to narrate the life of Theodosius from his early years. And listen, brothers, with all diligence, for this story is full of benefit to all who heed it. I beg again of you whom I have come to love not to condemn me for my ignorance. For being moved by love of this most righteous one, I have attempted to write down everything about him; and likewise being careful, lest Christ's words about the evil and slothful servant be applied to me: "Thou wicked and slothful servant, thou oughtest therefore to have put my money to the bankers and at my coming I should have received my own with interest." [3]

And moreover, it is not fitting, brothers, to conceal the miracles of the saints; especially since God spoke to his disciples thus: "That which I say to you in the darkness, tell in the light; and that which you hear in your ears, proclaim in the houses."

These things I want to write down for the benefit and the edification of my readers. Praising God for these things, accept the reward offered you. However, wishing to begin the confession, I first pray to the Lord, saying thus: "O my Lord, Almighty, giver of Grace, Father of Our Lord Jesus Christ, come to my aid and enlighten my heart to the understanding of thy commandments, and open my lips for the announcing of thy miracles and for the praising of thy holy saint. May thy name be sanctified; for thou art the only helper to those who trust in thee forever. Amen."

---

[2] Antonius: was one of the first monks who settled on the hills overlooking the Dnieper in the vicinity of Kiev. Here can be meant also Anthonius the Great (c. 250–350), the founder of Christian monasticism.

[3] A slightly modified quotation of Matthew 25:26–27.

II. THE CHILDHOOD OF THEODOSIUS

There is a town called Vasiliev, separated from Kiev, the capital city, by a distance of about thirty miles. In that city lived the parents of the holy one, living in the Christian faith and adorned with all manner of piety. They gave birth to this blessed child, and then on his eighth day brought him to the presbyter of God as is the Christian custom, to give the child a name. The presbyter, having seen the child and with the help of God perceiving that he would from youth wish to devote himself to God, called him Theodosius.[4] Then, when the child was forty days old, they solemnized his Christening. And he grew, nurtured by his parents; and the Grace of God was with him, and the Holy Ghost rejoiced in him from his youth.

Who can perceive the Grace of God? For lo, he selects the shepherd and teacher of the monks neither from among the wisest philosophers, nor from among the rulers of cities, but for this purpose—and for this may the name of the Lord be praised —one who was ignorant and coarse became wiser than philosophers. O secret mystery! That from where it was not to be expected, from there shone out to us the most radiant morning star! That from all countries, those having seen its shining hastened to it, despising everything worldly, sated by that light alone. O Grace of God! For he, first having designated and blessed the spot, created a pasture on which he wished to have his flock of pious sheep until he had selected their shepherd!

With his parents our blessed one settled in another city, Kursk,[5] the prince having willed it so; and moreover—I say—God had willed thus, so that there also the life of the valiant youth would shine out upon *us* as is fitting: from the East the morning star rises, gathering around itself many other stars, awaiting the Just Sun, Christ God, and saying: "Here am I, Lord, and the children whom I have nurtured with thy spiritual food; behold, Lord, my disciples! For lo, I have brought to thee those whom I have taught to despise everything worldly, and to love thee, the only God and Lord! Behold, O Lord, the flock of thine Orthodox sheep, for whom thou hast made me the shepherd and whom I have brought to thee, having kept them pure and uncorrupted."

Then the Lord said to him: "O good and true servant, having multiplied the talent given thee, receive in like manner the crown which is prepared for thee and enter into the joy of thy Lord."

---

[4] Theodosius means "dedicated" or "given to God," from Greek.

[5] Kursk: a city in southern Russia on the border of the prairie and the forest, northeast of Kiev.

And to the disciples he said: "Come, good herd of the valorous shepherd, Orthodox sheep, who for my sake have hungered and labored, receive the kingdom which has been prepared for thee since the creation of the world . . ."

And likewise let us also, brothers, strive to be zealous followers of the way of life of the blessed Theodosius and his disciples, of those whom he sent then before himself to the Lord, so that we too may be made worthy to hear the voice of the Lord Almighty, saying: "Come, therefore, blessed of my Father, receive the kingdom which is prepared for thee!"

And now let us return to the primary narration of the life of this holy youth.

Now he was growing in body and in spirit, being drawn to the love of God and going every day to the church of God, listening to the reading of the holy books with great attention. But still he did not draw near to children playing, as is the custom of youth, but disdained their games. His clothing was poor and patched. For this reason his parents many times tried to force him to dress in clean clothing and to go out to play with the children; but he did not obey them in this, but willed even more to be like one of the poor. In a similar manner he wished to enter into the study of the Scriptures with one of the teachers, and he did so; and soon he had learned all of the grammar. Soon everyone was amazed at the great wisdom and understanding of the child and at his rapid learning! Who can tell of his meekness and obedience which was evinced in his learning, not only toward his teacher, but toward the other students as well?

III. THE YEARS OF SPIRITUAL MATURING

When the blessed Theodosius was thirteen years old, his father came to the end of his life. Thenceforth he began to be more persevering in his works, as when he would go away with the serfs to the country and act with all manner of humility. But his mother would hinder him, not wishing him to do such things; and she would plead with him to dress again in clean clothing and to go out to play with his peers. For she would say to him thus: "Going about in this fashion thou bringest shame upon thyself and upon thy kin."

And because he did not obey her in this, she would often get angry at him and beat him; for she was as strong and solid in body as a man, and, indeed, if someone could not see her but only hear her conversing, he would begin to think she was a man.

Meanwhile, the blessed youth was considering how and in what manner he might be saved. Then he heard again about the Holy Land, where Our Lord Jesus Christ walked in the flesh; and he thirsted to go there and to worship there. And he prayed to God, saying: "My Lord Jesus Christ, hear my prayer and make me worthy to enter into thy holy places and to bow to them with joy."

And when he had thus prayed many times, lo there came pilgrims to that city. Having seen them, the blessed youth was glad, and having hastened, he bowed to them, kissed them lovingly, and asked them where they were from and where they were going. They answered thus: "We are coming from the holy places; [6] and if God wills it, we want to go back."

The holy one begged of them that they take him with them and make him a fellow traveler. And they promised to take him with them and accompany him to the holy places. Then the blessed Theodosius, having heard that which they promised him, was happy and went home.

When the pilgrims wanted to leave, they let the youth know about their departure. He, having gotten up during the night and not letting anyone know, secretly went out of the house, not taking with him anything except the clothing he was wearing, and even that was poor. And in that manner he went away behind the pilgrims. But benevolent God did not allow him, who from the maternal womb had been designated to be a shepherd to the Orthodox sheep in this country, to depart from this land; lest, the shepherd having gone, the pasture which God had blessed should become barren, and thorns and wolves should grow up in it and the herd become scattered.

After three days his mother, having found out and taking with her her other son who was younger than Theodosius, rode hurriedly a long way, and catching up with them, took Theodosius. And from rage and anger his mother grasped him by the hair and threw him upon the ground and kicked him with her feet. And, having severely reproached the pilgrims, she returned home leading her son tied like a villain. Being gripped by such great anger, even when they had arrived home, she beat him until she could no longer. And after this she led him to a room, tied him up, and locked the door as she left. The divine youth, however, accepted all these things with joy, and praying to God, gave thanks.

Then after two days, his mother came, released him, and let him eat. But still being gripped by rage, she placed irons on his legs and allowed him to walk about thus, taking care lest he

---

[6] Holy places: In Russia, as elsewhere in medieval Europe, places of pilgrimage were termed holy places.

run away from her again. And she made him walk in that fashion for many days.

After that, however, she again took pity on him and began with entreaty to persuade him not to run away from her, for she loved him very much more than her other children and for this reason could not bear living without him. And when he promised her that he would not leave her, she removed the irons from his legs, allowing him to do as he wished.

And so the blessed Theodosius returned to his former practice and was going every day to God's church. Then, seeing how many times Mass was not said because sacramental wafers had not been baked, he deplored such a condition greatly. Thus he resolved with his humility to dedicate himself to this task, and he did so. For he began to bake the wafers and to sell them; and when his sum would increase, he would give the profits to the poor and buy grain with the rest. Having ground the grain with his own hands, he would again make wafers. For lo, God so willed that pure sacramental wafers be brought into his church by a pure and uncorrupted youth.

Twelve years or more passed in this manner. All his peers would rail at him and reproach him because of his doing such work. But when the devil incited them, the blessed one would accept all these things with joy, in silence and with humility. For the villainous devil, hating goodness first and foremost, seeing himself being defeated by the humility of the blessed youth and not resting, wished to turn him from his good works: and lo, he began to incite the mother of Theodosius in order that she would prohibit his engaging in them. His mother, not being able to bear his being in such a shameful condition, began to speak to him lovingly: "I beg of thee, child, to quit these doings, for they bring censure upon thy family; and I cannot bear to hear from everyone the reproaches against thee because of them. It is not fitting for thee, a youth, to do such deeds."

Then with humility the divine youth answered his mother, saying:

Listen, O Mother, I beg of thee, listen! For Lord Jesus Christ lowered himself and was humble, giving us a model so that we for his sake should humble ourselves. And, moreover, he was abused and spat upon and smitten; and he bore it all for the sake of our salvation. Is it not much more fitting that we exercise patience so that we may receive Christ? And listen, my Mother, concerning my works. When Our Lord Jesus Christ lay down at the Last Supper with his disciples, having taken the bread and blessed it and broken it, he gave it to his disciples saying: "Take it and eat! This is my body, broken for you and for many for the remission of your sins." And if Our Lord himself called the bread his flesh, how much more fitting it is that I rejoice that the Lord has made me worthy to be the maker of his flesh!

Having heard these things, his mother was amazed at the wisdom of the youth; and from that time she began to leave him alone . . .

But the devil did not rest, inciting her to forbid such humility in the youth. After one year, having again seen him baking sacramental wafers and becoming blackened from the fire in the oven, she deplored it greatly. And from that time she began again to scold him, sometimes with caresses, sometimes with terror, and at other times beating him to make him forsake such work. The divine youth was in great sorrow concerning this and was confused as to what to do.

Then, however, having arisen secretly in the night and gone out of the house, he went to another city which was not far away and there lived with the presbyter and did his work according to his custom. After that, his mother, having searched in her own city and not having found him, grieved for him. Then after many days, having come to the aforementioned town and having searched, his mother found him in the house of the presbyter, and taking him, sped away, beating him, to her city.

And arriving home she locked him up, saying: "Henceforth thou wilt not be able to leave me. Because no matter where thou goest, I will come and find thee and will lead thee, tied and beaten, back to this city."

After that the blessed Theodosius prayed to God and went every day to the church.

He was humble in heart and meek toward all, so that even the governor of that city, having seen the youth in such meekness and mildness, grew to love him greatly and ordered that he attend him in the church. And he gave him a new garment to wear when he went. For several days the blessed Theodosius wore it, but it was as if he were carrying some sort of burden upon his back. Then, taking it off, he gave it to the needy, dressing himself in poor clothing. And so he went about in that way. The governor, however, seeing him thus, gave him still another garment which was better than the first, beseeching him to wear it. But he, having taken it off, gave away this one also. He did likewise many times, so that when the judge learned of it, he began to love him greatly, wondering at his humility.

After these occurrences, the blessed Theodosius, having gone

to one of the smithies, ordered him to forge an iron chain; and
taking it, he girded his loins with it and went about thus. And
although the iron was tight and gnawed into his body, he remained as though his body were suffering no injury from it.[7]

Then when many days had passed, on a holy day his mother
began to order him to dress in clean clothing for the service.
For all the notables of that city were attending a dinner at the
home of the governor, and it had been ordered that the blessed
Theodosius attend and serve. And for this reason his mother
persuaded him to dress in a clean garment, the more so since
she had heard what he had done.

And so while he was dressing himself in the clean garment,
being simple in mind and not minding her presence, she was
carefully watching, wishing to see more clearly; and lo, she saw
on his undergarment blood, which came from the gnawing of
the iron. Having become excited with anger against him and
having risen with rage and torn apart the undergarment on him,
beating him, she removed the iron from his loins. God's youth,
however, as if he had suffered nothing evil at her hand, dressed
himself and left, serving before the guests with all manner of
tranquillity.

Then, after some time, he heard in the Holy Gospel the words
of the Lord, saying: "If one does not leave his father or his
mother and follow after me, he is not worthy of me." And again:
"Come to me all who labor and are burdened, and I will comfort you. Take up my burden upon yourselves and learn from
me, for I am meek and mild in heart, and you will find peace
in your souls." And thus, having heard these things, the divinely
inspired Theodosius became excited with godly zeal and with
love and with the breath of God; and he was considering how
or where he might be tonsured and might conceal himself from
his mother.

IV. THEODOSIUS' EARLY YEARS IN THE CRYPT MONASTERY

By the will of God, his mother went away to the country; and
since she would spend many days there, the blessed one was
glad. Having prayed to God, he went secretly out of the house,
not taking with him anything at all except his clothing and a
little bread for his physical needs, and thus he set out toward
the city of Kiev.

For he had heard about the monasteries there. However, not

---

[7] During the Middle Ages it was a common practice in the Christian
West and East to mortify the flesh with a hair shirt, chains, or special
mail coat, which was worn directly on the body under the shirt.

knowing the way, he prayed to God that he might find travelers who would direct him to the desired road. And lo, by the will of God, there were coming along the road merchants in wagons with heavy burdens. The blessed one, having learned from them the city to which they were traveling, glorified God and walked along after them at a distance, not appearing to them. And when they would make a stop for the night, the blessed one would not approach within their eyesight, but would rest where he was, observed by God alone. And so traveling in this manner for three weeks, he reached the aforementioned city. Then, having arrived, he went about to all the monasteries, wishing to be a monk; and he begged them to accept him. But they, seeing the simplicity of that youth dressed in poor garments, did not deign to receive him. For God had so willed that he should be led to that very place to which he had been called by the Lord from his youth.

Then, hearing about the blessed Antonius,[8] who lived in a cave and who possessed a winged mind, he set out for that place. And, coming to holy Antonius and seeing him, he fell down and bowed to him with tears, pleading that he might remain with him. The great Antonius taught him, saying: "Child, dost thou see this cave, for it is a sorrowful place and more crowded than others, and I consider that, being young, thou wilt not be able to bear the sadness here."

For not only was he testing him by these words, but foreseeing with prophetic eyes that Theodosius would reward that place and found a glorious monastery for the gathering of a multitude of monks.

And the divinely inspired Theodosius answered him with emotion: "Know, blessed father, that the Omniscient Teacher, God, has led me to your holiness and willed to save me; and therefore, whatever thou orderest me to do, I will do."

Then the blessed Antonius said to him: "Beneficent God, child, has strengthened thee for this endeavor and for this place! Remain here."

And Theodosius again fell down and bowed to him, then the elder blessed him and ordered Nikon the Great to tonsure him, for he was a presbyter and an experienced monk. And he, taking the blessed Theodosius and shaving him according to the custom of the holy fathers, dressed him in a monk's garment.

Our father Theodosius then, submitting himself to God and

---

[8] Blessed Antonius: despite the fact that Antonius became the founder of the monastery, he lived in seclusion and did not interfere very much in the life of the monastic community.

to the holy Antonius, from that time forth dedicated himself to manual labor. He would remain awake all night praising God, driving away the burden of drowsiness, striving for physical moderation, with his hands doing his work, and keeping in mind constantly the words of the Psalm: "See my humility and my labor, and grant me absolution for all my sins." In this manner he would entirely humble his soul with moderation and mortify his flesh through labor and religious striving, so that the holy Antonius and the Great Nikon were amazed at his humility and obedience, at the great virtue and fortitude and courage in one so young; and they praised God greatly for all these things . . . .

Meanwhile his mother, having sought very much in her own city and in surrounding ones and not having found him, wept for him as for one dead, beating her breast cruelly. And it had been proclaimed throughout all that country that anyone who had seen the youth should come and let his mother know.

And lo, they came from Kiev and told her thus: "Four years ago we saw him walking in our city and wishing to be tonsured in one of the monasteries."

And having heard that, she, not tarrying or fearing the length of the journey, arrived in that city, walked around to all the monasteries searching for her son.

Later she was told that her son was with the holy Antonius in the cave; so she went there, and there she found him. And, lo, she began to call out the elder with deceit, saying thus: "Tell the holy one to come out, for lo, having hastened a long way, I have come wishing to converse with him and to bow to his holiness so that I also may be blessed by him."

The elder was informed about her, and he went out. And having seen him, she bowed to him. Then when they had sat down, the woman began to be very conversant, and later she declared the sin which was the reason for her coming and said: "I beg of thee, Father, tell me whether my son is here. For I have grieved much for his sake, not knowing whether he is alive or not."

And the elder, being simple in mind and not fathoming her lie, said to her thus: "Thy son is here; and do not grieve for his sake, for he is alive."

Then she said to him: "Why then, Father, may I not see him? For having traveled a long way, I have come to this city only to see my son, and then I shall go back to my own city."

The elder answered her: "If thou wishest to see him, go to thy house now; and I will come and let thee know whether he deigns to see anyone or not. Then on the morrow thou might come and see him."

Having heard this, she went away hoping to see him on the coming day.

The holy Antonius, having gone back into the cave, told all this to the blessed Theodosius, who, having heard it, grieved greatly that he had not succeeded in concealing himself from her.

On the second day the woman came again. But though the elder exhorted the blessed one to go out and see his mother, he did not wish to do so. Then the elder went out and said to her: "I have pleaded with him much, but he does not deign to come out to thee."

Thenceforth she began not to speak to the elder with humility, but cried out with anger: "So! Thou art the monk who has taken my son and hidden him in a cave and thou dost not want to show him to me. Bring my son out to me, monk, so that I may see him; for if I do not see him, I cannot bear to remain alive. Show me my son, or I shall surely die. For lo, I will kill myself before the doors of this cave if thou dost not show him to me."

Then Antonius in great sorrow went into the cave and begged the blessed Theodosius to go out to her. And he, not wishing to disobey the elder, did so. Seeing her son in such sorrow—for already his face had changed much from his great labor and mortification—and embracing him, she wept bitterly. Then having hardly composed herself, she sat down and began to persuade Christ's servant, saying: "Come home, child, and do freely whatever thou requirest for the salvation of thy soul, only do not separate thyself from me. And when I die, bury my body and then return to this cave if thou wishest. For I cannot bear to live not seeing thee."

But the blessed one said to her: "Then if thou wishest to see me every day, come to this city, and having entered one of the nunneries, take the veil. Coming here in that fashion, thou wilt see me. And moreover thou wilt receive salvation for thy soul. If thou dost not do this, then I tell thee the truth: from this time forth thou wilt not see my face."

With these and many other admonitions he spent the whole day exhorting his mother, but she did not wish to obey him in the least. And when she left him, the blessed one, having gone back into the cave, prayed fervently to God concerning the salvation of his mother and the turning of her heart to obedience.

And God heard the prayer of his saint. For concerning this the words of the prophet say: "The Lord is near to those who call on him in truth, and he does the will of those who fear him and hears their prayer and saves them."

For one day his mother came and said to him: "Lo, child, I will do all that thou hast ordered and henceforth I shall not return to my own city but, God willing, I shall go to a convent and there, having taken the veil, shall spend my remaining days. For lo, from thy teaching I have realized how worthless is this passing world."

Having heard this, the blessed Theodosius rejoiced in his soul and went in to tell the Great Antonius, who, having heard it, praised God, who had turned her heart to such repentance. And having gone out to her and taught her much that is useful for the salvation of the soul and having informed the princess about her, he admitted her to the convent named for Saint Nicholas. Here she took the veil and was dressed in the nun's habit; and living for many years in good confession, she died in peace.

This is the life of our Father Theodosius from his youthful years up to the time that he came to the Crypt Monastery. His mother related it to one of the brothers, by the name of Theodor, who was a cellarer with our Father Theodosius; and I, having heard all these things from him, have written them down for the memory of those who read them.

After that time a great many people would come to the Crypt Monastery to receive the father's blessing, and by the will of God many of them became monks. Thereafter, Great Nikon [9] and another caloyer, who used to be a monk at St. Minas Monastery [10] and was a noble before taking orders, left the monastery in order to live separately from the monastic community. Great Nikon himself went to Tmutorokan [11] where in a pleasant site near the city he founded a monastery, and this religious com-

---

[9] Monk Nikon, together with Antonius, was one of the first monks to live in the cave in the hills on the shore of the Dnieper. The brethren of the monastery particularly respected him and called him Great Nikon. There are reasons to believe that he was none other than the former Kievan metropolitan Hilarion, who took orders under the name of Nikon. In any case, Nikon was one of the first compilers of the Kievan Chronicle, which later was reworked into the *Primary Chronicle*. He worked on this codex from 1068 to 1073.

[10] It is difficult to ascertain which of the St. Minas Monasteries is meant here by Nikon.

[11] When, in 1073, Princes Sviatoslav and Vsevolod seized Kiev and forced their brother, Prince Iziaslav, to abandon the city, Monk Nikon also left Kiev and went to the Russian city of Tmutorokan, located in the northwest Caucasus on Taman Peninsula, across from the Crimea.

munity grew by the will of God, developing according to the
rules of the Crypt Monastery. Another monk, Ephraim the
Eunuch, also left the Crypt Monastery, went to Constantinople
and joined another monastery. He lived there until he was called
back to Russia and ordained bishop in the city of Pereiaslavl.[12]

In agreement with the desire of blessed Antonius, blessed
Theodosius was ordained priest and every day he celebrated the
Lord's Supper with the deepest humility. He was of an uncom-
plicated, pleasant, and quiet disposition, and he was imbued
with divine wisdom and Christian love for his brother monks,
who had now reached the number of fifteen.

In the meantime blessed Antonius, who used to live by himself, undisturbed, retired to a cell in the caves and appointed
Monk Barlaam abbot in his place. Thereafter, blessed Antonius
went to another mountain where he dug for himself a cave in
which he lived and never left, and where his venerable body
rests to this day.

Abbot Barlaam constructed over the caves a small church
devoted to Our Lady, Mother of God, and ordered that the
brethren gather there for prayer. Since that time the church of
the monastery could be seen by the people of the surrounding
countryside. Before they were hardly aware of the monks who
lived in the caves.

I shall now describe the simple life of these caloyers. Only
God knows the suffering which they endured in the narrow
spaces of the cave where they lived. The human mind is unable
to grasp it. The monks lived only on rye bread and water. On
Saturdays and Sundays they had some boiled rye. On some
occasions, however, even this food was lacking, and they had to
be satisfied with some cooked vegetables. They themselves
performed all the manual work, even weaving their vestments
and cowls and performing with their own hands all kinds of
work. In the city they sold the products of their labor in order
to buy rye, and what was bought was distributed equally among
the caloyers. At night each caloyer would grind his part of the
rye to bake bread, and early in the morning all monks would
celebrate matins, and then cultivate their vegetables in the garden. Later, returning to the church to praise God, they would
celebrate the hours and offer the Holy Eucharist. Afterward
they would eat their small amount of bread and every brother
would go back to his work. In this way they lived and worked,
imbued with the spirit of charity . . .

---

[12] Ephraim the Eunuch: probably a Greek. In medieval Byzantium
some monks practiced self-castration to avoid temptation of the flesh.

Our blessed Theodosius surpassed all other brethren in wisdom and obedience to the rules and used to take harder labor than the other monks, for he was strong and healthy . . .

He used to go to church earlier than everyone else; he would never leave his place, and would sing praises to God with a pure mind. He was also the last to leave the church. Therefore he was revered by the caloyers, who loved him as their father and praised his humility and obedience.

After a certain period of time the prince ordered Abbot Barlaam to leave the Crypt Monastery and appointed him abbot of the Monastery of St. Demetrius the Martyr. And the monks who lived in the caves got together and told blessed Antonius that they had elected Theodosius to be abbot of their monastic community. Our Father Theodosius, however, even in this position of authority did not change his habits or his humble way of living, for he always remembered the word of Our Lord: "Whosoever will be the greater among you, let him be your minister. . . ."

He built around the church a fence, and around the fence he built several cells, and in the year 6570 (1062) he went with his monks to live in this new monastery. From that time the monastery prospered and became widely famous as the Monastery of the Crypts.

After some years Abbot Theodosius dispatched one of his monks to Ephraim the Eunuch in Constantinople, requesting that the Rules of the Monastery of Studion [13] should be copied there and brought back to Kiev. Ephraim did what our blessed Father wished. Having received the Rules of Studion, Abbot Theodosius ordered these Rules to be read to the assembled monks, and from that time the monastery was ruled according to these Rules, and they are observed to the present day . . .

After evening prayers Abbot Theodosius would rest in his cell; however, he would never lie down, but sit in a chair, and after sleeping awhile would get up for another night of prayers and genuflections . . .

The prince and his nobles who had heard of the pious life of this monastery used to visit blessed Theodosius to make their confession to him and to receive from him spiritual guidance. Thereafter they gave Abbot Theodosius a certain part of their wealth for the construction of a church to accommodate the

---

[13] Monastery of Studion: one of the leading monasteries of Constantinople, which elaborated its own system of monastic rules and later a special type of Eastern liturgy.

monks. And they even gave the monastery a certain part of their lands, especially the religious Prince Iziaslav,[14] who in those years occupied his father's throne and was deeply attached to the blessed abbot and often used to send for him. Or he would go himself to the saint and return home provided with spiritual guidance. And since that time, by the prayers of his saint, God granted the monastic community an abundance of all goods.

The devil once inspired three princes who were brothers to start a feud. The two younger princes started fighting their elder brother, the religious Iziaslav, and forced him out of the capital city of Kiev. When the two brothers entered Kiev they sent for venerable Abbot Theodosius, praying that he would come to dinner with them and participate in their sinful counsel. Abbot Theodosius, who knew of the injustice accorded to Iziaslav, and being inspired by the Holy Ghost, gave an answer according to the Holy Spirit. "I shall not go to the feast of Jezebel and taste the fruit of murder covered with blood." And he added several other words of reproach to his letter and sent the messenger back to the princes . . .

One day the abbot wrote Sviatoslav a long message, reproaching him in the following words: "The blood of your brother cries out to God against you as the blood of Abel cried out against Cain." And the abbot quoted many cases of persecution, murder, and fratricide of olden times, and wrote about all these things which befitted the behavior (of Prince Sviatoslav). Having read this letter, Prince Sviatoslav became enraged, he cursed the just and roared like a lion and flung the message to the floor. Then the rumor spread that Theodosius would be jailed. The brethren became alarmed and prayed to our blessed Father Theodosius to retract his accusations. Many nobles came to the Crypt Monastery and warned Abbot Theodosius of the prince's wrath and asked him to stop accusing the prince. The nobles said: "Prince Sviatoslav wants to jail thee." Blessed Theodosius, hearing that he would be jailed, was seized by joy and replied: "Brothers, I am filled with joy. Nothing could be better for me in this life. What should I fear? To lose wealth or land? To be separated from my children? or my land (which I do

---

[14] Prince Iziaslav, son of Yaroslav the Wise, reigned in Kiev from 1054 to 1068 and from 1069 to 1083. He was a great benefactor of the monastery. In 1073 his brothers, Sviatoslav and Vsevolod, drove Iziaslav from Kiev. Iziaslav died in 1078 in the vicinity of Kiev, fighting on the side of his brother Vsevolod against the princes of Chernigov.

not have)? We have brought no earthly wealth into this world; all of us are born naked, and naked we are supposed to leave this world. Therefore I am prepared to be jailed or to meet death." After that time the abbot would accuse Prince Sviatoslav even more openly . . .

V. ABBOT'S DEATH

When Abbot Theodosius came to the end of his life, he was forewarned by God of the day he would go to rest, because death is the rest of the righteous. He asked all the brethren and even those who used to work in the field, or who were absent from the monastery for other duties, to come back to the Crypt Monastery. When all of them came together he told the bailiffs, the stewards, and the servants to fulfill their work with diligence and awe of God in obedience and charity. Shedding tears, he advised all of them on their behavior concerning their salvation and a way of life pleasing to God: to fast, to attend church, to show pious behavior at the church service, to have brotherly love and to obey. He asked the monks to love and obey not only their superiors, but also all who were their equals. Having said these things he permitted them to go.

Then the abbot returned to his cell and began to cry and to beat his chest and cried to God and prayed for the salvation of his own soul, his flock, and the monastery. The brethren walked to the court and started talking among themselves: "What did he say? Perhaps he wants to go away to some unknown place and live alone without us." (They talked in this way) because he already had intended to do this, but had yielded to the entreaties of the prince and the nobles, and particularly to the entreaties of the brethren. And now they thought that he had the same intention. Thereafter the illness of the blessed one became stronger and fever seized his body and he could not do anything but lie on his couch. The abbot said: "God's will be done. Whatsoever is his will shall be done to me. Lo, I entreat thee, my Lord, to have mercy on my soul that it may not succumb to the devil's malice. May thy angel have my soul and bring it to the light of thy mercy through all the trials of the darkness." Saying this, he became silent because he was no more able to talk. The brethren were in great sorrow and sadness because of his illness. For another three days he was not able to talk or look around, and many monks thought he had died. Only a few noticed that his soul had not abandoned his body. After three days he got up and addressed all the brethren who had gathered. "My brethren and fathers, I know that the time of my life has come to an end, that the time to leave this world has arrived. And this was announced to me by the Lord during Lent when I was in the cave. You have to decide whom you will appoint abbot in my place." Hearing this, the brethren were seized by sadness and wept bitterly. And thereafter the brethren left the cell, held a meeting, and selected the choir-master of the church, Stephan, as their future abbot. Next day our blessed Father Theodosius once more called the brethren to his cell and asked: "My children, did you decide who is worthy to become your abbot?" And all of them answered that Stephan was worthy to become abbot. And for a long time Theodosius instructed the brethren to obey their new abbot and then let them go, foretelling the day of his death. "On Saturday at the rise of the sun my soul will abandon my body." And once more he asked Stephan to come to him alone and taught him how to be the shepherd of his holy flock. And Stephan no longer left Theodosius, but humbly cared for him, for the abbot's condition was getting worse and worse. When Saturday came and the sun began to rise, the blessed one called all the brethren and began to embrace each one. And the brethren were shedding tears and groaned because they were being separated from their shepherd. But the blessed one told them: "My children and my beloved brethren, I embrace ye most heartily because I am going to the Lord, Our master, Jesus Christ. And here is your abbot whom ye yourselves wanted. Obey him and respect him as your spiritual father and fulfill all his orders. Be blessed by God who created everything by his word and by his wisdom. He will protect ye from evil and will help ye preserve your unshakable and firm faith through your unity and mutual love, in order to let ye stay together until your last breath . . ."

After he said these words he sent everyone away, remaining alone in his cell. But one monk who always served Theodosius followed him through a small hole in the wall (and he saw) the blessed one get up, bow deeply, pray, and shed tears to God for the salvation of his soul, asking all the saints to help him, especially praying to Our Holy Lady, Mother of God, and he prayed to her in the name of God, Our Lord and Savior, Jesus Christ, to help his flock and his monastery. And once more, after he finished praying, he stretched out on the couch, and after a while he looked to heaven and with a joyful countenance exclaimed: "Blessings to God, for it has happened. I have no more fear and I am happy that I am leaving this world." And one could think that, saying these words, the abbot

had a vision, because thereafter he straightened his robe,
stretched his legs, crossed his arms over his chest and gave up
his holy soul into the hands of the Lord and joined the flock
of the Holy Fathers . . .

Our Father Theodosius died in the year 6582 (1074) on the
3rd day of the month of May on Saturday, as he himself foretold. And he passed away after the rise of the sun.

c. Stories from the *Kievan Crypt Paterikon*

Most of the stories of this *Paterikon* come from the pen of
Simon, Bishop of Vladimir and Suzdal, who apparently began
his ecclesiastical career in the Crypt Monastery; and from the
pen of Polycarpe, a monk of the same monastery. Simon, who
became bishop in 1214 and died in 1226, wrote his narratives
as an appendix to his epistle to Polycarpe. In this epistle Simon
endeavors to reconcile Polycarpe, who was dissatisfied with his
life in the monastery, with his brethren and abbot, and to convince him that the monastery was the spiritual center of the land.
Apparently Polycarpe wanted to become a bishop and his relations with the other monks were rather strained. The portion of
the *Paterikon* written by Polycarpe was done some years later,
when he had become reconciled with the monastery. It is addressed to Abbot Akindin, and has about the same structure as
the first part—that is, an epistle with eleven tales about the
lives of the monks, but is in a style less personal than the work
of Simon. It was written for wide circulation both within and
without the monastery, whereas the work of Simon was meant
to be read only by Polycarpe.

In the thirteenth century both works were made into one,
and to them was added the story of "The Brethren of the Crypt
Monastery" (Damian, Jeremy, and Matthew) and "Isaac and
the Demons" from the *Primary Chronicle* by Nestor. Later, more
narratives were added to this *Paterikon*, and it became one of the
most popular collections of this genre in Russia.

Bishop Simon wrote the first four stories of this collection,
and the last one, "Marko the Gravedigger Who Was Obeyed by
the Dead," is the work of Polycarpe. The translations here presented are based on the text published by D. Abramovich, *Kievo-
Pecherskii paterik*, Kiev, 1931.

26. BISHOP SIMON: VIKING SHIMON AND ST. THEODOSIUS

THE BUILDING OF THE CHURCH OF THE HOLY VIRGIN OF THE CRYPT MONASTERY

And now I will come to the other stories. Everyone should know how, according to the will of God and the prayers and desires of the Holy Virgin, the beautiful and great Church of the Crypt Monastery, dedicated to the Holy Virgin, was founded and built. This is the church of the great abbey of all the Russian land, the monastery of St. Theodosius.

There was in the land of the Vikings [1] a certain prince whose name was Africanus, the brother of Yakun, who, when he and Prince Yaroslav were fighting against evil Prince Mstislav, lost his gold-embroidered mantle when he was fleeing from battle. This Prince Africanus had two sons, Friand and Shimon. After Prince Africanus' death, his brother, Yakun, drove his nephews from their patrimonies. And thus Shimon came to our faithful Prince Yaroslav. And Yaroslav received him with honor and sent him to his son, Vsevolod, appointing him to be the senior counselor to Vsevolod. And through this position Shimon gained great influence. The reason for Shimon's devotion to the holy Crypt Monastery is explained in the following narrative.

During the reign of Prince Iziaslav in Kiev, the Kumans came to the Russian land, this being in 6576 (1068). And the sons of Yaroslav, Princes Iziaslav, Sviatoslav, and Vsevolod, decided to attack them. And Shimon went with Prince Vsevolod. When they came to the great and holy Father Antonius and asked him for his blessing and prayers, the blessed monk opened his lips, which had been sealed for a very long time, and clearly foretold of their forthcoming demise. Then Shimon the Viking fell at the monk's feet and begged him to tell how he, Shimon, might escape this fate.

And the blessed monk told him: "My son, many of you will fall in battle, pierced by swords. And when many of you attempt to escape from the enemy, you will be pursued and struck down by weapons or drowned in the river. But you, my son, will escape, and later you will be buried in the church that you will build."

And the Russian regiments engaged in battle on the river Leta, and because of God's wrath the Christians were defeated

---

[1] Apparently Shimon came to Russia from Sweden.

and routed. And many *voevodas* [2] and warriors fell in battle. Among those who were hurt in battle was Shimon, who lay wounded. He raised his eyes to the heavens and there saw a great church, the same that he had seen once at sea. And, remembering the words of the Savior, he said: "Lord! Deliver me from bitter death through the prayers of your Most Holy Mother and the reverend fathers Antonius and Theodosius."

And at that moment a certain power took him from the clutches of death. He became cured of his wounds and soon found that all his family was safe and in good health.

And then he returned to the great Antonius and told him of this wonderful miracle, saying: "My father, Africanus, once made a cross on which was the figure of Christ with a girdle of gold that weighed fifty *grivnas*.[3] And on his head he placed a golden crown. When my uncle, Yakun, drove me from my patrimony, I took with me the girdle and the crown from this image of Jesus. And when I did so, I heard coming from the cross a voice that was directed to me, and it said:

" 'Man, never put this crown on your own head, but take it to the place that I have chosen. And there the Reverend Father Theodosius will erect a church in honor of my Mother. Place this crown in his hands and tell him to hang it over my altar.'

"And I fell to the ground, seized with awe, and I lay there motionless, as if dead, for a long time. Then I got up and went to a ship. When we were crossing the sea, there occurred a great storm, and we all feared for our lives. And I began to pray, 'Lord! Forgive me, for I am perishing because of the crown I took from your revered and holy image.'

"And I saw in the heavens a church, and I began to wonder what this vision meant. And then there came from above a voice that announced: 'This is the church that should be built by the Reverend Father Theodosius in the name of the Mother of God. And in this church you are to be buried.'

"And I saw the size and the height, and I measured it with the golden girdle and found it to be twenty times wider and thirty times higher, and the wall and the roof fifty times higher than the length of this golden girdle. And we all glorified God and, becoming consoled, we experienced great joy at having escaped a bitter death. Until now, I did not realize where the

---

[2] Military commanders.
[3] Old Russian unit of money.

church, shown me both at sea and at the river Leta where I was lying at death's door, was to be built. And then I heard from your revered tongue that I will be buried here in the church that will be erected."

And Shimon took out the golden girdle, and said: "Here are the measurements and the plan, and here is the crown that should be hung above the holy altar."

And Abbot Antonius glorified God, and told the Viking, "My child, from this day on you will never be called Shimon, but Simon."

And Antonius invited blessed Father Theodosius to come to him, and he told him: "Here is Simon who wants to build such a church." And Antonius gave Theodosius the girdle, crown, and plans. And from that day Simon loved holy Theodosius very much, and he gave him his wealth and estate for the needs of the monastery.

Once Simon came to blessed Theodosius, and after the usual talk he told the holy one, "Father, I ask you to give me a gift."

And Theodosius answered: "O my child, what can you, a powerful man, ask from me, a humble one?"

And Simon answered: "The gift I ask of you is most important, and beyond my power to obtain."

And Theodosius replied: "My child, you know how poor we are and that often we don't even have enough bread for the daily meal. And I know not what else we may have."

But Simon said: "If you want to give me this gift, you can do so, thanks to the grace that you have received from God, who called you a 'Reverend Father.' When I had taken the crown from the head of Jesus, he told me: 'Take it to the place that I have chosen. And there the Reverend Father Theodosius will erect a church in honor of my Mother.' And so I now ask you to give me your word that your soul will bless me both during our lives and after our deaths."

And the saintly father answered: "What you ask me is beyond my power, but if the church is built, and if after my passing the rituals and traditions are preserved in this church, then know that I shall dare to ask God. But now I know not whether my prayers would be acceptable."

And Simon said: "God is my witness that I was told about you by the purest lips of his holy image. Therefore, I beg you, pray for me, for my son, George, and for his descendants, in the same way in which you pray for your monks."

The saint promised this to Simon the Viking, and then added:

"I don't pray for my monks only, but for everyone who for my sake loves this holy monastery."

Then Simon bowed deeply to the earth, and spoke: "My father, I won't leave you until you have confirmed in writing what you have said."

Theodosius felt compelled to do so, since Simon loved him. And he wrote: "In the name of the Father, and of the Son, and of the Holy Ghost. . . ." And these words became the prayer which, from that time to this, is always placed in the hands of the dead. And since that time it has become the custom to put such letters in the coffins of the dead. No one did this before. And the following was written in the prayer: "Remember, me, O Lord, when thou comest into thy kingdom, and when thou judgest everyone according to his deeds, then permit, O Lord, that thy servants Simon and George remain on the right side of thy glory, and hear thy blessed voice saying: 'Come, O blessed of my Father, and inherit the kingdom that has been prepared for you since time immemorial.'"

And Simon asked: "My father, please ask the Lord also to absolve the sins of my father and my relatives."

And Theodosius raised his hands to the heavens and said: "Be blessed by the God of Zion, and you, and everyone to the last of your line, shall view the beauty of Jerusalem."

Simon received this holy blessing and this prayer as a priceless gift. Once he was a Viking, and now, thanks to the grace of God, he became an Orthodox Christian. He was instructed by our holy Father Theodosius, and, for the sake of the miracles performed by holy Antonius and Theodosius, he gave up his Western heresy and became a believer of the one true faith. And this he did with all his household and all his priests, and they numbered about three thousand. And Simon was the first to be buried in the church of the Crypt Monastery. Since that time Simon's son, George, also loved this holy place exceedingly. Prince Vladimir Monomakh sent George, the son of Simon, to the land of Suzdal, and entrusted to him his son, Yury. Many years later this Prince Yury became the ruler of Kiev, and he entrusted to George the land of Suzdal as if George were his own father.

27. BISHOP SIMON: THE COMING OF THE GREEK ICONOGRAPHERS FROM CONSTANTINOPLE TO ABBOT NIKON

Once, several Greek iconographers from Constantinople came to Abbot Nikon of the Crypt Monastery and began to complain,

saying: "Bring before us the men who hired us. We wish to have
a trial. They hired us to embellish a small church, and we made
the agreement in front of witnesses, but this church is very
large. Take back your gold (which we received as payment),
and we will return to Constantinople."

Abbot Nikon (not understanding of what they were speaking)
asked them: "Who were the people who made this agreement
with you?"

And the Greeks described these people and gave their names
as being Antonius and Theodosius.

But the abbot answered them, saying: "My children, we cannot bring them before you, for they departed this world ten
years ago. But they still continue to pray incessantly for us; they
steadily safeguard this church; they care for this monastery; and
they protect all those who live in it."

Hearing these words, the Greeks were awestruck. However,
they brought before the abbot numerous merchants, Greeks and
Abkhasians,[1] who had traveled with them from Constantinople
to Kiev. And the iconographers declared: "We made the agreement and accepted gold for payment from those who hired us in
the presence of these merchants. But since you, Abbot, do not
wish to bring to us those who commissioned us, or are unable
to bring them here, then show us their images so that our witnesses can see them."

When the abbot brought them the icons of Sts. Antonius
and Theodosius, the Greeks and Abkhasians, upon seeing them,
bowed deeply and said: "Verily, they are their image! And we
believe that even after death they still live and can protect, save,
and succor those who turn to them for aid." And they decided
to give the mosaic, which they had brought with them from
Constantinople to sell, for the embellishment of the altar.

And the iconographers began to confess their sins: "When we
arrived in our boats at the city of Kanev on the river Dnieper,
we had the vision of a mountain on which was a large church.
And we asked other travelers, 'What church is this?' and they
answered, 'It is the church of the Crypt Monastery in which you
are to paint the icons.'

"And, becoming angry,[2] we decided to go back, and started
down the river. But that same night there occurred a severe
storm on the river, and when we awoke the next morning we

---

[1] Abkhasians: a tribe in the western Caucasus.

[2] They were upset because having seen the size of the church they
realized that their work would have to be much more extensive than
they had expected.

found that we were at the village of Tripole, farther up the river, and that a certain power was pulling us always up river. And only with great difficulty were we able to stop our boat. And we remained there the whole day, contemplating the meaning of this event, since in one night, and without any rowing, we went up the river for a distance that usually requires three days of travel.

"The next night we again had the same vision of the church, and in the church was an icon of the Holy Virgin, and from this icon there came a voice announcing: 'Men! Why do you worry? Why do you not submit yourself to my will and that of my Son? If you do not obey, but try to escape, you, together with your boat, will be taken from this place and placed in the church. And know that you will never leave the monastery, but will there receive the tonsure, and will there end your days. But you will be granted mercy in the life eternal for the sake of the builders of the monastery, abbots Antonius and Theodosius.'

"And the next day, when we awoke, we once more attempted to escape, and made a great effort to row downstream; but the boat moved continually upstream. And soon it landed at the shore under the monastery, and of its own accord."

After the Greeks had finished their narration, they and the monks glorified God, the miraculous holy icon of his most Pure Mother, and the holy fathers Antonius and Theodosius. And actually, having become monks, the iconographers and builders did end their days in the Crypt Monastery. And they were buried near the altar, and their robes still hang there and their books are preserved in the monastery for the commemoration of this miracle.

28. BISHOP SIMON: JOHN AND SERGIUS

There were two men from this great city (of Kiev) who were very close friends, and their names were John and Sergius. Once, both of them went into the Church of the Crypt Monastery, which was built by the will of God. And there they saw that from the icon of the Holy Virgin there emanated a bright light, even brighter than the rays of the sun. And so they decided to pledge themselves to become spiritual brothers.

Many years later John became very ill and was on his deathbed, leaving a son, Zacharias, who was only five years old. Before his death John called for the abbot of the Crypt Monastery, and gave him all his personal wealth for distribution to the poor. The part that belonged to his young son, which consisted of one thousand *grivnas* of silver, and one hundred *grivnas* of gold, he left in trust with his spiritual brother, Sergius. John also asked his spiritual brother to care for his son, Zacharias, telling Sergius: "Give this gold and silver to my son when he comes of age."

When Zacharias was fifteen years old, he wanted to obtain his gold and silver from Sergius. But Sergius, incited by the devil, decided to keep the money for himself, and in so doing to lose his soul. Therefore he told the youth: "Your father gave his entire estate to God, and you should ask God for your gold and silver. He owes it to you, and, being merciful, perhaps he will return it to you. But I don't owe your father even a single gold coin, for he, having lost his mind, gave away all his wealth and left you in poverty."

Hearing these words, the youth became sad and once more he begged Sergius for his money, but this time asking for only one-half of his money, letting Sergius keep the second half. But Sergius began to reproach the son and the son's father in strong words.

Zacharias then attempted to obtain from Sergius at least one-quarter or even one-tenth of his money; but seeing that he would not receive anything from Sergius, he spoke to him, saying: "Come and avow in the Church of the Crypt Monastery, before the miraculous icon of the Virgin, the same icon before which you pledged to be my father's spiritual brother, that you received no money from my father."

And Sergius promised to avow before the icon that he had received neither one thousand *grivnas* of silver nor one hundred *grivnas* of gold from John. But as Sergius approached the icon to avow, an invisible power prevented him from nearing it. And suddenly he began to shout: "Holy angels and St. Theodosius! Enjoin this merciless angel not to slay me. Pray to the Holy Virgin to drive away the devils who attack me! Take your gold and silver! It is in a sealed vessel in my house!"

Everyone was seized with awe. And from that day it was forbidden to pronounce avowals on this icon. Men were sent to Sergius' house, and there they found the sealed vessel, and in it were two thousand *grivnas* of silver and two hundred *grivnas* of gold, for God had miraculously increased the fortune of the poor, knowing that Zacharias would give his fortune to the abbot of the Crypt Monastery. Zacharias remained at the monastery to the end of his days, and his fortune was used to erect the Church of St. John the Baptist. This church was dedicated to the memories of John and Zacharias, since their gold and silver had erected it.

29. BISHOP SIMON: PRINCE SVIATOSHA
OF CHERNIGOV

This blessed and faithful Prince Sviatosha, called Nicholas after he became a monk, was the son of Prince David and the grandson of Prince Sviatoslav. This prince came to the conclusion that all things in this vain life are illusive and that everything on the earth comes to its end and passes away, but that the blessings of the future life are eternal and everlasting and that the kingdom of heaven, which God has prepared for those who love him, is unending. And he relinquished his princedom together with all his honor, glory, and power, seeing no worth in all these things. And he came to the Crypt Monastery and became a monk. This happened in 6614 (1106) on the 17th day of February. All the monks who were living in the monastery at that time are witnesses to his virtuous life and his fulfillment of the vows of obedience.

For three years he remained in the kitchen working with his brethren. With his own hands he chopped wood for the preparation of meals, often carrying it on his shoulders from the river Dnieper. And his brothers, Iziaslav and Vladimir, were [hard] trying to keep him from such heavy labor. However, he asked and begged that they permit him to work at least one more year in the kitchen with his brethren. Thereafter, he was placed in charge of the monastery gates, for in every type of work he was skillful and diligent. He remained there, at the gates, for three years, never leaving except to attend church services. From there he was told to go and serve in the refectory. Finally, according to the will of the abbot and all the brethren, he was permitted to have his own cell, which he himself built. This cell is called Sviatosha's cell to this very day, and the vegetable garden, which he planted with his own hands, is also called after his name still. People say of him that no one has ever seen him idle. He was always occupied with some kind of work, and thus he earned his keep. On his lips permanently was a prayer to Jesus: "Jesus Christ, have mercy upon us." He never ate anything more than the monastery meals. He had considerable wealth, but he gave everything away to pilgrims and the poor and for the building of churches. Up to now there are many books given by him to your monastery. When he was still ruling, this blessed Sviatosha had a very skilled physician, Peter, who was from Syria. This Peter came with him to the monastery, but, seeing that the prince voluntarily accepted poverty and worked in the kitchen and at the gate, he left him and, settling in Kiev, became a doctor for many citizens of this city. This physician used to come often to Prince Sviatosha at the monastery and, seeing his bitter sufferings and endless fasting, tried to convince him to change his way of living, saying: "Prince, you should care for your health and not ruin your body with endless labor and abstinence. You will become so ill, that you will not be able to carry the burden which, for God's sake, you have voluntarily accepted. God does not desire unbearable fasting and labor, but only a humble and contrite heart. You are not accustomed to hardships such as you, working like a slave, must now endure. Your pious brothers, Iziaslav and Vladimir, feel that your poverty is a reproach to them. How could you turn away from such glory and honor to such wretchedness and how can you exhaust your body with such food? I wonder about your stomach; once sweet meals were too heavy for it, and now it accepts and endures simple herbs and dry bread. Beware, for sometime all your maladies will attack you at once, and you, deprived of resistance, will succumb, and I will not be able to help you. You will leave your inconsolable brothers to mourn after you. Also, your boyars, who once served you, hoped to become powerful and glorious with your help. Now they are deprived of your love, and they complain about you. They have built large houses for themselves, but they remain in them in great grief. You yourself have not even a place to lay your head, remaining in this backyard. They consider that you have become insane. Who among the princes has done anything of this nature? Did your blessed father, David, or your grandfather, Sviatoslav, do so? Or who among the boyars has acted in this way? Or who even intended to do anything similar, excepting Barlaam, who was the abbot here? And if you don't follow my advice, you will meet an untimely death."

So he used to talk with Prince Sviatosha, now Monk Nicholas, sitting with him in the kitchen or at the gate. And he was instructed to do so by Prince Sviatosha's brothers. But Prince Sviatosha answered him, saying: "Brother Peter, I have thought for a long time and I have decided not to spare my flesh so as to prevent it from arousing in me a new struggle. It is better to keep it submissive under the burden of heavy labor, for it is said: 'Strength is achieved through weakness,' and, 'These present temporary passions are nothing worse in comparison with the glory which will be revealed in us.' I thank God for he has liberated me from the slavedom of this world and made me the servant of his servants, these blessed monks. And my brothers had better look after themselves, for each man must bear his cross alone. They should be satisfied with having my patrimony

—all of what I had: my wife and children, the house and power, brethren and friends, serfs and estates, I gave up for Christ's sake so as to inherit eternal life. I became poor for the sake of God, so that I might gain God's favor.

"And even yourself, when you treat people, don't you prescribe refraining from excessive eating? To die for Christ would be a real acquisition of fortune for me. And sitting here in the backyard next to the refuse heap is the winning of a real kingdom. It may be that no prince has done as I do now. Then I will be the first example for them. Perhaps one of them will want to imitate my example and follow in my footsteps. As far as my life is concerned, it should not be of concern to you, nor to those who have asked you to come to me."

When the blessed prince was sick, his physician, Peter, usually prepared some medicine for the illness, such as severe heartburn or other pains, that had occurred to the prince. But before the physician could reach the prince, the prince was already cured. And he never permitted himself to be treated by a physician. And so it happened many times. Once, when the physician himself became ill, Prince Sviatosha sent him a messenger to say: "Don't take your medicine and you will be cured. And if you don't obey me, you will suffer bitterly."

But the latter, relying on his medical skills, drank the medicine, hoping to be cured of his illness; but instead of being cured, he almost died. And only the prayer of the blessed prince helped and cured him.

Another time the physician again became ill, and the blessed prince sent his messenger once more to say: "If you don't attempt to cure yourself, you will be completely recovered in three days."

The Syrian obeyed him, and on the third day he recovered, according to the words of the blessed prince. As soon as he had recovered, the blessed one asked him to come to the monastery, and there he enjoined the physician to become a monk, saying: "In three months from now, we shall part." With these words Prince Sviatosha predicted the death of the physician.

The Syrian misunderstood the prince's words, thinking that not his own death but that of the prince was nearing. He fell before the prince's feet and tearfully implored him, saying:

> *"Alas, woe is me, my lord and benefactor!*
> *Who will help me, a foreigner?*
> *Who will feed so many people who are hungry?*
> *Who will be the intercessor of the offended?*
> *Who will be merciful with the poor?*

Have I not told you, my prince,
that you will be mourned by all your inconsolable brothers?
You cured me not only through the words and power of God,
but also with the help of your prayers.
Where will you depart to, my good pastor?
Tell me what fatal illness you have,
and I will cure you.
And, if I cannot,
then my head shall be given for your head,
and my soul for your soul.
O my lord, don't leave me
without telling me how you learned of your death.
I would give my life for you.
If God has announced your passing away to you,
please pray to him that I might die in your place.
Where would I be able to mourn my loss,
if you leave me?
Should I do it here, at this refuse heap,
or at the gate where you live?
And what can you leave me if you die?
You yourself are almost naked, and when you die
you will be buried in your patched and tattered garments.
Help me through your prayers
as once prophet Elijah gave Elisha his mantle
to get through paradise
under the shelter of the wonderful house of the Lord.
Even the beast knows where the sun will rise
before it goes to its lair.
And the bird knows how to find its abode
and the turtledove knows how to find the nest
where it raises its fledglings."

But the blessed one answered him: "It is better to place one's hopes in the Lord than to rely upon many; God knows how to feed his creatures and how to protect and save his poor. My brothers should not worry about me, but about themselves and their children. I never wanted any treatment by a physician during my life, because when the hour of death has come the physician cannot help." And the prince went with the physician down into the crypt and dug a grave for himself, and he asked the Syrian: "Which of us wants this grave the more?"

And the Syrian replied: "It should come to pass as each of us desires. But you should live, and I should be buried here."

And then the blessed prince told him: "Let it be as you do desire."

The Syrian physician became a monk, and passed three months weeping incessantly both day and night. The blessed one consoled him, saying: "Brother Peter, do you wish that I should take you with me?"

And the physician answered tearfully: "I want you to release me and let me die in your place. Please, pray for me."

And the blessed prince told the physician: "Prepare for death, my son, and in three days you will depart to the Lord."

And after three days the physician took Holy Communion, lay down on his bed, adjusted his robes, stretched out his legs, and gave up his soul into the hands of the Lord, as it was predicted by blessed Prince Sviatosha.

Prince Sviatosha lived after this for another thirty years, never leaving the monastery again. And when he died, almost the entire city of Kiev came to his burial. Learning of blessed Sviatosha's death, his brother, Prince Iziaslav, sent a messenger to the abbot, asking that he be given the crucifix of Prince Sviatosha, his pillow, and the board upon which he had knelt.

The abbot gave them to the prince, saying: "It will renew your faith."

The prince accepted them and carefully preserved them at home. And he gave the abbot three pieces of gold so as not to receive this blessing of the abbot for nothing.

Once, this prince became so ill that all his family lost hope and, seeing that he was about to die, his wife, children, and boyars went to his chambers and remained with him. He raised up slightly and asked for some water from the well of the Crypt Monastery, and then he became mute.

In the meantime a messenger went to the monastery for the water. The abbot took Sviatosha's hair shirt,[1] put it first on the grave of St. Theodosius, and then gave it to the prince's messenger, telling him to put this shirt on Prince Iziaslav. Before the messenger had returned with the water and hair shirt, the ill prince suddenly uttered the words: "Go beyond the gates of the city and meet St. Theodosius and St. Nicholas."

And when the messenger returned with the water and the hair shirt, the prince exclaimed: "Nicholas—Nicholas Sviatosha!"

And the prince was given the water, and the hair shirt was placed on his body, and he recovered immediately. And everyone glorified God and his saints. And each time Iziaslav became ill, he would put on this hair shirt, and he always recovered. And in all battles he wore this hair shirt, and he remained unharmed. But once, a poor sinner, he dared not put on the hair

---

[1] Hair shirt: a shirt made of horsehair, and worn as a penance.

shirt, and he was slain in battle. And he was buried in this hair
shirt, as he had requested. And the brethren still remember
other great deeds of the saint. Until this day the monks of the
Crypt Monastery still hold blessed Prince Sviatosha in their
memory.

30. MONK POLYCARPE: MARKO THE GRAVEDIGGER
WHO WAS OBEYED BY THE DEAD

We sinners imitate the ancient writings on the saints. But the
ancient writers, with great difficulties, sought the saints in the
wilderness, in the mountains, and in the abysses. Some of these
authors have themselves seen these saints, while of other saints
they have heard stories of their lives, works, miracles, and
deeds, and have composed the *Paterikons,* which we read and in
which we enjoy spiritual narrations. I, an unworthy one, have
not yet been able to comprehend the truth of reason, and I have
seen nothing of this kind. I tell only what I have heard. This
narration was told to me by Bishop Simon, and I wrote it down
for you, my reverend father. I have never been in holy places,
nor have I seen Jerusalem nor Mount Sinai. Therefore I am unable to add anything to this narration for the purpose of embellishment, as is the habit of those who are clever with words.
I do not want to praise anything but this holy Crypt Monastery,
the monks who live therein, and the lives and miracles of the
latter. I shall rejoice when I remember them, for I, a sinner,
hope that the saintly fathers will pray for me. And here I shall
begin the narration concerning the gravedigger Marko.

St. Marko used to live in the crypt, and during his life there
the body of our father, Theodosius, was taken from the crypt
into the great holy church. This Marko dug graves in the crypt
with his own hands, and carried the earth away on his shoulders. He worked hard all day and all night to do these pious
deeds. Though he dug many graves for the burial of his brethren, he never accepted payment for doing so. If someone gave
him money, he would take it and distribute it among the poor
and crippled.

Once, according to his custom, he dug a grave and, laboring
very much, became tired. However, the grave was not sufficiently wide. It so happened that this very day one of the
brothers passed to God, and there was no grave available except
this narrow one. The dead man was brought to the crypt, but
because the grave was so very narrow he could not be placed
in it. And the brethren began to grumble at Marko, for it was

neither possible to adjust the dead man's robes nor to anoint him with holy oil. Marko, the monk of the cave, bowed to everyone with humility and said: "Forgive me, my fathers, but I could not finish the grave because of my poor health."

But the monks continued to reproach him still more. Then Marko addressed the dead man: "Brother, your grave is so narrow we cannot even anoint you with holy oil. Take the oil and anoint yourself."

The dead man raised up slightly, extended his hand, took the oil, and anointed his face and chest, making the sign of the cross. He then returned the vessel, adjusted his robes, lay down, and once more died. Awe and trembling seized everyone because of the miracle.

Some time later, after a long illness, another brother died. One of his friends cleansed the body with a sponge and went to the crypt to view the grave where his friend was supposed to lie. He asked Marko about the grave, and Marko answered: "Go to the dead brother and tell him, 'Wait until tomorrow, until I dig your grave, and then you can enter into rest.'"

But the brother, who had come to the crypt, said: "Brother Marko, I have already cleansed the dead man's body with a sponge. How can you now ask me to speak to him?"

Marko once again spoke to him: "You can see for yourself that the grave is not finished. I enjoin you to go and tell the dead man that sinful Marko tells him: 'Brother, live one more day, and then tomorrow you will pass to God in peace. When I have prepared a place for you, I will send for you.'"

The brother who had come to blessed Marko obeyed. When he returned to the monastery, all the brothers were standing around the dead man and were singing the usual hymns. The monk stood before the dead brother, and said: "Brother Marko has told me to tell you that your grave is not ready and that you should wait until tomorrow."

Everyone was astounded by these words. But as soon as they were spoken by the monk who had returned from Marko, the dead brother's soul returned to his body. The whole day and night he remained with his eyes open, but talked with no one at all.

The next day his friends once more returned to the cave to find out if the place was ready. And blessed Marko told them: "Go and tell the following to one who has become alive: 'Abandon this provisional life and pass into the life eternal. Here the place is ready for your body. Give your soul to God, and your body will be buried here with many holy brothers.'"

The brothers came and told all this to the dead one who had

come alive. Immediately the latter, in the presence of all who had come to visit him, closed his eyes and passed away. And he was placed with honors in the new place in the cave. And everyone wondered about this miracle. How could it be that, with just one word from blessed Marko, the dead would become alive, and then die once more after Marko ordered it?

Two other brethren in this great Crypt Monastery had since their youth been united by the great love in their hearts. They had the same thoughts and the same desires, which were directed to God. And they begged blessed Marko to prepare them a common grave where they would be able to lie together when God should order them to do so. Many years later the elder brother, Theophile, left the monastery on business. In the meantime the younger brother became ill and died and was laid in the grave prepared for him. Theophile returned only some days after the burial. Having learned of the death of his brother, he became very sad and, taking some other monks, went to the cave to see in which place the deceased was laid.

Having noticed that his brother was buried in a place that was higher than the place reserved for himself, he was seized by wrath, and began to complain to Marko, saying: "Why did you put him there? I am the older, and therefore should be put in the higher place. But you have buried him in my place."

Marko, the monk of the cave, being a humble man, bowed to Theophile, and said: "Excuse me, my brother, I have sinned before you." Then he said to the deceased: "Brother, give your place to your elder brother and lie down in the lower place." And immediately after these words of blessed Marko, the dead man got up in the presence of all the monks and lay down in the lower place. Everyone saw this terrible and awe-inspiring miracle.

Then brother Theophile, who had reproached Marko, fell to his knees and said: "Brother Marko, I have sinned by moving my brother from his place. Tell him to return to the original place."

But blessed Marko told Theophile: "God ended the enmity between us. He did so because you complained and so that you might be prevented from lasting enmity and evil feelings toward me. Even this soulless body has demonstrated its love to you, respecting your seniority even after death. I should like you to make use of your seniority by not leaving this crypt, but by lying down in this place. But you are not ready for passing away. Therefore, go and care for your soul. In some days from now you will be brought to this place. The resurrection of the dead is the work of God, whereas I am only a miserable sinner.

Look on your dead brother, who was not able to bear the reproaches with which you covered me. And he left you a half of the place that was prepared for both of you. God can raise the dead, but I cannot say, 'Go down and lie in the lower place,' and then say, 'Go up and lie in the higher place.' If you want him to go back to his former place, order it, and perhaps he will go back to the place he left before."

Having heard these words, Theophile became saddened, and he thought that he would be unable to walk back to the monastery. When he returned to his cell, he began to cry disconsolately. He distributed everything he had, and kept only his mantle and robe. From that time forth, he was in permanent expectation of death, and no one could bring an end to his bitter crying and no one could convince him to eat well.

At the beginning of the day he would say to himself: "I don't know whether I shall live till evening." When evening was approaching, he would cry and say: "What should I do? Shall I be able to live till morning? Many people who arose this morning were not able to live until evening, but were obliged to lie down and were unable to get up again. And what of me? For I was told by blessed Marko that my end was very near." And he spent each day mortifying his flesh with fasting, praying, and incessant weeping, expecting each day that his final hour was approaching. The expectation that his soul would soon be separated from his body exhausted him to such an extent that it became possible to count his ribs. Many people wished to console him, but this made him weep only the more. Finally, because of his incessant tears, he became blind. And so Theophile spent his days in great abstinence, thereby winning the Grace of God by his exemplary life.

When Marko learned the hour of his own passing to God, he asked Theophile to come, and he told him: "Brother Theophile, forgive me for having caused you great sadness, lo! these many years. Now I leave this world. Pray for me. If I receive God's mercy, I shall not forget you. Let us pray that we may see each other with our fathers, Antonius and Theodosius, in the next life."

And Theodosius answered tearfully: "Father Marko, why do you leave me here? Why don't you return my sight to me?"

Marko told him: "Brother, don't grieve. Thanks to God you have lost your physical sight, but you have won the insight for understanding him with your spiritual eyes. My brother, I was responsible for your blindness, for I prophesied your death. But I did so for the sake of your soul, for I wanted to turn your pride into humility, and God rejects neither the contrite heart nor the humble man."

And Theophile answered him, saying: "I know, my father, that I should have fallen dead for my sins when you raised my dead brother. But, because of prayers, the Lord gave me new life, hoping for my repentance. Now I beg you, please, either take me with you to the Lord or return my sight to me."

Marko replied: "There is no need for you to see this transitory world. Pray to the Lord that you may see his glory in the next world. Your hour will come, even if you do not wish it to. Nevertheless, I shall give you a foretoken of your passing. Three days before your death, you will regain your sight. And, passing to God, you will there see endless light and unspoken glory." And blessed Marko passed to God, being buried in the crypt in a grave he himself had dug.

This separation from Brother Marko added greatly to Theophile's suffering and increased his weeping. He shed whole torrents of tears, and the tears continually increased. He had a special vessel, and because his tears would always reappear when he began praying, he would put this vessel before himself so that his tears would fall into it. Some days this vessel would be full of tears, since every day Theophile expected the end of his life as blessed Marko had predicted. When Theophile felt that his day of passing to God was drawing near, he began to pray zealously, saying: "Our Lord who loves man, my God, my most holy King, you do not want the death of sinners; you anticipate their conversion to righteousness. You know our weaknesses, our gracious Comforter. You are health to the ill and salvation for the sinner. You are succor for the exhausted and an uplifting for the fallen. O Lord, I, an unworthy one, pray to you in this hour to show me your amazing Grace and to reveal to me the unfathomable depths of your mercy. Deliver me from temptation. Do not permit the enemy to overcome me in my ordeal, but give me strength for the sake of the prayers of your saints and our great fathers, Antonius and Theodosius, and for the sake of the prayers of all saints who have served you since the beginning of time."

And in this moment a beautiful youth appeared before him, and said: "You pray well, but why are you so saddened by the vanity of your tears?" And the youth, taking a vessel much larger than that which Theophile had, and which was filled with the fragrance of myrrh, said: "Here are the tears that have poured forth from your contrite heart during your prayers to God. All your tears that you dried neither with your hand nor with your robe nor with a cloth fell from your eyes to the earth. All of them, at the command of the Creator, I gathered and preserved in this vessel. Now I have been sent to you to announce tidings of joy. With joy will you go to the one who said: 'Blessed are they that mourn, for they shall be comforted.' " Having spoken these words, the youth disappeared.

After this, blessed Theophile asked the abbot to come to his cell, and he told him of the appearance of the angel and of the angel's words. He showed the abbot both vessels, one of which was filled with tears and the other with a fragrance that could not be compared to any other. And blessed Theophile asked that the contents of both vessels be poured over his body after his death.

Three days later, blessed Theophile passed to the Lord and was buried in the crypt near the grave of Marko the gravedigger. And when the contents of the angel's vessel were spread over his body, the entire crypt was filled with a wondrous sweet fragrance. And the monks also poured the contents of the vessel of tears over him, doing this so that he who had shed these tears might harvest the fruits of his labor.

D. APOCRYPHA

31. THE DESCENT OF THE VIRGIN INTO HELL

AFTER the Christianization of Russia under Prince Vladimir, canonical books, such as the Bible, liturgical texts, and the works of the early Church Fathers, circulated through the Russian land. In addition to these, a considerable number of apocryphal or noncanonical writings came to Russia. Patterned after the Bible and written at the time of the New Testament, they were never recognized by the Church. Among such works, *The Descent of the Virgin into Hell,* or, as it was called by Russians, *The Visitation to the Torments by the Mother of God,* is the most distinguished owing to its concept of divine mercy and the originality of its composition. "A visit to hell" was a subject common to both Eastern and Western Christianity, its most famous version being, of course, Dante's great poem *The Divine Comedy.*

The juxtaposition of eschatological concepts with the concept of divine mercy, as presented in this work, greatly influenced the Russian religious mind and was reflected in medieval Russian *vitae,* spiritual songs, and icons.

This translation is based on the text of a seventeenth-century manuscript that was revised and corrected by Professor N. K. Gudzy according to a twelfth-century manuscript, and it appeared in his *Khrestomatiia po drevnei russkoi literatury,* Moscow, 1955, pages 92–98. Some portions of this translation follow that of Professor L. Wiener.

The Holy Virgin wished to see the torments of the souls, and so she said to the Archangel, Michael: "I ask that you tell me all things which are upon the earth." And the archangel answered: "I shall tell you all things which are upon the earth, Blessed One, as you would have it." And the Holy Virgin asked him: "How many torments does the Christian race suffer?" And the archangel said: "Innumerable are those torments." And then the Holy Virgin replied: "Show me what is in heaven and upon the earth."

Then the archangel ordered the angels to come from the south, and hell was opened. And she saw those that were suffering in hell, and there were a great number of them and there was much weeping. And the Blessed Virgin asked the archangel: "Who are these that they suffer so?"

And the archangel answered: "These are those who did not believe in the Father, the Son, and the Holy Ghost, but forgot God and believed in those things which God created for our sakes. They called the sun and the moon, beast and reptiles, earth and water God. And they made gods out of the devils Troyan, Khors, Veles, and Perun, and they worshiped these evil devils. And even now they are possessed by evil darkness, and therefore they suffer such torments."

And the Holy Virgin saw great darkness in another place. And she asked: "What is this darkness and who are those who dwell therein?" And the archangel answered, saying: "Many souls dwell in this place." And the Holy Virgin said: "Let the darkness be dispersed that I may see the torment." And the angels who watched over the torment answered: "We have been enjoined not to let them see light until the coming of your blessed Son, who is brighter than seven suns." And the Holy Virgin was saddened, and she raised her eyes to the angels and looked at the invisible throne of her father and said: "In the name of the Father, and the Son, and the Holy Ghost! Let this darkness be dispersed that I may see this torment."

And the darkness was dispersed and seven heavens appeared and there was a great multitude of men and women. And there were loud weeping and wailing in this place. And seeing them, the Holy Virgin said, weeping: "What have you done, wretched and unworthy people? What has brought you here?" But there was no voice nor any answer from them. And the watching angels spoke: "Wherefore do you not speak?" And one who was tormented replied: "Blessed One! For ages we have seen no light and we cannot look up." The Holy Virgin, looking on them, wept bitterly.

And a tormented one, seeing her, said: "How is it, Holy Virgin, that you have visited us? Your blessed Son came upon the earth and did not ask us, nor did Abraham the Patriarch, nor Moses the prophet, nor John the Baptist, nor Paul the Apostle, the favorite of the Lord. But you, most Holy Virgin, are an intercessor and protector for the Christian people. You have prayed to God for us, but how did it come to pass that you have visited us, wretched as we be?"

Then the Holy Virgin inquired what was the sin of these tormented ones, and Michael answered: "These are they who did not believe in the Father, the Son, and the Holy Ghost, nor in you, Holy Virgin! They did not want to proclaim your name, nor that from you was born Our Lord Jesus Christ who, having come in the flesh, has sanctified the earth through baptism. It is for this that they are tormented in this place."

Weeping, the Holy Virgin spoke to them. "Wherefore do you live in error? Do you not know that all creation honors my name?" And when the Holy Virgin finished speaking, darkness once more fell upon them.

And Michael said to her: "Whither, Blessed One, do you wish to go now: to the south or to the north?" And when the Virgin replied that she would go to the south, there appeared cherubim and seraphim and four hundred angels who took the Holy Virgin to the south. And there the Holy Virgin saw a river of fire. There was a multitude of men and women who stood in this fiery river. Some stood in the river to their waists, some to their shoulders, some to their necks, and some above their necks. Seeing this, the Holy Virgin exclaimed in a loud voice: "Who are they that stand in the fire up to their waists?" And the archangel answered: "They are those that have been cursed by their fathers and mothers, and being so cursed, they are tormented here." And when the Holy Virgin inquired who were those who stood in the fire to their shoulders, Michael replied: "They are those who have cursed and indulged in lechery, and therefore are tormented in this place." And the Virgin asked: "Who are those that are in the fiery flame up to their necks?" And Michael answered, saying: "They are those who have eaten human flesh. For this they are tormented here." And the Holy Virgin then asked: "Those who are immersed in the fiery flame above their heads, who are they?" Michael the archangel replied: "They are those, Lady, who, holding the cross, have sworn falsely. Such is the power of the cross that it is worshiped with awe by the angels and they tremble before it. And so, when a man swears by the cross and then lies, he is punished by such a torment."

And then the Holy Virgin saw a man who was hanging by his heels, and worms were devouring him. And she asked the archangel who he was and what were his sins. And the archangel answered: "They are those who took interest on their silver and gold, and therefore they are tormented in this place."

And then she saw a woman who was hanging by one tooth, and various serpents came from her mouth and were devouring her. The Holy Virgin, seeing this, asked Michael: "Who is this woman? What is her sin?" And the archangel answered: "Lady, this one is she who used to say evil words and gossiped, which led to evil discourse among her neighbors, and therefore she is damned." And the Holy Virgin replied: "Blessed be the woman who does not give birth to such a sinner."

And then Michael said: "Holy Virgin, you have not yet seen the greatest torments." And the Holy Virgin replied: "Let us go and visit so that I may see all torments." And, when Michael inquired where she should like to go, the Holy Virgin asked to go to the north. And then seraphim and cherubim and four hundred angels took the Blessed One to the north where there was a great fiery cloud, and in this fiery cloud there were fiery places to lie down. In these places were a great many men and women. And the Holy Virgin, weeping, asked who these men and women were and what were their sins. And the archangel replied: "Lady, those are the ones who, during holy weeks, did not get up to attend the Easter Midnight Service, but lay in bed lazily as if dead. Therefore, they are tormented in this place." And the Holy Virgin asked: "And those who were not able to get up, are they also condemned as sinners?" And Michael answered: "Holy Lady, only those who cannot get up even when their house be in flame on all four sides do not sin when they do not go to church."

And the Holy Virgin saw a big iron tree with branches of iron on which there were iron barbs. On these barbs hung a great many men and women by their tongues. Seeing them, the Holy Virgin began to sob, and asked Michael who these people were and what was their sin. And the archangel replied: "These people are calumniators and gossipers who separate brother from brother and husband from wife."

And she saw women hanging by their fingernails, and fire came from their mouths and burned them. And serpents came out of the flames and tormented them. And they cried out, saying: "Be merciful unto us, for we are tormented beyond all other torments." And the Holy Virgin asked what were their sins. And Michael answered: "These are the widows of priests who did not revere the office of the priesthood, but married other men after the death of their priestly husbands."

And the Virgin saw other women who were lying in fire and were devoured by various serpents, and Michael said: "These are nuns from convents who sold their bodies for lechery, and therefore they are tormented."

And the archangel said to the Blessed Virgin: "Come hither, Holy Virgin, and I will show you the place where many sinners are tormented." And the Holy Virgin saw the river of flames. And the river appeared as if it were flowing blood and it covered the whole earth. In the middle of this river were a great many sinners. Seeing these, the Virgin wept, and asked: "What is their sin?" And the Archangel Michael answered: "These are the whores and the adulterers, those who listen to gossip, the matchmakers and calumniators, the drunkards, merciless princes, bishops, and archbishops, tsars who did not fulfill the will of God, the usurers who collected interest, and the lawbreakers." Hearing this, the Blessed Virgin wept, and said: "O these evil sinners, it would have been better if they had never been born!"

And Michael asked her: "Wherefore do you weep, Holy One? Have you never seen such great torments before?" And the Blessed Virgin answered: "Take me farther, that I may see all torments that are." And Michael asked: "Where do you wish to go, Blessed One, to the east or to the west, to the right into paradise or to the left where are the greatest torments?" And as soon as the Virgin replied that she wished to go to the left, there appeared seraphim and cherubim and four hundred angels and they took the Most Holy One to the east, to the left. And in the vicinity of the river there was a great darkness, and in the river there came many men and women, and it appeared as if the water were boiling. And great waves broke upon the sinners, and when the waves rose they drowned the sinners in a thousand feet of water, so that they were not even able to utter, "Righteous Judge, be merciful unto us!" And there was much gnashing of teeth in this place, since the sinners were devoured by the worms.

And seeing the Holy Virgin, the host of angels that watched over the sinners exclaimed in unison: "Holy, Holy, Holy! Holy God and you, Holy Virgin, we bless you and the Son of God born of you. For ages we have not seen light, but now, praise be to you, we have seen the light." And once more all of them exclaimed: "Rejoice, Blessed Virgin. Rejoice, Source of Light Eternal. Rejoice, Holy Archangel Michael and pray to Our Lord for the entire world, for we have seen the sinners who are tormented, and we are very saddened."

The Holy Virgin, seeing the angels saddened and filled with sorrow because of the torments of the sinners, began to weep. And all exclaimed in unison, saying: "It is good that you have come to this darkness, for now you have seen their torments. Most Holy Lady and Archangel Michael, pray for them." And she heard the sobs and voices of the sinners who raised their laments, saying: "God have mercy upon us!" And the Virgin said: "God have mercy upon them." And as soon as she had said this, the tempest on the river of fiery waves ceased. And the sinners gained the hope in a tiny mustard seed. And the Holy Virgin, seeing this, wept and said: "What is this river and of what are its waves?" And Michael answered: "This river is a river of hot pitch, and its waves are of flame. And the Jews are tormented here because they tormented Our Lord, Jesus Christ. And those who were baptized in the name of the Father, the Son, and Holy Ghost and still believed in demons and rejected

God and baptism are also tormented in this place. And those who committed lechery with their mothers and daughters, and those who murdered with poisons or who killed with weapons, or who strangled their children are tormented in this place. Because of such deeds they are tormented." And the Holy Virgin said: "They deserve this for their sins." And when she had said these words the fiery waves once again enveloped the sinners, and darkness betook them. And Michael said to the Holy Virgin: "There is no thought of God for those who are lost in darkness." And the Most Holy One said: "O evil sinners, the flame of this fire shall never become extinguished."

And then the Holy Virgin spoke, saying: "I have only one request. Let me also enter, that I may suffer together with the Christians, for they have called themselves the children of my Son." And the archangel said: "Rest yourself in paradise!" And the Holy Virgin replied: "I beg you, move the host of the angels that we may pray for the sinners, and God may accept our prayer and have mercy upon them."

The archangel replied, saying: "Great is the name of our Lord God. Seven times in the day and seven times in the night do we bring praises and worship Our Lady for the sake of the sinners. And we hope that Our Lord will listen to our prayers." And the Holy Virgin answered: "I beg you, order that the angelic host carry me to the heavenly height and take me before the invisible Father."

And the archangel so ordered, and there appeared cherubim and seraphim, and they carried the Blessed One to the heavenly height, and put her down at the throne of the invisible Father. She raised her hands to her Blessed Son and said: "Have mercy, O Lord, upon the sinners, for I have seen them, and I could not endure. Let me be tormented together with the Christians." And there came a voice to her which said: "I see nails in my Son's hands. How can I have mercy upon them?" And she said: "I do not pray for the infidel Jews, but for the Christians I ask thy mercy." And a voice again came to her, saying: "I see how they have had no mercy upon my brethren, so I can have no mercy upon them."

And the Holy Virgin again spoke, saying: "Have mercy, O Lord, upon the sinners, the creation of thine own hands, who proclaim thy name over the whole earth and even in their torments, and who in all places say, 'Most Holy Lady, Mother of God, intercede for us.' And when a child is born people say, 'Most Holy Virgin, help us.'"

Then the Lord spoke to her: "Hear, Holy Virgin! There is not a human being who does not praise thy name. I will not abandon them, neither in heaven nor upon the earth." Then the Holy Virgin asked: "Where is Moses the prophet? Where are all the prophets? And you, Fathers, who have never committed a sin? Where is Paul, God's favorite? Where is Sunday, the pride of the Christian? And where is the power of the pure cross through which Adam and Eve were delivered from their curse?"

Then the Archangel Michael and all the angels cried: "Have mercy, O Lord, upon the sinners!" And Moses wept aloud and said: "Have mercy upon them, O Lord, for I have given them thy Law!" And John wept and cried out: "Have mercy, O Lord, for I have preached thy Gospel to them." And Paul wept and said: "Have mercy, O Lord, for I carried thine epistles to the churches." [Here a fragment is missing, but it is apparent from the text that follows that God did not concede to the prayers of the Holy Virgin and the saints.] And the saints, hearing the voice of the Lord, did not dare to answer.

The Most Holy Virgin, seeing that she could not intercede and that God would neither listen to their pleas nor take mercy on the sinners, said: "Where is the Archangel Gabriel who announced to me: 'Rejoice, because you have heard the Father before all ages and he will take away his reproach among men?' . . . [fragment missing]. And where are the servants of the throne and where is St. John the Theologian? Wherefore did they not appear with us to pray for these Christian sinners? Don't you see that I shed tears for the sinners? Come, all angels which are in the heavens. Come, all righteous people acquitted by God, since you are given the right to pray for sinners. And come you, Michael, for you are the first incorporeal one and are next to the throne. Let us all pray to the invisible Father for mercy, and let us not move away as long as he will not have mercy unto the sinners."

And Michael bowed to the ground before the throne, and with him bowed all those who are in heaven and all the incorporeal angels. Then the Lord, seeing the intercession of the saints, became merciful for his Son's sake, and said: "Come down, my beloved Son, and listen to the prayers of the saints and appear before the sinners."

And the Lord came down from the invisible throne, and all sinners who were in the darkness exclaimed in unison: "Have mercy upon us, King of All Ages! Have mercy upon us, Son of God!"

And the Lord then said: "Hear all! I have planted paradise, and have created man in my own image, and made him lord over paradise, and gave him life eternal. But they have disobeyed me and sinned in their selfishness and delivered them-

selves unto death. And since I did not want to see deeds done
by hands which were forced by the devil, I came to earth and
became incarnate through the Virgin. And I was raised to the
cross to free them from slavery and the original curse. And I
asked for water, but I was given gall mixed with vinegar. My
hand created man and man put me into the grave. I descended
to hell and defeated the enemy and raised the selected ones.
And I blessed the river Jordan to save you from original sin, but
you did not care to repent for your sins. You became Christians
only in words, and did not keep my commandments. For this
you find yourselves in the fire everlasting, and I ought not to
have mercy upon you! But today, by the mercy of my Father
who sent me to you, and through the intercession of my Mother
who has wept much for you, and through Michael, the archangel
of the Gospel, and through the multitude of martyrs who have
labored much in your behalf, I give you from Good Thursday
to Holy Pentecost, day and night, for rest and for praising the
Father, and the Son, and the Holy Ghost!"

And they all answered: "Glory be to thy mercy!" Glory to the
Father, and to the Son, and to the Holy Ghost, now and forever.
Amen.

32. ADAM'S ADDRESS TO LAZARUS IN HELL

Among early Russian writings that cannot be dated with certi-
tude a very prominent place is occupied by *Adam's Address to
Lazarus in Hell*. Its style and content indicate that this work
was written in the Kievan era and probably in the same century
as the *Lay of Igor's Campaign*, with which it has many parallels.
Its origin is definitely apocryphal, but it is still difficult to determine whether the original text is Byzantine or Russian. The topic
of this work is Adam's address to Lazarus in hell before he had
been raised from the dead by Jesus. The address consists of two
rather different parts, the first being poetic and original, while
the second is composed of quotations from the Gospel, and
apparently has been corrupted by the scribes.

The final text has been established by M. Hruchevsky, who
divided the work into poetic lines. The translation offered here
was published anonymously in *The Slavonic Review*, Volume X,
1931, pages 246–252. Several stylistic corrections have been
made by the present editor.

Hear, heaven, attend, earth,
how speaks the Lord:
"I bore sons and exalted them,

and they have rejected me.
The ass recognizes his master's manger,
but my people have not recognized me.
And behold I will not give my glory to another
but will send my Word on earth
that I may save my people from the meshes of Satan."

"Brethren, let us today sing songs,
let us cast aside grief, and be full of joy,"
spoke David, seated in infernal hell,
setting his eyed fingers on the live strings.
And he struck the lute and said:
"For now has come a joyful time,
for now has come the day of salvation.
For I hear shepherds
playing the reed in the cave,
and their voice passes the gates of hell
and enters my ears.
And I hear the trampling of feet of Persian horses,
that carry the Magi with their gifts for him,
from their kings to the King of Heaven,
who has today been born on earth.
And him, brethren,
we have been awaiting for many days,
whose throne is heaven
and whose feet rest on the earth.
The maiden mother
wraps him in swaddling cloths
who wraps the heavens in clouds
and the earth in darkness.
And she speaks bending over him:
'O great and heavenly King,
how hast thou willed
to descend to us on the earth in poverty?
Hast thou desired this cave,
and this manger,
in which thou liest now?
And lo, how soon does the furious Herod
shake as he sharpens his sword against thee,
wishing to kill thee,
whose throne is heaven
and whose feet rest on the earth.'"

And Adam spoke
to those that were with him in hell:
"Come, ye prophets
and all ye just men,

let us send a message to the Lord,
into the living world,
to the Lord Christ
asking him with tears
whether he wishes
to release us
from these torments?"

And Isaiah and Jeremiah,
upbraiding hell
and his impotent power,
said to David:
"But who can carry the message
from us to him?
Gates of brass,
posts of iron,
locks of stone,
solidly sealed."

Then David spake to them clearly:
"Isaiah, Jeremiah, Aaron,
Ezekiel, Solomon,
Adam, Abraham, Isaac,
Jacob, Samuel, Daniel,
and all the seventeen prophets
attend to my voice:
Tomorrow will go from us
Lazarus the four-dayed,
friend of Christ.
He from us
will carry the message."

And hearing this, Adam,
first-created of men,
began beating his face
with his hands.
Groaning heavily,
he exclaimed and said:
"Tell the Lord about me,
Lazarus, glorious friend of Christ:
Thus cries to thee
thy first-created Adam:
Was it for this, Lord, thou createdst me
to be on this earth
for but a short age
only to condemn me
to be tormented in hell for many years?

Was it for this, O Lord, that thou madest the earth full?
For now thy beloved ones,
my grandchildren, lie in darkness
in the pit of hell—tormented by pain
and finding their joy in their grief.
They wash their eyes with tears
and gladden their hearts with grief
and are downcast exceedingly.
For on this earth
but a short while did we know prosperity,
and now in this sorrow
many years are we in duress.

For a short while was I king
of all God's creatures,
and now for many days
am I slave to hell
and captive to devils.

For a short while did I see thy light,
and now it is many a year
that I do not see thy bright sun
nor hear the stormy winds,
O Lord.

If I have sinned
worse than any man,
it is according to my deserts
thou hast assigned to me these torments,
I do not complain, O Lord.

But this is what fills me with pity—
I was created in thine image,
and now I am upbraided,
cruelly tormented by the devil,
who oppresses me, O Lord.

If I, Adam,
while I lived in nature,
broke thy divine commandment,
behold, O Lord,
Abraham, first Patriarch,
and thy friend
who for thy sake was ready
to sacrifice his son,
his beloved Isaac,
but thou saidst:
Through thee, Abraham, all the generations on earth shall be
    blessed.

*In what way has he sinned
that he should be tormented here in hell
and sigh heavily?
Descend, O Lord, for the sake of Abraham,
or has Abraham, too, sinned unto thee, O Lord?*

*And behold thy servants
Isaac and Jacob his son
lying in thralldom in the infernal hell.*

*And behold Noah, the just,
whom thou, O Lord,
deliveredst from fierce deluge,
and canst thou not deliver him from hell?
Or maybe he too has sinned
like myself?*

*And behold thy great prophet Moses,
who led the Jews through the Red Sea,
and spoke with thee on the Mountain of Sinai
and in the burning bush face to face,
in what way, O Lord, has he sinned
that he too should lie with us in the darkness of hell?
Or maybe, Moses, too, O Lord, has sinned unto thee?*

*And David, O Lord,
whom thyself exaltedst on earth
and gave him to reign over many men,
and he did make the psalter and lute,
in what way has he sinned, Lord?
But he too is tormented together with us in this hell,
and sighs, as he groans frequently,
or maybe he too has sinned
in the same way as myself?*

*And here, O Lord, is thy prophet Isaiah,
who from his mother's womb was lifted to heaven
and then returned into his mother's womb,
like as thou too, O Lord, didst descend into the womb of a
     maiden,
and he too, O Lord, is with us in hell,
or maybe Isaiah, too, has sinned, O Lord?*

*And here is thy great prophet Daniel,
son of Ezekiel the prophet,
who carried about a wooden rack in a frame,
who prefigured thy divine passion,
who smote the golden body in Babylon*

and was cast into the lions' den,
and he, Lord, is with us in hell
or maybe Daniel, too, has sinned, O Lord?

And here, Lord, is Solomon son of David
who erected for thee a house in Jerusalem
and cast two eagles of gold
like unto cherubim and seraphim,
and spake: If God is on earth,
the Holy Ghost will descend on the two eagles.
And the two eagles flew round the church
and ascended to heaven.

And here is John, great among prophets,
The Lord's Precursor, the Baptist,
who was born from the annunciation of Gabriel,
who from youth grew up in the wilderness,
eating wild honey.
In what way has he sinned, O Lord?
On earth he was dishonored by Herod,
and now together with us he is tormented in hell.

And here thy prophets complain,
Elijah and Enoch who pleased thee
more than all just men on earth.
No longer, O Lord, do we see
thy resplendent sun
nor thy gratifying light,
but instead are possessed by sorrow
and downcast with grief.
Or maybe the prophets too have sinned unto thee?

Is it for the sake of our sins that thou wilt not release us?
or art thou biding thy time?
If thou willst descend thyself,
thou alone knowest it.
But we are yearning men
and thou art long-suffering and without malice.
Come to us soon,
release us from hell and bind the devil,
that the mutinous Jews may know thee,
and we all may worship thee."

And hearing this the Lord went to Bethany, to Mary the sister of Lazarus and of Martha; and Mary and Martha, as soon as they heard that he was coming, hastened forth and falling at his feet and wiping his feet with their hair said: "Lord, if thou hadst been here, our brother Lazarus had not died." And the Lord said to Martha and Mary: "Your brother shall rise again."

And hell spake to the devil:

"I hear.
My soul is sad at having to release Lazarus,
and I am sore pressed to cast forth Adam."

And the Lord said to Mary and Martha: "Where have ye laid him?" And they came to the grave, and the Lord told them to take away the stone from the entrance of the grave. And Mary and Martha said: "Lord, by this time he stinketh, for he hath been dead four days." And the Lord said: "If ye would believe, ye should see the glory of God." And he lifted up his eyes and said: "Lazarus, come forth." And Lazarus rose at once, bound with grave clothes, and the Lord said: "Loose him."

And when Lazarus had risen from hell, he spake to the Lord: "Lord, thy prophets in hell cry unto thee, Adam the first-created and Abraham the Patriarch with Isaac his son and Jacob his grandson. David cries unto thee on behalf of Solomon his son, 'Lead us out of hell.'"

And the Lord spake to Lazarus: "Had it not been for David my beloved servant, I would have destroyed Solomon in hell." And the Lord descended to hell in person, and a multitude of heavenly warriors with him, Semiel, and Raguel, and Ismael, and Nanael, Tartarus, Gabriel, Michael, and all the angels advanced with the cross against hell, saying: "Lift the gates of eternity and let the gates of sorrow be taken, that the King of Glory may enter."

And the angels and the prophets spake: "The Lord is strong and terrible in battle, for he is the King of Glory. Let them be taken."

And the great king David spake: "When I was alive . . .[1] that the gates of brass be overthrown and the posts of iron be broken. And then will the Lord overthrow the gates of brass and break the posts of iron."

And the Lord spake to Adam: "This hand created thee from the beginning of time, and the same will lead thee out of corruption."

And then Jesus arose and said to his Apostles: "Go forth, preach to all lands, baptizing in the name of the Father, the Son, and the Holy Ghost, teaching to obey them . . ." And the Lord himself ascended to heaven and was seated on the right hand of the Father, and all over the earth is his glory, of Christ Jesus Our Lord.

---

[1] An apparent lacuna.

E. EPICS

33. THE LAY OF IGOR'S CAMPAIGN

WRITTEN on the occasion of Prince Igor's unfortunate campaign against the Kumans in 1185, the *Lay of Igor's Campaign* (*Slovo o polku Igoreve*) is unanimously acclaimed as the highest achievement in Russian literature of the Kievan era.

Igor was himself a well-known historical personality, a prince of Novgorod-Seversk (not to be confused with Novgorod "the great," the metropolis of northern Russia). Novgorod-Seversk, now a small city on the border between the Russian and Ukrainian S.S.R.'s, was at that time one of the Russian strongholds against the Kumans, nomads of Turkic origin who inhabited the prairie of southern Russia. Prince Igor (1151–1202), one of the leaders of Russian political and military activities of that region, began his campaign in 1185 to drive out these nomadic invaders, who, every year, would raid Russian territories, burn the cities, and take the inhabitants as slaves. Relying only on his own military forces and those of his relatives, Igor moved into the prairie with no support from the other Russian rulers. This campaign ended in defeat and in Igor's capture by the Kumans, although he later escaped from them.

Though much is known about Igor, practically nothing is known about the author of the *Lay of Igor's Campaign*. One can only presume that he belonged to Igor's court, was a warrior, and, as is evident from his *Lay*, was very familiar with the life and environment of the prairie. Even less can be said of the literary antecedents of the work and of the epic tradition previous to it. It is true that the writer of the *Lay* often mentions Boyan, a bard who apparently lived in the eleventh century, but no details are known either of his life or of his poetic works.

The *Lay* is a poetic masterpiece and a highly sophisticated literary work. The word "poetic" should not be understood here in its narrower sense, since the *Lay* is neither rhymed nor organized in verses, nor does it follow any metrical pattern. The rhythm and the length of the sentences to some extent replace verse organization. Besides rhythm, the poetic elements of the *Lay* comprise an extremely rich imagery constructed primarily on parallels with nature, symbolism, poetic address, and lyric lamentation. Among other devices, the author of the *Lay* employs the repetition of characteristic images, stylized descriptions of military action, assonance, and alliteration. Unfortunately, the last two are impossible to reproduce in translation. The structure of the *Lay* is by no means that of a narrative poem; and rather than being an epic tale, per se, it is much more a lament over the feudal discord in medieval Russia, a stern admonition to the princes responsible for the fratricidal feuds. The writer's forebodings of impending disaster in the Russian land proved to be true, for, only fifty years after Igor's defeat and the writing of the *Lay*, Russia was subjugated by the Mongol-Tatars and lost her independence for two hundred years.

Three distinct structural planes can be discerned in the *Lay*. The first concerns the destiny of Prince Igor, his campaign, defeat, and escape from the Kumans. This plane, the narrative core of the work, is somewhat clouded by invocations to the late bard, Boyan, reminiscences of past glory, and the allusive atmosphere of foreboding. The second plane consists of portents and lamentations over the outcome of the campaign and Russia's fate, such as the dream of Prince Sviatoslav of Kiev and the lament of Yaroslavna, the wife of Igor. The final plane consists of the author's admonitions to the princes to unite, and his censure of their feuding.

Unfortunately, the *Lay* was preserved in only one copy, discovered at the end of the eighteenth century and first printed in 1800. This single copy, which was subsequently destroyed in a fire in Moscow during the Napoleonic invasion in 1812, was itself defective, and so the first edition of the *Lay* was an unsatisfactory one reflecting the low standard of scholarship and interpretation of ancient manuscripts of that time. Many portions were apparently misread or misinterpreted, and in some places inadequately deciphered. Despite the efforts of generations of scholars and voluminous research, several passages in the *Lay* still remain extremely unclear, and have lent themselves to contradictory interpretations. In the present translation such passages have been placed in brackets.

The text that was used for the present translation of the *Lay of Igor's Campaign* is that revised by Dmitry S. Likhachev and published in the series *Literaturnye pamiatniki*, Moscow-Leningrad, 1950. However, the present translator has made wide use of the text and interpretations of Professor Roman Jakobson of Harvard University, who offers numerous and extremely ingenious explanations of certain unclear passages, while others have been interpreted in the light of such research as that on nature symbolism by N. V. Charlemagne as well as other scholars.

It must also be kept in mind that the present editor and translator, on several occasions, followed the suggestions of Professor Jakobson and has rearranged some unclear passages of the text that were probably misplaced by either a medieval scribe or by the publisher of its first edition. This rearrangement follows the edition of the *Lay* published under the title *La Geste du Prince Igor,* edited by Roman Jakobson, New York, 1948.

The *Lay*'s complex symbolism, structure, imagery, and philosophy require a more detailed commentary than any other medieval Russian work. Notes on the symbolism of the *Lay* and on Russian literary tradition appear at the bottom of each page, as well as comments pertaining to historical and geographical names specific to the work. Finally, references of a more general type can be found in the Introduction and in the Glossary.

The typographical arrangement and the chapter and stanza form given here are in agreement with authoritative publications of the *Lay* and also reflect this editor's feeling that they contribute to readability. For the sake of better understanding, some explanatory words have been added in parentheses and proper names have been preceded by the words "prince," "river," or "city."

I. INVOCATION

Might it not behoove us, brethren
to commence in ancient strains
the grievous lay of Igor's campaign,
    Igor, son of Sviatoslav?
Then let this begin
according to the events of our time,
and not according to the cunning of Boyan.[1]
For he, Boyan the Seer,
when composing a song for someone,
soared in his thoughts over the tree (of wisdom [2]),
ran as a gray wolf over the land,
flew below the clouds as a blue-gray eagle.

When he recalled the feuds of former times
he would let loose ten falcons upon a flock of swans.
    And the first swan overtaken
    was the first to sing a song
    to old Yaroslav,[3]

---

[1] Apparently a bard who lived in the eleventh century and who composed songs in honor of the Russian princes.

[2] Apparently this refers to the tree of wisdom or thought, a common symbol of Eastern mythology.

[3] Prince of Kiev from 1019 through 1054. He is considered the greatest ruler of Russia during the Kievan era.

    to valiant Mstislav,[4]
    who slew Rededia [5] before the Kasog regiments,
    and to handsome Roman,[6] son of Sviatoslav.

Boyan, however, did not let loose ten falcons
upon the flock of swans.
But rather he would lay his wise fingers
    upon the living strings
    and they sounded lauds to the princes.
Let us begin this narration, brethren,
from the old times of Vladimir [7] to this present time of Igor,
    who strengthened his mind with courage,
    who quickened his heart with valor
    and, thus imbued with martial spirit,
    led his valiant regiments
    against the Kuman land
    in defense of the Russian land.

II. PRINCE IGOR PREPARES HIS CAMPAIGN

Igor looked up at the bright sun,
and saw that all his warriors
became enveloped in darkness.[8]
And Igor spoke to his warriors:
    "Brethren and warriors!
    It is better to be killed in battle,
    than to become a captive.
    Let us mount our swift steeds, brethren!
    Let us view the blue river Don."

And the prince's mind was seized by ambition.
And the desire to drink from the great river Don
concealed the evil omens from him.
And he spoke:
    "I want to break a lance at the Kuman frontier.
    I want, O my Russians,

---

[4] Mstislav the Brave, the brother of Yaroslav the Wise and Prince
of Tmutorokan, a principality located on the Caucasian shore between
the Black and Azov seas.

[5] A prince of the Kasogs, now called the Cherkess, who was slain
by Mstislav.

[6] Roman the Handsome, a prince of Tmutorokan who was killed by
the Kumans in 1079.

[7] Apparently Vladimir the saint, the Christianizer of Russia.

[8] The author probably meant that the sun was eclipsed. An eclipse
of the sun occurred on May 1, 1185.

either to drink with you Don (water) from my helmet,
or to leave my head there."
O Boyan, the nightingale of yore!
If you were to sing the glory of the (Russian) campaign,
like a nightingale would you soar over the tree (of wisdom),
soaring in your mind up under the clouds
and singing the glory of both these ages.[9]
You would race along the trail of Trojan,[10]
over the prairies and the mountains.
And the (god Veles') grandson
would sing Igor's song (thus),
    "It is not a storm that has driven
    the falcons over the wide prairies.
    It is a flock of jackdaws
    racing toward the great river Don."

Or you, Boyan the Seer, grandson of god Veles, would sing:
    "Steeds neigh beyond the river Sula.
    Glory resounds in the city of Kiev.
    Trumpets blare in the city of Novgorod.
    Banners fly over the city of Putivl." [11]
Igor awaits his dear brother, Vsevolod.
This fierce aurochs, Vsevolod [12] (comes to him and) speaks:
    "My only brother, Igor,
    you are my only bright light.
    We are both the sons of Sviatoslav.
    Brother, order the saddling of your swift steeds,
    as those of mine are ready.
    They were already saddled at the city of Kursk.
    And my men of Kursk are famed as warriors.
    They were swaddled under trumpets.
    They were brought up under helmets.
    They were fed at lance point.
    The roads are known to them.
    The ravines are familiar to them.
    Their bows are taut,

---

[9] The glorious age of Vladimir and this age of Igor. (See "Invocation.")

[10] Trojan: the meaning of this word is not clear. It may refer to Trajan, Emperor of Rome (98–117), who campaigned in southern Russia, to a Slavic and Balkan deity, or the city of Troy.

[11] Novgorod-Seversk and Putivl: important cities in Igor's principality.

[12] Fierce aurochs Vsevolod: Igor's brother, who died in 1196, was prince of Trubchevsk and Kursk.

their quivers are open,
their sabers have been sharpened.
They race into the prairie like gray wolves,
seeking honor for themselves
and glory for their prince."

III. THE OMENS

Then Prince Igor set his foot in the golden stirrup
and rode into the open prairie.
The sun barred his way with darkness [13]
and night, moaning with tempest, awoke the birds.
The whistling of the beasts arose.
And the Div [14] arose and from the treetops it cried,
enjoining unknown lands to listen:
the land of the Volga,
the land on the Azov Sea,
the land at the river Sula,[15]
the city of Surozh,
the city of Kherson,[16]
and you, the idol of the city of Tmutorokan.[17]

The Kumans hastened by untrodden ways
to the great river Don.
Their carts squeak at midnight,
one may say, as dispersed swans.
Igor leads his warriors to the river Don.
The birds in the forests of oak portend his misfortune.
The wolves conjure the tempest in the ravines.
The screeching eagles call the beasts to the feast of bones.
Foxes bark at scarlet shields.
O Russian land! You are already far beyond the hills.

IV. THE FIRST DAY OF BATTLE: THE RUSSIANS ARE VICTORIOUS

Evening is slow to fade into night.
The glow of dusk disappeared.
Mist enveloped the prairie.
The song of the nightingale died out.

---

[13] Again the author wishes to say that the sun was eclipsed.
[14] A deity in the form of a bird that represented foreboding for the Russians.
[15] A tributary of the river Dnieper.
[16] Surozh and Kherson: Greek cities in the Crimea.
[17] Idol of Tmutorokan: probably a colossal idol that was held in veneration by the Kumans.

The daws began to caw.
Russian warriors barred the wide prairie
with their scarlet shields.
They seek honor for themselves
and glory for their prince.

Early in the morning of Friday
the Russians trampled the infidel Kuman armies,
and, spreading like arrows over the prairie,
they galloped away with beautiful Kuman maidens.
And with them they took:
    golds and brocades,
    and precious velvets.
With cloaks and coats and fur mantles
and with all kinds of Kuman finery
they began to bridge their way over the swamps and marshes.
The scarlet banner,
the white gonfalon,
the scarlet panache, and
the silver lance
were taken to brave Igor,
son of Sviatoslav.

Brave Oleg's [18] clan slumbers in the prairie.
They have flown far away.
They were born to be offended
    neither by the falcon,
    nor by the gyrfalcon,
    nor by you, the black raven,
    the infidel Kuman.
Khan Gza flees like a gray wolf.
Khan Konchak [19] shows him the way to the great river Don.

V. THE SECOND DAY OF BATTLE: THE VICTORY OF THE KUMANS

Very early on the second morn
a bloody dawn announced the day.
Black clouds arrive from the sea
and want to envelop the four suns.[20]
Blue lightning shows through the clouds.

---

[18] Oleg was the grandfather of Igor and prince of the principal city (Chernigov) in which Igor's domain was located.

[19] Gza and Konchak: Kuman khans.

[20] Four suns: refers to the four princes who lead the Russian armies: Igor, Vsevolod, Oleg, and Sviatoslav.

There is to be a mighty thundering.
The rain of arrows will come from the great river Don.
Here, on the river Kaiala,[21]
close to the great river Don,
lances will be broken
and swords will be dulled on Kuman helmets.
O Russian land! You are already far beyond the hills.

Here the winds, grandsons of god Stribog,
blow the arrows from the sea
against Igor's brave regiments.
The earth groans.
The rivers become turbid.
Dust covers the prairie.
The pennants announce:
> "The Kumans have come from the river Don
> and from the sea.
> They encircle the Russian regiments from all sides."
The devil's children bar the prairie with their battle cries.
The brave Russians bar it with their scarlet shields.

Fierce aurochs Vsevolod!
Your defense is firm,
Your arrows rain down upon Kuman warriors.
Your Frankish swords [22] clang on Kuman helmets.
Where you, fierce aurochs, gallop gleaming in your golden
    helmet,
there will lie the heads of infidel Kumans.
There Avar helmets [23] are cloven at your hands,
fierce aurochs Vsevolod.
What wound can matter, brethren,
to one who has forgotten honors and fortune,
and his father's golden throne in the city of Chernigov,
and the habits and ways of his dearly beloved
and beautiful wife,
the daughter of Prince Gleb? [24]

---

[21] The river at which Igor was defeated. Its location remains unknown but apparently it was a tributary of the Donets, itself a tributary of the river Don.

[22] Frankish swords or lances: weapons made of steel imported from Western Europe.

[23] Apparently helmets made in the Avar style. The Avars were nomads who in the seventh and eighth centuries lived in southern Russia and Hungary.

[24] The daughter of Prince Gleb, the ruler of Pereiaslavl-Seversk.

VI. CENSURE OF THE PRINCES' FEUDS

There were the eras of Trojan.
There passed the years of Yaroslav.
And there were the campaigns of Oleg,
Oleg, son of Sviatoslav.[25]
That Oleg fostered feuds with his sword
and sowed the Russian lands with arrows.
In the city of Tmutorokan
he used to put his foot in the golden stirrup
and its clinking could be heard by great Yaroslav,
who lived long ago.
And Prince Vladimir, son of Vsevolod,
would stop his ears in the city of Chernigov.[26]
And the dubious glory of Prince Boris,[27]
son of Vyacheslav,
brought him to his final Judgment,
and he remained in eternal sleep
on a burial shroud of green grass,
at the river Kanina
for offending brave and young Prince Oleg.

On the same river Kaiala Sviatopolk ordered
that his father be taken between two ambling Hungarian
    horses
at the river Kanina
to be buried in the Cathedral of St. Sophia in Kiev.[28]

Then, in the era of Oleg, son of misfortune,
the feuding spread and grew.
The fortune of god Dazhbog's [29] grandson was destroyed.
Human lives became shortened through the princes' discord.
In those days the plowman spoke but rarely,

---

[25] Igor's grandfather, Prince Oleg, son of Sviatoslav, and grandson of Yaroslav the Wise, was the prince in Volynia, then Tmutorokan, then Chernigov, and finally in Novgorod-Seversk. He was responsible for the fratricidal warring among the Russian princes. He died in 1115.
[26] So that he might not hear the clinking of Oleg's stirrup.
[27] Boris, son of Vyacheslav, was the first Russian prince to fight other Russian princes in alliance with the Kumans. Boris was killed in this campaign, while his brother, Oleg, escaped to the Kumans.
[28] Sviatopolk's father was killed in battle in 1078 and was taken to Kiev for burial. Slain warriors were carried in a carpet between two horses.
[29] Dazhbog: an ancient Russian deity; Dazhbog's grandson refers to the Russians. Veles and Stribog were also pre-Christian deities.

and the ravens often cawed, dividing corpses among themselves.
And the daws talked in their own tongue,
before flying to feed on corpses.

VII. THE RUSSIAN DEFEAT

And so it used to be.
There were battles and campaigns,
but there had never been such battle as this.
From early morning to night,
from evening to dawn
there flew tempered arrows,
swords rained down upon helmets,
Frankish lances resound,
and all this in the unknown prairie,
in the Kuman land.
The black earth under the hooves
was strewn with bones,
was covered with blood.
Grief overwhelmed the Russian land.

What noise do I hear?
What clinking comes to my ears
so early in the morning, before the dawn?
It is Prince Igor who has led away his troops.
He is saddened by the fate of his brother, Vsevolod.
They fought for one day.
They fought for another day.
At noon on the third day Igor's banners fell.
Here, on the shores of the swift river Kaiala,
the brothers parted.
The wine of this bloody banquet was drunk to the last drop.
The Russians gave their guests to drink from the same cup.
They died for the Russian land.
　　　The grass withered from sorrow,
　　　and the saddened trees drooped earthward.

VIII. THE AUTHOR'S LAMENTS

And now, brethren, unhappy times have arrived.
The prairie overwhelmed the Russian forces.
Grief reigned over the forces of god Dazhbog's grandsons.
Grief, like a maiden, entered the land of Trojan.
She splashed her swan wings at the river Don,
by the blue sea,
and splashing, she put an end to the times of good fortune.

The Kumans attack Prince Igor's army. The Russian horses fall from exhaustion. A miniature from the Radzivil Chronicle of the fourteenth century.

The princes' fight against the infidel came to an end.
And brother said to brother:
"This is mine,
and that also is mine."
And the princes began to argue about trifles,
calling them important matters,
and began to create discord among themselves.
The infidels from all lands began to invade
the Russian land and to win victory.

O too far toward the sea has the falcon flown, slaying birds!
And Igor's valiant regiments cannot be resurrected!
He is mourned by Grief and Sorrow,
and they spread across the Russian land.
[Shaking the embers in the flaming horn],[30]
the Russian women begin to lament, saying:
"No more, our dear husbands,
can you be envisioned in our thoughts,
nor can you reappear in our dreams,
nor can you be seen with our eyes,
and never again shall we jingle gold and silver."
And, brethren, the city of Kiev began to groan from grief,
and the city of Chernigov also, from their misfortune.
Anguish spread over the Russian land.
Deep sadness flew through the Russian land.
And the princes created discord among themselves.
The infidels, victoriously invading the Russian land,
levied a tribute of one *vair* from each household.

All this happened because Igor and Vsevolod,
two valiant sons of Sviatoslav,
once more revived evil forces
once subdued by their godfather (another), Prince Sviatoslav.[31]
This stern prince of Kiev
kept (everyone) in fear and awe,
for, as a tempest, his powerful regiments
and his Frankish swords defeated and attacked the Kuman
lands.
They trampled under Kuman hills and ravines,
made turbid Kuman rivers and lakes,

---

[30] A part of the mourning ritual (?).
[31] Sviatoslav III, the great prince of Kiev (1177–1194) and theoret-
ical ruler of all Russia. He was the cousin and godfather of Igor
and Vsevolod. In 1183 he defeated Khan Kobiak on the shores of the
Azov Sea and took him as a prisoner to Kiev.

dried out Kuman streams and marshes.
Like a tornado, he seized Khan Kobiak
from amongst his great iron regiments
on the shore of the sea bay.
And Kobiak fell in the city of Kiev,
in the hall of Prince Sviatoslav.

Now the Germans and the Venetians,
the Greeks and the Moravians
sing the glory of Prince Sviatoslav
and reproach Prince Igor,
who has lost his fortune on the bottom of the river Kaiala
and filled the Kuman rivers with Russian gold.
And here Prince Igor exchanged his golden saddle of a prince
for the saddle of a slave.
And the cities became saddened
and joy vanished.

IX. THE DREAM OF PRINCE SVIATOSLAV OF KIEV

Sviatoslav had a troubled dream
in Kiev, on the hills:
    "Early this night I was clothed in a black shroud
upon a bed of yew.
They ladled out for me
  a blue wine mixed with sorrow.
From the empty quivers of the infidel strangers
there poured large pearls into my lap.[32]
They comforted me.
And the beams of my gold-roofed palace
were already without girding.[33]
During the entire night, since evening,
the gray-blue ravens were croaking.
[And at the foothills of the city of Plesensk [34]
appeared a sledge,[35]
and this sledge was racing to the blue sea."]
And the boyars told the prince:
    "O Prince, sorrow has seized your mind.
    There were two falcons who flew

---

[32] Pearls were the symbols of forthcoming tears for the Russians.
[33] It was the custom among Russians to remove the girding of porches before removing the dead from a house.
[34] Plesensk was a fortified city in the Galician mountains. Probably the allusion here is to the funeral of the Galician warriors, countrymen of Igor's wife, who was the daughter of the prince of Galicia.
[35] In ancient Russia sledges were used for funerals.

from their father's golden throne,
either to conquer the city of Tmutorokan
or to drink the water of the river Don with their helmets.
But their wings were clipped by the sabers of the infidels,
and they themselves were put in irons.
It became dark on the third day.
The two suns [36] were eclipsed.
[Two purple columns [37] faded into the sea,
Two young moons—Oleg and Sviatoslav—became enveloped in darkness,[38]
On the river Kaiala darkness overcame the light,[39]
and the Kumans, like a brood of panthers,
spread across the Russian land.
And great violence came from the Hins.]
Already shame has eclipsed glory.
Already violence has defeated freedom.
Already the Div has descended to earth.
And now beautiful Gothic maidens [40]
have begun their song on the shore of the blue sea.
They jingle Russian gold.
They sing of the foreboding time (the time of Bus).
They glorify the revenge of Sharokan.[41]
And we, the army, are without joy."

And then great Sviatoslav let fall his golden words
mixed with tears, saying:
"O my young cousins, Igor and Vsevolod,
too early did you begin to disturb
the Kuman lands with your swords, seeking glory,
but you won it without honor,
for you spilled the blood of the infidels
without winning glory for yourselves.
Your valiant hearts are forged of Frankish steel
and are tempered in valiance.
What have you done to my silver-gray hairs?
No longer do I behold my powerful
and wealthy,

---

[36] Igor and Vsevolod.

[37] Apparently symbols of the two armies of Igor and Vsevolod.

[38] Young Prince Sviatoslav, Igor's nephew, and Igor's son, Prince Oleg.

[39] Darkness symbolizes the infidel Kumans, and light, the Russian army.

[40] In the twelfth century the Goths still maintained settlements in the Crimea, where they had penetrated in the third century.

[41] Sharokan: a Kuman khan defeated several times by the Russians.

and well-girded brother,
Yaroslav of Chernigov,[42]
nor his lords.
With his Moguts and Tatrans,
with his Shelbirs and Topchaks,
with his Revugas and Olbers.[43]
They used to defeat the regiments (of the infidels),
and without shields,
only with their knives and ancestors' war cries.
But you said:
   'Let us be valiant.
   Let us assume the glory of the past.
   Let us divide amongst ourselves
   the glory of tomorrow.'
What is there to wonder, brethren,
when an old man feels like a young one?
When a falcon molts, he chases birds high and away
and does not permit harm to come to his nest.
But there is great misfortune,
and the Russian princes are no help to me."

X. THE BARD APPEALS TO THE RUSSIAN PRINCES

THE APPEAL TO VLADIMIR, SON OF GLEB [44]

Gloomy times have arrived.
The Russians cry out at the city of Rim
under the Kuman swords.
Prince Vladimir is covered with wounds.
Grief and sorrow to you Vladimir,
son of Gleb.

THE APPEAL TO VSEVOLOD, PRINCE OF SUZDAL [45]

Great Prince Vsevolod!
Do you not intend to come from far away

[42] Prince of Chernigov and brother of Sviatoslav, Prince of Kiev.

[43] Moguts, Tatrans, Shelbirs, Topchaks, Revugas, and Olbers: apparently Turkic tribes, but their identification is not certain. They settled in the land of Chernigov, in the principality of Yaroslav.

[44] Vladimir, son of Gleb: In 1185 the Kuman Khans Gza and Konchak invaded the Russian land, destroying the city of Rim on the river Sula. During this invasion Vladimir Glebovich was mortally wounded.

[45] Vsevolod was called "the great nest" because of his numerous and powerful family. He was prince of Suzdal, a powerful principality in the vicinity of present-day Moscow, the latter being at that time only a small village in the Suzdalian territory.

to watch over your paternal golden throne?
For you, with the oars (of your fleet),
can scatter the river Volga into droplets.
With the helmets (of your army)
you empty out the river Don.
If you were here, then (Kuman) slave girls
would go for a *nogata,*
and (Kuman) male slaves for only a *rezana.*
And you can shoot over the dry land
with the fiery arrows,
with the courageous sons of Gleb.

THE APPEAL TO PRINCES RURIK AND DAVID [46]

O valiant Rurik and David!
Was it not your warriors who swam through blood
under the gilded helmets?
Was it not your army that roared like aurochs,
wounded by tempered swords in the unknown prairie?
Lords, set your feet in the golden stirrups
to avenge the outrage of the present day,
of the Russian land,
of Igor's wounds,
wounds of the daring son of Sviatoslav.

THE APPEAL TO PRINCE YAROSLAV OF GALICH [47]

O Yaroslav of Galich,
the prince of eight senses!
You sit high on your throne wrought of gold.
Your iron regiments defend the Hungarian mountains.
You bar the way to the (Hungarian) king.
You close the gates of the river Danube.
You hurl stones over the clouds.
Your law reigns up to the river Danube.
Your thunder resounds above the lands.
You keep the gates of Kiev open.
From your father's golden throne you shoot at the sultans
beyond the (Russian) lands.
Lord, shoot at Konchak, the infidel slave,

---

[46] Rurik and David: Princes of Belgorod and Smolensk who died
in 1215 and 1198. They were known for their courage during the
fratricidal wars.

[47] Yaroslav of Galich, Prince of Galicia (1152–1187). Igor's father-
in-law, he was called *Osmomysl* (eight-sensed) apparently because
of his abilities at ruling. His land bordered on the Kingdom of
Hungary, and he practically controlled the Danube River.

for the revenge of the Russian land,
for the wounds of Igor,
the wounds of the valiant son of Sviatoslav.

THE APPEAL TO PRINCES ROMAN OF VOLYNIA AND MSTISLAV OF GRODNO [48]

And you, daring Roman and Mstislav,
your courageous thoughts direct your minds to action.
In your bravery you soar to valiant deeds,
like a falcon over the winds,
which desires, in its daring, to surpass the bird.
Your iron men are under Latin helmets [49]
and they make the earth tremble,
and (they make) many nations (tremble):
> the Hins,
> the Lithuanians,
> the Deremelas,
> the Yatvags, [50]
> the Kumans.

(All of them) have dropped their lances
and have bowed their heads under your Frankish swords.

But Prince Igor, the sunlight has already dimmed for you.
And, by misfortune, the tree lost its foliage.
The enemies have already divided amongst themselves
the cities of the rivers Ross and Sula. [51]
The valiant regiments of Igor will not be resurrected.
The river Don appeals to you, Prince,
and summons the princes to victory.
O valiant princes, grandsons of Oleg,
you are ready for the battle.

THE APPEAL TO MSTISLAV'S SONS

Ingvar and Vsevolod and you three sons of Mstislav! [52]
You are six-winged falcons [53] of no mean nest.
You have not won your patrimonies by deeds of victory.
To what avail are your golden helmets,

---

[48] Roman (died 1205) and Mstislav (died 1226): Princes of Volynia, a region east of Galicia.

[49] Refers to the helmets of Latin or Western origin.

[50] Hins: probably nomads (Huns?). Deremelas and Yatvags: Lithuanian tribes who lived at the northwestern Russian border.

[51] Tributaries of the Dnieper.

[52] Princes of Volynia.

[53] Some of the Russian falcons have wings that have three distinct sections, and are therefore called "six-winged falcons."

your Polish lances and shields?
Bar the gates of the prairie with your sharp arrows
    for the Russian lands,
    for the wounds of Igor,
    the wounds of the daring son of Sviatoslav.

EVOCATION OF PRINCE IZIASLAV'S [54] DEATH IN THE BATTLE
OF GORODETS (1162)

No more do the silver streams of the river Sula
protect the city of Pereiaslavl.
And the river Dvina, which flows to Polotsk,
that city of stern men,
became turbid under the cries of the infidels.

Only Iziaslav, son of Vasilko,
rained his sharp arrows upon Lithuanian helmets
and tarnished the glory of his grandfather Vseslav.
And, having been worsted by the Lithuanian swords,
he fell upon the bloody grass
[(as if it were) the marriage bed,]
under the scarlet shields.

And Boyan said:
    "Prince, the wings of birds cover your warriors
    and the beasts already have begun to lick their blood."

Neither his brother, Briachislav,
nor the other brother, Vsevolod, was there (in battle).
And (you, Iziaslav) remained alone.
And you let drop from your valiant body,
through the golden necklace of a prince,
the pearl of your soul,
and voices became saddened,
and joy ceased to be.
And the trumpets mournfully resound at the city of Gorodets.

THE APPEAL TO PRINCE YAROSLAV OF CHERNIGOV AND
VSESLAV'S [55] HEIRS

O sons of Yaroslav and the grandsons of Vseslav,
lower your banners!
Put your dented swords into their sheaths!

---

[54] Prince Iziaslav was killed at Gorodets in a war between the Russians and Lithuanians.
[55] Vseslav (d. 1101): Prince of Polotsk who in 1067 attacked and burned Novgorod, but was defeated at the Nemiga River. In 1068 he became Prince of Kiev for seven months. The "maiden" he cast lots for was the city of Kiev. He was considered a sorcerer.

You do not deserve the glory of your ancestors,
since, through your feuding,
you brought the infidels into the Russian land,
into the domain of Vseslav.
Your warring brought Kuman violence (into Russia).

THE EVOCATION OF PRINCE VSESLAV THE SORCERER

During the seventh age of Trojan
Vseslav cast lots for the maiden he desired, and,
cunningly leaning on the lance,
he leaped to the city of Kiev and
touched the golden throne of Kiev
with the staff of his lance.
Like a fierce beast he leaped from Belgorod at midnight,
under the cover of blue mist.
[He managed to cast thrice a lucky lot:]
> he opened the gate of the city of Novgorod,
> he tarnished the glory of Prince Yaroslav, and
> he leaped like a wolf from [Dudutki] to Nemiga.

On the river Nemiga they built haystacks of heads.
They are threshed with steel flails
and lives are left behind on the threshing floor.
Souls abandon their bodies.
The bloody shores of the river Nemiga
> were sown with misfortune,
> were strewn with the bones of Russia's sons.

Prince Vseslav used to judge the people.
And, as prince, he ruled over the cities.
But, in the night, he prowled like a werewolf.
He was able to go from Kiev to Tmutorokan
before the cock could crow.
And, prowling as a werewolf, he crossed
the way of great god Hors.[56]
At the Church of St. Sophia of Polotsk
the bells tolled the matins for him,
and he could hear them in Kiev.
His magician's soul lived in a valiant body,
but he still often suffered miseries.
Of him Boyan the Seer said wisely in his refrains:
> "Neither a crafty man,
> nor a clever man,
> nor a clever bird,
> can escape divine judgment."

---

[56] God of the sun in ancient Russia.

O Russian land, you must mourn,
remembering your early age, your early princes.
And Vladimir of yore
could not be retained by the hills of Kiev.[57]
But now his banners have become the banners of Rurik,
and some of them have become the banners of David.
Thus, they are blown (by the wind) in different directions.

XI. IGOR'S WIFE, YAROSLAVNA, DAUGHTER OF PRINCE YAROSLAV OF GALICH, LAMENTS ON THE WALLS OF PUTIVL

At the river Danube lances sing their song,
but it is the voice of Yaroslavna which is heard.
Since morning, she sings like an unknown seagull: [58]
    "Like a seagull I will fly along the river Danube.
    I will dip my beaver-trimmed sleeve into the river Kaiala.
    I will cleanse the bloody wounds of my prince,
    on his mighty body."

Since morning Yaroslavna has lamented on the walls
of the city of Putivl, saying:
    "O wind, why do you, my lord wind,
    blow so fiercely?
    Why do you bring on your light wings
    Kuman arrows against the warriors of my beloved?
    Isn't it enough for you to blow under the clouds,
    to loll the ships on the blue sea?
    Why, my lord, did you scatter my joy
    over the feathergrass of the prairie?"

Since morning Yaroslavna has lamented on the walls
of the city of Putivl, saying:
    "O river Dnieper, son of Slovuta,
    it is you who have broken through
    the stone mountains [59] of the Kuman land.
    You lolled the boats of Sviatoslav
    (when he went) to meet Khan Kobiak's army.
    O my lord wind, loll my beloved
    and (bring) him to me that I might not
    send him my tears to the sea so early in the morning,
    at dawn."

---

[57] Because he unceasingly campaigned against his enemies.

[58] The seagull was considered to be the bird of mourning.

[59] Stone mountains: apparently a reference to the cataracts in the river Dnieper, and the surrounding rocky shores.

Since morning Yaroslavna has lamented on the walls
of the city of Putivl, saying:
> "O my bright and thrice bright sun!
> For everyone you are warm and beautiful.
> Why did you spread, my lord, your burning rays
> upon the warriors of my beloved?
> In the waterless prairie you parched their bows
> and closed their quivers with misfortune."

XII. PRINCE IGOR FLEES FROM KUMAN CAPTIVITY

The seas splashed at midnight
and the tornado rushes through the mist.
God shows the way to Igor,
the way from the Kuman land,
to the Russian land,
to his father's golden throne.

The glow of the sunset had faded.
Igor sleeps.
Igor keeps his vigil.
Igor's thoughts cross the prairie,
from the great river Don
to the small river Donets.
Beyond the river, Ovlur whistles,[60]
having caught a horse.
He warns the prince.
Prince Igor will not remain a prisoner.
The earth rumbled,
the grass rustled,
and the Kuman tents began to stir.
Prince Igor raced to reeds like an ermine,
like a white duck (he races) on the water.
He leaps to his swift steed.
He (later) springs from it, like a gray wolf.
He rushed toward the curve of the river Donets.
He flew under the clouds like a falcon
which kills geese and swans
> for lunch,
> for dinner,
> and for supper.

If Prince Igor flies like a falcon,
then Ovlur races like a wolf,

---

[60] Ovlur was Igor's faithful servant.

shaking off the chilling dew.
And both of them exhausted their swift steeds.

XIII. IGOR SPEAKS WITH THE RIVER DONETS

The river Donets speaks:
    "O Prince Igor,
    there will be no small glory for you,
    but dislike for Konchak,
    and joy for the Russian land."

And Igor spoke:
    "O my river Donets!
    There will be no small glory for you,
    for you have lolled the prince on your waves,
    for you have spread for him green grass
    on your silver shores,
    for you have enveloped him in your warm mists
    in the shadow of green trees,
    for your drakes watched over him on the water,
    and your seagulls on the streams,
    and your black ducks in the winds."

But different words came to him from the river Stugna.
Its stream is weak.
It has swallowed up other brooks and rivulets
[and, therefore, has grown wide at its delta.
It hid young Prince Rostislav.[61]
It concealed him on its bottom near its dark bank].
And Rostislav's mother mourned the young prince.
Flowers withered from sorrow,
and the saddened trees dropped earthward.

XIV. THE KUMAN KHANS PURSUE IGOR

It is not the magpies which have begun croaking,
it is Khans Gza and Konchak
who search for Igor's path.
At that time the crows did not caw.
The daws became silent and
the jackdaws did not chatter.
Only the snakes were crawling,
and the woodpeckers show the way to the river with their
    sounds.
The nightingale announces the dawn with its gay song.

---

[61] Prince Rostislav was drowned in 1093 at the age of twenty-two,
during a fording of the river Stugna, a tributary of the Dnieper.

And Khan Gza told Khan Konchak:
   "If the falcon fly to his nest,
   we will shoot at the falconet [62]
   with our gilded arrows."

And Khan Konchak replied to Khan Gza:
   "If the falcon flies to his nest,
   we will enmesh the falconet
   with the charms of a beautiful maiden."

And Khan Gza said to Khan Konchak:
   "If we enmesh him with the charms of
   a beautiful maiden,
   we will have neither the falconet
   nor the beautiful maiden,
   and (their) birds will start fighting us
   in the Kuman prairie."

XV. APODOSIS

And Boyan [the bard of olden times,
said of the time of Sviatoslav,
   of Yaroslav,
   and of Kagan Oleg:]
     "It is difficult for a head
     to be without shoulders.
     But it is also a misfortune
     for the body to be without the head."
And so it is difficult for the Russian land
to be without Prince Igor.
The sun gleams in the sky.
Prince Igor is in the Russian land.
Maidens sing on the Danube.
Their voices reach across the sea to Kiev.
Igor rides along the Borichev [63]
to the Church of the Holy Virgin of Pirogoshch.
The lands are jubilant.
The cities rejoice.
Once the glory of the princes of yore was sung,
now glory will be sung for the young.

---

[62] The term "falconet" refers to Igor's son, Vladimir, who remained
a prisoner of the Kumans.

[63] Borichev: a place on the Dnieper shore in the vicinity of Kiev
where a church was built in honor of the Holy Virgin of Pirogoshch.
This name comes from the name of an icon in a tower ("pyrios" is
Greek for "tower") in Constantinople.

Glory to Igor, son of Sviatoslav,
to fierce aurochs Vsevolod,
and to Vladimir, son of Igor.
Hail to the princes and the armies
who fight for Christendom against the infidel hosts.
Glory to the princes and to the army. Amen.

epigones
of the
kievan
school

(Mid-Thirteenth to Fourteenth Century)

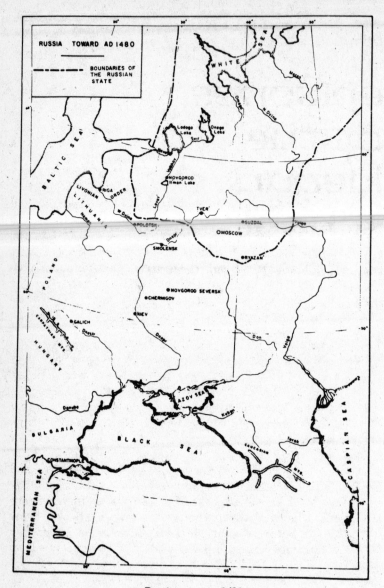

Russia ca. A.D. *1480*

A. MILITARY TALES

34. THE BATTLE ON THE RIVER KALKA

In 1223 the Mongols, united under Genghis Khan, invaded southern Russia for the first time. They came there more or less accidentally, returning to Central Asia after conquests in Persia and the Caucasus. (The Mongols became known to Russians by the name Tatar. The Tatars were actually a Mongolian tribe from which were taken the shock troops for the advancing Mongolian army.) After having defeated the Russian princes and their allies, the Kumans—who joined with the Russians the better to resist the invasion—the Mongols disappeared into the Central Asian steppes and deserts. They returned twelve years later, and this time they held the Russian land for more than two centuries. The report of this first decisive battle on the river Kalka is apparently of southern origin, and was incorporated into the *Novgorodian Chronicle* under the year 1224.

6732 (1224)   In the same year, for our sins, there came unknown tribes. No one knew who they were or what was their origin, faith, or tongue, and some people called them Tatars, while others called them Taurmens, and still others called them Pechenegs. Some say that these are the same people of whom Methodius of Patar spoke and that they came from the Yetrian Desert, which is between North and East. Methodius said that at the end of time there will appear those whom Gideon drove away, and they will conquer the whole land from the Tigris and Euphrates rivers to the Pontic Sea, with the exception of Ethiopia. Only God knows who these people are or from whence they came. The wise men, who understand the Books, know who they are, but we do not. Here we record them in memory of the misfortunes of the Russian princes that came about at their (the Tatars') hands. We have heard that they have conquered many lands and have killed many Yassians, Abkhasians, Kassogians,[1] and godless Kumans. And many Kumans were driven away and many others were killed, owing to the wrath of God and his Immaculate Mother. Much evil has befallen the Russian land at the hands of these Kumans, and therefore most merciful God desired that these godless Kumans, sons of Ishmael,

---

[1] Yassians, Kassogians, and Abkhasians were Caucasian tribes.

should die in order to revenge the Christian blood that was upon them, these lawless ones.

These Taurmens (Mongols) came across the whole Kuman land and came close to the Russian border. And the remnants of these godless Kumans under the leadership of Khotian and other princes came to the so-called Kuman Wall, where many were killed together with princes Daniil Kobiakovich and George. This Khotian was the father-in-law of Mstislav Mstislavich, the Russian Prince of Galich. And he (Khotian) arrived in Galich with greetings for his son-in-law, Mstislav Mstislavich, and all the other Russian princes. He brought them numerous presents: horses, camels, buffaloes, and girls. And he presented these gifts to them, and said the following: "Today the Tatars took away our land and tomorrow they will come and take way yours." And Khotian begged his son-in-law (for help). And Mstislav Mstislavich began to beg his brothers, the Russian princes, saying: "Brethren, if we do not help them, they will turn to the Tatars, and so later they (the Kumans) will be more powerful."

And hence, having deliberated for some time, they decided to start a campaign, responding to the appeals of the Kuman princes. And the warriors began to gather in their respective regions, and began a march against the Tatars after the whole Russian land was united. Soon the Russian army came to a place called Zarub on the Dnieper.

The Tatars, learning that the Russian princes had begun to march against them, sent their envoys to them, saying: "We hear that you, having followed the advice of the Kumans, do march against us. But we have neither occupied your lands nor your cities and villages, and we are not campaigning against you. We came because God let us conquer the godless Kumans who are our slaves and cattle herders. You should make peace with us. If the Kumans came to you, fight them and take all their belongings. We tell you this because we understand that they have done much harm to you and that is why we fight them."

The Russian princes paid no heed to these speeches, but killed the envoys and marched against the Tatars. They set up camp on the Dnieper in the vicinity of Oleshie. And the Tatars once again sent envoys, and they said the following: "You have listened to the Kumans and have killed our envoys. Come, then, though we have not occupied your lands, and it will be an injustice against God and everyone." And the Russians permitted the envoys to go away.

And Prince Mstislav Mstislavich forded the Dnieper and charged the Tatar outpost and took it with a thousand warriors.

The rest of the Tatars of this outpost escaped to the Kuman Hills under the command of Gwemia Beg. Since the Tatars found no assistance, they hid their leader, Gwemia Beg, underground so that he would not be killed. But they were attacked at that place by the Kumans, and Gwemia Beg was killed with the approval of Mstislav Mstislavich.

As soon as the other Russian princes learned of this action, they all crossed the Dnieper, and after nine days they came to the river Kalka. They sent the Kuman vanguard, under the command of Yarun, ahead, while the Russian princes and their armies set up camp. Yarun began fighting with the Tatars, but his Kuman warriors failed, and retreated in such haste that they galloped over the Russian camp and trampled it underfoot. And there was not time for the Russian forces to form ranks. And so it came to complete confusion, and a terrible slaughter resulted.

Mstislav, Prince of Kiev, having witnessed this misfortune, decided not to retreat, but took his position over the river Kalka. It was a rocky, rugged place on which he built a stockade and fought off the Tatars for three days. In this fortification with Prince Mstislav there remained his brothers-in-law, Andrew and Alexander of Dubrovich. The Tatar troops that besieged the fortification were led by Chigyz Khan and Teshu Khan. With the Tatars there were also a number of Brodniki [2] who were under the command of Ploskyn. This accursed commander pledged by the holy cross that Prince Mstislav and his two brothers-in-law would not be killed, but released for ransom. But this accursed Ploskyn lied, and he bound the princes hand and feet and turned them over to the Tatars. The princes were taken by the Tatars and crushed beneath platforms placed over their bodies on the top of which the Tatars celebrated their victory banquet. And the fortified camp of Mstislav was taken, and all his warriors were slain.

The other princes were pursued to the Dnieper, and six of them were killed there: Sviatoslav of Yanev, Iziaslav, son of Ingvar, Sviatoslav of Shumsk, Mstislav of Chernigov and his son, and George of Nesvizh. But Prince Mstislav Mstislavich, Prince of Galich, escaped by crossing the Dnieper, and he cut loose the boats from the shore to ensure his escape. Only one Russian warrior in ten lived through this battle; in returning to their homelands, many of these were killed by the Kumans for their horses and clothes.

---

[2] Russian outlaws and adventurers who lived on the prairie among the Kumans.

In such a way did God bring confusion upon us, and an endless number of people perished. This evil event came to pass on the day of Jeremiah the prophet, the 31st day of May. As for the Tatars, they turned back from the Dnieper, and we know neither from whence they came nor whither they have now gone. Only God knows that, because he brought them upon us for our sins.

35. ORISON ON THE DOWNFALL OF RUSSIA

The *Orison on the Downfall of Russia* is a well-known, poetic, but still obscure, Russian thirteenth-century literary fragment. It can be found in miscellanies that contain the *Tale of the Life and Courage of the Pious and Great Prince Alexander* [Nevsky], and precedes it in manuscripts. However, its style differs strikingly from the tale of Alexander Nevsky. It is very probable that it is the beginning of a longer orison or lamentation bewailing the conquest of Russia by the Mongols. It ends abruptly with the indication that a catastrophe befell Russia. Its style is both rhetorical and pathetic, and reflects a strong nationalistic spirit embittered by the catastrophe. One can presume that a longer description of the Mongol invasion originally followed this introductory part.

Although this orison was not written in verse, it can easily be divided into short rhythmic units, many of which rhyme, as for instance, lines three to eleven. The rhythm and diction of this work have many features in common with those of the *Lay of Igor's Campaign*. Since the author mentions the ruler at the time of the orison's writing as being Yaroslav (Great Prince of Vladimir, 1238–1246), it can be concluded that this work was composed no earlier than 1237, the year the Tatars invaded Russia, and no later than 1246, the year of Yaroslav's death.

This translation is based on the Russian text to be found in Yu. K. Begunov, *Pamiatnik russkoi literatury XIII veka*, "Slovo o pogibeli russkoi zemli," Moscow-Leningrad, 1965.

O Russian land, brightest of the bright,
most beautifully adorned,
thou art marvelous to us, with thy many beauties.
Marvelous are thy numerous lakes,
thy rivers and venerated springs,
steep mountains, high hills,
oak forests, beautiful fields,
many beasts and countless birds,

great cities, wonderful villages, and monastery gardens,
honorable boyars and countless lords,
Christian churches and stern princes.
Thou, Russian land, art rich in wealth
and in the Orthodox Christian Faith.
Thou spreadest from Hungary to Poland and Bohemia,
from Bohemia to the land of the Yatvags,
from the land of the Yatvags to the Lithuanians and Germans,
from the land of the Germans to Karelia,
from Karelia to Ustiug
where live the pagan Toymians,
and beyond the breathing sea,[1]
and from the sea to the Bulgars,
from the Bulgars to the Burtasians,
from the Burtasians to the Cheremiss, and
from the Cheremiss to the Mordvians.
All these vast areas and the people that live on them
were subjugated by God to the Christian people (of Russia)
and to Great Prince Vsevolod
and to his father, Yury, Prince of Kiev,
and to his grandfather, Vladimir Monomakh,
with whose name the Kumans frightened
their children in their cradles,
and in whose reign the Lithuanians
did not dare show themselves from their swamps,
and in whose reign the Hungarians fortified
the stone walls of their cities with their iron gates
so that great Vladimir might not pass through.
And at that time the Germans did rejoice
in being so far (from the Russians) beyond the sea.
And the Burtasians, Cheremiss, Votiaks, and Mordvians
worked hard to pay tribute to Vladimir the Great.
And even the Emperor of Byzantium, Manuel,
fearing lest Vladimir the Great take Constantinople,
was sending rich presents to him.

And so it used to be.
But now a great misfortune has befallen the Russian land,
the land that was once ruled by the great Yaroslav and
    Vladimir,
and is now ruled by Prince Yaroslav
and his brother, Yury, Prince of Vladimir. . . .

---

[1] The White Sea and Arctic Ocean, so-called because of the frequent fogs.

36. TALE OF THE DESTRUCTION OF RIAZAN

The *Tale of the Destruction of Riazan* is one of the most interesting and best written accounts of the invasion of Russia by
the Mongols under the leadership of Batu. Though the writer of
this tale called Batu "tsar," meaning emperor, Batu was actually
only a commander of the Mongolian armies that operated in
Europe. The Mongolian emperor resided either in Mongolia or
in northern China.

This story is contained in many manuscripts of the sixteenth
and seventeenth centuries. Apparently it once formed a part of
a miscellany that was composed and revised many times by the
clergy of the Church of St. Nicholas of Zaraisk, which, according
to legend, is located on the very spot where Princess Eupraxy
killed herself. The composition of this account, which in our
translation is divided into distinct parts, shows its heterogeneous
origins. The first contains typical chronicle entries slightly embellished by the usual phraseology of Old Russian military tales.
The story of the knight, Eupaty Kolovrat, is one of the oldest
examples of the Russian heroic tale and has several stylistic features to be found also in Russian *byliny*, or heroic epic songs.
Many features of this knightly epic resemble those of the deeds
of medieval knights in Western Europe. The joust between
Eupaty and the Tatar knight, Hostovrul, and Batu's respect for
the body of Eupaty Kolovrat and the survivors of his army,
would fit perfectly well into the knightly tradition of Western
Europe. Other details seem to be patterned after the *Lay of
Igor's Campaign*, such as the appeal by Great Prince Yury
Ingvarevich to the princes of Riazan. In the last part is included Prince Ingvar's remarkable "Lament," in which folklore
and biblical stylistics and themes are skillfully blended. It follows to a considerable extent the lament from the *Life and
Death of Grand Prince Dmitry Ivanovich*, which was written
in the fifteenth century.

It is evident that this is a fictionalized account of the destruction of Riazan and that it was actually written many years after
the events occurred. The author apparently used for his source
material a short account of the events and a list giving the
names of the princes of Riazan but not the dates of their deaths.
Therefore, the writer oversimplified the family relationships
among the Riazan princes and also mentioned several princes
who had actually died either before the battle or some time
after: i.e., Prince Vsevolod and Prince Oleg the Handsome are
mentioned as heroic defenders of the Riazan land. Actually,

Prince Vsevolod died in 1208 and Prince Oleg in 1258. Still, most of the facts and details given in this tale exactly correspond to information provided in other documents and chronicles. This lament was added considerably later, probably sometime between the beginning of the fifteenth century and the early sixteenth century.

This translation is based on the Russian text published by V. P. Adrianova-Peretts in *Voinskie povesti drevnei Rusi*, Moscow and Leningrad, 1949, pages 9–17, 18, and 19.

I. BATU INVADES RUSSIA

Within twelve years after bringing the miraculous icon of St. Nicholas from Kherson, the godless Emperor Batu invaded the Russian land with a great multitude of his Tatar warriors and set up camp on the river Voronezh in the vicinity of the principality of Riazan. And he sent his infidel envoys to the city of Riazan, to Great Prince Yury Ingvarevich, demanding tithes from everyone—from the princes and from all ranks of people. And they also demanded one-tenth of all the horses in the city. As soon as Great Prince Yury Ingvarevich learned of the invasion by godless Batu, he sent his envoys to the city of Vladimir, to the faithful and Great Prince George Vsevolodovich, asking that he either send succor against the godless emperor or come personally with his army. However, the great prince neither came personally nor sent help, since he had decided to fight Batu himself. And the Great Prince Yury Ingvarevich, having learned that he would receive no help from the Grand Prince of Vladimir, immediately sent to his kin for help, to Prince David Ingvarevich of Murom, to Prince Gleb Ingvarevich of Kolomna, to Prince Oleg the Handsome, and to Prince Vsevolod of Pronsk, and to other princes. And they started to deliberate as to how to satisfy the godless emperor with tribute. And the Great Prince Yury Ingvarevich decided to send his son, Fedor Yurevich, to Batu with many gifts and supplications that he not invade the land of Riazan.

Prince Fedor came to the Emperor Batu whose camp was on the river Voronezh. And he pleaded with the emperor. The godless, false, merciless emperor accepted the gifts and deceitfully promised not to launch a campaign against the principality of Riazan, but he bragged, and threatened to conquer all other Russian lands. And the emperor began to entertain the Riazan princes, and after this entertainment asked that they send their sisters and daughters to be his concubines. And one envious Riazan courtier told Batu that the wife of Prince Fedor belonged to the Byzantine imperial family and that she had a most beautiful body. Emperor Batu, who was false and merci-less, became excited, and told Prince Fedor: "Prince, give me your wife so that I may enjoy her beauty."

But Prince Fedor laughed at Batu's suggestion, and said: "It is not our Christian custom to bring to you, the godless emperor, our wives so that your lust may be satisfied. If you conquer us, then you will be the ruler of our wives."

The godless Emperor Batu felt offended, and became angry. He ordered the immediate death of Prince Fedor, and com-manded that his body be thrown in a field where it would be devoured by beasts and birds. And the retinue and the warriors of Prince Fedor were also put to death.

One of the servants of Prince Fedor, by name Aponitsa, man-aged to escape, and wept bitterly, seeing the body of his master. Having noticed that no one guarded the corpse, he took his be-loved master's body and buried it secretly. Then he hurried to Princess Eupraxy and told her that Emperor Batu had killed her husband. At that moment the princess happened to be on the upper floor of the palace with her infant son, Prince Ivan. When she heard from Aponitsa that her husband had been slain, she was seized with grief, and threw herself from the window with the child in her arms. And so both were killed.

When Great Prince Yury Ingvarevich learned of his son's death and of the deaths of his son's retinue and warriors, he fell to mourning with Princess Agrippina. And for a long time there were lamentation and sorrow throughout the city. As soon as the great prince recovered from his bereavement, he began to gather an army and to groom his regiments. When Great Prince Yury Ingvarevich saw his kin, his boyars, and his *voevodas* fearlessly and bravely astride their horses, he raised his hands to the heavens and said with tears in his eyes: "Save us, God, from our enemies and those that march against us. And preserve us from the faithless and make their way dark and difficult."

And then he said to his men: "O my lords and brethren! Since we have received from God his blessing, we must also accept his punishment. It is better, through death, to win eternal glory than to be under the power of the heathen. And I, your brother, am ready to sacrifice my life for the holy divine Church, for the Christian faith, and for the country of our father, Great Prince Ingvar Sviatoslavovich."

And then he went to the Church of the Assumption of the Blessed Virgin, and prayed there. And he cried before the icon of the Blessed Virgin and prayed to the great worker of miracles, St. Nicholas, and to his holy kin, Sts. Boris and Gleb. And for the last time he kissed Great Princess Agrippina. And he received the blessings of the bishop and the priests.

II. BATU DEFEATS PRINCE YURY

And they marched against the infidel Batu, and meeting him on the border of the principality of Riazan, attacked and began to fight both fiercely and bravely. And it was a terrible and awesome battle, and many of Batu's regiments were defeated. And Emperor Batu, seeing how fiercely and bravely did the warriors of Riazan fight, became frightened. But who can resist the wrath of God? Batu's forces were innumerable and invincible. Each Riazan warrior had to fight with a thousand of the enemy. And every two Riazan warriors had to fight with ten thousand of the enemy. And Prince Yury Ingvarevich saw the slaying of his brother, David, and exclaimed in anguish: "O my kind brothers and dear warriors, the flower of Riazan's troops, be brave and resist mightily. Our dear brother, Prince David, was the first to drink the bitter cup to the dregs, and we shall do the same."

And the princes and the warriors changed horses and once again began to fight fiercely. And they cut through the many strong lines of the Tatar regiments, fighting bravely and fiercely. And all the Tatar regiments were struck with awe upon seeing the bravery and power of the Riazan armies. And they fought with such intensity that even the earth began to moan, and confusion reigned in the ranks of Batu's armies. The strong Tatar regiments were hardly able to overcome the Riazan offensive. In this battle were killed Great Prince Yury Ingvarevich, Prince David Ingvarevich of Murom, Prince Gleb Ingvarevich of Kolomna, Prince Vsevolod Ingvarevich of Pronsk, and many other brave Riazan princes, powerful *voevodas*, and warriors. Heroes and brave warriors, the flower of Riazan's army, all drank the same bitter cup to the dregs, and fell on the field of battle.[1] And Prince Oleg was taken prisoner half alive. All of this happened according to the will of God and because of our sins.

And the Emperor Batu, seeing that numerous regiments of his army had been defeated, was seized by awe and grief. He began conquering the Riazan lands, ordering that everyone and everything be cut down and burned without mercy. And he lay low the cities of Pronsk, Belgorod, and Izheslavets, killing everyone in these cities without mercy. And Christian blood flowed like a great river. And all this because of our sins.

When Emperor Batu saw Prince Oleg Ingvarevich, the most handsome and bravest of the Riazan princes, dying from his

---

[1] None of the men of Riazan deserted the battlefield; all were slain.

grievous wounds, he wanted to heal his wounds and win him over to his faith. But Prince Oleg began to reprimand Batu, and called him godless and the enemy of all Christendom. And fire came from the evil heart of Batu, and he ordered that Prince Oleg be cut to pieces. And so he became the second Stephen the Martyr, having received the crown of suffering from the all-merciful God. And he drank his bitter cup to the dregs with all his brethren.

III. THE TAKING OF RIAZAN

The accursed Batu began the conquest of the land of Riazan, and soon approached the city of Riazan itself. They encircled the city and fought without surcease for five days. Batu changed his regiments frequently, replacing them with fresh troops, while the citizens of Riazan fought without relief. And many citizens were killed and others wounded. Still others were exhausted by their great efforts and their wounds. On the dawn of the sixth day the pagan warriors began to storm the city, some with firebrands, some with battering rams, and others with countless scaling ladders for ascending the walls of the city. And they took the city of Riazan on the 21st day of December. And the Tatars came to the Cathedral of the Assumption of the Blessed Virgin, and they cut to pieces the Great Princess Agrippina, her daughters-in-law, and other princesses. They burned to death the bishops and the priests and put the torch to the holy church. And the Tatars cut down many people, including women and children. Still others were drowned in the river. And they killed without exception all monks and priests. And they burned this holy city with all its beauty and wealth, and they captured the relatives of the Riazan princes, the princes of Kiev and Chernigov. And churches of God were destroyed, and much blood was spilled on the holy altars. And not one man remained alive in the city. All were dead. All had drunk the same bitter cup to the dregs. And there was not even anyone to mourn the dead. Neither father nor mother could mourn their dead children, nor the children their fathers or mothers. Nor could a brother mourn the death of his brother, nor relatives their relatives. All were dead. And this happened for our sins.

IV. EUPATY THE FEARLESS

Seeing this terrible letting of Christian blood, the heart of godless Batu became even more hardened, and he marched against the cities of Suzdal and Vladimir, intending to conquer all Russian lands, to uproot the Christian faith, and to destroy the churches of God. At that time a Riazan lord, Eupaty Kolovrat,

who was in Chernigov at the time of the destruction of the city
of Riazan, heard of Batu's invasion. He left Chernigov with a
small force and hurried to Riazan. When he came to the land of
Riazan he saw it devastated and the cities destroyed, the rulers
killed, and the people dead. And he rushed to the city of Riazan
and found it destroyed, the rulers killed, and the people slaughtered. Some of them were cut down, while others were burned,
and still others were drowned. And Eupaty wept with great
sorrow and his heart became angry. He gathered a small force
of seventeen hundred men who had been preserved by God
outside the city. And they hurriedly pursued the godless emperor. And with difficulty they caught up with him in the
principality of Suzdal, and suddenly fell upon his camp. And
there began a battle without mercy, and confusion reigned.
And the Tatars lost their heads from fear as Eupaty fought so
fiercely that his sword became dull, and, taking a sword from a
fallen Tatar, he would cut them down with their own swords.
The Tatars thought that the Russians had risen from the dead,
and Eupaty was riding through the ranks of the Tatar regiments
so bravely that Batu himself became frightened.

With great effort the Tatars managed to capture five men from
Eupaty's regiments, and then only because they were exhausted
from their wounds. They were brought before the Tatar emperor, and he asked them: "Why do you cause me such evil?"

The warriors answered: "We are of the Christian faith, knights
of the Great Prince Yury of Riazan, and from the regiment of
Eupaty Kolovrat. We were sent by Prince Ingvar Ingvarevich
to you, the powerful emperor, to honor you, to chase you away
with honors, and to render unto you all honors. Do not wonder,
Emperor, that we have not had time to serve up the bitter cup
to your entire army." And the emperor admired their witty an-
swers. And he sent his brother-in-law, Hostovrul, against Eupaty,
and with Hostovrul went strong regiments. Hostovrul bragged
to the emperor, and promised to bring back Eupaty alive.

Eupaty was encircled by Tatar troops because they wished
to take him alive. And Hostovrul rode out against Eupaty, but
Eupaty was a giant, and with one blow he cleft Hostovrul to
the saddle. And once more he began to cut down the Tatar
troops, and he killed many of Batu's best knights. Some were
cut down, while others were cleft to their waist, and still others
were cleft to their saddles. The Tatars became afraid, seeing
what a giant Eupaty was. And then they brought up catapults
and began showering rocks upon him. And they finally killed
Eupaty Kolovrat, but only with great difficulty.

Eupaty's body was brought before Batu, and the emperor sent

for his princes, lords, and commanders, and all marveled at the courage, power, and bravery of the Riazan warriors. And the lords, commanders, and princes told Batu: "We were in many battles with many emperors in many lands, but never have we seen such courageous heroes, and even our fathers never told us of such. They are winged people. They do not think about death, and they fight bravely and courageously on their horses, one against a thousand, and two against ten thousand warriors. None of them would abandon the battlefield alive."

And Batu looked at Eupaty's body, and said: "O Eupaty Kolovrat, you have honored us with your courage, and you, with your small army, have killed many knights of my powerful horde and have defeated many of my regiments. If such a knight would serve with me, I would keep him very close to my heart." And he gave up Eupaty's body to the remainder of the Riazan force that had been captured on the battlefield. And Batu gave orders that the prisoners should be released and that no harm should come to them.

V. PRINCE INGVAR BURIES THE DEAD

Prince Ingvar Ingvarevich (the brother of Great Prince Yury Ingvarevich of Riazan) returned from Chernigov, having been there with his relative, Prince Michael, at the time of the destruction of Riazan. And so he was preserved by God from the enemy of all Christendom. Prince Ingvar Ingvarevich found his fatherland devastated, and learned that all his brothers had been killed by the impure, lawbreaking Batu. And he came to the city of Riazan and found the city destroyed, and his mother and sisters-in-law, his relatives, and many other people lying dead. And he found the churches burned and all valuables taken from the common treasury of Chernigov and Riazan. When Prince Ingvar saw this great and enduring destruction he shrieked aloud in his sorrow, sounding as a trumpet summoning the army or as an organ resounding. And after these rending shrieks and horrifying lamentations, Prince Ingvar fell to the ground as if dead. With great difficulty and the help of water and a fresh breeze did he recover. And finally his soul did revive in his body.

Who would not so lament such a catastrophe? Who would not bewail the deaths of so many Orthodox people? Who would not mourn the death of so many rulers? Who would not mourn such a dispersion?

And Prince Ingvar searched through the bodies, and found the body of his mother, Princess Agrippina, and those of his brothers' wives. And he called a priest from villages that were preserved by God, and he buried his mother and the wives of his deceased brothers with great lamentations in place of the psalms and chants. And he cried and lamented terribly. And he buried the bodies of the other dead and he cleaned the city. And he had the city blessed by a priest and he gathered the few survivors and comforted them. And he lamented for a long time, thinking of his mother, his brothers, his relatives, and all the people of Riazan who had met such untimely deaths.

And all this happened because of our sins. There used to be the city of Riazan in the land of Riazan, but its wealth disappeared and its glory ceased, and there is nothing to be seen in the city excepting smoke, ashes, and barren earth. All churches and the cathedral were burned. And not only this city, but many others were conquered. There is neither the ringing of the church bells nor church services. And instead of joy, there are only uninterrupted lamentations.

And Prince Ingvar went to the place where his brethren were killed by the impious emperor Batu. Great Prince Yury of Riazan, Prince David of Murom, Prince Vsevolod of Pronsk, Prince Gleb of Kolomna, many other princes, boyars, *voevodas*, and warriors—indeed, all the best souls of Riazan—were lying on the barren earth and frozen grass. And they were covered with snow and ice, and no one cared for them. Beasts devoured their bodies, and a multitude of birds tore them to pieces. And they were lying together, even as they had fallen together. They all drank the same bitter cup to the dregs.

And when Prince Ingvar Ingvarevich saw this great number of corpses lying on the earth, he shrieked bitterly, like a trumpet resounding. He fell to the ground, and tears flowed from his eyes in a stream. And Prince Ingvar spoke in great sadness:

"O my dear brethren and warriors!
O my treasured lives!
How could you close your eyes
and leave me alone in such misfortune?
How could you disappear from my sight,
treasures of my life?
O my beautiful flowers!
O my unripened vineyard!
Why won't you speak to me, your brother?
Never again will you make my life sweet.
Why won't you look at me?
Why won't you talk with me?
How could you, fruitful gardens,
born of the same father,
and from the same womb of Great Princess Agrippina,

and fed by the same breast, forget me?
To whom have you forsaken me, your brother?
You did fade too early, my dear eastern stars.
You set so early, my dear suns.
You lie on this deserted land watched over by no one!
No one renders you honor or glory.
Indeed, your days of glory have dimmed.
Where is your power?
You, who used to be rulers of many lands,
now lie on this barren earth,
and your faces darken from decay.
O my dear brothers!
O my dear warriors!
Never again shall we share joys.
O my bright lights,
Why were you extinguished?
I have not had enough joy with you!
If God hears your prayers,
pray that I, your brother, might join you!
After days of joy have come those of tears and sorrow.
After pleasures and happiness,
have come lamenting and mourning.
O, why did I not die before you
so that I would not have had to see your deaths?
This is my bitter fate!
Do you hear my unhappy words that fall so sadly?
O mother earth!
O forest of oak, lament with me!
And how shall I describe these days
in which perished
so many rulers and warriors,
so many brave and dashing heroes of Riazan?
None returned,
but all drank the same bitter cup to the dregs.
My tongue does not obey me,
my lips close,
my sight darkens,
my strength ebbs,
for great is the sorrow of my soul."

And there was great sorrow and sadness, tears and sighs, fears and trembling, because of the evil ones that attacked our land. Great Prince Ingvar raised his hands to the heavens, and prayed tearfully:

"O Lord, my God,
I place my hope in thee.
Save and preserve me from my persecutors.
O my Most Holy Mother of Christ, my Savior,
don't forsake me in my hour of grief.
Boris and Gleb, our great martyrs and ancestors,
be of help to me in battle, lowly sinner that I am.
My brethren and warriors,
help me with your prayers in my struggles against the enemy,
these children of Hagar,
these grandchildren of Ishmael."

And then Prince Ingvar began to search among the bodies of the dead, and he took for burial the bodies of his brothers, Great Prince Yury, Prince Gleb of Kolomna, and of other princes related to him, as well as those of many other boyars and *voevodas* well known to him. And he transported the bodies to the city of Riazan, and buried them with honor. And the bodies of the others, which were lying on the devastated earth, he buried and had the last rites pronounced over them. Having buried all of them, Prince Ingvar then went to the city of Pronsk where he gathered the remains of his slain brother, the peaceful and Christ-loving Prince Oleg. And he ordered the body returned to the city of Riazan, and he himself carried the venerable head of Prince Oleg to the city. And he kissed it with respect, and placed the body in the same coffin with the body of Great Prince Yury. In the vicinity of this grave were buried the remains of Princes David and Gleb in a single coffin. And then Prince Ingvar went to the river Voronezh where Prince Fedor Yurevich had been killed at the order of Batu. And Prince Ingvar shed many tears over the body of Prince Fedor and he brought it to the city of Riazan, and in the vicinity of the icon of the great maker of miracles, St. Nicholas, he buried Prince Fedor together with his wife, faithful Princess Eupraxy, and his son, Prince Ivan. And he placed stone crosses over the graves. . . .

(A fragment has been omitted.)

Then faithful Prince Ingvar, whose baptismal name was Cosmas, took the throne of his father, Ingvar Sviatoslavovich. And he restored the land of Riazan and he erected churches and monasteries. And he consoled the settlers and gathered his people together. And he was a great joy for the Christians who, with the help of God's strong hand, had escaped the godless infidel, Emperor Batu. And he put Prince Michael Vsevolodovich of Pronsk in his father's patrimony.

37. THE HEROIC DEEDS OF MERCURIUS
OF SMOLENSK

After having conquered central and northern Russia, the Mongolian commander, Batu, began his advance into western Russia in 1237. However, because of the spring floods he was unable to take the city of Novgorod, and thus turned southward to the city of Smolensk. For some reason that remains indiscernible from historical writings, the Tatar troops were unable to capture Smolensk. From this event developed the charming legend of St. Mercurius of Smolensk, the heroic defender of his city. Written in a simple style characterized by redundancy, this is probably the most "medieval" of Russian legends. Contrary to this narrative, however, upon leaving the region of Smolensk Batu marched into southern Russia, where he devastated Kiev and other cities, and in 1241 he invaded Hungary. Defeating the Hungarians, he left Hungary so that he might return to Mongolia and participate in the selection of a new khan. The killing of Batu by King Stephen of Hungary, as mentioned in this tale, is the product of the writer's imagination.

The subject of *The Heroic Deeds*—the fight of a pious Russian knight against the nomadic invaders—was a common theme in Russian medieval epics, and various details have been supplied from early Christian and Byzantine hagiography. Very likely this legend grew out of the life of Mercurius of Caesarea (now Kaisaria, Turkey) and from the writings of Dionysius Pseudo-Areopagite. It was probably written in the late fourteenth century, and absorbed a considerable amount of Russian folklore elements.

This translation is based on the Old Russian text, edited by Professor M. O. Skripil, found in *Russkie povesti XI–XVI vekov,* Moscow, 1958, pages 106–107.

There used to live in the city of Smolensk a young man called Mercurius who was very pious, who studied God's commandments both day and night, who distinguished himself by his holy life, and who, because of his fasting and prayers, shone like the star which announced the birth of Christ to the entire world. He had a contrite soul and the gift of tears.[1] Often he would pray before the cross of Our Lord for the whole world, and he lived in the St. Peter's part of the city.

---

[1] Eastern Christianity considered the capacity for incessant tears during prayers to be a divine gift.

At that time the evil emperor Batu had conquered the Russian land, had shed rivers of innocent blood, and had tortured the Christians. This emperor came with a great army to the pious city of Smolensk, camped at a distance of twenty miles, burned many holy churches, killed many Christians, and began to prepare for the assault of the city. The people of the city were deeply grieved, and remained incessantly in the Cathedral of the Holy Mother of God. From all their hearts they prayed and worshiped. And, shedding tears, they asked Almighty God, the Holy Mother of God, and all the saints to preserve their city from evil. And God decided to preserve the city and its people.

In the Crypt Monastery, which was located in the vicinity of the river Dnieper outside the city, the sexton of the church had a vision of the Most Holy Mother of God. And she addressed him, saying: "O servant of God! Go at once to the cross where my servant, Mercurius, prays. And tell him, 'The Mother of God beckons you to come.'"

The sexton, going there and finding Mercurius praying to God before the cross, called to him by name, "Mercurius."

Mercurius answered: "What do you wish, my lord?"

And the sexton replied: "Go at once, brother. The Mother of God beckons you to the Crypt Monastery."

And when Mercurius, who was made wise by God, entered the holy church, he saw the Most Holy Mother of God sitting on the golden throne with the Christ Child in her arms and surrounded by the host of angels. Seized by awe, he fell at her feet and genuflected low before her.

And the Holy Mother of God raised him, and said: "Mercurius, my chosen one, I send you to take revenge immediately for the Christian blood which has been spilled. Go and defeat the evildoing emperor Batu and all his armies. Afterward, there will come to you a man with a handsome face. Give him all your arms, and he will decapitate you. Then take your head in your hands and return to your city. And there you will pass away and will be buried in my church."

Mercurius was saddened by these words, and, beginning to weep, he said: "O Most Holy Mother of God. How can I, a poor sinner and undeserving servant, be strong enough for such a deed? Is it possible, my Lady, that the heavenly hosts are not enough to defeat this evildoing emperor?"

Thereafter, Mercurius received her blessing, took up weapons and, bowing to the earth, went from this church. Outside the church he found a spirited steed and, mounting it, he left the city. With the help of God and his Holy Mother, he came to the regiments of the evildoing emperor, defeated the enemy, gathered together the Christian prisoners and, sending them back to his city, he courageously galloped over the regiments of Batu even as an eagle soars through the air. The evildoing emperor, seeing such a rout of his men, and being seized by great awe and fright, rapidly fled with a small retinue, not having achieved the smallest success in battle. From Smolensk, Batu fled to Hungary, and there this evildoer was killed by King Stephen.

And the handsome warrior appeared before Mercurius. The latter gave all his arms to him and bowed deeply before him. And the warrior severed his head from the body. Then the blessed one took his head in one hand and, leading his horse with the other hand, returned to the city decapitated. The people of the city, seeing this, were astounded by God's design. And when Mercurius came to the Molokhov Gate, he met there a certain maiden who was going to fetch water. When she saw the blessed one walking without his head, she began to abuse him vilely. But he lay down at this gate and offered up his most contrite soul to God. And his steed, at that moment becoming invisible, disappeared.

The archbishop of the city came with a large number of people carrying crosses and hoping to take the honorable body of this saint to the church, but they were unable to lift his body from the ground. Then there began a great wailing and weeping among the people because it was impossible to raise the body of the saint. Even the archbishop became greatly bewildered and began to pray to God. And there came a voice to him that announced: "O servant of God! Do not grieve. He will be buried by the Same who sent him to victory."

And the body of the saint remained there unburied for three days. In the meantime, the archbishop remained all these nights praying to God to explain to him this mystery. And he remained without sleep. Praying, he looked out through the window that faced the cathedral, and there he saw a great light as if it were the rising of the sun. And in this light the Most Holy Mother of God and the Archangels Michael and Gabriel came from the church. And, coming to the place where the body of St. Mercurius was lying, the Most Holy Mother of God raised the venerable body of the saint and brought it to her cathedral and placed it in a casket. And this body can still be seen there, attesting to the miracle and glory of Christ, our God, and spreading the fragrance of cedar.

The next morning, when the bishop went to matins in the cathedral, he saw there the wondrous miracle, the body of the saint lying in its place. And the people flocked to the cathedral, and, seeing this miracle, they glorified God.

38. SOFONY OF RIAZAN: ZADONSHCHINA

On September 8, 1380, Russian troops, under the command of the Great Prince of Moscow, Dmitry, defeated the Tatar armies, 300,000 strong, led by Mamai, Khan of the Golden Horde. It was the first time, after one and a half centuries of Tatar domination over the Russian land, that the Russians defeated the Tatars. This battle did not bring an immediate end to the Tatar Yoke, but it was a great victory for the Russians, both weakening the domination of the Tatars and fostering the unification of the Russian lands. Thus, it is not surprising that this important historical event is recorded in various literary works. Among them, the most interesting is the *Lay of Great Prince Dmitry Ivanovich and His Brother, Prince Vladimir Andreevich*, written by Sofony of Riazan. It is known in Russian as *Zadonshchina*, meaning "The Tale of Events Beyond the Don," because the battle took place not far from the Don River, on the Kulikovo prairie. *Zadonshchina* was the title used in one of several extant manuscripts of this tale.

The purpose of this poetic lay was not to give a detailed historical account of the background and development of this battle, one of the most memorable in Russian history. The author omitted a considerable number of events that were of importance to the final outcome of the conflict, and many others were consolidated for the sake of poetic unity. Instead, the author wished to give an epic account of the Russians' efforts, and to stress the importance of this, the first decisive victory over the Tatars.

For the basic patterns of this lay, Sofony of Riazan turned to the greatest poetic work of Kievan Russia, the *Lay of Igor's Campaign*. In many respects he imitated this work, using its symbolic parallelisms, metaphors, alliterative patterns, and poetic imagery. Some sentences are taken word for word from the text of the earlier *Lay* (*Slovo*). Still, Sofony of Riazan created a lay that is very different from that about Igor, not only in its historical perspectives and political conceptions but also in its structure and in the development of narrative line.

Like the author of the tale of Igor, Sofony of Riazan, in writing this work, had in mind not only a poetic account of the battle but also an appeal to Russian unity and Russian national feelings. But, whereas the *Lay of Igor's Campaign* is primarily a lyrical appeal, *Zadonshchina* has a very definite narrative scheme that gives a more realistic account of events. Unlike the

Lay, the lyrical elements in this work are minimized, and the reminiscences of past feuds, so central to the *Lay*, are practically absent. *Zadonshchina*, like the *Lay*, was written not in verse but in rhythmic prose consisting of clearly distinguishable units.

The present translation is based on the text edited by V. P. Adrianova-Peretts, which is itself based on various medieval manuscripts of the work. This text was published in *Voinskie povesti drevnei Rusi*, in the series *Literaturnye pamiatniki*, Moscow and Leningrad, 1949, pages 33–41. The division into chapters and stanzas, as well as the typographic arrangement, was made by the translator to facilitate reading.

PROEMIUM

Great Prince Dmitry Ivanovich, with his brother,[1] Prince Vladimir Andreevich, and his *voevodas*, attended a banquet at the house of Mikula Vasilievich. (And Prince Dmitry Ivanovich spoke, saying:)

"Do you know, dear brothers, that Emperor Mamai
invaded the Russian land at the swift river Don
and is advancing into the midnight land?
Let us go, brothers, into that midnight land,
the lot of Japheth, the son of Noah,
from whom has come most glorious Russia.
Let us ascend the mountains of Kiev
and view the glorious river Dnieper.
Let us view the entire Russian land
and toward the eastern land, the lot of Shem,
the son of Noah, from whom were born
the pagan nomads, the Moslem Tatars."

I. EXHORTATION

They have defeated the race of Japheth on the river Kalka.[2]
And since that time the Russian land has been sad.
And, from the battle on the Kalka to the defeat of Mamai,
the Russian land has been covered with grief and sorrow,
shedding tears and lamenting the loss of her children.
Princes, boyars, and all courageous men!
Let us leave our homes, our wealth, our women and children,
  our cattle,

---

[1] Prince Vladimir was actually his cousin, but among close relatives it was customary to call each other "brother."

[2] In most of the manuscripts the river is called Kaiala, but Sofony apparently refers to the river Kalka, the site of the battle with the Mongols in 1223, where the Russians (the race of Japheth) were defeated.

that we may receive glory and honor in this world.
Let us lay down our lives for the Russian land and the Chris-
tian faith.
First, the sorrow of the Russian land did I describe,
as it has been done before in the books.
Then, I have described my sorrows and my glorifications
of the Great Prince Dmitry Ivanovich
and his brother, Vladimir Andreevich.
Let us come together, brothers, friends, and sons
of the Russian land.
Let us knit word after word.
Let us bring joy to the Russian land
and cast sorrow on the eastern country, the lot of Shem.
Let us sing of the defeat of Mamai, the infidel.
Let us sing glory to the Great Prince Dmitry Ivanovich
and to his brother, Prince Vladimir Andreevich.

Let us say the following words:
  "It behooves us, brothers, to begin with new words
  the telling of the glorious tale of the army of Prince Dmitry
      Ivanovich
  and his brother, Prince Vladimir Andreevich, great-grand-
      sons
  of holy Prince Vladimir of Kiev."
Let us tell the tale in the tradition of yore.
Let us race in thought across the lands.
Let us remember the deeds of former years.
Let us glorify wise Boyan, the great bard of Kiev,
for he, wise Boyan, would put his nimble fingers
on the living strings and would sing the glory of
the princes of Russia, of Igor Rurikovich, the first Great Prince
    of Kiev,
of Great Prince Vladimir Sviatoslavovich and
of Great Prince Yaroslav Vladimirovich.
So let us glorify with our melodies and powerful lyrics
this Great Prince Dmitry Ivanovich
and his brother, Prince Vladimir Andreevich,
great-grandsons of those princes who devoted all their
bravery and efforts to the Russian land and the Christian faith.

II. THE RUSSIANS PREPARE FOR THE CAMPAIGN

Great Prince Dmitry Ivanovich and
his brother, Prince Vladimir Andreevich,
strengthened their minds with valor,
quickened their hearts with courage, and
imbued their thoughts with martial spirit.

And they gathered their regiments throughout the Russian
   land.
And they remembered the deeds of their great-grandfather,
Prince Vladimir of Kiev.

Skylark, joy of beautiful days!
Fly high into the beautiful blue sky.
Look on the powerful city of Moscow,
sing the glories of Great Prince Dmitry Ivanovich
and his brother, Prince Vladimir Andreevich.
The storm will bring the gyrfalcon
from the Russian lands into the Kuman prairie.
Steeds neigh in Moscow.
Glory rings out over all Russian lands.
Trumpets blare in Kolomna.
Drums resound in Serpukhov.
Banners are raised at the shore of the great river Don.
Bells resound in the great city of Novgorod,
but men of Novgorod remain in Holy Sophia, saying:
> "O brethren, we shall not have time to help
> Great Prince Dmitry Ivanovich."

It seems that eagles fly from the midnight land,
but they are not eagles.
They are Russian princes who fly together
to help Prince Dmitry Ivanovich and his brother,
Prince Vladimir Andreevich, telling them such words:
> "Lord, Great Prince, the infidel Tatars have begun ad-
> vancing into our lands.
> They take from us our patrimony.
> They camp on the river Mech,
> between the rivers Don and Dnieper.
> Our lord, we will go beyond the swift river Dnieper.
> We will win glory for our land in the tradition of old.
> We will gain memories for our youth.
> We will put our brave warriors to the test
> for the Russian land and the Christian faith."

And then Prince Dmitry Ivanovich said:
> "Brethren and princes of the Russian land,
> we are all descendants of Prince Vladimir of Kiev.
> Since our birth we have never permitted ourselves to be
> offended,
> neither by the falcon nor the gyrfalcon,
> nor by the black raven nor by the infidel Mamai."

If only the nightingale could sing the glories
of the two brothers of the Lithuanian land,

Andrew and Dmitry, the sons of Olgerd,
and of Dmitry of Volynia,
for these courageous sons, gyrfalcons in time of battle,
our brave army captains,
were swaddled under trumpets,
were brought up under helmets, and
were fed at lance point in the Lithuanian land.

And Andrew, son of Olgerd, spoke to his brother, Dmitry:
    "We are two brothers, sons of Olgerd,
    grandsons of Adiman, great-grandsons of Skolomend.
    Let us gather together our dear brethren,
    the nobles of brave Lithuania, bold and brave fellows.
    Let us mount on swift steeds.
    Let us view the swift river Don.
    Let us drink the water of the Don from our helmets.
    Let us test our Lithuanian swords on Tatar helmets,
    and our German javelins on the armor of the Moslems."

And Dmitry, son of Olgerd, said to him:
    "Brother Andrew, let us not spare ourselves
    in defense of the Russian land and the Christian faith,
    and in defense of the honor of Prince Dmitry Ivanovich.
    Already, brother, thunder resounds and clamor raises in
      the stone city of Moscow.
    But it is not thunder, brother.
    It is the clamor of the powerful army of Dmitry Ivano-
      vich.
    The brave Russian warriors thunder in their gilded armor
    and with their scarlet shields.
    Andrew, saddle your swift steed,
    for mine has been long saddled.
    Let us go, brother, into the open fields.
    Let us go, brother, and view our regiments."

III. THE COMING OF THE TATARS

Already from the sea there have begun blowing strong winds
into the mouth of the rivers Don and Dnieper.
And they have wafted great clouds over the Russian land,
and these clouds made the sunsets as scarlet as blood,
and blue lightning flashes through these clouds.
There will be great clamor on the river Nepriadva,
between the rivers Don and Dnieper.
Many men will fall on the field of Kulikovo,
and blood will be shed on the river Nepriadva.

The carts (of the nomads) have begun to creak
between the Don and the Dnieper.
The Tatars march into the Russian land.
Gray wolves follow after them
from the mouths of the Don and the Dnieper.
They howl on the river Mech and
they wish to advance into the Russian land.
But they are not wolves.
They are the infidel Tatars who wish
to march into the Russian land and conquer it.

The geese have begun to cackle on the river Mech.
Swans have begun to flutter their wings.
But it is not geese that cackle
nor swans that flutter their wings.
It is the infidel Mamai who has entered the Russian land,
and he brought his warriors there.
These winged birds have been brought by misfortune.
They fly high under the clouds.
Ravens croak and magpies speak in their own speech.
The eagles screech menacingly, wolves howl,
and foxes bark, waiting for bones.
O Russian land, you are far away beyond the hills.

IV. THE RUSSIAN ARMY MARCHES TO BATTLE

Already the falcon and the gyrfalcon
and the goshawks of Belozersk [3] race from the stone city of
    Moscow,
fly high under the blue sky,
ring their golden bells,[4]
and prepare to swoop down upon numerous flocks
of geese and swans.
And so the brave warriors of Russia prepare
to strike the great armies of the infidel, Mamai.

Great Prince Dmitry Ivanovich sets in the golden stirrup
and takes his sword in his right hand.
The sun shines brightly from the east,
showing him the road (to victory).
What rumbles? What roars so early before the dawn?
It is Prince Vladimir Andreevich
who prepares his regiments for battle
and leads them to the great river Don.

---

[3] Allusion to the princes of Belozersk.
[4] Hunting falcons had small bells attached to their talons.

And he speaks to his brother:
> "Prince Dmitry, Great Prince, don't yield to these Tatars,
> for these infidels destroy our fields and
> invade our fatherland."

Prince Dmitry Ivanovich speaks to his brother:
> "My dear brother, Vladimir Andreevich,
> we are two brothers.
> Our *voevodas* are appointed and our armies are well
>   known to us.
> We mount swift steeds and we wear gilt armor.
> We have Circassian helmets and Muscovite shields.
> We have German javelins and Frankish lances,
> and our swords are made of steel.
> The roads are known to us.
> The rivers are prepared for fording.
> The armies are eager to sacrifice their lives
> for the Christian faith.
> Our banners flap in the wind,
> and Russians seek honor and glory."

V. THE BATTLE BEGINS

Already the falcons, the gyrfalcons, and
the goshawks from Bélozersk swiftly cross the river Don.
And they strike against flocks of geese and swans.
They are Russian sons who strike against the great Tatar army,
And who, with their steel lances, clash against Tatar armors,
whose tempered swords sunder Tatar helmets,
on the prairie of Kulikovo,
at the small river, Nepriadva.

The earth became black from horse hooves.
The field became strewn with Tatar bones.
Much blood was spilled upon the field.
Strong regiments came together and clashed,
and they trampled the hills and the meadows.
The calm waters of rivers and lakes became stirred up.
The Div [5] called out in the Russian land,
calling all lands to listen.
And the glory of the Russian princes resounded,
from the roar of battle to the Iron Gates,
to Rome and to Kafa-on-the-Sea,

---

[5] A god or bird of misfortune that was mentioned in the *Lay of Igor's Campaign.*

to Tyrnovo and to Constantinople.[6]
O great land of Russia,
you have defeated Mamai on the prairie of Kulikovo.

The storm clouds began to gather
and from them shone lightning,
and thunder roared mightily.
It was the clash of the sons of Russia
with the Tatar infidels, for they seek revenge for Tatar
     offenses.
The gilt armor of the Russian princes gleamed.
Their steel swords rained upon the Tatar helmets.
It is not aurochs that roar upon the prairie of Kulikovo.
It is the wailing of Russian princes, boyars, and *voevodas* of
     Prince Dmitry,
and the princes of Belozersk who were massacred at the swift
     river Don.
And there *voevodas* Fedor Semionovich, Timofey Valuevich,
Andrey Serkizovich, Mikhail Ivanovich,
and a great many warriors were cut to pieces by the Tatars.
And their bodies lie on the shore of the river Don.
And then a boyar of Briansk, Monk Peresvet,
was ordered to the place where he was fated to meet death.
And Monk Peresvet said to Prince Dmitry Ivanovich:
     "It is better that we fall in battle
     than become slaves of these infidels."
And Peresvet, galloping on his horse,
filled the air with his battle cry.
And his armor gleamed as he called
to his younger brother, Osliabia:
     "Well, brother, it is time for those who are old
     to feel young and for the young to win glory
     by trying the arms of brave warriors."
And the brother, Monk Osliabia, answered:
     "Brother Peresvet, I already see that there
     will be heavy wounds on your body and
     that your head will lie on the feathergrass.
     I can see that my son, Jacob, will also lie in the green
         grass
     on the prairie of Kulikovo and for the defense
     of the Christian faith and revenge of the offenses
     done to Great Prince Dmitry Ivanovich."

---

[6] Iron Gates: a narrow canyon on the lower Danube; Kafa-on-the-
Sea: an Italian city in the Crimea; Tyrnovo: the capital of medieval
Bulgaria.

And at that time in the land of Riazan
at the river Don there was heard neither
the voice of the plowman nor of the shepherd.
Only the ravens cawed and the cuckoos cuckooed,
circling above the corpses.
And it was awesome and bitter to look about,
for the grass was covered with blood
and the trees bowed down to the earth in their sorrow.

VI. THE LAMENTATION OF THE WIDOWS

The birds began to sing their songs of sorrow.
And the princesses and wives of the boyars and *voevodas*
began to lament the deaths of their husbands.
Maria Dmitrievna, the wife of Mikula,
cried early in the dawn on the fortress wall of Moscow:
> "O river Don, my swift river,
> mountains crumble before you, and
> you flow to the land of the Kumans.
> O that you might bring me from there my lord, Mikula!"

And Fedosia, the wife of Timofey Valuevich, also lamented:
> "Joy has abandoned the glorious city of Moscow.
> Never again will I see my dear lord, Timofey Valuevich."

And Maria, the wife of Andrey,
and Xenia, the wife of Mikhail, lamented since dawn:
> "For both of us the sun has set in the glorious city of
>   Moscow.
> News of our relatives has come from the swift river Don
> and has brought great sorrow upon us.
> Russian knights have dismounted their swift steeds
> on the fateful prairie of Kulikovo."

And the Div cries under the Tatar sabers,
and there the wounded Russian knights weep.

And since dawn nightingales sing sadly
from the walls of the city of Kolomna.
But these sad songs are not sung by nightingales,
but by the wives of Kolomna who lamented:
> "O Moscow, Moscow, our swift river,
> why did you take our husbands from us to the Kuman
>   land?"

And they addressed their great prince, saying:
> "O our lord, why wouldn't you close
> the river Dnieper with your oars?
> Why wouldn't you empty the swift river Don
> with the helmets of your warriors?
> Why wouldn't you build a dam

on the river Mech from Tatar corpses?
Why wouldn't you close the gates of the river Oka,
that we might be preserved from the infidels,
for our husbands have succumbed in battle."

VII. THE DEFEAT OF THE TATARS

Prince Vladimir Andreevich, with the Prince of Volynia,
threw seventy thousand warriors from his right flank against
    the infidels.
And they rapidly struck down the infidel Tatars,
their golden helmets gleaming,
their tempered swords raining on Tatar helmets.
And Prince Dmitry praises his brother:
    "Brother, Prince Vladimir, you are our shield of iron
    in this time of evil.
    Don't let your regiments cease fighting.
    Don't give in to these evil Tatars.
    Don't pardon these traitors,[7]
    for these infidels destroy our fields
    and have killed most of our valorous army.
    O my brother, it is so sad to see
    so much Christian blood spilled!"
And then Prince Dmitry Ivanovich addressed his boyars:
    "Fellow boyars, *voevodas*, and sons of boyars,
    this is not a banquet for drinking sweet Muscovite mead.
    This is not a court in which to win higher ranks.
    This is the place to win glory for your names.
    This is the place where an old man must act as a young
        man,
    and the young man must win glory."

And it seemed that a falcon flew to the swift river Don,
but it was not a falcon that flew beyond the swift Don.
Prince Dmitry galloped with his regiments beyond this river.
And Prince Dmitry said:
    "Brother, Prince Vladimir,
    now is the time to drink of the cup.
    Let us attack the infidel army, brother,
    with our strong regiments."

And the princes advanced onto the field of battle.
Once more tempered swords rained upon Tatar helmets.
Now the infidels can protect their heads only with their arms.
The infidels begin to retreat swiftly from the princes.

---

[7] Apparently some of the Russian leaders hesitated in attacking the
Tatars.

Banners flap in the wind.
The infidels flee while Russian cries of victory cover the field.
Their gilt armor gleams.
The aurochs have taken the stronger position.

Indeed, the tide turned, and the Russian
regiments began to cut the Tatars to pieces.
And despair seized the infidels.
Princes fell from their mounts,
and Tatar corpses began to cover the field.
And blood flowed in a stream.
The infidels began fleeing on all sides.
They fled by impassable routes to the sea,
and they gnashed their teeth
and they clawed their faces in despair, saying:
 "Alas, brothers, we shall never escape to our land.
 We shall never again see our children.
 We shall never again caress our wives,
 but we must kiss the damp earth.
 We shall never again campaign against Russia.
 We shall never again receive tribute from the Russian
  princes."

And the Tatar lands began to mourn,
and sorrow and sadness covered the land.
And they lost their courage for campaigning against the
 Russian land.
Their joy disappeared.
The sons of Russia pillaged the Tatars of
cloths and silks, weapons and horses,
oxen and camels, wines and sugars,
jewelry and velvets, and they carried
the wealth of the Tatars to their wives.
Tatar gold jingled in the hands of Russian women.
Joy and happiness spread over the Russian land.
Russian glory was exalted,
while shame was brought upon the Tatars.
And the Div was enthroned, and the fear
of Russian princes spread over the earth.

O great princes of Russia,
fight the enemy with your valorous army.
Fight for the Russian land and the Christian faith,
fight against the infidel emperor, Mamai.

And the infidels threw down their weapons,
and they bowed their heads to the Russian sword.

Their trumpets stopped sounding, and their voices became
   saddened.

VIII. THE ESCAPE OF MAMAI

Like a gray wolf, the infidel emperor, Mamai,
ran away with his guards.
And he came to the city of Kafa-on-the-Sea.
And the Italians asked him:
   "Infidel Mamai, how did you dare to attack the Russian
      lands?
   Once Tatar power spread over the Russian forest land,
   but the time of Emperor Batu has long passed.
   Emperor Batu had four hundred thousand, and he
      conquered the whole Russian land,
   the whole earth, from the east to the west.
   And God punished the Russian land for its sins.
   But this time you, Emperor Mamai,
   came to the Russian land with a large army,
   with nine hordes and seventy princes,
   and yet you run away to the sea, and with only eight
      soldiers.
   And there is no one to pass the winter with you in the
      prairie.
   Did the Russian princes treat you so badly
   that there are no longer princes or commanders with you?
   Did they really become drunk with your own blood
      on the prairie of Kulikovo, on the feathergrass?
   Go away from us, infidel Mamai!
   Go from us, as you went from the Russian forest!"

IX. AFTERWORD

We love the Russian land as a mother loves her dear child.
The mother caresses her child and praises it for good deeds,
but she also punishes it for bad deeds.
In the same way, our Lord God
was merciful unto the Russian princes
who fought between the Don and the Dnieper,
unto the Great Prince Dmitry Ivanovich,
unto his brother, Vladimir Andreevich.

And so Princes Dmitry Ivanovich and Vladimir Andreevich
remained victorious on the bone-strewn prairie of Kulikovo,
on the river Nepriadva.
And Prince Dmitry Ivanovich said:
   "It is horrible, brethren, to see the earth
   covered with the corpses of Christians,

even as the field is covered with haystacks.
And it is horrible to see that the river Don
has flowed bloodred for three days."
And then Prince Dmitry Ivanovich commanded:
"Count how many *voevodas* perished,
count how many young men were killed."
And Mikhail, a boyar of Moscow replied:
"Our lord, Great Prince Dmitry Ivanovich,
we are missing forty boyars from Moscow,
twelve princes from Belozersk,
thirty *posadniks* from Novgorod,
twenty boyars from Kolomna,
forty boyars from Serpukhov,
thirty magnates from Lithuania,
twenty boyars from Pereslavl,
twenty-five boyars from Kostroma,
thirty-five boyars from Vladimir,
eight boyars from Suzdal,
forty boyars from Murom,
seventy boyars from Riazan,
thirty-four boyars from Rostov,
twenty-three boyars from Dmitrov,
sixty boyars from Mozhaisk,
thirty boyars from Zvenigorod,
and fifteen boyars from Uglich.
And altogether 253,000 Russian men were
cut down by the infidel Emperor Mamai.[8]
But God was merciful to the Russian land,
and still more Tatars fell on the battlefield."
And then Prince Dmitry Ivanovich addressed the dead:
"Fellow princes, boyars, and sons of boyars,
you have found peace everlasting here, between
the Don and the Dnieper, on the prairie of Kulikovo.
Here you gave your lives for the holy Church,
for the Russian land and for the Christian faith.
Forgive me, brethren, and give me your blessing
for this life and for the life everlasting."
And then Prince Dmitry Ivanovich addressed his brother:
"Let us go, my brother, Vladimir Andreevich,
back to the Russian land,
back to the glorious city of Moscow.
And let us rule there on our throne,
for we have won glory and veneration.
Glory be to God!"

---

[8] Actually, the Russian casualties were hardly higher than 100,000.

B. LIVES OF THE SAINT-PRINCES

39. TALE OF THE LIFE AND COURAGE OF THE PIOUS AND GREAT PRINCE ALEXANDER [NEVSKY]

THE heroic personality of Alexander, who was first Prince of Novgorod, then, after 1252, Great Prince of Vladimir and of all Russia, has inspired Russians from the thirteenth century to World War II, when the Soviet government established a military medal in his honor and bearing his name. Indeed, Alexander Nevsky managed to protect Russia's western borders in one of the most tragic periods of his nation's history—when the eastern part was overrun by the Mongols under Batu Khan. The original version of this *vita* was apparently written as a military tale by one of the warriors of his household who witnessed Alexander's last years of life. This version clearly reflects the military and feudal background of its writer, and its very title, "Tale of the Life and *Courage* of Prince Alexander," is unusual for a *vita*. Further, when the author decries the passing of his lord, his words reveal the fealty of a feudal warrior to his lord, for the author says: "A man may leave the house of his father but he cannot leave the house of his good lord; and if he has to, he should share the coffin with him." The details of the deeds of some warriors of Alexander's army also point to the origin of the author. Probably he knew many of the prince's warriors who distinguished themselves in the Battle of Nevá, such as Sbyslav, son of Yakun, and Misha, both known from the chronicles to be representatives of leading Novgorodian families.

Description of some episodes, several metaphors, and similes in this early version testify that it was patterned to some extent after a Byzantine knightly epic cycle known as "The Deeds of Digenes Akrites." [1] The original *Tale of the Life and Courage of the Pious and Great Prince Alexander* [Nevsky] was

---

[1] Digenes Akrites was the hero of a cycle describing the struggle between the Moslem Arabs and Christian Byzantines of Asia Minor in the ninth century A.D. "Akrites" means a "wandering frontier knight," and "Digenes" means "twice-born." According to legend, Digenes' father was a certain Andronikos, a Byzantine Christian; however Digenes for some time thought that his father was not Andronikos but a Moslem emir at whose court he had grown up and been educated. Hence his name, Digenes, "twice-born."

rewritten later, around 1280, by some ecclesiastic from the city of Vladimir. To the original text he added some deeds, quotations, and motifs from the Bible and, especially, from the Psalms, the First, Second, and Fourth Books of Kings, First and Second Chronicles, Isaiah, and the Apocryphal book of The Wisdom of Solomon. In most cases this second writer drastically rephrased the words of these quotations, as well as the original content, often replacing the names of heroes from antiquity and Byzantine history with those from biblical sources. This reworking is reflected clearly in the text that has reached us, for in some places it destroyed the *Tale*'s narrative and stylistic unity and resulted in an unsystematic rearrangement of the source material.

The *vita* is of special interest—being the first one about a prince, a defender of the country and of Eastern Orthodox Christianity. Early Russian *vitae* described the lives of monks or outstanding bishops and such martyrs as Boris and Gleb, who sought to imitate Christ. In the case of Alexander's *vita* the main protagonist is not necessarily a man distinguished by an exemplary Christian life but, rather, the defender of his "holy" nation against invaders of alien faiths who attacked Russia from "countries of the North, West, and East."

This translation follows a fifteenth-century text contained in the *Second Pskovian Chronicle* and published in *Pskovskie letopisi*, Volume II, Moscow, 1955, pages 11–16. The translator on some occasions used the editorial suggestions of Yu. K. Begunov, who prepared for publication another version of the same tale in *Izbornik*, Moscow-Leningrad, 1970, pages 328–342 and 739–742.

The words in brackets have been added by the translator to assist understanding.

By the will of Our Lord Jesus Christ, Son of God.

I, the unworthy and sinful servant of God, will try, despite my poor mind, to write the life of holy Prince Alexander, son of Yaroslav and grandson of Vsevolod.[2] I am glad to tell about his holy, noble, and glorious life in the same way as I have heard it from my father and other older people, as well as about the events I have seen myself, while I lived in his household and witnessed his life. For King Solomon says:

---

[2] Prince Alexander (1220–1263) was the son of Great Prince Yaroslav of Vladimir and grandson of Great Prince Vsevolod the Great Nest (1154–1212), who was instrumental in transferring the balance of power from declining Kiev in southern Russia to the city of Vladimir in the north, where a new capital of the Russian land developed.

"Wisdom cannot enter a deceitful soul.
And it will rise,
and it will watch in the middle of the roads,
and it will sit at the gates of the mighty." [3]

Although I am simple of mind, I will still start my work with a prayer to the Holy Mother of God, with the help of the holy Prince Alexander.

I. PRINCE ALEXANDER

By the will of God, Prince Alexander was born from the charitable, people-loving, and meek Great Prince Yaroslav, and his mother was Theodosia. As it was told by the prophet Isaiah: "Thus saith the Lord: I appoint the princes because they are sacred and I direct them."

It is really true, for without God's will there would not have been his rule.

He was taller than others and his voice reached the people as a trumpet, and his face was like the face of Joseph, whom the Egyptian Pharaoh placed as the next king after him in Egypt.[4] His power was a part of the power of Samson and God gave him the wisdom of Solomon and his courage was like that of the Roman King Vespasian, who conquered the entire land of Judea. Once, during the siege of the city Jeotapata, the burghers of the city made a sortie and defeated his army and Vespasian remained alone. But he still chased the enemy's army to the city gates and thereafter he jeered at his own army and reproached them, saying: "You abandoned me and left me alone." [5]

And so was this Prince Alexander: he used to defeat but was never defeated. Once, for the sake of seeing him, there came a powerful man from the Western Land, from those who call themselves "the servants of God," [6] because he wanted to see Alexander at the blossom of his life. He did so in the same way as did the Queen of Sheba, who came to Solomon to hear

---

[3] This text is a paraphrased version of the Apocryphal book, The Wisdom of Solomon, 1:4 and 6:14.

[4] A reference to the biblical story described in Genesis 41 ff.

[5] A reference to the description of the siege of the city of Jeotapata by Josephus Flavius in his *Great Roman-Jewish War*. Emperor Vespasian (A.D. 69–79) quelled the rebellion of the Jews.

[6] Servant of God: from the German "Gottesritter." The narrator speaks of Anders von Welven, the Great Master of the German Livonian Order, which at that time conquered Livonia, presently Latvia and Estonia.

his wisdom. And thus did this man,. whose name was Andreas. He saw Prince Alexander, returned to his people, and told them: "I went through many countries and saw many people, but I have never met such a king among kings, nor such a prince among princes."

II. DEFEAT OF THE SWEDES IN THE BATTLE OF NEVÁ IN 1240

The king of the Northern Country,[7] who was of the Roman faith and who had heard about the courage of Prince Alexander, pondered, thinking: "I will go and conquer Alexander's land."

And he gathered a great army and filled numerous ships with his regiments and he moved forth with great strength, being inspired by a martial spirit. He came to the river Nevá, and, carried away by his madness and filled with pride, he sent his envoys to the city, Novgorod, to Prince Alexander, saying: "If you can, resist me. I am already here conquering your land."

Upon hearing these words, Alexander's heart burned and he went to the Church of Holy Sophia, and, kneeling before the altar, he began to pray, shedding tears and saying: "Glorious and Just Lord, Great and Powerful God, God Eternal, who created heaven and earth, and who determined the boundaries of the peoples. Thou commandedst people to live without oppressing the other countries."

And remembering the song from the Psalter, he said: "O Lord, judge those who offended me. Smite those who set themselves against me and come to my aid with arms and shields."

Having finished his prayer, he got up and bowed to the archbishop and the Archbishop Spiridon blessed him and let him go. Leaving the church, he wiped his tears and began to encourage his regiments, saying: "God is in Truth, not in Power. Let us remember the psalmist who said: 'Some came with weapons and some came on horses, but we called the Lord God to our help and they were defeated and fell, but we got up and stood straight.' "

After having said this, he led his small troop against the enemy, even before the many other regiments came, because he relied upon the help of the Holy Trinity. It was a great sorrow that his honorable father, Yaroslav the Great,[8] did not know that his son, dear Alexander, was attacked; but Alexander didn't have time to send a message to his father because the enemy was nearing. Even many men from Novgorodian lands didn't have time to join him because the prince was in a hurry to start the campaign. On Sunday, July 15th—on the day when five

---

[7] The narrator gives the name of "northern land" to Sweden.
[8] See footnote 2 of this Selection.

hundred and thirty Holy Fathers who attended the Council of Chalcedon, as well as the holy martyrs, Kyrik and Julita, are remembered [9]—he moved against the enemies because he relied upon the help of the holy martyrs, Boris and Gleb.[10]

There lived in Izhora a certain notable who was the head of this land and whose name was Pelgusius,[11] and who was in charge of watching the seashore. He was baptized, but lived with his tribe, which remained pagan still; when he received Holy Baptism, he was named Philip. He lived very piously, fasting every Wednesday and Friday, and therefore, God wanted him to see on that day an awesome vision. Let us talk briefly about it:

After Pelgusius reconnoitered and determined the power of the enemy, he went to meet Prince Alexander to tell him about the enemy's camp and fortifications. Pelgusius remained on the seashore watching both roads, and therefore he did not sleep the entire night. And when the sun began to rise, he heard a loud noise from the sea and saw a moving ship, and in the midst of the ship stood the holy martyrs, Boris and Gleb, dressed in crimson vestments and embracing each other. The men rowing appeared as if in clouds.

And Boris said: "Brother Gleb, order them to row in order to help our relative, Alexander."

Pelgusius was awestruck by this vision and by these words of the martyrs, and he did not move until the ship disappeared from sight.

Soon thereafter Prince Alexander arrived. Pelgusius was full of joy when he saw Alexander and told only the prince what he had seen. And the prince said to him: "Do not tell this to anyone."

Thereafter, Alexander decided to charge the enemy at eleven o'clock in the morning [June 15th], and there was a great battle with those Roman Catholics, and he destroyed an endless number of them and with his lance even left a mark on the king's own face.[12] In this battle six men from Alexander's army dis-

---

[9] The Ecumenical Church Council of Chalcedon (A.D. 451). Sts. Kyrik and Julita are remembered on July 16.

[10] The story of Boris and Gleb, indirect forebears of Alexander Nevsky, is given in Selection 21.

[11] Pelgusius was the head of a local Finno-Ugric tribe and was converted to Christianity by the Russians.

[12] Under "Roman Catholic" the narrator meant the Swedes and Norwegians, who at that time belonged to the Roman church. The narrator gives the title "king" to Birger Jarl, regent of Sweden during the reign of the Swedish king, Eric.

tinguished themselves for their bravery because they fought courageously.

1. The first was the son of Alexis, Gabriel by name. He attacked a ship and, noticing there the royal prince [13] supported by two people, he rode onto the gangway. Everyone escaped from him back to the ship, but thereafter they turned and threw him and his horse from the gangway into the Nevá. With God's help he got out of the water uninjured, charged them again and fought courageously with the general, himself, who was surrounded by his warriors.

2. The second, a Novgorodian by name Sbyslav, son of Yakun, on several occasions charged the army and fought only with a battle-ax, no fear in his heart. And several were killed by him and the people marveled at his power and his courage.

3. The third, Jacob, a man from Polotsk,[14] was the prince's huntsman. He charged the enemy with a sword, fought courageously with them, and was praised by the prince.

4. The fourth one was a Novgorodian, by name Misha, who fought on foot with his detachment. He attacked the Latin ships and sank three of them.

5. The fifth, by name Savva, was from a junior regiment. He charged a big, golden-crowned tent and cut its pole. When the tent fell, Alexander's regiments were very much encouraged.

6. The sixth, also the prince's warrior, was called Ratmir. He likewise fought on foot and was encircled by many. He was wounded several times and died from these wounds. All this I have heard from my lord, Alexander, and from many others who participated in this massacre.[15]

There happened a miracle which reminds us of the one which took place in olden times, during the reign of King Hezekiah, when Jerusalem was attacked by Sennacherib, King of Assyria. Suddenly there appeared the angel of the Lord, who killed one hundred and eighty-five thousand Assyrian warriors, and when the next morning came their bodies were found there. The same occurred after Alexander's victory when he defeated the king: on the other shore of the river Izhora, which Alexander's regiments did not reach, there were found numerous enemy who were killed by the angel of the Lord. The remaining enemies escaped and they put the corpses of their warriors into

---

[13] Royal prince: apparently the son of Birger Jarl.

[14] Some troops from Polotsk participated in the Battle of Nevá.

[15] In this sentence the author testifies that he was a member of Prince Alexander's retinue.

ships and sank the ships in the sea, and Prince Alexander returned with victory, praising and glorifying his Creator.

III. CAMPAIGN OF 1242 AGAINST THE GERMAN LIVONIAN ORDER

The next year, after Alexander returned with victory, there
came once more the adversary from the Western Country,[16]
who built a fortress on Alexander's land. Alexander started a
campaign immediately and razed the fortress to its foundations.
Some of the enemy were hanged, some others were taken prisoner, and to some others he gave mercy, releasing them because
he was more merciful than anyone else.

The third year after his victory over the king,[17] during the
winter, Alexander campaigned with a big army in the German
country [18] in order to show them they should not brag, saying:
"Let us go and conquer the nation of the Slavs."

Indeed, they seized the city of Pskov, and appointed there
their own city officers. Alexander captured them, and liberated
the city of Pskov from the conquerors. And he destroyed the
country of the Germans and took an endless number of prisoners
and cut to pieces the others.

Thereafter several German cities [19] concluded a treaty among
themselves and decided: "Let us take Alexander. Let us take him
prisoner with our own hands." When the enemy approached
they were noticed by Alexander's scouts and Prince Alexander
put his regiments in battle formation and went to meet the
enemy. And the Chud Lake was covered with dead warriors of
both armies. [In this battle participated] the troops which his
father Yaroslav sent with Alexander's younger brother, Andrew.
In this way Prince Alexander had as many brave warriors as in
ancient times King David had mighty and strong ones. Alexander's warriors were instilled with the spirit of courage because
their hearts were the hearts of lions, and they decided: "O our
honorable Prince, it is time for us to sacrifice ourselves for our
country."

And Prince Alexander raised his arms to heaven and said:
"Judge me, my God, help me in my discord with this proud
people, and help me, my Lord, as in the ancient times thou

---

[16] Western Country: the Livonian Order of German Knights. See
footnote 6 of this Selection.

[17] This is a reference to Alexander's victory over the Swedes on the
river Nevá.

[18] German country: another designation for the Livonian Order.

[19] Most of the cities of Livonia were populated by Germans.

helped Moses to defeat the Amalekites, and as thou helpedst my forefather, Yaroslav, against the accursed Sviatopolk."

On Saturday [April 5th, 1242] when the sun rose, the two armies clashed. There was horrible bloodshed and such a noise from the breaking of lances and clanging of swords that one could think that the ice itself on the lake was breaking. And the ice itself was so covered with blood that it could not be seen. I was told [by a witness of the battle] that a godly regiment in the heavens came to help Alexander. And so the Germans were defeated with the help of God and the enemy fled and they were pursued and cut to pieces by his warriors so that one could think that these warriors were rushing through the sky. And the enemy did not know whither to escape, and God glorified Alexander here before all the regiments in the same way as Joshua, son of Nun, was glorified at Jericho. And God placed in Alexander's hands those who bragged: "Let us take Alexander with our own hands." And there was nobody to resist him in the battle.

Alexander returned home with great glory. And there were plenty of German prisoners who followed his regiments. And those who once called themselves "the knights of God" [20] were walking barefooted next to the horses of Alexander's warriors. When the prince approached the city of Pskov, the abbots and the priests in vestments and with crosses, as well as the entire population, met him before the city, praising God and glorifying their lord Alexander and singing songs:

"O Lord [once], you helped meek David to defeat the foreigners and [now] you helped our pious Prince Alexander to deliver the city of Pskov from the enemy with the help of the power of the Cross."

And then Prince Alexander said to the Pskovians:

"O ignorant people of Pskov!
If in the time of my grandchildren
you would ever forget God's [miraculous] deeds,
you would then follow the example of those Jews
who were fed by God in the desert with manna and quails
and who thereafter forgot their God,
who delivered them from the yoke of Egypt."

And since that time Alexander's name was glorified over all countries, up to the Sea of Egypt, to Mount Ararat, and on both sides of the Sea of the Vikings, and to Great Rome.

---

[20] See footnote 6 of this Selection.

IV. WARS WITH THE LITHUANIANS

At that time the people of Lithuania [21] began to expand and they started to sack Alexander's lands. But he campaigned against them, and defeated them. During one campaign he happened to defeat their seven armies, killed their numerous princes, and captured many. And his servants jeered at the enemies, attaching them to the tails of their horses, and from that time they [the Lithuanians] began to fear his name.

V. PRINCE ALEXANDER AND KHAN BATU

About the same time there was a certain powerful Khan [Batu] of the Eastern Country,[22] whom God let conquer many peoples from the Orient to the Occident; that Khan heard Alexander was very brave and courageous and he sent to him his own envoys, whom he ordered to say [to the Prince]: "Alexander, don't you know that God let me conquer many peoples? You are the only one who does not submit to my power; but if you want to preserve your land from calamity, come immediately to me to see the glory of my reign."

At that time, after the death of his father [Yaroslav], Alexander came to the city of Vladimir [23] with a large army. It was a redoubtable arrival and the news of it reached the very mouth of the Volga.[24] And the women of the Moabites [25] began to frighten their children, saying: "Alexander the Prince is coming."

But [in 1246] Prince Alexander decided to go to the Khan's

---

[21] Lithuanian and Indo-European people who lived in present-day Lithuania and the northern part of present-day Poland (Prussia) preserved tribal organization until the beginning of the thirteenth century when, under pressure from the German orders of Teutonic and Livonian Knights, they began to form a more tightly organized nation. The German knights fought them under the pretext that the Lithuanians were pagans, which they remained until the late fourteenth century.

[22] Eastern Country: the narrator's name for the Golden Horde, a part of the Mongolian empire, which extended from Vietnam and Korea to the Adriatic Sea, and which conquered Russia in the 1230s.

[23] After the death of Yaroslav, Alexander's brother, Andrew, became the Great Prince of Vladimir.

[24] The center of the Golden Horde was located at the mouth of the Volga River.

[25] Moabites: a Semitic tribe that lived in Palestine; see Genesis 19:37. Russians used this name to designate nomadic tribes, especially the Mongols.

Horde and the Metropolitan Archbishop Cyril [26] blessed him to do it. When Khan Batu saw him, he marveled at him and said to his dignitaries: "I was told the truth—that there is no other prince like Alexander."

And he rendered him due honor and let him go. Later, Khan Batu became angry with Alexander's younger brother, Andrew, and [in 1252] sent his general, Nevruy, to sack the Suzdalian land.[27] After Nevruy's invasion, Great Prince Alexander rebuilt the destroyed churches and the cities and gathered to their homes the people who had run away from the cities during the invasion.

The prophet Isaiah said about such [princes]:

"To be good for his country a prince is to be according to the
*   image of God, quiet, friendly, meek and peaceful,*
he should not seek wealth;
he should not be alien to the just life;
he should administer justice to orphans and widows;
he should like charity and not gold;
he should be good to his household
and hospitable to those who come to him from other lands.
God rewards such a prince during his life with his Grace,
for God wants to provide peace
not only to his angels but also to men,
whom he rewards generously with his Grace,
whom he teaches, and to whom he provides his Grace already
*   in this world."*

And God endowed [Alexander's] land with wealth and glory and extended his years.

VI. THE ENVOYS OF THE POPE

Once there came to him the envoys of the Pope from Great Rome [28] saying: "Our Pope spaketh the following: I have heard that thou art worthy and glorious and that thy land is great. Therefore I send to thee Golda and Gemond, two most wise out

---

[26] Metropolitan Archbishop Cyril was head of the Russian church from 1249 to 1287. He transferred his see from devastated Kiev to Vladimir.

[27] Nevruy's raid actually took place in 1252 when Batu died and Sartak ruled the Golden Horde.

[28] It could have been Pope Alexander IV (1256–1261) or Urban IV (1261–1264) who tried to involve Russia in an all-European coalition to fight the Mongols. Alexander refused to participate in it because he realized that Russia was too weak and open to Mongol retaliation.

of my twelve cardinals, to give you the opportunity of hearing their teaching about Divine Law."

But Prince Alexander, after consulting with his wise men, answered him, saying:

"From Adam to the Flood;
from the Flood to the confounding of the languages;
from the confounding of the languages to the birth of Abraham;
from Abraham to the crossing of the Red Sea by the children of Israel;
from the Exodus of the sons of Israel to the death of King David;
from the beginning of the reign of Solomon to the time of Augustus, the Emperor;
from the beginning of the time of Augustus to the birth of Christ;
from the birth of Christ to the Passion and Resurrection of the Lord;
from his Resurrection to his Ascension into heaven;
from his Ascension into heaven to the reign of Constantine;
from the beginning of the reign of Constantine to the First Council;
from the First Council to the Seventh Council,
all the happenings we know well, all of this [sacred history],
and we do not accept your teaching."

And they returned home empty-handed.

VII. THE DEATH OF PRINCE ALEXANDER

And his days lasted in great glory because Alexander loved the priests and the monks, and the poor, and because he respected the metropolitan archbishop and the bishops, and because he obeyed them as he would have obeyed Christ, himself. And there was at that time great violence from foreign peoples [of the Golden Horde]: they oppressed the Christians, forcing them to campaign in the ranks of the army; but Great Prince Alexander went to the Khan and beseeched him not to drive his [Russian] people into misery.[29]

In the meantime he sent his son, Dmitry, against the Western Land [to command the army in his absence] and with him he

---

[29] Alexander succeeded this time in convincing the Great Khan of the Golden Horde not to use Russian troops in his campaign. In later years, however, Russian armies were forced to lend a hand in the Mongol's conquest of China.

sent all his regiments and many warriors from his own household, telling them: "Serve my son as you used to serve me, not
sparing your life." And Prince Dmitry campaigned with this
large army and conquered some of the German lands and took
the city of Yuriev and returned to Novgorod with many prisoners
and great booty.

Returning from the Golden Horde, his father, Great Prince
Alexander, reached the city of Nizhny Novgorod and remained
there for several days in good health, but when he reached the
city of Gorodets he fell ill:

> *O woe to me, poor man.*
> *How am I able to describe the passing of my lord?*
> *How is it possible not to lose the eyes together with the tears?*
> *How is it possible not to have a broken heart from our sorrow?*
> *A man may leave the house of his father, but cannot abandon*
> *   the house of his good lord,*
> *and even if he has to, he should share the coffin with him.*

Great Prince Alexander, who was always firm in his faith in
God, gave up this worldly kingdom and became a monk because
it was always his greatest desire to receive these angelic orders
[before death]. God even permitted him to receive [the supreme
angelic orders of] the ascetic Schema.[30] And then he gave up his
soul to God and died in peace on November 12th [1263], on
the day when the holy Apostle, Philip, is remembered.[31]

[At his burial] Metropolitan Archbishop Cyril[32] said: "My
children, you should know that the sun of the Suzdalian land
has set. There will never be another prince like him in the
Suzdalian land."

And the priests and the deacons and the monks, the poor and
the wealthy, and all the people said: "It is our end." His holy
body was taken to the city of Vladimir. Metropolitan Archbishop
Cyril, with the entire clergy, with the princes and boyars and
the entire population, from youths to elders, met the body in the
city of Bogoliubovo with candles and censers. The people

---

[30] Schema: in Russian, "Skhima," second extremely severe vow in
the Orthodox Church that required complete repudiation of all ties to
worldly life. In the Middle Ages it was common usage among the
princes and aristocracy of Russia to take first monastic vows and the
Schema on their deathbed.

[31] Alexander died in Gorodets but his body was taken and buried
in Vladimir.

[32] Archbishop Cyril was aware of Alexander's importance in these
hard years of Russian history and supported him in his attempts to
unify Russia and come to terms with the Mongols.

crowded because everybody wanted to touch the honorable couch on which the holy body was lying. And there was crying and shedding of tears and such sighing as has never been before, so that even the earth quaked. On November 23rd, the day when Holy Father Amphilotheus is remembered, his body was laid in state in the Church of the Nativity of the Holy Mother of God in the Great Abbey.

And then there happened a wonderful miracle, which is befitting to be remembered. When the holy body was placed in the coffin, Sebastian the Cellarer and Metropolitan Archbishop Cyril wanted to open the hand [of the prince's body] to put into it the charter [with a prayer asking for the remittance of his sins]. But Alexander himself, as if he were alive, extended his hand and took the charter from the hand of the metropolitan archbishop. And they were so seized by awe that they had difficulty stepping away from the coffin. I heard this from my lord, the metropolitan archbishop, and his Cellarer, Sebastian.

Who would not marvel at this [miracle? Because Alexander] was dead and his body was brought from far away in winter.[33] So did God glorify his pious servant.

Glory be to God, who glorifies his saints, forever and ever. Amen.

40. NARRATIVE OF THE PIOUS PRINCE DOVMONT AND HIS COURAGE

The *vita* of Prince Dovmont grew to a large extent out of the *Tale of the Life and Courage of the Pious and Great Alexander* [Nevsky]. It is another story of Orthodox Russia's prince-defender against enemies of different civilizations and faiths. Many features of Dovmont's *vita* clearly indicate that its author used the original version of the *Tale of the Life and Courage of the Pious and Great Prince Alexander* [Nevsky] as a prototype for his work. The name of the Byzantine epic hero, Akrites, which disappeared from the final version of Alexander's *vita*, remains preserved here, and the characteristics of both princes are very similar. The author of Dovmont's *vita* even used the same biblical expressions to characterize his hero, and in both *vitae* the commanders of the inimical armies are wounded in the face by the lance of the holy prince.

Dovmont was a Lithuanian by birth and the prince of the Nalshenay land. He was a relative of the Great Prince of

---

[33] This final section of the *vita* was apparently added to the original version by Cellarer (Treasurer) Sebastian.

Lithuania, Mindaugas, who wanted to unify Lithuania and eliminate the feudal rulers. Dovmont participated in a conspiracy that led to the assassination of Mindaugas, but he escaped the revenge of the latter's son and went to Pskov, where he became the elected prince and defended the Pskovian land from the Lithuanians and German knights of the Order of the Sword in Livonia. The Pskovians venerated his memory and in the sixteenth century he was canonized by the Orthodox Church. Throughout the *vita* the author stresses Dovmont's merits in the defense of Orthodoxy.

The translation follows the text of the *vita* of Dovmont as it appears in the Sinod and Stroev manuscripts of the *Pskovian Chronicles*, Volume II, Moscow, 1955, pages 16–18 and 82–87. The words in brackets have been added by the translator to assist understanding.

In the year 6773 (1265) fratricidal strife began in Lithuania, and therefore the blessed Prince Dovmont,[1] together with his household, left his fatherland, the land of Lithuania, and escaped to the city of Pskov. This Prince Dovmont, a Lithuanian by birth, had been born a pagan and, according to the traditions of his fathers, used to worship idols; but God wanted to choose him to be among the newly converted and inspired the prince with the Grace of the Holy Spirit. And the Prince awakened from the sleep [of paganism], broke away from the worship of idols, and, together with his boyars, decided to receive Holy Baptism in the name of the Father, Son, and Holy Ghost. And he was baptized [in Pskov] in the Church of the Holy Trinity [2] and was christened Timothy. And there was great joy in the city of Pskov and he was chosen by the men of Pskov as the prince of their city.[3]

In the year 6774 (1266) Dovmont decided to campaign with three troops of ninety men each from Pskov. He invaded the Lithuanian lands and raided his [own former] principality. He

---

[1] The assassination of the Lithuanian ruler, Mindaugas, in 1263 led to the distintegration of state unity (see footnote 21, Selection 39, *Tale of the Life and Courage of the Pious and Great Prince Alexander*) and to war among the tribal princes.

[2] The Cathedral of Pskov was dedicated to the Holy Trinity, considered the protector of the city.

[3] Pskovians used to elect their princes. Dovmont was elected Prince of Pskov not in 1265, but in 1266. (The discrepancy in the dating of the event reflects a different beginning of the year in Russian medieval chronology.) After his baptism and election Dovmont married the granddaughter of Alexander Nevsky.

captured the Princess Gerden and her children, raided [her] principality, and turned back toward the city of Pskov with numerous captives. He forded the river Dvina, advanced another three miles and put up a hundred tents in a forest clearing. He left David, son of Jakun, grandson of Zhavr, with the Lithuanian [commander] Luva to guard the river Dvina. Sending away two troops of ninety men with the captives, he himself remained with the other ninety waiting for the pursuers.

Prince Gerden and his [vassal] princes were not in their land [during Dovmont's raid] and when they returned home they found that their principality had been raided. [Thereafter, Prince] Gerden, as well as Goitord, Lunila, and Yugailo, with seven hundred warriors, prepared themselves for war and undertook to pursue Dovmont. Gerden wanted personally to capture and cruelly execute Dovmont, and to cut the men of Pskov to pieces with broadswords. When they forded the river and stood on shore in formation [Dovmont's] sentries saw this big army and sent [men] to tell Dovmont: "The [Lithuanian] army has crossed the river."

And Dovmont said to David and Luva: "God and the Holy Trinity will help you for having seen them. You may go home!"

But David and Luva answered: "We will not retreat. We want to end our lives in glory together with the men of Pskov and spill our blood for the glory of the Holy Trinity and the Holy Church. Our lord prince, charge these pagan Lithuanians swiftly with your Pskovians."

And thereafter Dovmont said to the Pskovians: "Brethren, men of Pskov, I deem the older of you to be my fathers and the younger my brothers. In many lands I have heard of your courage. Now we have before us [the choice between] life and death. Let us fight, we men of Pskov, for the Holy Trinity, the Holy Church, the land of our fathers."

It was the day when great and glorious Leontius,[4] martyr for Christ, was remembered [and therefore] Prince Timothy [Dovmont] spake: "The Holy Trinity and the holy and great Leontius and the blessed Prince Vsevolod![5] Help us in this hour against

---

[4] It was the tradition in medieval Christianity to remember an event not by the date of the month but by the commemoration of a saint or a holiday in the church calendar.

[5] Prince Vsevolod Gabrial ruled Pskov from 1137 to 1138 and was the defender of Pskovian freedom against encroachment by the Novgorodian Republic, for which Pskovians venerated his memory as a local saint. The holy martyrs Leontius, Hepatius, Theodulus, and Aitherius are remembered on June 18th.

this evil adversary." And Prince Dovmont, together with the men of Pskov, rode [against the enemy] and, thanks to the help of Divine Power and the holy martyr Leontius, defeated seven hundred men, having only his own ninety [warriors]. In this battle there were killed the Lithuanian Great Prince Potort and many other princes; and many Lithuanians drowned in the river Dvina and some seventy of them floated on the Dvina to the Goidov Island and some floated to the other islands and many others floated down the river.

[Among the Russians] there was killed only one Pskovian man [a certain] Anthony, son of Lochek, brother of Smoliga, while all others remained safe, thanks to the prayer of St. Leontius, martyr for Christ, and all of them returned to Pskov with great joy and with rich booty. And there was great joy and gladness in Pskov because the Holy Trinity, the glorious Leontius, great martyr for Christ, and the blessed Prince Vsevolod, interceded with their prayers for the defeat of the adversary.

After [this victory] the blessed Prince Dovmont asked Great Prince Dmitry Alexandrovich to give in marriage his daughter Maria.

[In the next year] 6675 (1267) Prince Dovmont and his Pskovian men, with Novgorodian troops, went to aid his father-in-law, Great Prince Dmitry, and Prince Yaroslav to campaign against the Germans and they fought them in an open field at Rokover. And thanks to the intercession of Holy Sophia, the Wisdom of God,[6] they defeated the German regiment on Saturday before Lent, on February 18th. And he crossed the impassable mountains and attacked the Viruyans,[7] crossed their entire land, campaigned in the Land at Seashore, and returned home with a multitude of captives. And glory spread over the lands, and in all countries people feared the dread courage of Great Prince Dmitry, and his son-in-law Dovmont, and their warriors from Novgorod and Pskov.

In the year 6779 (1271). Some days later these godless Latins secretly [again] gathered their remaining forces, overran several [Russian] villages of the Pskovian lands, and retreated rapidly. Blessed Dovmont, however, could not stand this offense by the godless Germans. And with sixty Pskovian men in five boats, he started in pursuit of them. And thanks to the help of God, he defeated these eight hundred Germans on the river Miropovna.

---

[6] Here is meant Holy Sophia (Wisdom of God), to whom the Cathedral of Novgorod was dedicated and who was considered the protectoress of the city.

[7] Here apparently is meant an unidentified Lithuanian tribe.

And only two boats with Germans escaped to the island on the river. The blessed Prince Dovmont followed them to the island, set fire to the grass of the island, and some of these Germans ran away with burning hair, some of them were cut to pieces, and others were drowned in the water. And this happened, thanks to the intercession of the Holy Trinity, of the glorious and great warrior St. George, and the prayers of the blessed Prince Vsevolod. It happened on April 23rd, the day when the great and glorious martyr for Christ [8] is remembered. And they returned with great joy to the city of Pskov, and everyone was happy and gay in the city because the Holy Trinity and the holy warrior, great Christian martyr George, interceded for them.

In the year 6780 (1272). When the Great Master of Riga [in the Livonian Order] [9] heard about Dovmont's bravery, he assembled a large army and, without any blessing of God, he approached the Pskovians with ships, boats, cavalry, and catapults, intending to take the house of the Holy Trinity, capture Prince Dovmont, cut many Pskovian men to pieces with broadswords, and take others into captivity. Then, hearing that this big army of men had thoughtlessly begun fighting without the blessing of God, Prince Dovmont went to the Church of the Holy Trinity, placed his broadsword before the divine altar, fell on his knees, prayed, shed tears, and said: "O Lord God Almighty, we men are like the lambs of thy pastures; we invoke thy name—be merciful to the meek, save the humble, defeat the proud, and do not let your lambs abandon their pasture."

Thereafter Abbot Isidor and the entire clergy girded the prince with his broadsword, gave a blessing and let him go [to fight]. Dovmont, with great anger and bravery, did not even wait for the arrival of the regiments from Pskov but moved [against the Germans] with a small army of Pskovian men. He defeated them with the help of God, annihilated their regiments, and wounded the Great Master in the face. The Germans loaded the corpses of their warriors onto the boats to take them to their land, while the remaining force of them hastily retreated. This happened on the 8th day of the month of June, when the removal of the relics of Theodore the Stratilat is remembered. [10]

---

[8] On April 23rd, St. George, traditional patron of Christian warriors, is remembered.

[9] Here is certainly meant the Grand Master of the German and Livonian Order. See footnote 6 of Selection 39.

[10] St. Theodore the Stratilat (the General) is remembered in the Eastern Church on June 8th.

Soon after, still during his reign, the godless Latins once again came with forces to conquer the Pskovian land and take captives. Blessed Prince Dovmont could not stand this offense, moved against them with Pskovian men, campaigned in their land, and burned many fortresses. A short time later, in the month of September, there was an eclipse of the moon.

That same winter, on the first day of March of the year 6807 (1299) on the day when the holy martyrs Paul and Juliana are remembered, a strong force of Germans attacked a suburb of Pskov and killed many clerics. At that attack Basil, the Abbot of the Monastery of the Holy Savior, Joseph the Presbyter, Josaphat, Abbot of the Monastery of the Holy Virgin on the Sniatna Mountain,[11] and seventeen monks, calugers, nuns, many poor women, and little children were killed. But the men were saved by God. The next day the evil Germans surrounded the city of Pskov in order to capture it. Blessed Prince Dovmont did not wait for the arrival of the large army, and with his personal guard of Pskovian men and the troops of Ivan, son of Dorogomil, moved against the Germans. Invoking the help of the Holy Trinity, holy Peter, and holy Paul, he attacked them on the shore. There was a horrible battle as had never been before in the Pskovian land. The [German] commander,[12] himself, was wounded in the head and many of their officers were captured and sent to Great Prince Andrey. The other ones dropped their weapons and ran quickly away, fearing the bravery of Dovmont and his Pskovian men.

In that year there was an evil plague which killed the people. This Prince Dovmont was distinguished not only by his bravery given by God, but also by his love for God.

He was righteous with the people;
he adorned the churches;
he loved the clergy and the poor;
he spent holy days piously;
he helped priests and monks;
he gave alms to orphans and widows;
and as the prophet Isaiah spake:
"The ruler who is good to his country is righteous,
God-loving,
loves pilgrims,
is humble and meek
because he is created according to the image of God,

---

[11] The monastery of the Virgin on Sniatna Mountain was an important religious center in the vicinity of Pskov.

[12] Apparently a commander of the Livonian Knights.

for in this world the Lord loves not only his angels,
but generously shows his generosity
and his Grace to the world."

Thus the names of our princes became famous over all lands
and the armies of adversaries feared their names and they were
princes of princes and commanders of commanders. And their
regiments listened with awe to their voices, which sounded like
trumpets, and they always defeated and were never defeated.
And they defeated the armies [of the enemies] by their bravery
alone, as Akrites used to defeat [his enemies]. And so Great
Prince Alexander [13] and his son, Prince Dmitry, and their boyars and Novgorodians and their son-in-law, Dovmont, with his
men of Pskov, defeated the evil nations of Germany, Lithuania,
Chud,[14] and Korelia.[15]

Because of Hezekiah alone, Jerusalem was saved from capture
by the Assyrian King Sennacherib. For the same reason because
of Great Prince Alexander, his son, Dmitry, and his son-in-law,
Dovmont, the cities of Novgorod and Pskov were saved from
the attack of evil Germans.

After some time the blessed Prince Timothy's health became
shaken, he fell ill and from this illness he passed away into the
eternal life to appear before God. This happened on May 20th
when the memory of holy martyr Philoleus is remembered. And
he was buried by the whole clergy and by abbots and monks
and a great multitude of people shed tears and his body was
placed in the Church of the Holy Trinity, while hymns, songs,
and holy chanting were intoned. And there was a great sorrow
among the men, women, and children of Pskov. They regretted
their good master, blessed Prince Timothy, who for the sake
of the house of the Holy Trinity suffered on many days and
who fought together with the men of Pskov for the defense of
the Holy Trinity's house.

---

[13] Here in the *vita* is meant Prince Alexander Nevsky, who by this
time had died but was venerated as a protector of Russia and of
Orthodoxy. As mentioned above, Dovmont was his grandson-in-law.

[14] Chud: a Finno-Ugric tribe in the region of Novgorod.

[15] Korelia: Finno-Ugric territory north of the Nevá River.

C. HOMILETIC WORKS

41. SERAPION OF VLADIMIR: SERMON ON THE MERCILESS HEATHENS

SERAPION of Vladimir is one of the outstanding Russian writers of the first century under the Tatar Yoke. Probably of southern origin, Serapion was abbot of the Kievan Crypt Monastery at the time of the Tatar invasion, and later became Bishop of Vladimir, the capital city of the Vladimir-Suzdal principality. After the invasion, Vladimir became a new nucleus for Russian national life and culture. Bishop Serapion died in 1275.

The eloquent homilies of Serapion are distinguished by their highly rhetorical style, and are composed principally of short, rhythmic sentences. Very often these sentences are rhymed and show repetition of an initial word or syllable through several lines. These characteristics tend to convey a sense of poetic unity.

The first sermon is entitled *Sermon on the Merciless Heathens*. This term refers not only to the Tatars but also to those Christians who do not follow the commandments of God and are not charitable to their fellowmen. In the second sermon, *Sermon on Omens*, Serapion speaks of God's wrath, which has manifested itself in earthquakes, conflagrations, and the Tatars' invasion of the Russian land.

The old Russian texts used as the basis for this translation can be found in *Serapion Vladimirskii, russkii propovednik XII veka* by E. V. Petukhov, St. Petersburg, 1888.

Let us contemplate, brethren, Our Lord's love for men.
How does he try to bring us to himself?
What commandments does he place upon us?
What words does he chastise us with?
Yet, in spite of this, we do not turn to him.

He has seen our trespasses multiply.
He has seen us forsake his commandments.
Many admonitions have we heard from him.
Many fears has he inspired in us.
Many of his servants has he enlightened,
yet what man has become the better for all this?

Then he released upon us the merciless heathens,
violent heathens, people having mercy neither
for the young,

for the weak and aged,
nor for infants.
The wrath of the Lord has descended upon us
even as David said: "He cast upon them the fierceness of his
    anger."

The sacred churches were destroyed.
The sacred vessels were defiled.
The saints were trodden upon.
The prelates were victims of the sword.
The bodies of holy monks became food for birds.
The blood of our priests and brothers,
as if it were water, soaked into the earth.
The strength of our princes and *voevodas* has disappeared.
Our valiant warriors, seized with great fear, have fled.
Many of our brothers and our children
have been led into captivity.
Weeds overgrow our villages.
Our pride has been humbled.
Our serenity has vanished.
Our wealth was taken from us by the heathens,
inheriting the fruits of our labors.
Our land has become the property of foreigners.
Our land taken from us,
we became the objects of the jibes
of those who live beyond our lands.

Then we realized that
God's wrath is like a torrent from heaven.
Yet we brought his anger upon ourselves.
His favor abandoned us,
and we became deprived of his merciful vigilance.
And now there is no misfortune which will pass us by.
And now we are punished without surcease.
Yet we do not turn to God.
We do not rue our trespasses.
We do not forsake our malevolent ways.
We do not cleanse ourselves of sin,
forgetting the awesome castigation meted out upon our land.
Being reduced to paucity, we act grandiosely.
And therefore evil forces will not cease to torment us.
Envy has increased and wickedness has overcome us.
Pride has turned our heads.
Hatred for friends has taken root in our hearts.
Avarice for possessions has enslaved us
and does not permit us to have mercy upon orphans,

nor does it permit us to be human beings.
We are predatory beasts desiring flesh to appease their hunger.
Nothing would prevent us from seizing the possessions of
    others,
even if it came to killing.
But even the beasts are satiated, after having eaten,
but we cannot appease our greed,
for, when we have gained one thing,
we desire only another.

For wealth rightly come by, God will not be angered,
but as the prophet said:
    "The Lord looked down from heaven
    to see if they were any that did
    understand and seek God."
And he saw that they had all gone astray.
    "Have they no knowledge,
    these evildoers who eat up my people
    as if they eat bread?"

And Apostle Paul unendingly admonished:
    "Brothers, refrain from evil and dark deeds,
    for usurer-robbers will be judged with the idolaters."
And what did God say to Moses?
    "You shall not afflict any widow or orphan.
    If you do afflict them, and they cry out to me,
    I will surely hear their cry;
    and my wrath will burn,
    and I will kill you with the sword."

And now that prophecy has been fulfilled,
for didn't we perish by the sword
and not once, but twice?
What can we do to end the evils which oppress us?
Remember the words of the Holy Scriptures:
to love each other,
to be charitable to all men,
to love thy neighbor as thyself,
to keep the body pure
so that it will not be defiled by lechery;
to cleanse the body with penitence,
if it has been defiled,
to be free of haughtiness,
to render good for evil.

No one does the Lord hate more than the rancorous,
for they will say: "Our Father, forgive us our trespasses,"

yet they themselves will not forgive others.
It is clearly written: "And with what measure you mete,
so shall it be measured to you again."

42. SERAPION OF VLADIMIR: SERMON ON OMENS

The blessing of the Lord be with you!
Brethren, you have heard what the
Lord himself said in the Gospel:
>   "And there shall be signs in the sun,
>   and in the moon, and in the stars,
>   and there will be earthquakes in many places,
>   and famines."

This prophecy of Our Lord
has now been fulfilled in our days.
Many times have we seen the sun extinguished,
the moon darkened,
and the stars disquieted.
And recently with our own eyes
have we seen the quaking of the earth.[1]
Now the earth, firm and immovable from time immemorial
by the will of God,
is today moved, quaking because of our sins,
unable to withstand our evil ways.

We have obeyed neither the Gospel
nor the Apostles,
nor the prophets,
nor those enlightened in God's ways:
Basil and Gregory the theologians,
John Chrysostom,
and the other blessed Fathers
by whom the Faith was upheld,
the heretics were driven out,
and God made known to all the lands.
They have taught us without surcease,
but we are living in evil ways.

For this does God punish us,
bringing upon us calamities and earthquakes.
He no longer chastises us with words,
but punishes us with afflictions.

---

[1] According to the chronicles, an earthquake occurred in 1230, just six years before the Tatar invasion of Russia.

God has castigated us in all ways,
yet he has not dispelled our evil ways.
Now he shakes the earth and makes it quake,
wishing to shake, like leaves from a tree,
our evil ways from the earth.
If any should declare that there have been earthquakes be-
     fore,
I should not deny it.
But what has happened to us after the earthquakes?
Were there not famines, plagues, and numerous wars?
But we did not repent.
Thus, by the will of God,
there fell upon us a merciless people
who devastated our land,
took entire cities off to captivity,
destroyed our holy churches,
put our fathers and brothers to death,
and defiled our mothers and sisters.
Now, brethren, that we have experienced such calamities,
let us pray to the Lord, and repent,
lest we incur the wrath of God even more,
and thus bring upon us an even greater castigation.

Much is still wanting in our repentance and contrition.
If we turn from dissolute and merciless judgments,
if we turn from bloody usury,
and from greed, thieving, blasphemy, lies,
slander, malediction, denunciations, and other diabolical ways;
if we turn away from all these,
I know full well that good times will come to us,
both in this life and the next.
For the Lord himself has said:
     "Turn unto me, and I will turn to you.
        Refrain from all evil things,
        and I will keep all afflictions from you."
When will we turn from sins?
Let us spare ourselves and our children.
When have we seen so many deaths?
Many were taken away before they could care for their houses.
Many lay down to sleep in the evening,
never to rise again.
Be fearful of such a sudden death, brethren.
If we follow the ways of God,
he will comfort us with his solace,
he will cherish us as his own children,

he will remove the burden of our earthly grief,
he will give us peace in the next life,
where we shall know elation and unending joy
with those who do the will of God.

I have told you many things, brethren and children,
but I perceive that our afflictions will neither lessen
nor change, for many take no heed,
acting as if they deemed themselves immortal.
I am afraid that the prophecy of the Lord
will come to pass for such people.
If I had not told them of God's ways,
they would not have sinned in their ignorance,
but I have told them, and now
there can be no pardoning of their sins.
And so I repeat again to you
that if we do not change our ways,
we shall have no pardoning before God.

I, your sinful pastor,
have followed the command of the Lord
in giving his word to you.

D. EPISTOLARY WORKS

43. THE WRITING OF DANIIL THE PRISONER

The Writing of Daniil the Prisoner remains, together with the *Lay of Igor's Campaign* and the *Orison on the Downfall of Russia*, an enigmatic literary monument. It was extremely popular from the thirteenth to seventeenth centuries and there remain an astonishingly large number of manuscript copies, most of which differ from each other. Usually these manuscripts are classified into two groups. The first, called *slovo (orison)*, which is given here, is thought to have been written in the late twelfth century and to have been addressed to Prince Yaroslav Vladimirovich, who reigned in Novgorod in 1182, 1187–1196, and 1197–1199 (he was thrice invited by the Novgorodians and thrice "asked" to stop ruling them). The second group, usually called *poslanie* or *molenie (epistle* or *petition)*, was probably addressed to Prince Yaroslav Vsevolodovich, 1213–1236, of the northern city of Pereiaslavl. All preserved manuscripts were written much later, however—in the sixteenth and seventeenth centuries—and therefore their exact dates and determination of earlier versions still remain the object of scholarly speculation. No more than this work is known about Daniil himself, whom some investigators believe to have been a noble member of the prince's court; others, on the contrary, consider him to have been a commoner.

The work seems to be an address or petition in which the exiled or imprisoned Daniil asked the prince for help. It is heavily saturated with aphorisms, biblical and other quotations, sayings and proverbs, and it may be, consequently, just a collection of such quotations and sayings to which a skillful compiler has given the form of a personal address. It consists of three different elements: first, rhetorical, biblical quotations primarily from the book of Psalms and the book of The Wisdom of Solomon, with some citations from *The Bee*, itself a collection of aphorisms of Greek and Latin writers. Then, rhymed folk witticisms and satirical remarks are incorporated; and, finally, some information on the life of Daniil himself is included. The subject matter is extremely varied. The author speaks about his own wisdom and importance, flatters the prince, and pronounces moralistic commentaries on the epoch; in some versions sharp, satirical attacks on wealthy and powerful people, mean wives, and immoral monks can be found. The author skillfully inter-

weaves various stylistic elements: the lines and stanzas are
rhythmically organized, abounding in the original in assonance
and alliteration; and beginning with the second stanza comes the
anaphoric address, "O my prince, my lord."

The present translation is based on the text published by M.
N. Tikhomirov in *Trudy otdela drevnerusskoi literatury*, Volume
X, Moscow-Leningrad, 1954, pages 280–289. M. Tikhomirov
writes that the manuscript discovered by him very probably
reproduces the earliest and least developed of Daniil's writing,
and it seems to the editor that this thesis is most probable. Since
this version differs considerably from the better known *slovo*
and *molenie* texts, Tikhomirov suggested it be called merely
"writing," as the original author, himself, called it in the very
beginning of the work. The editor has arranged this text into
shorter lines that correspond to the rhythmic units of the Russian
text of the "writing." Some defective portions have been corrected on the basis of other manuscripts, and the last section,
placed in brackets, was taken from another text published by
N. N. Zarubin in *Pamiatniki drevnerusskoi literatury*, Volume
III, Leningrad, 1932. The identified quotations from the Bible
are italicized.

FROM THE BOOK CALLED THE BEE;

THE VERY IMPORTANT WRITING OF DANIIL THE "PRISONER";

To his great Prince Yaroslav Vladimirovich.

Let us announce the strength of our mind with the same power
as if we were blaring into golden-forged trumpets;
let us announce as silver cymbals;
let us sing our wisdom.
O God, my God, why hast thou forsaken me.
Awake my glory,
awake my psaltery and harp.
I will awake early.
I will confess.
I will open my mouth in parables and
I will proclaim my power;
for the heart of a wise man gets stronger in the body
through his wisdom.
My tongue is like the pen of a ready writer.
My friendly lips are as a streaming river.
Therefore I was compelled to write about the fetters of my
    soul,
with the same bitterness as the ancients that

dashed the little ones against the rock.
I am afraid, prince, that thou praisest me:
For I am as the unfruitful fig tree,
I have not the fruit of penitence,
for my heart is as a face without eyes,
and my mind as a black raven keeping vigil on the ruins.
I have wasted my life as the honorless Canaanite kings,
and destitution has covered me
as the proud pharaoh was covered by the Red Sea.
All of this I have written,
having been rescued from the face of my poverty
as Hagar from her mistress Sarah;
but having seen, O Lord, thy loving-kindness toward me
I have resorted to thy constant love.
For the Scriptures saith:
Give to him that asketh, open to him that knocketh,
in order not to be deprived of heaven.
For it is written:
Trust thy sorrow in the Lord and this will sustain you.

O my prince, my lord,
for I am as the weed which is growing in the shade of the
    wall
on which neither sun shines nor rain comes,
for I am offended by everyone,
because I am not protected by the fear of thy wrath,
as it were, by a sturdy bulwark.
Look not on me, O lord, as the wolf at the lamb,
but look on me as the mother at her child.
For, O lord, some are loved by God, but I am abandoned by
    him to cruel sorrow.
My friends and kinsfolk, these have renounced me,
for I did not set before them a banquet or many-varied viands.
For many are friends with me in fame,
however, only enemies are found in unhappiness:
With their eyes they weep for me,
but with their hearts laugh at me.
Therefore trust not in a friend, and rely not on a brother.
So said Solomon:
Give me, O Lord, neither riches nor poverty,
for if I am rich I will be puffed up with pride,
if I am poor I will conceive thieving and robbing.
Therefore, I appeal to thee,
O my prince, my lord,
I, who am possessed by poverty,
have mercy upon me, O son of Great Prince Vladimir.

I will not begin crying, sobbing like Adam for Paradise.
For, O lord, a rich man is known, and he has friends even in
    foreign cities.
But a poor man is hated even in his own city.
When a rich man speaks, everyone keeps silent,
and they extol what he says to the clouds;
but when a poor man speaks, everyone laughs at him.
For whose vestment is rich, his speech is honored.

O my prince, my lord,
deliver me from this destitution
as a bird from the snare, as a sheep from the wolf.

O my prince, my lord,
for I am as a tree along the road;
many chop it up and throw it into the fire:
So I am hurt by everyone,
for I am not protected by thy dread wrath.
As pewter disappears when it melts in a fire:
So does man when he lives in great poverty.
As no one can eat much salt,
so no one can stand much grief.
Gold is tested by fire, and a man is tested by grief.
Well-ground wheat gives fine bread.
A man tested by sorrow finds sober thoughts.
As a moth eats clothes, so does sorrow the man.
If someone helps a man in grief,
it is as if he offers him a cold drink for relief.
A bird makes happy the spring,
and a mother is made happy by her offspring.
Spring adorns the land with flowers,
and thou revivest the people with thy kindness.

O my prince, my lord,
show me thine image, for thy voice is sweet,
and thine image beautiful, thy lips shed sweetness.
But when thou art made happy by many viands,
remember thou me, with the dry bread of life.
Or when thou drinkest a sweet drink,
remember thou me, drinking warm water.
When thou liest on a soft bed under sable quilts,
remember thou me, O lord, lying under only one shawl,
dying from the cold and the raindrops, like arrows, piercing
    my heart.

O my prince, my lord,
be thy hand extended to the poor:

Just as the sea cannot be emptied by a cup,
so thy house will not be emptied by our supplications.
As the net holds not water in it but only fish,
so thou, O lord, should hoard neither gold nor silver,
but give it unto the people.
As velvet is admired for being embroidered with silk,
so thou, O prince, art admired by your many people.
They that trust in the Lord shall be as Mount Zion
which cannot be moved but abideth forever.
Often from confusion regiments perish,
and so many good regiments when without a good prince:
The psalteries are tuned with fingers, and the body strength-
    ened by sinews,
and an oak made strong by a multitude of roots,
and thus our city is made strong by thy rule.
A generous prince is a father to his servants
and many come to him abandoning their fathers and mothers.
Serving a good lord a man rises to freedom,
but serving an evil lord a man rises to more slavery.
A generous prince is as a river which flows through oak
    groves,
quenching the thirst of the people and cattle.
But a miserly prince is as a river bounded by shores of stone,
and no man can drink from it or water a horse at it.

O my prince, my lord,
do not take the bread from the wise poor man
or raise to the clouds a stupid rich man;
for a poor man is as gold in a vessel;
but a handsome, stupid, rich man is as a silken pillowcase
    stuffed with straw.

O my prince, my lord,
look not at my outward appearance but look at my inward
    appearance,
for I am dressed poorly, but I am plentiful with reason.
In growth I am but a youth, but old thoughts are in me,
and with these thoughts I have soared as an eagle in the air.
If thou sendest a wise man thou wilt have to explain little to
    him,
but if thou sendest a stupid man the same wilt thou have to
    follow after.
It is better to hear the rebukes of a wise man
than the instructions of a fool.
Give instruction to a wise man and he will become yet more
    wise.

There is no wheat on the edges of the field,
neither is there wiseness in the heart of a fool.
A girl ruins her purity with fornicating
and a man his manliness with thieving.

O my prince, my lord,
it is not the sea that sinks ships, but winds;
it is not the fire that makes red hot the iron, but the blowing
　　bellows:
And so a prince falls not into much evil by himself,
but because his advisors introduce him to it.
With good advisors advising the prince will attain a high
　　place,
but with fools advising he will attain a low place.
I myself, O lord, my prince,
have neither sailed the sea nor studied from philosophers.
But I am as the bee landing on beautiful flowers
and collecting honey in combs.
For I collect through books the delights of their words and
　　thoughts,
and I have collected them as seawater in a leather bottle.
I will not begin to talk much
for I will not be as the leather bottle
with holes spreading wealth to the poor.
But neither will I be like a millstone, for they satiate many
　　people,
but by themselves they cannot satiate.
Neither do I want to be hated by the world for my verbose
　　talk:
When a bird often sings they soon begin to hate it.

[You may say, O prince:
　　"Marry the daughter of a wealthy father-in-law,
　　then you can wine and then you can dine."
But it is better to get a fever:
　　Since from fever you can still recover,
　　but an evil wife will destroy you unto death.
For so it is said in folk parables:
　　An owl is not a bird among birds;
　　nor a hedgehog an animal among animals;
　　nor a crayfish a fish among fish;
　　nor a nanny goat a cow among cattle;
　　nor is a serf who works for serfs a good serf;
　　nor is a husband who obeys his wife a man among men.
　　It is the worst vice among vices to marry a mean woman
　　because of her dowry or the father-in-law's fortune.

And I prefer to see an ox in my house
than an evil-minded wife.
Even if one's wife has much gold
one may say: "It is hard to get this gold."
I would rather try to boil iron
than to live with a mean wife.
A mean wife is worse than an itch,
for your body would hurt and itch,
Would I see an old and mean-looking wife,
cross-eyed, like a devil
bigmouthed, big-toothed, and mean-tongued,
but looking steadily into the mirror,
I would tell her: "Don't look into the mirror,
but cure your mange."
An evil-looking wife should not stick to the mirror
because seeing her ugliness in the mirror on the shelf,
she will get disgusted with herself.

You may say, O prince: "You may become a monk."
But I have never seen a corpse riding a hog
nor a devil riding a woman.
Nor could I find a fig growing on an oak
nor velour in place of linden leaves.
I would prefer an end to my life
than to accept angelic orders and tell God a lie.
The lie is good for worldly life
but not for salvation.
One cannot lie to God
or betray our Creator.
Many people leave the world for the monastery,
but still return to lay life.
Just as the dog returns to the house of the master
and the beatings of the master.
Where there are banquets and dining,
there are monks, nuns, and wining.
There are people who have religious orders
but they often live in moral disorder.
And there are bishops who have high ranks
but they have the mean morals of cranks.]

O Lord, give our prince the power of Samson,
the bravery of Alexander,
the reason of Joseph,
the wisdom of Solomon,
now and forever.

the era of muscovite ornamental formalism

(Fifteenth to the Beginning of the Seventeenth Century)

A. LIVES OF SAINTS AND BIOGRAPHICAL TALES

44. EPIPHANIUS THE WISE: PANEGYRIC TO ST. STEPHEN OF PERM

THE names of Epiphanius the Wise, St. Stephen of Perm, St. Sergius of Radonezh, and the great painter Andrey Rublev signify the Russian spiritual and cultural revival of the late fourteenth and early fifteenth centuries. St. Sergius, and to some extent St. Stephen, gave a new impetus to Russian monasticism. St. Sergius became the holy patron of Muscovite Russia. His spirit of humility, his contemplation, and unending prayers inspired and comforted the Russian people of the late Middle Ages. The wonderful icons and frescoes of Andrey Rublev offered a harmonious and colorful expression of the spirit of complete serenity and humility. For the Russian people these icons became the finest achievement of religious art and the highest expression of Russian spirituality. A contemporary of Andrey Rublev, Epiphanius the Wise, described the lives of St. Sergius and St. Stephen. In these works he made wide use of new literary devices, and perfected a completely new style of writing. Thus a new page in Russian literary history appeared.

Epiphanius gives a consistent, detailed, and well-organized account of the lives of these two saints. His main purpose in writing these biographical works was not to give an account of the life and deeds of each saint, but to portray an ideal type of sanctity. He endowed the heroes of his *vitae* with a number of general traits that he describes in lengthy panegyrics, containing a great number of epithets. The literary style that Epiphanius the Wise perfected was termed "weaving of words" (*pletenie sloves*, in Russian). In this style sentences are nearly deprived of verbs, consisting almost entirely of the adjectives and nouns that characterize the deeds and humility of the saints. Another feature of Epiphanius' "word-weaving" is the abundance of neologisms formed by nouns or combinations of nouns and adjectives, such as "songbeautifier," rather than "beautifier of songs."

Particularly representative of this style is the *Panegyric to St. Stephen of Perm*. Stephen of Perm was a well-known fourteenth-century missionary who converted the Finnic tribe of Permians to Christianity. He also created a Permian alphabet, thus becoming the founder of the Permian written tradition. The text of the present translation is based on the Russian text of the

Life of St. Stephen of Perm published by V. G. Druzhinin in
*Zhitie sv. Stefana episkopa Permskago, napisannoe Epifaniem
Premudrym,* St. Petersburg, 1897.

The life of St. Sergius, which likewise abounds in epithets
and lengthy panegyrics, was reworked in the fifteenth century
by Pachomius the Serb. The present translation is taken from
the work *St. Sergius, Builder of Russia* by Nicholas Zernov. Zernov's text is based upon the *Vita of St. Sergius* published by
Archimandrite Leonid, Volume 58, St. Petersburg, 1885, P.D.P.I.
In view of the length of the text, Zernov eliminated the panegyrical passages and abbreviated some of the text's stylistic
ornamentation. The narrative part of the *vita* did not, however,
undergo any changes, and the overall continuity and spirit of the
work remain.

My father, lord, and bishop, although you have passed away,
I should like to sing your praises with my heart, with my
tongue, and with my mind. When you were alive, I often was
your annoyance, but now I am your panegyrist; and sometimes
I would argue with you about happenings and works, about
some verses or some lines, but now, remembering your enduring
patience, your great reasoning, and your blessed humility, I
humble myself; I cry, shedding tears.

And now, how shall I call you, my bishop?
    How shall I name you?
    How shall I appeal to you?
    How shall I announce you?
    How shall I regard you?
    How shall I proclaim you?
    How shall I praise you?
    How shall I esteem you?
    How shall I gratify you?
    How shall I present you?
    How shall I weave lauds to you?

Shall I call you a prophet,
since you prophesied prophetic prophecies,
and, like a prophet, explained the hopes of the prophets,
and among the people, faithless and unlearned,
you were a prophet?

Shall I call you an Apostle,
since you performed apostolic deeds
and, acting like an Apostle, following the examples of
    Apostles,
acted, following in the steps of the Apostles?

Shall I call you a lawgiver or a lawmaker,
since you gave the law to the lawless,
brought faith to the lawless,
and established the law among them?

Shall I call you the Baptist,
since you baptized many
who came to you to be baptized?

Shall I call you a preacher, since,
like a herald who announces in the town square,
you loudly preached the word of God to the heathens?

Shall I call you an evangelist,
since you proclaimed Grace to them
and the Holy Evangel of Christ,
and performed many deeds of the annunciator of Grace?

Shall I call you bishop,
since you were the great archbishop and the eldest
    bishop,
since you consecrated priests in your land,
and since you were above all other priests?

Shall I call you a teacher,
since you taught the heathens who had gone astray,
since you brought the faith to the heathens
and taught men who were unlearned?

Shall I call you a sufferer or a martyr,
since, like a martyr, you surrendered yourself
into the hands of men who were cruel in torturing,
since you were as a sheep among wolves,
since you accepted martyrdom, suffering, and torment?

And I, a great and unlearned sinner,
following the words that eulogize you,
do knit words and create words,
attempting to glorify you with words.
Gathering the words of praise,
and adding and weaving words,
I ask: How shall I eulogize you?
Shall I call you
    the pastor of those who have gone astray,
    the redeemer of those who have perished,
    the teacher of those who were enticed,
    the leader of those whose sight has been darkened,
    the cleanser of those who have been defiled,

the guardian of the soldiers,
the consoler of those who are afflicted,
the nourisher of those who hunger,
the provider for those in need,
the punisher of those who are simpleminded,
the sustainer of the offended,
the one who prays for others fervently,
the intercessor for the faithful,
the savior of the heathens,
the curser of demons,
the breaker of idols,
the destroyer of graven images,
the servant of God,
the upholder of wisdom,
the lover of philosophy,
the protector of chastity,
the defender of the truth,
the writer of books,
the creator of Permian letters?

Many epithets have you received, O Bishop!
Many titles have you won!
Many gifts have you deserved!
Many blessings have enriched you!

45. EPIPHANIUS THE WISE: THE LIFE, ACTS, AND MIRACLES OF OUR BLESSED AND HOLY FATHER SERGIUS OF RADONEZH

I. CHILDHOOD

Our holy Father Sergius was born of noble, Orthodox, devout parents. His father was named Cyril and his mother Mary. They found favor with God; they were honorable in the sight of God and man, and abounded in those virtues which are well-pleasing unto God.

Cyril had three sons, Stephen, Bartholomew, and Peter, whom he brought up in strict piety and purity. Stephen and Peter quickly learned to read and write, but the second boy did not so easily learn to write, and worked slowly and inattentively; his master taught him with care, but the boy could not put his mind to his studies, nor understand, nor do the same as his companions who were studying with him. As a result he suffered from the many reproaches of his parents, and still more from the punishments of his teacher and the ridicule of his companions. The boy often prayed to God in secret and with many tears:

"O Lord, give me understanding of this learning. Teach me, Lord, enlighten and instruct me." His reverence for God prompted him to pray that he might receive knowledge from God and not from men.

One day his father sent him to seek for a lost foal. On his way he met a monk, a venerable elder, a stranger, a priest, with the appearance of an angel. This stranger was standing beneath an oak tree, praying devoutly and with much shedding of tears. The boy, seeing him, humbly made a low obeisance, and awaited the end of his prayers.

The venerable monk, when he had ended his orisons, glanced at the boy and, conscious that he behold the chosen vessel of the Holy Spirit, he called him to his side, blessed him, bestowed on him a kiss in the name of Christ, and asked: "What art thou seeking, or what dost thou want, child?"

The boy answered: "My soul desires above all things to understand the Holy Scriptures. I have to study reading and writing, and I am sorely vexed that I cannot learn these things. Will you, holy Father, pray to God for me, that he will give me understanding of book learning?"

The monk raised his hands and his eyes toward heaven, sighed, prayed to God, then said, "Amen."

Taking out from his satchel, as it were some treasure, with three fingers, he handed to the boy what appeared to be a little bit of white wheaten bread of the Holy Sacrament, saying to him: "Take this in thy mouth, child, and eat; this is given thee as a sign of God's Grace and for the understanding of Holy Scriptures. Though the gift appears but small, the taste thereof is very sweet."

The boy opened his mouth and ate, tasting a sweetness as of honey, wherefore he said: "Is it not written, How sweet are thy words to my palate, more than honey to my lips, and my soul doth cherish them exceedingly?"

The monk answered and said: "If thou believest, child, more than this will be revealed to thee; and do not vex thyself about reading and writing; thou wilt find that from this day forth the Lord will give thee learning above that of thy brothers and others of thine own age."

Having thus informed him of divine favor, the monk prepared to proceed on his way. But the boy flung himself, with his face to the ground, at the feet of the monk, and besought him to come and visit his parents, saying: "My parents dearly love persons such as you are, Father."

The monk, astonished at his faith, accompanied him to his parents' house. At the sight of the stranger, Cyril and Mary

came out to meet him, and bowed low before him. The monk
blessed them, and they offered him food, but before accepting
any food, the monk went into the chapel, taking with him the
boy whose consecration had been signified even before birth,[1]
and began a recitation of the Canonical Hours, telling the boy
to read the Psalms.

The boy said: "I do not know them, Father."

The monk replied: "I told thee that from today the Lord
would give thee knowledge of reading and writing; read the
Word of God, nothing doubting."

Whereupon, to the astonishment of all present, the boy,
receiving the monk's blessing, began to recite in excellent rhythm;
and from that hour he could read. His parents and brothers
praised God, and after accompanying the monk to the house,
placed food before him. Having eaten, and bestowed a blessing
on the parents, the monk was anxious to proceed on his way.
But the parents pleaded: "Reverend Father, hurry not away,
but stay and comfort us and calm our fears. Our humble son,
whom you bless and praise, is to us an object of marvel. While
he was yet in his mother's womb three times he uttered a cry in
church during holy Mass. Wherefore we fear and doubt of what
is to be, and what he is to do."

The holy monk, after considering and becoming aware of
that which was to be, exclaimed: "O blessed pair, O worthy
couple, giving birth to such a child! Why do you fear where
there is no place for fear? Rather rejoice and be glad, for the
boy will be great before God and man, thanks to his life of
godliness."

Having thus spoken the monk left, pronouncing a dark saying that their son would serve the Holy Trinity and would lead
many to an understanding of the divine precepts. They accompanied him to the doorway of their house, when he became of
a sudden invisible. Perplexed, they wondered if he had been
an angel, sent to give the boy knowledge of reading. After the
departure of the monk, it became evident that the boy could
read any book, and was altogether changed; he was submissive
in all things to his parents, striving to fulfill their wishes, and
never disobedient. Applying himself solely to glorifying God,
and rejoicing therein, he attended assiduously in God's church,
being present daily at matins, at the Mass, at vespers. He
studied holy scripts, and at all times, in every way, he dis-

---

[1] According to an introductory passage here omitted, the future
spiritual life of St. Sergius was revealed to his mother shortly before
his birth.

ciplined his body and preserved himself in purity of body and soul.

Cyril, devout servant of God, led the life of a wealthy and renowned boyar, in the province of Rostov, but in later years he was reduced to poverty. He, like others, suffered from the invasions of Tatar hordes into Russia, from the skirmishes of troops, the frequent demands for tribute, and from repeated bad harvests, in conjunction with the period of violence and disorder which followed the great Tatar war. When the principality of Rostov fell into the hands of the Grand Duke Ivan Danilovich of Moscow, distress prevailed in the town of Rostov, and not least among the princes and boyars.[2] They were deprived of power, of their properties, of honors and rank, of all of which Moscow became the possessor. By order of the Grand Duke they left Rostov, and a certain noble, Vassili Kotchev, with another called Mina, were sent from Moscow to Rostov as *voevodas*. On arrival in the town of Rostov these two governors imposed a levy on the town and on the inhabitants. A severe persecution followed, and many of the remaining inhabitants of Rostov were constrained to surrender their estates to the Muscovites, in exchange for which they received wounds and humiliations, and went forth empty-handed and as veriest beggars. In brief, Rostov was subjected to every possible humiliation, even to the hanging, head downward, of their governor, Averky, one of the chief boyars of Rostov. Seeing and hearing of all this, terror spread among the people, not only in the town of Rostov but in all the surrounding country. Cyril, God's devout servant, avoided further misfortune by escaping from his native town. He assembled his entire household and family and with them removed from Rostov to Radonezh,[3] where he settled near the church dedicated to the Birth of Christ, which is still standing to this day.

II. THE HERMITAGE

Cyril's two sons, Stephen and Peter, married, but his second son, Bartholomew, would not contemplate marriage, being desirous of becoming a monk. He often expressed this wish to his

---

[2] Grand Duke Ivan Danilovich of Moscow (1301–1341), called Kalita ("Moneybag"), was the actual founder of the Muscovite state. He spread his reign over a considerable part of the land between the Oka and Volga rivers. Rostov was an important city of the Volga.

[3] Radonezh was a village that belonged to St. Sergius' family and after which his family was named. This village, some nine miles from the Monastery of St. Sergius, is the present-day industrial city of Zagorsk.

father, but his parents said to him: "My son, wait a little and bear with us; we are old, poor, and sick, and we have no one to look after us, for both your brothers are married." The wondrous youth gladly promised to care for them to the end of their days, and from henceforth strove for his parents' well-being, until they entered the monastic life and went one to a monastery, and the other to a convent. They lived but a few years, and passed away to God. Blessed Bartholomew laid his parents in their graves, mourned for them forty days, then returned to his house. Calling his younger brother Peter, he bestowed his share of his father's inheritance on him, retaining nothing for himself. The wife of his elder brother, Stephen, died also, leaving two sons, Clement and Ivan. Stephen soon renounced the world and became a monk in the Holy Mother of God Monastery at Khotkov.

Blessed Bartholomew now came to him, and begged him to accompany him in the search for some desert place. Stephen assented, and he and the saint together explored many parts of the forest, till finally they came to a waste space in the middle of the forest, near a stream. After inspecting the place they obeyed the voice of God and were satisfied. Having prayed, they set about chopping wood and carrying it. First they built a hut, and then constructed a small chapel. When the chapel was finished and the time had come to dedicate it, blessed Bartholomew said to Stephen: "Now, my lord and eldest brother by birth and by blood, tell me, in honor of whose feast shall this chapel be, and to which saint shall we dedicate it?"

Stephen answered: "Why do you ask me, and why put me to the test? You were chosen of God while you were yet in your mother's womb, and he gave a sign concerning you before ever you were born, that the child would be a disciple of the Blessed Trinity, and not he alone would have devout faith, for he would lead many others and teach them to believe in the Holy Trinity. It behooves you, therefore, to dedicate a chapel above all others to the Blessed Trinity."

The favored youth gave a deep sigh and said: "To tell the truth, my lord and brother, I asked you because I felt I must, although I wanted and thought likewise as you do, and desired with my whole soul to erect and dedicate this chapel to the Blessed Trinity, but out of humility I inquired of you." And he went forthwith to obtain the blessing of the ruling prelate for its consecration. From the town came the priest sent by Theognost, Metropolitan of Kiev and all Russia, and the chapel was consecrated and dedicated to the Holy Trinity in the reign

of the Grand Duke Simon Ivanovich,[4] we believe in the beginning of his reign. The chapel being now built and dedicated,
Stephen did not long remain in the wilderness with his brother.
He realized soon all the labors in this desert place, the hardships, the all-pervading need and want, and that there were no
means of satisfying hunger and thirst, or any other necessity.
As yet no one came to the saint, or brought him anything, for
at this time nowhere around was there any village, or house,
or people; neither was there road or pathway, but everywhere
on all sides were forest and wasteland. Stephen, seeing this, was
troubled, and he decided to leave the wilderness, and with it
his own brother the saintly desert-lover and desert-dweller. He
went from thence to Moscow, and when he reached this city
he settled in the Monastery of the Epiphany, found a cell, and
dwelt in it, exercising himself in virtue. Hard labor was to him
a joy, and he passed his time in ascetic practices in his cell,
disciplining himself by fasting and praying, refraining from all
indulgence, even from drinking beer. Alexis, the future metropolitan, who at this time had not been raised to the rank of
bishop, was living in the monastery, leading a quiet monastic
life. Stephen and he spent much time together in spiritual
exercises, and they sang in the choir side by side. The Grand
Duke Simon came to hear of Stephen and the godly life he led,
and commanded the Metropolitan Theognost to ordain him
priest and, later, to appoint him abbot of the monastery. Aware
of his great virtues, the Grand Duke also appointed him as his
confessor.

Our saint, Sergius, had not taken monastic vows at this time
for, as yet, he had not enough experience of monasteries, and
of all that is required of a monk. After a while, however, he
invited a spiritual elder, who held the dignity of priest and
abbot, named Mitrofan, to come and visit him in his solitude. In great humility he entreated him: "Father, may the
love of God be with us, and give me the tonsure of a monk.
From childhood have I loved God and set my heart on him
these many years, but my parents' needs withheld me. Now, my
lord and father, I am free from all bonds, and I thirst, as the
hart thirsteth for the springs of living water."

The abbot forthwith went into the chapel with him, and
gave him the tonsure on the 7th day of October on the feast

---

[4] Grand Duke Simon Ivanovich the Proud (1341–1353) was the
son of Ivan Kalita. Metropolitan Theognost, the former Metropolitan
of Kiev, lived in Moscow and was one of the upholders of the rise of
Muscovy.

day of the blessed martyrs Sergius and Bacchus. And Sergius was the name he received as monk. In those days it was the custom to give to the newly tonsured monk the name of the saint whose feast day it happened to be. Our saint was twenty-three years old when he joined the order of monks. Blessed Sergius, the newly tonsured monk, partook of the Holy Sacrament and received Grace and the gift of the Holy Spirit. From one whose witness is true and sure, we are told that when Sergius partook of the Holy Sacrament the chapel was filled with a sweet odor; and not only in the chapel, but all around was the same fragrant smell. The saint remained in the chapel seven days, touching no food other than one consecrated loaf given him by the abbot, refusing all else and giving himself up to fasting and prayer, having on his lips the Psalms of David.

When Mitrofan bade farewell, St. Sergius in all humility said to him: "Give me your blessing, and pray regarding my solitude; and instruct one living alone in the wilderness how to pray to the Lord God; how to remain unharmed; how to wrestle with the devil and with his own temptations to pride, for I am but a novice and a newly tonsured monk."

The abbot was astonished and almost afraid. He replied: "You ask of me concerning that which you know no less well than we do, O Reverend Father." After discoursing with him for a while on spiritual matters, and commending him to God, Mitrofan went away, leaving St. Sergius alone to silence and the wilderness.

Who can recount his labors? Who can number the trials he endured living alone in the wilderness?

Under different forms and from time to time the devil wrestled with the saint, but the demons beset St. Sergius in vain; no matter what visions they evoked, they failed to overcome the firm and fearless spirit of the ascetic. At one moment it was Satan who laid his snares; at another, incursions of wild beasts took place, for many were the wild animals inhabiting this wilderness. Some of these remained at a distance; others came near the saint, surrounded him and even sniffed him. In particular a bear used to come to the holy man. Seeing the animal did not come to harm him, but in order to get some food, the saint brought a small slice of bread from his hut, and placed it on a log or stump, so the bear learned to come for the meal thus prepared for him, and having eaten it went away again. If there was no bread, and the bear did not find his usual slice, he would wait about for a long while and look around on all sides, rather like some moneylender waiting to receive payment of his debt. At this time Sergius had no variety of foods in the wilderness, only bread and water from the spring, and a great scarcity of these. Often, bread was not to be found; then both he and the bear went hungry. Sometimes, although there was but one slice of bread, the saint gave it to the bear, being unwilling to disappoint him of his food.

He diligently read the Holy Scriptures to obtain a knowledge of all virtue, in his secret meditations training his mind in a longing for eternal bliss. Most wonderful of all, none knew the measure of his ascetic and godly life spent in solitude. God, the beholder of all hidden things, alone saw it.

Whether he lived two years or more in the wilderness alone we do not know; God knows only. The Lord, seeing his very great faith and patience, took compassion on him and, desirous of relieving his solitary labors, put into the hearts of certain god-fearing monks to visit him.

The saint inquired of them: "Are you able to endure the hardships of this place, hunger and thirst, and every kind of want?"

They replied: "Yes, Reverend Father, we are willing with God's help and with your prayers."

Holy Sergius, seeing their faith and zeal, marveled, and said: "My brethren, I desired to dwell alone in the wilderness and, furthermore, to die in this place. If it be God's will that there shall be a monastery in this place, and that many brethren will be gathered here, then may God's holy will be done. I welcome you with joy, but let each one of you build himself a cell. Furthermore, let it be known unto you, if you come to dwell in the wilderness, the beginning of righteousness is the fear of the Lord."

To increase his own fear of the Lord he spent day and night in the study of God's word. Moreover, young in years, strong and healthy in body, he could do the work of two men or more. The devil now strove to wound him with the darts of concupiscence. The saint, aware of these enemy attacks, disciplined his body and exercised his soul, mastering it with fasting, and thus was he protected by the Grace of God. Although not yet raised to the office of priesthood, dwelling in company with the brethren, he was present daily with them in church for the reciting of the offices, nocturnes, matins, the hours, and vespers. For the Mass a priest, who was an abbot, came from one of the villages. At first Sergius did not wish to be raised to the priesthood and especially he did not want to become an abbot; this was by reason of his extreme humility. He constantly remarked that the beginning and root of all evil lay in pride of rank, and ambition to be an abbot. The monks were but few in number, about a dozen. They constructed themselves cells, not very large ones, within the enclosure, and put up gates at the entrance. Sergius built four cells with his own hands, and performed other monastic duties at the request of the brethren; he carried logs from the forest on his shoulders, chopped them up, and carried them into the cells. The monastery, indeed, came to be a wonderful place to look upon. The forest was not far distant from it as now it is; the shade and the murmur of trees hung above the cells; around the church was a space of trunks and stumps; here many kinds of vegetables were sown.

But to return to the exploits of St. Sergius. He flayed the grain and ground it in the mill, baked the bread, and cooked the food, cut out shoes and clothing and stitched them; he drew water from the spring flowing nearby, and carried it in two pails on his shoulders, and put water in each cell. He spent the night in prayer, without sleep, feeding only on bread and water, and that in small quantities; and never spent an idle hour.

III. THE HUMBLE ABBOT

Within the space of a year the abbot who had given the tonsure to St. Sergius fell ill, and after a short while, he passed out of this life. Then God put it into the hearts of the brethren to go to blessed Sergius, and to say to him: "Father, we cannot continue without an abbot. We desire you to be our abbot, and the guide of our souls and bodies."

The saint sighed from the bottom of his heart, and replied: "I have had no thought of becoming abbot, for my soul longs to finish its course here as an ordinary monk." The brethren urged him again and again to be their abbot; finally, overcome by his compassionate love, but groaning inwardly, he said: "Fathers and brethren, I will say no more against it, and will submit to the will of God. He sees into our hearts and souls. We will go into the town, to the bishop."

Alexis, the Metropolitan of all Russia, was living at this time in Constantinople, and he had nominated Bishop Athanasius of Volynia in his stead in the town of Pereiaslavl. Our blessed Sergius went, therefore, to the bishop, taking with him two elders; and entering into his presence made a low obeisance. Athanasius rejoiced exceedingly at seeing him, and kissed him in the name of Christ. He had heard tell of the saint and of his beginning of good deeds, and he spoke to him of the workings of the Spirit. Our blessed Father Sergius begged the bishop to give them an abbot, and a guide of their souls.

The venerable Athanasius replied: "Thyself, son and brother, God called in thy mother's womb. It is thou who wilt be father and abbot of thy brethren." Blessed Sergius refused, insisting

(ABOVE) *St. Sergius. A portrait worked in embroidery of about 1450.* (BELOW) *St. Sergius and his monks build a fence around the monastery. A sixteenth-century miniature from the* Life of St. Sergius.

on his unworthiness, but Athanasius said to him: "Beloved, thou hast acquired all virtue save obedience."

Blessed Sergius, bowing low, replied: "May God's will be done. Praise be the Lord forever and forever." They all answered, "Amen."

Without delay the holy bishop, Athanasius, led blessed Sergius to the church, and ordained him subdeacon and then deacon. The following morning the saint was raised to the dignity of priesthood, and was told to say the holy liturgy and to offer the bloodless Sacrifice. Later, taking him apart, the bishop spoke to him of the teachings of the Apostles and of the Holy Fathers, for the edification and guidance of souls. After bestowing on him a kiss in the name of Christ, he sent him forth, in very deed an abbot, pastor, and guardian, and physician of his spiritual brethren. He had not taken upon himself the rank of abbot; he received the leadership from God; he had not sought it, nor striven for it; he did not obtain it by payment, as do others who have pride of rank, chasing hither and thither, plotting and snatching power from one another. God himself led his chosen disciple and exalted him to the dignity of abbot.

Our revered father and abbot Sergius returned to his monastery, to the abode dedicated to the Holy Trinity, and the brethren, coming out to meet him, bowed low to the ground before him. He blessed them, and said: "Brethren, pray for me. I am altogether ignorant, and I have received a talent from the Highest, and I shall have to render an account of it, and of the flock committed to me."

There were twelve brethren when he first became abbot, and he was the thirteenth. And this number remained, neither increasing nor diminishing, until Simon, the archimandrite of Smolensk, arrived among them. From that time onward their numbers constantly increased. This wondrous man, Simon, was chief archimandrite, excellent, eminent, abounding in virtue. Having heard of our Reverend Father Sergius' way of life, he laid aside honors, left the goodly city of Smolensk, and arrived at the monastery where, greeting our Reverend Father Sergius with the greatest humility, he entreated him to allow him to live under him and his rules in all submission and obedience: and he offered the estate he owned as a gift to the abbot for the benefit of the monastery. Blessed Sergius welcomed him with great joy. Simon lived many years, submissive and obedient, abounding in virtue, and died in advanced old age.

Stephen, the saint's brother, came with hs younger son, Ivan, from Moscow and, presenting him to Abbot Sergius, asked him to give him the tonsure. Abbot Sergius did so, and gave him the name of Theodore; from his earliest years the boy had been taught abstinence, piety, and chastity, following his uncle's precepts; according to some accounts he was given the tonsure when he was ten years old, others say twelve. People from many parts, towns and countries, came to live with Abbot Sergius, and their names are written in the book of life. The monastery bit by bit grew in size. It is recorded in the *Paterikon* —that is to say, in the book of the early fathers of the Church— that the Holy Fathers in assembly prophesied about later generations, saying that the last would be weak. But, of the later generations, God made Sergius as strong as one of the early fathers. God made him a lover of hard work, and to be the head over a great number of monks. From the time he was appointed abbot, the holy Mass was sung every day. He himself baked the holy bread; first he flayed and ground the wheat, sifted the flour, kneaded and fermented the dough; he entrusted the making of the holy bread to no one. He also cooked the grains for the *kutia,* and he also made the candles. Although occupying the chief place as abbot, he did not alter in any way his monastic rules. He was lowly and humble with all people, and was an example to all.

He never sent away anyone who came to him for the tonsure, neither old nor young, nor rich nor poor; he received them all with fervent joy; but he did not give them the tonsure at once. He who would be a monk was ordered, first, to put on a long, black cloth garment and to live with the brethren until he got accustomed to all the monastic rules; then, later, he was given full monk's attire of cloak and hood. Finally, when he was deemed worthy, he was allowed the "Schema," [5] the mark of the ascetic.

After vespers, and late at night, especially on long dark nights, the saint used to leave his cell and go the round of the monks' cells. If he heard anyone saying his prayers, or making genuflections, or busy with his own handiwork, he was gratified and gave thanks to God. If, on the other hand, he heard two or three monks chatting together, or laughing, he was displeased, rapped on the door or window, and passed on. In the morning he would send for them and, indirectly, quietly and gently, by means of some parable, reprove them. If he was a humble and submissive brother he would quickly admit his fault and, bowing low before St. Sergius, would beg his forgiveness. If, instead, he was not a humble brother, and stood erect thinking he was not the person referred to, then the saint, with patience, would

---

[5] See footnote 30 in Selection 39.

make it clear to him, and order him to do a public penance. In this way they all learned to pray to God assiduously; not to chat with one another after vespers, and to do their own handiwork with all their might; and to have the Psalms of David all day on their lips.

In the beginning, when the monastery was first built, many were the hardships and privations. A main road lay a long way off, and wilderness surrounded the monastery. Here the monks lived, it is believed, for fifteen years. Then, in the time of the Grand Duke Ivan Ivanovich,[6] Christians [7] began to arrive from all parts and to settle in the vicinity. The forest was cut down; there was no one to prevent it; the trees were hewn down, none were spared, and the forest was converted into an open plain as we now see it. A village was built, and houses; and visitors came to the monastery bringing their countless offerings. But in the beginning, when they settled in this place, they all suffered great privations. At times there was no bread or flour, and all means of subsistence was lacking; at times there was no wine for the Eucharist, or incense, or wax candles. The monks sang matins at dawn with no lights save that of a single birch or pine torch.

One day there was a great scarcity of bread and salt in the whole monastery. The saintly abbot gave orders to all the brethren that they were not to go out, or beg from the laity, but to remain patiently in the monastery and await God's compassion. He himself spent three or four days without any food. On the fourth day, at dawn, taking an ax, he went to one of the settlers, by name Danila, and said to him: "I have heard say that you want to build an entrance in front of your cell. See, I have come to build it for you, so that my hands shall not remain idle."

Danila replied: "Yes, I have been wanting it for a long while, and am awaiting the carpenter from the village; but I am afraid to employ you, for you will require a large payment from me."

Sergius said to him: "I do not require a large sum of money. Have you any mildewed loaves? I very much want to eat some such loaves. I do not ask from you anything else. Where will you find another such carpenter as I?"

---

[6] Grand Duke Ivan Ivanovich, son of Ivan Kalíta and brother of Simon the Proud, reigned from 1353–1359. His son, Dmitry, was the hero of the Battle of Kulikovo.

[7] The word "Christians" here refers to the Russians themselves; surrounded by Moslems, pagans, and un-Orthodox Christians, the Russians called themselves Christians. This is reflected in the Russian word for peasant—krest'ianin.

Danila brought him a few mildewed loaves, saying: "This is all I have."

Sergius said: "That will be enough, and to spare. But hide it until evening. I take no pay before work is done."

Saying which, and tightening his belt, he chopped and worked all day, cut planks and put up the entrance. At the close of day, Danila brought him the sieveful of the promised loaves. Sergius, offering a prayer and grace, ate the bread and drank some water. He had neither soup nor salt; the bread was both dinner and supper. And he distributed the loaves among the monks.

Several of the brethren noticed something in the nature of a faint breath of smoke issuing from his lips, and turning to one another they said: "O brother, what patience and self-control has this man!"

But one of the monks, not having had anything to eat for two days, murmured against Sergius, and went up to him and said: "Why this moldy bread? Why should we not go outside and beg for some bread? If we obey you we shall perish of hunger. Tomorrow morning we will leave this place and go hence and not return; we cannot any longer endure such want and scarcity."

Not all of them complained, only one brother, but because of this one, Sergius, seeing they were enfeebled and in distress, convoked the whole brotherhood and gave them instruction from Holy Scriptures: "God's Grace cannot be given without trials; after tribulations comes joy. It is written, at evening there shall be weeping but in the morning gladness. You, at present, have no bread or food, and tomorrow you will enjoy an abundance."

And as he was yet speaking there came a rapping at the gates. The porter, peeping through an aperture, saw that a store of provisions had been brought; he was so overjoyed that he did not open the gates but ran first to St. Sergius to tell him. The saint gave the order at once: "Open the gates quickly, let them come in, and let those persons who have brought the provisions be invited to share the meal"; while he himself, before all else, directed that the *bilo* should be sounded,[8] and with the brethren he went into the church to sing the *Te Deum*. Returning from church, they went into the refectory, and the newly arrived, fresh bread was placed before them. The bread was still warm and soft, and the taste of it was of an unimaginable strange sweetness, as it were honey mingled with juice of barley and spices.

---

[8] Bilo: a wooden or iron rod used to beat a gong, gongs being used in Russia instead of bells.

When they had eaten, the saint remarked: "And where is our brother who was murmuring about moldy bread? May he notice that it is sweet and fresh. Let us remember the prophet who said: 'Ashes have I eaten for bread and mixed my drink with tears.'" Then he inquired whose bread it was, and who had sent it. The messengers announced: "A pious layman, very wealthy, living a great distance away, sent it to Sergius and his brotherhood." Again the monks, on Sergius' orders, invited the men to sup with them, but they refused, having to hasten elsewhere.

The monks came to the abbot in astonishment, saying: "Father, how has this wheaten bread, warm and tasting of butter and spices, been brought from far?" The following day more food and drink were brought to the monastery in the same manner. And again on the third day, from a distant country. Abbot Sergius, seeing and hearing this, gave glory to God before all the brethren, saying: "You see, brethren, God provides for everything, and neither does he abandon this place." From this time forth the monks grew accustomed to being patient under trials and privations, enduring all things, trusting in the Lord God with fervent faith, and being strengthened therein by their holy Father Sergius.

According to an account by one of the elders of the monastery, blessed Sergius never wore new clothing, nor any made of fine material, nor colored, nor white, nor smooth and soft; he wore plain cloth or caftan; his clothing was old and worn, dirty, patched. Once they had in the monastery an ugly, stained, bad bit of cloth, which all the brethren threw aside; one brother had it, kept it for a while and discarded it, so did another, and a third and so on to the seventh. But the saint did not despise it, he gratefully took it, cut it out and made himself a habit, which he wore, not with disdain but with gratitude, for a whole year, till it was worn out and full of holes.

So shabby were his clothes, worse than that of any of the monks, that several people were misled and did not recognize him. One day a peasant from a nearby village, who had never seen the saint, came to visit him. The abbot was digging in the garden. The visitor looked about and asked: "Where is Sergius? Where is the wonderful and famous man?"

A brother replied: "In the garden, digging; wait a while, until he comes in."

The visitor, growing impatient, peeped through an aperture, and perceived the saint wearing shabby attire, patched, in holes, and face covered with sweat; and he could not believe that this was he of whom he had heard. When the saint came from the garden, the monks informed him: "This is he whom you wish to see."

The visitor turned from the saint and mocked at him: "I came to see a prophet and you point out to me a needy-looking beggar. I see no glory, no majesty and honor about him. He wears no fine and rich apparel; he has no attendants, no trained servants; he is but a needy, indigent beggar."

The brethren, reporting to the abbot, said: "We hardly dare tell you, Reverend Father, and we would send away your guest as a good-for-nothing rude fellow; he has been discourteous and disrespectful about you, reproaches us, and will not listen to us."

The holy man, fixing his eyes on the brethren and seeing their confusion, said to them: "Do not do so, brethren, for he did not come to see you. He came to visit me." And, since he expected no obeisance from his visitor, he went toward him, humbly bowing low to the ground before him, and blessed and praised him for his right judgment. Then, taking him by the hand, the saint sat him down at his right hand, and bade him partake of food and drink. The visitor expressed his regret at not seeing Sergius, whom he had taken the trouble to come and visit; and his wish had not been fulfilled. The saint remarked: "Be not sad about it, for such is God's Grace that no one ever leaves this place with a heavy heart."

As he spoke a neighboring prince arrived at the monastery, with great pomp, accompanied by a retinue of boyars, servants, and attendants. The armed attendants, who preceded the prince, took the visitor by the shoulders and removed him out of sight of the prince and of Sergius. The prince then advanced and, from a distance, made a low obeisance to Sergius. The saint gave him his blessing and, after bestowing a kiss on him, they both sat down while everyone else remained standing. The visitor thrust his way through, and going up to one of those standing by, asked: "Who is the monk sitting on the prince's right hand? Tell me."

The man turned to him and said: "Are you then a stranger here? Have you indeed not heard of blessed Father Sergius? It is he speaking with the prince."

Upon hearing this, the visitor was overcome with remorse, and after the prince's departure, taking several of the brethren to intercede for him, and making a low obeisance before the abbot, he said: "Father, I am but a sinner and a great offender. Forgive me and help my unbelief."

The saint readily forgave, and with his blessing and some words of comfort, he took leave of him. From henceforth, and to the end of his days, this man held a true, firm faith in the

Holy Trinity and in St. Sergius. He left his village a few years later, and came to the saint's monastery, where he became a monk, and there spent several years in repentance and amendment of life before he passed away to God.

IV. THE MIRACLES

We shall now turn to the miracles God performs through his elect. Owing to lack of water near the monastery, the brotherhood suffered great discomfort, which increased with their numbers and having to carry water from a distance. Some of the monks even complained to the abbot: "When you set out to build a monastery on this spot, why did you not observe that it was not near water?" They repeated this query with vexation, often.

The saint told them: "I intended to worship and pray in this place alone. But God willed that a monastery such as this, dedicated to the Holy Trinity, should arise."

Going out of the monastery, accompanied by one of the brethren, he made his way through a ravine below the monastery, and finding a small pool of rainwater, he knelt down and prayed. No sooner had he made the sign of the cross over the spot, than a bubbling spring arose, which is still to be seen to this day, and from whence water is drawn to supply every need of the monastery.

Many cures have been granted to the faithful from the waters; and people have come from long distances to fetch the water and carry it away and to give it to their sick to drink. From the time it appeared, and for a number of years, the spring was called after Sergius. The wise man, not seeking renown, was displeased, and remarked: "Never let me hear that a well is called by my name. I did not give this water; God gave it to us unworthy men."

A certain devout Christian living close by the monastery, who believed in St. Sergius, had an only son, a child, who fell ill. The father brought the boy to the monastery, and entreated the saint to pray for him; but while the father was yet speaking the boy died. The man, with his last hope gone, wept and bemoaned: "It would have been better had my son died in my own house." While he went to prepare a grave, the dead child was laid in the saint's cell. The saint felt compassion for this man, and falling on his knees prayed over the dead child. Suddenly the boy came to life, and moved. His father, returning with preparations for the burial, found his son alive, whereupon, flinging himself at the feet of God's servant, he gave him thanks. The saint said to him: "You deceive yourself, man, and do not know what you say. While on your journey hither your son became frozen with cold, and you thought he had died. He has now thawed in the warm cell, and you think he has come to life. No one can rise again from the dead before the Day of Resurrection."

The man however insisted, saying: "Your prayers brought him to life again."

The saint forbade him to say this; "If you noise this abroad you will lose your son altogether." The man promised to tell no one and, taking his son, now restored to health, he went back to his own home. This miracle was made known through the saint's disciples.

Living on the banks of the Volga, a long distance away from the Lavra,[9] was a man who owned great possessions, but who was afflicted incessantly, day and night, by a cruel and evil spirit. Not only did he break iron chains, but ten or more strong men could not hold him. His relatives, hearing tell of the saint, journeyed with him to the monastery, where dwelt the servant of the Lord. When they came to the monastery the madman broke loose from his bonds, and flung himself about, crying: "I will not go, I will not. I will go back from whence I came." They informed the saint, who gave the order to sound the *bilo*, and when the brethren were assembled they sang the *Te Deum* for the sick. The madman grew calmer little by little, and when he was led into the monastery, the saint came out of church, carrying a cross, whereupon the sufferer, with a loud cry, fled from the spot, and flung himself into a pool of rainwater standing nearby, exclaiming: "O horrible, O terrible flame." By the Grace of God and the saint's prayers he recovered, and was restored to his right mind. When they inquired what he meant by his exclamation, he told them: "When the saint wanted to bless me with the cross, I saw a great flame proceeding from him, and it seized hold of me. So I threw myself into the water, fearing that I should be consumed in the flame."

One day the saint, in accordance with his usual rule, was keeping vigil and praying for the brotherhood late at night when he heard a voice calling: "Sergius!" He was astonished, and opening the window of the cell he beheld a wondrous vision. A great radiance shone in the heavens; the night sky was illumined by its brilliance, exceeding the light of day. A second time the voice called: "Sergius! Thou prayest for thy children;

---

[9] Lavra was the name given a monastery that was independent of local bishops, being under the direct authority of the head of the Russian Church. There were four such monasteries in Russia.

God has heard thy prayer. See and behold great numbers of monks gathered together in the name of the Everlasting Trinity, in thy fold, and under thy guidance."

The saint looked and beheld a multitude of beautiful birds, flying, not only on to the monastery, but all around; and he heard a voice saying: "As many birds as thou seest by so many will thy flock of disciples increase; and after thy time they will not grow less if they will follow in thy footsteps." Anxious to have a witness of this vision the saint called aloud for Simon, he being the nearest. Simon ran to him with all haste, but he was not found worthy to behold this vision; he saw no more than a ray of its light, but even so was greatly astonished. Filled with awe and wonder at this glorious vision, they rejoiced together.

V. THE PATRIARCHAL CHARTER

One day some Greeks arrived from Constantinople, sent by the patriarch to visit the saint. Making a deep obeisance they said to him: "The all-powerful Patriarch of Constantinople, Philotheus, sends you his blessing," and they presented him with gifts from the patriarch, a cross and a "paramand," and also handed him a letter from him.

The saint asked: "Are you sure you have not been sent to someone else? How can I, a sinner, be worthy of such gifts from the most illustrious patriarch?"

They replied: "We have indeed been sent to you, holy Sergius." The elder went then to see the metropolitan, Alexis,[10] and took with him the missive brought from the patriarch. The metropolitan ordered the epistle to be read to him. It ran: "By the Grace of God, the Archbishop of Constantinople, the Ecumenical Patriarch Philotheus, by the Holy Spirit, to our son and fellow servant Sergius. Divine Grace and peace, and our blessing be with you. We have heard tell of your godly life dedicated to God, wherefore we greatly praise and glorify God. One thing, however, has not been established: you have not formed a community. Take note, blessed one, that even the great prophet and our father in God, David, embracing all things with his mind, could not bestow higher praise than when he said, 'But

---

[10] Metropolitan Alexis (1353–1378), the son of a boyar from Chernigov in southern Russia, was an outstanding Russian Church leader. He became adviser to Prince Ivan II and Prince Dmitry. Following the policy set by Metropolitans Peter and Theognost, he supported Moscow as the main center of Russian political and spiritual life, and fostered the unification of all Russian lands around Moscow.

now, however good and however perfect, yet, above all, is abiding together in brotherly love.' Wherefore I counsel you to establish a community. That God's blessing and his Grace be always upon you." The elder inquired of the metropolitan: "Revered teacher, what would you have us do?" The metropolitan replied: "With all our heart we approve, and return thanks."

From henceforth life on the basis of community was established in the monastery. The saint, wise pastor, appointed to each brother his duties, one to be cellarer, others to be cooks and bakers, another to care for the sick, and for church duties, an ecclesiarch, and a subecclesiarch, and sacristans, and so forth. He further announced that the ordinances of the Holy Fathers were to be strictly observed; all things were to be possessed in common, no monk was to hold property of his own.

His community having been established with much wisdom, the numbers of his followers soon increased. Also, the larger the supply of offerings to the monastery, the more hospitality was extended. No person in need ever left the monastery empty-handed; and the saint gave orders that the poor and all strangers were to be allowed to rest in the monastery, and no suppliant to be refused, adding: "If you will follow my precepts and continue in them faithfully, God will reward you, and when I leave this life our monastery will prosper and continue to stand with the Lord's blessing for many years." And to the present day it has remained standing.

VI. THE DISSENSIONS

Before long dissension arose; the devil, hating goodness, put about the idea of disputing the authority of Sergius.[11] One Saturday, while vespers were being sung, and the Abbot Sergius, wearing his vestments, was at the altar, his brother, Stephen, who was standing by the choir, on the left, asked the canonarch: "Who gave you that book?" The canonarch replied: "The abbot gave it to me." The other said: "What has the abbot to do with it? Did not I sit in that place before?" and adding other silly remarks.

Although the saint was standing by the altar, he heard what was said, but he kept silence. When they all came out of church he did not go to his cell; he walked away from the monastery,

---

[11] These dissensions were apparently caused by St. Sergius' desire to introduce a more disciplined and strictly enforced communal life in the monastery, which was in disagreement with earlier Russian monastic tradition.

unknown to all. When he arrived at the monastery of Mak-risch,[12] he asked the abbot, Stephen, if one of his monks could lead him to some desert place. Together they searched and finally discovered a beautiful spot close to a river called the Kerzhach. The brotherhood, hearing about the saint, took to visiting him, in twos and threes, and more. Our Father Sergius sent two of his followers to the Metropolitan Alexis, with the request for his blessing and permission to erect a church. Aided by divine favor, a church was erected in a short while, and many brethren gathered there.

Soon several monks from the Holy Trinity, unable any longer to bear the separation from their spiritual father, went to the metropolitan and said: "Holy lord, we are living like sheep without a shepherd. Command our abbot to return to his monastery, that he may save us from perishing and dying of grief without him."

The metropolitan dispatched two archimandrites, Gerasim and Paul, to the abbot with the message: "Your father, Alexis the Metropolitan, sends you his blessing. He has rejoiced exceedingly to hear that you are living in a distant wilderness. But, return now to the monastery of the Holy Trinity; those persons who were dissatisfied with you shall be removed from the monastery."

Whereupon, hearing this, the saint sent reply: "Tell my lord the metropolitan, all from his lips, as from those of Christ, I receive with joy and do disobey in nothing."

The metropolitan, glad at his prompt obedience, instantly dispatched a priest to consecrate the church to the Annunciation of the Immaculate and Blessed Virgin, Mother of God. Sergius selected one of his followers, called Romanus, to be the abbot of the new monastery, and sent him to the metropolitan to be raised to the priesthood. The saint then returned to the monastery of the Holy Trinity.

When the news reached the monastery that the saint was returning, the brethren went out to meet him. On beholding him it appeared as if a second sun were shining; and they were so filled with joy that some of the brethren kissed the father's hands, others his feet, while others seized his clothing and kissed that. There were loud rejoicing and glorifying God for the return of their father. And what of the father? He rejoiced with his whole heart at seeing this gathering of his flock.

---

[12] Makrisch was another monastery situated about twenty miles from the Monastery of St. Sergius.

VII. ST. STEPHEN OF PERM

Now Bishop Stephen,[13] a god-fearing and devout man, had for St. Sergius a deep spiritual affection. One day he was travelling from his episcopacy of Perm to the capital, Moscow. The road along which the bishop journeyed lay about seven miles from St. Sergius' monastery. When the godly bishop came opposite the saint's monastery, he stopped and said, bowing low toward the direction of the saint: "Peace be with thee, brother in God!" The saint, at this hour, was seated at table with his brethren. Perceiving in spirit what Bishop Stephen was doing, he rose from the supper table, stood for an instant in prayer, then bowing said aloud: "Be joyful, thou shepherd of Christ's flock; the peace of God be always with thee." At the end of supper his disciples inquired of him what he meant. He openly told them: "At that hour Bishop Stephen, going on his way to Moscow, did reverence to the Holy Trinity, and blessed us humble folk." He pointed out to them, also, where this had taken place.

One time, when Theodore,[14] son of Stephen, was with blessed Sergius in the monastery, he was taking part in the Divine Liturgy which was being sung by the saint, and with the afore-named Stephen, the saint's brother. Of a sudden Isaac, who had taken the vow of silence, saw a fourth person serving at the altar with them, of a bright, shining appearance, and in dazzling apparel. Isaac inquired of Father Macarius, who was standing by his side: "What miraculous apparition is this?" Macarius replied: "I do not know, brother; I see a fearful and ineffable vision. But I think, brother, that someone came with the prince." (Prince Vladimir was at this time in the monastery.) One of the prince's attendants was asked whether a priest had come with him; but, no, they knew of no one.

When the divine Mass was at an end, seizing a favorable moment, one of the brethren approached St. Sergius and questioned him. But he, anxious not to disclose the secret, asked: "What wonder did you see, brother? My brother, Stephen, was saying the Mass; also his son, Theodore, and I, unworthy as I am. No other priest whatever was serving with us." His disciples insisted, entreating the saint to reveal the mystery to them, whereupon he said: "Beloved brethren, what the Lord God has

---

[13] Bishop Stephen: refers to St. Stephen of Perm (see introductory commentary).

[14] Theodore was the son of Sergius' brother, Stephen. He later became the bishop of Rostov.

revealed can I keep secret? He whom you beheld was an angel of the Lord, and not only this time but every time I, unworthy as I am, serve with this messenger of the Lord. That which you have seen tell no one, so long as I am on this earth." And his disciples were astonished beyond measure.

VIII. ST. SERGIUS AND RUSSIA

A rumor spread that Khan Mamai was raising a large army as a punishment for our sins and that with all his heathen Tatar hordes he would invade Russian soil. Very great fear prevailed among the people at this report. The puissant and reigning prince, who held the scepter of all Russia, great Dmitry,[15] having a great faith in the saint, came to ask him if he counseled him to go against the heathen. The saint, bestowing on him his blessing, and strengthened by prayer, said to him: "It behooveth you, lord, to have a care for the lives of the flock committed to you by God. Go forth against the heathen; and upheld by the strong arm of God, conquer; and return to your country sound in health, and glorify God with loud praise."

The grand duke replied: "If indeed God assist me, Father, I will build a monastery to the Immaculate Mother of God." And with the saint's blessing he hurriedly went on his way. Assembling all his armies, he marched against the heathen Tatars; but, seeing the multitudes of them, he began to doubt; and many of his followers, not knowing what to do, were overwhelmed with fear. Of a sudden, a courier from the saint arrived, in all haste, with the message. "Be in no doubt, lord; go forward with faith and confront the enemy's ferocity; and fear not, for God will be on your side." Forthwith, the Grand Duke Dmitry and all his armies were filled with a spirit of temerity; and went into battle against the pagans. They fought; many fell; but God was with them, and helped the great and invincible Dmitry, who vanquished the ungodly Tatars. In that same hour the saint was engaged with his brethren before God in prayer for victory over the pagans. Within an hour of the final defeat of the ungodly, the saint, who was a seer, announced to the brotherhood what had happened, the victory, the courage of the Grand Duke Dmitry, and the names, too, of those who had died at the hands of the pagans; and he made intercession for them to all-merciful God.

---

[15] Grand Duke Dmitry, reigned 1363–1385, was the hero of *Zadonshchina*, and the first Russian prince to defeat the Tatars in a major battle.

The Grand Duke Dmitry returned to his country with great
joy in his heart, and hastened to visit holy, venerable Sergius.
Rendering thanks for the prayers of the saint and of the brotherhood, he gave a rich offering to the monastery and, in fulfillment of his vow, expressed his wish to build at once the monastery of the Immaculate Mother of God. After searching for a
favorable place, venerable Sergius fixed upon one by the banks
of the river Dubenka, and with the consent of the grand duke a
church to the Assumption of our Blessed Virgin Mother of God
was consecrated by St. Sergius. As abbot, the saint appointed
one of his followers, Sabbas by name, a man of exceeding great
virtue. A community was formed, and many brethren joined it.

Once again the Grand Duke Dmitry entreated St. Sergius to
come to Kolomna, to consecrate a site for the building of a
monastery to be dedicated to the Holy Epiphany. It was the
saint's custom to go everywhere on foot. Obedient to the grand
duke, he went to Kolomna, consecrated the site, and a church
was erected and, at the grand duke's request, he sent him one
of his disciples for the founding of the monastery, a priest-monk,
Gregory, a devout man and of great virtue. In time a stone
church was built, which is standing to this day.

Another time the illustrious Prince Vladimir begged St.
Sergius, likewise, to come to his part of the country, to the town
of Serpukhov, and consecrate a place by the river Nar, and dedicate a church to the Conception of the Immaculate Mother of
God. Once again the saint obeyed the request. This God-fearing
prince also begged him to send one of his disciples, Athanasius
by name. Although the saint found it hard to grant this request,
love prevailed, and he consented. Athanasius being a man of
rare virtue, exceedingly learned in Holy Scriptures—many valuable writings by his hand bear witness to him to the present
day—the saint loved him dearly. To him the saint entrusted the
founding of the monastery, and the forming of the community.
Aided by the prayers of the saint, the monastery was built, wonderful and beautiful, and named "On the Height."

But why pursue further the saint's planting of ecclesiastical
fruit? It is well known how many monasteries were founded by
God's own chosen servant. And, offspring of his offspring, burning bright as stars, they are everywhere radiating a serene and
wondrous life, and a blessing to all.

The Metropolitan Alexis, being old, and seeing his weakness
increasing, sent for St. Sergius. While they conversed, the metropolitan asked to have the cross with the "paramand" adorned
with gold and precious stones brought to him, to give it to the

saint; but he, bowing low in great humility, refused it, saying: "Forgive me, lord, I have worn no gold ornaments since childhood, wherefore all the more do I wish in old age to continue in poverty." The bishop insisted, and said: "I know, beloved, that thou art fulfilling a vow, but be obedient, and take this which we offer thee with a benediction." Further, he said to the saint: "Dost know why I sent for thee? I desire, while I yet live, to find a man able to feed Christ's flock. I have doubted of them all; thee alone have I chosen as worthy. I know with all certainty that, from the puissant prince to the lowliest of his people, thou art the one they want."

On hearing this the saint was deeply grieved, regarding honor for himself as a thing of naught, and he pleaded with the bishop: "Forgive me, lord, but this of which you speak is beyond my powers, and you never will find it in me. What am I but a sinner, and the least of men?" The bishop quoted many sayings from Holy Scriptures, but the saint, unyielding in his humility, said: "Gracious lord, if you do not wish to drive away my poverty from your Holiness, speak no more about my poor self, nor permit anyone else, for no one can make me otherwise."

The bishop, understanding that the saint would not yield, allowed him to return to his monastery. Before long the Metropolitan Alexis left this life, in the year 6885 (1378); and once more the princes implored the saint to accept the rank of bishop; but, firm as adamant, he would in no way consent. Then a certain archimandrite, Michael, was raised to the bishopric; but this man, with great presumption, not only invested himself with the episcopal robes but also proceeded to plot against the saint, in the belief that the venerable Sergius would put a check on his audacity, wishing to occupy the episcopal throne himself. Blessed Sergius, hearing of Michael's threats against him, remarked to his disciples that Michael, vaunting himself of his sacred appointment, would not obtain his wish, for, overcome by pride, he would not reach the imperial city. The saint's prophecy was fulfilled. On his way by boat to Constantinople,[16] Michael fell ill and died. Thereupon everyone regarded St. Sergius as one of the prophets.

---

[16] From the beginnings of the Russian Church until 1448, its head, who was first the Metropolitan of Kiev and later the Metropolitan of Moscow, was ordained by the Patriarch of Constantinople. After 1437, the year the Byzantine Church concluded its union, of short duration, with the Church of Rome, the Russian Church broke away and became independent.

IX. THE LAST MIRACLES AND THE
PASSING AWAY OF ST. SERGIUS

One day the blessed father was praying, as was his wont, before the image of the Mother of Our Lord Jesus Christ. Having sung the "Magnificat" of the Blessed Virgin, he sat down to rest a while, saying to his disciple, Micah: "Son, be calm and be bold, for a wonderful and fearful event is about to happen." Instantly a voice was heard: "The Blessed Virgin is coming." Hearing this the saint hurried from his cell into the corridor. A dazzling radiance shone upon the saint, brighter than the sun, and he beheld the Blessed Virgin, with the two Apostles Peter and John, in ineffable glory. Unable to bear so resplendent a vision, the saint fell to the ground. The Blessed Virgin, touching the saint with her hand, said: "Be not afraid, mine own elect, I have come to visit thee. Thy prayers for thy disciples for whom thou prayest, and for thy monastery, have been heard. Be not troubled; from henceforth it will flourish, not only during thy lifetime but when thou goest to the Lord, I will be with thy monastery, supplying its needs lavishly, providing for it, protecting it."

Having thus spoken, she vanished. The saint, in ecstasy, stood in trembling awe and wonder. Returning slowly to his senses, he saw his disciple, terror-struck, lying on the ground, whereupon he raised him up; but the other flung himself down at the feet of the elder, saying: "Tell me, Father, for God's sake what miraculous vision was this? For my spirit almost loosed its bonds with the flesh from so resplendent a vision."

The saint, so filled with ecstasy that his face glowed therewith, was unable to answer other than a few words: "Wait a while, son, for I, too, am trembling with awe and wonder at this miraculous vision." They continued in silent adoration until, finally, the saint said to his disciple: "Son, call hither Isaac and Simon." When these two came, he recounted to them all that had happened, how he had beheld the Blessed Virgin with the Apostles, and what a wonderful promise she had given him. Hearing this their hearts were filled with indescribable joy, and they all sang the "Magnificat," and glorified God. All night long the saint remained in meditation on this ineffable vision.

After a while, a Greek bishop came from Constantinople to Moscow, but, although he had heard a great deal about the saint, his doubt about him prevailed, for, he reasoned: "How can such a light have appeared in this savage land, more especially in these latter days?" He therefore resolved to go to the monastery and see the saint. When he drew near to the monastery, fear entered his soul, and as soon as he entered the monastery and beheld the saint, blindness fell upon him. The venerable Sergius took him by the hand and led him to his cell. The bishop, with tears, confessed his doubts to the saint, and prayed for the recovery of his sight. The gentle lover of humility touched his blinded pupils, and, as it were, scales fell from his eyes, and instantly he recovered his sight. The bishop proclaimed to all that the saint was indeed a man of God and that in God's mercy he himself had been deemed worthy to behold a celestial man and an earthly angel.

A moneylender, living near the saint's monastery, and who, like the strong in all ages, oppressed the poor, ill-treated a certain poor orphan, and, moreover, carried off his pig, which was being fattened, and without paying for it had it killed. The ill-used orphan went to the saint in great distress and, weeping, begged for help. The saint, moved by compassion, sent for the offender, convicted him of wrongdoing, and said: "My son, do you believe that God is a judge of the righteous and of sinners; a father to widows and orphans; that he is quick to avenge and that it is a fearful thing to come under the wrath of God?" Having reproached him and told him he must pay what he owed to the orphan, he added: "Above all, do not oppress the poor." The man, overcome by fear, promised to amend and to pay the orphan, then returned to his own house. Little by little the effect of the saint's rebuke grew faint, and he decided not to pay his debt to the orphan. And, thinking it over in his mind, he went as usual into his larder, where he found the pig half devoured and swarming with maggots, although it was midwinter. He was stricken with fear, and without delay paid the debt; and ordered the pig to be thrown to the dogs and birds to eat, but they would not touch it and clear the usurer of his offense.

Now, again, one day, the saint was reciting the Divine Liturgy with one of his disciples, venerable Simon, the ecclesiarch, of whom we have already spoken, when a wonderful vision was vouchsafed to Simon. While the saint was saying the liturgy, Simon saw a flame pass along the altar, illuminating it and surrounding the holy table; as the saint was about to partake of the Blessed Sacrament the glorious flame coiled itself and entered the sacred chalice; and the saint thus received Communion. Simon, who saw this, trembled with fear. The saint, when he moved away from the altar, understood that Simon had been deemed worthy of this miraculous vision, and telling him to approach, asked: "Son, why are you fearful?" The other replied: "Master, I beheld a miraculous vision; the Grace of the Holy Spirit operating with you." The saint forbade him to speak of it: "Tell no one of this which you have seen, until the Lord calls me away from this life."

The saint lived a number of years, continually chastening himself with fasting, and working unceasingly. He performed many unfathomable miracles, and reached an advanced age, never failing from his place at divine service; the older his body grew, the stronger grew his fervor, in no way weakened by age. He became aware of his approaching end six months before, and assembling the brotherhood he appointed his dearest disciple to take his place, one perfect in all virtue, following his master in all things, small of stature, but in mind a continual blossoming, whose name was Nikon. The saint exhorted him to guide Christ's flock with patient care and justice. The great ascetic soon began to lose strength and in September was taken seriously ill. Seeing his end, he again assembled his flock and delivered a final exhortation. He made them promise to be steadfast in Orthodoxy and to preserve amity among men; to keep pure in body and soul; to love truth; to avoid all evil and carnal lusts; to be moderate in food and drink; above all, to be clothed with humility; not to forget love of their neighbor; to avoid controversy, and on no account to set value on honor and praise in this life, but rather to await reward from God for the joys of heaven and eternal blessings. Having instructed them in many things, he concluded: "I am, by God's will, about to leave you, and I commit you to Almighty God and the Immaculate Virgin, Mother of God, that they may be to you a refuge and rock of defense against the snares of your enemies." As his soul was about to leave his body, he partook of the Sacred Body and Blood, supported in the arms of his disciples and, raising his hands to heaven, with a prayer on his lips, he surrendered his pure, holy soul to the Lord, in the year 6900 (1393), September 25th, probably at the age of seventy-eight. After his death an ineffable sweet odor flowed from the saint's body.

The entire brotherhood gathered around him and, weeping and sobbing, laid on its bier the body of him who in life had been so noble and unresting, and accompanied him with psalms and funeral orisons. The saint's face, unlike that of other dead, glowed with the life of the living, or as one of God's angels, witnessing to the purity of his soul, and God's reward for all his labors. His body was laid to rest within the monastery of his own creation. Many were the miracles that took place at his death and after, and still are taking place, giving strength to the weaker members of the community, deliverance from the crafts and wiles of evil spirits, and sight to the blind. The saint had no wish during his life for renown, neither in death, but by God's Almighty Power he was glorified. Angels were present at his passing into the heavens, opening for him the gates of paradise and leading him toward the longed-for blessings, into the peace of the righteous, the ever-looked-for glory of the Blessed Trinity.

46. PETER AND FEVRONIA OF MUROM

In Russian medieval literature the tale of *Peter and Fevronia of Murom* is a unique instance of a work in which some romantic elements are presented. The love between Peter and Fevronia is considerably spiritualized, however, emphasizing their faithfulness to each other both in this life and in life after death. In this respect, the story of Peter and Fevronia resembles that of Tristan and Iseult, although deprived of any amorous background. This tale can be divided into composite segments, as has been done in this translation. The first, and the most fantastic, part, "The Story of the Evil Serpent," echoes the widely spread motif concerning the effect of the blood of an evil serpent, a motif that can be found in the *Nibelungenlied*. The second section treats the miraculous healing of Prince Peter by a wise and fair maiden, a theme also to be found in both Eastern and European legends and fairy tales. The third part, "The Intrigues of the Boyars," unlike the preceding sections, contains a political polemic attempting to prove that the autocratic rule of a prince is superior to the rule of an aristocracy that leads to its own self-destruction through dissension. The conclusion of this work has hagiographic colorations. Peter and Fevronia appear here as devout and just rulers who care for their subjects, helping the poor and supporting the Church.

Unusual for a work describing the lives of saints—Peter and Fevronia actually were venerated as the saintly patrons of the city of Murom—is their last testament: to remain together in the same casket after death. Here, the elements of the purity and sanctity of the family supersede the usual ascetic tradition of hagiographic works.

Peter and Fevronia, in its language, symbolism, and its use of riddles (as in the speech of Fevronia), clearly reflects a folklore origin. The name Agric itself plainly shows this influence, for Agric was an invincible mythological warrior of Russian folk epics who possessed a magic sword with which he slew evil serpents and monsters.

The exact background of this story is not well known. Peter and Fevronia had been venerated in Murom since the middle of the fifteenth century, and they were both canonized in 1547 by

an All-Russian Church Council in Moscow. However, this narrative has never been included in the official collection of *vitae*
nor was it read in the Church. There are some indications that
the life of Prince David of Murom, who ruled there from 1203
to 1228, was the historical source for this work.

This translation is based upon the Old Russian text prepared
by Professor M. O. Skripil and published in the collection
Russkie povesti XV–XVI vekov, Moscow, 1958, pages 108–115.

I. THE EVIL SERPENT

There is in the Russian land a city called Murom. I was told
that this city was once ruled by a good prince named Paul. The
devil, hating everything good among men, sent a serpent to the
palace of Prince Paul's wife to seduce and debase her. And
when the princess was with the serpent, she saw him as he
really was, while it seemed to others who visited the princess'
palace that not a serpent, but Prince Paul himself was with the
princess. Time passed, and the wife of Prince Paul decided that
she could no longer hide her secret. She revealed what had
happened to her husband, for the serpent had already debased
her.

Prince Paul tried to think of what to do with the serpent, and
finally he told his wife: "I cannot discern how I am to deal with
this evil spirit. I don't know any means of killing it. But we
shall do the following. When you talk with him, ask him cleverly
whether he knows how he is destined to die. And when you
learn this, tell me, and you will not only be rid of this evil spirit
and its debauchery, of which it is disgusting even to speak, but
also in the next life you will gain the mercy of our righteous
judge, Jesus Christ."

The princess became gladdened by her husband's words, and
thought: It would be good if it would only happen so. And
when the serpent came, she began to converse slyly and cleverly
with it about various things, keeping in mind her intentions.
When it began to brag, she asked humbly and with respect:
"You certainly know everything, and so you must certainly know
to what kind of death you are destined."

And the great deceiver was himself deceived by the decep-
tion of the faithful wife and unknowingly betrayed his secret,
saying: "My death will come from Peter's hand and Agric's
sword." The princess, hearing this, concealed it firmly in her
heart. After the departure of this evil being, she told her husband, the prince, what the serpent had said. The prince, hearing
this, was unable to understand what was meant by the words
"My death will come from Peter's hand and Agric's sword." But,

since he had a brother named Peter, he summoned him and told him what his wife had learned from the evil serpent. Prince Peter, learning from his brother that the serpent gave his namesake as the cause of his death, began to think bravely of how to kill this serpent. Yet he was confused by the fact that he did not know what was the sword of Agric.

Prince Peter had the custom of going alone to church to pray. Once he came to the Church of the Elevation of the Holy Cross, which belonged to a convent beyond the city wall. There he was approached by a youth who asked the prince if he wished to see the sword of Agric. The prince, desirous of fulfilling his desire to kill the serpent, answered: "Certainly! Where is it?" And the youth asked Prince Peter to follow him, and he showed him a niche in the bricks of the altar in which a sword was lying. Faithful Prince Peter took the sword and went to his brother, Prince Paul, and told him everything. And from that moment Prince Peter began to wait for the opportunity to kill this evil serpent.

Each day he visited his brother and his sister-in-law. One day, after he had visited his brother, he went to the chamber of his sister-in-law, and there he once again found his brother, sitting with the princess. Leaving her room, he met a man from Prince Paul's retinue, and he asked him: "I was just in my brother's room and found him there. Then I went directly to my sister-in-law's chamber and again I found him there. How is this possible?"

And the man answered: "It is not possible, my lord. Prince Paul has not left his room since you left him." He went to his older brother's room and asked him: "When did you return to your room? When I left you, I went to the chambers of the princess without losing any time. And yet, when I came there, I found you next to her. I can't understand how you could get there before me. Therefore, I left there, came back here, and now once more I see that you were faster than I in getting here. I don't understand it."

Then Prince Paul explained to Peter that he had not left his room nor had he been with the princess during this time. Then Prince Peter understood what had happened. "All this is the witchcraft of this evil serpent. In my presence he assumes your image for his own so that he would not be killed by me. Brother, do not leave this room, for I am now going to your wife's chambers to fight the evil serpent. I hope that I will be able to slay it with the help of God."

Prince Peter then took Agric's sword and went to the princess' chambers, where he again found the serpent in the form of his brother. He struck it with the sword, and the evil spirit returned to its true form and died in convulsions. Before it died, however, its blood spilled on Prince Peter. The body of Prince Peter became covered with sores and ulcers from this blood, and the prince became gravely ill. He was attended by many physicians, but none was able to cure him.

II. THE HEALING OF PRINCE PETER

Having heard that there were many physicians in the region of Riazan, Prince Peter told his servants to convey him there. Weakened by his illness, Prince Peter was no longer able to mount his horse. When he arrived in the land of Riazan, he sent all the men of his retinue to look for physicians.

One of the young men of his retinue came accidentally to a village called Charity. In this village he approached the gate of a house in which apparently no one was at home. He entered the house and found no one. Finally, he entered a room in which he found a beautiful maiden who was weaving. Before her a hare was jumping and playing about. The maiden said to the young soldier: "It is indeed unfortunate when the yard is without ears and the house without eyes."

The young man didn't understand the meaning of these words, but asked where the master of the house was. The maiden answered: "My father and mother have gone alone to weep so as to pay their debt in advance, and my brother has gone to view death between his feet."

Once more the young soldier did not understand the maiden's words, and things appeared to be strange to him. He again spoke to the maiden: "I came to your place and I saw you weaving and a hare jumping about before you. Now I hear strange words from your lips which I cannot understand. First you told me that it is unfortunate when a yard is without ears and a house without eyes. Then you told me that your mother and father have gone to weep alone so as to pay their debt in advance and that your brother has gone to view death between his feet. I have not understood a word that you have told me."

The maiden smiled, and said: "Well, it is not too difficult to understand. You came into the house and found me sitting here weaving and dressed in house clothes. If we had a dog, it might have heard you and started barking. In such a case the yard would have had ears. If my brother were at home, he might have seen you coming here and warned me. In this case the house would have eyes. I told you that my parents went to weep alone so as to pay their debt in advance. Actually, they went to a burial and wept there. Once death has come to them, others will weep after them, and therefore they weep now to pay their debt in advance. As for my brother, I told you that he had gone to view death between his feet. Actually, he and my father climb trees and collect pitch. He went just now to climb trees, and when he does so, he must watch his feet so that he will not fall. If he should fall, it would be his death. Therefore I said that my brother had gone to view death between his feet."

The young soldier then said to the maiden: "I see that you are very wise. Please tell me your name." Upon learning that the maiden's name was Fevronia, the young soldier explained why he had come there: "I have come here on behalf of my lord, Prince Peter of Murom. My prince is sick and covered with sores and ulcers. He received these afflictions from the blood of an evil serpent which he killed with his own hands. Since that time many doctors have treated him, but none has been able to cure him. Therefore, he ordered us to bring him to this land, for he heard that there are many physicians here. But we know neither where they live nor what are their names."

Fevronia answered, saying: "The only one who can cure the prince is the one who would order that your prince be brought to this place."

"Who would that be? What do you mean by these words?" the young man inquired. "The prince will lavishly reward the physician who will cure him. Tell me the name of such a physician—who he is and where he lives."

The maiden then told him: "Bring your prince to this place. If he is kind of heart and not proud in answering my questions, he will be cured." The young soldier listened to these words and then returned to Prince Peter and told him in detail all that he had seen and heard.

Prince Peter then enjoined his retinue to take him immediately to this wise maiden. And they took him to the house wherein lived the maiden. The prince sent a page to the maiden asking: "Tell me, maiden, who is the man who can cure me? Let him cure me, and he will receive a large part of my wealth!"

Without hesitation the maiden answered the page: "I am the physician who is able to cure your prince, but I do not desire any part of his wealth. However, if I do not become his wife, I shall have no reason to cure him."

The page returned to the prince and repeated to him the words of Fevronia. Prince Peter did not take her words seriously, thinking that it would be impossible for a prince to marry the daughter of a man whose station in life was as low as that of one who collects pitch. And he instructed his page to tell the maiden that she must cure him, and that if she did, she would become his wife. The page repeated these words to the maiden. She then took a small pitcher and scooped up some leaven from a barrel and told the page: "Prepare a steam bath for your prince, and, after the bath, spread this leaven over the sores and ulcers on his body. But you must take care not to cover all of the scabs, but leave one uncovered. And then your prince will return to good health." The young man brought the ointment made from leaven to the prince, and the servants immediately prepared the steam bath.

While the servants were preparing the steam bath, the prince decided to learn how wise this maiden really was, for he had only the word of his servant in this matter. To this end he sent her a small bundle of linen, asking that she make him a shirt, towel, and pants from this linen while he was in the steam bath, and if she were successful, she would thereby prove her wisdom.

A servant brought the bundle of linen to Fevronia and repeated the command of Prince Peter. Fevronia, without any hesitation, ordered the man to climb up on the stove and fetch down a piece of dry wood. When the servant gave her the piece of wood, she marked off a piece one foot in length and ordered the man to cut off this piece. When the servant had done so, she told him to take the block to his master and ask him to make from it a spinning wheel and a loom, while she was combing the linen in preparation for making the shirt, pants, and towel.

The servant took the block of wood to Prince Peter and repeated Fevronia's request. The prince laughed, and said: "Go to Fevronia and tell her that it is not possible to prepare so many things from so small a block in so short a time."

Fevronia had anticipated this answer, and told the servant: "Well, if your prince is unable to make a spinning wheel and a loom from such a small piece of wood in so short a time, how can I, in return, weave a shirt, pants, and a towel for him from such a small bundle of linen, while he takes a steam bath?" When the page returned to the prince, he was astounded by the wisdom of her answer.

Then Prince Peter went into the steam bath, and his servants applied the ointment over the sores and ulcers, leaving only one scab uncovered, as was ordered by Fevronia. When Prince Peter left the steam bath, his pains left him, and the next morning all his body was clear and healed excepting the one scab that had been left uncovered. He marveled at the curing powers of Fevronia. However, since Fevronia was the daughter of one of lowly birth, Prince Peter did not wish to marry her. He did, however, send her luxurious gifts, but Fevronia would not accept them.

Peter returned to his native city of Murom with his body completely healed excepting the single scab. Soon afterward, however, more sores and ulcers began to spread from the single scab which had not been covered by the ointment. And then his whole body was once again covered with sores and ulcers. Seeing that his affliction had returned, Prince Peter decided to return to Fevronia once again to undergo the proven treatment.

He returned to Riazan and to Fevronia's house, and despite the fact that he was ashamed for not having kept his promise to marry her, he asked her to treat him once more. Fevronia was not the least bit angry, but said that she would treat him only if he decided to be her husband. This time the prince firmly promised that he would take her as his wife.

The maiden then prescribed the same treatment as before. And when he was healed again, Prince Peter took Fevronia for his wife. And in this way did Fevronia become a princess. And both of them went to Peter's native city of Murom, and there they lived extremely piously, closely obeying the commandments of God. Soon after their arrival in Murom, Prince Paul died, and Prince Peter became the sole ruler of the city.

III. THE INTRIGUES OF THE BOYARS

The boyars of the city of Murom did not find Princess Fevronia to their liking. They, under the influences of their spouses, resented the princess because of her common origin. However, because of her charitable deeds, she was extremely popular among the simple people, and they prayed to God for her. Once, one of the courtiers, wanting to bring strife between Peter and Fevronia, came to the prince and told him: "The princess usually gets up from the table when she is not supposed to do so. Moreover, before leaving the table, she picks up the crumbs as if she were hungry."

Prince Peter decided to see if these accusations were true. He ordered that Princess Fevronia sit beside him at the table. When dinner was over, Fevronia picked up all the crumbs and kept them in her hand as she was accustomed to doing since her childhood. Seeing this, Prince Peter caught her by the hand and told her to open her fist, but when she did so they found fragrant myrrh and incense in the palm of her hand. And from that day on, Peter never attempted to question his wife's deeds.

Many years later the resentful boyars came once again to Peter and said: "Our lord, we want to serve you honestly and want you as our ruler, but we do not want Princess Fevronia as our princess, nor do we want her to rule over our wives. If you are to remain, our lord, you must take another for princess. Fevronia may take her wealth and go away anywhere she may wish to go."

Blessed Prince Peter was of gentle nature and did not become angry, but promised to talk to Princess Fevronia to learn what she would say of this. The shameless courtesans then decided to organize a banquet. They became drunk at this banquet and began to talk arrogantly like loudly barking dogs. And they began to deny Fevronia's miraculous gift of healing, which she had received from God not only for this life but even for after death.

They began talking: "Our lady, Princess Fevronia, the whole city and all the boyars ask you to give back to us Prince Peter, because we want him."

Fevronia answered: "You can have him. Only speak with him."

Then the boyars all spoke at once, saying: "Our lady, all of us want Prince Peter to rule over us, but our wives do not want you to rule over them. Please, take as much wealth as you desire and go wherever you like."

Hearing these words, Princess Fevronia told them that she would do as they desired but that now she must ask them to do one thing that she desired. The boyars, who were not very clever, rejoiced, and thought that they would easily rid themselves of her. So they pledged to do as she asked. And Princess Fevronia said: "I want nothing from you but my husband, Prince Peter."

The boyars deliberated for a short while and then said: "If Prince Peter will have it this way, we will not contradict him."

They hoped that they would be able to choose another ruler if Prince Peter did not wish to break the divine commandment, for it is written in the Gospel of Apostle Matthew: "But I say unto you, that whosoever shall put away his wife, saving for the cause of unchastity, makes her an adulteress." And Prince Peter, following the commandment of Jesus, gave up his rule over the city of Murom.

The evil lords prepared boats for Peter and Fevronia, for the city of Murom was situated on the river Oka. And so they went down the river in these vessels. On the princess' boat was a courtier who, despite the fact that he was accompanied by his wife, was tempted by evil spirits and began to stare at Princess Fevronia with shameful thoughts. The princess immediately discerned his evil thoughts and exposed them to the man. Approaching him, she ordered him to scoop up water from the river on one side of the boat and drink it. When the man had done so, she ordered him to go to the other side of the ship and do the same. When the man had drunk the water, Fevronia approached him, and asked: "Tell me, did you find that the water tastes the same on both sides of the ship, or was it perhaps sweeter on one side than on the other?"

The man answered: "No, my lady. The water tasted the same on both sides."

Then she replied: "And so is the nature of all women. Why then do you want to leave your wife and think about another woman?" The courtier then realized that the princess possessed the gift of reading the minds of men. Becoming afraid, he gave up his evil intentions.

In the evening the boats docked, and when the travelers were disembarking, Prince Peter became seized with doubts as to whether he was right in giving up his rule in the city of Murom. His sagacious wife perceived his doubts, and comforted him, saying: "Do not grieve, my Prince, for merciful God, our Creator, who directs our life, will never forsake us to misfortune."

That same evening the servants began to prepare dinner for the prince. They cut down branches of some trees and, making a spit, put the kettle on. Princess Fevronia, who was walking along the shore, came upon these branches that had been cut from the trees. Seeing them, she said: "Bless them, for before morning these branches will grow into great trees with rich foliage." And so it happened, for when the travelers got up in the morning they found that these branches had grown into great trees with rich foliage.

And when the servants began to load the boats, there came a lord from the city of Murom, saying: "My lord, Prince Peter, I come to you in behalf of all the courtiers of the city of Murom. They ask that you do not desert them, your poor orphans, but that you return as ruler to your native land. Many lords of the city have perished by the sword. Each, wanting to become ruler of the city, killed the other. Those lords who have survived and all the rest of the people beg you to come back, my lord, and rule over us. And we will neither anger nor irritate you again. Some of our ladies did not wish to be ruled by Princess Fevronia, but now these ladies have perished in the feud. Those of us who remain alive do love her, and we beg you not to leave us alone, your humble servants."

Thus Prince Peter and Princess Fevronia returned to the city of Murom, and they ruled according to the commandments of God.

IV. THE PASSING AWAY OF PETER AND FEVRONIA

Peter and Fevronia always helped their people with alms and prayers. They treated all as if they were their own children. They loved everyone equally, and disliked only those who were proud or who exploited the people. Peter and Fevronia lay up their treasures, not on earth, but in heaven. They were real pastors of their city. They always ruled with truth and humility, and never with anger. They gave shelter to pilgrims, fed the hungry, and clothed the naked. And they helped the poor in their misfortune.

When death was nearing, Peter and Fevronia prayed to God that they both might die in the same hour. And they requested that they be buried in the same tomb and in a common coffin in which their bodies would be separated only by a partition. And together they took monastic vows, Prince Peter becoming Brother David, and Princess Fevronia, Sister Euphrosinia.

And it happened that, shortly before her death, Princess Fevronia was embroidering a figure of the saints on a coverlet for the chalice of the cathedral. And a messenger came from Prince Peter, now Brother David, saying: "Sister Euphrosinia, I am ready to die, and wait only for you, so that we may die together."

But Princess Fevronia, now Sister Euphrosinia, answered: "You should wait, my lord, until I finish the coverlet for the chalice of the holy cathedral."

Then Brother David sent another messenger, who announced: "I can wait for you only a short time." Shortly after, another messenger arrived, saying: "I shall soon depart this world. There is no time left for waiting."

Princess Fevronia was just finishing the embroidering of the coverlet, but, hearing these words, she placed the needle in the coverlet and wound up the thread she had been using. Doing so, she sent a message to Brother David saying that they would now die together. And, having prayed, they offered up their souls to God on Friday, the 20th day of June.

After their deaths, some of the people decided that Prince Peter should be buried in the Cathedral of the Holy Virgin, which was within the walls of the city of Murom, and that Princess Fevronia should be buried in the Church of the Elevation of the Holy Cross, which was outside the walls of the city. And they actually did so, saying that it was not becoming for a man and woman who had taken monastic vows to be buried in the same casket. The body of Prince Peter was put in a casket and was placed in the cathedral, where it was left overnight.

The body of Princess Fevronia was put in another casket and placed in the church outside the city walls. A tomb, which had been carved from a huge rock as a resting-place for Peter and Fevronia, remained empty in the yard of the Cathedral of the Holy Virgin.

The next morning the people went to the caskets of Peter and Fevronia and found them empty. The bodies of the holy prince and princess were found together in the tomb of stone, which they had ordered prepared for them. The people, not understanding the meaning of this event, once more placed the bodies in separate caskets. On the following day the bodies of Prince Peter and Princess Fevronia were once again found together in the tomb of stone. Since that time no man has dared to disturb their holy bodies, but left them in their common tomb in the yard of the Cathedral of the Holy Virgin, which is located in the city of Murom. And whoever touched with contrition the tomb wherein lie the holy relics of Peter and Fevronia always received comfort and healing.

47. THE LIFE OF ST. MICHAEL, A FOOL IN CHRIST

The life of Michael of Klopsko was one of the most popular hagiographic works of northern Russia in the fifteenth and sixteenth centuries. Some seventy ancient manuscripts containing different versions of this *vita* have been preserved, and they have been rewritten, re-edited, and expanded upon by various medieval writers. Michael of Klopsko was an actual historical person, known not only from his *vita* but also from chronicles and documents. He lived in the first half of the fifteenth century, came to the Monastery of the Holy Trinity in Klopsko, near the city of Novgorod, between 1408 and 1412, and died there between 1453 and 1458. This was a period of intense struggle within the Muscovite ruling dynasty—specifically, between the Grand Prince of Moscow, Vasily II (or the "Blind"); his cousin, Prince Dmitry Shemiaka; and the latter's brother, Vasily the "One-Eyed." The epithets "the Blind" and "the One-Eyed" indicate the cruelty of this struggle, as each cousin was responsible for the other's mutilation. Shemiaka's memory has become notorious because of his cruelty and perfidy; in fact, the name Shemiaka has become a synonym for injustice. His story will be found in the tale of *Shemiaka's Judgment*. In addition to the struggle for power among these cousins, the *Life of St. Michael* also reflects the desire of the Muscovite princes to unify Russia under their leadership and to incorporate the Novgorodian Republic into the Russian state.

Michael of Klopsko was one of the first Russian *yurodivy,* or "fools in Christ," as certain people were called who devoted themselves entirely to the service of God. They accepted voluntarily the role of a fool in order to be able to teach people the truth of Christ and also to speak the truth to the powerful princes and lords. These "fools in Christ" usually wore coarse linen frocks throughout the whole year, ate the barest minimum of food, and walked barefoot, even in winter. In their prophecies they often spoke truths in the forms of parables, and interesting examples of such can be found in this work.

This *vita* consists of a number of episodes that have been placed under subtitles for easier reading. The style of this work clearly recalls the simple, clipped language of the *Novgorodian Chronicle.* Many sentences are so curt that they often require additional words for comprehension, and any such added words have been placed in parentheses. Similar also to the *Novgorodian Chronicle* is the use of "in this same year" to introduce a new topic or episode. The style of "Michael Addresses the Novgorodian Republic," however, differs considerably from the anecdotal manner and abrupt, curt style of the rest of the story. One can surmise that this section was a late addition to this work and was of a political nature—that is, it was intended to show the people of Novgorod that God himself, speaking through the mouth of Michael, wished Novgorod to become incorporated into the Muscovite realm. In episode XII ("The Punishment of *Posadnik* Gregory") the narration is clearly satirical.

Some of these episodes are presented in the form of anecdotes, and are among the earliest examples of Russian satirical writing. Their language resembles that of later Muscovite satirical tales of adventure, especially *Shemiaka's Judgment.* Michael's *vita* offers an interesting instance of primitive biography written in simple, naïve language and consisting of disconnected episodes from the life of the saint.

This translation is based upon version B of the earlier text of the *Life of St. Michael of Klopsko* to be found in L. A. Dimitrieva's *Povesti o zhitii Mikhaila Klopskogo,* published by the Academy of Sciences of the U.S.S.R., Moscow and Leningrad, 1958, pages 99–110.

I. MICHAEL'S ARRIVAL IN KLOPSKO

St. Michael, a fool in Christ, came to the Church of the Holy Trinity in Klopsko in the time of Abbot Theodosius who later became archbishop of Novgorod.

St. Michael came to the monastery on the eve of St. John's Day. The priest Ignatius, who was officiating in the church,

began to cense it during the ninth hymn. Then he went to cense
the cells (wherein resided the monks). When the priest entered
one cell, the door of which was open, he found there Monk
Michael who was sitting in a chair before a burning taper. He
was copying the Acts of the Apostles. Ignatius became alarmed
(at the presence of this unknown monk), and, returning to the
church, informed Abbot Theodosius and the other monks of this.
The abbot then took the cross and the censer and himself went
to the same cell and found that the door of the porch of this
cell was closed. Therefore the abbot went to the window and,
looking in, also saw a monk who was sitting and writing inside
the cell. The abbot then began to pray, saying: "O Lord, Jesus
Christ, Son of God, be merciful unto us."

After he had said his prayers, the abbot addressed the monk:
"Who are you, my son, a man or a devil?"

And Michael answered with the same words: "Are you a man
or a devil?"

The alarmed abbot then ordered the tearing down of the
porch roof and the door to gain entrance to the cell. When
Abbot Theodosius entered the cell, he began to cense the icon
and the monk with thyme; and the monk, attempting to protect
himself with his hand from the incense, made the sign of the
cross. Theodosius once more asked him: "Who are you? Why
did you come to us? Where are you from? What kind of man
are you?"

But Michael, instead of answering, only repeated the words
of the abbot: "Who are you? Why did you come to us? Where
are you from? What kind of man are you?" And so the abbot
did not learn the name (of the newcomer).

A short time later, before the day of Christ's Transfiguration,
Prince Constantine and his wife came to the monastery to take
Holy Communion and to present a gift to the monastery on the
occasion of the holy day. On that occasion Michael was asked
to read from the Book of Job during the dinner given in the
refectory. Hearing his voice, Prince Constantine turned toward
him and, recognizing him, said: "Oh, is it you Michael, the son
of Maxim?"

But Michael countered: "God alone knows who I am."

Then Abbot Theodosius questioned the monk: "Well, my
son, why won't you reveal your name to us?"

But Michael simply replied: "God alone knows who I am."
But then he revealed his name as being Michael, and so he was
called by all from that day on. Prince Constantine, however,
asked the abbot and the monks to care for Michael because he

was his relative. From that time the abbot and the monks began to care for Monk Michael.

II. MICHAEL PREDICTS THE EVERLASTING SPRING

In this same year and in the three that followed, there was a great drought and the river Veriazh was entirely dried up. Toward the end of these years of drought Abbot Theodosius went to this dried-up river and noticed the following words written in the sand of the riverbed: "In this place will be the spring of everlasting water." Seeing this, the abbot asked Michael, who was accompanying him: "Tell me, son, what is that which is written here?"

And Michael answered: "Here will be the spring of water everlasting." And both Abbot Theodosius and Michael addressed their prayers of thanksgiving to God. And then they began to dig, and immediately water gushed forth from the earth. And since that time there has been a well in that place, and it still exists. As soon as the inhabitants of that region learned of it, they began to use it, and do so until this day.

III. MICHAEL PREDICTS THE TONSURING OF PROKHOR

A short time later, Michael told Abbot Theodosius: "We shall have guests."

And Theodosius asked Michael: "Son, what kind of guests shall we have?" But Michael did not explain who the guests would be. But when Abbot Theodosius and Michael left the church, they found three men standing in the monastery yard.

Michael told the abbot: "Invite them to the refectory, Father, that they might break bread with us."

And Theodosius told the strangers: "Let us go, my children, into the refectory that we may break bread."

One of the strangers answered: "Father, there are other friends with us."

And Theodosius told the man: "One of you must go and invite your other friends to have the meal with us."

One of the strangers then went for their friends, and he returned with thirty men who were in armor and with weapons and javelins. And they entered the refectory to break bread.

Theodosius and Michael addressed them: "Sit down, children, and break bread." All but two began eating.

Then Michael addressed those who were not eating. "It will not come to pass as you believe it will."

Actually, almost immediately after, both strangers who were not eating became ill. After the meal everyone who had eaten got up from the table, glorifying God and the Holy Trinity.

And one of the strangers gave the monastery one hundred squir-rel furs [1] (for the meal). And he said the following: "Father, care for our ill comrades. We leave you in peace."

And the two strangers remained ill for five days. One of them wanted very much to become a monk, and since Theodosius hesitated to tonsure him, Michael said to the abbot: "Tonsure him, Father, and he will be our brother." And so he took mo-nastic vows and received the name of Prokhor. And the other stranger recovered, and left the monastery.

IV. THE MIRACLE OF THE FILLED GRANARY

In this same year there was a famine throughout the land of Novgorod. And Theodosius and all his brothers became sad-dened, but Michael said to Abbot Theodosius: "Don't grieve, Father, but remember that Our Lord fed forty thousand men, besides the women and children, in the wilderness." And he convinced Abbot Theodosius that the monks should commence cooking rye in kettles and distribute it to pilgrims and travelers. But the monks began to grumble about this, being dissatisfied with Abbot Theodosius and with Michael. But Theodosius and Michael suggested to the monks: "Let us visit our granary."

And they learned that the granaries were overflowing and that the amount of grain did not diminish (even though many were fed from this grain). And they ordered that more rye be prepared so that they might continue to distribute it to the peo-ple without hesitation. And they glorified God, the Holy Trinity, and the blessed saints.

V. THE BUILDING OF THE CHURCH OF THE HOLY TRINITY

On the Saturday of St. Lazarus, Prince Constantine arrived at the Monastery of the Holy Trinity in Klopsko greatly saddened. And he told Abbot Theodosius and Monk Michael: "I am very sad now because my brothers do not wish to give me my share of the patrimony."

And Michael answered him: "Prince, don't grieve. You will yet come into possession of your estate. In a short time your brother will send for you. Pray to the Holy Trinity and build a stone church in its name, and in return the Lord will reserve a temple in heaven for you."

And then the prince asked Abbot Theodosius: "Do you have any craftsmen? I want to build a church of stone in honor of the Holy Trinity, the source of all life, to commemorate the memory of my parents and myself."

---

[1] Squirrel furs, or, as they are sometimes called, *vairs*, were a monetary unit in ancient Russia.

Theodosius sent for craftsmen, and there came craftsmen by the names of John, Clement, and Alexis. And the prince ordered these master craftsmen: "Build a church of stone in the honor of the Holy Trinity, the source of all life, and embellish it in the manner of the Church of St. Nicholas in Latki."

And the craftsmen answered: "We can do so, lord prince. And we are ready to serve you if God and the Holy Trinity will aid us." And they laid the foundation of the church on the day of the Commemoration of our holy Father Theodore Sekiot, April 22nd, 6931 (1423). And they began bringing the stone, but a mighty storm hindered them in their work, and they were able neither to bring the stones by the river nor to work on the walls of the church.

Then Michael said to the masters: "Pray to God for help, because the invisible power of God builds churches." And even as Michael spoke, God sent a helpful wind to fill their sails as they were going for the stone and when they returned with the stone.

For the consecration of the church, Prince Constantine came with his princess and the boyars and brought plenty of food and drink, because he was very glad. And, on the day of the holy martyr Tekla, September 24th, 6932 (1423), this Church of the Holy Trinity was completed, thanks to the blessings of Abbot Theodosius and the prayers of St. Michael. And Prince Constantine said to Theodosius and Brother Michael: "Father, thanks to your prayers I received the news from my older brothers that they will give me my patrimony."

And Theodosius and Michael answered: "Go in peace, our child, and they will meet you with friendship. Only, don't forget, our child, this house of God, the Church of the Holy Trinity, the source of all life, as well as ourselves, your poor servants."

And the prince promised: "All my life I shall never forget this house of God, the monastery, the Church of the Holy Trinity, and you, my poor brothers, who have prayed for me."

VI. MICHAEL PREDICTS ABBOT THEODOSIUS' ELECTION TO THE ARCHBISHOPRIC

This same year Simon, Archbishop of Novgorod, passed away. And Michael predicted to Abbot Theodosius: "You will be elected to the chair of the archbishop and will rule for three years, but you will also be deposed before you have become consecrated."

VII. MICHAEL'S MIRACULOUS APPEARANCES

On Tuesday of Holy Week during matins the brethren found that Michael was missing from the monastery. And at that very time he appeared during matins in the sacristy of the Cathedral of Holy Sophia of Novgorod, and he was there recognized after matins by Gregory, the *posadnik,* who addressed him, saying: "Come and break bread with us," and he ordered one of his men to attend him. And suddenly Michael was no longer there. But when in Klopsko the priest went that day to celebrate the liturgy in the monastery, Michael was already in the church. When the brothers left the church for the refectory, there arrived a man who was sent by the *posadnik* to inquire the whereabouts of Michael. And Michael was already there.

VIII. MICHAEL PREDICTS ALFIRY'S MISFORTUNES

This very day there was an argument between Alfiry, son of John, and Ivan Loshinsky, son of Simon, over the possession of land. And Michael predicted to Alfiry: "You will remain without hands and feet and you will become mute." And when Alfiry came to the Church of the Holy Virgin in Kurechka, he met Ivan, and said: "Brother Ivan, this land is mine," and he clapped his hands and his gloves dropped to the floor. When he bowed down to pick them up, a stroke hit him. His hands, feet, and tongue became paralyzed, and he could no longer speak.

IX. MICHAEL AND PRIEST NICEPHORIUS

And there was another prophecy made by Michael concerning a certain priest, Nicephorius, who had secretly stolen the venerable icon of the archbishop. And Michael said to this priest: "You will be dishonored." And from that time the priest lost his mind. And Michael ordered that they look in the stove, and there they found the venerable icon that had been stolen.

X. THE PROPHECY TO THE ARCHBISHOP

Archbishop Euthemius received the taxes due him from the monastery, but he wanted additional collections. And so he took a horse as black as a raven from the monastery. And Michael told the archbishop: "You will live but a short time, and you will leave everything behind." And soon the archbishop fell ill and passed away.

XI. MICHAEL AND ARCHBISHOP EUTHEMIUS II

In this same year, another Euthemius was elected to the archbishopric. For the three years that followed he was not consecrated. Once, the bishop came to Klopsko to help the monastery. During the meal at the table the archbishop asked Michael: "Dear Michael, pray to God for me that I should be invested by Great Prince Vasily."

The archbishop had a kerchief in his hand, and Michael snatched it suddenly from the bishop and placed it on the bishop's head, and said: "You will go to Smolensk and you will be consecrated to the archbishopric." And actually, the bishop did go to Smolensk and was there consecrated.

The bishop returned to Michael, and said: "God and the Metropolitan of Moscow gave me their blessing."

And Michael once again spoke to the archbishop: "You will be summoned to Moscow, and you will go there and you will submit yourself to the Great Prince and to the metropolitan."

XII. THE PUNISHMENT OF POSADNIK GREGORY

And the Monastery of the Holy Trinity at Klopsko was heavily oppressed by *Posadnik* Gregory. Once, on Easter Sunday, this Gregory came to Mass at the Church of the Holy Trinity of this monastery. When the abbot finished celebrating the Mass, he and the *posadnik* left the church. The *posadnik* stopped the abbot and the monks in the monastery, and addressed them: "Abbot, do not let your horses and cows into the meadows in the summer, for that is my land. Also, don't hunt or fish along river Veriazh, or in the marshes, or in the vicinity of my estates. And if your people come there, I shall order that their arms and legs be broken."

And Michael replied to the *posadnik:* "You yourself will lose your arms and legs, and, more than that, you will nearly drown in the river."

Once the abbot and Michael sent their men to the river and to the marshes. As the men of the monastery were pulling in the nets, the *posadnik* went to the river. He went up to the men of the monastery and followed them into the water. Chasing the fishermen, he hit one of them with his fist, and wanted to hit another one, but he missed and fell in the water, and nearly drowned. When his people came, he was nearly drowned, and they carried him home because he was unable to use his arms and legs, as was predicted by Michael.

Early in the morning he was brought to the monastery, but Michael forbade him to enter it and he forbade the monks to pray for him, to light a candle for him, or to mention his name in the liturgy. And Michael added, addressing the *posadnik:* "Don't bring us any food or drink; only leave us in peace."

The abbot and the monks were afraid that they had made a mistake by not praying for the *posadnik* or by not mentioning his name in the liturgy. In the meantime the *posadnik's* men decided to complain, and said: "We are going to complain to the bishop and to the authorities of the city of Novgorod, for you would neither pray for the *posadnik* nor mention his name during Mass." And they went to the bishop and to the authorities of the city of Novgorod—to Jacob Andreianov, Fefilat Zakharin, and John Vasiliev to lodge their complaint. And the bishop sent his archpriest and his archdeacon to Michael and Abbot Theodosius, saying: "Do pray for the *posadnik* during Mass, and celebrate special services for his recovery."

But Michael replied to the archpriest and the archdeacon: "We pray to God for the entire world, and not only for Gregory." (And then he addressed Gregory:) "Go to the other monasteries and there ask God's forgiveness."

And the *posadnik* began his pilgrimages to the monasteries, and he began to make gifts to them, as well as to the churches in the cities. His pilgrimages to monasteries lasted a year and one and one-half months. But nowhere, in any of these monasteries, did he find God's forgiveness.

Thereafter (returning to Novgorod), he sent a man to the bishop, saying: "My lord and my father, nowhere in the monasteries could I find help."

(The bishop answered:) "Go now, my child, to the Monastery of the Holy Trinity, and ask there the mercy of the Holy Trinity and of Monk Michael." And the bishop sent a priest (to Michael), and the *posadnik* went there personally. It was decided to hold a special service to the Holy Trinity and to celebrate the Mass. The *posadnik* was brought into the church in a carpet, but he was not even able to make the sign of the cross. The celebration of the service to the Holy Trinity began. And when they began to sing the hymn, the *posadnik* was able to move his hands, even though he had not been able to move his hands and feet for one year and one and one-half months. When the priest began reading the Gospel, the *posadnik* was already able to make the sign of the cross and to sit down. In the middle of the service he was able to stand, and so he remained standing until the end of the service. After Mass, everyone went to the refectory, and the *posadnik* addressed the monks during the meal: "Holy brothers, I wish you health and appetite."

But Michael countered: "Those who live by the sword shall perish by the sword." In such manner did Michael teach a lesson to Gregory the *posadnik*. And Michael added: "My child, be good to Michael and to the monastery."

XIII. MICHAEL AND DMITRY SHEMIAKA

A short time afterward Prince Dmitry Shemiaka visited Novgorod, and he came to the monastery in Klopsko that he might receive Michael's blessing. (And he said to Michael:) "Dear

Mikhailushka, I was chased away from my patrimony, and my enemies have driven me from the throne of the great prince." [2]

And Michael replied: "Every power is given by God."

"My dear Mikhailushka, pray to God to help me get back my patrimony, and to become once more the great prince," Shemiaka once again said to Michael.

But Michael answered only: "Prince, all you will get is a three-foot coffin." But Prince Dmitry, paying no heed to Michael's words, decided to begin another campaign to become great prince. But Michael said: "It is in vain, prince, for you cannot receive that which God does not wish you to have." And God did not help Shemiaka, and he escaped once more to Novgorod.

On Friday of the week of Pentecost, Prince Shemiaka returned to the monastery at Klopsko to bring gifts. He gave the brothers much food and drink. And to Michael he gave his own fur coat. When Prince Dmitry, accompanied by the abbot and the monks, returned to his boat, Michael patted the prince's head, and said: "The damp earth is already awaiting you." And he repeated these words thrice.

And the prince said: "My dear monk, I want to return to the city of Rzhev to my patrimony in Konstantinov."

But Michael added: "Prince, your desire will not be fulfilled."

And so it came to pass, for the prince died soon afterward.

XIV. MICHAEL ADDRESSES THE NOVGORODIAN REPUBLIC

Once, *Posadnik* John Nemir came to the monastery, and he asked the *posadnik:* "Why do you travel?"

The *posadnik* answered: "I have been at my wife's grandmother, Euphrosinia, and now I come to you to receive your blessing."

And Michael asked: "Well, my child, what kind of problems do you try to solve with women?"

John Nemir answered: "We expect that that great prince (of Moscow) will start a campaign against us. But we expect help from Prince Michael of Lithuania."

But Michael retorted: "Your Lithuanian prince will not be a help, but worse than nothing at all. Send your envoy to the Great Prince of Moscow right now, and sue for peace. If you don't come to an agreement with the Great Prince of Moscow, he will come with all his forces to Novgorod, and you will have no divine help. And the Great Prince of Moscow will camp at Bureguy. He will display his army along the river Shelon, and

---

[2] Shemiaka led a revolt against his cousin, the Great Prince of Moscow, and for a short time became the ruler of Muscovy.

he will jail many citizens of Novgorod. Some will be sent to
Moscow, some will be executed, and some will be forced to pay
tribute. And the Lithuanian prince will not fight for you, and
you will receive no help from him. Better that you send your
archbishop and *posadniks* to Moscow with a petition for peace
to the Great Prince. Better to pay him tribute; otherwise the
Great Prince of Moscow will return here, will take your city,
and will deprive you of liberty, and God will help him."

And so it came to pass as Michael said.

XV. MICHAEL'S DEATH

Michael had a simple way of living. He lived alone in his cell
and had neither a headboard and pillow nor a bed; neither
sheets nor covers, but he slept on the earth. He heated his cell
with dried horse manure and lived in the monastery for forty
and four years. The entire week he ate only bread and water.

Once Abbot Theodosius called Michael for Communion, and
after it Michael said: "Father, I would receive the Divine Sacrament from you."

And the abbot answered: "Have it, my child, and once more
take Holy Communion."

And all were astounded by these words. And Michael took
the censer and thyme and went to his cell. When everyone went
to the refectory, the abbot had food sent to Michael's cell. And
when the monks came to his cell and entered in, they found the
holy man lying as if asleep. And the fragrance of the thyme from
the censer near Michael was rising from the earth to the heavens. On January 11th, the day of our father, Theodosius of
Jerusalem, Michael was buried in the Monastery of the Holy
Trinity, the source of all life.

Glory be to God, now and forevermore.

48. THE STORY OF GREAT JOHN, ARCHBISHOP OF NOVGOROD THE GREAT; HOW, IN ONE NIGHT, HE WAS TAKEN FROM NOVGOROD TO THE CITY OF JERUSALEM, AND THEN RETURNED TO NOVGOROD THE GREAT THAT SAME NIGHT

This is one of the oldest Novgorodian legends. Bishop John was
a very popular Church leader in the middle of the twelfth century, and around him there arose a number of stories. When
Novgorod was threatened with incorporation into the Muscovite
realm in the middle of the fifteenth century, Bishop Euthemius
II (1430–1458) began collecting the legends and tales concerning the city's history and the deeds of its most outstanding

leaders. Most likely this account of Great John was re-edited by Pachomius the Serb after discovery of Bishop John's relics in 1439. Pachomius, one of the innovators of the literary style known as "weaving of words" (*pletenie sloves*), embellished this text with more biblical words, difficult and complex sentences, and its stylistic redundancy.

The motif of a demon confined in a vessel is found both in tales from the East, as for instance in *Tales of the Arabian Nights,* and in early Russian hagiography.

The story is not presented here in its entirety. It ends with an account of the procession of the people and clergy to the St. George Monastery to ask Bishop John to return. Bishop John forgives the people and returns to his see.

This translation is based on the text published by N. K. Gudzy in *Khrestomatiia po drevnei russkoi literatury,* Moscow, 1955, pages 207–209.

FATHER, MAY YOUR BLESSING BE WITH US

This story should not lapse into oblivion, for God Almighty, who placed John in the bishopric, permits people to be overcome by temptation. He does this to sanctify and glorify them, testing their mettle as one might test gold. God has said: "I will glorify those who glorify me." Wondrous is God among the host of his saints, and God himself glorifies them.

And Christ said: "I give you power over evil spirits."

Once, in the evening, John, Archbishop of Great Novgorod, went to recite his evening prayers, as was his custom. At that time there was a vessel filled with water near his cell, and the Reverend Father used it for his ablutions. Suddenly he heard someone struggling in the water of this vessel. Coming closer to the vessel, and realizing that this was the design of the devil, he read a prayer so as to confine the demon in the vessel. The devil wished to frighten the holy father, but he was defeated in this purpose by the firm adamant.[1] The devil wanted to get out of the vessel, but could not overcome this power. A short time later, the demon could no longer endure and so began to shriek: "Oh, what a miserable plight! I am burned by fire and cannot resist any longer. Let me go at once, O servant of God."

The bishop answered: "And who are you? How did you get in this vessel?"

This devil answered: "I am an evil demon and came to this

---

[1] Adamant was often used in Russian medieval literature as a symbol of firm strength, and in this case refers to the power of the cross.

place so that I might corrupt you, hoping that you would become frightened and cease your praying. But you confined me
so cruelly in this vessel, and here I am burned terribly by the
fire. O woe is me, a cursed one! How could I become tempted?
How could I get in this vessel? I am bewildered! Release me
now, you servant of God. I shall not return to this place again!"

And the evil demon shrieked so, that finally the bishop spoke,
saying: "For your daring I order that you this very night take
me from Novgorod the Great to the city of Jerusalem. And place
me before the church wherein is the Lord's Sepulcher. And this
very night you must bring me back to my cell, which you have
dared to enter. And only then shall I release you."

The demon promised to comply with the will of the bishop,
and said: "Please, only release me from confinement, you servant
of God."

Without releasing the demon from the power of the cross,
the holy bishop let the devil out of the vessel and said to him:
"Ready yourself and appear before me as a horse. Then I will
mount you and you will fulfill my request."

The devil, like a cloud of darkness, left the vessel and appeared as a horse before the cell door. The bishop went from
his cell and, having armed himself with the cross and Grace,
mounted the demon and that very night arrived in the city of
Jerusalem in which is located the Holy Sepulcher of the Lord
and the Tree of Life. Retaining his power over the demon, the
bishop forbade it to move from the spot where it stood. And
the demon, remaining under the power of the cross, was unable
to move away.

In the meantime the Reverend Father went to the Church of
the Holy Resurrection and, standing before the door of this
church, knelt and prayed. And the doors of the church opened
of their own accord, while the tapers and censers of the Lord's
Sepulcher began to burn. The bishop, shedding tears, thanked
God. And he venerated and kissed the Holy Sepulcher and the
Tree of Life and the other shrines. Then he left the church,
having fulfilled his longing. And the church doors closed after
him of their own accord.

The bishop found the demon standing in the form of a horse
and in the same place, as he had been ordered. And mounting
the demon, the bishop found himself that very night in his cell,
in the city of Novgorod the Great.

Leaving the saint's cell, the devil said: "O John, you forced
me to labor, carrying you in one night to Jerusalem and that
very same night carrying you back to Novgorod the Great. I was
bound to do so, by the power of the cross, as if I were bound

by shackles. I had to undergo many calamities. Reveal to no one
what has happened this night. If you do, I will lead you into
temptation. You will be tried and sentenced for lechery, abused,
and put on a raft in the river Volkhov." [2]

To prevent the abuse of the demon, Bishop John made the
sign of the cross.

The bishop had the custom of discussing problems of the
spirit with the honorable abbots, most learned priests, and God-
abiding men, since he considered it a necessity that he share
his wisdom with others and open to them the sublimity of the
Holy Trinity. He never tired of teaching men, and he often
told to them the occurrences of his own life, describing them
as those of another man. "I know," he told them once, "a certain
man who happened to go from Novgorod to the city of Jerusalem in one night, worshiped there at the Lord's Sepulcher, and
returned that very night to Novgorod the Great." The abbots
and the others were astounded.

But from that time on, and with the permission of God, the
demon began to lead the bishop into temptation. The people
had the vision many times of a harlot leaving the cell of the
bishop. Many officials of the city, who used to come to the
bishop's cell to receive his blessing, would see there a woman's
necklace of coins and also a woman's robe and sandals. And
they felt sore offended, and wondered what to say of this. But
all this was the design of this demon who expected that the
people would rise up against the bishop, would speak unjustly
of him, and would drive him from their midst.

The people took council with the officials, and declared: "It
is unjust for such a bishop, who is a whoremonger, to occupy
the apostolic seat. Let us go and drive him from our midst, for
about such people King David said: 'And words will pour forth
from the mouth of the flatterer and they will speak of righteousness, lowliness, pride, and destruction. This they do for they
worship the devil, even before the assembly of Jews.'"

But let us return to the narration. When the people came to
the cell of the bishop, the demon walked among the people,
and they saw him as a girl, leaving the cell of the saint. And
the people began to exclaim that she should be seized, but they
could not do so, although they followed her for a long time.

The bishop heard the cries of the people and came out to
them and said: "What has happened, my children?" But the
citizens paid no heed to these words, and told him what they

---

[2] Novgorod was situated on the river Volkhov, and the placing of
convicts on a raft in the middle of the river was a common punishment.

had seen, condemned him as a whoremonger, abused him, and, after wondering what should be done with him, they decided: "Let us put him on a raft in the middle of the river Volkhov so that he may float down the river and away from our city."

And so they took the ascetic, holy, and great bishop of God, John, to the great bridge which spanned the river Volkhov, led him down to the river, and put him on a raft. And so the dream of the evil demon was fulfilled. However, God's Grace shone on the face of the bishop, and his prayers to God overcame the demon's design. The demon had begun to rejoice, but when John, the bishop of God, was put on the raft in the middle of the river Volkhov, the raft immediately began to move upstream, although it was not driven by anyone. The raft on which the bishop was sitting was pushed upstream from the great bridge to the Monastery of St. George, and against a strong current. The bishop was praying for the people on the raft, saying: "O Lord, forgive them this sin, for they know not what they do."

And seeing this, the demon was abashed, and began to weep.

The people of Novgorod, seeing this miracle, rent their garments, returned, and said: "We have sinned; we have committed an injustice to this father, and we have condemned our pastor. We now know that this has happened through the designs of a demon."

B. LIVES OF THE SAINT-PRINCES

49. ORISON ON THE LIFE AND DEATH OF GRAND PRINCE DMITRY IVANOVICH

THE highly rhetorical *Orison on the Life and Death of Grand Prince Dmitry Ivanovich, Tsar of Russia,* was written either in the late fourteenth century shortly after Dmitry's death in 1389, or at the beginning of the fifteenth. In any case, it was already included in a Novgorodian codex of chronicles in 1448. The purpose of this work was to praise the prince who, in 1380, defeated the Golden Horde for the first time, paving the way for complete liberation from the Asian conquerors. It is very different from *Zadonshchina,* in which the Battle of Kulikovo Field was similarly glorified and, despite some borrowings from earlier literary works, it certainly belongs to the literature of the ornamental Muscovite style. The usual themes and stylistics of the military story are overshadowed here by the oratorical devices of the hagiographic eulogy and extremely interesting borrowings from the oral tradition. Among the latter, of particular beauty is the funeral lament of Princess Eudoxia, widow of the Grand Prince, the first lament to appear *in extenso* in Russian literature. In a remodeled version it reappeared in the *Tale of the Destruction of Riazan* (see Selection 36) written in the fifteenth or sixteenth century.

The most frequently used devices of the writer's poetic diction are extended and redundant epithets, short rhythmic sentences with frequent verbal rhyme—not always seen in the translation—and longer sentences with many subordinated clauses.

Several passages of the *Orison* recall the *Life of St. Stephen of Perm* by Epiphanius the Wise. It ends with a highly rhetorical glorification of the prince in which the author uses biblical imagery, comparing Dmitry with the patriarchs and prophets of the Old Testament. He finds that Dmitry surpassed Adam, Noah, Moses, and other prophets and biblical heroes in deeds and wisdom. In view of the close parallels between this specific passage and the more original work of Epiphanius, it has been omitted from this translation.

The spirit of Muscovite ornamentalism permeates the entire *Orison.* The author is not so much concerned with providing biographical information about Dmitry as with his exaltation and his role of Muscovite ruler. He even endowed Dmitry with the title, "tsar," actually assumed by the Muscovite dynasty only some hundred and eighty years after Dmitry's death. Thus, despite its folk motifs and heavy use of imagery, the story probably had primarily the political and propagandistic purpose of enhancing the role of the Muscovite ruler as a unifying power in Russia. Chronologically, Prince Dmitry's *vita* should go together with *Zadonshchina*, which describes his victory over the Tatars. The latter, however, being patterned after the *Lay of Igor's Campaign*, belongs to the category of "Epigones of the Kievan School," whereas the former is a typical example of "Muscovite Ornamental Formalism."

Some passages of the text were omitted for the sake of space. The translation follows the text published in *Polnoe sobranie russkikh letopisei*, Volume 6, "Novgorodskii svod," St. Petersburg, 1853, pages 104–111.

Grand Prince Dmitry was born of honorable and most esteemed parents, the Grand Prince Ivan Ivanovich and Grand Princess Alexandra. He was the grandson of Great Ivan Daniilovich, unifier of the Russian land; among his ancestors were holy Tsar Vladimir, who was the new Constantine and Christianized the Russian land, and who became a fruitful branch and a beautiful flower in the holy garden planted by God; he was also kin to Princes Boris and Gleb, with whom he is glorified for his piety. And he was carefully brought up in piety and reverence, and from his earliest infancy loved God.

When his father, Grand Prince Ivan Ivanovich, ended his life in this world and was taken into the heavenly gardens he left his son, Dmitry, who was still very young, only nine years old, as well as Dmitry's most beloved brother, Prince Ivan Ivanovich. Soon after this his mother, the Grand Princess Alexandra, passed away and he was left alone to rule the provinces of the Grand Principality (of Moscow) in glory and honor, thanks to the grace which was given him by God. And he took over the scepter of the dominion of the Russian land. Thus he ascended the throne of this earthly kingdom and his patrimony of the Grand Principality.

While he was still young he matured in spiritual matters,
and did not make empty talk,
and did not use shameful words,
and he shunned evil people,
and consorted always with honorable people,
and always listened with tender emotion to Divine Scripture,
and cared greatly for the churches of God,
and kept guard over the Russian land with his courage,

gentle and forgiving like a child,
he was mature in his judgment,
always dreaded by the enemy in battle,
and vanquished many enemies who raised themselves against
*   us,*
and fenced his glorious city of Moscow with splendid walls
and was renowned in all the world—
and he grew strong like the Cedars of Lebanon,
and flourished like a phoenix in the woods.

When he became sixteen years old he married Princess Eudoxia from the Suzdalian land, daughter of Grand Prince Dmitry Konstantinovich and Grand Princess Anna, and the entire Russian land rejoiced at this union. And even after marriage he lived in chastity and piety, because he cared for his eternal salvation. He ruled his earthly kingdom justly and with wisdom, but remaining faithful to the Heavenly King he did not pursue the pleasures of the flesh. Like a firm helmsman he directed his land even against the storms, escaping the waves, for he was inspired by High Providence. He ruled his tsardom with the same care by which a prophet tries to perceive Divine Will. And the glory of his name grew (with each year) just as did the glory of the holy and Grand Prince Vladimir. In the years of his reign the Russian land flourished in the same way as once did the promised land of Israel. With dread of his power he girded the whole land of Russia and from the Orient to the Occident his name was glorified. From sea to sea, from the rivers to the last frontiers of the universe his name was exalted. And the kings of this earth who heard of him marveled at him, but his enemies who lived around his frontiers envied him and incited Khan Mamai against him, saying: "Grand Prince Dmitry of Moscow calls himself Tsar of the Russian land and claims to be more honorable than thou, and he wants to oppose thy kingdom."

Mamai was advised by evil counselors who were of the Christian faith, but who acted as pagans, and he told his princes and advisors: "I will conquer the Russian land and I will destroy Christian churches, and I will convert them to my faith, and I will force them to worship my Mohammed, and where there are Russian churches I will build my mosques, and I will put my publicans in all Russian cities, and I will kill all Russian princes."

And he acted in the same way as King Og of Bashan acted, bragging before the Lord's Tabernacle of the Congregation in Shiloh, who perished there after having bragged.

And godless Mamai sent to Russia, ahead of his army, his

godless General Bigich, who moved up considerable forces with numerous Tatar princes from the Horde. Having heard about this, Grand Prince Dmitry Ivanovich went to meet him with large forces of the Russian land and fought the pagans at the river Vozha in the Riazan principality. And Our Lord and the Holy Mother of God helped Grand Prince Dmitry Ivanovich and the pagan sons of Hagar were humiliated. Some were cut to pieces, others escaped running. Grand Prince Dmitry Ivanovich returned after this great victory; he had defended his patrimony, the Russian land, from the invasion of the pagans.

Shameless Mamai was humiliated because in place of praise, dishonor met him. And he, himself, went with his armies into the Russian land, bragging that he would defeat the grand prince; and his heart was filled with evil lawlessness. Having heard it, Grand Prince Dmitry Ivanovich sighed from the depths of his heart to God and to his Holy Mother and said: "O Holy Lady, Virgin, Mother of God, Intercessor and Defender of the world. Implore thy Son to help me, a sinner, to be worthy of sacrificing my head and my life for thy Son's and thy name. I have no other patron, I have only thee, my Lady. . . ."

And Grand Prince Dmitry Ivanovich called the dignitaries and all the princes of the Russian land who were under his rule and told the princes of the Russian land and his dignitaries: "It is better, brethren, to sacrifice our lives for the Orthodox Christian Faith than

> For us to allow them (the Tatars) to devastate the holy
>   churches of God,
> or be dispersed over the face of the entire world,
> or let the pagans capture our wives and children,
> or let the pagans persecute us,
> because the Most Holy Mother of God will implore her Son
>   and our God (to help us)."
> And the Russian princes and dignitaries said,
> "O our lord, Russian Tsar!
> We promise thee to sacrifice our lives in thy service.
> And now for thy sake we will spill our blood
> and accept a second baptism in this blood. . . ."

And he (Dmitry) became filled with the courage of Abraham and prayed to God and to his servant, great saint and patron of the Russian land, holy wonder-maker Peter, and he went against the pagan Khan Mamai, the second Sviatopolk (as years before did Grand Prince Yaroslav Vladimirovich).

And he met the khan in the Tatar prairie on the river Don.
And they clashed like blue clouds,
and the weapons flashed like lightning on a day of rain,
and the warriors fought hand to hand,
and the blood flowed in the ravines,
and the river Don flowed mixed with blood,
and the Tatar heads rolled like stones,
and the pagan bodies were cut down like oaks,
and the angel of God saw many battles.
And the angel helped the Christians.
And many witnesses saw the angels helping the Christians.
And God helped Grand Prince Dmitry Ivanovich
and his kin, holy martyrs Boris and Gleb.
And the accursed Mamai fled from the vision of his face.
And as once thrice-accursed Sviatopolk disappeared from our
*   memory,*
so accursed Mamai ran into oblivion.

The Grand Prince Dmitry Ivanovich returned greatly victorious, like the victory of Moses over the Amalekites. And there was peace throughout the Russian land. And his enemies were humiliated, and other lands, who heard of the victory given him over the enemy by God, submitted themselves to him. And all dissenters and rebels in the tsardom perished.

Grand Prince Dmitry Ivanovich customarily loved children, as David, prophet and forerunner of (the Virgin Mary and Jesus Christ) Our Lord, loved the children of Saul; and this Grand Prince loved the innocent and pardoned the guilty; and as it is told in the Book of Job, he was a father to his people, eyes to the blind, feet to the lame; he was pillar and guardian of the (Christian) banner, and his just reign over his people was known to the entire world; by High Providence he was placed to rule mankind, to put straight all confusion in the world; he was a high-soaring eagle, a fire to scorch ungodliness, a bath to cleanse moral pollution, a threshing floor for purity, a gale dispersing the chaff, a resting-bed for those who worked for God, trumpet for sleepers, ruler of the peaceful, a victorious crown, a quiet haven for seafarers, a ship of welfare, a weapon against the enemy, a sword against violence, an indestructible wall, net for the wicked, firm ground, mirror of life, one who did everything with God's help and ruled in God, a humble mind, peace during a storm, a depth of understanding mind; he confirmed the princes of Russia in their principalities, was affable in commanding his dignitaries, never offended anyone, liked everyone equally, taught the young, gave generous alms to all, and enough to the begging hand. . . .

And here is what I will tell about his life: he preserved his body pure until his wedding, as the Church must be preserved from all abuse for the Holy Ghost; the Grand Prince often looked at the earth from which he came; his soul and mind, however, turned to the heavens in which he was predestined to rest. After this wedding he kept his body pure without sin. . . .

He lived with his Princess Eudoxia twenty-two years in chastity and their sons and daughters grew up in piety. He ruled over his patrimony, his Grand Principality, for twenty-nine years and six months and altogether he lived, beginning with his birth, thirty-eight years and five months. And he accomplished many deeds and victories and preserved his Orthodox Faith more than anyone else. Thereafter he became ill and was very sorrowful, but since his illness was very light the Grand Princess and his sons and his dignitaries greatly rejoiced. But his illness got worse. Pains came to his heart and his insides were very sore. And his body approached death. . . .

When the most pious, Christ-loving, honorable Grand Prince Dmitry Ivanovich of All Russia passed away, his face shone as fair as the face of an angel. And when the princess saw him dead on the bed, she cried with loud voice, and her eyes shed burning tears, and all her body became feverish, and she beat her chest with her hands. And she addressed him as a trumpet addresses an army, or like an organ which sounds most sweetly:

"How could you die, my beloved life?
How could you leave me a lonely widow?
Why did I not die before you?
O my tsar, how will I be able to greet thee and serve thee?
O my lord, where is thy honor and glory?
Where is thy reign?
Thou wast the ruler of thy Russian land,
now thou art dead and dost not rule anyone.
Thou broughtest peace to many countries,
and achievest many conquests.
Now thou art conquered by death.
Thy glory hath ended.
Thy sight seeth only decay.
How can I find joy without thee?
Thou hadst priceless vestments.

Now thou hast only a poor shroud.
Thou hadst the crown of a ruler,
now thou hast the cowl of the poor.
Thou hadst a beautiful palace,
now thou hast a casket!
O my fair light, why wert thou eclipsed?
If God hears thy prayer,
pray for me, thy princess.
I lived together with thee,
and I want to die with thee,
then youth will never abandon us,
and old age will never strike us.
To whom dost thou abandon me and thy children?
How couldst thou, light of my eyes, be extinguished?
Why dost thou not speak to me?
Lo, my beautiful flower,
which faded so early.
Lo, my fruitful vine,
no longer wilt thou give any fruit for my heart,
no longer any sweetness for my soul.
Why, my lord, dost thou not look at me?
Why dost thou not speak to me?
Or hast thou forgotten me already?
Why dost thou not look at me? at my children?
Why dost thou not answer them?
To whom hast thou abandoned me?
O my Sun, thou hast set too early.
O my beautiful Moon, thou hast perished too early.
O my rising star, why art thou setting already?
I did not have much time to rejoice with thee.
After joy came crying and tears.
After pleasure and happiness, sorrow and grief.
Why did I not die before thee?
So I would not see thy death and disappearance.
Canst thou not hear, my lord, my poor words?
Canst thou not be touched by my bitter tears?
The animals of this earth go to their dens,
the birds of the sky fly to their nests,
but thou, my lord, abandonest thy home.
What will I become?
I lost my lord.
Old widow, console me.
Young widow, cry with me.
The lot of a widow is more bitter than the lot of all people.
How can I bewail now?

How can I lament now?
My great God, King of Kings, be my Defender!
The Purest Lady, Mother of God,
do not abandon me or forget me in the days of my grief."
When Dmitry Ivanovich, prince of the Russian land,
commenced his eternal rest
the air became troubled,
the earth began to shake
and the people became sorrowful.
What can I call this day?
This day of sadness and grief,
of tears and sighs,
of great misery and misfortune? . . .

To whom may I compare Grand Prince Dmitry Ivanovich, Tsar of the Russian land, Ruler of a Grand Principality, Unifier of Christians? Come, my beloved friends of the Church, praise with words, praise dutifully the lord of the Russian land.

(Here is omitted a praise that follows the one in Epiphanius the Wise's *Panegyric to St. Stephen of Perm* [see Selection 44] and ends Prince Dmitry's *vita*.)

C. IDEOLOGICAL WRITINGS

50. THE TALE OF THE WHITE COWL

THE *Tale of the White Cowl,* which was to become the corner-stone of Russian medieval ideology, was written toward the end of the fifteenth century in Novgorod, apparently by Archbishop Genady and his co-worker and interpreter, Dmitry Gerasimov. The tale was conceived with the purpose of defending the sovereignty of the Novgorodian Church, in particular, and the Russian Church, in general, from encroachment by the Grand Duke of Muscovy, but it developed into an ideological work that glorified the prestige of Russian Orthodox Christianity. Later, in the sixteenth century, after the rise of Moscow to a position of power, there developed from this work the theory of Moscow being the Third Rome, which theory was clearly and concisely formulated by Monk Philotheus (*circa* 1510–1540) when he wrote: "All Christian realms will come to an end and will unite into the one single realm of our sovereign, that is, into the Russian realm, according to the prophetic books. Both Romes fell, the third endures, and a fourth there will never be." [1] This theory defined Moscow as the sole staunch defender of the Eastern Orthodox Faith, which, in the minds of Greeks, Russians, Southern Slavs, and other Eastern Europeans, was the only true Christian doctrine.

The background of this concept is a rather eclectic one, and can be traced to the Book of Daniel (7:27), in which the prophet announced that the final kingdom of the one true faith will come about and will never be destroyed. This concept of Daniel's was taken up by the Chiliasts (from the Greek, *chiliad,* meaning "a thousand"), who proclaimed the forthcoming King-dom of Christ that would last a thousand years.

In the Middle Ages the Irish philosopher John Scotus Erigena (ninth century) and the Italian theologian Joachim de Fiore (twelfth century) modified Daniel's original concept into the theory of the "three kingdoms," that is, the Kingdom of the Father who gave the Law (Old Testament), the Kingdom of

---

[1] The best discussion of the works of Monk Philotheus can be found in V. Malinin's *Starets Eleazarova Monastyria Filofey i ego Poslaniia,* Kiev, 1901. This quotation is to be found on page 45 in the appendix of Malinin's work.

the Son who brought Grace, and the final Kingdom of the Holy Spirit, of which the Apostles said: "Where there is the spirit of God, there is freedom." The theory of the final Kingdom of the Holy Spirit became known in Russia, and later formed the basis for both the *Tale of the White Cowl* and the Third Rome theory.

In the eyes of Archbishop Genady and Dmitry Gerasimov, Russia was predestined by God to be revealed as this last kingdom, the Kingdom of the Holy Spirit, which will endure until the Last Judgment. The authors of the *Tale of the White Cowl* combined this theocratic, utopian tenet with the Roman Catholic legend of the gift of the city of Rome to Pope Sylvester by Emperor Constantine (Emperor of Rome, 306–337). This legend laid the foundation for the secular power of the Pope of Rome and also for the independence of the pope from the emperor.

The *Tale of the White Cowl* underwent many revisions and is extant in several versions; however, its central theme remains the same in all: the White Cowl, the symbol of the radiant Resurrection and Orthodox Christianity, remained in Rome as long as the popes preserved the original teachings of Christ. But when the popes broke with the Eastern Church and developed their "Latin heresies," [2] divine power gave the White Cowl to the patriarch of Constantinople, which the Greeks of that time called the "Second Rome." When the Greeks began to "multiply their sins" and even began negotiating with the Pope of Rome, God punished them by letting their land be overrun by Turks. [3] The tale states that a century before the fall of Constantinople, God, who had predestined the last Orthodox nation, after the fall of Byzantium, to be Russia, commanded that the White Cowl be taken to the Archbishop of Novgorod, Vasily.

The present translation is based on the Russian text published by G. Kushelov-Bezborodko in *Pamiatniki starinnoi russkoi literatury*, Volume I, St. Petersburg, 1860, pages 287–303.

Since the translation given here is not the complete tale, it is essential to present a synopsis of the narrative up to the point where the translation begins.

---

[2] The Byzantines, and later the Russians, called the teachings of the Western Church "Latin heresies," since Rome proclaimed the primacy of the pope and used the Latin tongue exclusively for liturgical purposes.

[3] The actual conquest of Constantinople by the Turks took place in 1453, some thirty or forty years before the *Tale of the White Cowl* was written in Novgorod.

SYNOPSIS

The *Tale of the White Cowl* opens with the story of Emperor Constantine's illness, which could be cured neither by physicians nor by magicians. One such magician, who was violently opposed to Christianity, advised the emperor that in order to be cured he must bathe in the blood of three thousand infants killed expressly for that purpose. However, at the last minute Emperor Constantine, moved by the tears and wailings of the mothers of the children who were to be slain, canceled his plan, preferring to die rather than to kill children in order to restore his health. That very night the emperor had a vision of the Apostles Peter and Paul, who told him that Pope Sylvester, who was in hiding from his persecutors at that time, could show him a font of salvation, bathing wherein would cure him of this affliction. In recompense, the emperor was to grant new rights to the Christian Church and to support it as the national religion.

The tale continues that the emperor was cured, ended the persecutions of Christians, and even wished to grant the imperial crown to the pope. The pope most humbly refused to accept it. So the emperor gave him a white cowl, the symbol of the primacy of spiritual power over secular power and of the Resurrection, the color white representing the radiance of the Resurrection of Christ. Having given the supreme power in the city of Rome to the pope, Emperor Constantine then left the Eternal City and went to the ancient city of Byzantium, which was later renamed the "city of Constantine," or Constantinople. Thus did the Eastern, or Byzantine, Roman Empire come into being.

After the death of Pope Sylvester, the tale goes on to say, the White Cowl was highly revered by the popes of Rome. However, in the ninth century, when the West was ruled by Emperor Charlemagne and the papal see was ruled by Pope Formosus,[4] a schism arose between the Eastern and Western Churches. The Western Church, under the leadership of the pope, developed new teachings and doctrines that the Eastern Church considered to be "Latin heresies," particularly the doctrine of the primacy of the Pope of Rome over the entire Church. From that time on the popes ceased to revere the White Cowl, and finally decided to profane and destroy it. However, a miraculous power saved the White Cowl, and the pope was forced to send it to the Patriarch of Constantinople, the capital of the still-extant Eastern Roman Empire, or, as it is more often called, Byzantium.

---

[4] Pope Formosus reigned from 891 to 896. During his reign there began the first conflicts between Rome and Constantinople over the jurisdiction of the two branches of the Church.

The translation begins at this point in the tale—that is, with the arrival of the White Cowl in Constantinople.

At that time the Patriarch of Constantinople was Philotheos,[5] who was distinguished by his strict fasting and his virtuous ways. Once, he had a vision in the night of a youth from whom emanated light and who told him:

"Blessed teacher, in the olden times the Roman Emperor, Constantine, who, through the vision of the holy Apostles Peter and Paul, was enlightened by God, decided to give blessed Pope Sylvester the White Cowl to glorify the Holy Apostolic Church. Later, the unfaithful popes of the Latin heresies wanted to profane and destroy this cowl, but I appeared to the evil pope, and now this pope has sent this cowl to you. When the messengers arrive with it, you must accept it with all honors. Then send the White Cowl to the Russian land, to the city of Novgorod the Great with your written blessing. And there this cowl will be worn on the head of Vasily, Archbishop of Novgorod,[6] so that he may glorify the Holy Apostolic Cathedral of Holy Sophia and laud the Orthodox Faith. There, in that land, the faith of Christ is verily glorified. And the popes, because of their shamelessness, will receive the vengeance of God." And having spoken these words, the youth became invisible.

The patriarch awoke filled with awe and joy, and was unable to sleep throughout the remainder of the night. And he contemplated this vision. In the morning he ordered that the bells should sound the matins, and when day came he summoned the Church council and revealed his vision. And all praised God, perceiving that a holy angel had appeared to the patriarch. Yet they did not fully understand the meaning of the message. When they were still in council, and were filled with awe due to their great joy, there arrived a servant of the patriarch, and he announced to them that messengers had arrived from the Pope of Rome. The patriarch ordered that they be brought before him. The messengers came, bowed lowly to the patriarch, and gave him the message. The patriarch read the message and pondered it, praising God. He announced its contents to Emperor John who was reigning at that time and whose name

---

[5] Philotheos was patriarch of Constantinople from 1353 to 1355, and from 1364–1376.

[6] Vasily was archbishop of Novgorod from 1330 to 1342. In 1946 his grave was discovered and opened. In it were found both the White Cowl and the vestments embroidered with crosses that are mentioned in this tale.

was Kantakuzen.[7] And then he went with the entire council to meet the bringers of the divine treasure which lay in an ark. He accepted it with all honors, broke the seal, and took from the ark the holy White Cowl. He kissed it with reverence, and looked upon it with wonderment both for its creation and for the wonderful fragrance that emanated from it.

At that time the patriarch had diseased eyes and constant headaches, but when he placed the White Cowl upon his head, these afflictions immediately ceased to be. And he rejoiced with great joy and rendered glory to Christ, Our Lord, to Constantine's blessed memory for his creating this wonderful cowl for blessed Pope Sylvester. And he put the holy cowl on the golden salver that was also sent by the pope. He placed them in the great church in an honorable place until he could make a decision with the emperor's counseling.

After the White Cowl was sent from Rome, the evil pope, who was counseled by heretics, became angered against the Christian faith and was driven to a frenzy, extremely regretting his allowing the White Cowl to be sent to Constantinople. And he wrote an evil letter to the patriarch, in which he demanded the return of the White Cowl on the golden salver. The patriarch read this letter and, understanding the pope's evil and cunning design, sent him a letter in return that was based on Holy Scripture, and in it he called the pope both evil and godless, the apostate and precursor of the Antichrist. And the patriarch cursed the pope in the name of Our Lord, Jesus Christ, the holy Apostles, and the Church Fathers. And this letter came to the pope.

When the pope had read the letter and learned that the patriarch intended to send the White Cowl with great honor to the Russian land, to the city of Novgorod the Great, he uttered a roar. And his face changed and he fell ill, for he, the infidel, disliked the Russian land and could not even bear to hear of this land where the Christian faith was professed.

Patriarch Philotheos, having seen that the White Cowl was illumined with grace, began to ponder how he might keep it in Constantinople and wear it on his own head. He consulted with the emperor about the matter several times, and wanted to write to the other patriarchs and metropolitans to summon them to a council. After matins one Sunday, the patriarch returned to his chambers and, after the usual prayers, lay down to rest. But

---

[7] John VI Kantakuzen (or Cantacuzene) was Emperor of Byzantium from 1347 to 1354.

he slept but lightly, and in this sleep he saw that two men, who were unknown to him, came through the door. And from them there emanated light. One of them was armed as a warrior and had an imperial crown upon his head. The other wore a bishop's vestments and was distinguished by his venerable white hair.

The latter spoke to the patriarch, saying: "Patriarch! Stop pondering your wearing of the White Cowl on your own head. If this were to be, Our Lord, Jesus Christ, would have so predestined it from the founding of this city. And for a long time did divine enlightenment come from heaven, and then God's voice came to me and I learned that Rome had to betray God and embrace their Latin heresies. That is the reason I did not wish to wear this cowl upon my head, and thus I instructed other popes not to do so. And this imperial city of Constantinople will be taken by the sons of Hagar [8] because of its sins, and all holy shrines will be defiled and destroyed. Thus has it been predestined since the founding of this city.

"The ancient city of Rome has broken away from the glory and faith of Christ because of its pride and ambition. In the new Rome, which has been the city of Constantinople, the Christian faith will also perish through the violence of the sons of Hagar. In the third Rome, which will be the land of Russia, the Grace of the Holy Spirit will be revealed. Know then, Philotheos, that all Christians will finally unite into one Russian nation because of its Orthodoxy. Since ancient times and by the will of Constantine, Emperor of the Earth, the imperial crown of the imperial city is predestined to be given to the Russian tsar.[9] But the White Cowl, by the will of the King of Heaven, Jesus Christ, will be given to the Archbishop of Novgorod the Great. And this White Cowl is more honorable than the crown of the tsar, for it is an imperial crown of the archangelic spiritual order. Thus, you must send this holy White Cowl to the Russian land, to the city of Novgorod the Great, as you were told to do in the vision of the angel. You should believe and trust in what I say. And when you send it to the Russian land, the Orthodox Faith will be glorified and the cowl will be safe from seizure by the infidel sons of Hagar and from the intended profanation by the Latin pope. And the grace, glory, and honor which were

---

[8] Both the Byzantines and the Russians called all nomads, whether they were Turks, Mongols, or Arabs, the sons of Hagar. "Hagar" refers to the handmaid of the biblical patriarch Abraham.

[9] The Russians of that time used only one word, "tsar," for the English words "king," "King of Heaven," "emperor," and even "khan." Equally, the word "tsarstvo" was used to mean "realm," "empire," "tsardom," and the "Kingdom of God."

taken from Rome, as well as the Grace of the Holy Spirit, will be removed from the imperial city of Constantinople after its capture by the sons of Hagar. And all holy relics will be given to the Russian land in the predestined moment. And the Russian tsar will be elevated by God above other nations, and under his sway will be many heathen kings. And the power of the patriarch of this imperial ruling city will pass to the Russian land in the predestined hour. And that land will be called Radiant Russia, which, by the Grace of God, will be glorified with blessings. And its majesty will be strengthened by its Orthodoxy, and it will become more honorable than the two Romes which preceded it."

And saying this, the man of the vision who was dressed in a bishop's vestment wished to leave, but the patriarch, seized by great awe, fell before the bishop and said: "Who are you, my lord? Your vision has seized me with great awe; my heart has been frightened by your words, and I tremble to my very bones."

The man in the bishop's vestments answered: "Don't you know who I am? I am Pope Sylvester, and I came to you because I was ordered by God to reveal to you the great mystery which will come to pass in the predestined time." Then, pointing to the other man in the vision, he added: "This is blessed Emperor Constantine of Rome to whom I gave rebirth in the holy font and whom I won over to the faith of Our Lord, Jesus Christ. He was the first Christian emperor, my child in Christ, who created and gave me the White Cowl in place of the imperial crown." And saying this, he blessed the patriarch, and became invisible.

Waking up, the patriarch was seized with awe, remembering the words about the White Cowl and the conquest of Constantinople by the pagan sons of Hagar. And he wept for a long time. When the hour of the divine Mass arrived, the patriarch went to the church, fell before the icon of the Holy Mother of God, and remained lying there for some time. Then he arose, took the White Cowl with great reverence, kissed it piously, placed it upon his head, and then put it to his eyes and his heart. And his adoration for this cowl increased even more. And doing this, he wept. His clerics, who were around him and saw that he wept inconsolably, did not dare to inquire as to why he was weeping. Finally the patriarch ceased crying and told his clerics in detail of the vision of Pope Sylvester and Emperor Constantine. Having heard these words, the clerics wept sorrowfully, and exclaimed, "Thy will be done!"

The patriarch, mourning the forthcoming misfortunes of the

city of Constantinople and fearing to trespass the Divine Will, told them that he must fulfill the will of the Lord and do with the White Cowl as he was commanded to do. After having deliberated with blessed Emperor John, he took the White Cowl and the golden salver, put them in the aforementioned ark, sealed it with his seal, and, as he was commanded by the holy angel and blessed Pope Sylvester, put in his epistle with his blessings, and in it he commanded Archbishop Vasily and all other bishops who would follow Vasily to wear the White Cowl upon their heads. He added many other honorable and marvelous gifts from his clergy for the bishopric of Novgorod the Great. And he also sent vestments with their embroidered crosses [10] for the glorification of the Holy Apostolic Church. And all this was placed in another ark. And he gave these arks to a bishop named Eunemios, and sent him forth with both joy and sorrow.

In the bishopric of the city of Novgorod the Great was Archbishop Vasily who distinguished himself by his fasting and virtuous ways. Once, in the night, he prayed to God and then lay down to rest, but he slept but lightly, and had a dream in which he saw the angel of God. This angel of God, who had a handsome appearance and radiant face, appeared before him in the garb of a monk and with the White Cowl upon his head. With his finger he pointed to his head and in a low voice announced: "Vasily! This White Cowl which you see on my head is from Rome. In olden times the Christian Emperor Constantine created it in honor of Sylvester, Pope of Rome. He gave it to this pope to wear upon his head. But God Almighty did not permit the White Cowl to remain there because of their Latin heresies. Tomorrow morning you must go from the city with your clergymen and meet the bishop and messengers sent by the patriarch. And they will bring an ark, and in this ark you will find the White Cowl upon a golden salver. Accept it with all honors, for this White Cowl symbolizes the radiant Resurrection which came to pass on the third day. And from now, you and all other archbishops of this city will wear it on your heads. And I have come to you to assure you beforehand that all is as God wills it and to assuage any doubts you may have." And saying this, the angel became invisible.

Waking up, Archbishop Vasily was seized with awe and joy, pondering the meaning of the vision. The next morning he sent his clerics outside the city, to the crossroads, to see whether the messengers really would appear. In the vicinity of

---

[10] See footnote 4, p. 325.

the city the envoys of Archbishop Vasily met a Greek bishop who was unknown to them and who traveled to the city of Novgorod. They made a low obeisance and returned to the archbishop and told them all they had seen. The bishop then sent his preacher into the city to summon the clerics and the entire population. And he ordered the tolling of the bells, and both he and his clerics donned their vestments.

The procession had not gone far from the Cathedral of Holy Sophia when they met the aforementioned bishop, sent by the patriarch and bearing the ark that had been sealed by the patriarch, and contained the venerable gifts. He came to Archbishop Vasily, made a low obeisance before him, and gave him the epistles of the patriarch. They blessed and greeted each other in Christ's name. Archbishop Vasily accepted the epistles of the patriarch and the ark bearing the venerable gifts. And he went with them to the Cathedral of Holy Sophia, the Wisdom of God. There he put them in the middle of the church in an honorable place, and ordered that the patriarchal epistles be read aloud. When the Orthodox people, who were in the cathedral, heard these writings read aloud, they rendered glory to God and rejoiced with great joy. Archbishop Vasily opened one of the arks and removed the cover. And a wonderful fragrance and miraculous radiance spread through the church. Archbishop Vasily and all present were in wonderment, witnessing these happenings. And Bishop Eunemios, who was sent by the patriarch, wondered about these blessed deeds of God that he had witnessed. And they all rendered glory to God, and celebrated the service of thanksgiving.

Archbishop Vasily took the White Cowl from the ark and saw that it appeared exactly like the one he had seen on the angel's head in his vision. And he kissed it with reverence. At that same moment there came a sonorous voice from the icon of the Lord, which was in the cupola of the church, saying: "Holy, holy." And after a moment of silence there came the same voice, which thrice announced: "Ispola eti despota." [11] And when the archbishop and all those present heard these voices, they were seized with awe and joy. And they said: "The Lord have mercy upon us!" And the archbishop then ordered that all present in the church be silent, and he revealed to them his vision of the angel and his words concerning the White Cowl.

[11] "Ispola eti despota" is Greek for "Many years to the lord," or, more loosely translated, "Long live the bishop." The Russians used this expression during the Church service, and it was always pronounced in Greek.

And he told of his vision as it had happened and in detail, even as it was told to him by the angel in the night.

Giving thanks to God for sending this cowl, the archbishop went forth from the church, preceded by the deacons in holy vestments carrying tapers and singing hymns. And they proceeded with serenity and piety. And the people crowded round, jostling each other and jumping so that they might see the White Cowl on the archbishop's head. And all were in wonderment. Thus, in this way, thanks to the Grace of Our Lord, Jesus Christ, and to the blessing of his Holiness Philotheos, Patriarch of Constantinople, the White Cowl became a symbol upon the heads of the archbishops of Novgorod. And Archbishop Vasily was overcome with great joy, and for seven days he feasted all priests, deacons, and clerics of the city of Novgorod the Great. And he also offered food and drink to the poor, to monks, and to prisoners. And he asked that the prisoners be released. During the divine service he placed the holy and venerable gifts of the holy patriarch in the Cathedral of Holy Sophia with the blessings of all clerics. And the golden salver, on which the White Cowl was placed, was also deposited in the Cathedral of Holy Sophia during the Mass.

The messengers of the patriarch who brought the holy White Cowl were also shown great honor and they received many gifts. The archbishop sent gifts to the Emperor and Patriarch of Constantinople and sent the messengers forth with great honors. Thereafter, multitudes arrived from many cities and kingdoms to look upon, as if it were a miracle, the archbishop in the White Cowl. And they were in wonderment about it, and told of it in many lands. This holy White Cowl was created by the first pious Christian Emperor, Constantine, for blessed Pope Sylvester in the year 5805 (297). And this is the history of the holy White Cowl up to this day.

D. TRAVELERS' ACCOUNTS

51. AFANASY NIKITIN'S JOURNEY ACROSS THREE SEAS

AT THE beginning of the year 1466 Afanasy Nikitin, a merchant from the city of Tver', undertook a long business trip. Interested in trade with the Middle East, he wanted to explore such a venture personally. Sailing down the Volga, Nikitin soon reached the Caspian Sea on his way to Persia, from where he unexpectedly decided to go to India through the Indian Ocean. The first European ever to explore this country, Nikitin remained there for one and a half years out of his six years of travel, at the end of which he returned to Russia by way of Ethiopia, Arabia, Persia, Armenia, and the Black Sea. Fate did not intend him to return to his native Tver', however, for he died in Smolensk, leaving there his apparently uncompleted and unedited manuscript with the account of his travels.

Nikitin's Journey Across Three Seas—the Caspian, Indian, and Black—belongs to a well-known type of Russian literature, the travel description; however, where earlier accounts all dealt with pilgrimages to the Holy Land, this one is devoted to a business journey and exploration. Still, in many places Nikitin's report is imbued with genuine religious feeling, reflected in a number of lyric and pathetic digressions.

Exotic India obviously struck Nikitin's imagination. Although he spent only one-quarter of the six years of his travel there, he devoted three-fourths of his work to it. It seems that he wrote his notes while traveling from country to country and probably for this reason his observations are couched in a brief, sober, and documentary style. There are few elements of the fantastic, so characteristic of other European travel memoirs of the time, but personal experiences and impressions are given at greater length.

Three different levels can be discerned in Nikitin's work. First, descriptions of the lands he has seen and his adventures in them. He often writes in direct speech, a technique presently known in Russian criticism as "skaz," which is often used for narrative. Sometimes he even seems to answer the questions of an imaginary interlocutor.

Second, probably for the benefit of later travelers to India, brief and condensed information is given, such as distances between various cities and the economic conditions in countries he visited.

Third, especially in its beginning and conclusion, the work contains pious and lyric digressions that sometimes take the form of a prayer or appeal to the Creator, or an evocation to his beloved Russian land. Curiously, part of these digressions were written by Nikitin in the language of the Koran, or in the "basic Islamic" business dialect of the Near East in which Arabic, Turkic, and Persian words are interwoven. One may presume that he did this to protect his notes from unwanted readers. It may be added that some intimate and practical observations of Indian women are given in the same dialect.

The presence of Near Eastern linguistic and stylistic elements, together with descriptions of unknown, fairy-tale-like lands, lend Nikitin's story a particularly exotic touch. The writer obviously enjoyed the profuse use of foreign words and sonorous Oriental names of cities and lands, and played unremittingly with them.

This traveler from Tver' frequently demonstrates a religious tolerance most unusual for a fifteenth-century European. Stating that during his six years of travel in the Islamic lands and India he lost track of the Russian calendar, and therefore was fasting not on the days prescribed by the Christian church but with the Moslems, he exclaims: "(But) among all these faiths I still pray to God to protect me, . . . God is one, he is the King of Glory, Creator of Heaven and Earth." In another place he writes, "Gracious God, Gracious Lord Jesus, the Spirit of God. Thine is the peace. God is great. There is no God beyond Allah, the Creator." The statement that there is just one and the same God in Islam and Christianity, as well as the use in Christian prayer of the word, "Allah," so specific to Islam, are a most unusual and unexpected demonstration of religious tolerance in both medieval Russian and Western writing.

Nikitin's language is concise and expressive, containing hardly any poetic figures of speech. His economy of language and sentence organization resulted, however, in innumerable long, rhythmic passages, which this editor has attempted to reproduce in verse form. The rhythm conveys a particular easiness and charm to Nikitin's description.

The present translation follows the text prepared by the Academy of Sciences of the U.S.S.R. in 1948 under the title, *Khozhdenie za tri moria Afanasiia Nikitina*.

By the prayer of our Holy Fathers,
O Lord Jesus Christ, Son of God,
have mercy upon me,

thy sinful servant Afanasy, son of Nikita.
(Herewith) I have written about my sinful journey beyond
*   three seas,*
the first being the Sea of Derbent, or Sea of Caspia,
the second the Indian Sea, or Sea of Hindustan,
the third the Black Sea, or Sea of Istambul.

I. FROM TVER' TO PERSIA

I set off down the Volga from the Golden-Domed Cathedral of the Savior, from Grand Prince Mikhail Borisovich and from Bishop Gennady of Tver'. Upon arrival at Kaliazin, I received there the blessing of Abbot Macarius and the brethren of the Monastery of the Holy Trinity and the holy martyrs Boris and Gleb; thereafter, I proceeded to Uglich, and from Uglich to Kostroma, to Prince Alexander, bearing another permit to travel from the grand prince (of Muscovy), and he let me sail on unhindered. Nor was I hindered on my way to the city of Nizhny Novgorod, to its Lord Lieutenant Mikhail Kiselev, and its Keeper of the Tolls, Ivan Saraiev.[1]

Vasily Papin had already passed on, and for two weeks I had to await at Novgorod the arrival of Hasan Beg, the Tatar Shirvanshah's ambassador.[2] He was coming from Grand Prince Ivan with gerfalcons, of which he had ninety. And I journeyed with him down the Volga. We sailed freely past Kazan, the Horde, Uslan, Sarai, and Berekezan.[3]

And we entered the river Buzan.[4] There we met three Moslem Tatars, who gave us false information: "Khan Kasim [5] lies in wait for merchants down the river and with him there are three thousand Tatars." Hasan Beg, the Shirvanshah's ambassador, gave each of the three a coat and a piece of linen in order that they might lead us securely beyond Astrakhan.[6] And

---

[1] Kaliazin, Uglich, Kostroma, Nizhny Novgorod (now Gorky): cities on the upper Volga.

[2] Vasily Papin was ambassador of the Grand Prince of Moscow and Russia to the court of Shirvanshah, ruler of a Tatar state in the southeastern Caucasus. Hasan Beg was the Shirvanshah's ambassador to Moscow.

[3] Kazan, Horde, Uslan, Sarai, Berekezan: Tatar cities on the lower Volga.

[4] River Buzan: a branch of the Volga.

[5] Khan Kasim: ruler of a Tatar tribe on the lower Volga.

[6] Astrakhan, in the delta of the Volga, was a Tatar city in the fifteenth century, now a Russian city. Russians used to call its ruler "tsar" since he was a descendant of Genghis Khan.

they took the coats, but sent word to the Tsar of Astrakhan. I left my ship and with my companions boarded the ambassador's. The moon was shining as we passed Astrakhan. The tsar (of Astrakhan) sighted us and the Tatars shouted to us, "Don't run away." Then the Tatar Tsar sent his whole horde in pursuit of us, and for our sins we were overtaken at Bugun; [7] the Tatars shot one of our men, and we shot two of theirs. Our small ship was stopped by a weir, they seized her and at once plundered her; and all my luggage was in that small ship.

On the big ship we reached the sea, but ran aground in the mouth of the Volga. Thereupon the Tatars seized us and towed the ship back to the weir. There they took the big ship away from us, and led four Russian men away captive; having robbed us, they let us proceed to the sea. They did not let us sail upstream lest we should send word.

And we headed for Derbent on two ships, on one of them sailed Hasan Beg, the ambassador, with Persians and us, the Russians, ten men in all; and the other ship carried six Muscovites and six men from Tver'. A heavy storm overtook us at sea. The smaller ship was smashed against the coast near the little town of Tarki,[8] and the men went ashore; then came the Kaitaks,[9] and made captives of them all.

Upon reaching Derbent [8] we learned that Vasily Papin had arrived safe and sound, while we had been robbed. And I humbly petitioned him and Hasan Beg, the Shirvanshah's ambassador, with whom we had arrived, to plead for the men seized by the Kaitaks near Tarki. And Hasan Beg solicited for them and went to Bulat Beg. Bulat Beg dispatched a courier to Shirvanshah Beg to inform him that a Russian ship had been wrecked off Tarki and that some Kaitaks had come and taken her men captive and robbed their goods. And Shirvanshah Beg at once sent a man to his brother-in-law, Khalil Beg, Prince of Kaitak, to tell him this: "My ship has been wrecked off Tarki, and thy men have come and taken the men captive and stolen their goods, and wilt thou for my sake send the men to me and have their goods recovered, because those men have been sent to me; and if thou wantest something of me, send for it and I shall not refuse thee, my brother, only let them free for my sake." And Khalil Beg at once sent all the men to Derbent, whence they were sent to the Shirvanshah's headquarters.

---

[7] Bugun: a place on the shore of the lower Volga.

[8] Tarki: a city and principality on the north Caucasian shore of the Caspian Sea. Derbent: city on the shore of the Caspian Sea.

[9] Kaitaks: Turkic-Mongol nomads in the northern Caucasus.

We, too, went to the Shirvanshah's headquarters, and humbly begged him to grant us the wherewithal to reach Russia. But he did not give us anything because we were too many. And we wept and dispersed; those of us who owned something in Russia left for Russia, and those who had debts there went wherever they could; some remained at Shemakha, while others went to work at Baku.[10]

> As for me, I went to Derbent,
> and from Derbent to Baku,
> where an eternal fire is burning;
> and from Baku I crossed the sea to Chapakur,
> where I lived for six months;
> then to Sari, in the Mazanderan country
> where I lived for a month.
> Thence I proceeded to Amul,
> where I lived for a month,
> thence to Demavend, and from Demavend to Ray.[11]

There Shah Husain, son of Ali and grandson of Mohammed, was slain; he cursed them, and by his curse seventy towns were felled.[12]

> And from Ray I journeyed to Kasha,
> where I lived for a month,
> thence I journeyed to Nain,
> and from Nain to Yezd,
> where I lived for a month.
> And from Yezd I proceeded to Sirjan [13]
> and thence to Tarum, where cattle are fed
> with dates bought at four altins a batman.[14]

---

[10] Shemakha, Baku: important trade cities in the southern Caucasus. The eternal fire of Baku was fed by the local gas fields and maintained by Zoroastrian fire worshipers.

[11] Chapakur, Sari, Amul: cities in the North Persian province of Mazanderan. Demavend: a peak in the North Persian mountains, about 18,000 feet high. Ray: one of the most important trade and cultural centers of medieval Persia.

[12] Husain, grandson of Mohammed and particularly venerated by Shia Moslems of Persia, was assassinated in Kerbela, Iraq, but Iranian tradition ascribed this event to the city of Ray.

[13] Kasha, Nain, Yezd, Sirjan, Tarum, Lar, Bandar: cities in southern Persia.

[14] Altin: local coin. Batman: a weight measure.

II. IN INDIA

And from Tarum I journeyed to Lar,
and from Lar to Bandar.[13]
And that is where the harbor of Hormuz is, [15]
as well as the Indian Sea,
called the Sea of Hindustan in Persian.
And from Bandar it is four miles by sea to Hormuz.

And Hormuz lies on an island which is flooded by the sea twice a day. There I kept my first Easter, having arrived four weeks before the feast.

I have not above listed all the cities,
for there are many more great cities.
The sun at Hormuz is blazing hot,
and may burn one.
I stayed there for a month,
and in the first week after Easter
I sailed across the Indian Sea
on a dabba with horses.[16]
And it took us ten days to sail by sea to Muscat,
and four days to sail from Muscat to Dega.
From Dega we sailed to Gujarat,
and thence to Cambay,
where there are indigo and lac,
and from Cambay to Chaul.[17]
We left Chaul in the seventh week after Easter,
having reached it on the dabba in six weeks.

And that is where the land of India lies, and where everyone goes naked; the women go bareheaded and with breasts uncovered, their hair plaited into one braid. Many women are pregnant; they bear children every year, and have many children. The men and women are all black. Wherever I went I was followed by many people who wondered at me, a white man.

And their prince wears a dhoti
upon his head and another about his loins;

---

[15] Hormuz: important port on the Persian Gulf.

[16] *Dabba:* a type of sailboat, still used by the Arabs. Persians and Arabs exported horses to India on them.

[17] Muscat: a province in southeastern Arabia. Dega: location is unclear. Gujarat: province on the western coast of Hindustan, whose main port was Cambay. Chaul: an important port on the Malabar coast of India.

their boyars wear a dhoti [18]
round their shoulders and another about their loins;
their princesses wrap a dhoti
round their shoulders and another round their loins.
The servants of the prince and the boyars wear a dhoti
wound about their loins,
and carry shield and sword in their hands,
while others have spear or knives or sabers, or bow and arrows.

And all are naked and barefoot, and strong. And the women go bareheaded and with breasts uncovered; as for the little boys and girls, they go naked till the age of seven and do not hide their shame.

From Chaul it took us eight days
by land to get to Pali,
both are Indian towns;
and from Pali to Umra, another Indian town,
it is ten days,
and from Umra to Junnar, six days. [19]

And at Junnar there lives the Indian, Asad Khan, a servant of Malik-at-Tujjar; they say he has seventy thousand men from Malik-at-Tujjar. And Malik-at-Tujjar has two hundred thousand; for twenty years he has been fighting *kafirs;* sometimes they beat him, but he beats them more often. The khan is carried by men; he has many elephants and fine horses. He also has many men of Khorassan, [20]

Who are brought from the Khorassan land,
or Arabian land,
or from Turkoman land,
and from Jagatai land.

---

[18] Dhoti: a light textile material used for turbans or loincloths. Boyars: a Russian word that Nikitin uses for the designation of influential Moslem feudal lords in India.

[19] Pali, Umra, Junnar: cities in eastern Hindustan.

[20] Khorassan: in the time of Nikitin's journey most of northern and eastern India was under the rule of Moslem invaders of mixed Turkic-Persian stock. They were called Khorassanis since many of them came from the Persian province of Khorassan. They called local non-Islamic native populations "*kafir*" (an equivalent of "pagan" or Jewish "gentile"—people who are not of "our" faith). Muhammed Shah was the main Moslem ruler in Deccan, in central Hindustan. Malik-at-Tujjar: title for the local prime minister. Asad Khan was probably the local Moslem governor.

They are always brought by sea in *dabbas,* which are Indian ships.

And I, a sinful man, brought a stallion to the land of India. Thank God, I reached Junnar in good health, but the passage cost me a hundred rubles. The winter there set in on Trinity Holiday, and we spent it at Junnar, where we lived for two months; throughout four months there were water and mud everywhere, both by day and at night. That is the time of plowing and of sowing wheat and rice and pulse, and all the other foods. Wine is made in big coconuts and beer is brewed from *tatna.*[21] Horses are fed with pulse, and rice meal with sugar and butter is made for them; early in the morning they are also fed with cooked rice cakes. No horses are born in India, but oxen and buffaloes are. They are used for carrying persons and sometimes goods, they serve all purposes. The town of Junnar lies on a rocky island not built by man but created by God. It takes a whole day's uphill walk to go there, the path is narrow and two people cannot pass.

In India strangers put up at inns, and the food is cooked for them by hostesses, who also make the guests' beds (and sleep with them. If you want to have relations with one you pay two shetels, if not you pay to the inn only one shetel. But you may have close relations with her free of charge—their women like white men).[22]

In winter people there wear a dhoti round their loins, another about their shoulders, and a third round their heads. As for the princes and boyars, in that season they put on trousers, a shirt, and a caftan; they also wrap a dhoti about their shoulders, girdle themselves with another and wind a third around their heads.

Allah, abr Allah, Allah kerim, Allah rahim![23]

There at Junnar the khan took away my stallion. But when he learned that I was a Russian and not a Moslem, he said: "I shall give thee back thy stallion and pay thee a thousand pieces of gold, if only thou wilt adopt our Mohammedan faith. But shouldst thou not adopt our Mohammedan faith, I shall keep the stallion and exact a ransom of a thousand pieces of gold from thee." And he allowed me four days, till Our Savior's Day, during the fast [before the day of Assumption] of the Holy Mother of God. And the Lord had mercy upon me in his holy

---

[21] *Tatna:* palm bark from which beer apparently was made in India.

[22] Text placed in parentheses was written by Nikitin in Turkic.

[23] O God, Great God, True God, Merciful God!

day; he kept not his mercy from me, miserable sinner, and left me not to perish at Junnar among the godless. Hoja Muhammad of Khorassan arrived on the eve of Our Savior's Day, and I humbly begged him to plead for me. And we went to the khan in town and persuaded him not to convert me to his faith; he also gave back my stallion. Such was the miracle wrought by the Lord on Our Savior's Day. And so, my Christian brothers of Russia, those of you who want to go to the land of India must leave their faith in Russia and invoke Mohammed and only then go to the land of Hindustan.

I was deceived by godless Moslems; they had told me of an abundance of goods but I found that there was nothing for our country. All duty-free goods are for the Moslem country only. Pepper and dyes are cheap. Some take their goods by sea, others pay no duty for them. But we will not be allowed to take our goods free of duty. And the duty is high and, moreover, there are many pirates at sea. And all the pirates are pagans, not Christians or Moslems; they worship stone idols and are ignorant of Christ.

On the day of Assumption of Our Lady
we left Junnar for Bidar, a big city,
and it took a month to arrive at this city.
And from Bidar to Kulungir it is five days,
and from Kulungir to Gulbarga it is five days.[24]

There are many other cities
between these two big cities;
every day we passed through three cities
and sometimes even four cities;
there are as many cities
as there are kos.[25]

From Chaul to Junnar it is twenty kos,
and from Junnar to Bidar it is forty kos,
and from Bidar to Kulungir it is nine kos,
and from Bidar to Gulbarga it is nine kos.

At Bidar horses and various goods are sold;
brocade, silk, and all kinds of other goods are sold;
black people, too, are sold.
Nothing else is sold.

---

[24] Bidar (Bider), Kulungir, Gulbarga: cities in Deccan.
[25] *Kos* (*kov*): a measure of distance, varies from four to nine miles.

And all the goods come from Hindustan. As for food, nothing is sold but vegetables. There are no goods for the land of Russia.

All the Indian princes are from Khorassan, and so are all the boyars. And all the people of Hindustan go on foot and walk fast, and are all naked and barefoot; they carry a shield in one hand and a sword in the other. Some of the servants have long, straight bows and arrows. And they always fight mounted on elephants, sending the infantrymen forward, while the Khorassanis ride horseback, both they and their horses being in armor. As for the elephants, long hammered swords are tied to their trunks and tusks, each weighing a kantar; they wear steel armor, and carry castles upon their backs; and in each castle there are twelve men in armor, with cannons and arrows.

There is a place, the tomb of Sheik Ala-uddin at Alland,[26] where a fair is held once a year and whither people from all over the Indian country come to trade for ten days. It is twelve *kos* from Bidar. Horses are brought thither for sale, as many as twenty thousand head, and all kinds of other goods, too. It is the best fair in the land of Hindustan; all wares are sold or bought there on the day of celebration for the memory of Sheik Ala-uddin, during the Russian Feast of the Intercession of the Holy Mother of God. At the city of Alland there lives the *ghugguk*, a bird; it flies at night, crying "ghugguk"; whenever it settles on a housetop, someone dies in the house; and when anyone tries to kill it, it begins to spit fire. The snakes prowl at night, catching fowl; they dwell in the mountains or upon rocks. As for monkeys, they live in the woods; and they have a monkey prince who leads an army. And when anyone harms them, they complain to their prince, who sets his army upon the offender. Then the monkeys fall upon that town and destroy the houses and kill the people. They are said to have a very large army and to speak a tongue of their own; they give birth to many young, but the young that are not like their father or mother are left on the roads. Then people of Hindustan pick them up and teach them crafts; but some of them they sell, doing it at night lest they should flee back; and some they teach how to fight.[27]

Spring came with the Feast of the Intercession of the Holy Mother of God; it is in spring, two weeks after Intercession, that an eight-day feast is kept to honor the memory of Sheik

---

[26] Sheik Ala-uddin: local Moslem saint whose tomb is in Alland, an important marketplace.

[27] This is one of the rare instances when Nikitin relates local fantastic stories.

Ala-uddin. Spring, summer, winter, and autumn last three months each.

(A description of Bidar and its rulers is omitted.)

The sultan's palace has seven gates, with a hundred guards and a hundred *kafir* [28] scribes at each gate; some of them register those coming in and others, those going out; but strangers are barred from the palace. And the palace is very beautiful, with fretwork and gilt all over it, and its every stone is fretted and very beautifully painted in gold; and inside the palace there are sundry vessels.

A thousand men posted by the governor guard the city of Bidar by night; they are mounted, wear armor, and carry torches. I sold my stallion at Bidar; I had been keeping him for a year, and had spent sixty-eight fanams on him. Snakes fourteen feet long crawl along the streets of Bidar. I arrived at Bidar from Kulungir during the Fast of Advent, and sold my stallion on Christmas Day.

And I stayed at Bidar till Lent. There I came to know many Hindus and told them that I was a Christian and not a Moslem, and that my name was Afanasy, or Khoja Yusuf Khorassani in the Moslem tongue. They did not hide from me when eating, trading, praying, or doing something else; nor did they conceal their wives.

I asked them questions about their faith and they said to me: "We believe in Adam; and the *buts*, they say, are Adam and his whole kin." Altogether there are eighty-four faiths in India, and everyone believes in *buts*.[29] People of different faiths do not eat or drink together, nor do they intermarry; some eat lamb, fowl, fish, and eggs, but people of all faiths do not eat beef there.

(Further description of the marketplaces of Bidar is omitted.)

The Indians eat no flesh at all, no beef, lamb, fowl, fish or pork, although they have a great many pigs. They have two meals a day and eat nothing at night; they drink neither wine nor mead. They do not eat or drink with Moslems. Their food is poor, and they do not eat or drink with one another, not even with their wives. They eat rice and rice meal with butter, and various herbs, which they boil in butter and milk. And they eat everything with their right hand, never touching any food with their left; they never use a knife and have no spoons. When journeying, each carries a pot to boil food in. And they hide

---

[28] See footnote 20, p. 339.

[29] *But:* local Moslem word, from Buddha, for Hindi deities and idols. In any case, this word cannot be applied to Buddha since there were no Buddhists in the fifteenth century in India.

from Moslems lest they should look into the pot or at the food. And should a Moslem look at the food, the Indian will not eat it. When eating, some cover themselves with a kerchief, so that no one may see them.

And they pray facing eastward, in the Russian manner; they raise high both hands and put them on their head, and lie face downward on the ground and stretch out on it—that is how they worship. And when they sit down to take a meal, some wash their hands and feet and also rinse their mouths. Their temples have no doors, and face eastward; the *buts*, too, stand facing eastward. And when someone dies, they burn him and scatter the ashes over water. And when a woman gives birth to a child, it is her husband who receives it; a son is named by the father, and a daughter by the mother. In coming or going, they bow after the fashion of monks, touching the ground with both hands and saying nothing.

They go to Parvata [30] at Lent to worship their god; that is their Jerusalem, or Mecca in the Moslem tongue. And they all arrive naked, with but a cloth round their buttocks; the women are naked, too, save for a dhoti about their buttocks; some wear dhotis and pearl necklaces and many sapphires, and also gold bracelets and rings, in faith they do. And they go to the temples astride oxen, and each ox has its horns encased in brass, and wears about three hundred bells round its neck, and has its hooves shod. And those oxen are called "fathers." The Indians call the ox "father" and the cow "mother"; they use the dung as fuel to bake bread and cook their food, and smear their faces, foreheads, and bodies with the ashes. That is their symbol. On Sundays and Mondays they have one meal, by day.

From Parvata I came to Bidar two weeks before Ulu Bayram,[31] the great Moslem feast. And I do not know when Easter Sunday, the great day of the Resurrection of Christ, occurs, so I try to guess in the following way: Christian Easter comes nine or ten days before the Moslem Bayram. I have nothing with me—no book; we took books with us from Russia, but when I was robbed the books were seized, too. And I have forgotten what I knew of the Christian faith and all the Christian feasts; I do not know when Easter occurs, or Christmas, or Wednesday or Friday. And surrounded by other faiths, I pray to God that he may protect me:

---

[30] Parvata (or Shriparvata): a popular Hindi holy city and place of pilgrimage, with an extensive complex of temples.

[31] Ulu Bayram: one of two main Moslem holy days, the day when Abraham sacrificed his son, Isaac, to God.

O Lord God,
O God of Truth,
O thou that are merciful,
God my Creator,
thou art my Lord.
There is one God,
the Prince of Glory,
maker of heaven and earth. [original in Arabic]

And I am going back to Russia thinking that my faith is dead, for I have fasted with the Moslems. The month of March has passed, and for a month I have not eaten any meat, have fasted with the Moslems and eaten nothing fat, no Moslem food, and taken two meals a day—nothing but bread and water. And I have prayed to God Almighty, Maker of heaven and earth, and have invoked none but his name: the God who made us, the Merciful God, God Almighty.

And from Hormuz to Kalhat it is ten days,
and from Kalhat to Dega it is six days,
and from Dega to Muscat it is six days,
and from Muscat to Gujarat it is ten days,
and from Gujarat to Cambay it is four days,
and from Cambay to Chaul it is twelve days,
and from Chaul to Dabhol it is six days.

As for Dabhol, it is a harbor in Hindustan, the last of the Moslem harbors.

And to go from Dabhol to Calicut takes twenty-five days,
and from Calicut to Ceylon takes fifteen days,
and from Ceylon to Shabait takes a month,
and from Shabait to Pegu takes twenty days,
and from Pegu to China takes a month.[32]

And these are all sea voyages. And from southern China to northern China it is six months' journey by land and four days' sail by sea. May God adorn my shelter.

Hormuz is a great harbor. People from all over the world arrive there, and all kinds of goods are sold in its market. Whatever is produced on earth can be had at Hormuz. The duties, however, are high, one-tenth of everything.

And Cambay is a harbor whence ships sail all over the Indian

---

[32] Dabhol, Calicut, Shabait, Pegu: cities in India.

Sea, and it is rich in goods: *alacha*,[33] taffeta, coarse cloth, and indigo are always produced by everybody there, and also lac, cornelian, and salt. Dabhol is a very big harbor and horses are brought thither from Egypt, Arabia, Khorassan, Turkestan, and Old Hormuz; and it is a month's journey by land to Bidar and to Gulbarga.

And Calicut is a big harbor on the Indian Sea, and God forbid that any ship should pass by it; no one who sails past it will cross the sea unscathed. And it produces pepper, nutmeg, cinnamon, clove, spices, *adrak*,[34] and many kinds of herbs. And everything is cheap there; and slaves are very good; they are black.

And Ceylon is rather a big harbor on the Indian Sea, and there Father Adam stood on a high mountain.[35] And near Ceylon precious stones, rubies, rock crystal, agates, amber, beryls, and emery are found. Elephants are bred there and sold by the cubit, and ostriches, which are sold by weight.

And the harbor of Shabait on the Indian Sea is very large. There the Khorassani warriors are paid a salary of one *tanga* [36] a day each, both the big and the little. And when a Khorassani marries there, he is granted one thousand *tangas* by the Prince of Shabait, who, moreover, pays him ten *tangas* a month by way of salary, and as much for food. And at Shabait there are silk and sandalwood and pearls, and it is all cheap.

The harbor of Pegu is not small, and it is mostly Indian dervishes that live there. And there one finds precious stones— *maniks* [37] and sapphires and rubies. These stones are sold by dervishes. And the harbors of southern and northern China are very large, and there porcelain is made, and sold by weight at a low price.

From Bidar to Shabait it is three months,
and from Dabhol to Shabait by sea it is two months.

And there porcelain is made, and everything is cheap. And it takes two months to reach Ceylon by sea. And in Shabait one finds silk and pearls and sandalwood; elephants are sold by the cubit.

---

[33] *Alacha:* textile material made of cotton and silk.

[34] *Adrak:* local word for ginger.

[35] According to Ceylonese legend, Adam walked for the first time on earth on a Ceylon peak, later called the Peak of Adam. It is still an important place in Buddhist pilgrimage.

[36] *Tanga:* local coin.

[37] *Manik:* Hindu word for ruby.

In Ceylon there are monkeys, rubies, and crystals,
and in Calicut, pepper, nutmeg, clove, areca nuts, and dyes.
And in Gujarat there are indigo and lac
and in Cambay, cornelian.
And in Raichur diamonds are mined—old and new ones;
one pochka of diamond is sold at five rubles,
and if very good, at ten rubles;
one pochka of new diamond [38]
is worth only five kanis,
one of blackish color
is worth from four to six kanis,[39]
and a white diamond,
is worth one tanga.

Diamonds are mined in a rocky mountain; they are sold at two thousand gold pounds a cubit if the diamonds are new, or at ten thousand gold pounds if they are old. And the land belongs to Melik Khan, a servant of the sultan; and it is thirty *kos* from Bidar.

And the Jews hold Shabait to be their own, but that is a lie. The Shabaitans are not Jews, Moslems, or Christians; they have a different faith, the Hindu faith. They do not eat or drink with Hebrews or Moslems, nor do they eat any meat. Everything is cheap in Shabait, and silk and sugar are made there—very cheap. And in the woods there one finds wildcats and monkeys, and they attack people on the roads, so that, because of the monkeys and wildcats, no one dares journey at night.

And from Shabait to Cathay it is ten months by land, and four months by sea, on a big ship.

The horns of fattened deer are cut off because there is musk in them. But wild deer shed their horns in the fields or woods, and the horns give off an aroma, which, however, is not so fragrant because they are not so fresh.

In the month of May, I kept Easter at Moslem Bidar, in Hindustan. And the Moslems kept Bayram [40] on a Wednesday in the month of May; and I began to fast on the first day of the month of April.

O faithful Christians,
those who voyage to many lands,

---

[38] The "new" diamonds, or the diamonds from the so-called new mines in Raichur were less expensive. *Pochka:* local measure for precious stones.

[39] *Kani:* little coin, one sixty-fourth of a *tanga.*

[40] Bayram: Moslem Lent.

fall oft into sin,
and rob themselves of their Christian faith.
And I, Afanasy,
servant of the Lord,
have been yearning for my faith with all my heart;
Lent and Easter have already passed four times,
and yet I, sinner that I am,
know not when Easter or Lent or Christmas
or any other holy day comes,
nor do I know when it is Wednesday or Friday.
And I have no books,
for when I was robbed,
all my books were taken away from me.

And because of the many misfortunes I went to India, for I had nothing to take to Russia, no goods being left. The first Easter Sunday found me at Kain, the second at Chapakur, in the Mazanderan country, the third at Hormuz, and the fourth at Bidar, in India, with Moslems. And there I shed many tears for the Christian faith.

Melik the Moslem pressed me for a long time to adopt the Moslem faith. But I answered him:

"My lord, you perform your prayers,
and I perform mine;
you say five prayers,
and I say three;
I am a stranger,
but you are not."

But he said to me: "Indeed, albeit thou professest not to be a Moslem, neither dost thou know the Christian faith." And then I thought it over a great deal, and said to myself:

"Woe to me, miserable sinner,
for I have strayed from the true path
and knowing no other, must go my ways.
Almighty God, Maker of heaven and earth,
turn not thy face from thy servant who sorrows.
Shelter me and have mercy upon me,
O God who created me;
lead me not away, O Lord,
from the path of righteousness,
but keep me in thy true ways,
for I have of necessity

done nothing virtuous
for thy sake in my distress,
and have lived all my days in evil.
Four Easter Sundays have already passed
in the Moslem land,
but I have not forsaken the Christian faith;
and God knows what may yet happen.
In thee I trust, O Lord,
save me, O God!"

In Moslem India, at great Bidar, I watched the heavens on
Easter night; the Pleiades and Orion stood low at Easter, and the
Great Bear was headed eastward.

During the Moslem Bayram,
the sultan went forth in procession,
and was accompanied by twenty grand viziers
and three hundred elephants
clad in steel armor and carrying castles encased in metal.
And in each castle there were six men in armor,
with cannons and harquebuses,
and the biggest elephant carried twelve men.
Each elephant bore two large standards,
and had long swords tied to its tusks,
each sword weighing a kantar,
and heavy iron weights fastened to its trunk;
and between its ears sat a man in armor,
who drove it with a big iron hook.
And there also went
a thousand spare horses in golden harness
and one hundred camels with drummers,
and three hundred trumpeters
and three hundred dancers
and three hundred slave girls.
And the sultan wore a caftan studded with sapphires,
and a helmet with a huge diamond on the top;
and his sagadak [41] *was adorned with sapphires,*
and he had three sabers in gold scabbards,
and a golden saddle.
And a kafir ran before him
juggling with an umbrella,
and after him came many footmen.
He was also followed by a trained elephant

---

[41] *Sagadak:* a horseman's bow and quivver with arrows.

clad in damask,
with a big iron chain in its mouth,
with which it struck at people and horses
to keep them away from the sultan.
And the sultan's brother was borne in a golden litter,
and above him was a velvet canopy,
with a golden top set with sapphires.
And the litter was carried by twenty men.
And the sovereign was borne in a golden litter,
under a silk canopy with a golden top.
His litter was mounted on four horses
in golden harness.
And he was surrounded by a great throng,
and preceded by singers and many dancers.
And all had bared swords or sabers,
and shields and spears and bows,
long and straight;
and all the horses were in armor,
and bore sagadaks.
And some people went naked
save for a loincloth to hide their shame.

At Bidar, the full moon lasts for three days. And there are no
sweet vegetables there.

The heat is not strong in Hindustan;
it is strong at Hormuz and in Bahrein,
where pearls are found,
and also in Jidda and Baku
and Egypt and Arabia and Lar.
It is hot in the land of Khorassan, too,
but not so hot.
And it is very hot in Jagatai.
And it is hot in Shiraz and Yezd and Kashan,
but a wind blows there at times.
And in Gilan the heat is very great and sweltering,
and in Shemakha it is sweltering too.
It is not at Babylon (Baghdad),
and also at Homs and Damascus.
But it is not so hot at Aleppo.
And at Sivas and in the land of Georgia
everything is most plentiful.
And the Turkish land is very plentiful.
Walachia is also plentiful,
and all food is cheap there.
The land of Podolia, too,

abounds in everything.[42]
May God protect the Russian land!
There is no land in the world like it,
although the boyars in the Russian land are unjust.
May the Russian land be well ordered,
and may there be justice there.
Allah,
Khuda,
O God,
Tangri! [43]
In thee I trust, O God!
Save me, O Lord!
I know not my way!
Whither shall I go from Hindustan?

(A description of wars between local rulers has been omitted.)

III. RETURN TO RUSSIA

On the fifth Easter Sunday, I made up my mind to leave for
Russia. I set out from the city of Bidar a month before the
Moslem Ulu Bayram, according to the faith of Mohammed, the
Prophet of God. As for the great Christian feast, the Resurrec-
tion of Christ, I knew not when to keep it, and I fasted with
the Moslems, and broke my fast when they broke theirs. I kept
Easter at Gulbarga, twenty *kos* from Bidar.

And then I went to Gulbarga,
and from Gulbarga to Sheik Ala-uddin,
and from Sheik Ala-uddin to Kamendria,
and from Kamendria to Kynarias,
and from Kynarias to Suri;
and from Suri I went to Dabhol,
a harbor on the great Indian Sea.

Dabhol is a very large city, and people from the whole coast of
India and Ethiopia come together there. And there I, Afanasy,
a confounded servant of Almighty God, Maker of heaven and
earth, pondered over the Christian faith, the Baptism of Christ,
the fasts established by the Holy Fathers, and the apostolic
commandments, and I longed to go to Russia. And having

---

[42] Bahrein: islands in the Persian Gulf. Jidda: a port in Arabia.
Gilan: province in northern Persia. Homs and Aleppo: cities in Syria.
Georgia: a Caucasian state. Walachia: a province in present-day
Rumania. Podolia: a province in the western Ukraine.

[43] *Khuda:* God (Persian). *Tangri:* God (Turkic).

boarded a *dabba* and struck a bargain on the fare, I paid two gold pieces for the passage to Hormuz.

I boarded the ship at Dabhol three months before Easter Day—the Moslem Fast. And I sailed on the *dabba* across the sea for a month, seeing nothing, and it was not until the second month that I sighted the mountains of Ethiopia. Then all those on board exclaimed: "O God, it seems that we are doomed to perish here!"

And I spent five days in the land of Ethiopia. By the mercy of God, no evil befell us; we distributed much rice and pepper and loaves of bread among the Ethiopians, and they did not plunder the ships.

Thence I sailed to Muscat in twelve days,
and there kept my sixth Easter.
And I sailed to Hormuz in nine days,
and spent twenty days there.
From Hormuz I journeyed to Lar,
and spent three days there.
From Lar I journeyed to Shiraz in twelve days,
and spent seven days there.
And from Shiraz I journeyed to Aberkuh in fifteen days,
and spent ten days there.
And from Aberkuh I journeyed to Yezd in nine days,
and spent eight days there.
And from Yezd I journeyed to Isfahan in five days,
and spent six days there.
And from Isfahan I journeyed to Kashan,
and stayed for five days there.
And from Kashan I journeyed to Kum,
and from Kum to Savah.
And from Savah I journeyed to Sultaniya.
And from Sultaniya I journeyed to Tabriz.
And from Tabriz I went to Hasan Beg's camp
and stayed for ten days there,
because I could not continue my journey.
Hasan Beg has dispatched an army of forty thousand
against the Turkish (sultan), and they took Sivas;
they also took and burned Tokat,
took Amasya and sacked many villages.
And fighting, the army marched on Karaman.
And from the camp I journeyed to Erzincan,
and from Erzincan to Trebizond.[44]

---

[44] Cities mentioned in this paragraph are located in Persia or Armenia.

And I arrived at Trebizond on the day of the Intercession of the Holy Mother of God, and stayed there for five days. And having boarded a ship, I struck a bargain on the fare—one gold piece for the passage to Kaffa; and I was to pay a toll of one gold piece at Kaffa.

At Trebizond the *subasi* [45] and the pasha caused me much harm; they took all my luggage to their town on the mountain, and searched it thoroughly; they stole all the fine things that they found while seeking for papers, for I had come from Hasan Beg's camp.

By the mercy of God, I reached the third sea, the Black Sea, or Sea of Stambul in Persian. It took me five days to sail with a fair wind to Vonada, but there a strong northerly wind stopped us, and made us turn back to Trebizond. And we lay at anchor at Platana [46] for fifteen days because of the strong and fierce wind. We put to sea from Platana twice, but the fierce wind checked us. O God! I had nearly crossed the sea when the wind drove us to Balaklava, and then to Gurzuf, where we lay at anchor for five days.

By the mercy of God, I arrived at Kaffa [47] nine days before the Fast of Advent. O God, my Creator! By the mercy of God, I have crossed three seas. The rest God alone knows, God the Protector alone is aware.

(Nikitin ended his report with a long Christian prayer in Arabic.)

---

[45] *Subasi:* petty Ottoman officer or landlord.

[46] Platana: city on the southern shore of the Black Sea near Trebizond.

[47] Balaklava, Gurzuf, Kaffa: cities on the southern shore of the Crimea.

E. NEW MILITARY TALES

52. THE STORY OF STEPHEN BATHORY'S CAMPAIGN AGAINST PSKOV

FOR almost two centuries the primary objective of Muscovite Russia's foreign policy was to gain free access to the Baltic Sea in order to establish direct contact with the West and put an end to Russia's political and cultural isolation. On many occasions Russian armies had tried to capture the Baltic shores, which had been in the hands of the Teutonic Knights of the Livonian Order since the thirteenth century. In 1558 Ivan IV began a military campaign against this Order, and at first he was successful. When Sweden and the Polish-Lithuanian Empire came to the help of the Livonian Order, however, the Russian advance lost momentum. The war then became an exhausting, indecisive undertaking that lasted some twenty-five years. In its final stages Russia had to face the powerful coalition of Sweden, Denmark, Poland, Lithuania, and Hungary, the last three countries being united under the scepter of the energetic Prince of Transylvania, Stephen Bathory.[1] After 1578 Russia lost most of the lands she had conquered earlier, and by 1581 King Stephen Bathory was able to begin an invasion of Russian territory. Polish, Lithuanian, and Hungarian troops, supported by some German mercenaries, invaded Russia and advanced on the city of Pskov, Russia's principal stronghold in the northwest. After a long siege and many attempts to subdue the city, King Stephen Bathory was forced to abandon his plans for conquest, for the heroic defense of Pskov and his failure to take the city had undermined both the strength and morale of his Polish-Lithuanian forces.

The *Story of Stephen Bathory's Campaign Against Pskov* was written in the form of an epic in the late sixteenth century by a talented and erudite anonymous writer who displays an excellent command of the traditional, ornamental stylistics of his time. His account is at once dramatic and ironic, picturesque, and varied. His metaphors and literary devices ideally serve his purpose to present a solemn account of the heroism of the Russian soldiers. With considerable mastery and pointed irony,

---

[1] Stephen Bathory was also elected King of Poland and Lithuania in 1575. His wife was Anna, the last princess of the Polish dynasty of Jagellons. The author of this tale refers to Stephen as "King of Lithuania," although Poland and Lithuania were united under his scepter.

the author describes King Stephen Bathory's campaign, his courageous, boastful courtiers and knights who, long before the final outcome of the battle was in sight, bragged that they would capture Princes Vasily and Ivan Shuysky, the valiant defenders of Pskov. This tale betrays the strong national fervor of the writer, who was firmly convinced that God would help the "only truly Christian" Russian army, and grant it final victory over the "infidel" invaders.

The excerpts that follow were taken from the early seventeenth-century Russian text published by V. I. Malyshev in *Povest o prikhozhdenii Stefana Batoriia na grad Pskov*, Academy of Sciences of the U.S.S.R., Moscow and Leningrad, 1952, pages 56, 57, 59, 60, and 65–78.

. . . Dreadful and cruel times have come. The Polish and Lithuanian king, Stephen Bathory, approached the borders of the Russian land with numerous forces. The rumor has spread to Pskov that this Lithuanian king has already invaded the land of Pskov and has occupied the city of Voronoch, located sixty miles from the city of Pskov.

Similar to insatiable hell which opens its jaws to swallow its victim, so also did the Polish-Lithuanian king prepare to take the city of Pskov in the pincers of his regiments. Always livelier and swifter, this king's army, like an ominous and great serpent wriggling from its cave, moved in columns to Pskov, and threatened the Russians with its campfires, guns, and smoke. The Lithuanian king boasted that he would swallow Pskov, even before he reached it. He boasted that he would satiate all the reptiles, snakes, and scorpions of his army with the rest of the booty. This ominous serpent leaped at Pskov, wanting to hurl it to the earth with its wings and to sting the Pskovian men to death with its stinger. He boasted that he would plunder all the spoils of Pskov and take them to Lithuania and that he would swallow up the Pskovian land, dragging on its tail all those who remained alive to the Lithuanian land. The serpent already flattered itself with thoughts of victory over Pskov. . . .

Dark smoke rose from south of the God-protected city of Pskov. The Lithuanian armies approached Pskov, and their black shadows, like a cloud, fell over the white stone walls of Pskov. Still, the whole Lithuanian land could not make the city black. Smoke began to rise from the enemy camp, which was three miles away from the city, on the river Cherekh. The tsar's officers, who scouted at this river, rushed to Pskov to inform the tsar's boyars and *voevodas* that the first Lithuanian troops were already at the river Cherekh. The tsar's boyars and *voevodas* ordered the tocsin sounded, and gave the command to burn the settlement beyond the Velikaia [2] River in order not to leave behind any quarters for the enemies. And so, on the day of the holy martyrs Frol and Lavr, on August 18th, 7089 (1581), the siege of the God-protected city of Pskov began. The Lithuanian troops began crossing the river Cherekh, and soon afterward their regiments appeared at the gates of the city. The boyars and *voevodas* led their men in a sortie against the enemy troops. But the enemy demonstrated their weakness in this skirmish, beginning the siege with methods of flight, and not daring to approach the city. And for them this was a bad omen. . . .

On Friday, September 8th, the day of the Birth of the Holy Virgin, at five o'clock in the afternoon, the Polish and Lithuanian *voevodas*, captains, storm troops, and gaiduks [3] hurried joyfully and hopefully to storm the city of Pskov. The tsar's boyars and *voevodas*,[4] all warriors, and the citizens of Pskov saw from their walls that a large number of regiments were leaving the king's camp and moving toward the city with banners. The gaiduks were entering the trenches and tunnels, and the Russians understood that they were moving to storm the breaches in the fortress wall. The *voevodas* ordered that the tocsin, which was located on the city wall in the vicinity of the Church of Vasily the Great on the hill, be sounded to warn all people of Pskov that the Poles and Lithuanians had begun the storming of the city. The boyars and *voevodas* of the tsar, with all their warriors and *streltsy*, were ordered to their places, and stood in preparedness while the artillery received the command to open fire on the enemy regiments. The artillery fired incessantly on the enemy, destroyed many regiments, and killed many Lithuanians and Poles. And their corpses were covering the ground. Still the enemy was advancing to the fortress, fighting fiercely, daringly, and hopefully. The enemy advanced as if it were a great stream flowing toward the city. The enemy troops looked as terrifying as the waves of the sea. And an endless number of their sabers were glinting at the city as if they were lightning bolts.

In the Cathedral of the Life-Giving Trinity the clergy began the service, praying to God with tears and appealing to God for

---

[2] The city of Pskov is located on the Velikaia (Great) River.

[3] The gaiduks were mercenary infantry and shock troops.

[4] The city of Pskov was under the command of Princes Ivan and Vasily Shuysky, and Prince Andrew Khvorostinin.

the deliverance of the city. The Pskovian men took leave of their wives and children, and hurried to the breaches of the fortress wall, prepared to stave off the enemy, and in their hearts they pledged to God that they would defend the Christian faith and die for each other, for the city of Pskov, for their homes, for their wives and children, and never surrender. And they did as they promised.

At six o'clock of this same day they heard a noise comparable to that of approaching gigantic waves or of powerful thunder. And the entire enemy army howled and ran to the breaches in the fortress wall, covering themselves with their shields, rifles, muskets, lances, and other weapons, and thus appearing to be under a roof. The tsar's boyars and *voevodas* appealed to God for help, encouraged the Russian warriors with their battle cries, and began fighting the enemies on the fortress walls. The innumerable Lithuanian troops rushed to the fortress wall like a rampaging stream. But our Christian warriors remained as firm as the stars in the sky, and did not permit the enemy to scale the walls. Like powerful thundering, there arose a din of shouts, noises of the shooting of artillery and gunfire, and battle cries of the great multitude of warriors from both armies.

The Pskovian army barred the way of the Lithuanian army, but these lawless Lithuanian warriors fiercely and daringly scaled the wall. The enemy artillery made such large breaches in the wall that even the cavalry could go through them. And at the Virgin's Veil and the Hog Towers there was not a single place safe from the enemy's artillery and guns. The Russians had begun building new wooden walls of many stories for artillery, but they could not complete them because of the heavy enemy artillery barrage. And only their foundations were completed. Thus many enemy warriors were able to climb the city walls. Many of their captains and gaiduks scaled the Virgin's Veil and Hog Towers with their banners, shooting at our defenders from the tower windows and from behind their shields. The first to scale the wall and to remain on it were the enemy's veteran soldiers who were clad in steel armor and armed with the best of weapons. The tsar's boyars and *voevodas* and the entire Orthodox army resisted them firmly and unbendingly, fighting bravely and skillfully, and not letting the enemy into the city.

When the most glorified King Stephen saw that his choicest storm troops were on the walls of the city, that his captains and gaiduks had unfurled the banners of the Lithuanian army over the Virgin's Veil and Hog Towers, and that they opened fire against the city and against the Russian artillery to open the way for the taking of the city, his heart was filled with indescribable joy. And he looked hopefully forward to the taking of the fortress. He moved his headquarters closer to the city, into the church of Christ's great martyr, Nikita, which was situated one-half mile from the wall of Pskov.

His retinue, councillors, and beloved noblest aristocrats approached the king and spoke words of hope and praise to him: "Our lord and sovereign, you have done it. You are the conqueror and victorious ruler of the city of Pskov. Glory be to you. We beg you, extend your kindness to us and allow us to proceed to the fortress of Pskov, so that not only your captains and gaiduks will know the glory of having taken Pskov."

When the king heard how joyfully his noblemen and councillors expressed their readiness to fulfill his plans, joy overcame him. With a gay face and happy heart he told them, as if they were his brothers: "Well, my friends, if you show such intentions to fight, I shall also go with you and not stay behind, my friends."

But they answered: "O our sovereign, King Stephen! You will make your triumphant and glorious entry into this great city of Pskov, in the same way as the great king, Alexander the Great, made his glorious and triumphant entry into the city of Rome.[5] And in the same way as Alexander's courtiers met him in the city, so also shall we, your servants, meet you in the city of Pskov with a hymn of glory. And we will prepare for you the spoils of the city. And we will meet you with the Russian commanders of Pskov, whom we shall capture! And for a particularly cherished treasure, we shall meet you with the two captured boyars and *voevodas:* the first commander of Pskov, Prince Vasily Shuysky, and the glorious, strong, invincible, great, and courageous second commander, Prince Ivan Shuysky. And we shall put them both in irons before you. And you, our sovereign, will do what you please with them in order that they be punished for their unruly resistance to you."

Hearing this, the king permitted them to go to the walls of the fortress of Pskov with joy, telling them the following: "I knew, friends, that it always would happen as you used to predict, and so it will happen now. And you will accomplish what you intend to, for no one can resist you and your brilliant mind." And two thousand selected storm troops and personal guards of the king began the assault of the Hog Tower, which was

---

[5] Either the Polish nobles erred in their speeches or the author of this tale did, for Alexander the Great certainly was never at war with Rome.

already destroyed on their side, and they began shooting through the windows of the wall at the Christian people and at the Russian militia. Their bullets fell like drops of rain from a storm cloud, and flooded the Russian warriors. These bullets were killing the Christian people as if they were the stings of serpents. Other enemy troops stormed through the break in the Virgin's Veil Tower, and cleared the tower of Russian warriors, preparing the way for the final taking of the city.

The Russian *voevodas*, their soldiers, and the Pskovian militia firmly and courageously stood their ground. Some waited for the enemy with lances at the foot of the wall. The *streltsy* shot at the Poles with their muskets. Some of the noblemen shot with their bows, while still others hurled rocks or defended the city of Pskov in other ways. The Poles' artillery shot at the Russian army from the walls and the towers and, relieving tired troops with fresh ones, they shot incessantly and shouted, "Let's take the city of Pskov!"

The king often sent his messenger to them, inquiring whether the city had been taken, and ordered the commanders, captains, and the entire army to speed the taking of the city.

In the God-protected city of Pskov the *voevodas* and boyars of the tsar, with kindness and tears, urged their Christian warriors to fight heartily, and they, themselves, fought unyieldingly at the side of their troops. It was sad to see the heads of the Christian warriors falling to the earth like the ears of wheat torn from the ground and lying in one heap. Many soldiers fell from the many wounds inflicted by the enemy's weapons, from exhaustion, and from the incessant fighting. During the day it was extremely hot because of the burning sun. Only faith in God's protection and deliverance gave strength to the warriors.

In the city itself and in the Cathedral of the Life-Giving Trinity the clergy incessantly prayed with tears and moaning for deliverance of the city. When the clergy of the cathedral learned the news that the Lithuanians were already on the walls and in the towers, and that they had unfurled their banners and were shooting from the walls into the city, preparing their way, then Tikhon, the abbot of the Crypt Monastery, and Archpriest Luka, and all the deacons of the city began to weep with loud voices, extending their arms to the most holy icon. They fell to their knees. Like the streams of many rivers their tears covered the marble steps of the altar, and they began to pray with more fervor, asking the Holy Virgin to protect the city and its inhabitants. The noble ladies, who had gathered in the cathedral for the service, beat their breasts and prayed to God and the most Pure Virgin; they fell on the floor, beating the ground with their heads and crying for divine help. And in every house of the great and God-protected city of Pskov the women, infants, and children who remained at home fervently cried and prayed before the holy icons, beating their breasts and asking the Holy Virgin and all saints for help, and begging God for the forgiveness of their sins and deliverance of the city. And in all the streets of the city there was crying, moaning, and indescribable wailing.

The enemy troops were incessantly and steadily advancing. "Forward, friends!" shouted their officers. "Let us slay all the people of Pskov for their unsubmissiveness. Not even a memory of the Christian inhabitants of Pskov will remain. The shadow of death will engulf them, and nothing will be able to aid them in escaping from our hands."

But who can speak of the power of God? Who can praise his glory?

Blessed are those that fear God and follow his righteous ways, and who honestly enjoy the fruits of their labors.

Listen, all people of the universe.

Listen all sons of man.

Listen all rich and poor.

Come all saints of Russia to the Christian land to aid the city of Pskov.

You have prayed for us and have helped us through your prayers to God.

You protected the city of Pskov,

which verily I say unto you is the God-protected city.

Let us glorify and declare together the power of the Holy Trinity.

God is our protection and power; God is our aid in the sorrow befallen us.

Therefore, I verily say unto you,

that we have no fear, as the voice of the prophet announced it.

Great is God and greatly is he glorified in this city of God.

We recognize God, who is on his holy mountain,

when we are in misfortune and when he intercedes for us.

For our humility God did not forsake us

when the kings of the earth gathered to march on Pskov, saying:

"God has abandoned that city. Let us hurry and take it."

O Stephen Bathory, commander of the accursed, haughty, and evil Lithuanian nation,

and of all your insane army!
How can you say that no one will deliver this city?
The power of God is with us!
Our Protector is the God of Jacob, the God of the Glorified
      Trinity,
the One God who has three names, but whom we worship as
      One,
the Father, the Son, and the Holy Ghost.
We place our hope in him and we rely upon him.
But you, Bathory, do not know him with your lawless Latin
      heresies.
And you, Bathory, who place your own majesty before that
      of heaven,
hope to conquer the city of Pskov, relying on your multitude
      of forces.
Wait, accursed one! You will see what happens to your forces!
You will see whether there is One who can deliver us!
And what is the worth of all your proud bragging about the
      taking of Pskov?
Because of your pride, you will now experience humiliation.
And from the heights of arrogance, you will descend to the
      hell of shame.
And so will it happen to your army,
for the Lord has remembered us for our humility
and has delivered us from our enemies.
And the Lord has heard the prayers of his servants
and through the miracle of his unfathomable compassion,
his mercy was revealed,
and he delivered his people and showed clemency to his
      servants.

A bomb from the great gun called the Leopard, which was placed upon the Praise Bastion, hit the Hog Tower squarely. And the bomb killed a great many Polish and Lithuanian warriors. At about the same time, the tsar's boyars and *voevodas* ordered the exploding of a large quantity of black powder under this Hog Tower. And the overproud knights, courtiers, and nobles of the king, who had begged their king for permission to take the city of Pskov and bring in the Russian boyars and *voevodas* in irons, as it was previously mentioned, were blasted into the air according to God's design, and were thus slain by these Russian boyars and *voevodas*. And the corpses were so numerous that another tower might have been built with them. And the best of the royal nobles, who had boasted that they would bring the imprisoned Russian commanders to their king, remained under the ruins of the Hog Tower, prisoners of death until the Last Judgment. And the deep Pskovian moat was overflowing with their bodies.

The king learned this, when he asked: "Are my noblemen already in the castle?"

And his courtiers told him: "No, sire, they are under the walls of the castle."

And then the king asked: "Do my nobles fight behind the walls of the city and destroy the Russian forces?"

And they answered: "Sire, all your nobles have been killed in the Hog Tower or lie burned in the moat."

And the king was so bereaved that he wanted to run on his sword, as the pagans used to do, for his heart was bursting with sorrow. And he became wroth, and ordered his captains and storm troops who were fighting at the Virgin's Veil Tower to stand firm and take by any and all means the city of Pskov.

The tsar's boyars and *voevodas,* seeing the heavy and uninterrupted bombardment, the incessant storming, and realizing that many of their warriors had been killed or wounded, relied only upon the help of God. They sent for the holy and miracle-working icons and for the miracle-working relics of the faithful and great Prince Gabriel [6] who had once delivered the city of Pskov from the enemy. And they ordered that the icons be brought to the breach which had been made in the wall by the Poles. Once the holy icon of the Holy Virgin of Vladimir had protected the city of Moscow at the time of Tamerlane's invasion. Now another icon was brought to Pskov because of the invasion of King Stephen Bathory. While the icon of the Virgin protected the city of Moscow from the infamous lame man [Tamerlane], now another icon of the Virgin, which had been brought from the Crypt Monastery,[7] helped and protected Pskov. At that time the holy icon of Vladimir was brought to Moscow on the day of the Assumption of the Holy Virgin, and Tamerlane was defeated because he became afraid of this icon of the Pure Virgin, and fled with all his army from Moscow and

---

[6] Prince Gabriel, as well as Prince Dovmont, mentioned in the following paragraph, were rulers of Pskov in the twelfth and thirteenth centuries, and became known for their courageous defense of Pskov against the German Knights of the Livonian Order and Baltic tribes. See Selection 40, footnote 5.

[7] The Crypt Monastery mentioned here is west of the city of Pskov, and has preserved to the present its fortifications built by Ivan IV. The name of the monastery was apparently taken from the Kievan Cave (or Crypt) Monastery.

from Russia. This time the miracle happened in the glorious city of Pskov, on the very day of the venerable and glorious holy day of her birth.

When the holy, miracle-working icon of the Assumption of the Holy Virgin of the Crypt Monastery was brought from the Cathedral of the Holy Trinity with other icons, relics of Prince Gabriel, and other holy relics, divine protection invisibly appeared over the breach in the wall.

The Poles and Lithuanians were fiercely fighting against the Russians in the breaches of the wall and in the Virgin's Veil Tower. Together with the warriors, the Russian officers and commanders were fighting, preventing the enemy from breaking through into Pskov. And when the church procession moved from the cathedral with the icons, at the head of the procession, black-robed heralds rushed on their steeds; they were not soldiers, but the warriors of Christ. Among them were the cellarer of the Crypt Monastery, whose name was Arseny Khvostov; the treasurer of the Monastery of the Birth of the Holy Virgin in Snetegorsk, Jonah Naumov; and the abbot, Mantiry, who was known to everyone in Pskov. All three of these monks were aristocrats by birth and, before becoming monks, had been great warriors. Seeing the bloody battle, they rushed to the breach and, for the sake of God and their holy faith, called out in strong voices. And it seemed as if these voices were coming from the icons. They called to the commanders and to the whole Christian army: "Be not afraid. Let us stand firm. Let us charge against the Polish and Lithuanian forces. The Holy Virgin has come to our aid with all her mercy and protection, and with all the saints."

As soon as the words were heard that the Holy Virgin had come with all the saints to help the Russian commanders and warriors, the Russians felt that the Holy Virgin really gave them her blessing and protection, and thus their weakening hearts became firm and they became ready for heroic deeds. In their hearts they accepted the aid of the Holy Virgin, and all commanders, warriors, and the aforementioned monks cried out in unison: "O friends, let us die this day at the hands of the Lithuanians for the sake of Christ's faith and for our Orthodox tsar, Ivan of all the Russias! Let us not surrender to the Polish king, Stephen!" And they appealed also for the intercession of the holy protectors of Pskov, late Prince Gabriel, late Prince Dovmont, and Nicholas, the fool in Christ. And in their hearts they accepted their help, and the entire Russian Christian army stormed the enemy together, and they were fighting in the breach of the wall.

Thus, with God's and the Holy Virgin's help, and with the

intercession of the holy miracle workers, the Russians expelled the Polish-Lithuanian forces from the breach and, where recently stood the feet of the enemy, now stood the firm feet of the Christian warriors. And they continued to defeat the enemy, going beyond the walls of the city, while others fought with the Lithuanian troops who remained in the Virgin's Veil Tower.

When the Lord demonstrated the Christian victory over Pole and Lithuanian, and when the Russian troops repulsed the Lithuanian warriors, captains, and gaiduks from the breach in the wall, this news of the blessing of Christ spread throughout the entire city of Pskov, and reached the women who had been left at home. And the word that the enemy had been stopped through divine help spread from house to house. And the women were ordered to go take the Lithuanian artillery and the remnants of the Lithuanian and Polish weapons that remained in the city, and then to gather at the breach. And all the women of Pskov, who had remained in their homes in great sorrow, were seized with joy, forgot their womanly weaknesses, and gained the strength of men, hurried to the breach, and took from their homes weapons according to their strengths. Even before, at the beginning of the assault, some strong young women had been fighting against the enemy with arms. Now all, the young, the strong, and the weak, were running with ropes to pull the artillery pieces left by the enemy into the city. All of them rushed to the breach. And each woman wanted to surpass the others in her speed. A multitude of women gathered at the breach, and they were great help for the Christian warriors. Some of them, as I mentioned above, who were young and strong, fought with masculine courage against the Polish and Lithuanian forces, demonstrating their superiority over them. The others brought rocks so that the soldiers might hurl them at the Lithuanians both within and outside of the fortress. Others helped the warriors, and brought them water to quench their thirst, thus bringing back courage to their brave hearts.

This happened on Friday, on the Holy Day of the Holy Virgin's Birth. It was already evening, but the Polish and Lithuanians were still fighting in the Virgin's Veil Tower and were shooting against the Christian warriors in the city. Then the tsar's boyars and *voevodas* appealed to God for succor, called their troops together, and began the storming of the Virgin's Veil Tower. Men and women hurled themselves against the remaining enemy troops in the tower, fighting with all the arms given to them by God. Some shot muskets, while others were trying to smoke out the enemy from their hiding places. Others threw rocks at the Poles and Lithuanians, while still others poured boiling water upon them. Finally they put black powder under this tower also, and with God's help they blasted the remaining Lithuanians and Poles from the Virgin's Veil Tower. In this way, with the Grace of Christ, the stone wall of Pskov was cleansed of the evil Lithuanian feet. When night came, God sent light, and the remainder of the enemy was driven out from under the walls.

And then the Lithuanians and Poles began to flee from the fortress back to their camps. The Christian Russian warriors made sorties from the fortress, pursued them, cut them to pieces, and chased the others away. Those who remained in the moat were destroyed. Many were taken prisoner and brought back to the city, to the tsar's boyars and *voevodas* to be interrogated. Many enemy warriors were taken with banners, drums, and weapons. And many Russians returned to the city uninjured, and brought back with them enemy arms, special muskets, guns, and endless booty.

Thus, with God's blessing, through the infinite mercy of the Divine Trinity, and the prayers and intercession of the Holy Virgin, and in honor of her glorious birth, and for the sake of the holy, great miracle workers, the great city of Pskov was delivered from the Poles and Lithuanians. And at three o'clock in the night the Lord gave a great victory to the Christian army over the proud and lawless enemy.

[The final part of this work describes the fighting around Pskov until February 4th, 1582, the day when King Stephen Bathory lifted the siege of this fiercely embattled Russian fortress.]

F. EPISTOLARY POLEMICS

53. PRINCE ANDREW KURBSKY: FIRST EPISTLE WRITTEN TO THE TSAR AND GRAND PRINCE OF MOSCOW IN CONSEQUENCE OF HIS FIERCE PERSECUTION

PRINCE Andrew Kurbsky's first epistle to Ivan IV is a strong protest against Tsar Ivan's autocratic rule. Wishing to destroy the old feudal system of Russia, by which the princes were practically independent rulers of their appanages, Ivan IV began a systematic purge of the aristocracy in the late 1550s and many nobles died on the scaffold or in prison.

An outstanding statesman and military leader, Prince Kurbsky was a close friend and adviser of Tsar Ivan IV until the latter began his cruel struggle against the Russian feudal aristocracy. Kurbsky then broke with the tsar and fled to Lithuania, where he settled for the rest of his life. Kurbsky had belonged to the intellectual elite of sixteenth-century Moscow and had been a pupil and friend of the famous and erudite scholar-monk, Maxim Trivolis, called Maxim the Greek, who had come to Russia in the early years of the sixteenth century. Living in Lithuania, Andrew Kurbsky became a writer and translator and participated in the revival of Russian Orthodox literature in the Russian parts of Poland and Lithuania. His best-known work is his correspondence with Ivan IV, in which he sharply criticized the tsar's autocratic policies and his persecution of the aristocracy.

This translation of the letter was made by J. L. I. Fennell and was published in *The Correspondence Between Prince A. M. Kurbsky and Tsar Ivan IV of Russia, 1564–1579*, Cambridge University Press, 1955, pages 3, 5, 7, 9, and 11.

To the tsar, exalted above all by God, who appeared [formerly] most illustrious, particularly in the Orthodox Faith, but who has now, in consequence of our sins, been found to be the contrary of this. If you have understanding, may you understand this with your leprous conscience—such a conscience as cannot be found even amongst the godless peoples. And I have not let my tongue say more than this on all these matters in turn; but because of the bitterest persecution from your power, with much sorrow in my heart will I hasten to inform you of a little.

Wherefore, O tsar, have you destroyed the strong in Israel and subjected to various forms of death the *voevodas* given to you by God? [1] And wherefore have you spilled their victorious, holy blood in the churches of God during sacerdotal ceremonies, and stained the thresholds of the churches with their blood of martyrs? [2] And why have you conceived against your well-wishers and against those who lay down their lives for you unheard-of torments and persecutions and death, falsely accusing the Orthodox of treachery and magic and other abuses, and endeavoring with zeal to turn light into darkness and to call sweet bitter? What guilt did they commit before you, O tsar, and in what way did they, the champions of Christianity, anger you? Have they not destroyed proud kingdoms and by their heroic bravery made subject to you in all things those in whose servitude our forefathers formerly were? Was it not through the keenness of their understanding that the strong German towns were given to you by God? [3] Thus have you remunerated us, [your] poor [servants], destroying us by whole families? Think you yourself immortal, O tsar? Or have you been enticed into unheard-of heresy, as one no longer wishing to stand before the impartial judge, Jesus, begotten of God, who will judge according to justice the universe and especially the vainglorious tormentors, and who unhesitatingly will question them "right to the hairs [roots?] of their sins," as the saying goes? He is my Christ who sitteth on the throne of the Cherubim at the right hand of the power of the Almighty in the highest—the judge between you and me.

What evil and persecution have I not suffered from you! What ills and misfortunes have you not brought upon me! And what iniquitous tissues of lies have you not woven against me! But I cannot now recount the various misfortunes at your hands which have beset me owing to their multitude and since I am still

---

[1] The expression "the strong in Israel" echoes the current panegyrical political literature of the sixteenth century, extolling the absolution of the grand prince and the supremacy of Moscow, "the Third Rome," "the new Israel."

[2] A reference to the first wave of Ivan's persecutions which, according to Kurbsky (*Skazaniia Kn. A. M. Kurbskogo,* ed. N. Ustrialov [St. Petersburg, 1842], "Istoria . . ." Chapter VI, page 90), began "shortly after the death of Alexis Adashev and the banishment of Priest Sylvester," i.e., in 1560.

[3] The "proud kingdoms" destroyed by the "strong in Israel" in the fifties of the sixteenth century were the Tatar Khanates of Kazan (captured in 1552) and Astrakhan (captured in 1556). The "strong German towns" are the Baltic towns captured during the first three years of the Livonian War (1558–1560): Narva, Neuhausen, and Dorpat (1558); Marienburg, Ermes, and Fellin (1560).

filled with the grief of my soul. But, to conclude, I can sum-
marize them all [thus]: of everything have I been deprived; I
have been driven from the land of God without guilt [*lit.* in
vain], hounded by you. I did not ask [for aught] with humble
words, nor did I beseech you with tearful plaint; nor yet did I
win from you any mercy through the intercession of the hierarchy. You have recompensed me with evil for good and for my
love with implacable hatred. My blood, spilled like water for
you, cries out against you to my Lord. God sees into [men's]
hearts—in my mind have I ardently reflected and my conscience
have I placed as a witness [against myself], and I have sought
and pried within my thoughts, and, examining myself [*lit.* turning myself around], I know not now—nor have I ever found—
my guilt in aught before you. In front of your army have I
marched—and marched again; and no dishonor have I brought
upon you; but only brilliant victories, with the help of the angel
of the Lord, have I won for your glory, and never have I turned
the back of your regiments to the foe. But far more, I have
achieved most glorious conquests to increase your renown. And
this, not in one year, nor yet in two—but throughout many years
have I toiled with much sweat and patience; and always have I
been separated from my fatherland, and little have I seen my
parents, and my wife have I not known; but always in far distant towns have I stood in arms against your foes and I have
suffered many wants and natural illnesses, of which my Lord
Jesus Christ is witness. Still more, I was visited with wounds
inflicted by barbarian hands in various battles and all my body
is already afflicted with sores. But to you, O tsar, was all this as
naught; rather do you show us your intolerable wrath and bitterest hatred, and, furthermore, burning stoves.[4]

And I wanted to relate all my military deeds in turn which
I have accomplished for your glory by the strength of my
Christ, but I have not recounted them for this reason, that God
knows better than man. For he is the recompenser for all these
things, and not only for them, but also for a cup of cold water;
and I know that you yourself are not unaware of them. And
furthermore may this be known to you, O tsar; you will, I think,
no longer see my face in this world until the glorious coming of

---

[4] Evidently one of the commonest forms of torture employed by
Ivan IV. Kurbsky speaks of Ivan's torture in his *History*: "Are not the
various instruments of torture of the ancient torturers the same as
those used by our new torturer [i.e. Ivan]? Pans and stoves? Cruel
flogging and sharp nails? Red-hot pincers for lacerating human bodies?
Needles to drive under the fingernails . . . ? (p. 145)

my Christ. Think not that concerning these things I will remain silent before you; to my end will I incessantly cry out with tears against you to the Everlasting Trinity, in which I believe; and I call to my aid the Mother of the Lord of the Cherubim, my hope and protectress, Our Lady, the Mother of God, and all the saints, the elect of God, and my master and forefather, Prince Fedor Rostislavich, whose corpse remains imperishable, preserved throughout the ages, and emits from the grave sweet odors, sweeter than aromatics, and, by the grave of the Holy Ghost, pours forth miraculous healing streams, as you, O tsar, know well.[5]

Deem not, O tsar, and think not upon us with your sophistic thoughts, as though we had already perished, massacred [though we are] by you in our innocence and banished and driven out by you without justice; rejoice not in this, glorying, as it were, in a vain victory; those massacred by you, standing at the throne of Our Lord, ask vengeance against you; while we who have been banished and driven out by you without justice from the land cry out day and night to God, however much in your pride you may boast in this temporal, fleeting life, devising vessels of torture against the Christian race, yea, and abusing and trampling on the Angelic Form,[6] with the approbation of your flatterers and comrades of the table, your quarrelsome boyars, the destroyers of your soul and body, who urge you on to erotic deeds and, together with their children, act more [viciously] than the priests of Cronus. So much for this. And this epistle, soaked in my tears, will I order to be put into my grave with me, when I [shall be about to] come with you before the judgment of my God, Jesus Christ. Amen.

Written in Wolmar, the town of my master, King Augustus Sigismund, from whom I hope to receive much reward and com-

---

[5] Fedor Rostislavich, prince of Yaroslavl, Andrew Kurbsky's paternal grandfather to the ninth degree, ruled in Mozhaisk at the end of the thirteenth century. In 1294 he received the principality of Yaroslavl after marrying the daughter of Vasily Vsevolodovich, prince of Yaroslavl. He died in 1299 and was canonized in 1463.

[6] The Russian expression "to accept the Angel's form" is the equivalent of "to take monastic vows." In certain copies of the text there exists the following marginal note: "That is to say, he abuses the Angelic Form when he flies into a rage with certain people and then forces them to accept the monastic tonsure together with their wives and children, and condemns them to everlasting imprisonment in strong monasteries and dark cells, making the holy places fortresses of hell with the approbation of certain accursed and cunning monks."

fort for all my sorrow, by his sovereign grace, and still more with God's help.

I have heard from sacred writings that a destroyer will be sent by the devil against the human race, a destroyer conceived in fornication, the Antichrist, hostile to God; and now I have seen a counselor, known to all, who was born in adultery and who today whispers falsehoods in the ears of the tsar and sheds Christian blood like water and has already destroyed the strong and noble in Israel, as one in agreement with the Antichrist in deed.[7] It is not befitting, O tsar, to show indulgence to such men! In the first law of the Lord it is written: "A Moabite and an Ammonite and a bastard to the tenth generation shall not enter into the congregation of the Lord."[8]

54. IVAN IV: EPISTLE OF THE TSAR AND SOVEREIGN TO ALL HIS RUSSIAN TSARDOM AGAINST THOSE WHO HAVE BROKEN THE PLEDGE OF ALLEGIANCE, AGAINST PRINCE ANDREW KURBSKY AND HIS COMRADES, CONCERNING THEIR TREACHERIES

The epistle of Ivan IV, the Terrible, to Prince Andrew Kurbsky is one of the most impressive works defending the Byzantine-Russian concept of autocracy, which accepted the tsar as ruler by divine right. Ivan IV thus claimed the exclusive right to command the destinies of the state and his subjects, while considering himself responsible only to God for the fate of the state and its people. (Concerning Prince Andrew Kurbsky and the roots of this conflict, see the introduction to Prince Kurbsky's letter to Ivan.)

A dread tyrant who was merciless to his enemies, Ivan IV was at the same time a great ruler whose policies helped determine the future of Russia. By breaking the power of the aristocracy he ended the feudal system of medieval Russia and thus laid the foundation for a unified Russian state. His successes against the Tatars opened to Russia the nearly limitless territories of the Volga-Ural region and northern Asia, thus paving the way for future Russian expansion. Some one hundred and fifty years before Peter the Great, Ivan IV tried to open a window to

---

[7] This is probably a reference to Fedor Alekseevich Basmanov, who was a favorite of Ivan's at that time. He was, indeed, renowned for his cruelty, and is alleged by Kurbsky to have murdered his father. There is, however, no confirmation of his illegitimacy.

[8] See Deuteronomy, 23:2–3.

Tsar Ivan IV (the Terrible).
A late sixteenth-century Russian portrait.

Europe and to end Russia's isolation by winning an area on the Baltic shore from the Order of Livonian Knights.

Ivan IV was very well educated, was a forceful polemicist and writer, and even composed music. His style of writing is not restrained, but fierce, stinging, and merciless, and he did not hesitate to insult his enemies.

These excerpts from Tsar Ivan's letter to Prince Kurbsky, which grew into a rather lengthy treatise, have been translated by Leo Wiener.

Our God, the Trinity, who has existed since eternity but now as Father, Son, and Holy Ghost, has neither beginning nor end; through him we live and move about, through him kings rule and the mighty write laws. By Our Lord Jesus Christ the victorious standard of God's only Word and the blessed Cross, which has never been vanquished, have been given to Emperor Constantine, first in piety, and to all the Orthodox tsars and protectors of Orthodoxy and, insofar as the Word of God has been fulfilled, they, in eagle's flight, have reached all the godly servants of God's Word, until a spark of piety has fallen upon the Russian realm. The autocracy, by God's will, had its origin in Grand Prince Vladimir, who had enlightened all Russia through the Holy Baptism, and the great Tsar Vladimir Monomakh, who had received memorable honors from the Greeks, and the valiant great Tsar Alexander Nevsky, who had obtained a great victory over the godless Germans, and the praiseworthy great Tsar Dmitry, who had obtained a great victory over the sons of Hagar beyond the Don, then it passed to the avenger of wrongs, our ancestor, the great Tsar Ivan, the gatherer of the Russian land from among the ancestral possessions, and to our father of blessed memory, the great Tsar Vasily until it reached us, the humble scepter-bearer of the Russian empire.[1]

But we praise God for the great favor he has shown me in not permitting my right hand to become stained by the blood of my race: for we have not snatched the realm from anyone, but

---

[1] Roman Emperor Constantine (306–337) granted the rights to the Christians, and summoned the first Ecumenical Council of the Christian Church. Prince Vladimir Christianized Russia in 988 or 989. Vladimir Monomakh was the last prince of Kiev (1112–1125) to be recognized as the real leader by all Russian princes of the Kievan era. Dmitry, Grand Prince of Muscovy, was the victor over the Tatars in 1380. "The great Tsar Ivan" is Ivan III, unifier of northern Russia (1462–1505) and grandfather of Ivan IV. Vasily—Vasily III (1505–1533)—was father to Ivan IV.

by the will of God and the blessing of our ancestors and parents, were we born in the realm, were brought up there and enthroned, taking, by the will of God and the blessing of our ancestors and parents, what belonged to us, and not seizing that which was not ours. Here follows the command of the Orthodox, truly Christian autocrat, the possessor of many kingdoms—our humble Christian answer to him who was an Orthodox, true Christian and a boyar of our realm, a councillor and a general, but now is a criminal before the blessed, vivifying cross of the Lord, a destroyer of Christians, a servant of the enemies of Christianity, who has departed from the divine worship of the images and has trodden underfoot all sacred commands, destroyed the holy edifices, vilified and trampled the holy vessels and images, who unites in one person Leo the Isaurian, Constantine Kopronymos, and Leo of Armenia—to Prince Andrew Mikhailovich Kurbsky, who through treachery wanted to become a ruler of Yaroslavl.[2]

Wherefore, O prince, if you regard yourself to have piety, have you lost your soul? What will you give in its place on the day of the terrible judgment? Even if you should acquire the whole world, death will reach you in the end! Why have you sold your soul for your body's sake? Is it because you were afraid of death at the false instigation of your demons and influential friends and counselors? . . .

Are you not ashamed before your slave Vaska Shibanov,[3] who preserved his piety and, having attached himself to you with a kiss of the cross, did not reject you before the tsar and the whole people, though standing at the gate of death, but praised you and was all too ready to die for you? But you did not emulate his devotion: on account of a single angry word of mine, you have lost not only your own soul, but the souls of all your ancestors: for, by God's will, had they been given as servants to our grandfather, the great tsar, and they gave their souls to him and served him up to their death, and ordered you, their children, to serve the children and grandchildren of our grandfather. But you have forgotten everything and traitorously, like a dog, you have transgressed the oath and have gone over to

---

[2] Leo III the Isaurian (717–741), Constantine V Kopronymos (741–755), and Leo V, the Armenian, were Byzantine emperors who supported the heresy of the Iconoclasts and were posthumously condemned by the Orthodox Church.

[3] Vaska (Vasily) Shibanov, a faithful servant of Prince A. M. Kurbsky who delivered his master's letter to Ivan IV, and died after long tortures without betraying the prince.

the enemies of Christianity, and, not considering your wrath, you utter stupid words, hurling, as it were, stones at the sky. . . .

We have never spilled blood in the churches. As for the victorious, saintly blood—there has none appeared in our land, as far as we know. *The thresholds of the churches:* as far as our means and intelligence permit and our subjects are eager to serve us, the churches of the Lord are resplendent with all kinds of adornments, and through the gifts which we have offered since your satanic domination, not only the thresholds and pavements, but even the antechambers shine with ornaments, so that all the strangers may see them. We do not stain the thresholds of the churches with any blood, and there are no martyrs of faith with us nowadays. . . . Tortures and persecutions and deaths in many forms we have devised against no one. As to treasons and magic, it is true, such dogs everywhere suffer capital punishment. . . .

It had pleased God to take away our mother, the pious Tsarina Helen, from the earthly kingdom to the Kingdom of Heaven. My brother George, who now rests in heaven, and I were left orphans and, as we received no care from anyone, we laid our trust in the Holy Virgin, and in the prayers of all the saints, and in the blessing of our parents. When I was in my eighth year, our subjects acted according to their will, for they found the empire without a ruler, and did not deign to bestow their voluntary attention upon us, their master, but were bent on acquiring wealth and glory, and were quarreling with each other. And what have they not done! How many boyars, how many friends of our father and *voevodas* they have killed! And they seized the farms and villages and possessions of our uncles, and established themselves therein. The treasure of our mother they trod underfoot and pierced with sharp sticks, and transferred it to the great treasure, but some of it they grabbed themselves; and that was done by your grandfather Mikhaylo Tuchkov. The Princes Vasily and Ivan Shuysky took it upon themselves to have me in their keeping, and those who had been the chief traitors of our father and mother they let out of prison, and they made friends with them. Prince Vasily Shuysky with a Judas crowd fell in the court belonging to our uncle upon our father confessor Fedor Mishurin, and insulted him, and killed him; and they imprisoned Prince Ivan Fedorovich Byelsky and many others in various places, and armed themselves against the realm; they ousted Metropolitan Daniel from the metropolitan see and banished him: and thus they improved their opportunity, and began to rule themselves.

Me and my brother George, of blessed memory, they brought up like vagrants and children of the poorest. What have I not suffered for want of garments and food! And all that against my will and as did not become my extreme youth. I shall mention just one thing: once in my childhood we were playing, and Prince Ivan Vasilievich Shuysky was sitting on a bench, leaning with his elbow against our father's bed, and even putting his foot upon it; he treated us not as a parent, but as a master . . . who could bear such presumption? How can I recount all the miseries which I have suffered in my youth? Often did I dine late, against my will. What had become of the treasure left me by my father? They had carried everything away, under the cunning pretext that they had to pay the boyar children from it, but, in reality, they had kept it back from them, to their own advantage, and had not paid them off according to their deserts; and they had also held back an immense treasure of my grandfather and father, and made it into gold and silver vessels, inscribing thereupon the names of their parents, as if they had been their inheritance. . . . It is hardly necessary to mention what became of the treasure of our uncles: they appropriated it all to themselves! Then they attacked towns and villages, tortured the people most cruelly, brought much misery upon them, and mercilessly pillaged the possessions of the inhabitants. . . .

When we reached the age of fifteen, we, inspired by God, undertook to rule our own realm and, with the aid of Almighty God, we ruled our realm in peace and undisturbed, according to our will. But it happened then that, on account of our sins, a fire having spread, by God's will, the royal city of Moscow was consumed. Our boyars, the traitors whom you call martyrs, whose names I shall purposely pass over in silence, made use of the favorable opportunity for their mean treachery, whispered into the ears of a stupid crowd that the mother of my mother, Princess Anna Glinsky, with all her children and household, was in the habit of extracting men's hearts, and that by a similar sorcery she had put Moscow on fire, and that we knew of her doings.[4] By the instigation of these our traitors, a mass of insensate people, crying in the manner of the Jews, came to the apostolic cathedral of the holy martyr Dmitry of Saloniki, dragged out of it our boyar Yury Vasilievich Glinsky, pulled him inhumanly into the Cathedral of the Assumption, and killed the innocent man in the church, opposite the metropolitan's place;

---

[4] Princes Shuyskys were members of an influential and wealthy aristocratic family who actually ruled in Moscow during Ivan IV's childhood.

they stained the floor of the church with his blood, dragged his body through the front door, and exposed him on the market-place as a criminal—everybody knows about this murder in the church. We were then living in the village of Vorobievo; the same traitors instigated the populace to kill us under the pretext, and you, dog, repeat the lie that we were hiding from them Prince Yury's mother, Princess Anna, and his brother, Prince Mikhail. How is one not to laugh at such stupidity? Why should we be incendiaries in our own empire? . . .

You say that your blood has been spilled in wars with for-eigners, and you add, in your foolishness, that it cries to God against us. That is ridiculous! It has been spilled by one, and it cries out against another. If it is true that your blood has been spilled by the enemy, then you have done your duty to your country; if you had not done so, you would not have been a Christian but a barbarian—but that is not our affair. How much more ours, that has been spilled for you, cries out to the Lord against you! Not with wounds, nor drops of blood, but with much sweating and toiling have I been burdened by you un-necessarily and above my strength! Your many meannesses and persecutions have caused me, instead of blood, to shed many tears, and to utter sobs and have anguish of my soul. . . .

You say you want to put your letter in your grave: that shows that you have completely renounced your Christianity! For God has ordered not to resist evil, but you renounce the final pardon which is granted to the ignorant; therefore it is not even proper that any Mass shall be sung after you. In our patrimony, in the country of Liveand, you name the city of Volmir as belonging to our enemy, King Sigismund: by this you only complete the treachery of a vicious dog! [5] . . .

Written in our great Russia, in the famous, imperial, capital city of Moscow, on the steps of our imperial threshold, in the year from the creation of the world 7072 (1564), the 5th day of July.

---

[5] The city of Volmir, actually Volmar, was conquered by Ivan IV during the first phase of the Livonian War (see introduction to Selection 52, the *Story of Stephen Bathory's Campaign Against Pskov*), and later was claimed by the Polish King Sigismund.

the wane of medieval patterns and rise of the baroque

(*Seventeenth Century*)

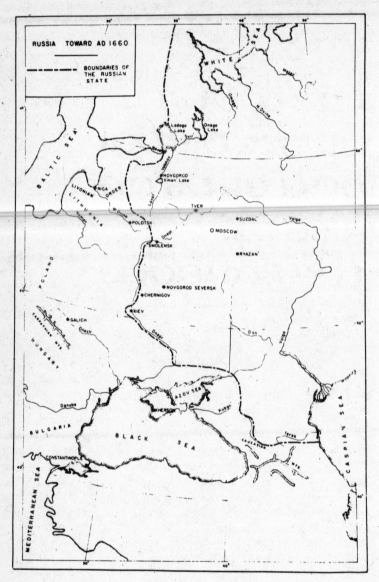

Russia ca. A.D. *1660*

A. HISTORICAL WORKS FROM THE TIME OF TROUBLES

55. AVRAAMY PALITSYN: PSEUDO-DMITRY

Soon after the death of Ivan IV, the Rurik dynasty, which had presided over Russia's destiny for seven hundred years, came to its end. Ivan had accidentally killed his eldest and favorite son, Tsarevich Ivan, and the throne was inherited by the physically and mentally debile Fedor. After reigning fourteen years, 1584 to 1598, Tsar Fedor died without leaving an heir to the throne. The dynastic crisis was aggravated by the fact that Ivan's youngest son, Dmitry, mysteriously perished in 1591. Rumors circulated that he had been slain at the order of Boris Godunov, Tsar Fedor's brother-in-law, a brilliant but ruthless statesman who wanted the throne for himself. Indeed, the Land Assembly, which was manipulated by Boris, elected him as Tsar of all the Russias in 1598. His reign was not a happy one, however, for Russia was plagued by famines and epidemics. Moreover, in 1602 a mysterious impostor appeared who claimed that he was Tsarevich Dmitry, the son of Ivan IV, declaring that he had escaped the knives of Boris' henchmen in 1591. The Poles, the age-old rivals and enemies of Russia, supported Dmitry and his claim to the Russian throne. He also received the blessing of the Pope of Rome, and in return Pseudo-Dmitry promised the Holy See that he would convert all Russia to the Roman Catholic faith. In 1604 he began his campaign against Tsar Boris, leading both Russian rebels and Poles. Upon the unexpected death of Boris Godunov, Dmitry entered Moscow and became tsar in 1605. Hated by the boyars because of his sympathy for the Poles and by the Russian clergy for his rapprochement with the Catholic Church, Pseudo-Dmitry was murdered in the following year. For the next seven years anarchy reigned while Polish and Swedish armies occupied a good deal of Russian territory. Even Moscow fell to the Poles, in September of 1610. Only in 1613, after the election of Michael, the first tsar of the Romanov dynasty, did Russia begin its rehabilitation under a stable and legitimate government.

These nine years, 1604 to 1613, years of crisis, great unrest, and foreign intervention, are usually called the "Time of Troubles," and they left a deep and indelible impression on the mind of Russia. Many writers who lived through these dramatic events left memoirs and analyses concerning this period. In most of them can be found a feeling of offended nationalism and fierce hatred toward the foreigners who had invaded the Russian land during these turbulent years. These writers are especially bitter toward the Poles and Catholics, who supported Pseudo-Dmitry, hoping, through him, to dominate all of Russia.

Among such writers Avraamy Palitsyn, a monk and cellarer of the powerful Holy Trinity–St. Sergius Monastery, left one of the best accounts of the events of the time. A member of a wealthy aristocratic family, Averky (Avraamy was his monastic name) was born about 1555, and, like many aristocrats of the day, served both in the civil service and in the army. In 1588 a courtiers' faction forced him to take monastic vows, thus excluding him for a time from political activity. As cellarer of the Holy Trinity–St. Sergius Monastery he participated in the patriotic and counterrevolutionary revival of 1610 to 1613, and as an influential leader he wrote his history (*skazanie*), which became one of the most popular accounts of the Time of Troubles, surviving in over one hundred extant manuscripts from the seventeenth century alone. Palitsyn died in the Solovki Monastery on September 13th, 1627.

The translations of Chapters IV and V of his work, *A Concise History Written in Memory of Past Generations*, are given here. These translations follow the text of *Skazanie Avraamiia Palitsyna*, edited by O. A. Derzhavina and E. V. Kolosova, Academy of Sciences of the U.S.S.R., Moscow and Leningrad, 1955, pages 110–115, 137.

ABOUT THE DEFROCKED MONK GREGORY AND THE DEATH OF TSAR BORIS

In the year 7113 (1605) a certain monk, whose name was Gregory and who was a scion of the Otrepiev [1] family, and who had been an addict of occult books and other evils, left Russia and went to the Polish Kingdom. Living there, he began to write subversive proclamations, sending them to all parts of Russia, in which he declared that he was the real Dmitry, son of the tsar. He would go from city to city, hiding himself and causing disturbances among the people of both realms. Then he was joined by fugitives from western Russian and Polish cities, by serfs whose time had arrived according to the will of the

---

[1] Pseudo-Dmitry remains one of the great enigmas of Russian history. His actual identity has remained unknown to this day. However, the government of Boris Godunov, as well as other opponents of the pretender, identified him as being Gregory Otrepiev, a scion of a wealthy and noble Muscovite family.

evil spirit, and by one village after another, and by one city after another, and finally all were tempted. However, his scheme was evident to many. Yet, what a great amount of evil did they cause! And until this day Russia is unable to be rid of this yoke. He and his followers in evil have done so many base deeds in Russia that no one could describe them all, even if he wrote for many years. In two years this unfrocked monk Gregory succeeded in winning over one-quarter of the entire universe, the entirety of Europe; and even the Pope of Rome wrote on his behalf to the entire West, presenting Gregory as an exile from his fatherland. And the Pope ordered the Polish king, Sigismund III, to start a campaign against Russia in order to take revenge for the impostor. Gregory joined the Catholics, that eternal enemy of Christians, and he gave them a written promise that he would bring entire Russia under the blessing of the Antichrist,[2] thus delivering all Russians to eternal death through the abomination of the Catholic Communion. And he would have done this, if the Lord hadn't overthrown his evil design. To him refer the prophecies of Ezekiel, for it is written: "You shall be fuel for the fire and your blood shall be in the midst of the land" (21:32).

Although Tsar Boris was not killed by this impostor, he died a sudden death in the summer of 7113 (1605) during the revolt brought about by Gregory, and all those upon whom Boris relied were dispersed along with his household.[3]

After Boris' death, this monk ascended the throne and called himself Tsar Dmitry. But from many witnesses we know that this Gregory was a simple monk, despite the fact that he wanted to become the Tsar of Russia. And he gathered together all the relatives of the murdered Tsarevich Dmitry [4] and many other people who had been deported by Tsar Boris. And those who did not wish to join him, he won over through his gifts. In such manner did he win over the nun Marfa, the mother of Tsarevich Dmitry and the wife of Tsar Ivan Vasilievich, Tsar of all the Russias. And so she called this impostor her son. And many of

---

[2] In the sixteenth and seventeenth centuries the Protestant West and the Orthodox East often called the Pope of Rome the Antichrist, and they claimed that the Pope served Satan. The Catholics, in turn, called the Protestants the servants of Satan and the Antichrist.

[3] When Tsar Boris Godunov died, his son, Fedor II, became Tsar of Russia. However, he was soon murdered by the impostor's supporters, and Pseudo-Dmitry ascended to the throne of Muscovy.

[4] Maria Nagoy was the last wife of Ivan IV. After the killing of her son, Tsarevich Dmitry, Boris Godunov forced her to take monastic vows. She did so under the name of Marfa (Martha).

the people of Uglich [5] who could have exposed him and even his real mother, Barbara, the wife of Bogdan Otrepiev, his brother's widow and son, and his uncle, Smirny-Otrepiev, did not. Therefore his uncle was sent to Siberia, and underwent many tribulations there. And there appeared many new martyrs: the nobleman Peter Turgenev, and Fedor Kolachev, who fearlessly exposed him, were beheaded in the central square of the imperial city of Moscow, after having undergone many tortures. When this Fedor Kolachev was led to the scaffold, he shouted to the crowd, saying: "You have accepted this servant of the Antichrist and you worship this messenger of Satan. But you won't understand this until you have perished because of it."

But the Muscovites only abused him and answered that he well deserved his execution. They paid no more heed to the execution of Peter Turgenev. Soon after these executions, Prince Vasily Shuysky [6] was also condemned to death on the scaffold for his exposures and intrigues, but the Poles, fearing his execution, asked the impostor to pardon him.

Soon after, following the evil impostor's advice, all metropolitans, archbishops, bishops, abbots, and all the leading clergymen with Patriarch Ignaty, as well as the princes and boyars with all the army commanders, obeyed him and signed the petition and sent ambassadors to the Polish Kingdom to ask the Lord of Sandomir to give his daughter to this impostor for his wife.[7] And all of them gave witness in their message that he was Dmitry, the real son of Tsar Ivan IV.

And even those who knew that he was Monk Gregory gave witness to this. Among them were Pafnuty, the Metropolitan of Krutitsa. When Pafnuty was abbot of the Miracle Monastery, this Gregory used to sing in his choir and then remained at the court of the Patriarch Job for one year, where he worked as a clerk. Soon after, he ran away to Lithuania because his heretical intrigues were exposed. And like a chariot of the pharaoh, he became involved in a plot, and after him the entire Russian state became insane, giving in to his temptations.

Now involved in this plot, this accursed, defrocked impostor got into a conspiracy with the *voevoda* of Sandomir when he

---

[5] Tsarevich Dmitry was killed in the city of Uglich in 1591, so it is quite natural that in 1605 many inhabitants of this city could have testified that Pseudo-Dmitry was an impostor.

[6] After Pseudo-Dmitry's death, Prince Vasily Shuysky became Russia's tsar, ruling from 1606 to 1610.

[7] Marina Mniszech, a daughter of a *voevoda* of Sandomir, became the impostor's wife in 1606 in Moscow.

lived at his house in Poland. And, following an evil path, this *voevoda* decided to give his own daughter, Marina, in marriage [to this pretender, and took her to Moscow] to the lawless celebration of her wedding, taking with him some six thousand selected troops. For the quartering of these Polish knights, not only were the houses of simple people taken, but even those of officials, courtiers, and the Nagoy family, the so-called relatives of the impostor. And in all good and noble places and houses heretical joy and violence spread.

This defrocked impostor, who was himself a sponsor of the crooked faith, feared that the same fate that befell Tsar Boris would befall himself. And therefore, coming and leaving the tsar's palace, and going to walk about the city, he surrounded himself with many guards. Before him and behind him there were marching armed soldiers with arquebuses, halberds, and other weapons. And this impostor would always walk in the center of them, while Russian courtiers and boyars had to follow far behind. Indeed, it was terrifying to behold so many glinting arms and shining armor. He selected his personal guardsmen, as well as the guards of his palace, only from among the Polish and German mercenaries. He permitted gamblers to gamble and cheat even in the tsar's palace. All his retinue and his common servants were clothed in finery as if they were bridegrooms, though no one knew what they had to celebrate. They loitered from street to street searching for pleasure and bedecked in purple finery and with gold and silver accouterments. And when they served the impostor, they adorned themselves with precious stones and pearls. And they did not want to look upon anyone who was humble. In such a way, the Poles were squandering the ancient treasures of Russia. And they used the silver vessels for carrying water and even in the bath, while they used silver and gold vessels for washing. And besides all this, they spread the seeds of the heretical dogma of Luther.

And no one dared to pronounce a word in the presence of the evil and fiercesome Cossacks.[8] And many an aristocrat shed tears, seeing the arrogance shown them by their serfs. The serfs could always claim that their masters had called Dmitry "an unfrocked impostor," and then such masters would always disappear. In all the Russian cities and in the venerated monasteries many laymen and monks perished. Some of them were imprisoned, while others were drowned, and the belly of a huge fish became their tomb. The impostor permitted both Jews and

---

[8] Many Don and Dnieper Cossacks, among whom were many runaway serfs, joined with Pseudo-Dmitry.

heretics to visit the holy and divine churches, and foreigners dared to enter the Cathedral of the Assumption of Our Holy and Honored Lady and to profane the miracle-working relics of the holy metropolitans, Peter and Jonas, leaning upon the reliquaries. And the unholy Poles entered the churches even with their weapons, but no one dared tell them a word, since resisting one of them could mean death.

Soon after, the accursed Roman pope sent a missal to the impostor reminding him of his promise to introduce into Russia the Roman Catholic form of Holy Communion and fasting on Saturday. This cursed, defrocked monk attempted to do as he was ordered, but when he wed his heretical bride, they were married in a divine Orthodox Church. But before marrying her, this cursed man corrupted many virgin nuns and even pious monks. And both he and the Poles were committing many shameful deeds. And the rebels and Cossacks who brought him to the throne enjoyed the fall of Christian virtues, seeing those shameful acts. And they offended people who were sad and grieved sorrowfully, calling them Jews and saying: "The tsar does as he wants, but, like Jews, you only complain about it." Even the Muscovites trod the path of perdition, did not repent before God, but enjoyed the gains from their speculations and, although bemoaning much, still cared primarily for the accumulation of wealth.

Becoming insanely proud, this defrocked monk and impostor ordered that his title be, "The most illustrious, invincible Caesar." This accursed man believed that by bearing the name of the Tsar he could win the highest and most sought-after of honors.

There was a high official at the court, whose name was Timothy Osipov, who was a person of pious behavior and disposition, and who gave little heed to this impostor's ambitions. This virtuous man saw that much harm was being done by this defrocked monk and his councillors. Seeing the unnatural and high title the impostor had given himself, this man realized that each man is mortal and possessed by passions and therefore should not call himself an "invincible Caesar," since only God is invincible. This Timothy Osipov was a man devoted to God, and he prayed piously and the fasts were strictly kept in his house. Once, after he had received the most wonderful and life-giving Communion—the pure flesh and blood of Christ, Our Lord, he went to the tsar's palace and daringly exposed the defrocked monk before the people, saying: "Verily, verily thou art Grishka Otrepiev, a defrocked monk, and not an 'invincible Caesar.' Thou art not Dmitry, the son of the tsar, but a slave to sin, and a heretic."

The defrocked impostor could not stand such a denunciation and shame, but ordered the man immediately executed. So ended the life and the heroic deed of this worthy martyr.

Once the impostor sent to the Khan of Crimea the most dishonorable of gifts. He ordered a fur coat made of swines' skins for the khan, and wrote him that he was preparing a campaign against the Crimea, the land of the southern sun, and that he himself would appear there soon to plunder the Crimean homes. And he ordered all Russians, as well as the Poles, to his service and to prepare the campaign against the city of Azov.[9] And he immediately sent a large corps of selected artillerymen to the city of Elets. He ordered that the army prepare to advance either by boats on the river Don or on land across the prairie. Rumors about these military moves spread to Constantinople, and the Turks began to prepare for the spilling of Christian blood. Some people claimed, I do not know whether it is true or not, that this defrocked monk wanted to arouse the Crimean Khan and the Turks, so that many Christian Russians would fall on the battlefield. It does appear that he was not really interested in victory over the sons of Hagar, but wanted rather to withdraw the Orthodox Russians in order that he might afterward settle the Muscovite realm with Poles. But the Lord himself did not allow this ambitious man's plan to come to fruition.

HOW THE DEFROCKED MONK PREPARED A PLOT WITH THE POLES TO KILL MUSCOVITES, BUT WAS HIMSELF KILLED BY THE MUSCOVITE BOYARS

This enemy, the defrocked monk, plotted with the heretics [the Poles] to massacre the Russian people of all ranks, beginning with the courtiers and ending with common officers. And he intended to have a great celebration with the shooting of artillery in the Pond Field at the Sretensk Gate. And when the people went to this celebration, then he would order the gate to be closed and all would be slain.

But this base plot did not come to fruition because two days before the celebration was to have taken place, and ten days after his improper wedding, this accursed man died an evil death, having reigned for one year. He used to say of himself that he was thirty-four years of age, but his friends, the demons, didn't give him many more years of life. And so the writing of

---

[9] The city of Azov, located at the mouth of the river Don not far from the Azov Sea, was an important Turkish-Tatar fortress at that time.

St. John Chrysostom, "Such is the honor which demons render to those who love them," was fulfilled.

After his death, the people of Moscow gave themselves to drinking in their joy, instead of rendering thanks to God. And everyone bragged about his deeds in murdering the impostor, Pseudo-Dmitry, and all boasted about their courage. But the people forgot to give thanks through prayer in the Church of the Holy Virgin for this most glorious victory. Once, a great miracle was performed by the most Pure Holy Virgin in Constantinople, but this miracle against the Persians and the Scythians occurred on the sea and beyond the walls of the city, and not within the city walls.[10] In Moscow, however, the miracle occurred within the city. This accursed heretic was able to keep everyone firmly in tow, and he was loved by everyone. And yet, on that day, by the command of God, everyone rose against him. And a great amount of heretical [Polish] blood was spilled in the streets of Moscow. But, instead of rendering thanks to the Righteous Avenger, the people were seized by insanity and pride. And therefore the wrath of God did not subside; but we the Russians did not recognize the divine plan and designs, and were not able to realize from what evils the Lord had delivered us.

56. AVRAAMY PALITSYN: ANSWER OF THE DEFENDERS OF THE HOLY TRINITY–ST. SERGIUS MONASTERY TO THE POLISH REQUEST OF SURRENDER

One of the most dramatic events of the Time of Troubles was the besieging of the Holy Trinity–St. Sergius Monastery by Polish and Lithuanian troops in 1609. After a long siege and many attempted stormings of the well-fortified monastery-fortress, the commanders of the Poles and Lithuanians, John Peter Paul Sapieha and John Alexander Lisowski, demanded the monastery's surrender. The commanders of the Russian troops defending the monastery, Prince Gregory Dolgorukov and Alexis Golokhvastov, together with Abbot Ioasaf and the leading elders, refused to capitulate, and answered the Polish and Lithuanian commanders in a letter that well reflects the bitterness, hatred, and fierce national feeling that reigned in both camps. For the defenders of this monastery, surrender to the Poles would not only have meant betrayal of the national cause

---

[10] The author refers to the so-called Miracle of the Holy Virgin's Veil which, according to the legend, protected the city of Constantinople against a Russian attack.

but also betrayal of the Orthodox Faith. There are reasons to believe that the letter was written by Avraamy Palitsyn himself, as he was certainly the most skillful writer in the monastery at that time.

The present translation follows the text of the letter contained in *Skazanie Avraamiia Palitsyna* edited by O. Derzhavina and E. V. Kolosova, Academy of Sciences of the U.S.S.R., Moscow and Leningrad, 1955, page 137.

To the proud commanders Sapieha and Lisowski! Your dark majesties and your warriors are the opposers of God, the abomination of dissolution, and know that you attempt in vain to lead us, a flock of Orthodox Christians, into temptation. You should know that even a ten-year-old Christian youth from the Holy Trinity–St. Sergius Monastery would laugh at your request. And as far as your letter is concerned, we spit on it upon receiving it. What man would, at the expense of his soul, prefer darkness to light, a lie to the truth, honor to dishonor, and freedom to bitter slave labor? How could we forsake our eternal, holy, and true Orthodox Christian Faith of the Greek confession and submit ourselves to the new heretical law which betrays the Christian faith and which was cursed by the four ecumenical patriarchs.[1] What would be our gain and honor in betraying our Orthodox sovereign and tsar [2] and submitting ourselves to our enemy, the impostor and rebel? [3] And you, people of the Latin faith, have become like Jews, and even worse, for the Jews didn't recognize the Lord and consequently crucified him. Yet how can we, who know our Orthodox sovereign, concede to your request to forsake our Christian tsar despite the fact that our grandfathers were born in the vineyard of our true pastor Christ and under the rule of a Christian tsar? And how can you attempt to tempt us with false kindness, vain flattery, and ill-gained wealth. We shall remain faithful to the pledge we gave on the cross, for we do not care for all the wealth in the entire world.

---

[1] The four patriarchs refers to the four patriarchs of the cities of Constantinople, Antioch, Jerusalem, and Alexandria who broke with the Pope of Rome owing to the latter's claim for primacy.

[2] Sapieha and Lisowski fought in the name of the second impostor, that is, the second Pseudo-Dmitry, while the monastery refused to capitulate in the name of Tsar Vasily Shuysky (1605–1610).

[3] This refers to the second Pseudo-Dmitry.

57. PRINCE IVAN M. KATYREV-ROSTOVSKY:
A DESCRIPTION OF THE TSARS AND THEIR FAMILIES

The Book of Annals, written by Prince Ivan M. Katyrev-Rostovsky, gives one of the best accounts of the Time of Troubles. Others who wrote about this first great national crisis in Muscovite Russia followed both the basic outline and the literary style found here. Since it gives a vivid description of this difficult time, the author remaining quite unbiased and keeping to the historical truth, it is an important source for historians. *The Book of Annals* is also significant for several innovations, such as the longer literary portraits of the heroes of the narrative, especially of the tsars and their families. *The Book of Annals* was as well one of the first Russian works to describe nature and the changes of the seasons superbly; the account of the coming of spring is particularly noteworthy. The author often used rhymed passages, and there are many rhymed couplets to be found throughout the text.

The reader will find in this selection from *The Book of Annals* the portraits of the tsars and their families. The translation follows one of the earliest extant manuscripts, published in *Russkaia istoricheskaia biblioteka*, Volume 13, St. Petersburg, 1912.

A SHORT DESCRIPTION OF THE MUSCOVITE TSARS,
THEIR PHYSICAL APPEARANCES, STATURES,
AND TEMPERAMENTS

[TSAR IVAN IV (THE TERRIBLE), REIGNED FROM 1530 TO 1584]

Tsar Ivan was physically unattractive, had gray eyes, a hooked and long nose, and was tall, lean, and with broad shoulders and chest. He had great physical prowess and was a person of great acumen, being well read, erudite, and very eloquent. He was fearsome to the enemy, and was always prepared to fight for the fatherland. He was cruel to his subjects given to him by the Lord, being always ready to spill their blood, and both merciless and daring at killing. He ordered that many people be slain, from infants to the aged; he laid waste to many of his own cities; and many clergymen were thrown into prisons and mercilessly executed at his orders. He committed many other evil deeds to his own people, deflowering many girls and women in his lust. This Tsar Ivan did many good things, however, and he cared very much for his armies, generously rewarding them from his treasury. Such was Tsar Ivan.

[TSAR FEDOR (IVAN'S SON), REIGNED FROM 1584 TO 1598]

Tsar Fedor was short of stature, and appeared as a man who constantly fasted. He was most humble, and greatly cared after his soul, standing before the icons and praying endlessly. He generously gave alms to the poor. He was not taken up with worldly matters, but concerned himself only with the salvation of his soul. And so, from his infancy to the very end of his days, his life was dedicated to matters of salvation; and thus God gave peace to his reign, brought his enemies in tow, and granted him a blessed epoch. Such was Tsar Fedor.

[TSAR BORIS (GODUNOV, BROTHER-IN-LAW OF TSAR FEDOR), REIGNED FROM 1598 TO 1605]

Tsar Boris shone in the full bloom of his handsome appearance, and he surpassed many people in his attractiveness. He was of average stature. He was a man of great intelligence, had a marvelous power of reasoning, and was a clever polemicist and eloquent orator. He was a faithful Christian, gave generously to the poor, and was a great builder. He spent much time on state affairs and he performed a great many marvelous deeds. He had, however, two great shortcomings, for he was not granted a certain virtue by God: he used to go too much to doctors, and he was obsessed by an insatiable desire for power. And he dared to slay those who should have been tsars before himself. And for such deeds he received divine retribution.

[TSAR FEDOR II, THE SON OF BORIS, WHO REIGNED SOME WEEKS IN 1605]

Tsar Fedor, the son of Tsar Boris, was a marvelous youth. He was so handsome that he blossomed like a flower in the meadow, having been created by God like a lily blooming in the fields. His eyes were large and black; his complexion was light and white as milk; his stature was average; and his body was slightly stout. He was brought by his father to the learned books, and he was clever and eloquent in polemics. And never did any senseless or coarse words come from his lips, but he was devoted to the Faith and to the reading of books.

[TSAREVNA XENIA (DAUGHTER OF BORIS AND SISTER OF TSAR FEDOR II)]

Tsarevna Xenia, Tsar Boris' daughter, was a maiden of wonderful spirit, physically very attractive, of light complexion, and had beautiful rosy cheeks, red lips, and big black eyes. From her there radiated graciousness. Being sad and shedding tears,

her graciousness would become particularly radiant. Her eye-
brows were thick and joined, and her body was supple, while
her skin was as white as milk. She was neither too tall nor too
short; her hair was black and long, covering her shoulders. She
was the most distinguished among maidens, and she was accustomed to reading books. She shone by her forceful and distinguished speech, and she did well in whatever she attempted.
She had a fondness for beautiful voices, and loved to listen to
church music.

[PSEUDO-DMITRY, REIGNED FROM 1605 TO 1606]

This defrocked impostor was of very short stature, but was
powerfully built and of great physical strength. His face did
not have the distinction of a tsar, but it was very common and
his body was covered with dark spots. But he was very witty
and was rather learned. He was a daring and eloquent speaker,
loved horse racing, was courageous in fighting the enemy, was
brave and strong, and cared greatly for warriors.

[TSAR VASILY SHUYSKY (THE HEAD OF THE POWERFUL AND ARIS-
TOCRATIC FAMILY OF BOYARS, HE ORGANIZED THE MURDER OF
THE PRETENDER, PSEUDO-DMITRY, AND WAS THEREAFTER ELECTED
BY THE BOYARS TO SUCCEED HIM), REIGNED FROM 1606 TO 1610]

Tsar Vasily was short of stature, physically very unattractive,
and had eyes that were dull, as if he were blind. He was rather
cultured, and his reasoning was sound and pointed. He cared
only for those people who brought him gossip and rumors about
people, and he used to receive such persons with a joyful face,
and with sweet pleasure, did he listen to them. He was given
to sorcery, and cared little for the military.

B. BIOGRAPHICAL WORKS

58. KALLISTRAT DRUZHINA-OSORYIN: THE LIFE OF YULIANIA LAZAREVSKY

THE *vita* of Yuliania Osoryin, called Lazarevsky after the village of Lazarevo, where she lived and died, was written in the first quarter of the seventeenth century by her son, Kallistrat Druzhina-Osoryin. Although written with the purpose of glorifying her holy life, this work is very different from the typical *vitae* of saints of medieval Russia. With the exception of the descriptions of rare miracles and the appearances of demons, Yuliania's biography much more resembles a narrative from a family chronicle than a hagiographic work. The biographer gives a detailed account of the domestic relations in Yuliania's family, and often remarks that the author, himself, and his family, witnessed her works and life. Yuliania was neither a nun who spent her life in a convent, nor a princess whose Christian charity and works gave her the halo of a saintly protectoress. She spent all her life with her family, and her biography is filled with the details of everyday events. Although her life was one of prayer and Christian piety, the fact that she remained all her life with her husband and children as a devoted wife, mother, and daughter-in-law distinguishes this *vita* from the usual hagiographies dealing with heroes who performed miraculous deeds or defended the Orthodox Faith, and who were usually either hermits, church leaders, or pious rulers. With this *vita* there began to appear in Russia a realistic, secular biography.

This narrative is written in plain language, completely devoid of the panegyrics, lengthy epithets, and stylistic embellishments that characterize Russian lives of saints. The present translation follows an early seventeenth-century text published by M. Skripil in *Russkaia povest XVII veka*, Moscow, 1954, pages 39–47.

In the days of the pious Tsar and Great Prince Ivan Vasilievich [1] of all Russia, there was at his imperial court a good and charitable man by the name of Yustin Nediurev, a housekeeper

---

[1] Ivan IV, or Ivan Vasilievich, usually called the Terrible or Dread. reigned over Russia from 1530 to 1584.

by rank.[2] He had a wife named Stefanida, equally devout and compassionate, daughter of a certain Gregory Lukin from the city of Murom. They led a pious and virtuous life, had several sons and daughters, and possessed considerable wealth and many serfs. To them was born this blessed Yuliania.

Her mother died when she was six years of age, and Yuliania was taken to the lands of Murom by her grandmother, who raised her in piety for six years. When the grandmother died, Yuliania's aunt, Natalia, wife of Putila Arapov, took, at the grandmother's behest, the young girl to her house. As the blessed Yuliania had loved God and the Holy Virgin since her very youth, she respected and honored her aunt and her aunt's daughters. She was humble and obedient, assiduous in prayer and fasting. Because of her fasting, she was much berated by her aunt and ridiculed by her cousins, who said: "O insane one! Why dost thou exhaust thy flesh and so ruin thy beauty, while thou art so young?" They urged her to take food and drink every morning, but she did not yield to them; rather she withdrew in silence, even though she accepted everything with gratitude and was obedient to all. She also refrained from laughter and games, as from her very childhood she was meek, silent, and obedient, and never rude or haughty. Although frequently urged by her companions to take part in games and frivolous songs, she did not comply, pretending confusion in order to conceal her virtues. Instead, she applied herself with great diligence to spinning and hoop embroidery, working late into the night. She also did all the sewing for orphans and ailing widows in the village, and supplied the sick and needy with all kinds of goods. Everyone admired her wisdom and devotion.

The fear of God dwelt in her. There was no church in the village, nor any closer than within some miles; so Yuliania had no chance to go to church in her maidenhood. Neither did she ever hear the reading of the Holy Scriptures, nor any preacher teaching salvation, but God himself instructed her in virtuous ways. When she was in her sixteenth year she was given in marriage to a virtuous and wealthy man, named Georgy Osoryin. They were married by a priest, Potapy, in the church of the righteous Lazar, in her husband's estate. This priest instructed them in the law of God according to the rules of the Holy Fathers, and she carefully listened to the teaching and instructions, carrying them out in her deeds. Her parents-in-law were still alive and, when they saw her of mature age and accom-

---

[2] The names of the relatives and other people mentioned in this *vita* are the names of real personages. He was the steward of a rich estate.

plished in virtue, they commanded her to take charge of the
whole household. She humbly obeyed them in all things, never
contradicting them, but respecting them and fulfilling all their
orders without fail, so that all marveled at her. Many people
tested Yuliania in conversation and she gave a seemly and reasonable reply to every question, so that all wondered at her
good sense, and glorified God. She prayed much every evening,
and made one hundred and more genuflections. Upon arising
each morning, she did the same, together with her husband.
When her husband would be away in the tsar's service in
Astrakhan [3] for a year or two, and sometimes even for three
years, she went without sleep all night, praying or working,
weaving or embroidering. She would sell her work and give the
price to the poor or for the building of churches; she gave many
alms in secret by night. During the day she managed the household and cared for widows and orphans as a true mother, min-
istering to them with her own hands and giving them to drink
and to eat. She provided the serfs, both men and women, with
food and clothing, and assigned them work according to their
strength. She called no one a rude name, nor did she command
anyone to pour water while she washed her hands, or to take
off her shoes, but did all this herself. She instructed and corrected foolish serfs with meekness and humility, taking the
blame upon herself and denouncing no one, but placing all her
hopes in God and the Holy Virgin. She called for help upon
the great wonder-worker Nicholas, and he assisted her.

One night in her husband's absence, as Yuliania arose for
prayer, as was her wont, she was seized with fear and great
terror by the attack of demons. Being young and inexperienced,
she was frightened, lay down on the bed, and fell fast asleep.
Then she saw many demons coming at her with weapons, saying: "If thou wilt not cease thy efforts, we will straightway
destroy thee." She prayed to God and to the Most Holy Virgin
and to St. Nicholas the wonder-worker. And St. Nicholas appeared to her, holding a large book; he dispersed the demons,
so they disappeared like smoke. Lifting up his right hand, he
blessed her, saying: "My daughter, take courage and stand firm
and do not be afraid of the demons' threats! For Christ hath
commanded me to guard thee from demons and from evil men."

---

[3] All Russian nobles were supposed to serve either with the army or
in the civil service. This service was not a permanent one, but each
noble could be summoned into the service as soon as the necessity
arose. The city of Astrakhan, where Yuliania's husband served, is
located at the delta of the Volga in the vicinity of the Caspian Sea.

Then she straightway awoke from sleep and clearly saw the
holy man leaving the chamber through the door, quick as lightning. Rising promptly, she followed him, and forthwith he became invisible; yet the anteroom of the chamber was securely
locked. Taking this as a message, Yuliania rejoiced, praising
God, and was more diligent in good works than before.

In a short time, for our sins God's wrath fell upon the Russian
land, and a great famine occurred, and many starved to death.
Yuliania gave many alms in secret; she began to accept food
from her mother-in-law for morning and midday meals, and gave
all to the poor and hungry. So her mother-in-law said to her:
"How comes it that thou hast changed thy custom? When there
was an abundance of bread, I was not able to make thee eat
early and midday meals, and now, when there is a dearth of
food, thou eatest!" Wishing to keep her secret, Yuliania answered: "When I did not bear children, I did not want to eat,
but when I started to bear them I grew weak and I cannot eat
my fill. Not only in the daytime, but many times in the night as
well I am hungry, but I am ashamed to ask." The mother-in-law
was glad to hear it, and sent her enough food not only in the
daytime but also at night, for in their house there was an
abundance of bread and of everything. However, while receiving
food from her mother-in-law, Yuliania did not partake of it herself, but gave all to the poor. When anyone would die, she hired
women to cleanse him, gave sheets to wrap the body, and
money for the burial. When any deceased whatever were buried
in their village, she prayed for the remission of their sins.

In a short time, there was a severe pestilence among the people and many died from the plague. Many locked their doors
so that those who were afflicted would not enter their homes;
and they would not even touch the garments of the ill. Yet,
secretly away from her parents-in-law, Yuliania healed many of
the afflicted, washing them in the bathhouse with her own
hands; she prayed to God for their recovery, and if they died
she prayed for their salvation, hired men to bury them, and
ordered the forty days' prayer.[4] When her parents-in-law, after
having been tonsured,[5] died in extreme old age, Yuliania buried
them with honor: she gave many alms in their memory, and
ordered many forty days' prayers. She also had the Mass cele-

---

[4] In the Orthodox Church special prayers are required for the dead
for forty days after their death.

[5] It was the custom in medieval Russia, especially among the
aristocracy, to take monastic vows shortly before the approach of
death.

brated for them and had meals served at her house for the priests, monks, and beggars every day during the forty days, and sent alms to the prisons. At that time her husband was serving for three years in Astrakhan, and she spent a great part of their wealth in almsgiving, not only in those days, but throughout these years, honoring the memory of her dead parents-in-law.

Having thus lived with her husband for many years in great virtue, according to God's commandments, Yuliania gave birth to sons and daughters. The devil, who hateth all good, sought to cause her strife, arousing frequent discord among the children and the serfs. Reasoning sensibly and wisely, Yuliania restrained them all, but the devil provoked a serf to slay the eldest son; then another son was killed in the service. Although she grieved, it was for their souls, and not because of their deaths. And she honored them with memorial Masses, prayers, and almsgiving. Then Yuliania begged her husband to give her leave to go to a nunnery. He did not let her go, but they agreed to live together yet have no bodily intercourse. She continued to prepare his bed as usual, yet she herself, after long evening prayers, would lie down on the stove without any bedding. She lay on firewood with the sharp edges against her body, and she put iron keys under her ribs, and on these she took little sleep until her serfs fell asleep. Then she would rise to pray throughout the night, until daylight, when she went to church for matins and Mass. She occupied herself diligently with handiwork and managed her house in a manner pleasing to God. She provided her serfs with sufficient food, and appointed each of them a task according to their strength. She cared for widows and orphans, and helped the poor in all things.

Ten years after their bodily separation, Yuliania's husband passed away, and she buried him reverently, honoring him with memorial Masses, prayers, the forty-day services, and alms. From then on, she rejected even more all worldly things that she might better care for her soul and emulate the holy women of old and, in this way, to please God. She prayed and fasted, went every day to church, gave unending alms, so that ofttimes not a silver coin remained in her house and she had to borrow in order to give alms to the poor. When winter came, Yuliania borrowed silver from her children for warm clothing, but gave even this money to the poor and she herself passed the winter without any warm clothes. She wore her shoes over bare feet, using nutshells and sharp potsherds instead of inner soles so as to mortify the flesh.

Once the winter was so cold that the ground cracked from

the frost, and for some time Yuliania did not go to church but prayed at home. It came to pass that once the local priest came alone to church very early and heard a voice from the icon of the Holy Virgin, which said: "Go and ask merciful Yuliania why she does not come to church and pray? Her prayers at home are also pleasing to God, but not so much as her prayers in church. However, let her be venerated, for she is already no less than sixty years of age, and the Holy Spirit resides within her!" The priest, being seized by awe, came forthwith to Yuliania, fell at her feet, asked her forgiveness, and told her of the vision. She treated him severely because he spoke of it in the presence of others. And she said: "Thou hast been tempted when thou spake of it; for how may I, a sinner, be worthy of such heavenly intervention?" And she adjured him not to tell anyone. Yet she herself went to church, prayed with warm tears, and venerated the icon of the Holy Virgin.

From then on, Yuliania even more devoted herself to God, going to church and praying every evening in the porch of the church, where there were icons of Our Lady and of St. Nicholas. One evening she entered it to pray, as was her wont, and suddenly the church was filled with demons who wanted to kill her with various weapons. But she prayed to God with tears, and St. Nicholas appeared to her. He carried a club and chased the demons away, so that they disappeared like smoke. Yet he caught one of them, and tormented it. He blessed St. Yuliania with a cross, and forthwith became invisible. Still the demon screamed, crying: "I have always made trouble for thee: I have aroused strife amongst thy children and slaves. Yet I did not dare to come close to thee because of thy charity, humility, and prayer." (For Yuliania incessantly said Jesus' prayer with beads in her hands; and whether she was eating or drinking, or doing anything, she said the prayer incessantly; even when she was asleep, her lips moved and her soul was aroused to the praise of God; many times we saw her asleep, and her hand was moving the beads.) The demon ran away from her, screaming: "A great disaster befell me now because of thee, but I will make trouble for thee in thy old age: thou wilt starve, instead of feeding others!" But she blessed herself with the sign of the cross, and the demon disappeared. She came to us sore afraid and changed in the face. Seeing her perturbed, we questioned her, but she did not tell us anything. Yet, not too long later, she told us secretly, and bade us to tell no one.

Yuliania lived as a widow for nine years and showed great goodness to everyone. She gave away much property as alms, retaining only the essential for home needs; she rationed food year after year and gave all surplus to the needy. She lived even until the reign of Tsar Boris.[6] At that time there was a great famine in the whole land of Russia—such that, in dire need, many partook of unclean meats and of human flesh, and untold numbers starved to death. In Yuliania's house there was great scarcity of food and of all necessary supplies, for the sown spring rye never sprouted, and both horses and cattle died. She implored her children and serfs that they in no way touch anything belonging to others, nor steal, and whatever cattle and clothes and vessels were left, she sold for rye to feed the servants. She also gave considerable alms, for even in destitution she did not discontinue her customary charity, but let no one asking for help go away empty-handed. She herself came to extreme need, and not a grain was left in her house; yet she was not alarmed but placed all hope in God.

That year Yuliania moved to another village, called Vochnevo, in the confines of Nizhny Novgorod, where there was no church closer than within some miles. Being afflicted with old age, and destitute, she did not go to church but prayed at home. That grieved her sorely, yet she remembered St. Kornily and other saints, and knew that praying at home did not harm them. When destitution increased in her house, she set the serfs free so they would not be exhausted by hunger. Those of them who were virtuous promised to endure with her, while others left, and she let them go with her blessing and prayers, being not the least angered. Then Yuliania commanded the remaining slaves to gather goosefoot and wood bark and, making bread therefrom, she lived on it with her children and the serfs. And through her prayers that bread was sweet. She continued to give to the poor and let no pauper go without; at that time the poor were innumerable. Her neighbors said to the beggars: "Why do you go to Yuliania's house? For even she herself is starving!" And the beggars told them: "We have walked through many villages and have received pure bread, but we did not relish it so much, for sweet is the bread of this widow." They called her this, for many did not know her name. And the neighbors, who had plenty of bread, sent to Yuliania's house to ask for some of hers, to try it, and they also witnessed that her bread was very sweet. They marveled, saying to themselves, "Her servants are good at baking bread," for they did not understand that the bread was sweet through Yuliania's prayer. Yuliania endured

---

[6] Tsar Boris, brother-in-law of the last representative of the dynasty of Rurik, Tsar Fedor, ruled from 1598 to 1605. During his reign there were both plagues and great famines in Russia.

this destitution for two years, and she neither grieved nor was troubled, nor complained, and did not sin with her lips, neither did she charge God foolishly. And she was not broken by poverty, but was more cheerful than in earlier years.

As her righteous passing drew near, Yuliania became ill on the 26th day of December and stayed abed for six days. In daytime she prayed as she lay in bed, and at night she arose to pray to God, standing without assistance and supported by no one, for, as she said: "Even from the sick God demands prayer." At daybreak on the 2nd day of January, she summoned her confessor and received the last rites. Then, sitting up, she summoned her children and serfs and instructed them in love, prayer, charity, and in the other virtues. She added this also: "Since my youth and with all my heart I have desired to take monastic vows, but because of my sins and wretchedness this was not granted to me. I was not worthy, being a wretched and lowly sinner, God willing it so; glory be to his righteous judgment." She commanded that a censer be prepared and that incense be put in it; she kissed all those present and bade them peace and forgiveness. She lay down, crossed herself thrice, and, having wound the beads around her arm, she spake her last, saying: "Praise God in all things! Into thy hands, O Lord, I commend my spirit. Amen!" And she surrendered her soul into the hands of God, whom she had loved since her youth. And all saw a golden halo around her head, such as is painted around the heads of the saints on icons. Having washed her, they laid her out in a storeroom, and that night they saw there light and burning candles, and a strong fragrance wafted from that storeroom. Having put her into an oaken coffin, they took her back to the confines of Murom, and buried her beside her husband at the wall of the church of the righteous Lazar, in the village of Lazarevo, which was three miles from the city. And this came to pass in the year 7112 (1604), on the 10th day of January.

They later erected over Yuliania a church in the name of Archangel Michael. A stove happened to be over her grave and, through the removal of ashes, the earth above her became thicker through the years. In the year 7123 (1615), on the 8th day of August, her son Georgy passed away, and they started to dig a grave for him in the porch between the church and the stove, for that porch had no floor. They found Yuliania's coffin intact and on top of the earth. It was in no way damaged, and they wondered whose it was, as for many years no one had been buried there. On the tenth day of the same month they buried her son Georgy next to her coffin, and went to his house to offer refreshments to the burial attendants. But the women who attended the funeral opened the coffin and saw it to be full of fragrant myrrh. Being seized with awe at that time, they did not reveal anything, but after the departure of the guests they related what had happened. Having heard this, we marveled. And when we opened the coffin, we saw even as the women had told us. We ladled out a small vessel of that myrrh and took it to the cathedral church of the city of Murom. In the daytime that myrrh looked like beetroot kvass, and at night it thickened, looking like crimson oil. We did not dare to open the grave and to view all the body. We saw only her legs and thighs intact, yet her head we did not see, because a log from the oven lay on the end of the coffin.

Next to the coffin there was an opening under the stove. In the night the coffin, by itself, moved toward the east. And, having gone the distance of two yards, it stopped at the church wall. This same night many people heard the ringing of the church bell. When they arrived, they saw nothing; only a fragrance emanated. Many people heard of it and came there to anoint themselves with the myrrh. And they received relief from various diseases. When all the myrrh had been distributed, a dustlike sand began to issue near the coffin. Those suffering of various ailments came and rubbed themselves with this sand and received relief. And even to this day they do so. And we would not dare to write this if there had been no witnesses.

59. THE LIFE OF ARCHPRIEST AVVAKUM
BY HIMSELF

A similar fate befell the most brilliant literary works of both the Kievan and Muscovite eras of Russian literature. Because of their nonconformity with the spirit of the Russian Church, both the *Lay of Igor's Campaign* and the *Life of Archpriest Avvakum by Himself* remained unavailable to the general reader, and therefore did not have a considerable influence on the further development of Russian literature. Once discovered, however, they fascinated the Russian reading public.

Born in 1621, Avvakum became a priest at the age of twenty. In the early 1640s he joined the revival movement of the Zealots of Piety, or Seekers After God (Bogoliubtsy), which attracted many representatives of the Russian Church at that time and which tried to breathe new life into Russian Orthodoxy. For several years both the government and the Church leaders supported this movement, but when the authoritarian and unbending Nikon became patriarch in 1652, he moved against this revival because he saw in its activities a threat to the authority of the hierarchy. Officially, the conflict arose over the re-editing of the missal and changes in the ritual, both of which Nikon revised to conform to those of the contemporary Greek Church. Avvakum and his followers advocated the ancient texts and rites that had originally been introduced into Russia from Greece some seven centuries earlier. The real core of the conflict, however, was different. Nikon sought the unquestioning submission of the Church to the authority of the patriarch, and received the support of Tsar Alexis and the state, since they also desired stronger controls over the Church by both the central ecclesiastic offices and the state itself. Avvakum and his followers, who represented the lower clergy and their parishioners, felt that the parish priests and local laity should have a greater voice in Church affairs. Moreover, in opposition to domination and disciplining of the Church from above, they proposed a genuine religious regeneration of the Church on the local level.

In 1653 Patriarch Nikon succeeded in deporting Avvakum, Ivan Neronov, and other leaders of the reform movement, and thus Avvakum spent some nine years in Siberia. He was permitted to return to Moscow in 1662, but his fierce defense of his principles led once more to his deportation to northern Russia and, finally, to his censure by the Church council. In 1666 he was condemned for his opposition to the ecclesiastic authorities and for upholding the ancient traditions of the Russian Church. The next year this condemnation was reaffirmed by a larger Church council, in which not only the Russian hierarchs participated but also the Greek patriarchs of Alexandria, Antioch, and Jerusalem. This time Avvakum and his followers, Deacon Fedor (Theodore), the monk Epiphany, and the priest Lazar, were deported to Pustozersk, a small settlement and fort in the extreme northeast of European Russia, about a hundred miles from the Arctic Ocean. They remained there some fifteen years, and during that time Pustozersk became the spiritual center of the Old Believer movement, as it was called. It was there that Avvakum's autobiography and his many treatises and epistles were written. In 1682 the government, which was unable to curb the spread of this movement, ordered that Avvakum and his three comrades should be burned at the stake.

The autobiography of Avvakum is certainly not the first Russian work in which an author describes his own life and deeds, but it is the most important one in Old Russian literature. Avvakum uses a simple but vigorous, clear, and laconic style in which there are hardly any of those stylistic devices of orna-

mentation that so characterized the literary works of his prede-
cessors and contemporaries. His narration is dynamic, and
reflects the active, unbending nature of the author. Avvakum
rarely used the solemn Church Slavonic literary language, but
turned to colloquial Russian. He does not hesitate to use crude
folk sayings that lend expressiveness to his style. A keen ob-
server and penetrating psychologist, he gives short, pointed,
sometimes ironic portrayals of his contemporaries, among which
perhaps the best are those describing his wife, Anastasia
Markovna, and Tsar Alexis.

The *Life of Archpriest Avvakum by Himself* is given here in
the translation by Jane Harrison and Hope Mirrlees, published
by Leonard and Virginia Woolf at the Hogarth Press, London,
1924. This work is given in its entirety except for the introduction, which does not deal at all with Avvakum's life but consists
rather of theological arguments and considerations, and also
excepting the final section describing "The Healing of Those
Possessed." For the convenience of the reader, the work has
been divided into chapters by the editor of this anthology. The
editor has also made some minor changes in personal and place
names, and the translation in many instances was re-edited.

I. FAMILY BACKGROUND

I was born in the Nizhny country, beyond the river Kudma,
in the village of Grigorovo.[1] My father was given to strong
drink; but my mother was given to fasting and prayer, and did
most constantly instruct me in the fear of God. Now one day at
a neighbor's I saw a dead ox, and that night, rising from my
bed, I wept abundantly for my soul before the holy icons, pondering mortality and how I too must surely die; and from that
day it became my custom to pray every night. Then my mother
was left a widow, and I, young that I was, an orphan, and we
were driven out by our kinsmen. My mother resolved that I
should marry. And I prayed to the Mother of God that she
would give me such a wife as should help me to win salvation.
And in that village there was a maiden, she too was an orphan,
who was wont to go continually to church, and her name was
Anastasia. Her father was the blacksmith Marko, exceedingly
rich, but when he died all his substance was wasted. So she lived
in poverty and she would pray to God that he might so compass it that she should be joined to me in matrimony; and he
willed that it should be so. At that same time my mother went

---

[1] The village of Grigorovo is in the Nizhny Novgorod (presently
Gorky) region on the right shore of the Volga.

to God, having first taken the veil, and died in the odor of
sanctity. And I, because of persecution, moved to another place,
and at the age of twenty I was ordained deacon and, after two
years, priest. When I had been a priest eight years, I was raised
to the rank of archpriest by Orthodox bishops, and this was
twenty years ago. And it is thirty years in all that I have been
in Holy Orders.

II. THE YEARS OF MISSION WITH "SEEKERS AFTER GOD" AND CLASHES WITH THE ADMINISTRATION (1640–1652)

And when I was still but a parish priest I had many spiritual
children—it would be five or six hundred souls in all. And never
resting, I, miserable sinner, in churches and houses and at cross-
ways, by towns and hamlets, even in the city of the tsar and in
the country of Siberia, was diligent during a period of some
twenty-five years in teaching and preaching the Word of God.
And in these days of my ministry a young woman came to
confess to me, burdened with many sins, guilty of fornication
and of all the sins of the flesh, and, weeping, she began to
acquaint me with them all, leaving nothing out, standing before
the Gospels. And I, thrice-accursed, though a leech, fell sick
myself. I inwardly burned with a lecherous fire, and that hour
was bitter to me. I lit three candles and fixed them to the
lectern and placed my right hand in the flame, and held it there
till the evil passion was burned out and, when I had dismissed
the young woman and laid away my vestments, I prayed and
went to my house, grievously humbled in spirit.

The time must have been midnight, and when I reached my
house I wept before the icons so that my eyes swelled; and
prayed diligently that God might remove from me my spiritual
children, in that the burden was too heavy for me. And I threw
myself upon the ground face downward, sobbing bitterly. And
as I lay I swooned and wist not how I was weeping, and in my
fancy I was transported to the banks of the Volga and gazed at
it with the eyes of my heart; and this is what I saw: On it were
sailing two stately ships of gold, and their oars were of gold,
and their masts were of gold and all was of gold; at the helm
of each was sitting a man, and I said: "Whose are these ships?"
They answered: "Luke's and Laurence's." Now these had been
two of my spiritual children, and they had set me and my house
on the path of salvation, and their end had been pleasing to
God. And after that I saw a third ship, not adorned with gold,
but pied with many and varied hues, red and white, and blue
and black and ash, so that the mind of man would be hard put
to grasp at the same time all its loveliness and excellence. And a

young man, all shining, sat at the helm steering, and I called out to him: "Whose ship?" and he who was on her answered: "Thine. Sail away on her with thy wife and children, if thou wilt persist." And I was seized with awe, and sitting there I pondered the meaning of the vision and of the sailing.[2]

And but a little time after this—as it has been written—*the sorrows of death compassed me, and the pains of hell gat hold upon me: I found trouble and sorrow.* A headman abducted her daughter from a widow, and I besought him to return the orphan to her mother; he scorned our prayers and raised up storms against me; he came to the church with a band of followers, and they crushed me to death. And I, having lain dead for half an hour and more, was brought to life by a wave of God's hand, and he was sore afraid and renounced the girl for my sake. Then the devil prompted him: he came to the church, he beat me and dragged me, clad in my vestments, along the ground by the legs, and while he did it I was praying.

And likewise another headman at another time became as a wild beast against me. Breaking into my house, he beat me and gnawed the fingers of my hand, like a dog, with his teeth; and when his throat was full of blood, then he loosened his teeth from my hand and, throwing me aside, went to his house. But I, blessing God, wrapped up my hand in a cloth, and started for vespers; and on the way he leaped out on me again with two small pistols and, standing close to me, fired from one of them and, by God's will, the powder exploded in the pan but the pistol missed fire. So he threw the pistol on the ground and in the same manner fired from the other, and God willed it should be in the same sort, for that pistol also missed fire. But I, praying diligently, with one hand signed him with the cross and bowed low before him; then began he to snarl imprecations, but I said to him: "Out of thy mouth, Ivan Rodionovich, let blessings proceed." And next he took from me my homestead and drove me out with violence, seizing all my goods, leaving me not even a morsel of bread to eat on the road.

During that time my son Prokopy was born, the same that today lies a prisoner with his mother dug into a pit in the earth. So I took my staff and his mother took the unbaptized infant, and we set off on our wanderings, whither God should lead us, and on the way we baptized our son, even as Philip of old baptized the eunuch.[3] And when in my wanderings I reached Mos-

---

[2] The symbol of the ship is very common in Russian literature, and usually symbolized the life of a man. It has a biblical origin.

[3] The episode described in the Acts of the Apostles, 8:27–38.

cow, I made straight for the tsar's chaplain, the Archpriest Stephen, and for Neronov, the Archpriest John, and they informed the tsar concerning me, and from that time began my acquaintance with the tsar.[4] And the reverend fathers sent me back whence I had come with royal mandates, and wearily I dragged myself home; but the walls of my house had been pulled down and I set to to rebuild them, and once again the devil raised up a storm against me. There came to my village dancing bears with drums and lutes, and I, though a miserable sinner, was zealous in Christ's service, and I drove them out and I broke the buffoons' masks and the drums, on a common outside the village, one against many, and two great bears I took away— one I clubbed senseless, but he revived, and the other I let go into the open country. And after that Vasily Petrovich Sheremetiev,[5] who was sailing up the Volga to Kazan to take over the governorship, took me on board, and he sternly reprimanded me and ordered me to bless his son who had a shaven face.[6] And when I saw that image of shame I would not bless him, but condemned him from the Scriptures. So my lord waxed terribly wroth and ordered that I should be flung into the Volga and, having inflicted on me many hurts, they cast me aside, but in later years their rough handling turned to friendliness, for we were reconciled one to another in the antechamber of the tsar, and my youngest brother was his lady's confessor. Thus does God fashion the lives of his people.

Let us return to earlier days: again another headman became as a wild beast against me; he arrived with his folk at my homestead and attacked me, shooting from bows and muskets; and I, the while, prayed to the Lord, calling to him in a loud voice: "Lord God! Make his heart gentle, and reconcile him to me by whatsoever means thou choosest." And he fled from my yard, driven out by the Holy Ghost. And that very night his folk came running and they called out to me with many tears: "Little father! Euphemy Stepanovich is near his end and he is most inconveniently screaming; he strikes himself and groans, and of his own accord he says: 'I want parson Avvakum, God will punish me because of him.'" And I felt it to be a trap. And

---

[4] Archpriest Stephen Vonifatiev was the confessor of the tsar. He and Archpriest Ivan Neronov were the leaders of the Zealots of Piety.

[5] The Zealots of Piety energetically fought these buffoons, or *skomorokhs,* traveling actors, singers, and bear trainers whose performances and songs strongly reflected the pre-Christian mentality.

[6] The shaving of a beard was considered sinful in Muscovite Russia. Vasily Sheremetiev was a wealthy and influential aristocrat and high official.

terror seized on the spirit within me and I prayed to God thus: "Thou, O Lord, who broughtest me out of my mother's womb, and out of nothing didst create me, if they are about to strangle me, then count me with Phillip, the Metropolitan of Moscow; [7] and if they are about to stab me, count me with the prophet Zachariah; [8] and if they are about to drown me, then deliver me from their hands, as thou didst Stephen of Perm." [9] And praying the while I betook myself to the house, even to the house of Euphemy. And when they had led me into the yard, out rushed his wife, Neonila, and seized me by the hand, and she said: "Come in then, dearie, my lord, my father! Come in then, light of our eyes!" And I answered: "Strange! Before it was 'Son of a whore'! and now it's 'My Father!' Christ wields a crueler scourge than he. Your good man has not taken long to own himself in fault." She led me into the bedroom. Euphemy leaped out of the featherbed, fell down at my feet, and howled and blubbered confused words: "Forgive me, my lord! I have sinned before God and before thee"; and he was all of a tremble. And I said in reply: "Dost thou wish to be healed?" and he, lying on the ground, answered: "Aye, good father!" And I said: "Stand up, God pardons thee." But he, sorely stricken, could not rise by himself, so I lifted him and laid him on his bed, and confessed him and anointed him with sacred oil, and his sickness departed. So Christ willed it. And the next morning they sent me back with honor to my home, and he and his wife became my spiritual children, excellent servants of Christ. Thus doth the Lord harden his heart against the proud, but he showers blessings on the meek.

And but a little time after this I was once again driven out of this place, so I betook me to Moscow and by God's will the tsar was pleased to appoint me Archpriest of Yurievets-on-the-Volga.[10] But I did not stay there long, but a matter of eight weeks. The devil prompted the priests and the peasants and the good wives; and they came to the patriarch's chancellery where I was occupied in business of the church and dragged me out of the chancellery (there would be nigh two thousand of them), and in the middle of the street they beat me with cudgels and stamped on me, and the good wives beat me with shovels; and,

---

[7] Phillip, Metropolitan of Moscow, was imprisoned and then slain by the order of Ivan IV.

[8] According to biblical tradition, the prophet Zachariah was slain in 520 by his enemies whose immorality he denounced.

[9] For Stephen of Perm, see introduction to Selection 44.

[10] Yurievets-on-the-Volga used to be an important market city in the province of Nizhny Novgorod.

for my sins, they flung me into a corner of a house. The captain
of the troops came rushing up with his soldiers, and seizing
me they galloped on their horses to my little home; and the
captain placed the soldiers round the house. But the folk came
up to it, and raised an outcry through the town, especially the
Jack priests and their Jills, whom I had rated for their whoring
ways, and they howled: "Death to the thief, to the son of a
whore, and we'll fling his body into the ditch, for the dogs."
And, on the third day, by night, having taken a short rest, I left
my wife and children and with two others made for Moscow by
way of the Volga; I would have taken refuge in Kostroma,[11]
but, lo! there too they had driven away their Archpriest, Daniel.
Ah, lackaday! The devil leaves no man in peace! I reached
Moscow; and went to Stephen, the tsar's chaplain; and he
grumbled at me: "Why," said he, "have you abandoned your
minster church?" And more trouble was awaiting me. In the
middle of the night the tsar came in to his chaplain for his blessing and he saw me there;—more vexation: "And why have you
abandoned your town?" And there were my wife and children
and household (some twenty souls in all) left behind in Yurievets
and I not knowing if they were alive or dead—yet another
burden on my heart!

III. CONFLICT WITH NIKON, AND THE ROUT OF THE "SEEKERS AFTER GOD" (1652–1653)

After that, Nikon, our friend, brought down the relics of the
Metropolitan Phillip from the Solovki Monastery,[12] and before
his arrival, Stephen, the chaplain, with the brotherhood [13] and I
with them, passed a week in prayer and fasting, concerning the
patriarchate, even that God might give us a shepherd fitted to
the saving of our souls. And the Metropolitan of Kazan and I,
we signed our names to a petition and gave it to the tsar and
the tsarina, concerning the chaplain Stephen, that he might be
made patriarch. But he did not wish it for himself and named
the Metropolitan Nikon. And the tsar hearkened to him and
wrote to Nikon to greet him on his arrival. "To Nikon, the
Right Reverend Metropolitan of Novgorod and Velikie Luki and

---

[11] Kostroma was an important merchant city on the Volga. Archpriest Daniel was the leading member of the Zealots of Piety in that
city, and he met with considerable difficulties there because he
denounced the morality of the city's people.

[12] In 1652 Tsar Alexis sent Nikon to bring the relics of Metropolitan
Phillip from the Solovki Monastery to Moscow.

[13] When speaking of brotherhood, Avvakum refers to the main
group of the Zealots of Piety in Moscow.

of all Russia, greetings," [14] and so forth. And when he arrived he played the fox with us, and it was bowings and scrapings and "Good morrow to you!" For he knew that he was to be patriarch and wished to remove all obstacles thereto. But I'll not waste my time telling all these cunning machinations. And when he became patriarch he would not so much as allow his friends into the Room of the Cross,[15] and now at last belched forth his venom.

In Lent he sent a pastoral letter to St. Basil's Church, to John Neronov. Now the latter was my spiritual father and I was lodging in his presbytery; and when he was absent I took the services; and at the time there was some talk of making me the successor to Silas, God rest his soul, at St. Savior's, but God willed not that it should be so and I myself was not overeager concerning it; I was well content to continue at St. Basil's: I used to read godly books to the flock, and they would come in great numbers. Nikon inscribed his letter with the year and the date, "According to the tradition of the holy Apostles and the Fathers, it is not seemly to make obeisance in church to the knee, it should be no lower than the girdle, and moreover it behooves you to sign yourselves with three fingers." [16] We met together and took counsel. It was as if winter was of a mind to come; our hearts froze, our limbs shook. Neronov entrusted his church to me and shut himself up in the Miracle Monastery, and he spent a week praying in a cell, and one day a voice came from the icon of the Savior: "The hour of tribulation has come; it behooves you to suffer and be strong." And, weeping, he recounted these words to me and to Paul, the Bishop of Kolomna, the same that afterward Nikon was to burn in the Novgorod country; [17] and then to Daniel the Archpriest of Kostroma, and also to all the brothers. Together with Daniel I wrote out excerpts from the Fathers concerning the manner to be used in crossing oneself and making obeisances, and we gave them to

---

[14] Before becoming patriarch, Nikon was Metropolitan of Novgorod and Velikie Luki.

[15] Room of the Cross: the official reception room in the patriarchal palace.

[16] As previously mentioned, the conflict between the Zealots of Piety, which was later to grow into the movement of Old Believers, and Patriarch Nikon originally grew out of the latter's changes in the Russian rites and missals. One of the most controversial changes was that of the two-fingered sign of the cross to a three-fingered one.

[17] Bishop Paul of Kolomna was a staunch upholder of old traditions and a resolute enemy of Nikon. Nikon deported him to the Novgorod region, and, according to rumor, had him burned.

the tsar. And many were the excerpts we had made. But he hid them, we know not where; I am of opinion that he gave them to Nikon.

And a little later Nikon seized Daniel in the monastery outside the Tver' Gates, and sheared him monk in the presence of the tsar, and tearing off his cassock and insulting him the while, had him taken to the Miracle Monastery and put in the bakehouse, and when he had suffered grievously there, he sent him to Astrakhan; and there they placed a crown of thorns on his head and cast him into a dungeon, where he died. After the shearing of Daniel, they seized another Daniel—he also was an archpriest, of Temnikov—and they confined him in the new monastery of St. Savior's. And in the same way with the Archpriest Ivan Neronov, Nikon took off his biretta in church and had him confined in the monastery of Simon, and later banished him to Vologda, to the walled monastery of St. Savior's, then to the fortress of Kola,[18] and in the end, after having suffered exceedingly, he recanted—poor soul; he signed himself with three fingers, and so died a heretic. Woe is me! Let every man stand firm and be ever on the watch lest his foot shall stumble. In the words of the Scriptures, these are surely evil days when even the elect yield to the blandishments of Antichrist. It behooves us to be exceeding strong in prayer to God, and he will save us and help us, for he is merciful and loves mankind.

And I, too, while I was celebrating vespers, was arrested by Boris Neledinsky and his musketeers, and together with me they arrested nigh on sixty souls and took them off to prison, and me they fastened with a chain for the night in the patriarch's court. And when the Sabbath dawned they placed me in a cart and stretched out my arms and drove me from the patriarch's court to the monastery of Andronicus, and there they put chains on me and flung me into a black dungeon, dug into the earth, and there I lay for three days, and I had nothing to eat or to drink in the darkness, as I sat there bowing myself to the earth against my chains, though I knew not, as I made my obeisances, which was east and which was west. No one came to me but mice and black beetles, and the crickets chirped, and of fleas there was abundance. And on the third day I was famished, that is to say, I wanted to eat, and after vespers someone was standing before me, I knew not whether he was man or angel, and to this day I know not. I only know this that he said a prayer in the darkness and, taking me by the shoulder, led me on my chain to a bench

---

[18] The city of Vologda is located in northern Russia. The fortress Kola is located in the extreme north not far from the Arctic Ocean.

and seated me on it and put a spoon into my hands and gave
me a little bread and some cabbage soup to sup—oh, but it was
tasty!—and he said to me: "Enough, let that serve you as restora-
tive." And, lo, he was gone! The door had not opened and yet
he was gone! Were he a man, it were a miracle; but were he
an angel? Then were there no cause for wonder, because for
such as he there are no barriers. In the morning came the archimandrite [19] with the brothers, and they led me away; they spoke
to me coaxingly, that I should yield to the patriarch, but I
thundered against them from the Scriptures and snarled at them.
They took off the big chain and put a small one on me in its
place, and set a monk as jailer over me; they ordered that I
should be dragged to church. In church they pulled my hair and
poked my ribs and pulled at my chain, and spat in my eyes.
May God forgive them in this life and the next! It was not they
themselves that did it, but Satan in his malice. I remained there
four weeks.

After me they next seized Login, the Archpriest of Murom. In
the monastery church, in the presence of the tsar, they sheared
him monk at Mass. At the time of the carrying round of the
Host, the patriarch seized the paten from the head of the archdeacon and placed it on the altar, together with Christ's body
and the chalice. Meanwhile, Therapont, the archimandrite of
the Miracle Monastery, was standing outside the choir before
the King's Gates. Woe is me that Christ's body should be
sundered, more impiously than ever by the Jews! When they
had shorn him they tore from him his kaftan and his outer garment. But Login was consumed with the zeal of God's fire; and
he defied Nikon and spat across the threshold to the altar
straight into his eyes; loosening his girdle, he tore off his shift
and flung it into the altar, into Nikon's face, and, oh, wondrous
to tell, the shift spread itself out and fell on the altar in such
way that it covered the paten as though it had been the corporal. And the tsarina was in church at the time. They put a
chain on Login and, dragging him from the church, beat him
with brooms and whips to the monastery of the Epiphany, and
thrust him into a dungeon for the night and set musketeers to
guard him strictly. But lo! in the night God gave him a new fur
cloak and a biretta; and in the morning they told Nikon, and
he, laughing, said: "I know that breed of sham saint!" and he
took from him the hat; but left him the fur coat.

At that time they led me again from the monastery on foot

---

[19] This refers to Therapont, the archimandrite, or abbot, of the
Miracle Monastery.

to the court of the patriarch's palace; and then again, spreading
out my arms and wrangling much with me, they took me away
from there also. And on St. Nikita's day there was a procession
with crosses, and as they were driving me in a cart we met the
crosses. And they drove me to the monastery church, that they
might shear me, and during Mass they kept me for a long time
on the threshold. The tsar rose from his place and going up to
the patriarch entreated him that he should not shear me, and
they took me away to the Siberia Office and handed me over to
the scribe, Tretiak Bashmakov, the same that today is suffering
for Christ—the elder Savvaty (for he took the cowl), he lies in
the monastery of New St. Savior's in a dungeon dug into the
earth: may God have mercy on his soul! and even in these days
he entreated me kindly.

IV. DEPORTATION TO TOBOLSK (1653–1655)

So they sent me then to Siberia with my wife and children,
and of the many and great privations on the way, had I the
time there would be much to tell. Dame Avvakum bore a child,
and still sick she was transported in a cart to Tobolsk; it was a
journey of 3,000 *versts*, and for some thirteen weeks we dragged
along in carts and by water and half of the way in sledges.[20]

The archbishop got me a church in Tobolsk. And there in
that church great afflictions found me out; five times in a year
and a half the *Tsar's Words* [21] were called out against me, and a
certain member of the archbishop's household, the scribe Ivan
Struna, outraged me. The archbishop was away in Moscow, and
in his absence he, taught by the devil, fell on me. He was
minded to torment without cause Anthony, the clerk of my
church. He, Anthony, gave him the slip and fled to me, in
church. But this Ivan Struna, having collected some others,
came to me that same day in church—I was singing vespers—
and came leaping into the church and seized Anthony in the
choir by the beard. I, in the meantime, had shut the church
doors and would let no one in, so Struna was alone and kept
twirling round like an imp of hell; and I, when I had finished
vespers, sat him down, Anthony lending a hand, in the middle of
the church on the floor and thrashed him soundly with a leather
strap for having made a riot in church; and the other rogues,

---

[20] One *verst* is about two-thirds of a mile. The city of Tobolsk is
located in western Siberia.

[21] The expression "Tsar's Words" meant that one person accused
another and, pointing to him, claimed he was involved in a conspiracy
against the tsar. It always led to the arrest of the accused man.

some twenty in number, fled, every man of them, driven away
by the Holy Ghost. And Struna having declared that he repented, I let him go in peace. But Struna's kinsmen among the
priests and monks raised the whole town against me, so that
they might compass my death. And in the middle of the night
they drove up in sledges to my homestead and broke into my
house, being of a mind to take and drown me; but a terror from
God fell upon them and drove them hence, and they fled away.
For a month was I tormented by their tricks, for they would
attack me in secret; and sometimes I would take refuge by night
in the church, and sometimes with the governor, and I would
beg that for safety I might be put in prison—but this they would
not do. Matthew Lomkov—the same that as a monk was called
Mitrophan, and later in Moscow was apparitor to the Metropolitan Paul—he kept close to my side; it was he that afterward
sheared me in the monastery church together with the deacon
Afanasy: but at that time he was a just man, though the devil
has now swallowed him. Then the archibishop returned from
Moscow, and, as was but meet considering his offense, thrust
Struna into prison with chains on him. For a certain man had
lain with his own daughter, and he, Struna, had accepted fifty
kopecks from the fellow and had let him go without punishment.
And the lord bishop ordered him to be fettered, and he bethought him of that affair with me. For he, Struna, went to the
governor and his men in their office, and said the *Tsar's Words*
against me. And the captain allowed a petty squire, Peter
Beketov, to go bail for him. Woe is me! Misfortune entered the
gates of Peter's dwelling place, and it grieves my soul. The archbishop took council with me, and, in accordance with the rubric,
on the first Sunday in Lent he started cursing Struna for the
sin of incest in the great church. And that same Peter Beketov
came to church, and rated the archbishop and myself, and
within an hour, on his way home from church, he went mad,
and he died a bitter and an evil death. And his grace and I, we
ordered his body to be flung into the street to the dogs, and
the townsfolk mourned him and his sin; for three days they
importuned God diligently that on the Day of Judgment he
might be pardoned. Through pity for Struna he had brought this
dire calamity upon himself, and on the third day his grace and I
read the office over his body. But enough of this woeful business!

V. THE HARDSHIPS OF TRAVELING TO DAURIA (1655)

At this time an edict arrived, ordering that I should be taken
from Tobolsk to the Lena, in that I had condemned Nikon

from the Scriptures and pronounced him a heretic.[22] At that time a letter came from Moscow telling how two brothers, who lodged in the tsarina's apartments at the top of the palace, had both of them died of the plague, together with their wives and children, and many also of their friends and kinsfolk; God was pouring forth the vials of his wrath on the kingdom. But they, wretched men, knew not this and continued making disturbance in the church. Then Neronov spoke to the tsar, saying: "The visitation for schism is threefold: plague, the sword, and division." And thus has it come to pass in our days, even now; but the Lord is merciful. When he has punished us to bring us to repentance, then has he mercy on us and, driving away the ills of our souls and bodies, he giveth quietness. I preach Christ and my hope is in him; I confidently await his mercy and I believe in the Resurrection of the Dead.

So once more I got into the boat that had been assigned me —as I have said before—and sailed toward the Lena. And when I reached Eniseysk I was met by another edict, wherein I was ordered to get me to Dauria [23]—it would be more than twenty thousand *versts* from Moscow—and to give myself over to Afanasy Pashkov as chaplain to his troops that numbered six hundred men, and, for my sins, he was a fierce hard man, and it was ever his custom to burn folk and torture them, and beat them, and many times did I try to persuade him to desist, and now I was in his hands, and from Moscow came an order from Nikon that I was to be tormented.

On our journey from Eniseysk, it would be on the great Tunguska River, a storm sank my raft. It foundered completely in midstream and it was full of water and its sail was in tatters, only the deck remained above water, all the rest was under water. My wife, bareheaded [24] as she was, managed, I know not how, to drag the children out of the water on to the deck, but I, looking up at the sky, cried out: "O Lord! Save us! O Lord! Help us!" And by God's will we were driven to the shore; but why multiply words?

From another raft two men were wrenched away and drowned in the water. After that, when we were come to ourselves, we set out once more on our way.

---

[22] This was the result of Struna's *Tsar's Words* against Avvakum.
[23] Dauria was a region in eastern Siberia in the vicinity of Lake Baikal and which the Russians intended to conquer.
[24] It was unseemly for a married woman to be without a kerchief on her head.

VI. FIRST DIFFICULTIES WITH PASHKOV (1655-1656)

When we came to the Shaman rapids, diverse folk came sailing out to meet us, and with them were two widows; one of them was aged about sixty; and the other was older, and they were traveling by boat to a nunnery where they were to take the veil. And this Pashkov was minded to send them back, and to give them by force in marriage; and I said to him: "It is against the canons of the church to give such women in marriage." And in lieu of heeding my words and letting the widows go, he waxed angry and devised how he might torment me.

In other rapids—called the long rapids—he set about driving me from the raft. "You bring bad luck," says he, "to the raft. You're a heretic," says he; "off with you to the mountains! It is not for such as you to keep company with Cossacks." Alackaday! The mountains were high, the ravines impassable, there was a stone crag that stood there like a wall—you'd crick your neck before you saw its top. In these mountains great serpents were to be found, and in them dwelt geese and ducks with red feathers, and black crows, and gray jackdaws; in these mountains were also eagles, and hawks, and gerfalcons and guinea fowl and pelicans, and swans and other wild things in plenty, every variety of bird. Moreover, on these mountains many wild beasts wandered at liberty: wild goats, and deer and bison, and elk, and boars, and wolves, and wild sheep—clearly to be seen but not to be caught.

Pashkov was of a mind to turn me out into these mountains to live with beasts and birds, and I wrote him a little letter that began thus: "O man! Fear God who sits on the Cherubim and gazes into the abyss; before him tremble the celestial powers and every creature including man; thou alone despisest him and doest things that are not seemly," and so forth. It was a long letter; and I sent it to him. And some fifty men rushed on me; they seized my raft and hastened toward him, who was distant some three *versts;* and I stood there, boiling some porridge for the Cossacks and I fed them with it; and they, poor souls, ate of it and trembled, and some of them, looking at me, began to weep for me. They dragged up the raft; the executioners seized me and led me before him. He was standing with drawn sword, shaking with rage; he began to speak to me, saying: "What are you? A parson, or an unfrocked one?" And I answered: "I am Avvakum, the archpriest; speak! what is your business with me?" Then he roared like a wild beast, and struck me a great blow first on one cheek and then on the other, and then again on the head, and knocked me off my feet; and seizing his leather sword-strap struck me, where I lay, thrice on the back, and then, tearing off my shift, gave me seventy-two strokes on my naked back with the knout. And I kept saying: "O Lord Jesus Christ, Son of God! Help me!" And this I kept repeating without pause, so that it was bitter to him, in that I did not say, "Have mercy." At each stroke I said a prayer, but in the middle of the flogging I screamed to him, "You've beat me enough, I say"; so he ordered that it should stop. And I said to him: "Why do you beat me—do you know?" And he ordered them to beat me again on the ribs; and then they stopped; and I was trembling all over, and I fell. And he ordered them to drag me off to the raft that carried the money bags: they put fetters on my hands and feet and flung me onto the deck. It was autumn, the rain fell on me all night, and there was a pool where I was lying. When they were beating me it did not hurt because of the prayers I was saying; but now, as I lay, the thought came to me: "Son of God, why didst thou permit them to beat me so sorely? Look thee, Lord, I was championing the widow, consecrated to thee. Who shall judge between thee and me? When I was living as an evil man, thou didst not chastise me thus; but now I know not in what I have sinned." Aye! There was a righteous man for you, another dung-faced Pharisee, wishing, forsooth, to judge the Almighty! If Job spoke in that fashion it was because he was a perfect and an upright man; and, moreover, he knew not the Scriptures, for he dwelt outside the Law in a barbarian land, and it was through Creation, not through Revelation, that he learned to know God. But I, in the first place, was a sinful man, and, in the second place, I was learned in the Law and the prophets and was fortified by the Scriptures in all my goings: *We must, through much tribulation, enter into the Kingdom of God*; and yet had I reached such a pitch of folly. Woe is me! How came it that the raft did not founder with me in the water? Then my bones began to ache, my veins to grow rigid, my heart to palpitate, verily, I was dying; the water began to splash into my mouth, then I heaved a sigh, yea, I repented before the Almighty, for, verily, the sweet Lord of compassion remembers not against us our former transgressions when once we have repented of them; and once more I ceased to feel the pain.

In the morning they flung me onto a small craft and carried me away. Then we came to the great rapids of the Padun, where the river is a *verst* in breadth, and there are three exceeding steep reefs stretching across the whole of the river, and, except you find the passages between them, your boat will be shattered into splinters. They brought me into the rapids: above was rain and snow, and they flung over my shoulders nought but

a mangy little kaftan; the water flowed over my belly and my
spine—my poor body was in sorry plight. They took me out of
the raft and, skirting the rapids, they dragged me over the
stones in fetters. Verily I was in a sad plight, but with my soul
it was well; I was no longer peevish with God. Once again there
came into my head the words spoken by the prophets and the
Apostles: "*My son, despise thou not the chastening of the Lord,
nor faint when thou art rebuked of him.*

"*For whom the Lord loveth he chasteneth, and scourgeth
every son whom he receiveth. If ye endure chastening, God
dealeth with you as with sons; for what son is he whom the
father chasteneth not?*"

And with these words I comforted myself.

And after that they brought me to the fortress of Bratsky, and
flung me into a dungeon, and gave me straw to lie upon. And
there I lay till Advent, in a freezing tower; these are the seasons
when winter reigns, but God kept me warm, and that without
garments. Like a poor dog I lay on the straw; and sometimes
they fed me, and sometimes they did not; there were many mice
and I would strike at them with my biretta—the fools had not
given me a stick; I lay all the time on my belly, my back was
covered with sores, and of fleas and lice there was abundance.
I would fain have cried on Pashkov to pardon me; but it would
have been contrary to God's will, it was ordained that I should
endure. Then they moved me to a warm hut, and there I dwelt
in fetters with hostages and dogs the whole winter; and my wife
had been sent with the children some twenty *versts* away. And
all the winter her serving-wench, Xenia, tormented her with her
tantrums and complaints. After Christmas my son Ivan, who was
still but a little lad, stole away from home that he might dwell
with me; and Pashkov ordered him to be flung into the freezing
dungeon where I lay; dear little lad, he spent the night there and
was nigh froze to death; and in the morning Pashkov ordered
him back to his mother and I saw him no more; it was all he
could do to drag himself home to his mother from the frostbite
on his hands and feet.

VII. THE DAURIA CAMPAIGN (1656–1662)

In spring we set out once more. There remained but scant
provision, for the first store had all been robbed—books and
garments and other sundries had all been taken; but the second
store remained. I came near again to drowning on the Lake of
Baikal; I was made to pull a towing rope on the Khilok River,
and upstream it was mighty hard going. And there was no time
for eating nor for sleeping; for a whole year I suffered from the

hardships of water travel; the folk kept dying, and my feet and belly were blue. For two summers we journeyed by water and in the winter we were towed along by haulage. And, as I have said, on this same Khilok for the third time I came nigh to drowning. My boat was sucked by the current from the shore, and the boats of the other folk stayed where they were, but mine was caught up and carried away. My wife and children had remained on shore, and the boat bolted with the steersman and me! she was pitched and tossed on the swirling water, but I climbed onto her and cried out: "Help, Blessed Virgin! Thou art our hope and defense. Let me not be drowned!" Sometimes my feet would be in the water and sometimes I would scramble to the top; she was carried on for a *verst* and more, and then the folk stopped her and she was shattered to fragments. Aye, what could one do if Christ and the Immaculate Mother of God so willed it? And I climbed out of the water laughing, but the folk were weeping, and they spread out my garments on the bushes— cloaks of satin and taffetas, and sundry trifles: for I still had a store of such things in chests and coffers, but from that day they were rotted. But Pashkov was fain to give me another flogging. "You're making yourself a laughingstock," said he. And once again I importuned the sweet Mother of God: "Our Lady! Soothe thy fool!" And she, our hope, did soothe him, and he began to concern himself about me.

Our next stage was the Lake of Irgen. There is there a haulage and in the winter we began hauling; he took from me my workmen, and would not permit me to hire others, and we had small children—many mouths and none to fill them; this poor hapless wretch of an archpriest set to fashion a dog sleigh for himself and started hauling. That spring we began to sail down the Ingoda River—it was the fourth summer of my journey from Tobolsk. They were floating logs for the building of houses and towns. There began to be nothing to eat, the folk began to die of hunger and from ceaseless working in the water; shallow was the river, heavy were the rafts, merciless were the taskmasters, stout were the sticks, gnarled were the cudgels, cutting were the knouts, cruel were the sufferings—fire and rack; the folk were so spent with hunger that let him, Afanasy, but start tormenting one of them, and lo! he was dead on his hands. Ah, me! What a time! It would almost seem that he was out of his mind. There remained to Dame Avvakum one Moscow gown that had not been rotted with damp. It would have fetched twenty-five rubles and more in Moscow; but in these parts they gave us four sacks of rye for it, and we dragged on for another year, living on the Nercha River, and keeping ourselves alive with the roots and herbs that grew on the banks. One after another the folk died of hunger, and he saw to it that none of them ran away, and they were circumscribed within a small space, and they would wander over the steppes and fields, digging up grasses and roots, and we with them. And in winter we would live on fir cones, and sometimes God would send mare's flesh, and sometimes we found the bones of stinking carcasses of wild beasts left by the wolves, and what had not been eaten up by the wolves that did we eat; and some would eat frozen wolves and foxes—in truth, any filth that they could lay their hands on. A mare foaled, and, in secret, the starving folk devoured the foal together with the caul. And Pashkov got wind of it, and he flogged them with his knout to the point of death. And another mare died, and desperation seized them all, inasmuch as they had pulled the foal out of her, stealing a march on nature. When nought but the head had as yet emerged from the womb, they tore it out, yea, and they began to eat the blood that came away with it. Ah, me! What a time! And two of my little sons died from these sore straits, and roaming the hills and the sharp rocks with my children that survived, naked and barefoot, living on grass and roots, what did I not endure? And I, sinful man, partook willy-nilly of mare's flesh and foul carrion and the flesh of birds. Woe for my sinful soul! Who will pour water on my head and unseal for me the fountain of tears, even that I may weep for the poor soul that is mine, which I have been destroying with my daily appetites? But in Christ's name a great lady helped us, the captain's daughter-in-law, Eudokia Kirilovna, and also his, Afanasy's, wife, Thekla Semenovna; in secret they would give us some comfort against a death from starvation. Without his knowledge they would sometimes send us a piece of meat, sometimes a circular loaf, sometimes flour and oats, as much as ever they could, and sometimes one of them would save up ten pounds of flour and some coins and sometimes twenty pounds and hand it over to us, and sometimes she would rake out the chicken's food from the trough. My daughter, the hapless lass Agraphena, would go in secret under her window. And it was both pitiful and laughable! Sometimes, without the lady's knowledge, they would chase the child from the window, and sometimes she would come home burdened with a nice little store; at that time she was still but a child, but now she is twenty-seven. My poor little maid! She dwells unwed with her younger sisters by the Mezen, living from hand to mouth and weeping; and their mother and brothers lie buried in a dungeon in the earth. But what would you? Let every man endure great tribulation for Christ's sake! With God's help let even that which

has been ordained come to pass, and let us suffer tribulation for
the sake of the Christian faith. The archpriest used to love
keeping company with the great; now love in place of that, poor
wretch, and endure even to the end; for it is written: *"Better is
the end of a thing than the beginning thereof."* Enough of this:
let us return to the previous matter.

We continued in the land of Dauria in dire straits some six
or seven years, but during some of these years there would at
times be some little balm, and he, Afanasy, slandering me,
ceaselessly sought my death. And during these lean years he
sent me of his own accord two widows—they were servants in
his house and dear to him—Mary and Sophia, clothed about
with an unclean spirit; many times had he tried spells and in-
cantations upon them, but it had availed him nought; and
tongues had begun to wag concerning the matter, whereupon
the imp of hell would start tormenting them most cruelly, and
they would twist themselves and shriek. He summoned me and,
bowing to me, said: "I pray you take them home with you and
physick them with prayer to God; God will hearken to you."
And I answered him: "My Lord! What you ask of me is beyond
my powers. By the prayers of the Holy Fathers of our Church
all things are possible to God." So I took the poor souls home—
if it was presumptuous in me may I be forgiven. I had had some
experience in such matters in Russia. Three or four persons possessed by an unclean spirit had, in former times, been brought
to my house, and with the prayers of the Holy Fathers I had
cast out the imps of hell by the action and will of the living
God and of Our Lord Jesus Christ, Son of God, Light of the
World. I had sprinkled them with tears and with water and
anointed them with oil, chanting prayers the while, in the name
of Christ, and the holy magic of these things had driven the
imps out of these persons, and they had been healed—not by
any virtue in me—by no means; but by their own faith. Of old
time an ass was made the instrument by which a blessing came
to Balaam,[25] and by a lynx a blessing came to Julian the martyr,
and by a stag to Sisinius: they spoke with a human voice. God
whensoever he chooses triumphs over Nature's laws. Read the
life of Theodore of Edessa; there will you find that a harlot
raised a man from the dead; in the *Christian's Pilot* [26] it is written: *"Not for all men are the gifts of the Holy Ghost, but all
men can he leaven, excepting only heretics."*

So they brought me these two women that were possessed;

---

[25] See the Book of Numbers, Chapter 22.
[26] The *Christian's Pilot* was a Byzantine codex of canon law.

and I, as the custom is, myself fasted and would not let them
eat, and I prayed and anointed them with oil and tried every
remedy I knew. And the good wives returned to health and to
their right minds; and I confessed them and administered the
Sacrament to them; and they tarried in my house, praying to
God, for they loved me and would not go home. And it came to
his knowledge that they had become my spiritual daughters;
and he was angered against me, more fiercely than before, and
he was fain to burn me alive. "You have wormed out of them
in the confessional," said he, "private matters concerning me."
And how, forsooth, can one administer the Sacrament to a man
if one has not first confessed him? And if you do not administer
the Sacrament to the possessed, you'll in no wise succeed in
casting out of them the imps of hell. A devil is not a muzhik, forsooth, that he should fear the stick; what he fears is the Cross
of Christ, and holy water and holy oil, but before the Body of
Christ he flies. Without the Blessed Sacrament I cannot heal; in
our Orthodox Faith there is no Communion without Confession;
in the Roman faith they pay no heed to Confession; but to us,
the Orthodox observers, this is not seemly, and for us the Sacrament of Penance must ever first be sought. And if in your need
you cannot have a priest, then confess your sins to some discreet
brother, and, beholding your contrition, God will pardon you;
and then, having read through the Canon of the Mass before
communicating, keep by you some reserved Sacrament. And,
whensoever you are away on a journey or engaged in traffic or
whatever it may be that takes you far from a church, if you
have first given sighs of contrition to the Lord and have confessed to your brother, as has been said above, then may you
partake with a clear conscience of the Blessed Sacrament and all
will be well, if you have first fasted and read through the Canon
of the Mass: take then a little casket and spread a napkin in it,
and light a candle, and pour a little water into a cup, and ladle
some out in a spoon, and place with prayer a portion of Christ's
Body in the water in the spoon, and cense it all with a censer;
and weeping say out loud the whole of the prayer that begins:
"O Lord! I believe and confess that thou art Christ, the son of
the living God." (It is written in the Canon of the Mass.) Then,
throwing yourself on the ground before the icon, ask for forgiveness and, standing up, kiss the holy image; and, having
signed yourself, communicate with prayer, and drink a little of
the water and pray again to God, saying: "Now glory to Christ!"
Even if you die the minute after, it will be well with you.
Enough of that matter, you yourselves know that it is good
counsel. Now I shall go on with the story of the women.

Pashkov took the poor widows away from me, and in lieu of gratitude he gave me harsh words. He hoped that Christ had settled the matter once and for all; but they began to rave worse than before. He shut them up in an empty outhouse and allowed no one access to them; then he summoned a monk to them, but they flung logs at him, and he scuttled away. I sat at home weeping, and I knew not what to do. I did not dare to go up to the big house, for he was mighty wroth with me; so in secret I sent them holy water, and told them to wash themselves and drink a little of it, and, poor souls, their sufferings were eased a little. And in secret they stole off to me, and I anointed them with oil in the name of Christ, and once again God granted that they should be healed, and they returned home; and by night they would escape to me in secret to pray to God. And they became exceeding good churchwomen; they put aside vanities and began to follow all the observances of the Church; and afterward in Moscow they went with their lady to dwell in the nunnery of the Ascension. Glory to God for them!

And then from the Nercha River we began to journey back to Russia; for five weeks we traveled on the naked ice in sledges. I was given two sorry nags for my children and my baggage, while myself and Dame Avvakum, we made our way on foot, stumbling over the ice. The country was barbarous, the natives were hostile, so we feared to get separated from the others, and yet we could not keep up with the horses—for we were a hungry, weary pair; and my poor old woman tramped along, tramped along, and at last she fell, and another weary soul stumbled over her, and he fell too; they both screamed, and were not able to get up. The man cried out: "O good wife! O my lady! Your pardon!" and my old woman answered, "Fie, gossip! Would you crush me to death?" And I came up, and she, poor soul, began to complain to me, saying: "How long, archpriest, are these sufferings to last?" And I said: "Markovna! till our death." And she, with a sigh, answered: "So be it, Petrovich; let us be getting on our way."

VIII. THE STORY OF THE BLACK HEN

And we had a pet, a black hen, and she laid two eggs a day to feed the children, by God's will, helping us in our need; it was God's doing. But when they were carrying out the baggage to the dog sledge, she was crushed to death, for our sins, and to this day whenever I think of that hen my heart aches for her. I know not if it were a hen or miracle: all the year round she laid two eggs a day, and we would not have taken a hundred rubles for her—nay, we would have spat on them! mere dross!

And that hen, God's living creature, fed us, and she would take her meals with us, pecking at the porridge of fir cones in the caldron, and pecking at the fish, and in exchange she gave us two eggs a day. Glory to God, who fashions all things well! And we had come by her in no ordinary way. My lady's hens had one after another turned blind, and they began to die, whereupon she gathered them into a basket and sent them to me. "And may it please you, Father," said she, "to pray over the hens." And I considered: she was a lady bountiful to us, she had children, and she had need of the hens. So I chanted a prayer and blessed some water and sprinkled the hens and censed them. Then I went to the forest and fashioned them a trough from which to eat, and sprinkled it with holy water, and sent the whole baggage back to her. And by a wave of God's hand the hens were healed, because of her faith. And it was from that same brood that our hen came; but enough of this matter; it was not the first miracle that Christ had brought to pass. Already Kosma and Damian had blessed and healed both men and cattle in the name of Christ.[27] God has a use for everything: cattle and fowls —they were created for the glory of his pure majesty, and also for the sake of mankind.

IX. AT LAKE IRGEN

So we made our way back to Lake Irgen. My lady had pity on us and sent us a little basket of wheat, so we had our fill of frumenty. Eudokia Kirilovna was a lady bountiful to me, but the devil set her quarreling with me in this manner: she had a son whose name was Simeon; he had been born in that place. It was I that had churched the mother and baptized the child, and every day they would send him to me for my blessing and I, having signed him with the cross and sprinkled him with holy water, would kiss him and send him home; he was a fine healthy child and I loved him like my own. But the little lad began to ail, and I was away from home. And in a moment of pettiness of spirit she was vexed with me and sent the child to a medicine man. And I, when I learned of it, was angry with her, and a wide breach came between us; the little boy began to ail still more, and his right hand and foot dried up, so they were like little sticks. She grew ashamed; but she knew not what to do, and God oppressed her still further. The little one became sick unto death, and the nurses came to me weeping and I said to them: "If the goodwife is a baggage, then let her keep herself

---

[27] Kosma and Damian were considered the saintly protectors of men and cattle, and possessing miracle-working powers for healing.

to herself." For I was waiting that she should repent. I saw that the devil had hardened her heart, and I bowed down before the Lord God, praying that he might bring her to her right mind. And the Lord, the God of Mercy, softened the rich soil of her heart, and early next morning she sent to me her second son, Ivan; with tears he begged forgiveness for his mother, walking round the stove and bowing before me; and I was lying on the stove, naked, under a covering made from birch bark, and Dame Avvakum was lying within the stove, and the children anywhere. It was raining at the time; we had no covering, and our winter quarters were dripping, so we were in sorry straits. And I said to him, bringing him low: "Tell your mother that she must ask forgiveness of Aretha, the medicine man." Then she brought the sick child to me and I ordered her to lay him before me, and they were all weeping and bowing themselves. And I arose and got me my stole out from the mess and dirt and found some holy oil, and, praying to God, I censed the boy and signed him with the sign of the cross. And God granted that the child was healed, both in his hand and foot. And I sprinkled him with holy water and sent him to his mother. Consider, thou who hearkenest to my story, what great things were compassed by a mother's penitence; it both physicked her own soul and healed her child. What then? It is not only today that God is with penitents. On the morrow she sent us fish and pies; and they were apt to our need, for we were starving; and that day we made our peace, she and I. When we had journeyed back from Dauria, she, sweet lady, died in Moscow, and I buried her in the nunnery of the Ascension.

And Pashkov himself learned of the affair with the boy, for she told him. I went to him and, bowing low before me, he, Pashkov, said: "God bless you! You have acted like a true priest; remember not our sins against us." And at that time he sent us no small store of food.

X. THE TRIBULATIONS OF THE MONGOLIAN EXPEDITION (1661)

But in a very short space he was minded to torture me— hearken how it came about. He was sending his son, Eremy, off to fight in the kingdom of the Mongols, and with him some seventy-two Cossacks and some twenty natives. And he made a native to "*shamanit*," [28] that is to say, to tell their fortune, as to whether they would prosper and return home victorious. And in

---

[28] *Shamanit'*: the shamans were Siberian pagan priests and medicine men. Avvakum gives to this word a verbal infinitive ending, thus *shamanit'* means to perform pagan rites.

the evening that wizard—it was near my winter quarters—
brought a live sheep and began to work magic over it: he rolled
it to and fro for a long space and then he twisted its head and
flung it away. Then he began to jump and dance, and invoke
devils, and, giving great screams the while, he flung himself
upon the earth, and foamed at the mouth; the devils were press-
ing him, and he asked them: "Will the expedition prosper?" And
the devils said: "It will return with much booty, having gained
a great victory." And the captains were glad; and all the folk,
rejoicing, cried: "We will come home rich!" Oh, lackaday! It
was bitter then, and even now it is not sweet to think upon. I,
a bad shepherd, made my sheep to perish; from vexation of
spirit I forgot the words of the Gospel, when the Sons of Zebe-
dee counseled Our Lord concerning the stubborn villagers,
saying:—

*"Lord, wilt thou that we command fire to come down from
heaven and consume them, even as Elias did?"*

*But He turned and rebuked them, and said, Ye know not what
manner of spirit ye are of.*

*For the Son of Man is not come to destroy men's lives, but to
save them. And they went to another village.*

But I, accursed, did not so. In my poor room I cried with a
great cry to the Lord, "Hearken to me, my God! Hearken to
me, King of Heaven! Sweet Lord! Hearken to me! Let not one
of them return home; and dig a grave for every one of them
yonder! Lay on them an evil fate, O Lord! Bring them to destruction, so that the devil's prophecy may not be fulfilled." And
many like words did I say, and in secret I prayed to God concerning it. They told him that I was praying thus, but he did
but snarl abuses at me. Then he sent off his son with the captain; they rode off at night, directing their course by the stars.
And I was seized with pity for them, for my soul foresaw that
they would perish; nevertheless, I continued praying for their
destruction, and some of them, as they passed, called out goodby
to me, and I called back, "You will die yonder." And, as they
rode off, the horses under them began to whinny, and the cows
that were there to low, and the sheep and goats to bleat, and
the dogs to howl, and the natives to howl, like the dogs. Terror
seized them all. With tears Eremy sent me word, "that it may
please my lord and spiritual father to pray for me." And I was
seized with pity for him, for he had been my secret friend and
had suffered for my sake. When his father was flogging me with
the knout, he had tried to dissuade him, so that his father had
chased him with drawn sword. And when they arrived after me,
at other rapids, those of the Pandun, forty rafts all got through

the straits in safety; but his, Afanasy's own raft, though her rigging was excellent and six hundred Cossacks had been set to build her, yet were they not able to get her through: the waters overcame them, or rather God was punishing him: all the crew were sucked into the water, and the raft was hurled against a rock; the waters splashed up against it, but did not flow into it. It is marvelous to watch God's lessons to the foolish! He himself was on the shore, and his lady was on the raft, and Eremy began to speak, saying: "Father! God will punish you for your sins; you flogged the archpriest with that knout unjustly; it is time to repent, my lord!" But he roared at him, like a wild beast, and Eremy, dodging behind a fir, clasped his hands and repeated the *Lord have mercy upon us.* But Pashkov, having seized a ringed musket, one that never missed, from an attendant, took aim at his son and pulled the trigger, and by God's will the weapon missed fire. Then, having adjusted the powder, he fired again, and again it missed fire. And he did the same a third time, and the third time, also, it missed fire. So he flung it on the ground, and the attendant picked it up and threw it out of the way, and it went off of its own accord.

And Pashkov sat him down on a chair and, leaning on his sword, he came to his right mind, and beginning to weep, he said: "I have sinned, accursed that I am, I have spilled innocent blood, I flogged the archpriest unjustly, God will punish me." It was strangely, strangely in accord with the words, *God is slow to anger and swift to hearken.* For because of his repentance the raft floated away from the reef; its prow was toward the water; and they pulled it from the shore and it leapt out into a lower level of the water. Then Pashkov called his son to him, and entreated him, saying: "Forgive me, Eremy, you spoke truly!" and he, running up, and bowing before his father, said: "It is God, my lord, that will forgive you; for I myself am guilty before God and before you." And he took his father's hand, and led him away. Eremy was a righteous-minded man, and a virtuous one; already was his own beard gray, and yet he honored his father exceedingly, and feared him, and according to the Scriptures it is seemly so to do, for God loves the children that honor their fathers. Come then, hearkener to my story! Is it not true that Eremy had suffered for my sake, and for the sake of Christ and his Law?

And all this was recounted to me by the helmsman of his, Afanasy's raft, by name Gregory Tielnoy. Let us return to the previous matter.

They went away, then, from me, and rode off to the wars;

and pity seized me for Eremy, and I began to importune God Almighty that he might protect him. Time passed and they were expected home from the wars, and the day came fixed for their return, but they came not; and during three days Pashkov refused me admittance to his house. And at last he prepared a torture chamber, and had a fire kindled; he wished to torture me. And I was repeating prayers for my latter end, for I knew what manner of cook he was and that few came out alive from his roasting. And I sat waiting in my house, and I said to my wife, who was weeping, and to my children, "God's will be done! For whether we live, we live unto the Lord; and whether we die, we die unto the Lord." And lo! at that moment I saw two executioners come hurrying in to seize me. Marvelous are the acts of the Lord, and unspeakable the counsels of Almighty God! Suddenly Eremy himself, wounded, comes riding along by the little path that goes past my house and garden, and he calls out to the executioners, and makes them turn back with him; and he, Pashkov, left the torture chamber and came toward his son, staggering like a drunk man from grief. And Eremy, bowing low to his father, acquainted him with all that had taken place: how all his troops had been slaughtered, no single man surviving; and how a native had led him, through wild and lonely places, away from the Mongolian people; and how, without food, they had wandered over stony mountains and through the forest for seven days, having nought to eat but one squirrel; and how a man in my image had appeared to him in a dream and had shown him the path, and whither he must journey; and how he had leaped up and gone on his way rejoicing. When he had recounted all to his father, then I came in to greet him. But Pashkov rolled his eyes at me—the very spit of a white polar bear, and he would have gobbled me up alive, only the Lord did not grant that it should be so—and, drawing in his breath, he said: "What think you of your handiwork? How many men, think you, have you caused to perish?" But Eremy said to me, "Father Avvakum! for Christ's sake, get thee gone, and do not bandy words with him." And I went.

For ten years he had tormented me, or I him—I know not which. God will decide on the Day of Judgment.

A change of post came for him, and for me a letter; we were ordered back to Russia. He went away and did not take me with him, for in his heart he was saying: "If he travels back alone, then surely the natives will slay him." He and his guns and his folk, they sailed away on rafts, and, on my own journey back, I learned from the natives that they were a timid, trem-

bling crew. And I, a month afterward, having assembled the
aged, and the sick, and the wounded, whatever there was there
of useless folk (there would be ten of them, and I with my wife
and children would bring it to seventeen), got into a boat, and,
putting our trust in Christ and fixing the cross to our prow, we
started on our way, wherever God should lead us, fearing nothing. I gave the book, the *Christian's Pilot,* to the clerk, and he
gave me a fellow for steersman in exchange; and he manumitted
my friend Basil, the same that was wont to denounce folk to
Pashkov and was the cause that much blood was shed, and he
sought my life also. And at one time, having flogged me, he
fastened me to the stake, but once again God kept me safe; and
when Pashkov was gone the Cossacks wished to flog him to
death, but I begged him off for Christ's sake and gave the money
for his manumission to the clerk, and carried him back to Russia,
from death to life. Poor soul, may he repent his sins! Aye, and
I took back with me another lousy spy of the same kidney; him
they did not wish to give up to me, and he fled from death to
the forest, and, coming upon me on the path, he flung himself
into my boat, for he was pursued and had nowhere to turn. And
I, forgive me, acted cunningly. As Rahab, the harlot of Jericho,
hid Joshua the son of Nun, so did I hide him, making him lie
down at the bottom of a chest, and I flung a coverlet over him,
and ordered my wife and daughter to lie on the top of him; they
sought him high and low, but they would not disturb my wife
from her place, and all they said was, "Rest in peace, Mother
Avvakum! You have had enough to endure, as it is, my lady."
And I—for God's sake forgive me—I lied that day, and I said:
"He is not here"—I was loth to give him up to be slain. And
when they had searched they went away empty-handed, and I
carried him back to Russia. Elder and servant of Christ! [29] forgive me, then, in that I lied that day. How think you, it may be
that it was not a very grievous sin? It would seem that Rahab
the harlot did likewise, and the Scriptures praise her for it; give
judgment, then, for God's sake: and if I acted sinfully, then
pardon me; but if I acted in accordance with the traditions of
the Church, then is it well. See, I have left a space for you, and
do you, with your own hand, write in either forgiveness or penance for me and my wife and my daughter, for we all three
shared in the cheat—we saved a man from death that he might
repent before the Lord. Judge us then so that we shall not be

---

[29] These words are addressed to Avvakum's cellmate and spiritual
father, Epiphany.

judged for it by Christ on the Day of Judgment; write in a few words, I pray you:—

God pardons thee and blesses thee in this life and the life to come, together with thy helpmeet Anastasia, and thy daughter, and all thy house: thou hast acted rightly and justly. Amen.[30]

So be it then, my elder. God bless you for your graciousness. But enough of this.

The clerk gave us sacks of corn to the value of thirty silver pieces, and a cow, and five or six sheep, and dried meat, and this we fed on for the summer, as we sailed on our way. The clerk was a good soul; he had been sponsor to my daughter Xenia, who had been born in the days of Pashkov, but Pashkov would not give me myrrh and oil, so she had to stay long unchristened; but when he was gone I christened her (I myself churched my wife and baptized my children),[31] and the clerk and my eldest daughter were the gossips, and I was the parson. In this manner, then, I also christened my son Afanasy, and both confessed my own children and administered the Sacrament to them during the Mass I said at Mezen, and I myself communicated, but I did not administer it to my wife: there are instructions concerning this in the rubric, wherein we are bade so to do. But as to my excommunication, it came from heretics and, in Christ's name, I trample it under foot, and the curse written against me—why, not to mince my words, I wipe my arse with that; if the heretics curse me, the saints of Moscow— Peter, and Alexis, and Jonah, and Phillip—*they* bless me; and in accordance with their books, with a clear conscience I believe in and serve my God; but the apostates I loathe and curse: they are God's enemies and, living in Christ, I do not fear them. Were they to heap stones on me then, secure in the tradition of the Fathers, I would lie in peace beneath these stones—how much more so beneath the thorny, knavish curses of Nikon! Tush! Why multiply words? All we need do is to spit on their doings and their ritual, and on their newfangled books, then all will be well. Our following discourse will be pleasing to Christ and the Immaculate Mother of God, so enough of their knavery. Pardon me, good Nikonites,[32] for having abused you; live as ye

---

[30] This last passage is written into the manuscript by Epiphany, who read the manuscript and made some addenda.

[31] Under ordinary circumstances, it was prohibited by the canons of the Orthodox Church to baptize one's own children.

[32] Nikonites: refers to the supporters of Nikon.

will. As for me, I am now about to take up again my tale of
woe, so go your ways in peace. For twenty years God has willed
that I should be tormented by you, and should it be for twenty
more, then will I endure it, in the name of the Lord our God
and of our Savior Jesus Christ. Enough of this. I have wandered,
as it is, far enough from my story—let us return to it.

So I left Dauria; the food began to grow scarce, so I prayed
together with my company, and Christ gave us a roebuck, a
huge beast, and on him we lived till we reached Baikal. There,
by the lake, we came on Russian folk—a settlement of sable-
hunters and of fishermen; they were right glad to see us, dear
souls, and we them, and they dragged us and our boat to shore,
and led us far inland to the hills. There was a dear lad called
Terenty, and he and his comrades gazed on us, and we on them
—dear souls—with tears of joy. And they snowed meat and drink
on us, as much as ever we needed. They brought me some forty
freshwater sturgeons, saying: "There, Father! God sent them
into our fishery for you. Take them all." I, bowing to them,
blessed the fish and bade them take them back, saying: "What
need have I of so many?" They entertained me there and, from
dire need, I accepted from them some provision. Then, having
repaired our boat, we let out our sails, and prepared to cross the
lake. But the lake grew rough, so we took to our oars. In that
place the lake is very broad—it must be a hundred or at least
eighty *versts*. When we stood to the shore there sprang up a
tempest and we were forced to find a shelter from the waves
on the shore. The place was surrounded by high mountains: I
have wandered over the face of the earth 20,000 *versts* and
more, but never have I seen their like. On their summit are
tents and earthen huts, portals and towers, stone walls and
courts, all neatly fashioned. Onions grow on them and garlic,
bigger than the Romanov onion, and exceeding sweet to the
taste; there also grows wild hemp, and in the gardens fine grass
and exceeding fragrant flowers, and there is great quantity of
birds—geese and swans that fly over the lake like snow. And
there are fishes—sturgeon and trout, sterlet and salmon trout and
whiting and many other kinds; it is fresh water and in that
mighty ocean lake there are sea calves and great sea hares. I
saw none such during all the time that I was living on the
Mezen,[33] and the fish in it are of a great weight, the sturgeon
and salmon trout are exceeding fleshy—they are not for frying,
for it would be naught but fat. And all this has been fashioned

---

[33] Mezen was a small city in northern Russia to which Avvakum
was deported in 1664, remaining there until 1665.

by our sweet Christ for man, so that, with a mind at last at rest, he might give praise to God. But such is man that he is given to vanity, and his days go by like a shadow: he leaps, like a goat; he blows himself out, like a bubble; he rages, like a lynx; he seeks to devour, like a serpent; when he looks on the comeliness of his neighbor he neighs like a foal; he is crafty, like a fiend; when he has eaten his fill then, like a heathen, he falls asleep, without saying his prayers; he puts off repenting till his old age and then he vanishes; we know not where,—whether it be to light or darkness: it will be shown on the Day of Judgment. Forgive me; I myself have sinned more than other men.

XI. THE STAUNCH PROTOPOPITSA [34]

So we reached Russian settlements, and I was informed concerning the Church, and like Pilate, I saw that I *"could prevail nothing, but that rather a tumult was made."* My mind was troubled and, sitting down, I began to ponder what I should do —should I continue preaching God's Word or should I hide myself? For I was tied by my wife and children. And seeing that I was troubled, my wife came up to me, timidly, delicately, and said: "How comes it, my lord, that you are troubled?" And I acquainted her with all my thoughts. "Wife! What must I do? The Winter of Heresy is at the door; am I to speak or to hold my peace? I am tied by you!" And she said to me: "Lord have mercy! What are you saying, Petrovich? Have I not heard, have you not read, the words of the Apostle: *Art thou bound unto a wife? seek not to be loosed. Art thou loosed from a wife? seek not a wife.* I and the children, we give you our blessing, continue preaching the Word of God as heretofore, and take no thought for us until such time as shall seem good to God; when that time comes, remember us in your prayers; Christ is strong and he will not abandon us. Get thee gone, get thee gone to church, Petrovich! Unmask the Whore of Heresy!" And I bowed myself to the earth before her, and shook myself free from the blindness of a troubled mind and began once more to preach and teach God's Word in the towns and in all places until such time as I could boldly tear the mask from the heresy of Nikon.

In Yeniseisk [35] I wintered, and having sailed through the summer again I wintered in Tobolsk; and on my way as far as Moscow I cried aloud in every town and in every village, in churches and in marketplaces, preaching the Word of God and teaching

---

[34] Protopopitsa: the wife of a protopope, or archpriest.

[35] Yeniseisk: A Russian outpost and merchant city in central Siberia on the Yenisei River.

and laying bare the snares of the ungodly. And thereon I came
to Moscow. Three years was I in coming from Dauria, and it
took me five years traveling upstream. We journeyed ever eastward amid native tribes and habitations. Much might be said of
that. Sometimes we fell into the hands of the natives; at Ob, the
mighty river, in my presence they put to death twenty men
who were Christians. And they were minded to do the like to
me, but they let me go altogether. And again on the Irtysh River
there was standing a company of them—they were lying in am-
bush for our men of Berezov to slay us—but I knew it not and
I went up toward them. And when I was come up to them I put
in to the bank. In a moment they were round about me with
their bows, and I, I tell you, went forth to embrace them as
though they were monks and I spoke and said: "Christ be with
me and with you too." And they entreated me kindly and they
brought their wives to my wife. And my wife dissembled with
them, as in the world they are wont to employ flattery; and the
womenfolk were kindly and we felt it: when the womenfolk are
good, then under Christ all is well. The men hid their bows and
arrows. I bought some bear's flesh from them and they let me
go free. As I was saying, I was come to Tobolsk. And the folk
were astonished thereat, for Bashkirs and the Tatars were scour-
ing all Siberia. But I, trusting in Christ, went through their
midst. And when I had reached Verkhoturié,[36] Ivan Bogdano-
vich, my friend, was astonished at me. "How did you ever get
through, archpriest?" And I made answer: "Christ brought me
through, and the all pure Mother of God brought me through. I
fear no man, only Christ do I fear."

XII. BACK IN MOSCOW: JOYS AND DISPUTES (1664)

Thus did I come to Moscow, and as though I were an angel
of God the tsar and all his boyars received me gladly. I went
to see Theodore Rtishchev,[37] he came himself from his home, received my blessing and began to speak of many things: for three
days and three nights he suffered me not to go home, and thereafter he informed the tsar concerning me. His Majesty gave

---

[36] Verkhoturié was a Russian city in western Siberia almost in the
foothills of the Ural Mountains.

[37] Theodore (Fedor) Rtishchev was a statesman and personal friend
of Tsar Alexis. He actively participated in church affairs and from
1645 to 1653 was a member of the Zealots of Piety. He remained
faithful to Nikon after the latter's break with this movement. He was
well known for his support of the arts, learning, and charitable
activities.

command to place me at his side and spake kindly to me. "Art thou well in health, archpriest?" said he. "God bade me see thee again." And I in answer kissed his hand and pressed it, and myself said: "God lives and my spirit lives, your Majesty! but for what is before us that God will ordain." And he sighed softly and went whither he had need. And other things happened, but what need to speak of it? That too passed by. He bade them place me in the guesthouse of a monastery in the Kremlin, and when he passed my door going out on expeditions he often gave me greeting, bowing low, and himself would say: "Bless me," said he, "and pray for me"; and one time he took his fur cap from his head and let it fall as he was riding on horseback. He used to slip out of his carriage to come to me and all his boyars kept bowing and scraping, crying: "Archpriest, bless us and pray for us." How shall I not grieve for such a tsar and such boyars? It grieves me to think how good they were, they gave me place wheresoever I wished, and they named me their confessor, that I might be made one with them in the faith. But I held all these things to be but vanity. And I gained Christ and was mindful of death, how all these things pass away.

And this was revealed to me in Tobolsk when I was half asleep. "Watch, I bid thee, that thou be not a branch cut off." I leaped up and fell before the icon in great terror, and I spake and said: "Lord, I will not go when they chant in newfangled fashion, my God." I was at early Mass in the cathedral on the name day of the tsarina. I was jesting with them in that Church in the presence of the officials, and from the moment of arrival I took notice whether they mixed the elements in triple or in twofold wise, and standing at the altar by the sacrificial table I abused them, and with time I got used to them, so I ceased from abusing them. Such was the bitter spirit of Antichrist that stung me.

Thus did our sweet Christ make me afraid and said to me, "*After so great suffering wilt thou perish?* Watch, lest I hew thee off as a dry branch." I went not to Mass, but I went to sup with the prince, and I told him all, every word. A kind boyar prince, Ivan Andreevich Khilkov, began to weep. Woe is me, accursed one, that I forget so great mercy of God!

When I was at Dauria and I labored as a fisherman, I went in the winter to my children, and I went along the lake on snowshoes; there was no snow but great frosts, and the ice froze well-nigh the thickness of a man. I began to want to drink, and I suffered much from thirst. I couldn't go on, I was midway in the lake, I couldn't get to the water; the lake was eight *versts*. I began to look up to heaven and to say: "O Lord, thou didst cause water to flow in the desert for the thirsty people of Israel, then and now art thou; give me to drink by whatever means seem good to thee. O Lord my God! Woe is me. I know not how to pray, forgive me for the Lord's sake. Who am I, a dead dog?" The ice gave a crack beneath me and split up to either side across the whole lake and came together again, and a great mountain of ice rose up, and while this was going on I stood in my accustomed place, and looking toward the east, I bowed twice or thrice, pronouncing the name of the Lord in a loud voice from the depths of my heart. God had left me a small hole in the ice, and I, falling down, slaked my thirst. And I wept and was glad, praising God. After that the hole in the ice joined up and I, rising up, bowed down to the Lord and then again ran along the ice whither I must needs go to my children. And in my other wanderings it often happened to me like this. I was either walking along, dragging my sledge or catching fish or cutting wood in the forest, or whatsoever I might be doing, I always recited my office at the regular time, whether it was morning Mass or evening, at the hours it was the custom; if I chanced to be among other people none could hinder me, but I would stand upright and none of my companions with me, for they did not love my office, and when they were there it was impossible for me to carry it out, and I, going away from among men, would go through it in a shortened form, either under a hill or in a wood, beating with my head against the earth, and sometimes I would weep and feel wounded. But if there should be people with me I would place the icon on the sledge rail and I would recite the office right through, and some would pray with me, but others would cook their porridge; and when I am going in my sledge on Sundays to the guesthouses I sing the whole church service, and on festival days when I am driving in a sledge I will sing, and often on Sundays as I go along I would sing. And when I do it very persistently, sometimes I would grumble though only a little, for my body was ahungered and would fain eat, and was athirst and would fain drink, and likewise my spirit, O Father Epiphany, desires spiritual food: It is not the hunger for bread that destroys a man nor the thirst for water, but the great hunger of a man when he lives without praying to God.[38]

If thou art not weary of listening to this thy servant of Christ, I, a sinner, will make known to thee this too, how often in the land of Daur, from loss of strength and from hunger I could not

---

[38] Another direct address to Epiphany, Avvakum's confessor and fellow inmate in Pustozersk.

keep my rule, only a little of it could I keep, only the evening psalms and the midnight office at the first hour, but more than that I could not: I dragged myself about like a poor beast. I was grieved about that office of mine, but I could not take it up. You see by now I had got so weak. But sometimes I went to the forest for wood, and while I was away my wife and children would sit on the ground by the fire, my daughter with her mother, and they would both cry. Agraphena, my poor unhappy one, was then not yet grown up. I came back from the wood— the child was sobbing hard. She could not speak for her tongue was fast bound, but she sat there and whimpered to her mother, and the mother looked at her and cried. But I breathed heavily and came near to the child with a prayer and said: "In the name of the Lord I bid thee speak to me and tell me why thou weepest." And she jumped up and bowed before me and began to speak clearly thus: "I do not know who it is, my lord father, but there is a Shining One within me and he held me by my tongue and he would not let me speak to mother, and because of it I cried. But he said to me, 'Tell your father that he should recite his office as he used to do, and then ye all go forth again to Russia, but, if he does not keep his rule, about which he is himself troubled, then in this place ye shall all die, and he shall die with you.'" At that time another thing of that sort was said to her, that there would be an edict to fetch us, and how that many of our friends had perished in Russia; all this came to pass. I was to say to Pashkov that if he sang the morning and evening office then God would give fair weather, and the corn would grow and there would be constant rain, and they sowed wheat on a small plot a day or two before Peter's day, and immediately it sprouted and was all but rotted by the rains. I spoke to him about the evening and morning office and he set to do this. God sent fair weather, and the corn ripened immediately. What a miracle! It was sown late but it ripened early.

And again, poor man, he began to practice cunning arts about God's doings—the following year he sowed much, but an unwonted rain poured down, and the water overflowed from the river and drowned the plowed fields and washed everything away, and it washed away our hut, and until that time there had never been water there, and the natives wondered. Mark you, as he went his way, so God moved in his mysterious way. At first he laughed at the news, but afterward, when the child wanted to eat, he betook him to tears—and then I sought not to slacken about my office. Enough of this have I spoken; let us return to our first subject. We must needs remember all these things and not be forgetting them, so as not to lay aside any of God's

doings in negligence and waste and not to alter them for the
pleasure of this age of vanity.

Now I will tell of what was done at Moscow. They said that
I was not at one with them. His Majesty bade Rodion Streshnev [39] persuade me that I should hold my peace. And I did his
bidding. The tsar is set over us by God, and at this moment was
kindly disposed toward me. So I hoped that little by little he
would come to a better mind. They promised me on Simeon's
day to place me at the printing office to correct books, and I
was exceedingly glad, for that pleased me better than to be the
tsar's confessor. I wanted something better than the confessional.
I waited on him. He sent me ten rubles and the tsarina sent me
ten. Luke, the confessor, sent me ten, and Rodion Streshnev also
ten, and our old friend Theodore Rtishchev then ordered them
to slip into my hat sixty rubles from his official salary, but about
that I was to say nothing! Each man put his hand in his pocket
and brought out every manner of thing. I lived in the house of
my dear one, Theodosia Prokofievna Morozova,[40] and didn't go
out inasmuch as she was my spiritual daughter. And her sister,
Princess Eudoxia Prokofievna, was my daughter also. My dear
ones, martyrs for Christ! And I was ever in the house of Anna
Petrovna Miloslavskaia.[41] God rest her soul! And I went to
Theodore Rtishchev's house to dispute with the Nikonites, and
so lived about the space of half a year. And I saw that I prevailed nothing but that rather a tumult was made; again, I began to grumble, and I wrote to the tsar many things to the effect
that he should earnestly seek for the ancient piety and defend
from heresy our common mother Holy Church, and on the patriarchal throne he should place a shepherd of the Orthodox Faith
in place of the wolf and apostate Nikon, him that was an evildoer and a heretic. And when I had got ready the letter I had
no more strength left in me: and I sent it forth on the journey
to the tsar by my spiritual son Theodore, the Fool in Christ,
which Theodore they strangled at Mezen, hanging him upon
the gallows tree. Now he in all boldness approached the tsar's

---

[39] Rodion Streshnev: a relative of the tsar's wife and his councillor
in Church affairs.

[40] Theodosia Morozova: a lady-in-waiting to the tsarina, and widow
of an influential boyar. She remained a faithful supporter of Avvakum.
She and her sister, Eudoxia Urusova, were arrested in 1670 for their
support of the Old Believer movement, and both died in prison
in 1672.

[41] Anna Miloslavskaia: a relative of the tsarina, and an influential
supporter of Avvakum.

carriage, and the tsar bade him sit down with the letter near the great entrance: he did not perceive that the letter was from me. And afterward, having the letter from him he bade let him go. And he—God rest his soul!—after staying a while with me again went into the church in the presence of the tsar and began to play the fool as though he was half-witted. The tsar was angry and bade them send him away to the Miracle Monastery. There Paul the archimandrite bade them put fetters on him, and by the will of God the fetters brake to pieces upon his legs before the people. But he, God rest his soul! my friend! crept into the burning stove in the bakehouse after the loaves and sat on the grating with his naked rump and picked up the crumbs in the stove to eat of them. Then the monks were affrighted and told the archimandrite Paul who is now metropolitan. He acquainted the tsar with this, and the tsar came to the monastery and ordered them to let him go with honor. He again came to me, and from that day on the tsar began to look askance at me. He was ill pleased that I began again to speak. He would have liked me to hold my peace but that was not my way. And the bishops, like goats, began to leap up against me, and they plotted to send me in banishment from Moscow, for many of the Christians had come to me and perceiving the truth they would not walk in the service of a lie. And from the tsar there came to me the accusation: "They tell me that the bishops bring complaint against thee; they say because of thee the churches are empty. Go again," said he, "into banishment." Thus spake the boyar Peter Mikhailovich Saltykov.[42] And they brought me to Mezen, and many good people gave me this and that in the name of Christ. And everything remained, only they took me with my wife and my children and my household. From town to town I taught the people of God and denounced them, the spotted beasts. And they brought us to Mezen.

Having endured for half a year, they took me again without my wife to Moscow, and my two sons journeyed with me, Ivan and Prokopy. But my wife and the rest were all left at Mezen. And having brought us to Moscow they took us at first away to the Pafnutiev Monastery,[43] and there they sent us a letter, and they spake thus and thus: "Wilt thou so long vex us? be reconciled to us, dear old Avvakum!" But I refused as though they were devils. And they flew in my face.

---

[42] Peter Saltykov was a boyar who energetically opposed Avvakum and his movement.

[43] Pafnutiev Monastery: a monastery in the vicinity of Moscow that often served as a prison for clergymen.

Then I wrote them an answer with much violence of words,
and I sent it by Kosma, a deacon of Yaroslavl, who was a clerk
of the patriarchal court—Kosma in public tried to overpersuade
me, but in private he upheld me, speaking thus: "Archpriest, do
not desert the ancient rites; a· mighty man wilt thou be with
Christ if thou wilt endure to the end—do not look to us for we
are ruined." And I to him made answer that he should again
stand for Christ. And he said: "I cannot. Nikon has led me
astray." And to speak shortly, he had denied Christ before
Nikon, in that he had no strength to stand firm, my poor Kosma.
I fell to crying; I blessed him, unhappy one—after that I had no
more dealings with him; let God deal with him as seems good
to him.

XIII. PREPARATIONS FOR THE TRIAL (1664–1666)

Thus having remained ten weeks in Pafnutiev in chains, they
took me again to Moscow, and in the Room of the Cross the
bishops held disputation with me. They led me to the cathedral
church, and after the Elevation of the Host they sheared me and
the deacon Theodore, and then they cursed us and I cursed
them back. And I was heavy at heart for the Mass. And after I
had stayed for a time at the patriarchal court, they took us by
night to Ugresha,[44] to the monastery of St. Nicholas—and the
enemies of God shaved off my beard. What would you? It is like
unto wolves not to pity the sheep; they tore at my hair like dogs
and only left one forelock—such as the Poles wear on their foreheads. They did it carrying me not along the road to the monastery but by the marshes and the quagmires that people might
not see me. They themselves saw that they were behaving as
fools but they did not wish to cease from their folly; the devil
had darkened their minds, why should one reproach them? It
was not them or they would have been otherwise. The time had
come spoken of in the Gospel. *"It must needs be that offenses
must come,"* and another evangelist saith: *"It must needs be
that offenses come, but woe unto him by whom offense cometh."*
Look thou that readest! Our misery was of necessity, we might
not escape it! For this cause God doth let loose offenses and
even that the elect may be inflamed and that they may be made
white, even that temptations be made manifest in us. Satan has
asked and obtained from God our bright shining Russia, that
he might purple it with martyr's blood. Well, hast thou imagined
this, O devil, and to us it is sweet to suffer for Our Sweet Lord.
They kept me at Nicholas' in a cold room for seventeen weeks.

---

[44] Ugresha: a village in the vicinity of Moscow.

There I had a visitation from God; read of it in the letter to the tsar. And the tsar came to the monastery and paid a visit to my prison cell and gave a groan and then left the monastery; it seems from that that he was sorry for me, the will of God lay in that. When they had shorn me there was a very great disturbance among them with the tsarina, God rest her soul! She, sweet lady, detected me at that time and asked to have me released from prison, as to which there is much to be said; God forgive them! As to my sufferings I do not hold them answerable, neither now nor hereafter; it sufficeth me to pray for them, be they alive or be they dead. The devil set discord between us but they were ever good toward me. Enough of this.

And poor Prince Ivan Vorotynsky [45] came there without the tsar to pray, and he asked to be admitted to my prison cell. But they would not let the hapless man in. I could only, looking through the window, weep over him. My sweet friend feared God, he was Christ's orphan. Christ will not cast him away. Thus always was Christ on our side, and all the boyars were good to us, only the devil was malicious and what could we have done if Christ had left us? They beat my dear Prince Ivan Khovansky [46] with rods and they burnt Isaiah,[47] and the lady Theodosia Morozova they brought to ruin, and they killed her son and tortured her and her sister Eudoxia, beating them with rods; and they parted her from her children and divorced her from her husband, and him they say, Prince Peter Urusov,[48] they married to another wife. But what was there to do? Let them torture those dear ones, they will go to their heavenly bridegroom. In every wise God will cause to pass this troublesome time and will call to himself the bridegroom to his heavenly palace, he the true Sun, our Light and our Hope. Let us turn again to the one first matter.

After this they took me again to the monastery of Pafnutiev, and there, having shut me up in the dark room, and put fetters on me, they kept me for well-nigh a year. There the cellarer Nikodemus was good to me at first, but he, poor fellow, smoked of tobacco of which more than that sixty *poods* they seized

---

[45] Prince Ivan Vorotynsky: member of a wealthy aristocratic family who supported Avvakum and his movement.

[46] Prince Ivan Khovansky: a member of a conservative family that lent its support to Avvakum.

[47] Isaiah: the majordomo of the boyar, Peter Saltykov. He was burned for his faithfulness to the Old Belief.

[48] Prince Peter Urusov: the husband of Princess Eudoxia Urusova, and brother-in-law of Theodosia Morozova.

when they searched the house of the Metropolitan of Gaza,[49] and they seized a lute too and other hidden things of the monastery on the which they played and made merry withal. It is a sin to speak of it, forgive me; it was not my business, let him look to it, to his own Lord he must stand or fall. This is just by the way. With them there were well-beloved teachers of Holy Writ. I asked of this Nikodemus, the cellarer, on Easter Day, in order that I might rest because of the holiday, that he would bid them open the door that I might sit on the threshold, and he abused me and refused me savagely as he willed. And after that he came into my cell he fell suddenly ill, they anointed him with oil and gave him the last sacraments and then and there he died. That was on Easter Monday, and before, on the night of Tuesday, there had come to him a man in the semblance of myself with a censer, and in shining vestments, and having censed him and taken him by the hand he moved himself and was healed. And he came to me with the servitor by night into the dungeon. And as he came he said: "Blessed is this dwelling —what a dungeon doth it contain—how blessed is this dungeon —what sufferings doth it hold! blessed are those bonds. . . ." And he fell before me and clasped my chain and said: "Forgive me, for God's sake! forgive, I have sinned before God and before thee. I have insulted thee, and for this God hath punished me." And I spake: "How hath he punished thee? Instruct me!" And he, "Thou thyself," said he, "didst come to me and didst cense me; thou didst have pity on me and didst raise me up. Why dost thou deny it?" And the servitor standing there said: "Yes, my Lord and Father, he took thee by the hand and led thee from the cell, and bowed down before thee, and thou didst go hence." And I charged him that he should say nothing to any man concerning this secret thing. And he questioned me how henceforth he might live for Christ. "Ah," said he, "dost thou charge me to go forth into the desert?" But I forbade him and would not suffer him to give up his stewardship, if only in secret he would preserve the ancient tradition of his fathers. And he bowed low and went away to his own place and on the morrow at meat he told it to all the brotherhood. And the people ceaselessly and with boldness pressed in to see me, asking for a blessing and for my prayers, and I taught them from Holy Writ and I healed

---

[49] Metropolitan Paisy of Gaza (Palestine): a Greek bishop who came to Russia in 1662 and became very influential at the court. He was the ideological leader of the opponents of Avvakum and the Old Believers, and was well known for his lack of scrupulousness and his participation in suspicious mercantile operations.

them by the Word of God. At that time I had some enemies, but these were reconciled to me. Alas, when shall I quit this life of vanity? It is written: "Woe to him when all men speak well of him." In very truth I know now how I may endure to the end; of good deeds there are none now; but I glorified God. That he knows and with him it rests.

Thither there came to me in secret Theodore with my children; he that was strangled, God rest his soul! and he questioned me thus: "How wouldst thou have me walk? Shall I go in my shift in the old fashion or shall I put clothes upon me? The heretics," said he, "are seeking me, they would fain bring me to ruin. I," said he, "was at Riazan under guard at the archbishop's palace at the court, and he, Hilarion,[50] did grievously torment me: there was scarce a day when he did not beat me with cords and he kept me bound in iron fetters, compelling me to partake of the new communion of Antichrist. And I said, 'I could not,' and I prayed in the night and wept and spake: 'O Lord, if thou dost not save me, they will cause me to commit abomination and I shall perish. What can I do?'" And weeping much he said suddenly, said he: "My father, all my chains fell rattling from me, and the door was opened of its own motion. And I," said he, "bowed down to God, and I went forth. I came to the outer gates and the gates were opened. I went straight forth along the road to Moscow. It was scarce daylight," said he, "when they gave chase on horseback; three men passed quickly by me and they did not see me, and I," said he, "trusting in Christ, went on my way onward. But," said he, "very soon they came upon me and they were snarling at me; said they, 'The son of a whore has escaped, where may one take him?' And again," said he, "they passed by me and did not see me. And I," said he, "again betook me to thee and asked whether I should go again to be tortured or whether I should don clothes and live in Moscow." And I, a sinner, bade him don clothes and not to hide himself from the hands of the heretics. They strangled him in Mezen, hanging him upon the gallows tree. Eternal be his memory together with Luke Lavrentievich. My well-beloved children! They suffered for Christ. Glory to God for them. And Theodore accomplished an exceeding mighty deed above measure; by day he played the Fool of Christ, and all night long he wept and prayed. I know many good men, but I had never yet beheld such an ascetic. He lived with me in Moscow about half a year, but I was still ill—two of us lived in

---

[50] Hilarion, Bishop of Riazan: a former friend of Avvakum's who became a staunch supporter of Nikon and the modernists. Theodore was a "Fool in Christ."

the same chamber with him and at the most he would lie an hour or two and then he would get up, and then he would go through a thousand genuflections and would seat himself on the ground, or else, standing up, he would weep for some three hours; meantime I would continue lying and sometimes sleep, but sometimes I was restless, and when he had his fill of violent weeping then he would come up to me and say: "How long wilt thou continue lying? Come to thyself. Thou art a priest. How are thou not ashamed?" And I could not rise though he lifted me up, saying: "Stand up, my sweet father!" And he pulled at me somehow or other. And he bade me say prayers as I sat, and he kept bowing down instead of me. He *was* my friend in very truth! He was sore vexed by his sufferings: at one time his intestine issued forth from him three yards in length, and at another five yards, and his guts were measureless—and it was both pitiful and laughable. At Ustiug for five years he froze barefoot in the frost with only his shift. I saw him myself. Then he became my spiritual son, and when I came from Siberia he ran up to my church in the stall in order to pray; he spoke thus: "When," said he, "one first began to thaw after the frost and get warm, my father, it was very hard to bear"; said he, "one stamps with one's feet on the brick floor as though they were wooden legs, and on the morrow they did not hurt."

He had with him there in his cell a Psalter of those newly printed. He knew but little as yet of those newfangled things. But I told him all, word by word, concerning the new books— and he snatched at the book and hurled it into the stove. And he cursed all these newfangled ways. And he was exceeding zealous for the faith of Christ. But why speak many words? As he began, so he ended. And his great virtue lay not in idle words, as is with me, miserable man, for whom he died pleading to God.

A good man, too, was my dear old Afanasy, my spiritual son —his name in religion was Avraamy—whom the apostates baked to death in Moscow on the fire, and like unto bread of sweet savor he was offered to the Holy Trinity. Until he took the cowl, he went about barefoot with only his shift, both winter and summer, only he was milder than Theodore and fell short of his asceticism. He dearly loved weeping, and weeping he would go about and with whomsoever he spoke his words were soft and sweet as though he wept. Theodore was very zealous and suffered much concerning the work of God. In every way he would weary himself to bring sin to light and to destroy it. But enough of them! As they lived, so they died, for Christ Jesus Our Lord.

XIV. THE CHURCH COUNCIL OF 1667 AND THE FINAL SCHISM

I will tell you yet more of my wanderings when they brought me out of the Pafnutiev Monastery in Moscow and placed me in the guesthouse, and after many wanderings they set me down in the Miracle Monastery, before the patriarchs of all Christendom, and the Russian Nikonites sat there like so many foxes. I spoke of many things in Holy Writ with the patriarchs. God did open my sinful mouth and Christ put them to shame. The last word they spoke to me was this: "Why," said they, "art thou stubborn? The folk of Palestine, Serbia, Albania, the Wallachians, they of Rome and Poland, all these do cross themselves with three fingers, only thou standest out in thine obstinacy and dost cross thyself with two fingers; it is not seemly." And I answered them for Christ thus: "O you teachers of Christendom, Rome fell away long ago and lies prostrate,[51] and the Poles fell in the like ruin with her, being to the end the enemies of the Christian. And among you Orthodoxy is of mongrel breed; and no wonder —if by the violence of the Turkish Mohmut you have become impotent, and henceforth it is you who should come to us to learn. By the gift of God among us there is autocracy; till the time of Nikon, the apostate, in our Russia under our pious princes and tsars the Orthodox Faith was pure and undefiled, and in the church was no sedition. Nikon, the wolf, together with the devil, ordained that men should cross themselves with three fingers, but our first shepherds made the sign of the cross and blessed men as of old with two fingers, according to the tradition of our Holy Fathers, Meletina of Antioch, Theodoret, the blessed Bishop of Cyrene, Peter of Damascus, and Maxim the Greek;[52] and so too did our own synod of Moscow, at the time of the Tsar Ivan, bid them, putting their fingers together in that wise, make the sign of the cross and give the blessing, as of old the Holy Fathers Melety and others taught. Then in the time of Ivan, the tsar,[53] there were the standard-bearers, Gury and Varsanophy, wonder-workers of Kazan, and Phillip the Abbot of Solovki among the Russian saints."[54] And the patriarchs

---

[51] Here Avvakum quotes the *Tale of the White Cowl* (see Selection 50), which became one of the ideological foundation stones of the Old Believer movement. He was addressing Greek members of the council.

[52] Maxim the Greek was a Greek scholar whose writings were often quoted by the Old Believers.

[53] This refers to Tsar Ivan IV.

[54] Sts. Gury and Varsanophy were Orthodox missionaries among the Tatars after the taking of Kazan. St. Phillip, Abbot of Solovki, later Metropolitan of Moscow.

fell to thinking, and our people began to howl like wolf cubs
and to belch out words against their fathers, saying: "Our Russian holy men were ignorant, and they understood nothing, they
are unlearned folk," said they. "How can one trust them? they
have no letters." O Holy God! How hast thou suffered so great
reviling of thy holy ones? I, miserable one, was bitter in my
heart, but I could do nothing. I abused them as hard as I could,
and I spake as follows: "I am pure, and the dust that cleaves
to my feet do I shake off before you, as it is written: 'better
one if he do the will of God than a thousand of the godless.' "
Then louder than before they began to cry out against me:
"Away with him, away with him; he hath outraged us all"; and
they began to thrust at me and to beat me. And the patriarchs
themselves threw themselves on me; about forty of them I think
there must have been. Great was the army of Antichrist that
gathered itself together. Ivan Uvarov seized me and dragged at
me, and I cried aloud: "Stop, do not beat me!" Then they all
sprang back and I began to speak to the interpreter, the archimandrite, thus: "Say to the patriarch, the Apostle Paul writes:
'For such a high priest became us, who is holy, harmless, and
so forth,' but ye, having sorely mishandled a man, how then can
ye straightway perform your office?" Then they sat down. I went
away to the door and lay down on my side. "Ye sit down," I
said to them, "but I lie down." At that they laughed. "The archpriest," said they, "is a silly fellow, and does not show honor
to the patriarchs." And I said: "We are fools for Christ's sake.
Ye are great and we without honor; ye are strong and we are
weak." After that, again, the authorities came to me and began
to talk with me on the question of the Alleluias: Christ put it in
my heart and I put them to shame for their Romish heresy,
through Dionysios the Areopagite, of whom mention has been
made before. And Euphemy, the cellarer of the Miracle Monastery, spake: "Right art thou," said he, "there is no more to be
said." And they took me along to chain me.

Then the tsar sent an officer with musketeers and they took
me to the Vorobiev Hills.[55]

There was the priest Lazar and the monk Epiphany, an
elder.[56] They had been shorn and were ill treated as though they
were village peasants, my dear ones. A wise man when he did

---

[55] Vorobiev, or Sparrow Hills: hills in the vicinity of Moscow where
Moscow University is now located.

[56] Father Lazar and Monk Epiphany were condemned, together
with Avvakum, by the Council of 1667. Both of them, as well as
Avvakum and Deacon Fedor (Theodore), were deported to Pustozersk, and burned in 1682.

but see them must needs fall aweeping when he looked at them. Well, let them suffer! Why grieve for them! Christ was better than them, and against him, Our Sweet Lord, evil was wrought by the forebears of the Nikonites, Annas and Caiaphas. No wonder, for they followed after an exemplar—we must grieve for them, poor things! Woe to the hapless followers of Nikon! They have perished of their own wickedness and their stubbornness of soul!

Then they brought us from the Vorobiev Hills to the guesthouse of the Andreevsky Monastery to the Savin suburb, and as though we were robbers, followed after us and left us not, nay, even when we relieved nature. It was both pitiable and laughable, as though the devil had blinded them.

Then again we were taken to the St. Nicholas Monastery at Ugresha. And there the tsar sent to me the officer Yury Lutokhin, that I might bless him, and we had much converse concerning this and that.

Then again they brought me to Moscow, to the guesthouse of the Nikolsky Monastery, and they demanded of us yet again a statement of the true faith. After that there were sent more than once to me gentlemen of the bedchamber, diverse persons, Artemon and Dementy.[57] And they spake to me in the name of the tsar: "Archpriest!" they said, "I see thy life that it is pure and undefiled and pleasing unto God, I and the tsarina and our children, be entreated of us." The envoy wept as he spake, and for him I weep always. I was exceeding sorry for him. And again he spake: "I beg of thee, hearken to me. Be thou reconciled with the patriarchs." And I said: "Even if God will that I should die, I will not be joined together with apostates. Thou art my tsar, but they, what have they to do with thee? They have lost their tsar and they have come here to gobble you up. I—say I—will not cease to uplift my hands to heaven until God give thee over to me."

The last word I got from the envoy was, "Wherever," said he, "thou shalt be, do not forget us in thy prayers." And I, sinful one, now, as far as I may, pray to God for him.

XV. BANISHMENT TO PUSTOZERSK

After scourging my friends, but not me, they banished us to Pustozersk. And I sent from Pustozersk to the tsar two letters,

---

[57] This refers to Artemon Mateev and Dementy Bashmakov. They were important bureaucrats and close councillors of Tsar Alexis. The latter was the head of *Tainy Prikaz* (Department for Secret Affairs) under Alexis.

the first not long but the other longer, what I had said to him,
that I wrote also in the letters, and also certain signs of God,
which had appeared to me in my prison. Who reads will understand. Also a letter written by the deacon was sent to Moscow
by me and the brotherhood as a gift to the True Believers. The
book was an answer of the Orthodox and was a conviction of the
heresy of the apostates—in it was written the truth concerning
the dogmas of the Church. Further, two letters had been sent by
the priest Lazar to the tsar and the patriarch, and of all this we
got a present. In Mezen of my household they hanged two men,
my spiritual children, the aforenamed Theodore, Christ's Fool,
and Luke Lavrentievich, servants of Christ. Luke was a dweller
in Moscow, the only son of his mother, who was a widow; he
was of the guild of tanners, a youth of twenty-five years. He
came to Mezen, to his death, with my children. And when there
was a general slaughter in my house, Pilate asked him: "And
how do you, my man, cross yourself?" And he made answer with
all temperance: "I do believe and do cross myself so, placing my
fingers as doth my spiritual father, the archpriest Avvakum."
And Pilate ordered them to put him in the dungeon, and there
to put a noose round his neck, and he hanged him on a railing.
And so he passed from earth to heaven. Greater than that what
could they do for him? And if he were but a youth, he acted
like an old man. He went his way to the Lord. Well were it even
for an old man did he win through like that.

At this time the order was given to hang my two sons after
the flesh, Ivan and Prokopy, but they, miserable ones, were
weaklings and never thought them to lay hold on the crowns of
victory. Being soon afraid of death they made submission, and
so they buried them alive in the earth with their mother for
third. There was a death without death for you. Repent as ye
sit there, while the devil concocts something else! That death
be terrible is not wonderful! Time was when even Peter, dear
friend of Christ, made denial and went out and wept bitterly,
and for his tears he was forgiven, and for my children it is not
wonderful that, because of my sins, weakness was permitted
them. Well and good! So be it! Christ is mighty to save us all
and to have mercy upon us.

Thereafter the deputy, Ivan Elagin, was with us in Pustozersk,
having come from Mezen, and he received from us a statement,
and this was it: "Year and month," and again: "We keep the
tradition of the Holy Fathers unaltered, and we proclaim as
accursed Paisy the Patriarch of Palestine with his fellows as an
assembly of heretics," and besides there were said there a few
words about Nikon, the fabricator of this heresy. For this they

brought us to the scaffold, and when they had read the sentence they took me away without scourging me to the dungeon. They read me the edict: "Let Avvakum be put into an underground prison within the palisade and let there be given to him bread and water." But I spat on this and I desired to die, refraining from food, and I ate nothing for about eight days or more. But then my brethren bade me eat.

At the same time they took the priest Lazar, and cut out his whole tongue from his throat, but little blood flowed and soon stopped. And he spoke again without his tongue. Moreover, having placed his right hand upon the scaffold, they cut it off at the wrist, and the hand that had been cut off, lying upon the ground, of its own motion placed its fingers after the ancient use, and lying thus long time before the people, the poor thing made confession, and even unto death did not betray the sign of salvation. Even I am amazed at that; the lifeless thing convicts the living. And on the third day I felt in his mouth with my hand; it was all smooth, and there was no tongue, but it did not hurt. God had granted that with good hap it had healed up. In Moscow they had cut out his tongue and then there was some of it left, but now it was all cut away. But he spoke clearly for the space of two years as though he had a tongue. And when he had completed two years there was another wonder—in the space of three days his tongue grew again to its full size, but that it was a little stumpy, and again he spake, instantly praising God and railing at the apostates.

At this time they seized a hermit priest, an anchorite of strict rule, Epiphany, an elder, and cut out the whole of his tongue. And they cut off four fingers of his hand. And at first he spoke thickly, and at this time he prayed to the Virgin, the Mother of God, and there appeared to him in the air two tongues, that of Moscow and the present one. Now he, taking up one, put it in his mouth, and from that moment began to speak purely and clearly, and the whole tongue fitted itself into his mouth. Great are the works and unspeakable are the judgments of the Lord! He sendeth forth his judgments and again he healeth and hath mercy. But what availeth many words? God is an old hand at miracles. Out of nothing he brings life, and shall he not at the Last Day raise up all flesh in the twinkling of an eye; and who may discern concerning this thing? God is after this wise: he createth what is new and he reneweth what is old. In all things glory be to him!

At this time they seized the deacon Theodore. They cut out the whole of his tongue, but left a little bit in his mouth, having cut it slantways across his throat. It healed just as it was at the

time, but later on it grew again as it was before. It stuck out a
little way from the lips, but stumplike. And they cut off his
hand across the palm. By the gift of God it all healed, and he
spake clearly and cleanly as before.

Then they covered us up with earth. There was a framework
in the earth, and above the earth a second framework, and then
again round the whole of it was a fence with four locks, and
they set a watch to guard all the doors. Now we, both here and
everywhere in dungeons, sing songs before the Lord Christ, the
Son of God, such as Solomon sang when he beheld his mother
Bathsheba: "*Thou art good, my fair one, thou art good, my beloved. Thine eyes burn like a flame of fire, thy teeth are as white
as milk; the shining of thy face is brighter than the sun's rays,
and altogether thou shinest like unto the day in its strength.*"

Then Pilate journeyed from us, and having settled his business at Mezen he returned to Moscow. And others of us were
burned and baked. They burned Isaiah to death and afterward
burned Avraamy and other defenders of the Church—the most
of them did he undo. God will count the number of them. A
wonder is it that they would not come to their right mind. They
think to establish the faith by fire or the knout and gallows tree!
Which of the Apostles taught them that? I know not. My Christ
did not teach his Apostles that fire and knout and gallows tree
should lead to the faith. But it was said to the Apostle by the
Lord thus: "*Go ye into all the world and preach the Gospel to
every creature; he that believeth and is baptized, the same shall
be saved.*" See now, my reader, Christ calls us to come if we
will, but he does not bid the Apostles to burn with fire and to
hang on the gallows tree them that are disobedient. The Tatar
god Mahmud [58] in his books wrote thus: "We bid ye lay low with
the sword the heads of them that obey not our law and tradition." But Christ never gave such like command to his disciples,
and these teachers, it is plain, are themselves Antichrists; they,
who, leading men to the faith, destroy them and give them over
to death—they bring forth works like unto their faith. It is
written in the Gospels: "*A good tree cannot bring forth evil fruit,
neither a bad tree good fruit. Every tree is known by its fruit.*"
But why speak many words? "No Cross, no Crown." He that
will be crowned, for *that* he had not need to go to Persia. We
have our Babylon at home. Come, True Believer! Name thou
the name of Christ, standing in the midst of Moscow, cross thyself with the sign of the Savior our Christ, with two fingers
as we have received from the Holy Fathers. Lo! here at home

---

[58] This refers to Mohammed, the Prophet of Islam.

for thee is thy Kingdom of Heaven. Glory to God! Suffer tortures for the placing of thy fingers, reason not much, but I with thee am ready to die for this and for Christ. If I am a foolish man and one without learning, yet this I know, that all the traditions of the Church, handed down to us by the Holy Fathers, are holy and incorrupt. I keep them even unto death, as I received them. I will not falsify the eternal boundaries—that which was laid down before our days, let it so remain to all eternity, but, O thou heretic, do not tamper with things, touch not the sacrifice of Christ, lay not thine hand on the cross, nay, stir not even the corporals! And they have planned with the devil to misprint books and falsify everything, and to alter the sign of the cross in the church, and on the wafers. Within the altar they have banished the priestly prayers, they have altered the "Lord have mercy upon us," and in baptism they bid to invoke the Evil One. I would fain spit in his eyes and in theirs! And round about the font the Evil One leads them against the course of the sun, and in like fashion they consecrate the church, and when they solemnize marriage they lead the married counterclockwise; plainly they do this in hostility. And in baptism they do not abjure the Evil One. How should they? They are his children and they do not desire to abjure their father. But why multiply words? Woe is me for the True Believer! Every spirit that is exalted is brought low. As Nikon, the hound of hell, spake, so did he do. "Print the books, Arsen,[59] anyhow, only not after the ancient fashion." And so he did! More than that, one cannot alter things. It behooves every man to endure for this, even unto death. May these damnable ones be accursed, with all their devilish imaginations: and to them whom they made to suffer in their souls, may theirs be threefold eternal remembrance.

For this I ask forgiveness of every True Believer. Some things that I have said were perhaps best unsaid—but I may read through the Acts of the Apostles and the epistles of Paul. The Apostles proclaimed concerning themselves that God was working through them. "Not unto us but to our God be the praise." And I am of no account. So spake I again and again. "I am a man that is a sinner. Wanton am I and a ravisher, a thief and a

---

[59] Arsen, a learned Greek, came to Moscow in 1649, and was invited to become a professor there. However, it was soon discovered that he had managed to become a Catholic three times, once a Moslem, and then, finally, Orthodox. For these successful conversions he was deported to Solovki Monastery. In 1652 Nikon invited him to revise the Russian missal, and this participation by Arsen in the re-editing of the holy books was largely responsible for the disrepute into which Nikon's reforms fell.

robber, the friend of publicans and sinners, and to every man am I a hypocrite accursed." Forgive me and pray for me; to you who read me and who hearken am I bound more than to any. I know not how to live and what I am doing that I tell to men. What matter that they talk vanity of me, in the days of judgment they shall all know of my deeds, whether they be good or evil. But if I be unlearned in speech, yet am I not in thought; I am untaught in rhetoric and in dialectic and in philosophy, but the mind of Christ is our guide within us, as the Apostle saith, *though I be rude in speech yet not in knowledge.*[60]

XVI. CONCLUDING REMARKS TO THE MONK EPIPHANY

And now, my elder, thou hast heard full much of my babbling, and I bid thee, in the name of the Lord, write thou also for thy servant in Christ, how the Mother of God kneaded this devil in her hands and gave him over to thee, and how the ants ate thee in thy secret parts, and how something devilish set fire to the Word and how the cell was burned to ashes, but all within it were safe and sound.[61] And how thou didst cry aloud to heaven: and other things thou dost remember to the glory of Christ and the Mother of God. Hearken to what I say; if thou dost not write to me I shall be sorely angered! Thou lovest to hear of me; of what thou art ashamed, tell me if even a little. The Apostles, Paul and Barnabas, were wont to set forth, in the assembly at Jerusalem, before all, what sights and wonders God had wrought by them among the Gentiles (see Acts 34 and 42), and the name of the Lord Jesus was magnified. And many who believed came to them, making confession and telling their deeds. And much of this is written by the Apostles and in the Acts. Fear not to tell me, only keep thy conscience straitly; seek not thine own glory, but speak thou for Christ and the Mother of God. Let thy servant in Christ read and rejoice. When we die, then shall this be read and we be remembered before God, and we will pray to God for them who read and who hearken. They shall be our people. They shall be there with Christ, and we shall be theirs forever and ever. Amen.

---

[60] Here a fragment about the "Healing of Those Possessed" is omitted.

[61] Here Avvakum once more addresses his cellmate Epiphany, who later also wrote an autobiography.

C. SECULAR TALES

60. SHEMIAKA'S JUDGMENT

Shemiaka's Judgment is one of the oldest Russian satirical stories with a purely fictitious plot. Indeed, the name "Shemiaka" can be traced back to the middle of the fifteenth century when Dmitry Shemiaka, prince of the northern city of Galych (not to be confused with Galich, capital of the southwestern province of Galicia), waged his endless feud against his cousin, Vasily III, Great Prince of Muscovy. The proper name "Shemiaka," however, subsequently became quite popular in Muscovite Russia, and there is no definite indication that the hero of the tale can be actually identified with Prince Dmitry Shemiaka or any other real historical figure.

The language and structure of the tale, its elements of popular satire and folk riddles, bring *Shemiaka's Judgment* somewhat closer to the oral folk tales (*skazki*) than to any literary narrative. Many Russian, Byelorussian, and Ukrainian tales and fairy tales about an unjust judge commonly employ the same motifs of crimes and court decisions that can be found in this tale. *Shemiaka's Judgment* satirizes Russian court mores of the sixteenth and seventeenth centuries, when judges often thought that their decisions should be a source of personal income. In those centuries this tale became extremely popular, and there have been preserved innumerable prose and verse versions of it.

The present translation follows the text of a seventeenth-century manuscript published by M. Skripil in *Russkaia povest XVII veka*, Moscow, 1954, pages 140–142.

In a village of Russia there lived two peasant brothers. One was rich and the other poor. The rich one for many years lent money to his poor brother, but could not end his destitution.

Once the poor brother came to the rich one and asked him to lend him his horse because he hadn't one for bringing in wood. The rich brother did not want to give him the horse, and said: "On many occasions I have lent you money, but I cannot improve your condition." But he did lend him the horse, and then the poor brother asked to borrow the harness. The rich brother felt offended, and began to abuse his brother, saying: "You! You don't even have your own harness," and he didn't give him the harness. The poor man left the house of the rich brother, took his own sledge, and attached it to the horse's tail. He then went to the forest and later returned to his house, but he forgot to take out the gate spike. The sledge got caught on the spike and could not move. He flayed the horse with the knout, and the horse pulled with all its might, finally tearing away its own tail. When the poor brother brought back the horse and the rich brother saw that it no longer had a tail, he began to abuse his poor brother for having ruined his horse. And he refused to take the horse back, but went to the city to lodge a complaint with the judge, Shemiaka.

And the poor brother, seeing that his brother went to court, followed him, because he knew that if he did not come of his own volition, he would be obliged to pay an additional fee to the court messenger.

And both of them stopped for the night in some township not far from the city. The rich brother went to pass the night with the parson of the township because the parson was an acquaintance of his. The poor man also came to the parson's, and, arriving there, went to sleep in an upper bunk. The rich brother began to tell the parson about the misfortune concerning his horse, and explained why he was going to the city. And then the parson began to sup with the rich brother. The poor one, however, was not invited. As the poor hungry brother looked from the upper bunk to see what the parson and his brother were eating, he fell from the upper bunk, accidentally crashing onto the cradle of the parson's infant son, killing him.

And then the parson went with the rich brother to the city to sue the poor brother for the death of his infant son. As they came to the city wherein lived the judge, the poor one was following them. They were walking over a bridge to the city. At that time one of the inhabitants of the city was transporting his father in a cart to a steam bath under the bridge in order to wash him. The poor brother, who knew that he must expect the worst from his rich brother and from the parson, decided to commit suicide. He jumped from the bridge into the moat in order to kill himself; but the moat was dry, and in jumping he accidentally fell on the old man and killed him. He was seized and brought before the judge.

The poor man began to think how to avoid the misfortune of a penalty and how to bribe the judge. But since he couldn't find anything in his pocket, he took a stone and wrapped it in a kerchief and put it in his hat and presented himself to the judge. And now the rich brother lodged his complaint against him, requiring a compensation for his horse, and began to explain the case to the judge. Shemiaka listened to the complaints, and told the poor man, "Answer." The poor brother didn't know what to say. He took out of his hat the wrapped stone and showing it to the judge, bowed deeply. The judge, thinking the poor man promised him a bribe, told his rich brother: "Since he tore away the tail of your horse, don't accept the horse from your brother as long as the tail will not grow back. But as soon as the tail grows back, at that time take from him your horse."

And then began the second trial. The parson began to sue the poor brother for the death of his infant son, because the poor man had crushed his son. The poor brother once more took from the hat the same bundle and showed it to the judge. The judge saw it, and thought that in the second trial the poor man promised another bundle of gold. And he told the parson: "Since he crushed your son, give him your wife until a child is born from him. And at that time take back from him your wife and the child."

And then began the third trial, for the crushing of the son's old father by jumping from the bridge. The poor one, taking the wrapped stone from his hat, showed it for the third time to the judge. The judge, hoping that the poor man was promising him a third bundle of gold for this, the third trial, told the son of the old man: "Go onto the bridge, while the man who killed your father remains under the bridge. And you must jump down from the bridge and kill him in the same way in which he killed your father."

When, after the trial, the plaintiffs left the court with the defendant, the rich brother began to claim his horse from the poor brother. But the latter told him: "According to the judge's decision, as he told you, I will return the horse to you when its tail grows back." So the rich one gave him five rubles in order to get back the horse, even though it had no tail. The poor brother accepted the five rubles, and returned the horse to him.

Then the poor one, according to the decision of the judge, claimed from the parson his wife in order to have a child with her, and having had the child, to return the wife with the child to the parson. But the parson began to beg him not to take his wife. For this concession the poor man took ten rubles from the parson.

Then the poor one told the third plaintiff: "According to the judge's decision, I will stand under the bridge while you go on the bridge and jump on me in the same manner in which I jumped on your father."

And the plaintiff thought, if I jump on him, probably I will not crush him but myself, and he began to plead with the poor man, and gave him some money in order not to be obliged to jump on him. In this way the poor man got money from all three of them.

The judge sent a servant to the defendant, ordering him to get from the latter the three bundles that had been shown him. The servant told him: "Give me that which you showed to the judge from your hat. He has ordered me to take it from you."

And the latter, taking the wrapped stone from under his hat, showed it to the servant. "Well, but that is a stone," said the servant.

The defendant said: "Yes, it is for the judge. I would have killed him if he hadn't tried me to my advantage."

The servant came back and told everything to the judge. And the judge, after listening to the servant, said: "I thank and praise God that I tried him to his advantage. If I had not done so, he would have killed me."

And the poor man returned home, being overjoyed and praising God.

61. THE TALE OF SAVVA GRUDTSYN

The *Tale of Savva Grudtsyn* is a work characteristic of a transitional period when the new currents that were appearing in Russian literature modified previously well-established patterns. The story of Savva's life, which describes his adventures, his illicit affair with the wife of his father's close friend, and his military deeds during his service in regiments commanded by foreign soldiers according to Western tactics, reflects the new way of life and the new mentality of Muscovite Russia. Still, some elements of the earlier Russian hagiographic tradition persist, especially at the conclusion of the tale.

The basic theme of this work is the struggle between good and evil, illustrated by the fall of a man and his eventual redemption through repentance. Thus the *Tale of Savva Grudtsyn* has several thematic parallels with the poetic tale of *Misery-Luckless-Plight*. The style of *Savva Grudtsyn* is equally transitional, combining solemn, archaic language and syntax with new, colloquial expressions and idioms.

It is worth noting that this tale begins in the Time of Troubles, when the Polish intervention in Russia during the period 1605 to 1613 undermined the foundations of the old order in Russia. As in other Russian tales of the seventeenth century, most of the characters belong to well-known aristocratic and merchant families. The Grudtsyn-Usovs and the Vtorys were important merchants in northern Russia; the boyars Streshnev and Shein are well known from Russian history; and, finally, the tsar himself shows interest in Savva and actually influences the hero's destiny. The plot is certainly fictional and complex, but it does give vivid and realistic details of the life of a patriarchal Russian family of that time, of the life of the military, and of the mores of Muscovite society. The author was decidedly not a member of the literati of that period, for, despite the use of both archaic and colloquial expressions, his art is rather limited, and he often repeats word for word certain descriptions, speeches, and conceptions.

The translation follows an early eighteenth-century manuscript published, with some corrections, by M. Skripil in *Russkaia povest XVII veka,* Moscow, 1954, pages 82–102.

This is a most truthful and true tale which has come to pass in these days and which reveals how God, who loves man, revealed his love to the Christian people. I wish to tell you, brethren, this most wonderful tale which is filled with awe and horror, which deserves inexplicable astonishment, and which explains the patience of our man-loving God who, awaiting our conversion, brings us to salvation through the most inexplicable of deeds.

On a day in 7114 (1606) God allowed, because of the multiplication of our sins, the God-offending apostate, heretic, and unfrocked monk Grishka Otrepiev [1] to attack the Muscovite state and to win the throne of the Russian land in a most robber-like, un-tsarlike manner. Also, at that time Russia was invaded by the increasing bands of faithless Lithuanians and Poles who performed all kinds of base deeds and who caused great misfortune to the Russian people in Moscow and in other cities. Because of these Lithuanian and Polish attacks, many people abandoned their homes and fled from city to city.

In the year 7114 (1606), in the city of Great Ustiug, [2] there lived a citizen named Foma, by surname, Grudtsyn-Usov, whose descendants still reside in that city. Seeing much anarchy and base deeds of the lawless Poles in Russia, this Foma decided to forsake the city of Great Ustiug, to live no longer in his home, but to migrate with his wife to the city of Kazan on the lower

---

[1] Grishka, or Gregory, Otrepiev was a pretender to the Russian throne who claimed to be Prince Dmitry, the son of Ivan IV. See introduction to Selection 55. At that time Poland and Lithuania were united into one dominion, which explains the author's calling the foreign troops Polish in one case, Lithuanian in another.

[2] The city of Great Ustiug is located in northern Russia, between Moscow and the White Sea. In the seventeenth century it was an important merchant city.

Volga, for in this city on the lower Volga there were no base
Lithuanians or Poles.

And Foma and his wife lived in the city of Kazan until the
beginning of the reign of the God-fearing sovereign, Grand
Duke, and Tsar of All Russia, Michael Fedorovich. Foma had
an only son, Savva, who was twelve years old. It was Foma's
custom to make frequent business trips, traveling up and down
the Volga, sometimes going to Solikamsk,[3] sometimes to the city
of Astrakhan, and sometimes beyond the Caspian Sea to the
land of Persia. He also taught his son, Savva, so that he might
learn to attend to his business promptly and diligently, since
after Foma's death his only son would inherit his estate.

After some time, Foma decided to sail to Persia and began
the loading of his goods into the usual ships. He also loaded
other boats with customary goods and ordered his son to sail to
Solikamsk, there to learn the merchant's trade with all diligence.
Having bidden farewell to his wife and son, Foma set out on
his journey. Some days later, his son, Savva, sailed to Solikamsk
in the ships his father had ordered loaded. Having reached the
city of Orel, which is in the Usolsk region, he docked and, following his father's orders, went to live at the inn of a certain
respectable man. The innkeeper and his wife, remembering the
loving kindness of Savva's father, for he had done them many
favors, cared with diligence for the son, rendering him many
services and even treating him as their son.

In this city of Orel there lived a citizen, Bazhen Vtory by
name, who was both famous and well known. He was already
old in years and was known in many cities for his virtuous way
of life and for his wealth. He had befriended and was well
acquainted with Savva's father. Having learned that the son of
Foma Grudtsyn had come to this city from Kazan, he thought
to himself: Since his father and I share much love and friendship, why should I neglect the son by not inviting him into my
home, to live with me and to eat at my table?

Having come to this conclusion, when Bazhen saw Savva
walking in the street he invited him to his house, saying: "My
dear friend, Savva, do you know that your father and I share
much love and friendship? Why did you neglect me by not
coming to abide in my home? This time, do not disobey me, but
come and live in my house and break bread with me. And, for

---

[3] Solikamsk and Orel are located in the same region as Great
Ustiug. The city of Astrakhan is located at the delta of the Volga. It
was the main trading center for commerce with Persia and other
countries of the Near East.

the love of your father, I shall receive you even as if you were
my own son."

Hearing these words from Bazhen, Savva was very happy to
be received into the house of such a famous man, and he bowed
low before him, and made haste to move from the inn to
Bazhen's house. And there he lived, enjoying all the comforts,
and rejoicing.

This old man, Bazhen, had a young wife who had never been
married before, but who was Bazhen's third wife. The devil,
that enemy who hates all things not vile in the human kind,
having seen this man's virtuous way of life, decided to bring
strife into his house by inducing Bazhen's wife to have sinful
relations with the young man. Thus the wife began to seduce
him into sin with tempting words. Human nature knows how
to lead the mind of a young man into iniquity. And thus Savva,
influenced by the flattery of this woman, or, better to say, by
the devil's envy, was led to the sin of adultery. They sinned
endlessly, but still they were unable to satiate their desires. And
Savva remained for a long time in such a sinful relation with
her. They sinned even on Sundays and on holy days and, having
forgotten all fear of God, they wallowed continuously, like
swine, in the filth that is sin. And for a long time they remained
in such insatiable lust, like beasts.

When the holy day honoring the Ascension of Our Lord Jesus
Christ neared, Bazhen Vtory took the young man and went to
vespers in the holy church, this being on the eve of that holy day.
Then they went home again and, after the usual supping, went
each to his own bed, giving thanks to God. As soon as the God-
loving man, Bazhen Vtory, had fallen soundly asleep, his wife,
incited by the devil, got up secretly from her couch, went to
the young man's bed, woke him, and compelled him to wicked
adultery. Though young, Savva was seized by the fear of God,
as if pierced by an arrow. And, fearing God's judgment, he
began to ponder, asking himself: How could I do such a wicked
deed and on such a great holy day?

And having thought thusly, he wished to be rid of her and,
taking an oath, said to her: "I do not want to lose my soul
forever by profaning my body on such a great holiday."

But she, in the grip of an insatiable carnal desire, tried to
force him by her caresses and threats to submit to her. But try
as she would, she could not force him to yield to her desire.
And some kind of divine power helped him. When this evil
woman saw that she could not bring the youth to do her bidding, she at once became seized by a wicked rage. Hissing like
a fierce serpent, she went away from his bed. Then she began

to ponder how she might destroy him through a magic potion. And she decided to fulfill her evil intention of destroying him without delay.

And she did as she had decided. When the bells announced matins, God-loving Bazhen quickly got up from his bed, woke the young man, Savva, and went with him to the morning service to glorify God. They listened to the liturgy with attention and with the fear of God, and then they returned home. When the hour of the sacred liturgy arrived, they returned to the holy church with joy so that they might hear the glorification of God. In the meantime, this accursed woman carefully prepared a magic philter for the youth, for she, like a serpent, wanted to spit poison at him.

When the holy liturgy was ended, Bazhen and Savva left the church, intending to go home. However, the *voevoda* of the city invited Bazhen to take dinner with him. And he asked, concerning the youth: "Whose son is this and where is he from?"

Bazhen answered that he was Foma Grudtsyn's son from Kazan. Thereafter, the *voevoda* invited the young man to his home, for he had known Savva's father well. So they went to the *voevoda's* house and, as was the custom, ate together with the others, and afterward returned home.

Arriving home, Bazhen ordered that wine be brought out so that they might drink in his home to honor the holy day. He was not in the least aware of his wife's evil scheme. When the wine had been brought in, she poured it into a cup and offered it to her husband. He drank it and gave thanks to the Lord. Then she poured more and drank it herself. Then she poured out the poisoned philter she had prepared, and offered it to Savva. He drank this base potion without any apprehension or hesitation, for he expected no evil deed from her, thinking that she harbored no ill will toward him. But as soon as he had drunk it, a fire began to burn in his heart. And he thought to himself: I have drunk many drinks in my father's house, but never such a wine as this one.

When he had finished the drink, he began to grieve in his heart and to long for a woman. The wife, like a fierce lioness, looked furiously at Savva and showed him not the least friendliness. But she began rather to slander the young man to her husband, saying base words and ordering her husband to drive the youth from their house. God-fearing Bazhen, although he took pity on the young man, was finally ensnared by his wife's cajolery and ordered the youth out of his home, accusing him of various failings. And the youth went away from the house with great sorrow and grief in his heart, lamenting and grieving the evil deeds of that woman.

He went back to the house of the innkeeper where he had previously lived, and the innkeeper asked him by what fault he had left Bazhen's house. And Savva answered: "I did not wish to live longer with those people, for I did not have enough to eat."

But he continued to grieve for and long after this woman. And, because of his grief, his handsome face began to wane and his flesh to waste away. Seeing the youth so grieving and lamenting, the innkeeper could not ascertain what had happened.

Now in the same city there was a magician who, through sorcery and charms, could tell why and to whom sorrow had come. He was also able to divine who would live and who would die. The innkeeper and his wife, who were sensible and cared greatly for the young man, summoned this sorcerer secretly, for they wished to learn why the youth grieved so. The sorcerer came and, consulting his book of magic, told them the truth: "The youth has no sorrow for himself, but longs only for the wife of Bazhen Vtory, since he has fallen into sinful adultery with her. But he became ashamed of her, and since that time he has grieved, longing for her."

The innkeeper and his wife, hearing this from the sorcerer, did not believe him, because they knew Bazhen Vtory to be a pious and God-fearing man who could not be involved in such an affair. Savva, however, continued to lament incessantly and to long for that accursed woman. And from day to day he wasted away, as if he were afflicted by some overwhelming bereavement.

Once, Savva left the city and went into the fields, wishing to take a walk to alleviate his longings and grief. He went walking alone, seeing no one before him nor no one behind him, and thinking of nothing in particular, but only grieving and lamenting his separation from that woman. Then there came into his mind an evil thought, and he said to himself: "If someone, man or devil, would do something so that I might take sexual pleasure with this woman, then would I serve even the devil."

And coming to such an idea, as if he had lost his mind, he continued walking through the field, but a short distance behind him he heard a voice that called him by name. He turned around and saw a youth who was dressed in fine garments and was running swiftly toward him, entreating him with his hand to wait. And the youth came up to Savva. It must be said that this was not a youth, but the enemy and the devil who searches for ways to destroy human souls.

The youth came up to Savva and, after they had bowed to each other, said: "Brother Savva. Why did you run from me? I have awaited you a long time, hoping that you would come to me and would have brotherly love for me. I have known you for a long time, and I know that you are of the Grudtsyn-Usov family of the city of Kazan. And if you wish to know me, I may say that I am also from the city of Great Ustiug. And since, by birth, I can be considered your brother, you should become my brother and friend from this time on. And never leave me, so that I can be of help to you in all things."

Savva, hearing such words from his false brother, that is to say, from the devil, became very happy to find a relative in such a distant and unknown land. And they kissed each other with love and went together through the wilderness. And the devil said to Savva: "Brother Savva, wherefore do you grieve? Why do you destroy your youthful beauty?"

Savva avoided the questions, however, telling him that he was afflicted by a malady.

The devil cunningly smiled and said: "Why do you conceal the truth from me? I know your ailment, but what would you give me if I were to cure you of it?"

And Savva answered: "If you actually know the affliction I bear in my heart, then I shall believe that you can help me."

The devil replied: "In your heart you long for the wife of Bazhen Vtory, since you are deprived of her love. What would you give me if I once more united you with her and she once more loved you?"

Savva answered: "In such a case, I shall give you all the merchandise and wealth of my father and all my profits! Only cause me to be once more with this woman."

The devil laughed and retorted: "Why do you tempt me? I know that your father actually is very rich. But you are not aware that my father is seven times richer than yours. What are your goods to me? Only give me a short note, and I shall fulfill your desire."

The youth was very happy, thinking to himself: The wealth of my father will remain intact, and I shall give him the letter and write whatever he wants.

The youth did not know what misfortune he was bringing upon himself. Actually, he did not read or write well. O the madness of youth! Thus he was ensnared by a woman's treachery and, for her sake, he was going to the devil.

Hardly had the devil spoken these words about the letter, when the youth happily promised to give him the letter. The false brother, that is to say, the devil, quickly took paper and ink from his pocket, gave them to the youth, and ordered him to write the letter. Savva still did not fully know what he was writing, but began to write senselessly. And by this letter Savva renounced Christ, the True God, and gave himself in the service of the devil. Having written the letter in which he rejected God, he gave it to the devil, his false brother.

Thus, they both arrived in Orel. Then Savva asked the devil: "Tell me, my brother, where you live, so that I may know your house."

The devil laughed, and said: "I have no particular house anywhere, but wherever it is convenient, there do I spend the night. However, if you wish to see me often, look always for me in the Horse Market, since I sometimes live there when buying horses. Now, go to the shop of Bazhen, and I know that you will be gladly invited to live in this house."

Savva, following the words of his brother, the devil, happily ran to Bazhen's shop. Bazhen, upon seeing Savva, eagerly invited him into his house, saying to him: "Master Savva! What wrong have I done you? Why did you leave my house? I pray you, come back now and live in my house. I am truly happy, for the love of your father, to have you here as if you were my own son."

Hearing such words from Bazhen, Savva was overcome with joy, and quickly entered Bazhen's house. And when the youth had entered, the wife, being incited by the devil, met him with joy and greeted him, giving him a welcoming kiss. The youth was ensnared in the woman's flattery, that is to say, by the devil, and was once more drawn into the sinful net with that accursed woman. From that time on, he remembered neither the holy days nor Sundays. He lost his fear of God, and wallowed with her constantly in the sin of lechery, as if he were a swine.

After quite a time had passed, there came a rumor to Savva's mother in the city of Kazan to the effect that her son was living an unrighteous and sinful life and that the father's wealth that was with him had all been squandered in lechery and drunkenness. Hearing such things about her son, the mother began to grieve profoundly, and wrote him a letter in which she urged him to return to his father's house in the city of Kazan. When the letter arrived, he read it, and laughed, paying it no heed. The mother sent him a second and a third letter in which she besought and entreated him to return home immediately from Orel to the city of Kazan. Savva, however, did not obey his mother's commands and entreaties, but, paying no heed to anything, continued only to persevere in his sinful passions.

Some time later, the devil took Savva and went with him

beyond the city of Orel into the fields of the countryside. As soon as they had left the city, the devil said to Savva: "Do you know who I am? You were fully convinced that I am of the Grudtsyn family, but it isn't so. Now, out of love, I shall reveal the truth to you. Don't be afraid, and be not ashamed to call me your brother, for verily I do love you as a brother. But if you wish to know who I am, I am the son of a king. Let us go farther, and I shall show you my glory and the wealth of my father!"

Having said these words, he led Savva to a certain hill and showed him a fine city a short distance away. Its walls and roofs were of pure gold, and gleamed.

And the devil said to Savva: "This city is the work of my father. Let us go and bow down before my father. And now, take the letter you gave to me and present it to my father, and you will be given a great honor by him."

And having said these words, the devil returned the letter in which Savva had renounced God.

O the madness of youth! Didn't he know that there was no kingdom near the Muscovite state that was not under the sway of the tsar? If only he had made the sign of the cross, then all these devilish temptations would have vanished like a shadow.

When they approached this chimerical city and came up to the city gates, they were met there by youths with dark faces and in vestments and belts decorated with gold. These youths bowed to them, rendering honor to the king's son, who was actually the devil, and also greeting Savva. When they entered the courtyard of the king's palace, they were met there by more youths, who wore still more brilliant raiment than the first ones they had met. And these youths also bowed to them. Then they entered the king's palace and were met by still more youths, who surpassed each other in their proud dignities and their magnificent vestments. And they also rendered honors to the king's son and to Savva.

Entering the palace, the devil said: "Brother Savva, wait here for me awhile. I shall go and announce you to my father, and I shall later take you to him. When you appear before him, think of nothing and have no fears; only give him the letter." Having said this, he passed into the inner chambers, leaving Savva alone. In a short while he returned, came to Savva, took him by the hand, and led him before the Prince of Darkness. The Prince of Darkness was sitting on a high throne embellished with gold and jewels. He was distinguished by his proud glory and his magnificent raiment. Round his throne, Savva noticed a large number of winged youth, the faces of some being blue, while the faces of others were red, and still others had faces as black as pitch. Savva appeared before the king, fell to the floor, and genuflected before him.

The king asked him: "From whence do you come? What is your plight?"

The senseless youth presented him with his God-rejecting letter, and said: "I have come, great King, to serve you."

That ancient serpent, Satan, accepted the letter, read it, turned toward his dark-faced warriors, and said: "Although I accept this youth, I know not whether he will remain faithful to me." Then he summoned his son, Savva's false brother, saying to him: "Go to another room, and have dinner with your brother."

Both bowed to the king, went to another room, and began to dine. They were served unimaginably aromatic dishes, and the same kind of drink. Savva marveled, and said that he had never partaken of similar dishes or of similar drinks in his own father's house.

After the meal, the devil took Savva, and together they left first the king's courtyard and then the city. And Savva asked his brother, the devil: "Tell me, brother, who were those winged youths who surrounded your father's throne?"

The devil smiled and answered: "Aren't you aware that many nations serve my father—the Indians, the Persians, and many, many others. Don't wonder about this and don't hesitate to call me your brother. From now on I will be your younger brother. However, when I tell you to do something, you must obey me. And I shall render you all kinds of good services."

Savva promised to be obedient, and the devil became so confident that, when they had arrived back in the city of Orel, he left Savva alone and went away. Savva still went to the house of Bazhen Vtory and continued to indulge in his sinful lechery.

In the meantime, Savva's father, Foma Grudtsyn, returned to Kazan from Persia, having been very successful in his business. As usual and as is due, he gave a kiss to his wife and then inquired about their son, asking whether he were still alive. And she answered him, saying: "I have heard from many people about him. After you left for Persia, he went to Solikamsk, and from there to the city of Orel. And since then, he sins and, as people say, has squandered all our wealth and has dissipated his health in drunkenness and in lechery. And on many occasions I have written him asking that he return home from there. But not once has he answered my letters, and so I don't know whether he is alive or not."

Hearing this from his wife, Foma was in a quandary. Then he

sat down and penned a letter to Savva, beseeching him to return
without delay to the city of Kazan. "I would like, my child," he
wrote, "once again to see your handsome face, for I haven't seen
you in a long time."

Savva, having received and read the letter, paid it no heed
and did not even think of returning to his father. He wished
only to indulge in his insatiable lust. Foma, seeing that his letter
had accomplished nothing, ordered boats and goods prepared
for sailing, and began his travels to Solikamsk, telling his wife:
"I shall myself look for our son, and bring him back to our
home."

As soon as the devil learned that Savva's father was traveling
to Solikamsk, he decided to take Savva from Orel. So he told
Savva: "Brother Savva, how long are we going to remain in this
small town? Let us visit other cities and have a good time there.
Then we can return here."

Savva did not contradict him, but said: "You are right,
brother. Let us go. But we should wait for a short while, since
I want to obtain some money for my merchandise."

But the devil prevented him from doing so, and said: "Haven't
you looked upon my father's glory? Aren't you aware that he
has estates everywhere? Wherever we go, we shall have as much
money as we need."

Thus they left the city of Orel, and their departure was known
to no one, neither to Bazhen Vtory nor to Bazhen's wife. In one
night Savva and the devil covered the distance of two thousand
miles, from the city of Solikamsk to the city of Kozmodemiansk [4]
on the river Volga. And the devil said to Savva: "In case you
should meet someone you know, and this person should ask
from whence you have come, you should answer that you came
from Solikamsk and have spent three weeks traveling to this
place." And Savva did as he was told, following the devil's order.

They passed several days in the city of Kozmodemiansk, and
then the devil and Savva covered the distance from the city of
Kozmodemiansk to the village of Paul's Ferry (Pavlov Perevoz)
on the river Oka in one night. They arrived there on Thursday,
which was the market day. Walking through the market, Savva
noticed a very old beggar who stood dressed in repulsive rags.
This man observed Savva carefully, and then began to weep.
Savva left the devil's side for a short time and went up to the
old man, wishing to learn what caused him to cry. Approaching

---

[4] The city of Kozmodemiansk is located on the upper Volga, north
of Moscow.

the old man, Savva asked him: "Wherefore do you grieve? Why
do you weep so incessantly?"

And the beggar, who was a holy elder, answered: "My child,
I cry because you have lost your soul. You don't realize that you
have lost it, but you have voluntarily turned to the devil. Do
you know, my child, with whom you walk and whom you call
your brother? It is not a man, but the devil who walks with you
and who hopes to bring you to the very pit of hell."

As soon as the old man had spoken these words, Savva turned
toward his false brother, or, better to say, to the devil. The
devil was standing a short way from him and was threatening
Savva and gnashing his teeth. The youth left the holy elder and
went up to the devil. The devil began abusing him, and said:
"Why do you talk with such an evil destroyer of souls? Aren't
you aware that this base elder has brought many people to their
downfall? He noticed your Sunday clothes and wanted to win
you by flattery, to take you away from the crowd, and then to
strangle you with a cord and steal your clothes. You will be lost
without me, if I abandon you."

After saying these words, the devil took Savva from that
village. He went with him to a city called Shuya,[5] and they
remained there together for a time.

In the meantime, Foma Grudtsyn came to the city of Orel
and began inquiring about his son's whereabouts, but no one
was able to give him any information. Everyone had seen his
son in the city before Foma had arrived, but then he suddenly
disappeared without telling anyone of his departure. Some said
that the son was frightened by the father's arrival, because he
had squandered his father's wealth, and had therefore disappeared. Especially astounded by Savva's departure were Bazhen
Vtory and his wife. And Bazhen told Foma: "He spent the night
at our place and the next morning he went away. We waited
for him to come to dinner, but since that morning he has not
reappeared in this city. And neither myself nor my wife knows
where he has disappeared to."

Foma shed many tears, and lived for a time in Orel waiting
for his son, but since his expectations went unrequited, he
returned home. And he told of the unhappy case to his wife.
Together they grieved and lamented the disappearance of their
only son. Foma Grudtsyn grieved for a long time, and then he
entered into his Father's House. And his wife remained a widow.

While the devil and Savva were living in the town of Shuya,

---

[5] The city of Shuya is located between Moscow and Nizhny Novgorod (which is now called Gorky).

the pious and great sovereign, Tsar, and Grand Duke, Michael Fedorovich, the Autocrat of All the Russias, sent his army against the city of Smolensk [6] to fight the King of Poland. According to the tsar's decree, soldiers were to be recruited throughout all Russia. For the recruiting of such soldiers, *Stolnik* Timothy Vorontsev was sent from the city of Moscow to Shuya. And he recruited soldiers and drilled them every day according to military regulations. Savva and the devil used to go and watch the drills. Once the devil told Savva: "Brother Savva, would you like to serve the tsar? Let us volunteer for the army."

Savva answered: "Well, brother, you are right. Let us serve." And so they joined the ranks of the army and began to go together for drilling. The devil gave Savva such a talent for military studies that he very soon surpassed the old soldiers and even the commanders. The devil himself served as Savva's orderly, and cared for Savva and carried his weapons.

When these recently recruited soldiers were transferred from Shuya to Moscow, a German colonel continued their training.[7] When this colonel came to inspect the newly recruited soldiers during drill, he noticed a very young man who behaved most properly, who acted by the regulations, and who was faultless in his military deportment, and who surpassed many old soldiers and commanders in his studies. He was astounded by Savva's acumen, called him aside, and inquired about his background. Savva told him the whole truth. The colonel took a liking to Savva, called him his own son, and gave him his hat, decorated with precious stones, from off his head. And he entrusted to Savva three companies of recruits. And so Savva began to drill and to instruct them in place of the colonel.

The devil secretly approached Savva and told him: "Brother

---

[6] The city of Smolensk, some 250 miles west of Moscow, was an important fortress on the Russian-Polish frontier in the seventeenth century. It was lost to Poland during the Time of Troubles. In the years 1632 to 1634, Russia was at war to win back this important city. The Russian armies were under the command of Boyar B. M. Shein. The author erroneously called him Feodor Ivanovich Shein. Tsar Michael Fedorovich, the first Romanov to be tsar, reigned from 1613 to 1645.

[7] Since the sixteenth century, the Russians had begun hiring foreign instructors to drill and equip their armies according to the requirements of contemporary military science. They preferred to hire German and English instructors because they were Protestants and not Roman Catholics. They preferred Protestants because Russia was constantly at war with Poland, which for centuries had been an outpost of Catholic expansion.

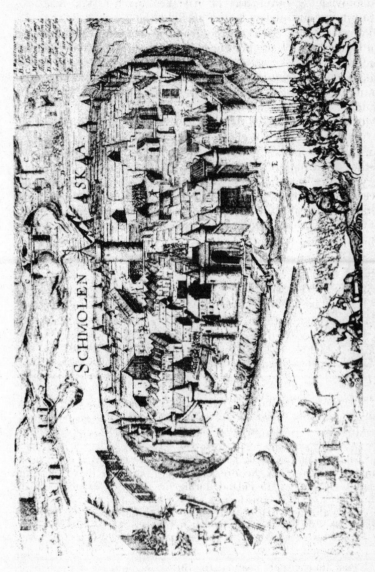

The siege of Smolensk by the Poles, 1604–1610. An early seventeenth-century engraving.

Savva, in case you don't have sufficient money to pay your soldiers, tell me and I shall bring you as much as you need, so as to prevent complaints and dissatisfaction among your troops."

And all Savva's soldiers were always quiet and peaceful, while in other companies there were complaints and disorder because the soldiers were dying of starvation and from the lack of clothing and provisions. Among Savva's troops the soldiers were peaceful and well organized, and everyone marveled at Savva's acumen.

Once, the tsar himself learned of Savva. At that time in Moscow was the very powerful boyar and brother-in-law of the tsar, Simeon Streshnev.[8] When this boyar learned of Savva, he ordered that he be brought to him.

When Savva came, Boyar Streshnev asked him: "My youth, do you want to be received in my house and to receive considerable honors from me?"

Savva bowed and replied: "I have a brother, my lord; I will ask him. If he orders me to do so, I will serve you with pleasure." The boyar had no objections, and permitted Savva to go and ask his brother.

When Savva came and told everything to his false brother, the devil, the devil answered him angrily, saying: "Why do you wish to disregard the tsar's service and become a servant of the tsar's servant? You are now in an important position and you have become favorably known to the tsar. No, you mustn't do this, but let us rather serve the tsar. When the tsar learns of your faithful service, you will be promoted by him to the higher ranks."

By the order of the tsar, all recruits were distributed among the regiments of *streltsy*[9] in order to swell their ranks. Savva was quartered in the city at the house of Jacob Shilov, a *streltsy* captain of the Zimin regiment. His house was located in the Ustretenka neighborhood of the Earthen City. This captain and his wife, who were pious and decent people, highly respected Savva for his acumen.

The regiments were readied in Moscow for the campaign, when one day the devil came to Savva and told him: "Brother Savva, let us go ahead of the regiment to Smolensk to see what

---

[8] Boyar Simeon Streshnev was a well-known Russian statesman of the second half of the seventeenth century. The author of this tale erroneously ascribed to him an active part in the first half of the seventeenth century.

[9] *Streltsy* (sing., *strelets*) were professional infantrymen who were armed with muskets, halberds, and sabers. This standing infantry was first organized by John IV.

the Poles are doing there, how they have fortified the city, and what kind of weapons they have." In one night they went from Moscow to Smolensk. Coming there, they remained in the city for three days and three nights, being invisible. There they saw and inspected all things and saw how the Poles were fortifying the city and how they were placing grenades in the places of possible storming. On the fourth day in Smolensk, the devil revealed himself and Savva to the Poles. Upon seeing them, the Poles became alarmed and began to chase after them, trying to catch them. The devil and Savva escaped from the city, fled to the river Dnieper, and the river parted before them and they crossed the river as if it were dry. The Poles opened fire on them, but did not succeed in injuring them. And they marveled, saying: "They, who have sojourned in our city, are demons in men."

However, Savva and the devil returned to Moscow and once again were quartered with this same Captain Shilov. When, at the tsar's command, the regiments marched from Moscow against Smolensk, this Savva and his brother went with the soldiers. The commander over all regiments was Boyar Feodor Shein.

On the way to Smolensk, the devil told Savva: "Brother Savva, when we arrive in Smolensk a giant Polish knight will ride out from the city, and will challenge one of our soldiers to a joust. Don't fear him, but go against him. I know and I assure you that you will defeat him. The next day there will come another giant from the Polish ranks who will seek to joust. Once again you must go against him, and I know that you will defeat him also. When the third day comes, the third Polish knight will ride forth from Smolensk. Don't fear him, but go against him, and you will defeat him. You will be wounded by him, but I shall cure you of your wounds." So Savva was advised. And the regiments came to the city of Smolensk and set up camp in a good place.

As the devil had said, there rode forth from the city of Smolensk a most terrifying warrior who rode on his horse and looked through the Muscovite ranks for an adversary. But no one dared to oppose him. But then Savva announced that he would do so, saying: "If I had a good, spirited steed, I would go to fight against this enemy of the tsar." And when his friends heard of this, they told his intentions to the boyar. The boyar ordered that Savva be brought before him and that he be given a good steed and a weapon, but the boyar thought that the youth would perish at the hands of such a terrifying giant. Then Savva, as he was ordered by his brother, the devil, galloped against this Polish knight, quickly defeated him, and brought him and his horse to the Muscovite regiments. And Savva was praised by all.

The next day there rode forth from Smolensk another glorious warrior who was in search of an adversary among the Muscovite armies. And once more Savva rode out, and defeated the knight. And everyone was stunned by his daring. However, Boyar Shein became wroth with Savva, but he concealed his rage in his heart.

On the third day, there once more came a warrior from the city of Smolensk, and this knight was more glorious than the previous two, and was looking for an adversary. Although Savva was afraid to ride against such a terrifying warrior, he followed the devil's order and immediately rode against him. And then this Pole furiously charged Savva and wounded him in his left thigh with his lance. Savva recovered, however, charged this Pole, killed him, and brought his body and horse into the Russian camp. He terrified the Poles in Smolensk, while the entire army was stunned. Then the Polish sortie commenced, army clashed against army, and the battle began. And the flank of the Russian army, in which Savva fought with his brother, was winning, and the Poles turned their backs, and fled. The devil and Savva killed an endless number of Poles, but they themselves were not injured by anyone.

When Boyar Shein learned of the courage of this youth, he could no longer conceal the wrath in his heart, but summoned Savva to his tent, and asked him: "Tell me, my youth, from which family are you and whose son are you?" And when Savva told him that he was the son of Foma Grudtsyn of Kazan, the boyar began to abuse him with all kind of crude words, and told him: "Why did you need to take part in such mortal combat? I know your father and your relatives. They are immensely wealthy. What is the reason for your forsaking your parents' home to come here? Was it persecution or poverty? I tell you, don't delay any longer, but return to the house of your parents and remain there, living in abundance with your parents. If you don't obey, and I hear about you once more and learn that you have remained here, then you will perish without mercy. I will order that you be beheaded!" Saying this to the youth, the raging boyar left him. And the youth left the tent in great sadness.

When he had left the tent, the devil asked him: "Why are you troubled about this? If people do not want our services here, we shall return to Moscow and live there." And soon after, they left Smolensk for Moscow, and there they continued to live in the house of Captain Jacob Shilov. The devil spent the day with Savva, while in the evening he would go to his abode in hell where he dwelt according to the ancient evil customs.

After a considerable length of time, Savva fell ill, and his illness was so severe, he was at death's door. The wife of the captain was a wise, God-fearing woman. She cared for Savva and told him on many occasions that he should summon a priest so that he might take Holy Communion and confess his sins. "You should do this," she said, "for you may die suddenly without having had the last rites."

Savva rejected her advice because, as he said, "My illness is certainly grave, but not fatal." His condition worsened from day to day, and the captain's wife incessantly urged him to take the last rites, because, as she said, "You may die without having taken them."

Finally Savva was forced by this God-loving woman to summon a priest. The captain's wife sent for a priest from the Church of St. Nicholas which is located in the Rooks' neighborhood. The priest came to the ill man without delay. He was of a mature age, with great experience, and was very devout. When he came to the bedside of the ill man, he began to pronounce prayers before Confession, as is the custom. When the other people had left the room, the priest began to confess the sick man.

Suddenly Savva noticed that the room had become filled with a multitude of demons. His false brother, who was actually the devil, came with these demons, but this time he was not in the image of man, but in his true bestial form. The devil, who remained behind the crowd of demons, was in a frenzy of rage, gnashing his teeth, and showing Savva the God-rejecting letter Savva had given him in the vicinity of Solikamsk. And the devil told the ill man: "Look at this, you perjurer, do you realize what it is? Did you write this or do you believe that by repenting you can escape us? Oh, no, don't think that, for I will move against you with all my forces." And the devil told him this and other evil threats. The sick man evidently heard them and was at first frightened, but later he relied upon the power of God and confessed everything in great detail to the priest. The priest, although he was a man of the holy life, also became frightened, since no one but he and Savva were in the room. And he was deafened by the great uproar that came from the multitude of demons, and only with great difficulty did the priest finish confessing the sick man. Then he left for home without saying anything to anyone.

After the confession, the evil spirit assaulted Savva and began to torture him mercilessly. One minute the devil was beating him against the wall; another minute he was throwing him from the couch to the floor; then he throttled him until Savva began to gasp and foam came from his mouth; then he tortured him with many different kinds of torture. The aforementioned captain, who was also a pious man, saw with his wife that the youth was assaulted and tormented by the devil. And they grieved and bemoaned the fate of the youth, but were unable to help him in any way. From day to day the assaults and torments of the devil became fiercer, and those who witnessed them were terrified.

The master of the house, who saw the unusual fate of this youth and who realized that, because of his courage, the youth was known to the tsar himself, decided with his wife to inform the tsar. They decided to do it because they had a close relative in the tsar's palace. As soon as the man had decided this, he sent his wife to her relative, telling her to inform the relative about everything and asking that she inform the tsar immediately. And he added: "In case the young man dies in such miserable plight, there may be litigation for not having informed the tsar."

His wife, without delay, hastened to her relative and told her exactly what she was ordered to say by her husband. Hearing these words, her relative was profoundly moved, grieved over the fate of the youth, and became sad at the situation of her relatives, fearing that this matter might bring them trouble. Therefore, without any delay, she went from her house to the tsar's palace and told the members of the tsar's court of these happenings. When the tsar heard about this youth, he showed mercy on him. He told the courtiers who were before him to send two sentries to the house of the captain where the sick man lay, whenever the daily changing of the sentries took place.

The tsar said: "They should watch over this youth with care so as to prevent him from killing himself by throwing himself into the fire or into the water, when he loses his senses because of the demons' torments."

And the pious tsar ordered that meals be sent daily to the sick man, and asked that the sick man appear before him in his palace as soon as he was cured. And so it was done. However, the sick man remained for a long time under the devil's sway.

The first of July arrived, and on those days the youth was particularly tormented by the devil. Finally he fell asleep, and while he was sleeping he began to talk as if he were awake and he shed tears from his exhausted eyes. And he said: "O Most Merciful Lady, Queen and Holy Virgin, have mercy upon me,

Portrait of a Russian boyar.
A seventeenth-century painting.

Our Lady, the Queen of Queens. I do not lie, I do not lie, but I shall do as I pledge."

The members of the captain's household and the sentries who watched him were astounded when they heard these words spoken by sick Savva, and they said: "He has a vision."

When the sick man woke from the sleep, the captain came to him, and said: "Tell me, lord Savva, what kind of words did you speak while shedding tears in your sleep?"

And tears flowed steadily from Savva's eyes, and he said: "I saw that my couch was approached by a Lady from whom emanated light, and who shone with indescribable grace, and who was wearing a purple vestment. With her were two men distinguished by their venerable white hair. One of them was in an archbishop's vestment, while the other was wearing the robes of an Apostle. And I believe that they were none other than the Holy Virgin, the friend of the Lord, John the Theologian, and Metropolitan Peter, the ever vigilant guardian of our city, Moscow, and the most glorious archbishop of bishops. I know well their images from the icons. And the Lady from whom emanated light said: 'What has happened to you, Savva? Why are you so full of sorrow?'

"And I said to her: 'I am full of sorrow, my Lady, because the Son of our God is wroth with me, and because you, the Intercessor for the Christians, are wroth with me.' And, smiling on me, she said: 'What do you think? How can you escape such a plight? How can you get your God-rejecting letter from hell?' And I told her: 'It cannot be done, my Lady, except with the succor of your Son and through your infinite mercy.' And she told me: 'I shall implore my Son and God in your behalf; only, you must follow to the word what I shall tell you. I shall deliver you from this misfortune, if you will decide to take monastic vows.'

"And so I vowed to her tearfully in my dream, and these were the words that you heard. And then she told me: 'Listen, Savva! On the holy day of my icon in my cathedral of the icon of Kazan, come to my church that is on the main square in the vicinity of the Rag Market. And then I shall perform a miracle for you in the presence of all.' And after this, she became invisible."

The captain and the sentries who kept watch over Savva marveled greatly upon hearing his words about his vision. And the captain and his wife began to ponder how they should inform the tsar of this vision, and decided to send their relative to inform the courtiers in the tsar's palace and let them tell of the vision to the tsar. When the aforementioned relative came

to the captain's house, they told her of Savva's vision. When she
learned of this, she went immediately to the tsar's palace in
order to inform the courtiers in the tsar's palace and to let them
inform the tsar of Savva's vision. When the tsar learned of it,
he marveled greatly.

When, on July 8th, the Holy Day of the Icon of the Blessed
Virgin of Kazan arrived, there was a church procession with
holy icons and sacred crosses from the Cathedral of the Assumption of the Holy Virgin to the Holy Virgin of Kazan. In this
procession participated the great sovereign, tsar, and grand
duke, Michael, the holy patriarch, with the bishops, and a great
many courtiers. And the tsar ordered that sick Savva be brought
to this church. Then, by the tsar's order, the ill man was rapidly
brought on a carpet to the Church of the Holy Virgin of Kazan
and was laid before the entrance to the church.

When the holy Mass began, ill Savva was assaulted by the
evil spirit, and the devil began to torment him ferociously, and
Savva called in a loud voice: "Help me, my Lady and Holy
Virgin! Help me, my Queen of Queens, the Mother of God!"
And when the choir began to sing the Song of the Cherubim,
people heard a sound like thunder, and there came a voice announcing: "Savva! Get up and come into my church!"

Then he got up from the carpet on which he had been
brought, as if he had never been ill. He quickly came into the
church, fell on his knees before the Icon of the Blessed Virgin
of Kazan, and prayed, shedding tears. At the same moment
there fell from the cupola of the church the God-rejecting letter
of Savva that he had given to the devil at Solikamsk. And all
writing was erased from the letter, as if nothing had ever been
written there. And then the same voice repeated: "Savva! Here
is the letter you wrote, and now fulfill my commandment, and
don't commit the sin of disobedience." And he arose, picked
up the letter, and, shedding tears, spoke in a loud voice before
the icon: "O Most Blessed Mother of God, Intercessor for all
Christians, who prays for us to her Son and to our God, absolve me of my sins and save me from the very pit of hell. And
I will fulfill what I have pledged."

When the tsar, the patriarch, and all who were there heard
this and witnessed this most marvelous miracle, they thanked
God and his Most Holy Mother, and greatly marveled about
such divine mercy that had delivered him from the very pit of
hell. And, after the Divine Liturgy, they began to glorify God,
and the entire clergy gave a service of thanksgiving for the
miracles that were performed before all.

Thereafter, the church procession with the holy icons and

sacred crosses left the church and went to the cathedral. And the tsar returned to his palace rejoicing over this miracle, and thanking God. And Savva returned in good health to the house of the aforementioned Captain Shilov, and never again did he suffer from his disease. The captain and his wife saw this, marveled greatly, and thanked God for his great mercy for all men.

Savva remained living for a short time in the house of the captain. Then he distributed all his wealth to the poor and to the churches, and left for the Monastery of the Miracle of Archangel Michael, which is called the Miracle Monastery and which is located in the vicinity of the Cathedral of the Venerable and Glorious Assumption of the Most Holy Virgin. There he took his monastic vows, and remained laboring, fasting, and praying incessantly and thus pleasing God. There he lived for many years, and passed to the Lord in peace. And he was buried in this monastery.

62. FROL SKOBEEV, THE ROGUE

Hardly any work of Russian seventeenth-century literature reflects so strikingly the drastic changes in both the way of life and the mentality of the Muscovite Russian as does the tale of *Frol Skobeev, the Rogue*. This story reveals the thorough secularization of Muscovite writings and the break with the traditions of the Age of Faith. The religious and moralistic tone in literature have vanished altogether. The solemn, ornate style, with an abundance of archaic Old Church Slavonic words, has given place to colloquial Russian and simple, short sentences. The subject itself of a rogue portrayed against the background of everyday Russian life was completely novel in Russian literature at that time, and the description of Frol Skobeev's life lacks the traditional clichés that dominated earlier biographical and hagiographic works. Amorous and erotic motifs now make their appearance. This work is a bitter satire on the new man who is shown as a rogue and cunning operator, and whose final success announced a new age for both Russian society and literature.

In some versions of this tale, the action takes place around 1680, the time when the customary barriers between the old, aristocratic boyars and the new gentry were crumbling, and the anonymous author gave the names of actual historical personages to his characters. The Skobeevs were small provincial squires of that time. Lovchikov actually did belong to the court and was a *stolnik* in the 1670s and 1680s. Only the name of

Ordyn-Nashchekin, a famous statesman and diplomat during
the reign of Tsar Alexis Mikhailovich, was slightly modified to
Nadrin-Nashchekin. Still, it appears that the plot does not depict
actual happenings, but reflects rather the new atmosphere and
social trends in Muscovite Russia.

The present translation follows the oldest extant version of
this tale, a manuscript written in the late seventeenth century
and published by M. Skripil in *Russkaia povest XVII veka,*
Moscow, 1953, pages 155–166.

Some interesting passages indicating the further development
of satirical and erotic themes in later versions of this tale have
been interpolated from a manuscript published by N. K. Gudzy
in *Khrestomatiia po drevnei russkoi literatury,* Moscow, 1956,
pages 415–425. These interpolated passages have been placed
in brackets.

In the district of Novgorod there lived the nobleman Frol
Skobeev. In the same district were the estates of *Stolnik* [1]
Nadrin-Nashchekin; and the *stolnik's* daughter, Annushka, was
living at these Novgorodian estates.

Frol Skobeev, learning about the *stolnik's* daughter, came to
the decision that he should marry her as soon as possible. But
since he could not get to meet her, he decided to become acquainted with the steward of estates of Nadrin-Nashchekin. And
so he began to visit him at his home. Some time later, Frol Skobeev happened to be at the steward's home when Annushka's
nurse came to this steward. Frol Skobeev learned that the nurse
lived with Annushka. When the nurse left to return to her mistress' home, Frol followed her and gave her a present of two
rubles. And the nurse said to him: "My lord Skobeev, the favor
you show me is beyond my service, for I haven't yet rendered
you any service." And returning home to her mistress, the nurse
said nothing to her of this matter. Frol spent a time at the
steward's house, and then went home.

When the time of the Christmas holidays arrived, during
which there is much merrymaking and the girls often have pre-
texts to pass the time gaily, the daughter of *Stolnik* Nadrin-
Nashchekin, Annushka, told her nurse to go to all noblemen who
had young daughters and whose estates were in the vicinity and

---

[1] *Stolnik:* an important rank at the Russian court in Moscow. At
official banquets and receptions the *stolniks* served the tsar at the
table. They usually were members of the aristocracy, and were often
high officials in various governmental agencies or commanders in the
army.

ask them to come to Annushka's party and have some fun. The
nurse went and asked all the daughters of noblemen, and they
all promised to come to Annushka's party. Since the nurse knew
that Frol Skobeev had a young sister who was unmarried, she
went to Frol's house and asked his sister to come to *Stolnik*
Nadrin-Nashchekin's house, to Annushka's party. The sister told
the nurse: "Wait a moment and I will go and ask my brother.
Then I will tell you what he has decided."

The sister went to Frol and told him: "The nurse of *Stolnik*
Nadrin-Nashchekin's daughter has arrived, and asks that I come
to Annushka's party."

Frol Skobeev told his sister: "Go and tell this nurse that you
will go, but with another girl, a nobleman's daughter."

The sister pondered on what her brother had told her to tell
the nurse. However, she did not dare to disobey her brother,
and told the nurse that she would go that very evening with the
daughter of another nobleman. Then the nurse returned to her
mistress, Annushka.

In the meantime Frol Skobeev began to speak with his sister,
saying: "Well, sister, it is time for you to get dressed to go to
the party." When his sister began to don feminine attire, Frol
ordered her: "Sister, bring me also a girl's attire. I shall don it,
and we shall go together to Annushka, the *stolnik's* daughter."

The sister was very much afraid that people might recognize
him, and then certainly there would be much trouble for her
brother, for the *stolnik* was much liked by the tsar. Still, she did
not dare to disobey her brother, and she brought him the attire
of a girl. Frol, having dressed himself as a girl, went with his
sister to Annushka, the *stolnik's* daughter.

There had already gathered many daughters of noblemen,
but no one was able to recognize Frol in his feminine attire.
Then the girls began to play parlor games, and enjoyed themselves. Frol also played the games, and was not recognized by
anyone. Finally Frol left the room for his needs, and was accompanied through the corridor by the nurse, who carried a
taper. On leaving, he told her: "Oh, my dear nurse, there are
many girls here, and many of them ask services of you, but none
of them would give you any gift for such services." Still the
nurse did not recognize him. Then Frol gave her five rubles,
which she accepted gratefully.

Seeing that the nurse still did not recognize him, Frol fell
on his knees and explained to her that he was a nobleman, Frol
Skobeev, and that he had come in feminine attire so that he
might marry Annushka. When the nurse realized that he really
was Frol Skobeev, she became frightened and did not know

what to do. Still, remembering both of his generous gifts, she said to him: "Well, my lord Skobeev, I am ready to do everything you may ask, in view of your gracious generosity."

Returning to the place where the girls were enjoying themselves, she spoke not a word about Frol Skobeev, but soon after she told her mistress: "Well, girls, you have had enough of these games. I suggest you play another game, one that was played when I was young."

Annushka did not wish to disobey her nurse, and said only: "Well, my dear nurse, we shall play the games according to your desires."

And the nurse told them of her game, saying: "Please, dear Annushka, play the role of the bride." Pointing to Frol Skobeev, she said: "And this girl will be the bridegroom." And then she led the two into a nice chamber, to the bed, as a bride and bridegroom are usually led after the wedding. The girls accompanied them to the bedroom and then, leaving the two alone, went to the rooms in which they had been playing their parlor games. And the nurse ordered the girls to sing loudly so that they might not hear any cries coming from the bedchamber. And Frol Skobeev's sister was very much afraid, fearing that her brother might get into trouble.

Lying with Annushka on the bed, Frol told her that he was a nobleman, Frol Skobeev, from the district of Novgorod, and not a girl. Annushka was seized by great fright. But Frol, despite the fact that he was himself afraid, became daring and forced her to submit to his will. Thereafter, Annushka begged Frol not to bring shame upon her by telling of this to others. Later on, when the nurse and the girls returned to the chamber where Frol and Annushka were, they realized from Annushka's expression that something had happened. [Annushka had undergone a tribulation she had never before experienced.] However, the girls still did not recognize Frol Skobeev, for he was again in feminine attire. But Annushka took her nurse by the hand, led her away from the girls, and said to her: "What have you done to me! The one who was with me was not a girl. He is a man, Frol Skobeev."

However, the nurse answered: "I tell you the truth, my gracious lady, when I say that I was not able to recognize him. I thought that he was a girl like the others. If he has committed such a shameful deed, we can kill him and hide his body in some secret place, for we have plenty of servants."

But Annushka took pity on Frol Skobeev [because she had begun to care for him, having lain with him in the bedchamber]. And she told the nurse: "Well, nurse, let it be this way, for never again shall I regain my chastity."

Thereafter, all the girls, as well as Frol Skobeev, went to the reception room, and all enjoyed themselves until late into the night. Afterward, all the girls went to bed. And Annushka went to bed with Frol Skobeev [telling herself, "I wouldn't be able to find a better girl with whom to sleep." And they enjoyed themselves throughout the night with carnal pleasures. And since that time a profound pity for Frol Skobeev dwelt in Annushka's heart. And only with great sorrow did she part from Frol Skobeev.].

In the morning, when everyone had got up, the girls returned to their homes. Frol Skobeev also wanted to leave with his sister, but Annushka, who permitted all the others to go, kept Frol Skobeev in her house. Frol Skobeev remained at Annushka's house for three days, always in feminine attire, so that he might not be recognized by the house servants. And he and Annushka enjoyed themselves, and only after three days did Frol go home with his sister. Before leaving, Annushka gave Frol three hundred rubles. Frol [returned home, overjoyed, and from that time the destitute Skobeev became richer, and began to live like a wealthy man and] began to have banquets with his fellow noblemen.

Some time thereafter, *Stolnik* Nadrin-Nashchekin wrote from Moscow that Annushka should come to Moscow because there were many noble young men, sons of *stolniks,* who were seeking her hand in marriage. [Although Annushka was most unwilling to do so,] she did not want to disobey her father. And so she soon left for Moscow. And when Frol Skobeev learned that she had gone to Moscow, he became confused, knowing not what he should do. Although he was a nobleman, he was quite poor, and made his living working in Moscow soliciting litigations at the court.[2] He decided [to mortgage his estate, which was just a wasteland, and] to go to Moscow in order to take Annushka as wife. He began to make preparations for his trip to Moscow, although his sister was greatly grieved, not wanting him to go.

Frol Skobeev [took leave of his sister and] said: "Dear sister,

---

[2] These solicitors were not formally trained, for there were no formally educated lawyers in Muscovite Russia. The functions of lawyers were performed by professional legal solicitors who represented their clients at the court and in governmental agencies. Many of these solicitors, however, gained positions of great influence in government administration.

don't grieve over anything. Maybe I will lose my life, but I will not give up Annushka. I will be either a colonel or a corpse. If things happen according to my plans, I will not leave you in need. However, in case misfortune occurs, please don't forget me in your prayers." And having made all the preparations, Frol went to Moscow.

Arriving in Moscow, he took quarters in the vicinity of *Stolnik* Nadrin-Nashchekin's mansion. The next day Frol Skobeev went to Mass, and in the church he met Annushka's nurse. After the liturgy was over, Frol Skobeev left the church and awaited the nurse. When the nurse came out from the church, Frol Skobeev approached her, bowed deeply, and asked her to announce his arrival in Moscow to Annushka. [The nurse promised to support him.] Coming home, she told Annushka about Frol's arrival. Annushka became very happy, and told her nurse to take him twenty rubles when he went to Mass the next day. And the nurse did as she was told.

Stolnik Nadrin-Nashchekin had a sister who had taken vows in the Maiden's Convent.[3] Once the *stolnik* went to visit his sister in the convent. When he came there, the sister met him with all due honors. And the *stolnik* passed a long time with his sister. They had many conversations, and once the sister asked the brother to permit her niece to visit her, since she had not seen her niece in many years. *Stolnik* Nadrin-Nashchekin promised to permit his daughter to visit her at the convent. The sister added: "I would only ask you to give the necessary order in your home so that your daughter may come whenever I send my carriage, even if you yourself are not at home."

Some time later, *Stolnik* Nadrin-Nashchekin and his wife had to go to visit some friends, and he ordered his daughter: "In case my sister, your aunt, should send her carriage from the convent, please go to her." And he then went with his wife to visit the friends.

Annushka asked her nurse to go immediately to Frol Skobeev and to tell him that he should procure a horse and carriage as soon as possible and come to her house, saying that he was sent from the Maiden's Convent by the *stolnik's* sister for Annushka. The nurse went to Frol Skobeev and repeated the commands of her mistress.

When Frol Skobeev heard this, he didn't know what to do and whom to deceive in order to obtain a carriage, for all noble aristocrats knew that he was a poor nobleman and a great cheat,

---

[3] The Maiden's Convent: the proper name of a convent in the vicinity of Moscow.

able only to solicit litigations. But he thought of a certain *stolnik* named Lovchikov who had always been very kind to him. Therefore he went to this Lovchikov and had a long talk with him. Finally Frol began to beg Lovchikov to lend him his carriage and horses [so that he might go and look for a fiancée. Giving in to his requests, Lovchikov lent him his carriage and a coachman.]. Frol went to his quarters and gave the coachman drinks until he was completely stupefied. Then he dressed himself in the lackey's clothes, sat on the coach box, and went in the carriage to the home of *Stolnik* Nadrin-Nashchekin to get Annushka. There he was recognized by Annushka's nurse, who told Annushka that her aunt had sent her carriage for her from the convent. Annushka readied herself, sat in the carriage, and went to Frol's quarters.

In the meantime Lovchikov's coachman had awakened, and Frol, realizing that the coachman was not sufficiently drunk, gave him more to drink. He then put him in the carriage, sat on the coach box, and returned to Lovchikov's mansion. Arriving there, Frol opened the gate, drove the carriage into the yard, and left it there. When Lovchikov's servants found the carriage in the yard and the coachman inside, stupefied from drink, they went to Lovchikov and told him that the carriage was in the yard and that the coachman was dead drunk. Yet no one could learn who had brought the carriage and horses into the yard. *Stolnik* Lovchikov ordered the putting up of the horses and carriage in the stables, and added: "It's all right. At least the horses were not sold. What can one expect from Frol Skobeev?" In the morning Lovchikov asked the coachman where he went with Frol Skobeev, and the man answered: "I remember that we went to his quarters, but I do not actually know where I drove and what I did."

Soon afterward *Stolnik* Nadrin-Nashchekin returned from his friends and asked to see his daughter. He was told by the nurse that Annushka, by his order, had gone to the convent to his sister, since the sister had sent her carriage for her. Nadrin-Nashchekin answered, "Well, that's all right."

Thinking that his daughter lived with his sister in the convent, Nadrin-Nashchekin did not go for a while to his sister. In the meantime Frol and Annushka married. When Nadrin-Nashchekin finally did go to see his sister at the convent, and passed some time there without seeing his daughter, he remarked to his sister: "Well, sister, I haven't seen Annushka here." The sister answered: "Brother, don't joke. What can I do if you don't honor my requests? I asked you to send her to me, but ap-

parently you don't trust me. As for myself, I haven't had time
to send my carriage for her."

Stolnik Nadrin-Nashchekin replied: "My dear lady and sister,
of what are you speaking? I don't understand a thing you have
said, because Annushka left for your convent a month ago when
you sent the carriage and horses after her. At that time I was
visiting friends with my wife. She was permitted to go, as I
ordered it so."

But the sister explained: "Brother, I have not sent a carriage
and horses for her, and neither has Annushka ever been in this
place."

Nadrin-Nashchekin grieved profoundly for his daughter, and
cried bitterly, for she had vanished without leaving the slightest
trace. Returning home, he told his wife that Annushka had disappeared and was not at the convent with his sister. And then
he began to question the nurse, asking who had come and with
whom Annushka had left. The nurse answered: "A coachman
came with a carriage and said that he had come from the
Maiden's Convent for Annushka. And Annushka left with him,
according to your order."

The *stolnik* and his wife were greatly grieved, and wept
bitterly. The next morning the *stolnik* went to the tsar to tell
him that his daughter had vanished into thin air. The tsar
ordered that the disappearance of the *stolnik's* daughter be
made public, and he made the following pronouncement: "In
case someone is keeping her secretly and does not come forward
and admit it, this man will be sentenced to death when she is
found."

Hearing this, Frol Skobeev didn't know what to do. Finally
he decided to go to *Stolnik* Lovchikov, for this *stolnik* had always been good and kind toward him. When Frol came to
Lovchikov, they had a long conversation during which Lovchikov asked, "Have you taken a bride?" And when Frol answered
that he had, the *stolnik* asked: "And did you marry a wealthy
wife?"

Frol answered: "Up to now I haven't seen much wealth, but
we shall see what the future holds."

And *Stolnik* Lovchikov told Frol: "Well, Mr. Skobeev, now
you must start living in upright ways. Stop soliciting. It would
be much healthier if you were to live in your own domain."
Thereafter, Frol began begging *Stolnik* Lovchikov to intervene
for him.

Lovchikov answered: "Well, if it is a decent cause I shall
intervene for you, but if it is something dishonest, don't be
angry with me."

Frol then revealed to Lovchikov that he had married *Stolnik* Nadrin-Nashchekin's daughter and that she was staying at his place.

Lovchikov answered: "You did this on your own, so accept the responsibility for it on your own."

But Frol threatened: "If you don't intervene for me, you also may be made responsible! I can testify against you, since you lent me the carriage and the horses to take her away. If you hadn't lent them to me, I wouldn't have been able to do it."

Lovchikov became very confused, and answered: "You are a real rogue! What are you trying to do to me? How can I intervene for you?" And then he suggested that Frol should go on the next day to the Cathedral of the Assumption of the Holy Virgin, for Nadrin-Nashchekin would be there for the Mass.[4] "After the Mass," he continued, "all of us will be standing together at St. John's Square. In this moment come and fall before the feet of Nadrin and tell him about his daughter. And I shall try to intervene on your behalf."

Frol Skobeev went the next morning to the Cathedral of the Assumption of the Holy Virgin and saw that *Stolnik* Nadrin-Nashchekin and several other *stolniks* were praying there. All of them, as was their wont, gathered after Mass before the Bell Tower of John the Great[5] in John's Square. Nadrin-Nashchekin talked of his bereavement caused by the disappearance of his daughter. Lovchikov discussed the matter with him and was trying to convince him that he should be merciful no matter what happened. While they were talking, Frol Skobeev approached them and bowed to the *stolniks*, as was his custom, since they all knew him. Paying no heed to the others, Frol Skobeev fell to the feet of Nadrin-Nashchekin and began begging for forgiveness, saying: "My merciful lord and the first of the *stolniks!* Forgive me my guilt as if I were your humble slave who had daringly made an altercation with you!"

Nadrin-Nashchekin was already of advanced age and therefore had poor eyesight, and so could not recognize the man before him. He then drew Frol up with the handle of his cane, and asked: "Who are you? Tell me about yourself. What do you want from us?"

---

[4] In the seventeenth century the Cathedral of the Assumption of the Holy Virgin, which is located in the Kremlin, was in the center of the area of Muscovite governmental agencies.

[5] The Bell Tower of John the Great is the highest of the campaniles in the Kremlin. It was built by John IV, and, like the Cathedral of the Assumption of the Holy Virgin, was in the center of the area of governmental agencies.

But Frol repeated only, "Absolve me of my guilt."

Lovchikov came nearer, and said: "Before you stands Frol Skobeev, a nobleman who asks you to absolve him of his guilt."

Then Nadrin-Nashchekin exclaimed: "Get up, you rogue! For a long time have I known you, you rogue and knave! Tell me what has happened, you scoundrel! So you have once more got yourself into a predicament. If it is not too bad, I will help you. But if it is really base, then do as you want. For a long time I have told you, rogue, to live decently. Now get up and tell what is your evildoing."

Frol got up from before the *stolnik's* feet and informed him that his daughter was at his place and that he had married her. Having heard that his daughter was Frol's wife, the *stolnik* began to sob, and lost consciousness. When he had slightly recovered himself, he began to rage: "What have you done, rogue? Do you know who you are? Who are you? Your evildoing cannot be forgiven. How could you, such a rogue, dare to wed my daughter? I will go to the sovereign and ask that he punish you for this offense which is such a great affliction for me, you rogue!"

Lovchikov, for the second time, came near Nadrin-Nashchekin and tried to convince him not to go to the tsar, saying: "You had better go home and explain this to your spouse and then do your best as you both shall decide. You cannot undo what is already done. And he, Frol Skobeev, can find no shelter from your wrath."

Stolnik Nadrin-Nashchekin followed the advice of Lovchikov, and took his carriage and went home. In the meantime Frol Skobeev went to his house and told Annushka: "Well, Annushka, I don't know what will become of us. I have told your father of our marriage."

Stolnik Nadrin-Nashchekin came home, went to his wife's chambers, and, bitterly weeping and sobbing, told her: "My wife, my wife! Do you know what? I have found Annushka!"

And the wife asked him: "And where is she, Father?"

And Nadrin-Nashchekin told his wife: "That thief, rogue, and knave, Frol Skobeev, has married her."

When his wife heard these words, she knew not what to do, but only grieved deeply for her daughter. And both of them began to weep bitterly and to reprove their daughter. And knowing not what they should do, they cursed their daughter. When they had become calm, they began to ponder, and they deeply regretted the fate of their daughter. Finally they decided: "We must send a servant to learn where this rogue lives and if Annushka is still alive or not." And so they summoned a servant and ordered him to find the house of Frol Skobeev and to learn about Annushka and whether she was still alive and eating well.

When the servant came to the house of Frol Skobeev and Frol noticed that a man from his father-in-law's house had come into the yard, Frol told his wife to go to bed and to behave as if she were very ill. Annushka did as her husband willed. When the man, who was sent by her parents, entered the house and bowed deeply, as was the custom, Frol asked him: "What man are you and what is your business?" The man told Frol that he was sent by *Stolnik* Nadrin-Nashchekin to find out whether Annushka was in good health or not.

And Frol Skobeev told him: "Do you see, my friend, what kind of health she enjoys? This is the result of her parents' wrath, for, as you know, they reprimand her and curse her. They should at least give her their blessing."

The man bowed, left Skobeev, and returned to his master, *Stolnik* Nadrin-Nashchekin. And the *stolnik* asked him: "Did you find their quarters? Did you find Annushka? Is she alive or not?" The man answered that Annushka was very ill and would hardly remain alive much longer. And he asked them to send their blessings to their daughter. The *stolnik* and his wife grieved deeply and pondered what they should do with this rogue and knave.

Finally, the mother spoke: "Well, my friend, there is little we can do. Apparently God himself has willed that such a rogue be our daughter's husband. We, my friend, must send them the icon with our blessings. When our hearts become more merciful, then we shall see them." And they took down from the wall an icon decorated with gold and precious stones that were worth five hundred rubles. And they sent it with a servant, directing him to tell Annushka to pray to it and to tell Frol Skobeev not to sell the icon and then squander the money.

The servant took the icon and went to Frol Skobeev's house. Frol Skobeev saw the man coming, and told his wife: "Get up Annushka!" She got up and sat down with Frol. The servant entered the room and gave the icon to Frol. The latter accepted it, put it in its due place, and told the servant: "Such is the power of parental blessings. As soon as they had sent their blessings, God helped Annushka, and she recovered. And now, thanks be to God, she is in good health."

The servant returned to his master, told him that he had given the icon to Annushka, that her health had much improved, and that Annushka thanked her parents. The man then went to his lodgings.

Stolnik Nadrin-Nashchekin began to deliberate with his wife concerning their daughter. And they became sorry for her. The mother asked: "What should we do, my friend? Certainly this rogue will starve Annushka. How can this dog provide for her, when he himself is hungry? We must send her some provisions in a six-horse carriage." And so they sent provisions and a list of such to Frol Skobeev. Frol ordered that the provisions be put in an appropriate place without looking at the list. And he ordered the *stolnik's* servant to thank the parents for such gifts.

And from that time, Frol Skobeev lived like a wealthy man, and often visited important personages. And everyone wondered about Frol Skobeev and how he could have dared to carry through this affair.

Only a month later did the hearts of the parents become merciful to Frol and his wife. And they sent a man to them asking that they come to their house for dinner. And the man came and asked that they come that very day for dinner. And Frol answered the man, saying: "Report to the father that we are ready to come today to his grace." Frol and his wife dressed and went to the house of Frol's father-in-law, *Stolnik* Nadrin-Nashchekin. And when they came to the father-in-law's house, Annushka went to her father and fell before the feet of her parents. When Nadrin-Nashchekin and his wife saw their daughter, they began reprimanding her and visited their parental wrath upon her. But looking upon her, they began to weep bitterly because she had married against the will of her parents. Finally, their wrath subsided and they forgave her and ordered that she sit with them. But to Frol Skobeev they said: "And you, rogue, why are you standing? Sit down here. How can you, such a rogue, be married to our daughter?"

But Frol answered only: "Well, my lord and father, it was the will of God." And all sat down at the table, but *Stolnik* Nadrin-Nashchekin ordered the servants not to admit any visitors to the house, saying: "In the event that someone does come and asks if the *stolnik* is home, tell them that he is not, since I do not want to have other people see that we are eating with our son-in-law, that knave and rogue, Frol Skobeev."

After the meal, the *stolnik* asked: "Well, rogue, how will you make your living?"

And Frol answered: "Well, you know that better than I. I know only how to make my living by soliciting litigations."

And the *stolnik* told Frol: "Well, rogue, stop your soliciting. In the district of Simbirsk I have an estate on which there are three hundred peasant families. You, rogue, can have it for your own, and live there permanently." Then Frol Skobeev and his wife bowed deeply and thanked the parents for this gift. But the *stolnik* said: "Don't bow, rogue. Better that you prepare the deeds to this domain."

Frol and Annushka remained only a short while longer at the parents' home, and then left. But on their way, *Stolnik* Nadrin-Nashchekin ordered that they return, and asked: "Well, rogue, how will you get supplies? Do you have any money?"

Frol answered: "Well, my father, you yourself know what kind of money I have, but perhaps I should sell the peasants on this estate."

Stolnik Nadrin-Nashchekin replied, saying: "No rogue, don't sell them. I shall give you some money. Take it." And he ordered that three hundred rubles be given to him. Frol Skobeev took the money and returned to his quarters.

Some time later he received the deeds to this estate. *Stolnik* Nadrin-Nashchekin eventually was to make Frol Skobeev the heir of all his capital and domains. After the death of his father, Frol Skobeev married off his sister to the son of another *stolnik*, while Annushka's nurse remained living with Annushka and her husband in great honor to the end of her days.

D. POETRY

63. IVAN FUNIKOV: MESSAGE OF A NOBLEMAN
TO A NOBLEMAN

AT THE end of the last century N. K. Nikolsky accidentally found an interesting letter from a Russian nobleman, Ivan Funikov, to one of his friends, probably another local noble landowner. From its text it can be deduced that the letter was written around 1607 during the Time of Troubles, in the region of the central Russian city of Tula, south of Moscow. It relates the hardships of Funikov, apparently taken prisoner by his rebellious peasants, who, after the fall of the first false Dmitry, became organized under a cunning, daring, and able serf, Ivan Bolotnikov.

In the main part of this letter, written in hilarious rhymed verse, Funikov jokes about his misfortunes. This rhymed missive is probably the oldest-known example of ironical verse in Russian literature and it strongly resembles the later recorded jokes and couplets of the popular jesters, the *skomorokhs*. Funikov makes light of his hardships and adventures, and from his own admissions it appears that he was an enterprising Casanova being punished primarily for his conquests of the peasant girls. Part of the letter follows the *skomorokh's* tonic couplet, based on three main stresses per line, also characteristic of Russian folk songs. The rhymed endings, however, are unusual for Russian folklore and probably reflect either *skomorokh* jokes or the influence of Western verse, which began to penetrate Russia in the Time of Troubles.

The text of this letter is taken from I. I. Smirnov's book, *Vosstanie Bolotnikova 1606–1607*, Moscow, 1951, pages 541–543. The beginning and the end have not been translated because they are not versified and are written in the conventional epistolary style. For convenience the original line structure has been somewhat modified.

. . . Now I live dolefully, in straitened condition,
but I never, milord, forget your generous disposition.
But, milord, the Tula brigands
so mutilated my hands
that now by their looks
they are not unlike hooks.
And then, thrown into a cell,

I was forced there to dwell,
and narrow was my cot
and grief and melancholy were my lot.
And a burlap mat was sent,
but my sleep was not content.
Nineteen weeks sat I there,
looking out from that cell,
but the muzhiks, like loathsome Polacks,
led me twice to the executioner's ax.
For indiscretions at some former hour,
they wished to throw me from the tower.
And I was tortured with torments well conceived,
but the truth from me they ne'er received.
"Tell the truth," they say,
"and lie in no way."
And on my knees, what's more,
I fell to the floor and to them swore:
"I have no rye,
I cannot lie,
yea, verily, forsooth,
I speak the truth."
But my story they do not believe,
and from their tortures I find no reprieve,
but, alas, their evils could not be mitigated
and my hide not once, but twice, with the knout was lacerated.
And, sinner that I am, God knows,
milord, from my plight know I no repose.
Bathing is foolish,
the bathhouse-keeper mulish,
my body was stripped
and I was cruelly whipped.
Shedding tears like rain
could naught assuage my pain.
Show me, milord,
how to heal myself again,
and I shall with even great ardor
pray for you God's beneficence
that he will strengthen you, yea, lord,
and so do ever hence.
And seeing my name in your handwriting,
my eyes brimmed with tears,
and I was astounded by the strength
of your wisdom at such young years.
And thanks to your kindness, having supped on fish at Prince
    Ivan's board,

I prayed to my God for you again, milord.
And waking and sleeping, indeed, so I always do,
and thus, to repay your kindness, do I pray to God for you,
and everyone says: "See," they say, "what good he does."
To write a great deal am I sorely tempted,
but because of the great trouble I am nearly demented.
Torn to pieces and all of a heap
ruined completely and white as a sheep.
Not a single possession was left me to keep,
and they burned down my estate to the very last board.
The soldiers reaped all the rye
and away they did fly.
Now, living in a cellar, round a homemade stove we do huddle
    for heat
and only remnants of boot-legs are on our feet,
and even these are worn to a shred.
God is my witness, milord, they left not a thread,
or horse, or cow, or even a handful of seed
for the making of bread.
All I had left was one old cow,
and even she wasn't well somehow.
God clearly sees
we're on our knees.
He well doth know
our affairs are low.
God commanded we should bear it out
and not grieve and not pout.
But to you, milord,
I appeal,
calling your name,
without fear or shame,
I most humbly bow . . .

64. MISERY-LUCKLESS-PLIGHT

The origin of *Misery-Luckless-Plight* has not been exactly
determined, and it is of mixed genre. Found in a single copy
that apparently was prepared in the eighteenth century, this
tale-poem, in its content, philosophy, and language, belongs to
the middle of the seventeenth century, when the problem of
religious regeneration became so acute during the period of the
movement of the Seekers After God (see Selection 59) and the
Great Schism. Its theme is the salvation of a sinner. The story
is in blank verse, and seems to have been written by a man well
acquainted with both the ancient Russian tradition and oral

folk poetry. The use of recurrent descriptions, its imagery, and repetition of traditional nature symbols and metaphors (for example, "The youth flew as a clear falcon," or "Misery after him as a gray hawk") relate the work to both the written and folklore traditions. The meter of four stresses is close to that of the historical *bylina*, and the psychological depiction of the prodigal young man seems to indicate that the author was familiar with religious literature. The writer's originality lies in the fact that his portrayal of the youth is distinctly different from the stereotyped characterizations of hagiographic writers.

For the present edition Leo Wiener's translation of the poem has been used. For readability, however, it has been divided into songs and stanzas, and the original Russian verse form has been retained. The translation has been partially revised.

I. THE NATURE OF MAN

By the will of the Lord, our God, and our Savior,
Jesus Christ, Almighty
from the beginning of the age of man.
In the beginning of this passing age
God created heaven and earth,
God created Adam and Eve.
He ordered them to live in holy paradise,
and gave them this divine command:
He told them not to eat the fruit of the grapevine,
from the great tree of Eden.

But the human heart is unthinking and unruly,
and Adam and Eve were tempted.
They forgot God's command,
ate of the fruit of the grapevine,
from the great and wonderful tree,
and for that great transgression of theirs,
God's wrath rose against Adam and Eve.
And God drove Adam and Eve from the holy paradise of
    Eden.
He settled them upon the lowly earth,
blessed them that they might grow and multiply,
and told them to appease their hunger through their own
    labor
from the fruits upon earth.

God gave them this commandment:
there should be weddings and marriages
for the propagation of the race of men,

and for having beloved children.
But the human heart was senseless and disobedient;
from the very start it was not submissive,
looked with disdain at the father's instruction,
did not obey the mother,
was untrue to the advice of friends.

Then there came a weak and wretched race
that turned to reckless deeds
and began to live in turmoil and wrong,
and discarded humility of spirit.
And God grew wroth with them,
and imposed great calamities upon them,
and permitted that great misery be accorded to them,
and immeasurable shame,
evil plight,
fiendish visitations,
and evil, immeasurable nakedness,
and endless poverty and extreme want.
And he did it to humble us, to punish us,
to lead us on the path of salvation.
Such is the nature of man from his very birth from father and
   mother.

II. PARENTS' ADMONITION

The youth had reached the age of discretion and absence of
   wantonness.
His father and mother loved him much,
and they began to teach and instruct him,
to prepare him for good deeds:

> "Dear child of ours,
> listen to your parents' instruction,
> listen to their saws,
> good and cunning and wise,
> and you will not be in want,
> you will not be in great poverty.
> Go not, child, to feasts and carousings;
> do not seat yourself on a high place;
> drink not two beakers at once;
> be not tempted by good, beautiful women, fathers' daugh-
>   ters.
>
> "Lie not down in the backyards.
> Fear not the wise man;
> fear the fool

lest the fools lay hands on you
and take off your costly garments,
and cause you great shame and dishonor,
and expose you to the scorn and empty prattle of men.
Go not, my child, to the dice-players and innkeepers,
and keep no company with tavern-goers.
Make no friends with the foolish and simple.
Steal not, rob not,
nor deceive, nor tell a lie, nor do wrong.
Be not tempted by gold and silver;
collect not unrighteous wealth.

"Be not a witness to false swearing,
and think no evil of father and mother
or any other man—
that God may protect you from all evil.
Dishonor not, child, the rich and the poor,
but regard them all alike.
Keep company with the wise and sensible,
and make friends with friends you may rely upon,
who will not deliver you to evil."

III. THE EMANCIPATION

The youth was then young and foolish,
not in his full senses, and imperfect in mind;
he was ashamed to submit to his father
and bow before his mother,
but wanted to live as he listed.
If the youth earned fifty rubles,
he found easily fifty friends,
and his honor flowed like a river;
the youth gained many friends for himself,
and they accounted themselves of his race.

And the youth had a trusted friend:
he named himself his plighted brother,
and he tempted him with tempting words;
he called him to the tavern yard,
led him into the hall of the inn,
brought him a cup of good wine,
handed him a beaker of heady beer,
and spoke to him the following words:

"Drink, my bosom friend, brother of mine,
to your joy and happiness and health.
Empty the cup of good wine

and follow it by a glass of sweet mead.
And if you drink, brother, until you be drunk,
lie down to sleep where you have drunk—
depend upon me, your plighted brother.
I shall sit down and keep watch over you:
at your head, dear friend,
I shall place a beaker of sweet mead,
by your side I shall place good wine,
and near you I shall place heady beer,
I shall watch well over you, dear friend,
and shall take you back to your father and mother."

At that time the youth depended
on his plighted brother; he did not wish to disobey him.
He settled himself near the heady drinks,
and emptied a cup of green wine,
followed it by a glass of sweet mead,
and he drank also the heady beer.
He drank until he lost his senses,
and where he had drunk, there he fell asleep;
he depended upon his plighted brother.

The day was inclining toward night
and the sun was in the west,
when the youth awoke from his sleep.
The youth looked all around him;
all the costly garments had been taken from him,
his shoes and stockings were all gone,
his shirt even was taken from him,
and all his property was stolen.
A brick was lying under his unruly head;
he was covered with a tavern sackcloth,
and at his feet lay ragged shoes;
at his head his dear friend was no more.

And the youth stood up on his bare feet
and began to clothe himself:
he put on the ragged shoes,
covered himself with the tavern sackcloth,
covered his white body
and washed his white face.
Sorrow entered the youth's heart,
and he spoke the following words:

"Though God has granted me a good life,
I have now nothing to eat or drink!
Since my money is gone,

even the last half-farthing,
I have not a friend,
not even half a friend.
They no longer account themselves of my race,
all my friends have disappeared!"

IV. THE EXPATRIATION

The youth felt ashamed to show himself
before father and mother,
and his race and family,
and to his former friends.
He went into a strange, distant, unknown land.
He found a court, a town in size,
and a house in that court, a palace in height.
In that house was given a splendid feast;
the guests drank, ate, and made merry.

The youth came to the splendid feast,
made the sign of the cross over his white face,
bowed before the miraculous icons,
made his obeisance to the good people
on all four sides.

And when the good people saw the youth,
how well he made the sign of the cross,
how he acted according to the written rule,
they took him by the hands,
seated him at the oaken table,
not in the best place, nor in the worst,
they seated him in a middle place,
where the younger guests were seated.

And the feast was a merry one,
and all the guests at the feast were drunk and merry and
    boastful;
but the youth sat, not merry at all,
gloomy, sorrowful, joyless,
and neither ate, nor drank, nor made merry,
nor boasted of anything at the feast.
Said the good people to the youth:

"Wherefore, O good youth,
do you sit, not merry at the feast,
gloomy, sorrowful, joyless;
you neither drink, nor make merry,
nor boast of anything at the feast.
Or has the cup of good wine not reached you,

or is not your seat according to your father's worth?
Or have small children insulted you?
Or are our children not kind to you?
Or foolish and unwise people made light of you, youth?"

But the good youth remained sitting, and said:

"My lords and good people!
I will tell you of my great misfortune,
of my disobedience to my parents,
of my drinking at the inn, about the cup of mead,
the tempting drinking of heady wine.

"When I took to drinking the heady wine,
I disobeyed both father and mother;
their blessing departed from me;
the Lord grew wroth with me
and to my poverty were added
many great and incurable sorrows
and sadness without comfort,
want, and misery, and extreme wretchedness.

"Want has tamed my flowery speech;
sadness has dried up my white body.
For this my heart is not merry,
and my white face is sad, and my eyes dim.
I have lost my paternal honor,
and my youthful valor has left me.
My lords and good people!
Tell me and teach me how to live in a strange land,
among strange people,
and how to find dear friends!"

Said the good people to the youth:

"You are a sensible youth!
Be not haughty in a strange land;
submit to friend and foe,
bow to old and young,
tell not of the affairs of others,
neither what you hear nor see.
Flatter not friends or enemies;
have no tortuous fits,
nor bend as a cunning snake;
be humble before all
but withal keep to truth and right—
and you will have a great honor and glory.
When people will find you out

> they will respect and honor you
> for your great truth,
> your humility and wisdom—
> and you will have dear friends
> who will call themselves your plighted brothers."

V. TEMPTATIONS OF MISERY-LUCKLESS-PLIGHT

And the youth went hence into a strange land
and began to live wisely,
and through his great wisdom acquired greater wealth than
    before.
He looked out for a bride according to custom,
for he wished to marry.
The youth prepared a splendid feast,
according to his father's worth
and as best he knew,
and invited the honored guests and friends.
But through his own sin,
by God's will and the devil's temptation,
he boasted before his honored guests
and friends and plighted brothers.
A boastful word is always rotten,
and self-praise brings the destruction of man.
"I, a youth, have gained more possessions than ever!"

Misery-Luckless-Plight heard the young man's boasting
and spoke the following words:

> "Young man, boast not of your fortune,
> praise not your wealth!
> I, Misery, have known people
> who were wiser and richer than you,
> but I, Misery, have outwitted them.
> When a great misfortune befell them,
> They struggled with me unto their death;
> they were worsted by their luckless plight—
> could not get away from me, Misery,
> until they took their abode in the grave,
> and I covered them forever with the earth.
> Only then they were rid of nakedness,
> and I, Misery, left them,
> though Luckless-Plight remained upon their grave."

And again it cawed ominously:

> "I, Misery, attached myself to others,
> for I, Misery-Luckless-Plight,

cannot live empty-handed; I, Misery,
wish to live among people
from whom I cannot be driven away with a stick;
but my chief seat and paternal home
is among the carousers!"

Spoke gray Misery the miserable:

"How am I to get at the youth?"

and evil Misery devised cunningly
to appear to the youth in his dream:

"Young man, renounce your beloved bride,
for you will be poisoned by your bride;
you will be strangled by that woman;
you will be killed for your gold and silver!
Go, young man, to the tsar's tavern,
save nothing, but spend all your wealth in drink;
doff your costly dress, put on the tavern sackcloth.
In the tavern Misery will remain,
and evil Luckless-Plight will stay—
for Misery will not gallop after a naked one,
nor will anyone annoy a naked man,
nor has assault any terrors for a barefooted man."

The young man did not believe his dream,
but evil Misery again devised a plan,
appeared as the Archangel Gabriel,
and stuck once more to the youth for a new plight:

"Are you not, youth,
acquainted with poverty and immeasurable nakedness,
with great paucity and dearth.
What you buy for yourself is money wasted,
but you, a brave fellow, will still survive!
They do not beat, or torture naked people,
or drive them out of paradise,
or drag them down from the other world;
nor will anyone annoy a naked man,
nor has assault any terrors for a naked man!"

VI. THE LAST TRIAL

The young man believed that dream:
he went and spent all his wealth in drink;
he doffed his costly dress,
put on the tavern sackcloth,
covered his white body.

The youth felt ashamed to show himself to his dear friends.
He went into a strange, distant, unknown land.
On his way he came to a swift river.
On the other side were the ferrymen
and they asked for money to ferry him across;
but the youth had none to give,
and without money they would not take him across.
The youth sat a whole day,
until evening, and all that day until compline
the youth had nothing to eat,
not even half a piece of bread.
The young man arose on his swift feet,
and standing, he fell to grieving,
and he spoke the following words:

> "Woe to me, miserable Luckless-Plight!
> It has overtaken me, young man,
> has starved me, young man, with a hungry death.
> Three unlucky days have I passed,
> for I, young man, have not eaten half a piece of bread!
> I, young man, will jump into the swift river:
> swallow my body, swift river!
> And eat, O fish, my white body!
> And that will be better than my shameful life;
> will I ever be able to escape the hands
> of Misery-Luckless-Plight?"

At that hour Misery leaped from behind a rock
near the swift river;
Misery was barefooted and naked
and there was not a thread upon it,
and it was girded with a bast thong,
and it called out with a mighty voice:

> "Wait, young man, you will not escape from me, Misery!
> Jump not into the swift river,
> nor be in your misery doleful!
> Though you live in misery, you need not be doleful,
> because a doleful man would die in misery!
> Remember, young man, your former life;
> how your father spoke to you, and your mother instructed
>   you!
> Why did you not then obey them?
> You would not submit to them,
> and were ashamed to bow to them,
> but wanted to live as you listed!

But he who will not listen to the good teaching of his
   parents
will be taught by me, Misery-Luckless-Plight!"

Luckless-Plight spoke the following speech:

"Submit to me, impure Misery;
bow before me, Misery, to the damp earth,
for there is no one wiser in the whole world than I,
   Misery;
and you will be ferried across the swift river,
and the good people will give you to eat and drink."

The young man saw his inevitable calamity,
and he submitted to impure Misery,
bowed before Misery to the damp earth!

The good fellow went ahead with a light step over the steep,
   fair bank,
over the yellow sand.
He went happy, not at all doleful,
for he had appeased Misery-Luckless-Plight.
And as he went, he thought a thought.
   "Since I have nothing,
   I need not worry about anything!"
And as the youth was not sorrowful,
he started a fair song,
a mighty, sensible song it was:

"Sorrowless mother has borne me:
with a comb she combed my little locks,
dressed me in costly garments,
and stepping aside shaded her eyes
and looked at me:
'Does my child look well in costly garments?
In costly garments my child is a priceless child!'
Thus my mother always spoke of me!
And then I learned and know it well,
that a costly gown cannot be made without a master,
nor a child be comforted without a mother,
nor a drunkard ever become rich,
nor a dice-player be in good renown,
and I was expected by my parents to be handsome
but was born to be penniless!"

The ferrymen heard the good fellow's song,
took the young man across the swift river,

and took nothing from him for the ferrying.
The good people gave him to drink and to eat,
took off his tavern sackcloth,
gave him peasant's clothes.
And these good people spoke to him:

> "You are a good fellow,
> so go to your home,
> to your beloved, respected parents,
> to your father and mother dear,
> take leave of your parents, father and mother,
> and receive from them the parental blessing!"

From there the youth went to his home.
When he was in the open field,
evil Misery had gone before him;
it met the youth in the open field,
and began to caw above the youth,
like an ill-omened crow above a falcon.
Misery spoke the following words:

> "Wait! you have not gone away from me, good fellow!
> Not merely for a time have I, Misery-Luckless-Plight,
> attached myself to you;
> I shall labor with you to your very death!
> And not I, Misery, alone, but all my relatives,
> and there is a godly race of them:
> we are all gentle and nice,
> and he who joins our family will end his days among us!
> Such is the fate that awaits you with us.
> Even if you were to be a bird of the air,
> or if you went into the blue sea as a fish,
> I would follow you at your right hand."

The youth flew as a clear falcon,
and Misery after him as a white gyrfalcon;
the youth flew as a steel-blue dove,
and Misery after him as a gray hawk;
the youth went into the field as a gray wolf,
and Misery after him with greyhounds;
the youth became the feather grass in the field,
and Misery came with a sharp scythe,
and Luckless-Plight railed at him:

> "You, little grass, will be cut down;
> you, little grass, will lie on the ground,
> and the boisterous winds will scatter you!"

The youth went as a fish into the sea,
and Misery after him with close-meshed nets,
and Misery-Luckless-Plight railed at him:

> "You, little fish, will be caught at the shore,
> and you will be eaten up and die a useless death!"

The youth went on foot along the road
and Misery at his right hand.
It taught the youth to live as a rich man by killing and
   robbing,
so that they might hang the young man for it,
or might put him with a stone in the water.
The youth bethought himself of the road to salvation
and at once the youth went to a monastery to be shorn a
   monk,
and Misery stopped at the holy gates—
and will no longer cling to the youth.

And this is the end of the story of life:
Lord, preserve us from eternal torment,
and give us, O Lord, the light of paradise!
Forever and ever, amen!

Three Poems from the Collection of
Baccalaureus Richard James

65. RAID OF THE CRIMEAN TATARS

In 1619 a young British scholar, baccalaureus Richard James,
visited Russia and brought back to England six short poems, or
songs, which he had transcribed phonetically in Russian, using
Latin letters. F. Buslaev, the first scholar to study and publish
them, believed that they were specimens of Russian folklore,
but contemporary scholars believe that all of the poems were
written by an unknown Russian poet of the early seventeenth
century. The use of rhymed verses, completely uncharacteristic
of Russian folklore of the time, their vocabulary—which betrays
an author well-versed in the Russian literary language—as well
as their subjects strongly confirm the latter opinion. The poems
reflect political events of the time, and one of them, "Ode on
the Return to Moscow of Filaret, Tsar Mikhail's Father," even
deals with an event that occurred in the same year as the tran-
scription of these poems.

The first is about the second raid against Moscow by the Khan of Crimea, Devlet Girey. In 1571 the Tatars of Crimea, under Khan Devlet, cleverly circled Russian armies guarding the access to Moscow and attacked and burned the Russian capital. Over a million Russians perished during this raid, and hundreds of thousands of prisoners were captured by the Tatars, later to be sold on the Middle Eastern and Mediterranean slave markets. In 1572 Devlet repeated his raid, but was defeated by Russian troops under Prince M. Vorotynsky. Out of a hundred and twenty thousand Tatar warriors, only twenty thousand returned home. The poem depicts the Tatars' hope of inflicting a final blow on Moscow and of conquering the other Russian cities. The "seventy Apostles" mentioned in the poem are the Muscovite churches, dedicated to seventy pupils of Christ, and the expression "Holy Fathers" refers to the churches dedicated to the three theologians of the early Christian Church: St. Basil the Great, St. Gregory the Theologian, and St. John Chrysostom (Golden Mouth).

The second poem voices the feelings and lament over her fate of Princess (Tsarevna) Xenia, the daughter of Tsar Boris Godunov. After the death of Tsar Boris, when the impostor, Pseudo-Dmitry, seized Moscow and became tsar, he abused the daughter of his enemy and then sent her to a convent in Ustyuzhna-Zheleznaia, in northern Russia, where she was forced to take monastic vows.

The last of the poems offered here from the James Collection is an ode glorifying the return from a Polish prison of Metropolitan Filaret (who soon became Patriarch), father of Mikhail Romanov, the first tsar of the dynasty that was to rule Russia until the revolution of 1917. Fedor (Filaret was his monastic name) Nikitich Romanov had been captured along with other Russian aristocrats by the Poles during the Time of Troubles, and only after the Russian-Polish armistice of 1618 was he permitted to leave the Polish-Lithuanian Condominium and return to Moscow.

The texts of the "Raid of the Crimean Tatars" and "Ode on the Return to Moscow of Filaret, Tsar Mikhail's Father" follow the translations by Leo Wiener, and the text of the "Lament of Boris Godunov's Daughter" is taken from W. R. Morfill's *Story of Russia*, New York and London, 1890. These texts have been revised by the editor of the present volume.

Not a mighty cloud has covered the sky,
nor mighty thunders have thundered:

Whither travels the dog, Crimea's khan?—
to the mighty Tsardom of Muscovy.
> "Today we will go against stone-built Moscow,
> but coming back, we will take Riazan."

And when they were at the river Oka,
they began their white tents to pitch.
> "Now think a thought with all your minds:
> Who is to sit in stone-built Moscow,
> and who is to sit in the city of Vladimir,
> and who is to sit in the city of Suzdal,
> and who will hold the old city of Riazan,
> and who will sit in the city of Zvenigorod,
> and who will sit in the city of Novgorod?"

There stepped forward Divi Murza, son of Ulan:
> "Listen, our lord, Crimea's khan!
> You, our lord, shall sit in stone-built Moscow,
> and your son in Vladimir,
> and your nephew in Suzdal,
> and your relative in Zvenigorod,
> and let the equerry hold old Riazan,
> but to me, O lord, grant Novgorod:
> There, in Novgorod, lies my luck."

The voice of the Lord called out from heaven:
> "Listen, you dog, Crimea's khan!
> Know you not the Tsardom of Muscovy?
> There are in Moscow seventy Apostles,
> besides the three Holy Fathers.
> And there is in Moscow still an Orthodox tsar."

And you fled, you dog, Crimea's khan,
not over the highways, nor the main road,
nor following the black banner.

66. LAMENT OF BORIS GODUNOV'S DAUGHTER

There weepeth a little bird,
a little white quail:
> "Alas, that I so young must grieve!
> They wish to burn the green oak,
> to destroy my little nest,
> to kill my little ones,
> to catch me, quail."

In Moscow the Princess weepeth:
> "Alas that I so young must grieve!
> for there comes to Moscow the impostor
> Grishka Otrepiev, the defrocked monk,

who wants to take me captive,
and having captured make me a nun,
to send me into the convent.
But I do not wish to become a nun,
to go into a monastery:
I shall keep my dark cell open,
to look at the fine fellows.
O our beautiful corridors!
who will walk over you
after our life as the tsar's family
and after Boris Godunov?
O our beautiful palace halls!
who will be sitting in you
after our life as the tsar's family
and after Boris Godunov?"
And in Moscow the Princess weepeth,
the daughter of Boris Godunov:
"O God, our merciful Savior!
wherefore is our Tsardom perished—
is it for father's sinning,
or for mother's not praying?
And you beloved palace halls!
who will rule in you,
after our life as the tsar's family?
Fine stuffs of drawn lace!—
shall we wind you around the birches?
fine gold-worked towels!
Shall we throw you into the woods?
fine earrings of hyacinth
shall we hang you on branches,
after our life as the tsar's family,
after the reign of our father,
glorious Boris Godunov?
Wherefore comes to Moscow the defrocked monk,
and wants to break down the palaces,
and to take me, princess, captive,
and to send me to Ustyuzhna Zheleznaia,
to make me, princess, a nun,
to place me behind a walled garden?
Why must I grieve,
as they take me to the dark cell,
and the abbess gives me her blessing?"

67. ODE ON THE RETURN TO MOSCOW OF
FILARET, TSAR MIKHAIL'S FATHER

The Tsardom of Muscovy was happy
and all the holy Russian land.
Happy was the sovereign, the Orthodox tsar,
the Grand Duke Mikhail Fedorovich,
for he was told that his father had arrived,
his father Filaret Nikitich,
from the land of the infidel, from Lithuania.
He had brought back with him many princes and boyars,
he had also brought the boyar of the tsar,
Prince Mikhail Borisovich Sheyn.
There had come together many princes, boyars, and
    dignitaries,
in the mighty Tsardom of Muscovy:
They wished to meet Filaret Nikitich
outside the famous white stone-built Moscow.
'Tis not the beautiful sun in its orbit—
'tis the Orthodox tsar that has gone out,
to meet his father dear,
Lord Filaret Nikitich.
With the tsar went his uncle,
Ivan Nikitich the boyar—
    "The Lord grant my father be well,
    my father, Lord Filaret Nikitich."
They went not into the palace of the tsar,
they went into the cathedral of the most Holy Virgin,
to sing a holy Mass.
And he blessed his beloved child:
    "God grant the Orthodox tsar be well,
    Grand Duke Mikhail Fedorovich!
    And for him to rule the Tsardom of Muscovy
    and the holy Russian land."

68. EPIC OF SUKHAN

One of the most interesting and important genres of Russian
folklore is the Russian heroic epic, known under the name of
starina, or *bylina* (happenings of the past). The *starina* glorified
either the heroes of the earliest period of Russian history—the
time of Prince Vladimir, who Christianized Russia and laid the
foundation of a Christian Russian state in the eleventh century,
or the heroes of Novgorodian Russia. The latter group of *starinas*

deals with a later period, the blossoming of the Novgorodian Republic in the fourteenth and fifteenth centuries.

It is not known exactly when the *starinas* originated. Some of their themes go back even farther than the time of Vladimir and are probably a survival of pre-Christian, pagan Slavic folklore. Most of the Vladimir cycle, however, probably dates from the eleventh to thirteenth centuries, taking its present form only in the fifteenth century. Russian folklorists started to record the *starinas* only in the middle of the eighteenth and early nineteenth centuries, when they were still widespread among the population of remote northern and eastern Russia. The tradition of the *starina* lasted until the early twentieth century and some of the most interesting were recorded in the region between Leningrad and the White Sea in the early Soviet period. The survival of the Russian epic tradition into modern times is very rare in Europe. Only in Serbia have the old heroic songs been preserved as long as in Russia.

The Kievan cycle of *starinas* centered around Prince Vladimir of Kiev, and resemble the Arthurian cycle. Both treat the defense of a Christian state against pagan invaders; both are centered around a Christian ruler; and in both the heroes (knights or *bogatyrs*) are often more heroic and valorous than the king or prince himself. The best known *bogatyr*-heroes of the Kievan cycle are Ilia Muromets, Olesha Popovich, and Dobrynia Nikitich, the last-named apparently having lived in the late tenth century, and he was probably Prince Vladimir's uncle. These valorous, fearless warriors, the dreaded fighters against the nomads, who acted largely as individuals, were known under the name "bogatyr." All nomadic invaders are called "Tatars" generally in the *starinas*.

Sukhan was a lesser *bogatyr*, but the *starina* of the following text is one of the oldest, probably written down in the midseventeenth century. It preserved very well the main characteristics of the *starina* style.

This text was discovered in 1948 by Vladimir I. Malyshev, Senior Research Associate of the Russian Academy of Sciences, and was published under the title, *Povest' o Sukhane*, Moscow-Leningrad, 1956, pages 135–139. The arrangement into rhythmic lines was done by Professor Malyshev.

In the city of Kiev
in the time of the elder Prince Monomakh Vladimirovich,
there was a rather old *bogatyr*,
more than ninety years old.

And he really liked the joys of falconry [1]
and did not quit this joy even in his later days.
It happened that he went with a red gyrfalcon
to the holiday of the Beheading of John the Baptist.
Before he arrived at the swift river Dnieper-Slautich [2]
he came upon many swans in a backwater.
And the *bogatyr* began to wonder at this:

> *"In this little backwater*
> *I came upon neither geese nor ducklings,*
> *but now I see many swans,*
> *and all of this has a reason.*
> *I will go, and go; I will see the swift river Dnieper-*
> *Slautich."*

And so Sukhan rode to the swift Dnieper-Slautich,
and already the Dnieper River was disappearing in the yellow
sands.
Sukhan stood, lost in thought.
At this time a man rode along the other shore,
and he dragged behind him a lance with a pennant
and he shouted in a loud voice:

> *"Thou, there, Sukhan Damantevich!*
> *Thou who art famous among the great bogatyrs of Kiev,*
> *you do not know what is happening in this place,*
> *already for nine days*
> *he has been moving across the swift Dnieper—*
> *he, Tsar Azbuk Tovruevich,*
> *and with him seventy princes,*
> *and with every prince*
> *there are seventy-two thousand men,*
> *not counting the right flank*
> *and the left flank and the forward guard.*
> *There are a good many people with him, countless*
> *numbers.*
> *And our ancestors served the princes*
> *and each spring they were ready for the Tsar's service,*
> *and this service was well known to you, bogatyr of Kiev."*

He spoke this word and went away.
Sukhan stood, becoming sorrowful,

---

[1] Falconry was one of the most popular sports in Old Russia. Tsar
Alexis Mikhailovich, the seventeenth-century ruler, particularly enjoyed it and wrote a book of rules for this noble sport. See Selection 76.

[2] A south Russian river, the Dnieper in this *starina* is given the
patronymic, "Slautich." The same name for this river is also found in
the *Lay of Igor's Campaign*. "Slautich" means "son of glory," from
"slava" ("glory").

and he let fly the gyrfalcon far away from his hand,
and he threw down the gauntlet to the ground.
The joys of falconry were lost to Sukhan,
and in their place there came the service to the Prince.

>And Sukhan said: *"Because of my sins I left my home*
>>*without arms,*
>*forgetting bows and sabers and all my military weapons.*
>*I should have gone to Kiev for military weapons—*
>*and so in Kiev the number of* bogatyrs *would have in-*
>>*creased,*
>*and so I would not have remained*
>*alone in my old age."*

And Sukhan rode to the green oak forest,
and came upon a fresh-green stump,
and he pulled it out with its roots,
and rode away without having time to clean it off.
And as he rides out of the green oak forest
he sees something white, but it is not the white stones of the
    mountains
but the armor of all those regiments.
And the *bogatyr* cannot count all the people.
The *bogatyr* began to pray to God:

>*"O Holy Lady, Mother of God!*
>*Appease my mad craving,*
>*Subdue my sinful heart.*
>*The pagans boasting with pride have come*
>*to capture the Russian land,*
>*to destroy the Christian faith,*
>*to demolish God's churches,*
>*to defile the holy places.*
>*O Holy Lady, Mother of God!*
>*Because of my sins I left without arms*
>*forgetting bows and sabers*
>*and all my military weapons.*
>*I have only a fresh-green stump,*
>*and I didn't even have time to clean it."*

And the *bogatyr* began to cry
and hot tears began to fall.

He began to shout, he charged them (the Tatars),
the oak-stump whistled in the *bogatyr's* hand,
the lances got broken,
the Tatar shields splintered,
the helmets shattered on the ground along with Tatar heads.

And the Tatars began to form a wagon-box.[3]
But Sukhan Damantevich said:
> *"Those Tatars who have not been in Russia,*
> *those who have not met Sukhan,*
> *those who still have not heard about him in their hordes*
> *   in their youth;*
> *and now, now they do not dare fight with me without a*
> *   wagon-box."*

Sukhan kicked his horse
with his steel spurs,
his horse jumped across the wagons,
came amidst the Tatar wagon-box.
And Sukhan hit a Tatar with the stump
and he hit them on all four sides of the wagon-box.
Wherever Sukhan turned around
there would be Tatar skeletons.
He struck all these Tatars.
And Sukhan rode to the shore of the swift Dnieper-Slautich,
and shouted with a loud voice:
> *"Tsar Azbuk Tovruevich:* [4]
> *Order your warriors to wait for me a bit,*
> *I will bring you many reminders from Kiev,*
> *from the Tsar and Grand Prince Vladimir,*
> *and to all your princes and Tatars,*
> *and to your mirzas and ulans without exception.*[5]
> *Because of my sins I left without arms,*
> *and even my stump broke at the root;*
> *only one little piece remained."*

And he said these words
as he swam across the swift Dnieper.
Tsar Azbuk, seeing his own death unavoidable,
having no means to kill this *bogatyr*,
ordered three catapults loaded,
a spear into each catapult.
And swiftly they rushed toward the deep ravine,
and quickly loaded the three catapults,
a spear into each catapult.
And Sukhan swam across the swift Dnieper,

---

[3] Wagon-box: all nomadic peoples of south Russia used to form a wagon-box, a square or circle of wagons from behind which they would fight, protecting their camps.

[4] Tsar Azbuk Tovruevich: Russians often called the Tatar khan "tsar" since he was a descendant of the Mongol emperor, Genghis Khan. It is difficult to identify Khan Azbuk exactly.

[5] *Mirzas, ulans*: Tatar or Mongol nobles and officers.

but did not reach the other shore with his bit of stump.
And the Tatars shot one catapult and missed,
shot from another and missed,
they shot from the third—
and killed the *bogatyr*, hitting his valiant heart;
they cut the heart-vein.
But the *bogatyr* forgot the mortal wound,
shouted, charged
and killed all the Tatars.
And only then the *bogatyr*, feeling the mortal wound,
quickly began to hurry to the city . . .

(Break in the text)

[Prince Vladimir] saw the mortal wound
and sent for many doctors,
and ordered a Mass for recovery in Holy Sophia,[6]
for the health of Sukhan.
And the sovereign began to honor Sukhan
with his gracious words:
 "*How many cities and patrimonies do you want, dear
  Sukhan,
 for with this I thank you for your great service.*"
And Sukhan bowed low to the ruler:
 "*Enough, my lord, I do not need cities or patrimonies.
 Give me, lord, your servant, a gracious word and a fare-
  well.*"
And it was his last word.
And in this hour he became silent.
It was not a golden trumpet that trumpeted,
but it was the mother of Sukhan who cried:
 "*O you, dear Sukhan, they called a carouser
 and you drank with great pleasure,
 but now you have outdone yourself.
 I don't weep because I see you dead,
 I weep for your bravery and true courage,
 that you attained manhood,
 when you died in the service of your sovereign.*"
And she carried him into a stone cave.
 "*Here, dear mortal Sukhan—life eternal.*"

---

[6] Holy Sophia: the main cathedral in Kiev, built in the first part of
the eleventh century by Prince Yaroslav the Wise. "Sophia" means
"wisdom" in Greek.

69. PRINCE IVAN KHVOROSTININ: AUTOBIOGRAPHICAL VERSES

Prince Ivan Khvorostinin (1585? to 1625) was one of the most controversial Russian writers of the first quarter of the seventeenth century. Scion of an ancient noble family and the son of the valiant defender of Pskov against King Stephen Bathory, Ivan Khvorostinin appeared at the Muscovite court quite early. He later became one of the intimate friends of Pseudo-Dmitry, who became tsar in 1605. After the fall of this impostor, Khvorostinin was banned from Moscow, but some years later he reappeared as commander of one of the armies that fought against the Poles in southwestern Russia. It seemed at the time that this talented aristocrat had a brilliant career before him, but his debauchery, dissoluteness, and unorthodox behavior caused him difficulty once more. He was apparently very unhappy in Moscow society, for he often criticized his surroundings, and complained that there weren't any clever people there, or anyone worth being acquainted with. In one of his satirical verses, he claimed:

> *"These Muscovite people*
> *cultivate much rye,*
> *but live only by the lie."*

Such verses aroused the indignation of the court, and a new investigation of his case showed that he wanted to flee to the West, to Italy, and that he denied such basic dogmas of the Orthodox Church as resurrection after death, and the Trinity. He apparently followed the teachings of the Unitarians. This early Russian Westernizer was then sent to the Monastery of St. Cyril where, in 1623, he decided to recant, and was then permitted to return to Moscow. Soon after his return he wrote his monumental *Exposition Against the Blaspheming Heretics,* in which he ambitiously attacked both the Roman Catholic and Protestant churches. This poetic Exposition, which is 1,333 verses long, is written in rhymed couplets. His verses have no meter, and the line varies from six to fourteen syllables. This first Russian poem of considerable length deserves attention not only because of its size, but also because of the great variations in rhyme and the autobiographical elements of its final part. In this last section Prince Khvorostinin bitterly complained of the unfaithfulness of his servants and friends, who apparently informed the government of his unorthodox behavior and thinking. Besides this religious poem, he was the author of a number

of other historical and polemical works in which he displayed a
skillful command of contemporary literary devices and in which
he often introduced rhymed passages.

The following translation of the final part of the *Exposition
Against the Blaspheming Heretics* is based on the text published
in *Letopis zaniatii arkheograficheskoi komissii,* Volume XVIII,
St. Petersburg, 1907, pages 77–80.

Look, reader, upon the Roman mores
and be faithful to God's glories.
Do not look for truth in any foreign creeds.
Do not betray the Holy Fathers' deeds.
Take care, for the Western Church's revelations
can certainly destroy our foundations.[1]
The Western Church is dark both day and night,
and bitter fruits grow like a blight.
Their Eighth Council [2] did many wrong deeds,
betraying many of the Holy Fathers' creeds.
They want to condemn us to evil torments,
and they give their warriors heretical armaments.
The wave of their wrath is great,
but ever shall I their teachings berate.
I have wanted to bequeath something to my nation,
which is built upon a holy and Christian foundation.
But there were many evildoers,
who have confused our blessed rulers.
I have wanted to lend my hand to the work of salvation,
and for the destruction of their heretical creation.
But in place of ink, I had to use tears
and in irons I found the end of my career.
In prison I passed many days,
for a long time I did not see the sun's rays.
I have wanted to escape their evil gold,
and for such, never have I my soul sold.
I was forced to hide from treacherous detestation,
and thus could not continue my affirmation.
As an army commander I was always brave,
not wanting to bring my friends to the grave.

---

[1] Under the expression "Western Church" Prince Khvorostinin
means both the Catholic and the Protestant churches.

[2] Eighth Council was the first council of the Western Christian
Church, which is considered by the Catholics an Ecumenical Council;
but it is not recognized by the Eastern Orthodox, who did not take
part in its works.

On him who knows my heart have I always relied,
and he has always been my friend, true and tried.
His commandments I have never rejected,
but to his protection have I myself directed.
And before the time of my misfortune,
I had always rejected a heretical fortune.
I did so by the Holy Scriptures,
and following the Holy Fathers' strictures.
I have remained the faithful son of my faith
and firmly stood for the Eastern Church's Grace.
It was not my wont to debate with the ignorant,
nor did I care for their argument.
By much misfortune have I been accosted,
but by the absence of friends I was sore exhausted.
And no one would fain take a stand for me,
but only the Lord his help granted me.
I have written many words against the enemy of the faith,
and still I was thrown into such a bitter place.
Many a friend denounced my writing
and launched against me bitter fighting.
They took me from my holy task,
and not a word of thanks could I ask.
As a heretic was I condemned,
and thus my task came to a bitter end.
Look upon their evil doings,
and contrite hearts be not eschewing.
Even my servants became my enemy,
thus depriving me of all serenity.
They took away their comfort and support,
and prepared against me the trial in court.
Their lawless hatred of me was evil,
and they prepared me for my burial.
They did so, for they belong to a kind most base,
worse than if they were of a devilish race.
They spewed their poisons at me,
and in their betrayal did agree.
Their weapons were denunciations,
spreading against me calumniations.
O Lord, our God, show your might
and judge whether they or I be right.
You alone know of all my devotions
and you will divine the truth in their motions.
They were fed on my bread,
yet they turned my good deed to one of dread.
Yet sweeter than the sweetest flower

is being in the Lord's power.
Let the work of my slaves be cursed,
let us hope their design be dispersed.
Don't throw pearls before swine,
for they will be defiled, whether they be yours or mine.
And I underwent many hardships because of my slaves,
and they nearly brought me to the brink of the grave.
They forgot the words of Christ's admonitions
and I could not escape their evil intentions.
Their words were as ensnaring as a spider's web,
and their hatred was like an evil web.
Over them I was placed by my Creator,
by God was I placed over these evil traitors.
I stood alone against this evil horde,
but I was raised above them by my dear Lord.
But they became my bitter enemies,
and they profaned their own souls with their calumnies.
To win their own freedom,
they wanted to escape their serfdom.
They hurled their words like arrows against their lord,
and I wonder about those who approve such a horde.

70. THE ORDERLY OF COLONEL THEODORE ZAY: A LOVE LETTER FROM THE YEAR 1698

The accidental arrest of a certain Savva Kartsev, who was suspected of participating in political conspiracy, preserved in the archives of the Russian police a love letter written by the orderly of Colonel Theodore Zay. The letter was written for the colonel's son, who had recently married without parental consent, and was to be delivered by Savva Kartsev to the wife of this young man. The intervention of the police prevented its delivery, but preserved the letter for posterity. The rhymed couplets of this letter demonstrate a new poetic vogue, and the meter, epithets, and vocabulary resemble the love songs of Russian folklore.

This poem is translated from the text published by L. Maikov in *Ocherki po istorii russkoi literatury XVII i XVIII stoletii*, St. Petersburg, 1889, page 230.

To the most glorious light which has ever appeared before
    my eyes,
to the nicest person whom I advise.
May my beloved live for many a year,
and not forget the pledge given me here.
Do not forget our pledge taken before the Lord,

when we exchanged rings of our future concord.
At that time we had our wedding crowns on our heads,
crowns of gold for the commemoration of the happy, holy
    event.
Do not forget me in your prayers,
for I shall forget you never.
And I am so sad without you,
that I could fly from here as if I were a bird,
and I would come to you, my beloved.
We could lock ourselves in our chambers,
and confide in each other's secrets.
O my dear, blue flower, the beloved of my life!
What did I do when I came to my lord-father
and when I saw my lady-mother?
When I looked into their eyes,
I saw that our joy was beshadowed.
I awaited kind words from their graces,
but their words betrayed my faith.
"You can marry
someone with considerable wealth,
but you should marry her that we would care for,
and whom you should love.
You should marry a girl from the house of a Muscovite
    nobleman."
But I, my dear nightingale, only thanked them for their
    advice,
and now I send you this love letter with my best regards.

71. PETER KVASHNIN: DEAR BROTHER

Around 1680 Peter Kvashnin, a member of an ancient and
noble family, wrote about fifty lyric poems, some of which are
more than a hundred lines in length. This poetry was first published in 1932 by M. N. Speransky, who thought it was the
product of Russian folklore. But the form, vocabulary, and unusual epithets, as well as partially rhymed lines, seem to prove
that the poems are instead the personal creations of Kvashnin
or of one of his friends. Only in a few aspects do they follow the
folklore tradition. The fact, also, that many of them are unfinished would indicate that they are the product of Kvashnin's
own poetic creativeness. All the poems have a common topic,
that of painful and unrequited love, and are imbued with
despair.

The translations of the two poems given here are based on

M. N. Speransky's texts published in *Izvestiia Akademii Nauk U.S.S.R.*, Volume 7, 1932, pages 721–724.

The subject of the first poem is the tender love of a sister for her brother.

It was not a she-turtledove that cooed with a turtledove.
It was a sister that spoke with her brother.
And speaking with her brother, the sister
began to praise the darling little brother:
"Oh, my dearest little brother, my fond heart,
my dearest of friends, my beloved.
I cannot cease my enjoyment of looking upon you.
You are my precious darling, beautiful as an apple.
You are handsome, my fair brother, like a poppy blossom.
You appear, my young, dear brother, as a cherry.
When I don't see you, my brother,
I could die from sorrow.
And I remember my brother,
but I can only sigh after him.
And I dream steadily of him,
my friendship for him is firm."
The sister speaks with her brother,
and the sister begins to lament:
"Bitter is my life, my brother,
for I hear nonsense and senseless rumors.
Why do those people hate me?
O God, judge those who envy us,
who want to abuse me, a young girl,
and who want to separate me from my brother.
I should rather lose my honor
than be separated from my brother.
Even if they spread calumnies about me,
I shall never forsake my brother. . . ."

[This poem is unfinished.]

72. PETER KVASHNIN: I THOUGHT

I thought, I pondered,
I followed the reasoning of another,
and I said no to my love, straight to his face.

[A hiatus of several lines]

And he decided to take a young wife, a maiden fair.
Oh, come to me, my beloved, on the eve of your wedding!

I shall give you, my beloved, a beautiful linen shirt,
a shirt adorned with muslin.
I waited for my dear friend the whole day until evening.
And my beloved came to me
early in the morning, when a beautiful sun had risen.
And you, my nurses and servants, bring me my trunk with
    iron bars.
And open this trunk with the iron bars,
and take from it two steel knives
for me and for my friend.
Since I could not keep him with me,
you had better open his white breast.
And then he, my beloved, will belong
neither to me, nor to my sister,
nor to that strumpet who separated us.
But you, my beloved, will belong to our mother, the damp
    earth.
And only an oaken board will preserve my secret.

73. SIMEON POLOTSKY: ODE ON
THE BIRTH OF PETER I

No Russian writer of pre-Petrine times achieved such a successful career primarily on the basis of his literary talent as
Simeon Petrovsky Sitnianovich (1629–1680)—called Polotsky,
because he came from the city of Polotsk. A West Russian by
descent, Polotsky studied in the Kievan Academy and became
the most outstanding representative of Polish scholastic school-
ing and literature in seventeenth-century Moscow. He wrote his
early verses in West Russian, Polish, and Latin, but after his
arrival in Moscow began to write in archaic Church Slavonic.
In Moscow he became the tutor to Tsar Alexis' children and the
first Russian court poet. Following the Polish and West Russian
tradition of his time, he wrote his poetry according to the
method of syllabic versification, which requires that each line
have either eleven or thirteen syllables with a caesura in the
middle and feminine couplet rhyme. His poetry is primarily
panegyric and didactic, and either celebrates some important
court and political event or exposes some shortcoming of contemporary life. Polotsky tried to bring to the Russians the pattern and motives of Western—better to say, Polish—literature.
His language is heavy and cumbersome but his choice of new
topics and rather skillful command of syllabic versification won
him the admiration of the tsar and the court and established
for over half a century the reign of syllabic poetry in Russian

literature. He was extremely prolific and was the first Russian
poet to see his verses in print.

The following texts of Polotsky's verses are taken from N. K.
Gudzy, *Istoriia drevnei russkoi literatury,* Moscow, 1966, page
503 (excerpts from the "Ode on the Birth of Peter I"), and
from S. Polotsky, *Izbrannye sochineniia,* Moscow, 1953, pages
7–8, 15.

The month of May ushers forth unto us great rejoicing,
Prince Peter's birth a crown upon its progress placing.
Yesterday great Tsargrad by evil Turks was taken,
in her today sweet hope and freedom's song awaken.
The conqueror is here, her vengeance now to give her,
our great imperial city this day to deliver.
O Constantinograd! Arise in exultation!
Sophia, lift your lamps on high in celebration.
Today, born unto us, as Orthodox Tsarevich,
comes the Great Prince of Moscow, Peter Alexeevich.

74. SIMEON POLOTSKY: THE LAW

Locked up in a chest the medical arts grow seedy,
providing not the slightest succor to the needy.
Gold, too, when under lock and key's insistence
brings the merchant not the slightest assistance.
The Law in like wise lies powerless in stagnation
without the State's diligent preservation.

75. SIMEON POLOTSKY: THE MERCHANT CLASS

The merchant class can hardly keep from sinning.
The Evil Spirit to his ways is winning,
great greed the merchant's soul is e'er infesting,
his entire life with gross misdeeds investing.
First, every merchant's greatest desire
is to buy things for less and sell them higher.
Great sin abides in the raising of prices;
with small profit only is one sinless.
The second sin of merchants is False Promise,
seduction of the buyer their sole premise.
The third sin be the merchants' dubious pledges,
as numerous as the sand grains at the oceans' edges.
Their fourth sin on criminality verges
when, often, in weighing, the merchant perjures.
When purchasing, their scale shows less than's in it,

yet when they sell, their scale extends its limit.
By wetting down their goods some merchants show their
   cunning
or by adding bad merchandise to the scale's summing.
In such a deed one sees the merchants' sin's commission.
God forbade such acts but finds in them no contrition.
Adding of interest is the fifth sin dire
when higher prices for term payment they require.
Some seek through sales on credit, extra money off it,
and reaping higher prices, in such business profit.
In false claims of worth is the sixth sin constituted
when poor products for good ones are oft substituted.
The seventh sin be defects of a product hiding
and selling them as good, the buyer thus deriding.
The eighth is concealment, all aspects not disclosing,
and thus bad transactions on the buyer imposing.
Often merchants make their sales in improper lighting
the buyer into blindness thus benighting.
O you Sons of Darkness in evil thus abiding.
Abusing your neighbors, toward your own bad end sliding.
Shady business practices lead to Darkness Eternal,
deprived of the Lord's Light in punishment infernal.
Give up this black business, forsake these acts of thieving.
Then will you to heaven climb and God's Grace be achieving.

76. TSAR ALEXIS MIKHAILOVICH: THE RULES OF FALCONRY—NEW REGULATIONS AND ORGANIZATION FOR FALCONRY STEERAGE

SEVENTEENTH-CENTURY Russia, with its revolutions, Time of Troubles, social upheavals, and great Church schism seems to many historians to have been primarily a land of anarchy and disorder, lacking any clear and purposeful thought. The lives and writings of many Russians during the reigns of Tsars Michael (1613–1645) and Alexis (1645–1676) show, however, that there were not a few people who admired order, harmony, and systematic organization. There is little doubt that Tsar Alexis, himself, was such a systematic and well-organized man. The study of his political papers, archives, and personal correspondence, as well as *The Rules of Falconry,* below, show that he was a calculating, reserved person who loved harmony and beauty above all. It should not be forgotten that Alexis was also the tsar who strengthened Russia and helped to pave the way for the ensuing transformation of Old Muscovy into the vast empire forged by his son, Peter I (the Great).

The following passages are taken from the introduction to Tsar Alexis' *New Rules of Falconry* written in 1656. It is not certain whether this work was actually written by Tsar Alexis, but the concluding words of the Introduction were written in his own hand and would tend to substantiate the conclusion that either he dictated the whole text to scribes or furnished instructions for its composition. In any case, this preface clearly reflects the tsar's own concepts of harmony, orderliness, and beauty. It offers an interesting picture of Muscovite aesthetics: that harmony is the best expression of beauty. This fundamental Platonic concept became especially popular in Russian thought in the late sixteenth century thanks to Maxim Trivolis, an outstanding Greek scholar known in Russia under the name, Maxim the Greek (1470–1556). After the Time of Troubles when Maxim's writings became widely read, his tenets of perfect orderliness and harmony came to influence seventeenth-century Muscovite thought. In the following excerpts this fondness for harmony and orderliness found a practical application in the rules for the medieval sport of falconry.

This translation follows P. I. Bartenev's edition of *Sobranie pisem Tsaria Alekseia Mikhailovicha,* Moscow, 1856, pages 89–92.

INTRODUCTION

The Sovereign Tsar and Great Prince, Alexis Mikhailovich, autocrat of all Great and Little and White Russia, has decreed this new model and rules for the honor and exaltation of His Majesty's beautiful and glorious sport of falconry.

And in accordance with His Majesty's decree let there be nothing done without stateliness, or without well-regulated and beautiful order; and let all things have their honor and their place and their model regulated by writ, because, though a thing be small, if it be in due form honored, well proportioned, harmonious, stately, no one will blame it or find fault with it; everyone will praise, everyone will honor and admire, that even such a small detail is honored and regulated and ordered in due measure. For honor and order are accorded to each detail, great or small, for this reason honor strengthens it and increases its importance; good order places it, announces its beauty and admirableness, harmony makes it acceptable; without honor nothing will become firm and strong; disharmony destroys it and leads to slackness. So let every reader read this and understand, and acquire knowledge and praise, but not blame me, the author.

What is important in all activities? Measure, harmony, consistency, strength; then in it and around it, stateliness, proportion in relations, good order. Nothing, unless it be well proportioned and have all the aforedescribed qualities, can become stable and strong.

You, most of all, should read this book of the beautiful and glorious sport, assiduous and wise huntsmen, that you may perceive and comprehend many good and reasonable things. If you read it with understanding, you will find in it much for your solace and for your good; if not, you will inherit much that is joyless and evil.

I pray and beseech you, wise, noble, and praiseworthy huntsmen, become experienced in all that is good; first of all in stateliness, honesty, orderliness, in the regulations of falconry for the headmen, and for the birds and for the men; then seek your joy in the field and savor this joy in the right time. And let your hearts be joyful and let not your minds be oppressed by your sorrows and griefs.

For greatly does this field sport ease weary hearts, and greatly does this bird-hunting amuse the huntsman with joyful mirth and exhilarate him. Endlessly glorious and admirable is the preying of the gyrfalcon. Astonishing and heart-comforting is the hunt of young hawks. Most attractive is the movement and preying of the peregrine falcon.

Beautiful to look at and exhilarating is the high flight of the falcon. Cunning is the flight and attack of the tercel. Beautiful also is the flight and attack of the merlin. Next to these, pleasing and joyful is the hunting of a well-bred hawk, his way of flying to the water and of approaching the bird.

The foundation of all sport is the discernment of the huntsman for season and time, and the selection of the birds according to their prey. But for the true huntsman there may be no question about season and time. It is always time, and the weather is always fine to take the field.

Be sportsmanlike, amuse yourself with this good sport and enjoy it joyously and heartily and gaily, for it is good to keep away all sorrow and sadness. Choose your days, ride out often, let the bird fly on a catch, without sloth and relaxation, that the birds might not forget their predatory and beautiful art.

O my glorious councillors, my true and able huntsmen, be joyful and mirthful, let your hearts enjoy and appreciate this goodly and gay sport in all years to come.

(This is signed in His Majesty's hand):

These maxims are for your souls and bodies; but never forget truth and justice, and benevolent love and martial exercise; one must have enough time for work, and some hours of frolic.

(These introductory remarks are followed by
the elaborated rules of falconry steerage.)

A SHORT GLOSSARY OF RUSSIAN TERMS USED IN THIS ANTHOLOGY

I. CURRENCY AND MEASURES

Grivna An old Russian unit of money equivalent to the old English pound. It was in the form of a silver ingot.

Kuna From the Russian word for marten. A monetary unit, there being twenty-five *kunas* in a *grivna*.

Nogata A unit of money, there being twenty *nogatas* in a *grivna*. It was a *vair*.

Rezana A *vair*. There were fifty *rezanas* in a *grivna*.

Ruble A Russian monetary unit since the fifteenth century. Equal to about one English pound at that time.

Vair Squirrel furs used as a monetary unit in ancient Russia.

Versta or *poprishche* Units of measure equal to about two-thirds of a mile.

II. RANKS AND TITLES

Bogatyr An epic hero of Russian historical songs, *starinas*, a kind of superman-warrior.

Boyar A member of the upper nobility in Old Russia, also a member of the Boiarskaia Duma (Council of Boyars), a council that assisted the prince or tsar. The members of this council were appointed by the ruler, but selected only from a restricted number of the highest ranking aristocratic families.

Metropolitan The head of the national Orthodox Church, in particular head of the Russian Church until the end of the sixteenth century. Since the end of the sixteenth century the term has come to denote an archbishop in charge of a large diocese.

Posadnik An elected high official in the cities of early Kievan Russia and in both the Novgorodian and Pskovian republics until the fifteenth century. Similar to rank of commissioner.

Sotnik An officer who commanded a *sotnia*, a company of one hundred men. A centurion.

Stolnik A high official at the tsar's court or of the civil administration.

Strelets (pl. *streltsy*) Professional infantrymen. The corps of *streltsy* was created in the sixteenth century.

Tysiatsky An elected commander of the army in the earlier Kievan period and in the Novgorodian and Pskovian republics.

Voevoda A high-ranking officer either in the civil administration or in the army. A rank equivalent to that of general or governor.

III. MISCELLANY

Bylina or *starina* Old Russian epic songs whose heroes were *bogatyrs*. The *byliny* were divided into two cycles. One, the Kievan cycle, dealt with the eleventh-century ruler, Prince Vladimir of Kiev, and its most popular legendary *bogatyrs* were Ilya Muromets, Dobryni Nikitich, and Alesha Popovich. Some of the *byliny* of this cycle, however, were of even earlier, pre-Christian origin. The other cycle, the Novgorodian, probably developed later, from the thirteenth to the fifteenth century, and its main hero was the merchant-*bogatyr*, Sadko.

Kut'ia A special grain meal that was prepared either on Christmas Eve or for a memorial dinner after a funeral.

CHRONOLOGY OF RUSSIAN HISTORY AND CULTURE

Seventh Century B.C. Occupation of the southern prairies of Russia by the Scythians, and the founding of Greek cities on the northern shore of the Black Sea.

Third Century A.D. Goths occupy the southern prairie of Russia.

Fourth Century The Huns penetrate into Europe from Asia, thus causing the Great Migration. The Antes (Slavs?) founded a state in what is present-day southern Russia.

Ninth Century Appearance of the Viking (Varangian) tradesmen in Russia.

862 The legendary founding of the Russian state by Rurik.

907 Oleg's first campaign against Constantinople.

955 Olga travels to Constantinople, and accepts baptism there.

988 or 989 The Christianization of Russia by Prince Vladimir.

Early Eleventh Century The Kumans drive out the Pechenegs from the southern prairies of Russia.

Circa 1040 The oldest known Russian literary work, the *Sermon* of Luka Zhidiata, bishop of Novgorod (1036–1060).

1019–1054 The reign of Yaroslav the Wise.

Circa 1050 The writing of the *Primary Chronicle* begins.

1113 Monk Nestor ends the writing of the *Primary Chronicle*.

1113–1125 The reign of Vladimir Monomakh, the last great prince of the Kievan Period submitted to by the other Russian princes.

1185 Igor's unfortunate campaign against the Kumans.

1186(?) The writing of the *Lay of Igor's Campaign*.

1223 Russians are defeated by the Mongols at the river Kalka.

1237–1240 The Mongol conquest of Russia.

1261 The beginning of the Muscovite branch of the Rurik dynasty.

1283–1304 Daniel, Prince of Moscow, founder of the Muscovite state.

1326 Metropolitan Peter, the head of the Russian Church, moves his office to Moscow.

1328 Ivan Kalita receives the title "Great Prince of Russia."

1314–1392 St. Sergius of Radonezh, the founder of monasticism in northern Russia.

1380 Russia defeats the Tatars at the Battle of Kulikovo.

1386(?) The writing of *Zadonshchina*.

1420 The death of Epiphanius the Wise, author of the lives of St. Sergius and St. Stephen of Perm.

1427 or *1430*   Death of the greatest Russian painter of the medieval era, Andrew Rublev.

1462–1505   The reign of Ivan III, the unifier of northern Russia.

1533–1584   The reign of Ivan IV.

1550–1570   The compilation of *Chetii Minei* (*The Book of the Lives of Saints*), of the *Book of Grades,* and Nikon's *Illustrated Codex.*

1598   The death of Tsar Fedor, and the consequent end of the Rurik dynasty.

1598–1605   The reign of Tsar Boris Godunov.

1605–1613   The Time of Troubles.

1613–1645   The reign of the first Romanov, Tsar Michael.

1620–1630   Avraamy Palitsyn, Ivan M. Katyrev-Rostovsky, and Ivan Khvorostinin write their works on the Time of Troubles. Probable time of the writing of the *Life of Yuliania Lazarevsky.*

1645–1676   The reign of Tsar Alexis.

1653   The first reforms of Patriarch Nikon.

1663   Simeon Polotsky comes to Moscow. Beginning of Russian syllabic verse.

1667   The Church Council of Moscow and the consequent schism within the Russian Church.

1672   *Esther,* the first Russian play, is staged in the tsar's theatre.

1673   Avvakum writes his *Life.*

1682–1725   The reign of Peter I, and the consequent westernization of Russia.